The Lost Warrior

First of the Return of the Lucca Trilogy

Neil Lynn Wise

fear nought
PUBLISHING

Fear Nought Publishing
A division of Fear Nought Productions LLC
1025 Black Lake Blvd. Ste. 3A, Olympia, WA 98502, USA.
Website: http://www.publishing.fearnought.net

Manufactured in the USA
First published in USA 2001
Second Edition published in USA 2009

ISBN-10:   0-9824855-1-4
ISBN-13:   978-0-9824855-1-4

Cover Illustration by Trevor Hart

CONTENTS

MITHREDATH
SAXHAVEN
UNEXPLORED EASTERN STEPPES
IMMER
RAGOULGUARD
RAVENGLASS
SHIELDAIG
DRAGONBACK
NAGEFF
ARGURION
KARRIMDOR
MONS NEGRA
AVALON
KRANG FERE
BARRIER LIFT
CNOC THOR
LOTHAR
MOGDA THAL
CRAIG PHADRIG
SKULL
OTHA
ZARXIEN
MAR SUR

CHAPTER ONE

SAXHAVEN

In the spring of 6012 AF, a man stood on a cliff overlooking the city of Saxhaven. The breeze ruffled his hair and stirred the grass at his feet, coming from the valley before him and rising toward the soaring mountains at his back. To his left, the evening sun bathed the cliffs in silent fires, and overhead a titanic silver ring arched from horizon to horizon, dully reflecting the blue of the sky. A quarter moon, ghostly and faint in the light of day, hung in the southern sky.

The man studied the city below. Saxhaven's founders had chosen a gorge in the lower mountains for their city, surrounded on three sides by sheer cliffs and craggy peaks. Those same mountains gave birth to the Saar River, which flowed through the gorge, its icy, clear waters tumbling past the city walls. Part of the river's flow had been diverted to form a moat. A large aqueduct also tapped the river, entering the city from the rear, supplying the people with water. Ancient and massive, Saxhaven was built of heavy stone blocks cut from the mountains. Double walls rose above the moat, the space between the walls designed as a killing ground, while a single wall encircled the rest of the city. The palace keep towered above all else, protected by an inner wall and on the roof of the keep, black and white pennants snapped in the stiff breeze. The keep overlooked the central plaza, and streets ran from the plaza, like the spokes of a wheel. Multi-storied stone houses, inns, and shops lined the narrow cobblestone streets. The man could see the doll-like figures of people walking the streets.

The traveler looked to his right, away from the city. The gorge that held Saxhaven opened up into the wide valley of Saarland, which extended to the Sarlassan Sea, a distance of nearly 1700 stadia, probably ten day's ride on horseback. Mountains hemmed the flat river valley on either side, the evergreens cloaking the foothills giving way to rolling swales thick with clusters of oaks and lush grass.

1

Spring flowers dotted the grasslands, the yellow of arrowleaf, the red of death star, and the deep purple of nightlark. Tilled fields covered the valley floor near the city, brown squares on the green carpet. A straight line of stone led from the gates of Saxhaven across the valley, the road to the port city of Androssar. In the distance, the man could just make out the stone and thatch buildings of the village of Helmsdale.

The howling cry of a rock ape echoed through the mountains, and the man turned to look up at the snow capped peaks behind him. He had observed several bands of apes in his journey out of the mountains. In the wild, the beasts were generally harmless, unless a particularly hungry pack encountered a lone traveler. They had not bothered him.

His eyes roamed the mountain vista. Massive summits, majestic and remote, looming high into the sky; the range was called Mithredath, the Perpetual Mountains. For most people, a forbidding wilderness of rock, snow and ice, torn by blasts of freezing wind and the unstoppable fury of avalanches, inhabited only by the most tenacious of creatures. For him, a place of healing and refuge, peace and safety, a sanctuary in which to forget the past. He gazed at the mountains a while longer, remembering the people and place he had left behind, then resolutely turned away, facing the future and the task before him.

The man sighed deeply and began his descent.

Early the next morning, the traveler followed a muddy track leading from the woods toward the city gates. He approached a lone woodcutter with his wagon, and observed the man attempting to repair a wheel, apparently broken by a rock hidden in the mud. Small logs filled the wagon, one of which the woodcutter had positioned as a lever to raise the wagon. He had a block ready to shove under the axle, but the wagon was too heavy for him to lift alone. The woodsman struggled and cursed, his face sweaty in the cool air. At the front of the wagon, a gaunt horse waited patiently in its harness, thankful for the rest.

The traveler stopped and watched for a moment. The scent of

the freshly cut logs filled the air, mixing with the smell of mud and horse. The horse flicked an ear toward him, but did not turn its head.

"Can I help?" he asked, speaking in Saarish, the local language.

The woodcutter jumped and dropped his lever, then turned to glare at the speaker. He studied the stranger suspiciously, seeing a large man, heavily built, wearing boots with scratched and dusty leather leggings that reached nearly to his knees. The man wore gray wool pants, a bulky brown overshirt, laced at the throat, and a hooded cloak that hung down to mid-thigh. He carried a battered traveling pack, and did not appear to be armed, except for a lacquered wooden staff.

The stranger wore the cloak of an Iosian monk, but the woodcutter had never seen this man before. He looked like he had traveled a long way, and yet he spoke Saarish. The woodcutter decided he had no time or energy for such mysteries.

"You're wasting your time, monk. My soul's already lost and I've no money for penance or alms," the woodcutter growled, and then gazed in frustration at the wagon. "And I need more than prayer."

The other man laid aside his staff, moved to a corner of the wagon and lifted it with a steady pull, his face reddening slightly from the strain. He nodded toward the block.

"Place the block. The state of your soul is between you and Iosus," the big man said.

Amazed at the man's strength, the woodcutter shoved the wooden block under the axle, and then stood up, his grimy hands clenched on the wagon. He would not look at the traveler, who had stepped away from the wagon, retrieved his staff, and now watched him silently.

"May Iosus bless you, monk," the woodcutter finally said.

"Blessing on you, freeman. May you get a good price for your wood," the monk replied.

The woodcutter laughed harshly, and turned away. The monk stared at him a moment longer, then continued on toward the city.

As he walked, the monk studied his surroundings. He noticed that the road to Androssar remained nearly empty. A squalid collection of tents and crude shacks littered the area before the city gates. The people living in the settlement appeared starving and desperate. Their garbage and waste lay piled everywhere, the smell filling the air. Some of the squatters stared at the traveler as he passed, fear in their gaunt faces, and several dirty faced women called out crude suggestions, baring bony shoulders and legs to entice him.

The monk ignored them, pulling up his hood and moving quickly through the settlement toward the city. As he neared the far end, two men rose from beside a small cooking fire and approached. The men glanced toward the city guards lounging by the gate, and then came closer; searching for signs of money or valuables the monk might be carrying. They kept their hands out of sight, hovering near hidden weapons, and they looked willing to commit robbery or murder, in plain view of the city guards.

The monk stopped and faced the two men, and they peered at his face, half hidden by the hood. After a moment of tense stillness, something about the stranger's eyes made them change their minds, and they retreated, cursing under their breath. They went back to their meager fire, watching as the monk continued toward the gate.

The monk crossed the bridge over the moat, his boots thumping on the wood. He pulled his hood closer as he neared the gate, but the guards paid no attention, laughing and casting dice in the dirt near the outer gate. One of the soldiers held a half empty bottle of liquor. Two mounted men rode in from the road to Androssar, and the monk kept the riders between him and the guards as he entered the gate.

He stepped to one side just inside the gate, and gazed up at the battlements of the inner wall. Those stones held many memories for him. With a last look at the guards, he walked across the space between the walls and through the inner gate.

He wandered the city, observing the conditions there, missing nothing. The cobblestone streets were in need of repair, the fronts of most of the houses and shops dirty and unkempt. People hurried past him, faces strained and eyes downcast, although a few glanced at him curiously, as if surprised to see an Iosian monk. A dismal pall of fear and despair hung over the entire city.

Groups of soldiers sauntered by, shoving through the crowds, arrogant and bold, and the monk avoided these. He made his way past several intersections, obviously familiar with the city's streets, and stopped before a simple building, surrounded by a low wall and an unkempt garden. The monk gently set aside the tottering gate and strolled through the garden. He found the building's entry closed and barred. He reached into his clothing and placed a gold coin in the empty basin near the door. He bowed his head for a moment and then turned away.

The stranger soon arrived at an inn. He watched it for a while from across the street, and then went inside. He stood beside the door, letting his eyes adjust to the gloom before going further. A heavy bar with stools stretched along the far side, beyond the tables and chairs scattered around the single room. A stairway led to the rooms above, and the monk could see a back door behind the bar. A few patrons were present, eating breakfast, but the fireplace lay empty and cold. The monk thought of the woodcutter with his wagon full of wood.

The big man crossed the room, moving between the tables and diners, who cast furtive glances as he passed. He approached the bar, and leaned his staff against it, letting the pack slip to the floor. A bartender watched him without interest, while a young man rummaged through some bottles at the far end of the bar.

"Is Argyle here?" the monk asked, still speaking in Saarish.

The bartender leaned back against the racks of bottles, folding his arms. His eyes flicked toward the young man, who looked up at the question, then came over.

"I thought the Guard ran you monks out of town. What're you doing here?" the young man asked.

"I'm looking for Argyle," the stranger said.

"Argyle's dead. Been dead for years. I'm his son Dason. Who're you?" the young man demanded.

The monk shoved back his hood and stared at the young man. "Dason? Little loud-mouthed Dason?" he asked.

The bartender hid a smirk, and Dason bristled. The others in the room watched closely, anticipating trouble. Dason walked up to

5

the monk, only the bar separating them.

"I said who are . . . ," "he began, and then stopped short at a voice from the stairs.

"Never mind, Dason. Who asks for Argyle?"

The monk turned to look at the man on the stairs. He saw an older man, stocky and balding, with the look of the military about him.

"An old friend," the monk said. "I wasn't aware he'd died."

The man on the stairs glanced at the bar's patrons, and then motioned toward the upper rooms. "Join me upstairs. We'll talk," he said.

The monk retrieved his staff and pack and climbed the stairs, while Dason glared after him. The other people in the room watched him go, and then returned to their breakfast. All but one, a man who got up from his table and left.

The stocky man led the monk to a room and once he had firmly closed the door, he motioned the stranger to sit at a small table. The other man took a chair opposite him, and leaned across the table, studying the stranger. The monk was clean-shaven, with strange gray eyes and brown hair. A scar etched his left eyebrow, and scars also lined the man's hands.

"I'm Harkon, Argyle's brother. Did you serve with him?" Harkon asked.

The monk's eyes narrowed. "What makes you ask that, Harkon?" he asked.

Harkon leaned back in his chair. "You dress like an Iosian monk, but move like a soldier. You're not from Saxhaven, even though you speak good Saarish. Argyle was a soldier, before he retired and bought this inn," he said.

"How long ago did he die?" the monk asked, his eyes distant.

"Five years. The winter of 6007," Harkon answered.

"How did he die?" the monk asked.

"In bed, quietly," Harkon said.

"How old was he, anyway?" the monk asked.

"He'd just turned 420," Harkon replied.

The monk smiled, and then his face turned somber. He looked

6

at Harkon. "What's happened to Saxhaven? It's not as I remembered it," he said.

Harkon shook his head. "You're right. Saxhaven's changed. So before I say anything else, I want to know who I'm talking to," he said.

"My name's Morgan, and I did serve with Argyle in the Raavs," the monk answered.

"The Raavs. The only Morgan Argyle ever spoke of was Morgan Caeda, the Commander of the Seventh Legion," Harkon said, and then looked skeptically at the stranger. "And you're obviously not him."

Morgan raised his eyebrows. "Obviously," he agreed.

"Argyle was in the Seventh. Was that your Legion too?" Harkon asked.

"I was a Raav, and Argyle and I were comrades in arms. I can't tell you any more right now," Morgan said.

"Oh, you can't? You come into my home, claim to be my dead brother's friend, and start asking questions. I don't know you! You could be anyone," Harkon said, then stood up. "I should throw you out in the street."

Morgan did not move, only looked at the man threatening him. Harkon had been a soldier most of his life, and had faced death many times. However, what he saw in Morgan's eyes made him sit down, his face slightly pale.

"Locha!" Harkon muttered. "Go ahead, ask your questions. If you're one of Malissa's spies, fine, I'm tired of being afraid. It's ruining my retirement."

"Who's Malissa?" Morgan asked.

"The Sagamore's Consort," Harkon said.

"Llorgau has a concubine? What does Llewelyn think of that?" Morgan asked.

"His wife's dead," Harkon said.

"How did that happen?" Morgan asked.

"She died the same year Malissa arrived. Rumor has it she was poisoned," Harkon said.

"Poisoned? By who?" Morgan asked.

7

"No one knows. The Sagamore interrogated many, but never found the killer. We all miss the Sagess, Llorgau most of all," Harkon said.

"Llewelyn dead. Poor Llorgau. He loved her so," Morgan said. "When did this Malissa come to Saxhaven?"

"The fall of 6006," Harkon answered.

"What else do you know about her?" Morgan asked.

"Nothing. I only saw her once, at the Sagamore's side. I don't know anything about the politics of Court, but everything changed after she came," Harkon said.

"What of Dachar, general of the Sagamore's army?" Morgan asked. "And Tarn?"

"Dachar? He's been exiled. And Tarn, the late Captain of the City Guard, we found him dead in one of the streets he was supposed to make safe. That's when I quit the Guard, and joined Argyle in his retirement," Harkon said.

"What else can you tell me?" Morgan asked.

"Llorgau seldom appears in public anymore, he stays in the keep with that woman, while the city rots in corruption. The people bear the weight of ever increasing taxes and abuses by the Guard and the army. The government deals harshly with any protest or complaint. They hung five people recently ---for 'treason'. Relations with Androssar are the worst they've ever been, and trade is nearly at a standstill.

I don't know how much longer this can go on. I was born and raised in this city, and served in the City Guard most of my life. I hate what's happening here," Harkon said, his shoulders slumping. He looked old and tired. "So, do what you will with me. I don't care anymore. "

Morgan leaned across the table and gently laid his hand on Harkon's shoulder. "I'm not in league with Malissa. You've nothing to fear from me," Morgan said.

"I'll believe that when I wake up tomorrow, still alive and free," Harkon said.

"What of Antony?" Morgan asked.

"The Ambassador? I think he's still alive, although I haven't seen him for a long time," Harkon said.

"I went to the temple," Morgan said.

Harkon laughed bitterly. "The Guard closed the temple of Iosus and threw the monks out of the city, almost a year ago." he said.

"Why?" Morgan asked.

"Who knows? I'll wager Malissa was behind it though," Harkon said.

Morgan stood, slipping out of his monk's cloak. "I don't think I should wear this any longer. Do you have another I could buy?" he asked.

Harkon measured the big man's frame with his eyes. "Nothing that would fit you," he said.

Morgan rolled up the cloak and stuffed it in his pack. "Is the market in the central plaza still open?" he asked.

"Barely. Few can afford to buy. Do you want some breakfast?" Harkon asked.

Morgan sighed. "I don't seem to have much of an appetite this morning. Thank you anyway," he said.

"What're you going to do now?" Harkon asked, looking up at Morgan.

"I need to talk with some old friends," Morgan said.

As Morgan walked toward the door, Harkon spoke. "I was right, you're no monk. And you seem to be personal friends with the entire Court of Saxhaven. Who are you?" he asked.

"It's safer that you don't know. Thank you for the information," Morgan said.

"Beware the whims of Locha, the god of ill fortune. He's the true ruler of this city," Harkon said bitterly.

Morgan turned in the doorway. "I serve Iosus, and fear only Him," he said.

Morgan stood at a cloth merchant's table in the central plaza, examining a dark cloak with a hood. The cloak was plain and worn but still serviceable. The merchant, a small man with grizzled hair, watched him closely.

"This will do. How much?" Morgan asked.

"A fine cloak. Two silvers?" the vendor said hopefully.

"One," Morgan countered automatically.

The merchant glanced at Morgan's simple attire, and then nodded. "One," he agreed.

Morgan donned the cloak, and slipped his pack over one shoulder. As he dug into his pouch for the coin, Morgan surveyed the passersby and the keep, which rose high in the midday sun. He remembered the plaza crowded with vendors, selling various wares, the air filled with good natured haggling and laughter. Today, the area lay nearly empty, dotted only with scattered clusters of people, their bargaining tense and strained, the prices low. A woman with a child huddled to Morgan's right, selling bread. She had a basket of twelve loaves. The child looked hungry, and the woman seemed determined yet near despair. In better days, she had been quite lovely. Her cup of coin sat almost empty; evidently the people of Saxhaven could barely afford bread.

A group of Guardsmen made their way through the plaza, people drawing away as they passed, glaring at the soldiers with thinly veiled hatred. Seeing them, Morgan tossed the coin to the merchant, and pulled up his hood. He made a show of closely inspecting a bolt of cloth. The merchant glanced at the approaching Guardsmen, then quickly pocketed the silver and began to extol the virtues of the cloth Morgan had chosen. As they passed, the Guard officer, a foppish sergeant, noticed the woman with the bread. The sergeant swaggered over to her table, and grabbed a piece of bread. Ignoring her protests, he took a large bite.

"Good bread. Have some," he said as he began tossing loaves to the soldiers.

They laughed and caught the bread, passing it amongst themselves. The corporal, an older man, was the only one who refused the bread. He looked disgusted with their behavior.

The woman held out the coin cup. "You've taken my bread, now pay for it," she said.

The sergeant laughed. "We don't pay for anything. We take what we want," he said as he tore the cup from her grasp. "In fact, you pay us for protection, you worthless hawker."

The woman's momentary defiance collapsed. "Please don't do this. That's all I have. My son is hungry. If you take my money and my bread, he'll starve," she pleaded.

With a half eaten piece of bread in one hand, and the coin cup in the other, the sergeant looked down at the child, who sat under the table, gazing up at him with wide eyes. Wrinkling his nose in disgust, he kicked at the child, who scrambled away, to hide behind his mother.

A small crowd gathered, watching in tense silence, their eyes burning. The Guardsmen divided their attention between the people and the actions of their officer.

"Leave my child alone, you coward," she said.

Seeing he now had an audience, the sergeant did not want to let this insult pass. Throwing the bread at the woman, he drew his sword and held it under her trembling chin. The crowd murmured angrily, drawing closer, and the soldiers began to get nervous, wishing their sergeant would stop before things got out of hand.

The cloth merchant noticed Morgan watching the Guardsmen and the woman, his eyes hard. The man leaned closer to Morgan and whispered. "You don't want to get involved. It'll only be trouble for you. You can't help her."

Morgan grimaced. "I can't just stand by and watch this."

The sergeant poked the woman with his sword, and laughed as she recoiled from the point. "Tell me why I shouldn't kill you and your spawn right now. Beg for your life and I might spare you. After all, it was good bread," he said.

Morgan placed a second silver on the bolt of cloth. "Thank you for your discretion, kind sir. May your business prosper," he said to the merchant.

"May Iosus be with you," the man said, as Morgan picked up his staff and turned.

The Guardsman poked the woman again. "Well, what'll it be?" he asked.

A new voice interrupted the officer's fun. "Pay the woman for the bread and leave her alone."

11

The sergeant turned to look, his sword still at the woman's throat. He saw a man standing nearby, in a dark cloak, with the hood up. He could not see the man's face, but the intruder had no weapons, only a walking staff. The staff was a head taller than the stranger, and fairly thick, but still no match for a Guardsman's sword. "Be off with you, man. You've no business here. I'll do what I want with this woman," the sergeant said.

The officer turned back to the woman, and did not even see the staff coming. The rod of lacquered wood struck his sword hand, and the sword fell onto the table. Next, the staff hit him behind the knees, and as he fell, the final blow cracked against his chin, snapping his head back. His helmet clattered to the stones of the plaza, and he collapsed senseless. The cup fell from his hand, the coins spilling out, one rolling between the feet of the nearest Guardsman. The soldier shook off his surprise and ran forward, drawing his sword, but the staff caught him in the face, and he landed in the arms of his comrades. Morgan stood poised, ready to continue. The woman had not moved, she stared open mouthed, while the crowd cheered and moved even closer. The Guardsmen were not sure what to do; the townspeople looked ready to join in the attack.

The old corporal shoved his way to the front, and held up a hand toward Morgan.

"Don't do this, man. The people will fight, and there'll be a bloodbath. Malissa will order more hangings. For their sakes, stop," he cried.

Morgan studied the man, noting the lean frame and hawklike features with the prominent nose. He recognized the scar on the lined neck. "Taskin, is that you?" he asked.

The corporal stiffened, and the other Guardsmen peered curiously over his shoulder. "Yes, I'm Taskin. Who're you?" he asked.

Morgan lowered his staff and swept back the hood. Taskin stared at him for a moment, frowning, then his eyes widened. Tension hung in the air.

"You?! It can't be. You're dead," he gasped.

Morgan shrugged. "I'm back," he said.

Taskin ignored the questions of his squad. "Stay clear," he ordered them. "You don't want to fight this one."

Several of the Guardsmen glanced at their fallen comrades, about half convinced of the truth of Taskin's statement.

Taskin stepped toward Morgan. "Will you surrender to me? To avoid the deaths of innocent people?" he asked.

Morgan hesitated a moment, then handed him the staff. "To you, Taskin, for old time's sake," he said.

The crowd murmured angrily and surged forward, but Morgan held up his hands, raising his voice. He spoke with authority, as one who was used to giving orders and having those orders obeyed. "No, not today. Wait. Your day will come. Go home," he said.

The crowd hesitated, and Morgan spoke even louder. "GO HOME!"

With many backward looks, the crowd began to disperse, and the Guardsmen breathed a sigh of relief. Morgan bent, tore loose the sergeant's coin pouch, and tossed it to the woman. No one moved to stop him.

CHAPTER TWO
MALISSA

Somewhere deep within Llorgau's palace keep, Morgan stood before a pair of massive doors, made of ornately carved dark wood. Guards flanked the doorway. One of the soldiers escorting him pounded the heavy metal knocker on the wood. Stone and shadows swallowed the sound.

Morgan waited, outwardly impassive. After he surrendered to Taskin, he had asked to see Antony, the Sagamore's Ambassador. Instead, soldiers had taken him to guest quarters in the palace, where servants asked for his clothes and belongings, and requested that he bathe and dress in other garments they provided. They had taken his pack, cloak, and staff, and Morgan had done as they asked. He glanced down at his new clothes with distaste. He had not spent much time in courts and palaces, and felt uncomfortable in such silken finery. Oh well, he thought, it's better than prison rags and chains.

Something odd occurred while he was dressing. A woman servant had entered, supposedly to take his original garments. As she picked up his clothes, she leaned close to him and whispered "pain is freedom." The statement made no sense to him, and he decided she was either slightly addled or had strange personal preferences. The doors before him began to open, and he put the incident out of his mind.

A woman servant stood in the doorway, thin and homely, her face etched by constant fear. The servant beckoned him to enter, and as he passed the guards, he noticed they were looking at him with an odd mixture of jealousy and pity. He wondered what he was about to face.

The heavy doors closed firmly behind him, and the servant vanished. He studied the room, seeing a large chamber, with fireplaces at either end. Both held roaring blazes, making the room uncomfortably warm, and Morgan began to suspect where all the wood was going, and why the woodcutter could not get a fair

14

price. Thick shutters covered the windows on the far wall and only a glimmer of daylight filtered through them, leaving the room lit mainly by the fires.

The fireplace to his right had a large stone hearth, covered with thick furs. Two of the ugliest beasts he had ever seen crouched on the hearth---large, vicious looking brutes with loose, almost hairless hides, and grotesquely wrinkled faces, split by mouths full of teeth. They had no real ears, just holes in the sides of their heads, and wore metal collars, that glinted redly in the firelight. The things watched him hungrily, their tails twitching. They appeared to be some form of cat.

Deciding the "cats" did not seem inclined to attack him immediately, Morgan turned to look at the rest of the room. A large, sunken bath filled with soapy water lay before the other fireplace, steaming in spite of the room's warmth. A massive bed on a raised dais in the center of the chamber dominated the entire room. A canopy spread over the bed, supported on corner posts.

Rugs and furs covered the floor of the chamber, and tapestries lined the walls. The firelight cast strange shadows on the hangings, but he could tell the scenes depicted were mainly sexual in nature. He pushed gently against the doors, watching the cats as he moved, but found the exit firmly locked. He could see doorways leading into other rooms, and he decided he would investigate.

As he stepped away from the main door, he noticed a strange smell. An exotic, somehow stimulating scent, it had a powerful effect on him. He was aware that his breathing had deepened and his heart was beating faster. He rubbed sweaty palms on his pants, leaving damp streaks. His skin tingled and he felt tense.

Something moved in the shadows behind the bed, and as he peered into the darkness, a figure came out of the gloom, moving languidly toward him. In the firelight, it appeared to be a woman in a sleeveless black dress, her eyes covered with a mask. She had long, absolutely white hair that flowed down her back and moved like waves of cream as she walked. Morgan felt his eyes drawn to the dress. From a collar around her neck two narrow strips of cloth crossed over her full breasts and attached to a band that hung low

15

around her slim waist. Her stomach was bare and he could see the shadow of her navel in the reddish light. The lower part of the dress fell in a cascade of black cords, dangling from the waist band nearly to the floor. As she moved, the cords parted, revealing the white skin beneath. Her bare feet sank into the plush rugs, but as she moved Morgan noticed her toenails were painted with some dark pigment. She wore no jewelry but delicate golden anklets.

The flashes of pale thigh and the curve of her breasts and stomach caused a disturbing reaction, and Morgan tore his eyes from the lush, voluptuous body, trying to concentrate on her face. The mask covered the woman's eyes and nose, but Morgan could see that her sensuous lips had been painted the same color as her nails.

Morgan took a deep breath, trying to clear his head, but only succeeded in drawing in more of the intoxicating fragrance. The scent he had noticed earlier was even stronger now, and it seemed to be coming from the woman herself, as if she wore some heavy perfume. The aroma clung to his nostrils and suddenly he could not think of anything but the woman. She seemed to glide across the rugs, her body moving with undulating grace. An arm's length away, she stopped. Morgan ached to reach out and touch her, to feel that white skin. He clenched his fists, rigid with the strain of holding himself back. Morgan did not understand what was happening to him. He had never reacted to any other woman like this.

Her hidden eyes regarded him. Dimly, he thought it strange that he could not see the whites of her eyes through the holes of the mask, but an overwhelming urge to kiss those beautiful lips swept the thought away.

"Morgan," the woman said, her voice a throaty purr. "Are you a strong man, Morgan? I need strong men."

When she spoke, he could see her teeth and tongue between the full lips. He stood trembling, drinking in her perfume, while she reached out and touched his cheek. Her strangely cool fingers left a trail of fire as they slid across his face, then she cupped his jaw in her hand. Her touch sent a tingling thrill through him. He glanced down at her painted fingernails, where they tickled his cheeks, then looked at her face. The woman tilted her head curiously, and pursed her lips.

"I haven't seen eyes like that in a long, long time," she remarked, her voice suddenly distant.

She leaned closer, and Morgan almost gasped at the intensity of her fragrance. "Could it be?" she breathed.

The woman shook her head, the ivory locks caressing her pale shoulders. "No. They're all gone," she said, a hint of sadness in the husky voice.

The woman slid her hand from his face, down his throat, until her icy fingers lay on the pulsing vein at the base of his neck. She closed her eyes, a flash of white behind the mask, and drew in a deep breath, savoring something. As she inhaled, Morgan became painfully aware of her perfect bosom, straining against the straps of her dress.

"So much . . . life," she said hungrily. "More than any other I've tasted in this land of fragile shadows. You're a rare prize, Morgan."

In spite of her beauty, something in her voice sent a shiver down Morgan's spine.

She gently took his hand, drawing him toward the nearest fireplace, and Morgan found he had no strength to resist. His whole world narrowed to those slender fingers and that cool palm. A small part of him knew that something was terribly wrong, that this woman was not what she seemed, but evil and dangerous. She was a very attractive woman, but there was something more, some reason for his sudden passion. He tried to follow that thought, but the smell and feel of her made thinking so hard, and his body was taking control. He wanted to react with sheer, animal instinct, to caress, to enjoy, to drink in this woman and all she had to offer. By the time they reached the hearth, he did not care about anything else.

The woman hissed at the cats, and they slunk away. The jarring sound alarmed him, but the feeling soon faded, as she eased him down on the furs before the fire. She knelt down beside him, between him and the fire, and then slowly unbuttoned his shirt. He made no attempt to stop her, helpless under her touch. She pushed the shirt aside, caressing the skin of his chest, her cool hands stoking raging fires within him. He lay shivering on the hearth, paralyzed, his eyes locked on the woman.

17

Then she slid her glorious body on top of him, her white hair cascading over them. As she moved, the black cords of her skirt parted, and he could see the long curve of her thighs. His heart was hammering now and he found himself nearly gasping in anticipation. He wanted to grab her and crush her to him, but his arms would not move. The feel of her was sheer ecstasy, the odd coldness of her skin only heightening the sensation. She put one hand on his chin, turning his head toward the fire, and he could feel her cool breath on his neck, then her lips. This close to the fire he should be roasting, but he felt almost chilled.

Something deep inside of him cried out. Torn between desire and revulsion, longing and fear, wild abandon and restraint, he prayed. Iosus, save me from myself, he cried silently. This is wrong, yet I want it so!

Her tongue touched the skin of his neck and he fought to hold onto any rational thought. His rising passion threatened to engulf him, to swallow him whole, and bear him away in a flood. He realized he was staring at the fireplace grating, an arm's length away. The grating glowed with the heat of the fire, and the servant's words came back to him. "Pain is freedom."

The woman writhed sensuously, bearing down on him, pushing him deeper into the furs. She turned his face to hers, lowering her parted lips. He knew that when she kissed him, he was finished. Blindly, he reached out with his right hand, guided by the heat. His straining fingers seized the hot metal of the grate and pain lanced through him.

He came back to himself in a rush, and before the storm of desire took him again, he pushed her roughly away, rolling free. Panting and shivering, his seared hand clutched to his chest, he scrambled to his feet. The woman lay on the furs, startled into immobility, and behind him he could hear the sudden growling of the cats.

Before she could move, he reached down with his good hand, and tore the mask free. Two black holes in a twisted white face glared up at him. Her eyes were large and completely black, and he remembered a famous quote---"the eyes are the window to the

18

soul." If that was true, then this creature's soul was pure evil.

Hissing in rage, the woman surged to her feet. Shuddering, Morgan dropped the mask and stumbled away, while the woman crouched before the fire, fingers hooked into claws, lips twisted in a snarl. He could see himself in those midnight eyes, a small figure reflected in their dark wetness. The two cats stalked closer, snarling like their mistress, circling around behind him.

Morgan turned and made for the shuttered window, like a drowning man striving for air. The cats retreated from his advance. The scent of her still filled the room, and he knew before long he would not care that she was not human, and would again welcome her embrace.

He seized the shutters, tearing them open with a rending of wood and metal. The contact brought a new burst of pain from his burned hand, and then the clean sun and sweet fresh air bathed him. He swallowed great lungfuls, trying to wash away the taint of her evil perfume. His head began to clear, and he could control the trembling of his limbs, but he felt so tired and cold, a coldness that reached his soul. He concentrated on the pain in his hand, using it as an anchor.

When he felt strong enough, he turned to face her. The woman had regained both her mask and her composure. She flung back her stark locks, and sharply gestured at the cats, who crouched, still growling deep in their throats. The woman stepped forward, carefully avoiding the shaft of sunlight that had invaded her domain. She held out her hand.

"Morgan, don't be afraid. Come back to me. You just startled me. I won't hurt you. You'll only feel pleasure. I want you, Morgan. I . . . need your strength," she said softly.

Morgan leaned against the window ledge, shaking his head firmly. He still could not trust his voice. Even knowing what she was, he longed to go to her. Morgan realized this must be the woman Malissa. No wonder Saxhaven had fallen before her. She could easily bring a kingdom to ruin.

Loud voices came from the hall, then a pounding of the knocker, and Malissa whirled.

"Go away!" she cried. "We're not to be disturbed."

A hesitant voice came through the panel. "Lord Antony wishes to speak with your . . . guest. He says it's urgent."

Malissa stalked to the doorway, speaking through the wood. "Secondus, send him away," she ordered.

A startled shriek came from the hallway, and the doors burst open. Malissa leaped back to avoid the swinging valves, and the cats bounded to her side. A huge man stood in the entry, regarding Malissa with cold eyes. She retreated from him and the sudden light, both repellent to her. Another man joined the first, this one of normal size, with long blond hair, and drooping mustaches, dressed in impeccable court fashion. He held a pinch of snuff to his nose and inhaled deeply, then shook his golden locks and favored Malissa with a wicked grin.

"My sincerest apologies, noble courtesan, but I truly do need to speak with Morgan right away. It's of the utmost importance. We're old friends and have much to discuss," he said in a powerful, flowing voice.

Malissa advanced on Antony, avoiding the giant. Even the snarling cats would not approach the huge man. "I was questioning this stranger, whom you claim as friend. I think he's a spy, disguised as an Iosian monk, sent by our enemies in Androssar. Or an assassin, on a mission to slay the Sagamore," she said.

Antony took another pinch of snuff. "I can assure you, madam, my friend is no spy or assassin. Although I fear he's in grave danger, and in need of my counsel," he said.

"I will have him questioned, and executed, and there's nothing you can do about it," Malissa hissed.

Antony shook his head solemnly. "I've taken the liberty of notifying our Sagamore that his comrade in arms has returned. Llorgau wishes to grant him audience, tomorrow morning," he said, and then his face brightened. "Perhaps we can discuss your concerns with Llorgau then."

The Ambassador paused for effect. "Did you know that Morgan and his Seventh Legion stood by Llorgau against the Targ when they laid siege to Saxhaven? Oh, I forgot. That was before your time, maybe 5972. Well, anyway, a grand, epic event," he said.

Malissa tried to calm herself. "I will talk to Llorgau, about you and your friend, then I'll have you both tortured and hung in the plaza," she said.

Antony's fluid voice took on a hard edge. "Malissa, you do me wrong. I'm privy to your secrets. It would be unfortunate if everyone else knew them, now wouldn't it?" he asked.

Malissa turned away. She pointed a finger at Morgan, who had not moved from the window. "You're mine! I will have you . . . all of you. Don't think this fool can save you," she said, and then stalked toward one of the interior doorways, the cats at her heels.

"Anise, get those people out of my chambers. And close that window," she snarled.

The homely servant appeared from nowhere, and eased past Morgan to the window. She pried the battered shutters closed, and the room darkened.

Antony gestured urgently at Morgan. "We best get you out of here, friend. This place isn't overly healthy," he said.

Morgan did not need a second invitation. He walked quickly to the door, forcing his leaden legs to move, still shivering. He nodded at the giant in passing.

"Greetings, Caestus. Good to see you again," he said.

Caestus gave him a gap toothed grin as Morgan stepped into the hallway. Secondus, the palace chamberlain, stood there, white-faced and wringing his hands. Several women soldiers dressed in white and gold watched the palace guards, hands near sword hilts, but the guards did not seem inclined to challenge them. Caestus pulled the doors closed.

"Antony, she'll have me killed," Secondus said, obviously terrified.

Antony put an arm around the quaking official. "I'll speak for you, Secondus. The only thing you have to fear is that strange illness of yours, which I fortunately have been able to keep in remission. Now go on about your duties. Leave this matter to me," he said.

As the chamberlain departed, Antony turned to Morgan and studied him a moment.

21

"It really is you," he finally said. "We thought you were dead. The lost warrior has returned."

Morgan gripped Antony's arm. "Thank you, my old friend. I owe you once again," he said.

Antony glanced at Morgan's burned hand. "I see you got my message. I'm glad the information proved useful," he said, then flashed a bright smile, and pointed down the hall. "Let's go to my quarters. You must be famished, after all that stimulation. We can exchange tales of these past twelve years."

Antony's female bodyguards moved in around them, and Caestus lumbered along in the rear.

The Ambassador nodded at Morgan's exposed chest. "And cover yourself. You're distracting my guards," he said.

Morgan looked down at his open shirt, then reddened slightly and pulled it closed. The soldiers on either side hid their smiles.

Morgan sat at a heavy oak table in Antony's chambers, his feet propped on its grained surface, wearing his traveling clothes once again. The monk's cloak lay over a nearby chair, and Morgan still had the old cloak he purchased in the plaza, now in his pack. He had finally gotten warm again, but he still felt unnaturally tired. His burned hand was tightly bandaged, and he held a mug of light ale in his good hand, the remains of a meal before him. Antony stood by the modest fire, guarding himself against the evening chill. They were alone.

Morgan waved his mug at the tapestries and collection of antiques and curios scattered about the room. "You not only survive, Glossauric, you prosper. Your skill at intrigue remains after all these years," he said.

Antony smiled, his face thoughtful. "Glossauric, Golden Tongue. I haven't heard that name in a long time," he said.

"We always gave you a chance to talk the enemy into surrendering, before we started killing them. You saved a lot of lives that way. The ultimate ambassador. A special gift," Morgan said.

Antony walked over and sat down beside Morgan. "You never returned from Mogda Thal. Argyle said you were dead," he said.

22

Morgan took a long drink. "First, I need to know the situation here. Then I can decide how much it's safe to tell you," he said, then paused. "I stopped at Argyle's inn and spoke with his brother."

"Argyle. He was one of the lucky ones, still sane when they found him floating down the Seir, crowded into a boat with a handful of other gibbering wretches. He couldn't tell us what'd happened at Mogda Thal, although some of the others raved of a horrible sound that drove men mad. When he recovered, Argyle used his severance pay to fix up the family inn and retired," Antony said.

"Short retirement. Seven years," Morgan said.

"He had a full life. I'm sure Harkon told you he died quietly in his sleep. It could've been much worse," Antony said.

"Much worse," Morgan said, his face haunted.

Morgan bumped his bandaged hand on the table and the pain reminded him of Malissa. "Harkon told me the trouble here all started with Malissa, and that Llewelyn died about the same time. How did Malissa become the Sagamore's Consort?" he asked.

As if the question chilled him, Antony got up and walked back to the fire, stroking the box of snuff on his arm. "Many say she is the incarnation of Luras," he said.

"The goddess of lust? I can well believe that. She's certainly not Viras," Morgan said.

"The twin goddesses. Love and lust. The same and yet so different," Antony said, then paused, staring into the flames. "Malissa came one night in the fall, riding through the dead leaves with her retainers, a cold, bitter wind at her back. May Iosus curse that night. Veiled and robed, she demanded to see Llorgau and for some reason, he granted her private audience. After the usual precautions, the guards took her to his chambers. They were only alone a short time, but he seemed bewitched after that.

Llorgau quartered the strangers in the palace keep, and sent for Malissa the next night, and the next and the next, like he couldn't get enough of her. At first, everyone thought he was just lonesome for a woman's company, but his relationship with Malissa soon became an unnatural obsession. Before long, Llorgau had created the office of Consort, and things began to change, including the

23

Sagamore. He became moody and unpredictable, and the woman was with him always. Llorgau's friends sought to counsel him, but he drove them away. He wouldn't listen to any doubts about Malissa. He became paranoid, claiming that everyone was trying to take her for themselves. That was ridiculous. No one even knew what the woman looked like; she still wore veils and robes. One by one, those with influence were summoned to Malissa," Antony said.

Antony sniffed, and blew his nose on a lace kerchief. "I had a raging sinus infection when Malissa sent for me, and I couldn't smell anything. I believe my affliction saved me. Malissa came to me without veil or robe, scantily clad in some alluring wisp of cloth. Despite the mask and the soulless eyes, I found her a beautiful, intensely desirable woman, but she wasted her more arcane wiles on me, in my congested state. Already suspicious of her, I didn't let her near me, and I made an enemy that day. Anyone Malissa couldn't control either died or was exiled. I'm about the last of the old retainers left," he said.

Morgan had a disturbing thought. "And Secondus? Has she . . .?" he began.

Antony nodded. "Even the ancient Chamberlain has felt her touch," he said.

"How did you survive?" Morgan asked. "She even seems to fear you."

"As you know, I'm a dabbler in pharmacology. After that first encounter, I realized her scent was her most deadly weapon, and I sought to combat it. I managed to avoid her until I'd developed a special brand of pungent snuff, that I administer when in her presence. It seems to work. Caestus, as you may remember, is a eunuch, a former harem guard. He seems to be immune to Malissa's charms. She fears him, regards him as something unnatural.

I also enlisted women as my personal guard, and honed their fighting skills until the palace guards fear them also. Using my pharmacological arts, I created slow acting poisons that I secretly administered to key persons in the keep, such as Secondus. As long as they behave, I supply the antidote. But should something happen to me, they know they face a slow, painful death. They've been most cooperative, much to Malissa's chagrin," Antony concluded.

"What is Malissa? She's not human," Morgan said.

Antony sighed. "Have you ever heard of the Hedonae?" he asked.

Morgan frowned. "Weren't they a race of beings that supposedly fed on the life force of others? But they're a myth, they don't really exist," he said.

"No, they exist. The total lack of body pigment, the black, soulless eyes, the intoxicating scent---Malissa bears all the signs. She is Hedonae. The scent is a type of body secretion, that arouses the passions of men, but has no effect on women. I've also seen her victims," he said.

"Victims?" Morgan asked.

"Her touch drains life energy, and the transfer peaks during sexual intercourse. Did you notice how cool her skin is, did you feel cold after touching her?" Antony asked.

Morgan nodded. "It was hot in the room at first, then I was cold," he said.

"She uses her scent to drive men mad with desire, and when they couple with her, she . . . feeds on them. Too much time in her arms, and you die, drained dry. She's terribly addictive, and once you surrender, there's no return. Your life is in her hands. Pain brings temporary relief, but few men can resist her for long," Antony explained.

Morgan shuddered. "I wanted her so badly. I could think of nothing else. She's incredibly dangerous," he said.

Antony nodded. "Llorgau didn't have a chance. He was grieving and vulnerable after Llewelyn's death, and Malissa was undoubtedly in his bed the first night. Since then, he lives at her sufferance," he said.

"Did Malissa kill Llewelyn?" Morgan asked.

"I think so, but I've not been able to prove it. The poison was quite exotic and we could find no antidote," Antony said.

"Llewelyn dead. I remember her so full of life. Llorgau must have been devastated," Morgan said.

"You'll see him tomorrow, but prepare yourself. He's not the

25

man we knew. He barely eats or drinks, he cares for nothing but Malissa. She's also poisoned his mind, and he trusts no one. He thinks all but Malissa plot against him. He even had the Iosian monks driven away, when they tried to confront him. He'll rarely grant me audience, and then listens to little I say. I fear he's lost," Antony said.

"What about these victims you spoke of?" Morgan asked.

"Malissa's appetite for life is voracious. If she were feeding on Llorgau alone, his life would be snuffed out in a single night. So she prowls the castle halls, seeking other prey. A procession of strong young men has entered that room you saw, and not returned alive. One night she grew careless, and left the palace in search of sustenance. My agents followed her to a noble's home, where she met with his seven sons in their father's absence. When she left, just before dawn, my people searched the house, and found three of the sons dead. The other four lay comatose, nearly drained dry.

My agents alerted me, and we hid the bodies. Their appearance was such that all would know her true nature, were I to reveal them. Malissa goes hooded and robed in public, and few know what she really is. If the general populace knew the truth, they wouldn't bear her, regardless of Llorgau's wishes. She would probably be burned at the stake," Antony explained.

"So why didn't you expose her?" Morgan demanded.

Antony shook his head. "I feared for Llorgau. As I said, he's deeply addicted. Were he to lose Malissa suddenly, he might die. He's still my Sagamore and I couldn't take chances with his life," he said.

"What happened to the bodies?" Morgan asked.

"We tried to preserve them, but failed, so I burned the bodies. And then I devised a cunning plan," Antony said mysteriously.

"What?" Morgan asked.

"A bluff. Malissa believes I keep the bodies in a stasis chamber. Malissa's efforts to find the rumored chamber have proved fruitless. I hold her hostage with a lie," Antony said.

"How does she know of stasis chambers? They're rarely found anymore, and I know of none that still functions," Morgan said.

Antony frowned. "Good question. I have no answer," he said.

26

Morgan stood, and began pacing the room. "You always were the subtle and patient one. I've no use for court intrigue and plotting. I'd just cut off her head, and deal with the consequences. Is there no defense against her?" he asked.

"My snuff has proven effective; it seems to overwhelm her scent. I continue my research, and I'll find a way to help Llorgau. There must be some antidote to her poison. She has other weaknesses. She cannot bear the cold for long, and sunlight quickly burns her pale skin. Her eyes are sensitive to light. I'm also trying to starve her, keep the men away from her. The best defense is to avoid her as much as possible, especially in confined spaces where her scent is concentrated. She can control the secretion and doesn't waste it in the open," Antony explained.

"How'd you know I was in Saxhaven?" Morgan asked.

Antony smiled wickedly. "Malissa and I have spies everywhere, and they immediately noticed the return of an Iosian monk. Disguising yourself as a member of that sect was ill-advised, as you probably realize now. After your arrest in the plaza, I learned of your true identity. I managed to send you my cryptic message through a serving maid, and when I heard Malissa had summoned you to her chambers, I came as quickly as I could. I'd regret losing another friend to that white witch," Antony said.

"Was I followed?" Morgan asked. "Did you know of all my activities?"

Antony summed up his intelligence. "You went to the temple of Iosus, then to Argyle's inn, talked with Harkon a while, then headed for the plaza," he said.

Morgan winced. "Then Malissa knows all that as well. I fear that Harkon and corporal Taskin are in danger," he said.

"They are, but I've already taken measures in that regard. I'll protect them as best I can," Antony assured him.

"Thank you," Morgan said.

"Well, now you know my situation. Can you tell me what happened to you?" Antony asked.

"As you can see, I survived the massacre at Mogda Thal, although sometimes I wish I hadn't. I have few memories, mainly nightmares. Considering your precarious position here, that's about all I can tell you," Morgan said.

"Precarious? I thought I was doing quite well," Antony said.

"I don't need to lecture you on the intricacies of court intrigue and the art of deception. I can't tell you anything more," Morgan said.

"No, I understand," Antony said, and then glanced at Morgan's cloak. "When did you become an Iosian monk, or is it just a disguise?"

Morgan sighed. "I'm not really a monk, although I now serve the Maker," he said.

"I'm pleased to hear that. I prayed for you a long time," Antony said.

Both men were silent for a while, and then Morgan spoke.

"What became of the siege of Droghelda and the Crusade?" he asked.

"You left in the spring of 6000, taking the Seventh to join Imperius in the march on Mogda Thal. Max and his Eighth, along with Korl and the Ninth, continued the siege through half of the summer. Droghelda hadn't fallen, and without warning an army of trolls and Immortals charged out of Aijalon, pinning our forces between two hostile groups. We were expecting Imperius' triumphant return from the Mhoul capital and instead we were faced with an army who taunted us with stories that Imperius and his men were all dead. The siege of Droghelda turned into a strategic withdrawal. We retreated to the Barrier Lift and made our stand there, at the foot of the cliffs. The fighting was fierce and merciless, but when it was over, the Immortal advance had been turned, and they retreated. However, Droghelda still stood, and the Eighth and Ninth were broken, a mere remnant had survived. The survivors returned to Saarland, and the eastern frontier has been relatively quiet ever since," Antony explained.

"What did Max do after I disappeared?" Morgan asked quietly.

"As soon as he could, he went to look for you. He'd heard reports of the fate of Imperius' Legions, but refused to believe you were dead. He booked passage on a freighter from Androssar to

Lothar, figuring that was the fastest way to reach the Mhoul capital. He chartered a small frigate at Lothar, but the ship was attacked by buccaneers in the Kuulian archipelago. He killed half of the pirates before they took the ship, but they finally captured him," Antony said.

"They managed to take him alive?" Morgan asked.

"Yes. Evidently the Kuulian buccaneers are nearly as vicious as your friend Max," Antony replied.

"What did they do with him?" Morgan asked.

"When they realized who he was, Commander of the famed Eighth Legion and all, they decided to hold him for ransom. They locked him in a tower at one of their secret bases, but before the buccaneer Captain could even convey his ransom demand, his ship sank in a skirmish with a Zarxien privateer. No one else knew where Max was being held, and he languished there for three years, in a small, dark cell. He finally escaped his cell, and slaughtered most of his guards before they begged for a truce. The survivors pledged themselves to Max and, nearly five years after he left, he sailed into Androssar in a Kuulian corsair.

After all the years that had passed, he lost hope of ever finding you, and by the time he'd returned, the Raavs had been decommissioned and disbanded. Imperius and the lost Legions never returned, only scattered survivors had been found, and most of those were insane, driven mad by something at Mogda Thal. The ex-Raavs scattered, finding employment where they could, selling their skills. I returned to Saxhaven, to be Llorgau's Ambassador. Max came here too," Antony said.

Morgan leaned forward. "Is he still alive?" he asked.

"Yes, Maximilian, Le Morte Kahn, the Lord of Death, has held his namesake at bay. He's guarding the few caravans that still ply the road between Saxhaven and Androssar," Antony said.

"I owe him an apology, for all I put him through," Morgan said.

"He generally avoids Saxhaven, and gets his supplies at Helmsdale. He knows he wouldn't be safe here," Antony said.

"Where is he now?" Morgan asked.

"First, we need to prepare for our audience with Llorgau. If

29

that doesn't go well, you may have to leave in a hurry. I'd prefer you to ride out slowly and with proper dignity, not like a criminal," Antony said.

CHAPTER THREE
LLORGAU

Palace guards ushered Morgan into Llorgau's study early the next morning. The room was dimly lit, and a fire crackled on the hearth. Heavy curtains covered the windows, and the firelight played across the Sagamore's beloved books, now dusty tomes that lined the walls. Llorgau had been a scholar as well as a warrior, and he sought knowledge, whenever the duties of state allowed. The other furniture in the chamber consisted of a large writing desk, a globe of the planet Kalnaroag, and a table and chairs. Hangings and maps covered the stone walls, and a thick rug lay over the floor tiles. A figure sat facing away from the door, huddled in a padded chair near the fire, a blanket pulled tightly under his chin.

"Morgan. Is it really you?" Llorgau asked, his voice so thin and weak Morgan barely recognized it.

"Yes, Sagamore," Morgan responded.

Llorgau let the blanket drop slightly and gestured. "Come around here where I can see you," he ordered.

Morgan walked to the fireside, the heat of the fire making him sweat.

Llorgau leaned forward, peering at him in the shadows. "You seem little changed after all this time. Although you wear a monk's cloak. Have you become a religious man?" he asked.

"I have considered it, Sagamore," Morgan said softly.

"Your Iosian brethren forced me to send them away. I regret that," Llorgau said, then looked closer at Morgan. "What happened to your hand?"

Morgan looked down at his bandages. "I got too close to something I shouldn't have," he said.

Llorgau frowned and sagged back in his chair. "You talk in riddles, like everyone else around here. You used to be more blunt, Morgan," he said.

Morgan stared at Llorgau. Despite Antony's warning, the Sagamore's appearance shocked him. Morgan remembered Llorgau as a great bear of a man, with wild, shaggy locks and a full beard. He used to have a powerful, vital presence, a born leader of men. He had always been full of energy, seldom resting, ever active.

The man that sat before him now was but a withered husk of the Llorgau he had known. The Sagamore had lost most of his hair and beard, only a few scattered wisps remained. His face was thin and drawn, and dark circles rimmed his bloodshot eyes. The hand and arm that lay above the blanket looked like bones wrapped in skin. Despite the heat, Llorgau trembled slightly, as if chilled.

Llorgau met Morgan's gaze, then dropped his eyes. "I know. I've changed since you last saw me. I've not been . . . well," he said.

Uncomfortable in the stifling heat, Morgan slipped out of his cloak, and laid it on the windowsill. The fact that he had been summoned to the Sagamore's study and not the throne room was a good sign, as was the fact that they met alone. Perhaps he could help his old friend. He was determined to try.

"I heard about Llewelyn. I grieve with you," Morgan said gently.

Llorgau sighed, a desolate sound. "They killed her, Morgan. She died in my arms," he said in a broken voice.

"Who killed her?" Morgan pressed.

"I don't know," Llorgau said. "She was poisoned, but I could find no clues, no real suspects."

Llorgau paused, remembering. "Llewelyn liked you, Morgan. You saved her husband's life, and his city. If you and Maximilian hadn't brought your Legions in time, the Targ would have swept over us like a wave. Those vicious savages and their trained rock apes overwhelmed my troops, we couldn't stand against them," he said.

"Without you to lead them, Saxhaven would've fallen before we got here," Morgan said.

"Sometimes I hear the rock apes howling in the night," Llorgau said, then fell silent, alone with his memories. Morgan waited quietly.

"Your Legions closed on them from the rear, and then we fought side by side. We finally drove them back to their mountains, after you killed their leader.

Llewelyn was so grateful. She wanted you to marry our daughter Maelin at the victory feast, but you refused. Those were good times. Family and friends, the joy of battle, my books. All gone now," Llorgau said sadly.

"What happened, Llorgau? What's brought you to this? Your people hungry and desperate, the fields not planted, squatters living at your doorstep, the city guards slovenly and ill-disciplined, abusing the citizens, all the old retainers gone. You've even changed your colors, I didn't recognize the banners flying from your keep," Morgan said.

"My wife was murdered. My daughter's left me, went to Carnac to study. I changed my colors the day Llewelyn died. All my old allies began to plot against me, and I had to exile them or have them executed. Androssar tries to starve us, cutting off trade, and bandits harry the few caravans. The people have grown fat and lazy, and refuse to work or pay their taxes.

And I'm always so tired, and cold. It's hard to even get up in the morning, although I don't sleep. The nightmares keep me awake," Llorgau said.

Morgan realized something else was missing from the room. "Where's Brutus?" he asked.

Llorgau gazed sadly at the hearth, where the Sagamore's dog used to lay, warming himself. "I sent him with Maelin, Malissa didn't care for him," he said. "She prefers cats."

Morgan squatted down, looking into Llorgau's face. "And what of Malissa?" he asked.

Joy and pain washed over the Sagamore's face. "She's all I have left. She is my life now. She's the only one I can trust," Llorgau said.

"Are you sure, Llorgau? Do you truly know her?" Morgan insisted.

The Sagamore raised his eyes briefly, and then looked away. "At times, I wonder. Part of me fears her. She makes me feel so strange- -a rapture that always turns to greater hunger. I've never known anyone like her," Llorgau said.

"You wanted me to speak plainly. Please hear me, Sagamore. Malissa is evil. She's killing you, draining away your life little by little. She also kills your city and your people. Let me help you," Morgan pleaded.

"Even if that were true, it's too late. I can't live without her.

33

And she cares for me, needs me," Llorgau said, his eyes haunted.

Morgan laid his hand on Llorgau's emaciated arm. "She feeds on your life, like a parasite. That's why you're so weak, so thin, so tired. You're not sick. It's Malissa that's doing this to you," he said.

Llorgau stood up, brushing aside Morgan's touch, the blanket falling to the floor. For a moment, his old power flared. "No. Do not slander Malissa. Whatever she is, she's a part of my life now. I will not give her up," the Sagamore said.

Morgan rose to his feet. Llorgau still towered over him, in spite of his stooped shoulders. "Even if you die? Even if evil rules your city? Even if Malissa leads you into war with Androssar? Cast her out! Free yourself, and Antony and I will help you. We can bring back the good times," Morgan urged.

Llorgau's face softened slightly. "Forgive me, old friend. I know you mean well. But the old days are gone, never to be recovered. We'd be fools to long for them overmuch. And it's too late for me, I'm lost already. I'll do what I must to keep her," he said, then took a deep breath. "I have an audience to conduct. Wait for me in the throne room."

Morgan picked up his cloak and walked toward the door. Llorgau's eyes brushed past the cloak. "Morgan," he said.

Morgan turned at the door. "Yes?" he asked.

"Will you pray for me?" Llorgau asked.

"I'll pray for you, Sagamore," he said softly.

Morgan stepped into the throne room---a long chamber, lined with heavy columns, the large stained glass windows near the ceiling aglow with the morning sun. A throne sat at the far end, on a raised dais with steps, and an aisle led to the throne, colored tiles marking the path. The sunlight cast shadows across the ancient stones, and glistened from the armor of the palace guards standing by the columns. The room echoed hollowly as Morgan walked toward the dais. Two groups of figures clustered silently near the throne, hatred crackling between them.

To Morgan's left stood Malissa, her cold beauty hidden beneath cloak and hood, her dark eyes flashing through the mask. Even robed, she avoided the shafts of sunlight in the room. To his annoyance, Morgan found that he was disappointed she had covered herself. A deep part of him longed for those alluring white curves, and that icy, thrilling touch.

Morgan forced himself to study Malissa's companions. He knew Secondus the chamberlain, and the other two looked familiar, by their trappings the General of the Army and the Captain of the Guard. One of the ugly cats squatted near Malissa.

Morgan joined the other group, which consisted of Antony and two of his female bodyguards. The women warriors watched everyone carefully, hands near their weapons. Antony wore his usual elegant finery, topped off with a scarlet cape.

"Greetings, Morgan," Antony whispered. "How was your private audience?"

Morgan grimaced. "It's worse than I thought. He doesn't even care what happens. All he wants is her," he said.

Antony gazed at Malissa, who turned away to speak with the general. "Mankind has a perverse tendency toward self-destruction and some forms of evil call to us most powerfully, against all reason. I know how he feels," Antony said.

Morgan sighed. "That's the worst of it. I can't say I would be any different, in Llorgau's place. We're a wretched species," he said.

Antony looked at Morgan and smiled. "Save for the grace of Iosus, Yfel would triumph, and we'd all drown in our own sins," he said.

Morgan nodded, and then indicated the two soldiers with Malissa. "Who're the new general and captain?" he asked.

Antony bowed with a flourish, raising his voice. "Morgan, let me present General Trang and Captain Borak," he announced.

Trang and Borak glared at Antony, and Morgan watched them while Antony continued. "You remember the former Colonel Trang, who Llorgau exiled to the frontier garrison at Malakal Pass. Seems he had some personal preferences unacceptable in polite society. Too good a soldier to court martial, he was merely hidden away in the mountains. At Malissa's request, Llorgau returned him to Saxhaven and gave him Dachar's position.

Borak lay in the dungeon, suspected of treason against the Crown, until Malissa had him pardoned and made Captain of the City Guard," he explained.

Trang glowered at Antony. "If you weren't such a coward, always hiding behind that maimed giant, and your women, I'd call you out and kill you," he said.

Antony smiled grimly, smoothing his mustaches. "I'd welcome a fair fight, General. However, I've no desire to sprout an arrow in my back while I fence with you. A pity. We'll have to get our satisfaction elsewhere," he said.

Trang started to step forward, but Malissa touched his arm. He stopped and gazed down at her. The look on his face told Morgan he'd already been with her. Borak also bore the mark of her touch. Two more slaves to her wicked charms.

The arrival of Llorgau interrupted any further conversation. The guards at the Sagamore's entryway stiffened, and Secondus hurried to announce him. Llorgau brushed past the chamberlain, climbed the dais steps, and sat heavily on the throne. He wore formal robes of state, and bore the crown and sword of the Sagamore of Saxhaven. Morgan could still see glimmers of the past glory, faded and tainted now.

Malissa glided over to Llorgau and knelt at his feet, one white hand stroking his bare leg above the boot. Llorgau trembled slightly at the touch, his eyes clouding, as his breathing deepened. He looked down at her, momentarily forgetting all else.

Antony coughed politely, and Llorgau reluctantly turned from Malissa. "My Sagamore, you summoned us?" Antony asked.

The Sagamore stole one last longing glance at Malissa, then faced Antony and Morgan, his features set and tense. "We have serious charges to consider. Morgan, step forward," he ordered.

Morgan moved to the foot of the throne, and Llorgau continued. "You've been accused of espionage and possible conspiracy against the throne. What do you have to say for yourself?" he asked.

"May I ask who my accusers are?" Morgan asked.

Llorgau looked at Malissa again. "That's not important. However, if you must know, Malissa supplied the information," he admitted.

"What information?" Morgan pressed.

Malissa spoke, her voice a deadly purr. "Loyal citizens came to me, revealing your meetings with known conspirators, and your plots against my Sagamore," she said.

"Known conspirators?" Morgan asked.

Malissa smiled, her teeth flashing in the hood. She continued to stroke Llorgau's flesh, spreading her poison. "The man Harkon, and a member of the City Guard, a Corporal Taskin. They spy for Rulda of Androssar and seek Llorgau's life. Can you deny you met with them?" she asked.

Morgan looked at Antony, who shrugged. "I met with Harkon, who plots no evil. His brother Argyle was my old friend. We served together in the Raavs. Taskin arrested me for assaulting his Sergeant," Morgan said.

Borak spoke. "This man tried to start a riot in the plaza, speaking against you, and he admits he assaulted an officer," he said.

"He's a veteran warrior, a former Raav Commander. Who better to spy out our defenses, to betray us to Androssar?" Trang added.

"And he comes disguised as an Iosian monk. The first place he went was the old temple. The Iosians are known traitors. What more do we need?" Malissa asked.

Llorgau studied Morgan. "Is that why you came back, after all this time? To betray me?" he said, then sat back in his throne, looking weary and alone. "I shouldn't be surprised. All the others have turned against me. I even have my doubts about Lord Antony here."

Antony joined Morgan. "You know neither Morgan nor I would ever betray you. I've served you loyally since my return, and you owe your life and your city to Morgan," he said.

Morgan stopped Antony with a touch. He met Llorgau's eyes. "You know me, Llorgau. Would I do these things?" he asked.

The Sagamore of Saxhaven sat silently, regarding his old friend, and then suddenly withdrew his leg from Malissa's touch, startling her. He smoothed his robes, covering his bare skin, while Malissa

37

drew back, stiff with rage.

Finally, he spoke. "I can't believe it, knowing you as I do. And yet Malissa has no reason to speak falsely. Treason and espionage are punishable by death. I can't ignore these serious charges, but Saxhaven owes you a debt, Morgan. Therefore, I pronounce you exile. Leave this city by sundown, never to return. Should you violate this decree, your life is forfeit," he said.

The Sagamore turned to Antony. "You have served me well, but in these days I can trust no one completely. I'll be watching you, Lord Antony. If I ever find reason to brand you traitor, my judgment will be swift. Never forget that," he said.

Llorgau stood. "This audience is concluded. Malissa, attend me," he commanded.

The Sagamore descended the dais steps. Malissa clutched his arm possessively, looking back over her shoulder at Morgan and Antony, her face promising ill. The cat skulked in her wake.

Morgan and Antony sat on their horses, just outside the city gates. Morgan wore his monk's cloak, and had strapped his pack and staff to the saddle. Antony's bodyguard exchanged taunts with the guards at the gate. The sun hung near the western horizon.

"Well, what now?" Antony asked.

"I want to see Max. After that, I have something I must do," Morgan said.

"While you were gone, did you miss any of the old life, your friends?" Antony asked.

Morgan shook his head sadly. "I'm not worthy of my old friends. Like Llorgau, I'm not the man I once was," he said.

Antony smiled. "As before, you fight yourself hardest of all. I still see the man I knew," he said.

Morgan said nothing, only gazed across the valley. The shadows lengthened.

"You better go. It's almost sundown," Antony said.

Morgan gripped his friend's hand. "Thanks for the horse, and everything else. It was good to see you again," he said, then paused. "I did miss you. I'm glad I could come back."

Antony gazed down the valley. "I wish I could go with you. But I'm needed here," he said.

"I know. Find a cure for Llorgau, and do what you can for Harkon and Taskin. They're good men," Morgan said.

"I will. There's something of Llorgau left in that shell. He knew exactly what he was doing when he exiled you. He had to get you away from Malissa, send you beyond her reach. He couldn't free himself, so he saved you instead. He also knew enough to agree when I suggested sending Maelin off to Carnac, and to take Brutus with her. Maelin and Llorgau fought terribly after Malissa arrived, and Malissa saw her as a threat. It was just a matter of time before Malissa took some action, and both Llorgau and I feared for Maelin's safety.

Maelin planned to ask the centaurs at Carnac about Malissa and her father's condition. There has to be an antidote to Malissa's spell, and if anyone can find a cure, it'll be the equisapiens. If all else fails, I'll kill Malissa and pray that Llorgau survives the withdrawal," Antony said, then paused. "You should see Maelin now. She's grown into a beautiful woman, not the little girl you almost married."

Morgan smiled. "Nothing stays the same, does it? Those days don't seem so far away," he said, then paused. "She was always fond of you."

"Maelin?" Antony asked. "A childhood fantasy, that's all."

"As you point out, she's not a child anymore," Morgan said.

Antony sighed. "No, she's not. And I sent her away. I'll probably never see her again," he said.

The two men sat silently for a time, while the far hills swallowed half of the sun.

"Give my greeting to Max when you see him. I miss his ready wit and sharp tongue," Antony said. "Although I was never completely comfortable around him. He had a dark side that disturbed me. He could be absolutely merciless, destroying life without thought or remorse. If I didn't know better, I'd say he lacked a soul."

Morgan smiled grimly. "He has a soul. He proved that when he traveled half a continent in search of a lost friend. I'll give him your greeting, although I don't think I'll tell him the rest," he said.

Antony nodded. "That would be wise. And more healthy for me," he remarked.

"Farewell, Antony. I'll return some day. Watch your back," Morgan said.

"Always. Iosus be with you," Antony returned.

Morgan nudged his horse into a trot, and soon its hooves clattered on the ancient stones of the road to Androssar, also known as the Khundlu Mata, the Passage of the Sagamores.

Antony turned his horse, and gazed at his city, reddish in the light of the dying day.

CHAPTER FOUR

MAXIMILIAN

A figure knelt by the small fire, a thin man, with long tangled hair and a beard, drinking from a soiled cup. He needed a bath, and his clothes were old and patched, his boots worn. A saber and knife hung from his belt. He shivered in the chill night air, and moved closer to the fire, spreading a rough, callused hand over the flames. The remains of the evening meal surrounded the fire, and a large black pot still rested on the coals. A small pile of firewood lay nearby.

They had built their fire in a clearing in the oaks, on a ridge above the road to Androssar. A breeze stirred the trees' branches, rattling them like bones, and the small clusters of new leaves glistened wetly in the firelight. Other men lay scattered through the trees, huddled in cloaks and blankets, with horses tethered near the men, their saddles beside them. A single battered tent had been pitched at the edge of the clearing. A ring of guards surrounded the camp, standing quietly in the trees, listening for any sound other than the wind.

The rising moon cast spidery shadows across the clearing, and the arch across the sky glowed coldly in the moonlight, a river of silver flowing through the brilliant stars. In the valley below, on the far side of the road, other fires burned. The firelight illuminated the heavy wagons resting there, drawn into a defensive circle. Dark figures moved amongst the wagons.

The man at the fire emptied the mug, and tossed it down beside the fire. A shadow moved over the grass, and he turned, thinking it was one of the sleepers, risen to warm himself by the fire. What he saw made him leap to his feet with a curse, and he clawed for his sword.

A tall stranger in a monk's cloak stood before him, silent in the moonlight. The newcomer's hood was up, his face hidden. The man with the sword, seeing the stranger alone and apparently unarmed, relaxed somewhat. He lowered his sword and uttered a hissing call. The monk did not move or speak, but stood with arms folded, hands

41

deep in the flowing sleeves of the cloak.

In response to the call, the flap of the tent folded back, and another man emerged---tall and thin, with rugged features and deep set eyes. He carried a drawn sword, studying the scene before him.

"Colm, check on the sentries," he said, his voice coarse.

Colm nodded and moved into the trees, glancing back over his shoulder at the stranger. The man from the tent stepped closer to the monk and gestured toward the trees with his sword point.

"You alone?" he asked.

"Yes. I mean you no harm," the monk said. "I merely wish to warn you."

The man with the sword looked around, his eyes narrowing. "Warn me?" he asked.

"Of your death, if you don't leave here immediately," the monk said.

The other man walked to the monk, and laid his sword point on the monk's chest. "Should I fear you, all alone in the night?" he demanded.

As if in answer to his question, Colm returned, giving the monk a wide berth. "Watch him, Malek," Colm warned. "He knocked out two of the guards. They're alive, but still down."

Several other men joined them, roused from sleep by the sound of voices. They had their swords out, and muttered questions to each other. Malek ignored the others, flipping back the monk's hood with his sword. The monk did not flinch, his strange gray eyes boring into Malek's.

"Who are you?" Malek asked, his voice tense.

"I am what I appear to be. Don't fear me; fear the man who guards the caravan below. The one you intend to attack later tonight," the monk said calmly.

Malek peered at the man's face in the moonlight. "I don't think you're a monk. You don't look like a monk, and no monk could get past my guards. I ask you one last time, who are you? And how do you know our plans?" he asked.

"Who I am is not important. As to your plans, your intent is obvious," the monk retorted.

42

Malek slapped his sword against the monk's chest in annoyance. "All right, it doesn't make any difference who you are, since I'm going to kill you. Who guards the caravan?" he asked.

"Ever heard of Maximilian, also called Le Morte Kahn?" the monk asked.

Malek frowned. "Sounds familiar. Should I know it?" he asked.

The monk cocked his head, curious. "You're not from around here, are you?" he asked.

"No, we're hillmen, from the north," Malek said.

The monk nodded. "Ah, that explains much. You do know of the Raavs?" he asked.

"Yes, but they were disbanded years ago," Malek said suspiciously.

"Maximilian was a Commander in the Raavs," the monk explained.

The hillmen exchanged nervous glances. They knew of Raav mercenaries and their famed Commanders.

"So what?" Malek growled. "For a man with little time left, you sure waste it."

"You know of the trollwars, also called the Crusade, when Imperius led the Raavs against Mogda Thal? Of the destruction of the troll fortress at Tchoga?" the monk continued.

Malek stepped back, his sword point drooping. "Everyone knows about that. It's legend in the entire west," he admitted.

"Maximilian and his Legion helped take the fortress. He killed the trollmother. He was also at the siege of Saxhaven, when the Targ came down," the monk said.

Malek's mouth dropped open, and then he closed it with a snap. Some of the other men backed away, looking around in fear.

"That Maximilian!? The one the Targs called the Dark Slayer?" someone exclaimed.

The monk nodded. "Yes, that Maximilian. That's who guards the caravan down there," he said.

"He and that brute Morgan killed hundreds of Targ when they came with their Raavs. Drove them away from Saxhaven, back up into the mountains. I heard that Morgan killed the Targ chief with his bare hands, broke his neck," Malek said, remembering the stories.

"Still want to proceed with your raid?" the monk asked.

Malek glanced toward the fires of the caravan below. "You're mad. Why would Maximilian waste his time herding some caravan? He's off leading an army somewhere," he protested.

The monk shrugged. "I warned you. If you attack that caravan, you'll all die," he said.

Colm snorted. "We're forty to their twenty. Who cares who leads them? We're hungry, and they carry food and gold to some noble in a castle," he said.

Malek turned on him. "You fool. Haven't you been listening? If Maximilian is down there, he could kill us all himself," he snapped.

"It's up to you. Ride away now or die. I'm telling you the truth," the monk said firmly.

Malek studied the monk's face and his piercing eyes, then sheathed his sword. "Strike camp! We ride!" Malek ordered.

The hillmen ran to obey, but Colm remained. "What about the caravan? Are you going to run away, on this madman's word?" he demanded.

Malek locked eyes with Colm. "Whatever's in that caravan, is it worth all our lives? I say no. We're leaving. Now!" he said.

Colm stalked off, shaking his head. Malek's tent collapsed, and men hastily stuffed it into a pack saddle, then they soon dismantled the rest of the camp. Someone brought Malek his horse.

As he mounted, the monk spoke again. "You seem to be honorable men. Why are you here, raiding caravans?" the monk asked.

Malek looked down at him. "The Targ are on the move again. They drove us from our homes, burned our villages, killed our women and children, and then hunted the survivors with their trained apes. We fled the hills, and now we do what we must to survive," he said bitterly.

"I'm sorry for your loss. But this isn't the way," the monk said.

Malek sighed. "I know. We're ill-suited to this cowardly thievery. We'll have to try something else," he said.

"Your men seem well trained. You could sell your fighting

44

skills. Many of the towns and cities are hiring guards, in this time of unrest," the monk suggested.

"Perhaps. Thank you for the warning," Malek said as he turned his horse away.

His men mounted their horses, leaving only the fire and the trash. Malek stopped, looking back at the monk.

"You never did tell me your name," he called.

The monk raised his hood. "My name is Morgan," he said.

Malek peered at his face in the dimness. "Morgan? Morgan Caeda?" he asked.

Morgan sighed. "Yes, that brute Morgan," he said.

Malek's eyes widened. "I picked a fine place to begin my career as a brigand. This valley is riddled with walking legends," he said.

He spurred his horse violently, and the startled animal leaped ahead, galloping through the trees. Malek's men hastened to follow, and the sound of running horses soon faded into the night.

"Iosus be with you," Morgan called after them.

A ring of shadowy figures crept through the night, closing in on the abandoned camp. Morgan sat by the fire. He had tossed the rest of the wood on it, and the flames crackled, rising high in the darkness. Morgan held his hands toward the fire, easing the chill. The staff lay across his lap and he had his hood drawn close about his features. His pack lay behind him, and he had tied his horse at the edge of the clearing.

Asa, the first moon, moved across the stars, and the second moon, Mora, brightened the dark horizon to the north, highlighting the jagged line of peaks. The approaching men kept to the shadows, moving silently, but when they came within sight of the empty clearing, one of them raised a hand. The other men stopped, and their leader dropped his hand, stepping into the moonlit meadow. The rest waited, motionless and poised.

The man walked across the clearing, approaching Morgan from the rear. He moved with effortless grace, and made no sound, floating over the ground like a predatory animal. He stopped behind the monk, just out of reach, studying the campsite.

45

The monk spoke. "Hello, Max. What took you so long?" he asked.

The other man circled Morgan, moving around to face him. The fire crackled between them.

"Stand and show yourself," Max said.

Morgan set aside the staff, rose to his feet, and eased back the hood. The firelight played across his features, and Max stepped forward, looking up at the taller man.

"You're dead. But I don't believe in ghosts," Max said, then paused and looked closer. "You look older."

Morgan laughed. "I feel older. But, then again, I'm not the one sneaking up on an empty camp. Forty men fled on horseback, and you weren't even aware of it. Perhaps we're both slowing a bit," he said.

Max shook his head. "You are Morgan. No one else talks to me like that. For your information, we came up here to see why they had fled," he said.

Max signaled his men, and they entered the clearing, gathering near the fire. They stared at Morgan.

Max waved a hand at Morgan. "Meet my old friend, Morgan Caeda. Back from the dead," he said.

The men with Max shuffled and muttered, drawing back a step, watching Morgan closely. They had obviously heard of him.

Max kicked a piece of trash into the fire. "Where did the bandits go? Did you run them off all by yourself?" he asked.

Morgan shrugged. "I told them who was guarding the caravan. That's all it took," he said.

Max kicked at the fire again. "This was the first action we've seen in a long time. And now you've ruined it. They must have been strangers. None of the locals will come anywhere near my caravans," he complained.

Morgan nodded. "They were hillmen, driven down by the Targs. They seemed honorable men, reduced to desperate means," he said.

"Honorable men, you say? Then it's just as well I didn't have to kill them," Max said sarcastically, then paused, brightening. "The

46

Targs? Are they campaigning again?"

"Not really campaigning, just stirring about, restless," Morgan said.

Max stared into the fire, his eyes distant. "Now that was a battle, when we saved Saxhaven from the Targ," he said, and then looked into Morgan's eyes. "A long time ago, and different men. Come on down to the camp, old friend. You owe me an explanation."

Morgan crouched on a low stool near the fire, drinking a mug of warm sasich. Morgan's cloak lay across a cask beside him, along with his pack and staff. Max stood on the other side of the fire, holding a bottle of stout liquor. Around them the caravan slept, save for the sentries. Max's soldiers lay on the ground under the stars, while the merchants and drivers slept in the wagons. The heavy, boxlike wagons sat in a circle, with the horses in a roped off area to one side. All three moons chased each other across the sky, and the night held no sound, save for the crackling of the fire and the sighing of the wind.

Morgan studied his old friend. A head shorter than Morgan, lean and supple, Max had black hair and a closely trimmed goatee that contrasted sharply with his pale skin. Handsome in a classical sense, his eyes lent a coldness to his face---dead eyes, like pale blue holes in a mask. Few could look into Max's eyes and not know fear.

The most striking thing about Max was the way he moved. Inhumanly graceful and fluid in his actions, incredibly fast, his lean muscles deceptively powerful, he reminded Morgan of a mountain panther stalking its prey.

Max wore dark clothing, as usual, and carried two short swords. He undoubtedly carried other hidden weapons. Morgan had never known him to be unarmed. He seemed little changed by the twelve years since Morgan had last seen him, a new scar or two, but otherwise the man Morgan remembered.

Morgan glanced at the wagons. "What're they carrying?" he asked.

"Mostly food and supplies. Evidently Saxhaven hasn't bothered to do any farming the last couple of years. Some fat merchant out of Androssar figured he could make a profit on the starving people of Saxhaven. If the starving bandits don't steal it all first," Max said.

Max took a drink from his bottle, and exhaled, clearing away the choking fumes of the liquor. He waved his bottle at Morgan's mug.

"Still the moralist, I see. Only sasich, ales, and meads, or maybe a sip of wine. No strong drink. Spare the women, mercy to your enemies. Nobility and honor, " Max remarked, with a faint smile that did not reach his eyes.

Morgan sighed. "As before, I prefer other vices---pride, selfishness, impatience . . ." he began.

Max interrupted. "Excessive introspection, self-deprecation, brooding melancholy. Yes, I remember you well," he said.

"The name you gave me has remained. I'm still known as Morgan Caeda, the Killer, even after all these years," Morgan said.

"Well, nobody knew who your parents were. You needed something other than just Morgan," Max said.

"And now no one remembers your real name," Morgan said with a wicked grin.

"No one living," Max warned.

"Don't worry. I'll not reveal your terrible secret. At least until a more opportune time," Morgan said.

"Be careful. Even friendship has its limits," Max said.

Morgan sat silently, thinking back. Max watched him a while, then spoke.

"I went after you. And ended up spending three years locked in a tiny dark cell on some barren island," Max said, then looked up at the starlit sky and took a deep breath. "I still hate to be inside."

Morgan met Max's eyes. "I know. Antony told me. I owe you a great debt," he said.

"You at least owe me an explanation. Why didn't you come back? Or send some word that you were still alive?" Max asked, his voice flat.

Morgan stared into the flames. "I couldn't face any of you," he said.

Max took another drink, and corked the bottle. "I ran into Argyle in Saxhaven, after I got back. He said what happened at

48

Mogda Thal was so terrible he couldn't even remember it. Something had destroyed seven Legions of Raavs and left no sane man with any memory of it. He thought Imperius had been killed, and he also said you were dead," he said.

"I made him swear he would say that, when I left him in the boat," he said.

"Where did you go? You just vanished," Max asked.

"After the massacre, the first clear memory I have is floating down the Seir with Argyle. There were others in the boat, but they were mad, screaming and crying, raving about impossible, horrible things, things that couldn't be true. Somewhere upriver of Kalixalven, I steered the boat to shore and got out. I couldn't live with the nightmares. I wandered into the mountains to die," Morgan said.

"But you didn't die," Max said.

Morgan hesitated, and then spoke. "The Mons Monachus found me, and I've been with them ever since," he said.

Max stared at Morgan. "The mythical Monachus of Khulankor? You said you left the madmen behind."

"One of their patrols found me, a starving wretch, nearly frozen. They took me to the monastery, and nursed me back to health. I spent twelve years with them," Morgan said.

Max frowned. "You really believe that," he said.

"It happened," Morgan assured him.

Max walked over to the cask and examined Morgan's cloak. "Where did you get this?" he asked.

Morgan glanced over at the cloak. "A gift from Sebastian," he said.

"Who's Sebastian?" Max asked.

"A mentor, trainer, and friend. One of the Monachus," Morgan responded.

"Trainer in what?" Max asked. "Prayer?"

Morgan laughed. "No, not exactly. Sebastian was Master at Arms, and led the Saan, the monastery's defensive force," he said.

"Well, that's good to hear. I was afraid you'd gone pacifist on me. I don't think I could bear that," Max said, then picked up the staff. "I assume this serves some purpose other than a crutch."

"With one of those, Sebastian could hold his own against swords, axes, spears, almost anything," Morgan said.

Max put down the staff and folded his arms. "How about arrows, at three hundred paces?" he asked.

Morgan held a straight face. "Plucked them from the very air," he said.

Max stared at him, then snorted. "I see your sense of humor hasn't changed," he said.

"He also taught me some hand fighting techniques," Morgan added.

"In case you lost your crutch? You need a real weapon," Max said, then went to one of the wagons and returned with a wrapped object. He handed it to Morgan.

Morgan set the mug on the ground, and unwrapped the package, revealing a sword with a heavy, slightly curved blade, suitable for slashing or thrusting, and a cross bar carved as twin dragon heads, their bodies curling together to form the two-handed hilt. The large pommel weight balanced the heavy blade, with its long blood groove. Above the cross bar two words were inscribed into the blade---"Lex talionus." The weapon had been carefully cleaned and oiled, and appeared still serviceable, despite signs of heavy use.

Morgan set aside the wrappings, and stood. He felt the familiar weight and balance, and then moved through a series of thrusts and parries. The sword felt like a part of him, and he wielded it with powerful grace, the large blade moving as if nearly weightless.

Max watched with a critical eye. "Argyle gave it to me. I don't know why I kept it. For old times' sake, I guess. Lex talionus, the sword of Morgan Caeda," he said.

Morgan did not respond, but continued to slice the air with his old weapon. "I was always fascinated by your meat cleaver form of combat. No style, but nothing stood in your way," Max commented.

Morgan returned to the stool, and sadly rewrapped the sword. "I miss her, but she brings back too many bad memories," he said.

"Bad memories? Of us? The battles we fought together?" Max asked.

Morgan shook his head, as he handed the bundle back to Max.

50

"You don't understand. I was sick of all the violence, the bloodshed and the dying. I wanted to be free of it, so I swore an oath. To never again raise a sword against my fellow man. Thank you, but I can't accept. She's not a part of my life anymore," he said.

Max stared at Morgan. "You have changed. For the worse. I'll keep this for you. When you come to your senses, you can have it back. I just hope your foolhardy oath doesn't get somebody killed, like me," he said.

"I appreciate you taking care of her for me," Morgan said, then paused. "I also want to apologize for what I put you through. I should've let you know, somehow."

Max shrugged and laughed harshly. "What happened to me was my own fault," he said. "Forget it."

Max returned the sword to the wagon, then pulled a stool near the fire and sat down. Neither man spoke for a while.

"You said you came through Saxhaven. I hear the city has fallen on hard times," Max finally said.

"The city's a disaster, and Llorgau's a withered remnant of the old Sagamore, under the spell of a white witch. Llorgau exiled me, because of her. Antony hasn't changed much, still able to talk his way off the executioner's block," Morgan responded.

"That's what I've heard. Did you see Malissa?" Max asked.

Morgan shivered, not from the cold, and studied his bandaged hand. "I saw more of her than I should have. She's pure, poisonous evil," he said.

Max chuckled. "All women are evil. Best the night before a battle, and for a night or two after a hard field campaign. Exquisite vessels, delightful curves, as long as you don't drink too deeply of the wine within. I hear Malissa's quite the beauty," he said.

Morgan looked at Max, his eyes haunted.

Max blew out his breath. "Whew. She must be really something, to tempt you," he said.

"She's not human. She's Hedonae," Morgan said, then paused, staring into the fire. "At first I felt tired and drained, but now I feel stronger than ever. Strange."

"You always were attracted to the wrong kind of women," Max

51

commented.

"It wasn't like that at all," Morgan muttered.

"I only saw Malissa once, but I heard the stories, and decided that was another reason to stay out of town. Sounds like I made the right decision," Max said.

"Yes, you did," Morgan said, suddenly refocusing on Max. "Antony has a hard task before him. But for the grace of Iosus, Llorgau and Saxhaven are lost."

"Well, if anyone can save them, it's Antony. Court intrigue is Glossauric's specialty. He thrives on it," Max said.

"He asked me to convey his greetings," Morgan said.

Max smiled. "I've seen him once or twice in Helmsdale. We talked of old times, and shared some good memories." He suddenly frowned. "Were you followed? Did Malissa send anyone after you?"

Morgan shook his head. "I left Saxhaven at sundown, and got off the road as soon as I was out of sight of the city, then traveled through the oak groves. No one followed. I saw your fires and rode up on the ridge to study the camp. That's when I discovered the hillmen," he said.

Max fixed Morgan with an intent look. "Why did you come back?" he asked.

"I did miss my friends, even though I was trying to forget everything else," Morgan said.

Max waited a moment, but Morgan offered nothing further. "You didn't answer my question. Why'd you leave the monastery? Did you get thrown out?" Max asked.

Morgan lowered his eyes, gazing into the fire. "The Monachus wanted me to do something for them. Nothing you need to concern yourself with," he said.

Max stood up. "Look. It's late and I'm tired. Tell me what's going on!" he demanded.

After a long pause, Morgan spoke. "As you know, the Mons Monachus and the Mhoul are ancient enemies. The Mhoul are plotting something, and the Monachus asked me to find out what it was. To scout for them," he said.

"What's the plan?" Max asked.

Morgan frowned. "I only get information as I need it," he said.

"Closed orders? I always hated that. So you don't have a plan, what do you know?" Max asked.

"I'm supposed to go to Aquarquff. Then I'll find out more," Morgan said.

Max put his hands on his hips, and looked up at the silver arch. "I hear Taurus was hauling short runs out of Androssar, staying near the coast during the winter storms. He can take us to Aquarquff. We can reach Androssar in a few days of hard riding," he said.

Morgan stared at Max. "We?" he asked.

Max regarded him, like a simple child. "Have you been listening to yourself? You disappear for twelve years, and then come back, talking of legendary mountain fortresses and mysterious missions against the Mhoul. I think it more likely you've been locked in an asylum and just escaped. Why would you be any less crazed than the other survivors from Mogda Thal?

Look what happened last time I let you go off alone, and you were sane then. Besides, I'm dying of boredom. The bandits around here are all cowards, they won't fight me. If you're not insane, then here's an opportunity for adventure, with deadly enemies and no plan whatsoever. That at least doesn't sound boring," he said.

Morgan shook his head. "I can't ask you to join me. I don't know where I'm going, what I'm facing, what my chances are," he protested.

Max threw a piece of wood on the fire, and sparks shot up into the darkness. "You didn't ask me, but I'm going, unless you think you can stop me?" he asked.

Morgan stood up. "I won't try to stop you. You're my friend, and I can use your help. I didn't come here expecting to enlist you. I just wanted to see you, and thank you for coming after me," he said.

"Fine. We leave at first light," Max said, then glanced at Morgan's cloak and frowned. "Did you really become an Iosian monk?" he asked.

"I now follow Iosus the Maker," Morgan admitted.

Max shrugged. "You were always half religious, looking for some higher meaning in life. I hope it makes you happy," he said.

53

"It has," Morgan said. "You should try it."

"No thanks. I know what life is like. I just face it. I don't need religion," Max said, then turned and walked toward one of the wagons. "Sarx, wake up!"

A head poked out of the wagon. "What?" a man asked sleepily.

"You're in command. I quit. Make sure the wagons get safely to Saxhaven. If anything happens to them, you'll answer to me. Give my pay to Lord Antony," Max said as he turned toward a second wagon. Sarx stared after him, rubbing his eyes.

Max soon returned with a leather bundle, which he carefully opened, unrolling the supple material across a table. An amazing array of weapons nestled in the bundle's felt lined pouches, and Morgan joined Max, looking down at the deadly collection. Max unbuckled his sword belt and set it aside.

"Ordinary steel's fine for the local bandits, but when one faces the Mhoul, ebonite is best," Max stated firmly.

Morgan suppressed a smile as Max slid a sword from its pouch. Slim, tapered, and relatively short, the sword had been forged of some black metal that absorbed rather than reflected the firelight. The sword had a simple, yet sturdy basket hilt made of the same dark material. Max set the blade down and drew out its identical mate. He buckled on a new belt, and flicked the two blades through the night, enjoying their lethal feel.

Morgan watched the dark blades. Light yet nearly unbreakable, ebonite made a perfect metal for sword blades. Unfortunately, it was also nearly impossible to acquire an ebonite blade. An alloy developed by the Empire, before the Fall of Craig Phadrig, the secret of its making had been lost to all but a few. Even if one knew how to fashion the material, even fewer had access to the special forges required to work the metal. Max had paid a Sagamore's ransom for the blades, after searching for years.

Morgan turned his attention back to the arsenal on the table. He touched one of the weapons laying there, a long recurve bow, nearly as tall as Max, made of layers of some dark, lacquered wood.

"Stryker," Morgan whispered, the name bringing back a flood of memories. Max picking off enemies at impossible distances, firing

54

arrow after arrow with deadly precision, and driving shafts through armor, the knights crashing from their horses. Max killing trolls, or dropping gargoyles from the skies over a battle.

Max sheathed his blades, and checked Stryker's arrows, making sure the arrowheads were properly protected in the quiver. The sight of the weapons reminded Morgan of something else, and he went to his pack and pulled out a wrapped object. He gave it to Max.

"Something from Khulankor, in case I found you again," he explained.

Max unwrapped the object, finding a small dagger, in a dark sheath. Max drew it out of the sheath, staring at the black blade, and the crystal sphere that adorned the hilt. Inside the sphere a spark of light flickered, and grew brighter. Max looked at Morgan.

"The blade is ebonite, worked at the smithys of Khulankor. The globe is a form of Luminarae," Morgan said softly.

Max gazed in wonder at the weapon. "Luminarae?" he asked.

Morgan smiled. "The fire of God. One mote from a collection of beings that live in Khulankor. Sometimes the monks find these spheres and attach them to weapons or armor, as a sort of talisman," he said.

Max peered at the point of light in the sphere, tapping it, and the mote flared in response. "Is it alive?" he asked.

"Yes," answered Morgan.

"It's like an egg," Max said, then suddenly frowned. "The mother's not coming after it, I hope."

Morgan laughed. "It doesn't have a mother. It's . . . I can't explain it," he said.

Max shook his head. "I wouldn't believe it, if it wasn't looking back at me. Maybe you aren't crazy after all," he said.

"I told you the truth. You'll just have to trust me," Morgan said.

Max examined the blade. "It is ebonite. The Monachus have ebonite?" he asked.

"A little, and they have the forge to work it," Morgan said.

"Could they make swords?" Max wondered.

"If they had enough raw materials, although I never saw an

ebonite sword while I was there," Morgan said.

"It's priceless. They gave this to you?" Max asked.

"Sebastian did," Morgan said.

"And you're giving it to me?" Max asked.

"Yes, to match your swords," Morgan said.

Max replaced the dagger in its sheath and slipped the weapon into a hidden pocket under his left arm. He looked at Morgan. "A fine gift. Thank you," he said, and then paused. "I'm glad you're not dead."

"Good," Morgan said.

Max seemed suddenly uncomfortable, and turned away. "See you in the morning," he said as he gathered his weapons and returned to the wagon.

Morgan stayed by the fire, pulling a small book from his pack, and read for a while, his eyes following the fine print in the flickering firelight. He closed the book and stared at the symbols on its cover, remembering his last day with Sebastian at Khulankor

CHAPTER FIVE

KHULANKOR

Morgan and Sebastian were on a balcony overlooking a mountain valley. Morgan leaned against the balcony railing, gazing down. The sun's warmth and light cascaded down through the massive peaks. A chill spring breeze wafted over the two men, playing in the chimes above the balcony. Far below a stream wound its way through the white carpet that lingered in the valley, a silver thread glinting in the sun. Before long that stream would be a raging torrent, gorged by the melting snows. A few stunted trees dotted the valley, darker green against the blaze of the snowdrifts and the exposed patches of alpine heather. The first blossoms of the year flecked the heather with motes of color, purple and red. The brooding cliffs that formed the valley walls stood silent and remote, as if pondering the new life emerging at their feet.

Morgan closed his eyes, reaching out with his other senses. He could feel the warmth of the sun on his face, tempered by the cool breeze. He could hear the tinkling of the chimes, the distant chatter of the stream, and somewhere, the angry rumble of an avalanche or rockfall. The scent of sun-kissed stone touched his nostrils, mingled with the faint tang of incense from somewhere inside the monastery.

He raised his eyes to the mountain peaks, those incredible masses of rock and snow and ice. He shifted his gaze to the glaciers, broken titans that hung dying in the sun, their life bleeding away into the waterfalls at their feet. As always, he could not help but admire the awesome majesty of the mountains, as they thrust up into the cobalt of the sky, a dome split by a swath of silver. Gallinor, the Bridge of the Gods, the metallic arch seemed to blur at the edges, as if it were dissolving in the blue sea of sky. The entire scene reminded Morgan of a fantastic tapestry spread by some cyclopean artist, unreal in the hazy distance.

A movement caught his eye, and he spotted a herd of mountain goats stepping carefully across a talus slope, their white coats contrasting with the dark gray of the rocks. A shadow flitted past them, and Morgan squinted up at a circling eagle, its wingtips spread against the thin air.

Sebastian sat in a chair behind Morgan, his ever present staff leaning against the railing. Sebastian was a massive man, thick through the chest, with arms and legs like barrels. His huge shoulders merged into the heavy skull, leaving little room for a neck, and a thick beard covered most of his face, black as midnight. In fact, hair covered most of Sebastian, from the curly mop on his head to his bushy eyebrows and his shaggy body. Some thought the monks had merely grafted the brain of a man into the body of a mountain bear and called it Sebastian. His voice matched his body, large and striking.

Normally, someone so large would be slow moving, but Morgan knew better. As Master of Arms for Khulankor, Sebastian had learned to use his size to good advantage---every movement spare and calculated. A wizard with the staff, he could hold his own against any hand weapon. Besides the staff, Sebastian had developed expertise with the sword, knife, spear, pike, and bow. Morgan had been a fighting man all of his life, and he had never met a more skilled warrior than this monk. Except maybe one, a small dark man who had shared his childhood. A man he had left behind, years ago.

Sebastian possessed a heart as large as his body. When the Monachus had found Morgan, wandering half mad through the mountains, with winter coming on, they had brought him to the monastery at Khulankor, and Sebastian had personally taken over his care. The huge monk had tended to him daily, until his body had healed. Morgan's tormented mind took longer, but the love of the Monachus and the peace of the mountains eventually restored him. An occasional echo of pain in his eyes remained the only outward sign of his ordeal. Sebastian had then taken his former patient on as a pupil, teaching him many things.

A ball of light floated over Sebastian's right shoulder, the Luminarae that seldom left his presence. The sphere glowed dull red now, nearly quiescent, except for a rhythmic throbbing, like the beating of a small heart. The strange creatures fascinated Morgan, and while the older inhabitants of Khulankor had grown used to them, no one really understood their nature or their purposes.

Despite centuries of observation and study, the Luminarae remained as mysterious as the mountains that surrounded Khulankor.

Morgan had always loved the mountains, even as a boy in the foothills of Saarland, and the peaks around the monastery had been a balm to his tortured soul. He took long hikes, climbing high into the mountain passes, soaking in the majesty that surrounded him, and eventually such calculated splendor had led him to the Maker, called Iosus by the Mons Monachus. Iosus had filled a place in his life that nothing else could touch, and he realized that the awe inspiring grandeur of the mountains, the peace of the lonely peaks, the joy of life, and even the love shown him by Sebastian, were mere reflections of Iosus, the creatures bore the mark of the Maker.

Seeing that he had started the journey toward knowledge of the Maker, Sebastian had given him a small book, the Codex of Khulankor. Sebastian said that men from another world brought the original copy to Khulankor, the same who had introduced the monks' ancestors to the worship of Iosus. These men came from a planet called Terra, in the Sol system. An entire Order of monks had devoted themselves to reproducing the original Codex by hand, until now several hundred copies existed. Sebastian regarded the Codex as the autobiography of the Maker, the revelation of a personal God to his people. Morgan had read from the book daily, learning to treasure its words, and discovering many truths about the Maker in its pages.

Morgan had rekindled another love in these mountains. Countless books filled the libraries of Khulankor, from all countries and ages, and he spent long hours there, pouring over the endless words. Sebastian had already read most of the books, and they discussed their reading often.

Morgan had not neglected his body, while his mind and soul were healing and feeding. He trained almost daily with the Saan. Sebastian led the Saan, and he worked Morgan harder than most. The exercise kept him in good condition, which was satisfying to an active man like Morgan. Lately, a strange restlessness had intruded, but the continual practice of the fighting arts seemed to soothe him.

Morgan sighed. These last twelve years had been good, but

now he had to leave, to return to the world that had nearly destroyed him, mind, body, and soul.

"I hate the thought of leaving," Morgan said.

Sebastian smiled, his beard splitting to reveal rows of white teeth. "We've had some grand times, haven't we?" he said.

Morgan turned to face him, leaning on his elbows at the railing. "This has been paradise for me," Morgan said.

"Just the smallest glimpse of what Iosus has for us in the future," Sebastian said.

Morgan looked up at the white buildings of Khulankor, nestled in the craggy peaks. "A glimpse I will never forget. I've found true peace here," he said.

"The world below used you badly, and you experienced some horrible things. I can't imagine what you went through," Sebastian said.

"You should know. You listened to my ravings long enough," Morgan said.

"Your torment grieved me deeply, but Iosus has healed you. As for leaving, maybe now you understand our brothers the Insula, who would prefer to forget the world and linger here forever," Sebastian said.

"It's tempting, but I knew it couldn't last," Morgan said. "I guess I always knew."

"I wouldn't have asked you to return, if I didn't think it was necessary," Sebastian said.

"I know," Morgan said.

They were silent for a time, lost in their own thoughts, while the breeze toyed with the chimes hanging nearby, their tinkling music lending a magical quality to the scene. Finally, Morgan spoke.

"Now that I've decided to go, what can you tell me of my task?" Morgan asked.

"As I said before, we fear the Mhoul are planning some great evil, and we need more firsthand information. We need someone who knows the world below, who knows its ways and its people, and can defend himself from its dangers. You were the best choice for that role. You'll be our eyes and ears, to spy upon the Mhoul. We're

60

well aware how dangerous the enemy is, and we've taken precautions. One of your strongest weapons will be your mind. We'll plant information in your memory centers, and then set guards on it, so that not even the Mhoul can retrieve it. If you're captured, they'll want to question you, rather than kill you, and there'll be no answers to their questions. Does this make sense?" Sebastian asked.

Morgan nodded. "Yes, but I think my best defense is to avoid capture altogether," he said.

Sebastian laughed. "That is always the first line of defense," he agreed.

"How will I contact you?" Morgan asked.

"Direct communication, at least on any regular basis, would be too dangerous, for both of us. The Mhoul have methods of intercepting and tracing our transmissions. As you travel, pay your respects at the Iosian temples along the way. That's all I can say," Sebastian said, and then paused. "You'll be like a stone thrown into a pond. We'll watch where the ripples go, what rises to the surface in response, and act accordingly," Sebastian explained.

"When do I leave?" Morgan asked.

"Soon. First you'll undergo surgery to implant the necessary information," Sebastian said.

"How's that done?" Morgan asked.

"I'm not an expert in such things, but I understand that most memory is chemical. The surgeons will be placing some very special chemicals in your brain, liquid memory. The memories will be triggered by certain visual stimuli," Sebastian explained.

"Then what?" Morgan asked.

"After you've recovered from the implants, you'll sleep again, and we'll place you at your point of departure. You'll be provided with money and travel supplies," Sebastian said.

"So I'll never know the exact location of Khulankor. I was lost when I came here, and I'll be asleep when I leave," Morgan said.

"Yes. That's best for everyone. You'll have to trust us, Morgan, as you trust the unseen Iosus. We've planned your journey, and will take every measure possible for your success and safety. I wish I could tell you more," Sebastian said.

"I understand, and I do trust you," Morgan said.

"We'll miss you. I believe you've made Khulankor a better place," Sebastian said.

Morgan frowned. "I know of one who'll not miss me," he said.

Sebastian shook his head sadly. "Try to forgive Michael. He sees you as a threat, both to himself and the monastery. I don't know where the poor boy got such foolish notions. I suppose I should reprimand him, but he's been a model pupil in all other respects."

"No, don't do that. Then he'll hate me all the more. I just don't understand him," Morgan said. He paused, and then shifted uncomfortably.

"What's bothering you?" Sebastian asked.

"My oath. To not use a sword against men. Was that wrong?" Morgan asked.

"That's between you and Iosus. What do you think?" Sebastian asked.

"I don't know. I swore the oath before I knew I was going back. It seemed right at the time. I wanted to put the past behind me," Morgan said.

"Do you wish to be released from your oath?" Sebastian asked.

Morgan sighed. "No, what's right doesn't change. But I don't want to do anything to jeopardize my mission, and a sword would be useful," he said.

"Don't fret, boy. Trust in Iosus. He'll show you the way." Sebastian paused. "Although it's been my experience that we humans are more interested in oaths, and rules, and taboos than Iosus. His law is love and justice, anything beyond that is suspect," he said.

"Is it love to kill?" Morgan asked.

"Sometimes love requires us to kill, but more often it's justice. If a child is about to be killed by a rock ape, is it love to let it happen? If a murderer is brought to trial, is it love or justice to set him free, to kill again? Is it love or justice for us to let the Mhoul enslave the world? Your question has no simple answer," Sebastian said.

They were silent again, enjoying the warm sun. "I wonder

what's become of my old friends," Morgan said.

Sebastian shrugged. "Seek them out. They may be able to help you in your journey."

"I'll do that," Morgan said.

"Antony's in Saxhaven, and we have some disturbing reports from that city. Why don't you start there?" Sebastian said.

"Saxhaven," Morgan repeated, his eyes distant.

CHAPTER SIX
THE DEMENTED BOAR

The two men stood in the middle of one of Androssar's waterfront streets, studying the inn before them. Max had been in high spirits ever since they left the caravan; the prospect of another adventure with his old friend had given him new energy.

Max waved his arm. "There it is. The Demented Boar. Finest dining and atmosphere in Androssar. Not to mention a variety of elegant liquors for the discriminating palate," he said.

Morgan folded his arms and squinted up at the inn, a large, two-story structure fronted with ornate stonework. Narrow alleys separated it from a noisy brothel on one side and a weapons shop on the other. Several second story balconies with folding doors hung over the street, and two large windows flanked the main entrance, although boards covered the window to the right. The front door, a massive construction of wood and iron strapping, stood half open, and sounds of laughter and general revelry came from within, echoing in the narrow street. The smell of baking bread wafted from the inn, mixing with the odor of ocean and stone. A huge stuffed boar with bulging eyes and worn yellow tusks balanced precariously on a beam above the door, the light from the setting sun painting the boar's hide with a reddish hue. The sign bearing the inn's name hung below the beam, creaking to and fro in the sea breeze.

Morgan pointed at the giant swine. "Where'd that thing come from?" he asked.

Max rubbed his bearded chin thoughtfully. "As best I remember . . . Gunter, the innmaster, served as a royal huntsman for the House of Rulda, until an encounter with this magnificent specimen forced him into early retirement. The beast was mad and had attacked the Sagamore's son, but Gunter saved the boy's life, and in gratitude Rulda gave him a small fortune as a retirement pension. He used the money to buy this place, about three years ago. Most of the clientele are mercenaries, soldiers, and seamen, and it's Taurus' favorite. If he's in town, he'll be here. If he's not, someone will know where he is, " Max said.

Max led the way with Morgan trailing along, skeptically surveying the boarded window and nearby brothel. Once inside, the two men threaded their way through scattered tables and groups of diners, Max returning several shouts of greeting from acquaintances. Seeing a group of local seamen, Max stopped to inquire into Taurus' whereabouts, while Morgan went to a corner table and sat down with his back to the wall.

Morgan studied the dining room, his thoughts wandering momentarily. Harkon and Taskin had ridden into the caravan camp just as Morgan and Max were leaving. The two men bore a message from Antony, suggesting they ride together, at least as far as Androssar. Malissa had been in a black rage since Morgan escaped her, and she was searching for victims, so Antony had decided the only way to protect Harkon and Taskin was to send them out of the city.

In spite of the fear and tension in Saxhaven, and conflicts with his arrogant nephew Dason, Harkon was determined to enjoy his retirement, and did not want to leave. Only the serious threat of torture and death convinced him. Taskin, on the other hand, knew his days in the Guard were numbered and was sick of the abuses on the populace. Consequently, he was not hard to convince when contacted by Antony's agents.

As soon as the four reached Androssar, they had stabled the horses. Morgan left his pack and staff at the stable, and went to pay his respects at the local Iosian temple. He talked briefly with one of the monks, but if the Monachus had agents at the temple, no one approached him with any messages. When he returned, Harkon and Taskin had gone to contact friends and relatives, so Max and Morgan went to find news of Taurus.

Morgan turned his attention back to the room around him. Globes suspended from ornate stanchions dimly lit the large dining room, which was filled nearly to capacity by exactly the kind of crowd Max had predicted---a hard looking group, heartily drinking, cursing, and swapping stories. A scantily clad woman gyrated on a raised platform in the center of the room, dancing to the beat of an enthusiastic band clustered in a corner. Several drunken sailors leaned against the stage, and the dancer deftly avoided their groping arms. A riot of smells filled the inn---spices, liquor, leather, bread, fish, sweat, and the pungent smoke from the wood fired ovens.

Max soon joined Morgan at the table. "Taurus took a load of tanned hides north to Skorn. He should be back any day now," he said as he sat down.

"Good," Morgan said absently, still studying the other patrons of the inn.

Max banged his fist on the table, yelling for the innmaster. A tall, gaunt man with a bald head and bushy eyebrows appeared at the bar, and Max caught his attention. The innmaster took a pitcher and two mugs from a serving tray and limped over to their table. As he approached, Morgan noticed a long scar running diagonally across his face and a shortage of fingers on his right hand. The old man had paid dearly for his retirement.

"Greetings, you hired killer," growled the innkeeper.

"No killing yet this trip, you old robber," Max said as the man set the mugs and pitcher on the table.

Gunter glanced at Morgan, taking in the monk's cloak. "Strange company . . . you get religion?" he asked Max.

Max leaned forward and whispered. "This is the mad monk Morgan. Ever hear of him?" he asked.

Gunter frowned. "Is he dangerous?" he asked.

"No, he's turned pacifist," Max assured him.

Gunter saw the look on Morgan's face. "I think you're in danger," he said to Max.

"No, he's harmless enough," Max said, and then tapped his temple. "But he is slightly mad, so I'm escorting him on his pilgrimage."

Gunter raised his eyebrows skeptically and sighed. "Oh well, it's your business. Just don't start any brawls this time, Shiva injured my bouncer last week and I haven't been able to find a replacement," he said and then glanced at Morgan. "Well met, Father."

Morgan nodded to him as the old man turned and made his

way back through the crowd. Gunter sent a serving girl their way and Max ordered massive quantities of bread and stew, then he filled their mugs with the chilled ale.

"Do you know this Shiva?" Morgan asked.

Max frowned. "Local boy with a hard life. A former wrestler turned bad. Huge, ugly, all muscles and scars, nubbins for ears, and only a few teeth left. His nose has been broken so many times it looks like a lump of clay. These days he makes his living beating up people. I hear he has quite a reputation as a fighter," he said.

"Have you had any trouble with him?" Morgan asked.

"He's still alive," Max responded grimly.

Morgan nodded. "That answers my question."

The server soon returned with a kettle of stew and two bowls, and a plate of hot bread. As he ate, Morgan watched the room. A woman just entering the inn drew his attention. She stood for a moment in the shadows near the entrance; her hood pulled low, carefully looking over the crowd. Morgan peered at her in the dim light. A stained and dusty traveling cloak muffled her figure, and she wore equally scuffed and soiled boots. Despite its tears and blemishes, Morgan could tell the cloak was made of expensive cloth.

The woman walked quickly across the floor to a side table, and dropped into a chair against the far wall, keeping the hood up. She waved down a servant and was soon eating stew and bread. She had paid for the meal with coins from a belt pouch. Hampered by the hood, she finally brushed it back and Morgan got a look at her face. She was a beautiful woman with tanned skin, and long brown hair pulled back into a braid. She had slightly slanted eyes that gave her an exotic look, and a regal bearing, softened only slightly by her fatigue.

The woman paused in her eating and looked around the room. She spotted Morgan watching her and frowned, searching his face. Morgan found himself fascinated by her eyes. They studied each other a moment longer, and then the woman heard a noise at the door and glanced that way. What she saw there made her stiffen. Morgan followed her gaze to a pair of men that had just entered, hard looking men with cold eyes, who also bore evidence of several days'

67

travel. The newcomers discovered the woman almost immediately, but made no move toward her, merely stood waiting by the door. In the next few moments, seven more men came into the inn and positioned themselves about the room, covering all the exits. After her initial reaction, the woman resumed her meal, evidently too tired and hungry to even care about the others.

Max had noticed Morgan's preoccupation and was disturbed by the set of his companion's face. "You're getting that look again. Like you're about to intrude into other people's affairs," Max whispered between mouthfuls.

Morgan nodded toward the woman. "The men that just came in are chasing that woman. Have been for several days, by the looks of them," he replied without taking his eyes off the scene.

Max took a drink of ale and wiped his mouth on a sleeve. "Forget it," he advised. "She's probably from next door."

Morgan glared at him. "The brothel? That's ridiculous. Look at what she's wearing, how she carries herself. She's no prostitute," he said.

"It's none of our business. What about your great mission for the Mons Monachus? You don't have time to rescue strangers," Max said, waving a soggy piece of bread for emphasis.

The arrival of two more men interrupted further debate. The first, a huge man, wore an open vest and loose pants stuffed into the tops of his grimy boots. Aside from heavy leather wrist braces, he bore no arms or armor. The second man, short, fat, and bald, with piglike eyes and an arrogant manner, wore gaudy clothes and carried an ornate sword. The shorter man appeared to be the leader of those who hunted the woman.

Max's eyes grew hard as he stared at the second man, his meal forgotten. "I think you're right, my friend. This woman definitely needs rescuing," he said.

Morgan had also recognized the man and he smiled grimly. Both men rose quietly to their feet.

The fat man swaggered over to the woman's table, and squeezed into a chair, the woman staring at him with obvious hatred. Two of the other men moved in behind her, and the giant loomed over

68

them all. The leader of the hunters leaned forward and whispered earnestly, trying to convince the woman of something. She shook her head defiantly, then abruptly stood up, shouting for him to leave. Her strong voice cut through the noisy room, and people nearby became aware of the argument, some watching with interest. The innmaster noticed as well, leaning on the bar and biting his lip, fearing destruction of property.

The fat man sighed and motioned to his men, who stepped up to the woman, reaching for her arms. She did not wait for them, but drew two daggers and attacked. The man on her left staggered back, with his hands clamped around the dagger in his stomach. He sat down heavily on a table, staring at the blood oozing between his fingers, and then crumpled to the floor. His companions made no move to help him. The woman's right hand flashed toward their leader. He jerked back with a gasp, a bright line of red appearing across his throat. The fat man clutched at his neck and stood up, swearing enthusiastically. His double chin had saved his life, the dagger merely slicing through a layer of fat.

The remaining man at the woman's back overcame his shock and moved, grabbing and firmly pinning her arms. Seeing her helpless, the fat man reached out and struck her viciously across the face. The woman sagged with the force of the blow, the dagger slipping from her hand to clatter on the floor. A thin trickle of red beaded from her lips. Her attacker smiled and daubed at his throat with a silk cloth. He glanced down at the blood on his cloth and, angered at the sight, raised his hand to strike the woman a second time.

A voice came from behind him. "Don't touch her again."

He froze at the sound, his hand dropping. He did not turn around, but his piglike eyes shot questions to his hireling, who stood staring over the leader's shoulder.

The fat man swallowed and spoke. "Mind your own business. This matter doesn't concern you," he said roughly.

By now the clamor of the inn had died down as more and more diners became aware of the conflict. Gunter waved to the dancer and she left the stage, fending off the admiring seamen to disappear through the back door. The band smoothly folded up their gear and settled farther back into their corner. When the music and dancing stopped, most of the diners turned their attention to the new show.

"You better leave. The woman stays," the challenger responded firmly.

The stocky leader could not stand it any longer and whirled, to be confronted by a lone monk standing with folded arms and hood pulled forward, shadowing the man's face. The giant stepped up and towered over the newcomer, glancing uncertainly at his employer.

"What're you going to do, monk? Call down lightning from the sky or maybe just pray us to death?" the fat man scoffed.

The monk made no reply and he lost patience. "Leave us, before I have Shiva throw you out!"

He started to turn back to his captive, but the monk interrupted him quietly. "I warned you, Thugmonger Wald," he said, sliding back his hood.

At the sound of his name, Wald turned and stared peevishly at the monk's features, a puzzled look slowly giving way to growing fear. His eyes widened in horror as realization struck him.

"You?!" he cried. "I heard you were dead!"

The innkeeper craned his neck for a better look at the monk's features, and other diners stared at the monk, whispering comments. Max spoke from where he now leaned against the bar.

"He did die, Wald, and Iosus, with His strange sense of humor, sent him back as a monk," he said.

Wald whirled toward the speaker, and immediately recognized Max. With a curse, he leaped behind the giant and began yelling frantically to his men. One of Wald's men, a lean man with a drooping mustache and cruel eyes, stepped to his side and whispered hoarsely.

"What's the matter with you?" he said. "It's ten against two, and the monk's not even armed."

Wald grabbed his arm, not taking his eyes from Morgan and Max. "Double your money, Cull, if I get out of this inn alive," he said.

Cull stared down at his employer. "You're daft, man. Let's take the woman and get out of here," he said.

70

Wald signaled to the man holding the woman, who started edging toward the door, the half conscious captive swaying in his grip. Wald backed away, making sure he kept the giant between him and Morgan.

"We're leaving now. Don't make me hurt the woman," Wald threatened.

Cull matched Wald's pace, sliding his sword clear of its sheath, while the giant leaned forward, spreading his arms wide to block any pursuit. Anticipating trouble, the seasoned crowd melted away from the immediate area, and the more timid patrons quietly slipped out the door.

Morgan rested a hand on a heavy chair. "The woman stays," he said, his voice bearing such a harsh edge that Thugmonger faltered in his retreat.

"Shiva, kill the monk! You men, get the other one!" Wald howled as he turned and bolted for the door.

The man with the woman stumbled after Wald, while Cull prepared to guard their retreat. Four of Wald's men drew their swords and leaped at Max, who vaulted effortlessly onto the bar. Two more of Wald's men slipped into the crowd, to wait for an opening. Gunter backed away, throwing up his hands in despair.

With surprising speed, Shiva reached for Morgan. Lifting the heavy chair one-handed, Morgan slammed the giant's arms aside and shoved the chair savagely into the man's face, knocking him backwards onto a table. The table collapsed under Shiva's weight, enfolding him in a mass of plates, mugs, and food.

Morgan charged after Wald, just as the woman recovered enough to trip her captor. Both fell heavily to the floor, and Cull backed over them to stay next to Wald. The other man got to his feet, slammed the woman into a chair and drew his sword. He lunged at Morgan, who jerked back from the blade. Morgan blocked a second thrust with his arm, and then drove his foot into the man's stomach. The man fell sprawling into a group of diners, who scattered, letting him fall to the floor. A rough looking man seated in a nearby chair brought his heel down on the forehead of Wald's man, bouncing his head on the hard wooden floor. Wald cursed and ran for the doorway, with Cull close behind him.

As Morgan followed, a pair of huge arms dropped around him. Shiva squeezed, intending to crush Morgan's ribs. Before Shiva's hold could fully tighten, Morgan jerked his hips to one side and chopped deeply into the giant's groin with the edge of his hand. Shiva grunted in pain and leaned forward, struggling to maintain his grip. Morgan met Shiva's descending face with the back of his head, breaking Shiva's nose once again. The giant recoiled in agony, and Morgan wrenched his arms free. He reached over his head; grabbing double handfuls of Shiva's hair, then bent forward and heaved the huge man into another table.

One of Wald's men saw his chance. He darted out of the crowd, intending to stab Morgan in the back with his dagger. Someone shouted a warning, but Morgan saw him coming. The monk caught the man's arm and broke it like a dry stick. Morgan picked up the writhing man and threw him onto the giant, who still struggled to rise. The two men collapsed in a heap on the floor.

Meanwhile, Max had drawn his swords and engaged his four attackers. He leaped and danced, the twin blades blurring in the dim light. His assailants slashed and stabbed, but their attacks met only air or one of the black blades. As he fought, Max commented on his opponent's lineage and physical characteristics. His abuse caused the four men to curse him and redouble their efforts. Max moved along the bar top until he had his back to the far wall, allowing the men to approach from only three sides.

Wald made one last desperate attempt, motioning for Cull to grab the woman. Cull's attention was focused on Morgan and Max, and he did not notice she had recovered from Wald's blow. As he reached for her, the woman slammed a mug into his face. With one hand over his bleeding cheek, Cull stumbled on a chair and fell.

"Triple pay for whoever kills these two!" Wald yelled to the survivors of his men.

The woman threw the mug at Wald, but he managed to duck it, and ran out the door. Seeing Wald in full retreat, Cull dropped his sword and scrambled after him on his hands and knees, not rising until he was safely outside. The giant roared and tossed the other

72

man aside, getting to his feet.

Max spoke from his vantage point on the bar. "I think you've angered the giant. Watch yourself," he advised.

"I can handle this," Morgan said.

The giant charged, grabbing an overturned chair as Morgan turned to face him. Shiva swung the chair with an audible grunt, but Morgan ducked under the chair. His fists thudded twice into the giant's ribs, with force enough to stagger him. Stepping back, Shiva stared at Morgan, amazed at the monk's strength. Morgan glared back, shaking the pain from his bandaged hand. Shiva swung the chair again, but missed Morgan a second time. Morgan snapped a punch to the giant's head, rocking it to one side. Shiva's vision blurred and he stumbled back several steps, and then threw the chair at Morgan. Morgan dodged the chair but the giant charged in, clasping his hands together. He brought both fists down on Morgan, angry enough to drive him through the floor. Morgan managed to sidestep the attack, but Shiva kicked him in the ribs, doubling him over. The giant seized Morgan and threw him onto the stage, but Morgan tore himself free and rolled out of reach. He fell off the far side of the stage and lay on the floor, trying to breathe. The giant moved around the stage, raising a booted foot to crush the gasping monk. Morgan wrapped his legs around the giant's, and then twisted, throwing Shiva on his face. As the giant collapsed, Morgan bent forward and drove his elbow into the back of Shiva's neck, slamming his forehead into the floor.

Morgan scrambled to his feet, but Shiva rose almost immediately, even though blood welled from his brow. The giant ran forward, swinging both fists. Morgan avoided the blows, but Shiva leaped on him, and the two men crashed into another table, which overturned with their weight. Morgan seized the giant's arms, and heaved up with his legs, using their momentum to throw Shiva over his head. The giant landed heavily on his back in the ruins of the table. Both men got up, but Morgan moved first, kicking his opponent in the stomach. Shiva swung wildly, but Morgan ducked under his arm and danced aside, punching the giant in the temple. Shiva staggered, and Morgan snapped a kick to the back of his knee. As Shiva rocked backwards, Morgan drove the heel of his hand into his face. The giant sagged to his knees, and then Morgan stepped away and kicked him in the back of the head. Shiva toppled, but somehow managed to get up again. Groggily waving his arms before him, Shiva stumbled backward toward the unbroken front window.

"Not that window, use the other one!" Gunter yelled in vain.

Morgan stepped forward, braced himself, and kicked high, driving his heel into the giant's jaw. Shiva crashed through the window to land in a heap in the street. He lay motionless as pieces of glass and window frame clattered down around him.

Seeing Morgan's victory, Max yelled, and his attackers stepped back uncertainly, their chests heaving with exertion. Max stood untouched by the battle, while blood and sweat covered his four opponents.

Max studied his opponents, as if seeing them for the first time. "Have we begun to play?" he asked. "I think not."

Max lunged with blinding speed, his two swords twisting to disarm the nearest assailant. He sent the man sprawling with a kick to the head, and attacked another of his adversaries. Before he could even lift his sword, a second man staggered back with a deep gash across his forehead. The last two men turned and ran for the back door, shoving past the startled innkeeper. Max bounded along the bar after them, encouraging them on to greater speed. The man with the slashed forehead, seeing that Max now blocked his escape, attacked in desperation. Max turned and parried two thrusts, and then the man's sword fell from a badly sliced hand. Max lashed out with a boot that caught the man in the chin, slamming him into a shelf of mugs. Man, mugs, and shelf all collapsed to the floor.

Without warning, Wald's last able-bodied man burst from the milling crowd with his sword leveled at Max's back. Morgan and several others yelled warnings and Max whirled. The attacker slumped over the bar and slid to the floor, his slashed throat leaving a bloody trail. Frowning slightly, Max watched him fall, his black blades stained red.

The crowd gave a lusty cheer for the entertainment. Max bowed, Gunter groaned, and Morgan stood holding his bandaged hand, looking slightly embarrassed. Several soldiers clapped Morgan on the back as they picked their way through the debris to relocate their scattered meals.

"Good fight," remarked one.

"It's about time someone stood up to Wald and his monster. Shiva's killed six men. I didn't think anyone could beat him," said another.

"You monks are tough. Maybe I should convert," laughed a third.

Max jumped down from the bar, wiping his swords clean with a cloth, while Morgan gingerly probed his abused midsection. The woman they had rescued dropped into a chair, holding a cold mug against her bruised lip.

People replaced tables and chairs, picked up mugs at random, and were soon calling for refills. Gunter hastened to respond, hustling about behind the littered bar. Others dragged the dead and wounded through the back door, and serving women brought out buckets and mops to clean the floor. The band was soon playing again as if nothing had happened.

Max walked over to Morgan, shaking his head. "You took some chances with the giant. You should've just killed him," he said.

Morgan held up a hand. "Later. Let's see to the woman," he said.

The woman looked up at their approach, and the men paused, staring at her. Even with her swollen mouth, and the travel stains, she was very attractive. Morgan noticed her eyes were a deep blue.

She spoke first, breaking the spell. "I thank you for helping me, but if you're expecting some reward, there is none. The money for the meal was the last I had," she said.

Max waved at Morgan. "He did it for honor, and I for revenge. We had an old score to settle with Master Wald," Max said.

Hearing something, Max walked over to the broken window and looked out, leaving Morgan alone with the woman.

Morgan seemed at a loss for words. "Is . . . there anything else we . . . can do?" he finally managed.

The dusty beauty locked eyes with him for a moment, deciding something. "No, you can't help me . . . I must be going," she said, then began looking around. "Where are my daggers?"

A keening whistle split the night outside, answered from a distance. Max stepped quickly away from the window to join them.

"Night watch on their way . . . and Shiva's gone. We better depart, unless you want to spend the night explaining things to the watch captain," he said.

The woman looked alarmed and gathered her cloak around her as if to leave. Without a word, Morgan and Max grabbed her and hustled her toward the rear of the inn, ignoring her protests. Gunter blocked their way.

"Who's going to pay for all this damage? I'm nearly ruined! And now you want to leave me with two dead men and four wounded to explain to the watch?" Gunter said, and then turned on Morgan. "And you! Pacifist, he says! Thaar help us if you ever turn militant."

Max looked sternly at the innkeeper. "Payment you ask! Who stopped the drunken sailors from stealing your best dancer last Festival? Who talked the Kuulians out of scalping you when you didn't serve their captain first? Who caught the disgruntled customer trying to burn the inn? Next time, I'll let the brigands have this place! And don't give me that nonsense about explaining to the watch. By the time they show up there won't be any dead or wounded and everyone here will suffer memory loss!" he said.

Gunter deflated a bit and began muttering and growling. "Well, just get out of here! I don't want any more trouble! Out! Out!" he ordered.

He herded the three of them out the back door into a dim hallway. Once inside the hall, he lowered his voice just long enough to say, "Back stairs . . . third room on the right . . . don't let anyone see you." With a final wave of his arms, Gunter the innkeeper left them.

CHAPTER SEVEN
CELESTE

Morgan, Max, and the woman entered the room. Max closed and bolted the door. The room had two beds with small night stands, two chairs and a curtained alcove containing a huge bathtub, a wash basin, and a toilet. A lighted globe sat on one of the night stands, and another one hung overhead. Throw rugs covered the hardwood floor, and a curtained window overlooked the alley. In spite of his grumbling, Gunter had evidently given them one of the more expensive rooms.

Max moved immediately to the window and glanced out, then pulled the curtains closed. Morgan sat on one of the beds, rubbing his side, but the woman stayed by the door, wary in the presence of two men she hardly knew. She touched the empty dagger sheaths on her forearms, again regretting that she had not retrieved her weapons.

Max returned to stand before Morgan, ignoring the woman. "Are you injured?" he asked gruffly.

"No, but my ribs will be sore for a few days," Morgan said.

"What were you doing down there? Why didn't you just kill Shiva? The man I knew twelve years ago would've finished him quickly," Max said, his voice low and hard.

Morgan lowered his eyes. "I didn't want to kill him," he said, then looked up and met Max's gaze defiantly. "And what about you? You only killed one."

Max waved a hand in dismissal. "Those fools were no threat. No sense killing in public without a good reason. The only one that did press me, I killed. Shiva could've seriously injured you," Max said, then glanced at the woman, lowering his voice even more. "Is this how it's going to be? You won't use a sword, you won't kill? If you keep this up, you know what's going to happen? You will fail, and I'll get killed trying to fight for both of us. You better just go back where you came from, so they can send someone more dependable.

Those we fight have no honor, and they have no rules. If you oppose them, they'll kill you without a thought. You know them, what they're capable of. If you bind yourself with foolish oaths, we're doomed.

I'll stay with you, but unless you look beyond your selfish codes, we'll both die, without accomplishing a thing. So make up your mind, decide what's more important," Max said.

The woman had been staring at them during their conversation, plainly alarmed at what she heard. Morgan started to reply, but she interrupted him.

"What asylum did you two escape from?" she said, as she turned to open the door. "I'm better off alone, than with two madmen."

Morgan stood. "Wait. I'm sorry if we disturbed you. You're safe with us. If you go out there, Wald and his men will find you," he said.

The woman stopped and leaned her head against the door, obviously exhausted.

She sighed. "I know what Wald wants. You two might be preferable, at least you hate Wald," she said. "I'm so tired."

Max threw a last sharp look at Morgan, and then stepped toward the woman. "If you're going to stay, we might as well know your name. I'm Maximilian," he said gently.

The woman turned slowly, leaning against the door. Her beautiful eyes had dark circles under them and her swollen lip looked painful. She studied Max a moment, and then spoke. "I'm Celeste. From Skara Thrae," she said.

Max pointed to Morgan. "And this is the mad monk Morgan. You were right, one of us did escape from an asylum," he said.

Morgan glared at Max. "Will you stop that? We're trying to make her feel more secure, not scare her away," he said.

Celeste smiled, and then frowned with the pain in her lip. "Well met, gentlemen. Thank you again for helping me. I hope you don't regret it," she said.

"As long as it inconveniences Wald, we'll never regret it," Max said with an evil grin.

"How do you know him?" Celeste asked.

Max glanced at Morgan. "It's a long story," Morgan said.

A soft knock at the door startled Celeste, and she jumped away from it. Max and Morgan stepped to either side of the door. Morgan gently moved Celeste behind him.

"Who is it?" Max whispered.

A husky voice came from the hall. "It's Alta. With hot water and towels. Open the door, you murdering blackheart."

Max unbolted the door and stepped back. "Gunter's wife," he said to Celeste with a grin.

The door swung open. A heavy set woman waited in the hall, carrying an armload of towels, and behind her stood four serving maids, with buckets of water. There was no one else in sight.

Alta frowned at Max. "Your water's getting cold," she said.

Max bowed and gestured for the women to enter. "A hot bath sounds wonderful. Do come in, fine maidens," he said.

Alta brushed past him, tossing the towels on the bed, while the maids carried the buckets to the bathtub. Alta shook her finger at Max.

"Don't give me your fancy talk, Maximilian. You two nearly destroyed our inn. Gunter wanted to leave you up here, cold and dirty," she said.

Max looked hurt. "But we were engaged in a heroic act. Isn't that worth a few spilled platters?" he asked.

Alta looked at Celeste. "You poor dear, you look exhausted. Why don't we get you a room to yourself? Then you can take a long hot bath without these two brutes trying to peer around the curtain," she said.

"She's safer with us," Morgan said.

"And we promise not to look," Max added.

Celeste shook her head. "No, they're right. I don't want to impose on you further. I'll be fine," she said.

Alta laid a hand gently on Celeste's arm. "It's your choice. Take a bath then. Before the water chills. If you need anything, let me know," she said.

"Thank you. You've no idea how much I appreciate that," Celeste said.

Alta turned on Max and Morgan. "And you boys be good. If you bother her, you'll answer to me," she warned.

With a swirl of heavy skirts, Alta left the room, the serving maids trailing in her wake. Max moved to the door.

"That woman is not to be trifled with. Poor Gunter," he said. "Well, if Celeste gets the first bath, I'll go check on the horses. And warn our friends if I see them. Remember Morgan, don't peek."

Morgan started to protest, but could not think of a good reason. Was he afraid to be alone with the woman? He closed his mouth.

When Max had gone, Morgan closed and bolted the door. Celeste turned to him. "If you don't mind, I'll take that bath now," she said.

For some reason, Morgan felt very nervous around her. He glanced at her, fascinated by those exotic eyes and flawless skin. "Sure. I'll be . . . over here," he stammered.

Celeste looked at him out of the corner of her eye, as if amused by his discomfort, then slipped out of her cloak, and laid it over a chair. Under the cloak, she wore sturdy traveling clothes, woolen pants and a long sleeved shirt with a vest, well made but stained and worn. In spite of the bulky clothing, it was obvious she had a slim, athletic figure.

Deliberately, Morgan turned away and lay down on the bed, staring at the ceiling. Celeste sat on the chair, and pulled off her boots and socks. She wriggled her sore toes in relief.

"Can you toss me a towel?" she asked as she took off her vest.

Morgan groaned, but sat up and threw her a towel. She caught it deftly and stood up, then slung the towel over one shoulder and took out the braiding in her long brown hair, shaking it loose. In spite of the dust, the rich colors glistened in the lamplight, the heavy locks cascading over her shoulders in a wave. Morgan watched for a moment, and then swung his feet over the edge of the bed.

"Maybe I should . . . wait outside," he said uncertainly. Where was Max, he thought to himself. What was taking him so long?

Celeste looked at him innocently. "Whatever for? There is a curtain, after all. No sense in you standing in the drafty hall," she said, and then paused. "Besides, I'd really rather not be alone right now."

Morgan lay back on the bed. "All right, I'll stay. Just get on with it," he grumbled.

Celeste laid the towel on the floor near the alcove, and slid back the curtains around the bath. She poured the water into the tub, and stirred the water with her hand.

"I'll hurry, so there's some warm water left for you," she said.

Morgan closed his eyes, forcing away the image that flashed into his mind. First Malissa, and now he was thinking improper thoughts about some woman he did not even know. He had been in the mountains too long.

Another knock came from the door, and Morgan moved quickly across the room. Celeste watched him, admiring the power and flow of his movements. She found him handsome, in a rugged sort of way, and now that they were alone, he seemed gentle and boyishly uncertain. Although there was nothing gentle about him when he fought. Alta had returned, this time with a bundle of clothing and another bucket of water.

"I'm guessing at your size. These may be a little small. But those other clothes need washing and mending," Alta said, looking at Celeste.

She took the clothes to Celeste, and set the bucket by the curtain.

"Thank you," Celeste said.

As she left, Alta glanced at Morgan, briefly studying his face. Something she saw there made her smile, and Morgan did not like the way she smiled. He closed the door firmly behind her, and went back to the bed.

Celeste closed the curtains, and Morgan could hear the rustle of clothing as she undressed, then the splashing of water and a deep sigh. Morgan tried to ignore the sounds she made.

Celeste's voice broke his concentration. "Are you the mad monk Morgan?" she asked.

"No. Don't listen to Max," Morgan said.

"Where are you from?" she asked.

"Max and I were both raised in Saarland. A village called Falmount, in the northern foothills," he said.

More splashing came from the alcove. "So you've known each

other since childhood?" she asked.

"We've spent most of our lives together, until recently," Morgan answered.

"Until you went to the asylum?" she asked.

"There was no asylum," Morgan said patiently.

"Are either of you married?" she asked without warning.

Morgan grimaced. Brash woman. "Uh . . . no. Our profession didn't suit a family life," he said.

"What is your profession, by the way? I thought you were a monk," she asked.

A complicated whistle from the hall saved Morgan from that question. He returned the signal, then went to the door and unlocked it. Celeste poked her head out of the curtain, damp brown locks framing her face. She was even more attractive wet.

"Who's that?" she asked.

Before Morgan could answer, Max strode into the room, carrying their packs, his weapons bag, and Morgan's staff. He stopped and stared admiringly at Celeste.

"Do you need me to wash your back?" he asked.

Celeste wrinkled her nose. "You mind your manners, Maximilian. I'm . . . a lady," she said, and then closed the curtain. "Although Morgan didn't even offer."

"Ah, well. That's Morgan. The ideal bodyguard, " Max said, then looked at Morgan and grinned. "How come you always get to guard the . . . lady?"

Morgan frowned back, shaking his head. "What did you see out there?" he asked, eager to change the subject.

Max flopped down in a chair. "The Guard has come and gone. They've done their duty and are none the wiser. The horses are fine. We can sell them just before we leave. I saw Harkon, and told him what happened here. He'll warn Taskin," Max said, then paused. "They're thinking of coming with us."

"What?" Morgan asked.

"They're afraid of . . . your jilted lover, even here," Max began.

"She was not my lover," Morgan spit the words out, glaring at Max.

"Taskin thinks she might send an assassin after them, or threaten their relatives in Androssar. He figures the farther away they are, the better. Harkon's still whining, but I think he agrees with Taskin," Max said.

"Harkon and Taskin are old men. They should be enjoying retirement somewhere. Not risking their lives on someone else's business," Morgan said.

Max shrugged. "Taskin served with us. The best years of his life were spent under our command. Harkon was in the City Guard and Taskin says he's a good man, despite his complaining. Besides, it's more dangerous for them here. Leaving them behind could be a death sentence," he said.

Morgan realized the splashing from the tub had stopped. He frowned and shook his head at Max, nodding toward the bath.

Max looked at the curtain. "Enjoying your bath, princess?" Max asked.

Celeste did not respond or even move for several moments. Max and Morgan exchanged glances.

"What did you call me?" Celeste asked quietly.

"What? You mean princess?" Max responded.

"Why'd you call me that?" Celeste asked, her voice flat and cold.

Max looked puzzled. "No reason. Just a bit of flattery. I'm sorry if it offended you," he offered.

Celeste did not speak again, just quickly finished her bathing. Max looked quizzically at Morgan, who shrugged.

They heard Celeste get out of the bath and soon she shoved the curtain back and stepped into the room. With the smudges and dirt gone, and wearing clean clothes, she was even more entrancing. The new clothes were slightly small, accenting her figure. Celeste glanced at them, tugging at her tight shirt, suddenly uncomfortable under their gaze. She picked up her old clothes and folded them by the door. Morgan and Max watched her without speaking, puzzled by the sudden change in attitude. Celeste now seemed tense and wary, and suspicious of them. It bothered Morgan, but he couldn't think of anything to say.

In fact, no one spoke much the rest of the evening. Max and

Morgan bathed while Celeste sat on one of the beds, combing her long hair. She was apparently exhausted, but fighting sleep for some reason. When she finished with her hair, she lay down, and the next time they looked at her, she was asleep. Morgan walked over to the bed and carefully placed a blanket over her. She stirred uneasily at the touch, making a frightened little sound in her sleep. Morgan looked at her for a moment.

When he left her, he saw Max watching him. "Be careful, friend. This is no time to find a woman," Max said softly.

Morgan sighed. "I know. Who gets the other bed?" he asked.

Max checked the bolt, then wedged one of the chairs against the door, and sat down on the second bed. "You're the hero on the quest. You take the floor. Tomorrow we can figure out who Celeste is and what to do with her," he said.

CHAPTER EIGHT
THE PRINCESS

Max slipped out early the next morning. Morgan heard him leave, and looked over to Celeste's bed, from where he lay on the floor, his head propped up on his pack. She was awake, and watching him. She lifted the corner of the blanket.

"You?" she asked.

Morgan sat up and nodded. "You fell asleep and looked cold," he said.

Celeste smiled. "Thank you," she said.

"Do you feel better?" Morgan asked.

She stretched luxuriously, and Morgan looked away.

"Yes, much better. It seems like it's been days since I ate or slept. A meal, a hot bath, and a good night's sleep, it's done wonders for my disposition," she said.

Morgan sat up and retrieved a small pouch from his pack. He went to the wash basin, where he removed the bandages from his hand. He washed the wound carefully, and then applied some ointment from his pouch.

"What happened to your hand?" Celeste asked.

"A burn," Morgan said.

He pulled out a length of new bandage. Celeste threw back her blanket and came to him. "Let me help you," she said.

Morgan shook his head, trying to place the wrapping one handed. "No, I can do it," he said.

Celeste plucked the cloth from his hand. "Men. Give me your hand," she ordered.

Morgan sighed, yielding his hand, and Celeste examined the burn.

"When did this happen?" she asked.

"A few days ago," Morgan said.

"Are you sure?" she asked. "This was a serious burn, but it's already half healed."

Morgan shrugged. "I heal fast," he said.

85

"You must," she said. "Then again, the mentally ill sometimes lose track of time."

"Are you going to wrap it or not?" Morgan asked.

Celeste chuckled and expertly replaced the bandage. She had obviously wrapped wounds before. Morgan stood tensely, trying not to get lost in her clean, fresh scent.

"It looks like you grabbed something hot. Whatever were you doing?" she asked.

"Saving my soul," Morgan said without thinking.

Celeste glanced at him. "Was this some bizarre religious ritual, or are you really crazy?" she asked.

"I'd rather not talk about this," Morgan said.

Celeste finished the wrapping and tied off the cloth with a tight knot. Morgan was extremely conscious of her soft touch and how close she stood.

She stepped back, examining her work. "There. Is it too tight?" she asked.

"No, thank you," Morgan said, and then retreated a pace or two, putting a safe distance between them.

Max returned, carrying a tray laden with food.

"Breakfast is served. Good morning, Celeste. How did you sleep?" he said brightly.

"I slept well, thank you. What's for breakfast?" she asked.

She walked over and looked at the tray, which Max had balanced on one of the night tables. Next to the hot bread, steaming porridge, and cups of sasich lay her two daggers, carefully cleaned and oiled. She snatched them up, and slid them into their hidden sheaths.

She patted the weapons. "A woman feels half dressed without her daggers. Be sure to thank Gunter and Alta for me," she said.

Max glanced at Morgan, raising his eyebrows. "A woman after my own heart," he said.

Morgan regarded Celeste thoughtfully. "Max, you don't have a heart," he remarked.

Max picked up a chunk of bread. "Hey, stab me and I bleed like anyone else," he said.

Morgan laughed. "I can't remember the last time anyone

86

managed to stab you," he observed. "Although many have tried."

They sat on Max's bed and ate, engaging in idle conversation. When they had finished eating, Celeste went back to her bed, and sat down, propping herself up against the headboard. Morgan sat on Max's bed, and Max slumped in a chair.

"As I said before, we need to know more about you," Morgan began.

"No, you first. I'm a woman, alone. You have me at a disadvantage. Before I tell you any more, I want to know who you are," Celeste said.

"I'm not sure how much we can tell you, without endangering you. We have some powerful enemies," Morgan said.

Celeste held up a hand, and for the first time, Morgan noticed her ring. It looked old and expensive.

"All right, let's do it this way. I'll sum up what I already know, and you can fill in the gaps. Morgan's unnaturally strong, and experienced in hand to hand fighting, even though he's supposedly a monk. Max is an excellent swordsman, and his swords appear to be made of ebonite. I've only seen ebonite once before, and I know it's rare and expensive.

Max and Gunter spoke of several recent experiences, so evidently Max has been in this area for a while. You two know each other from childhood, and were raised in the Saar valley. Neither of you are married, although Morgan is apparently not a celibate." Morgan tried to protest, but Celeste silenced him with a sharp gesture.

"No, let me finish. You can correct me after I'm done. Max hasn't seen Morgan until recently, after a period of twelve years. Max said he was in an asylum, but Morgan denies it. Morgan used to be a swordsman as well, but for some reason has now given up killing. Maybe it's the religious influence, or dementia, a death wish.

I would guess you both are, or were, mercenaries, and the friends you mentioned, Harkon and Taskin, are also soldiers. You've evidently made some powerful enemies; someone more than just jilted lovers and Thugmonger Wald. You plan a trip, and your friends have decided to go with you. How am I doing?" Celeste asked.

Max shook his head. "You're quite observant, Celeste. I'll have to watch what I say in the future," he said.

Morgan was bothered by something else. "Malissa was not a jilted lover," he said, his face flushing.

"Malissa. Well, at least I know her name. Who is Malissa? Is she beautiful?" Celeste asked.

Morgan ground his teeth, realizing he had said too much.

"I've only seen her once, and she wore a mask, veil, and heavy robes," Max said, then pointed to Morgan. "But he claims to have seen much more, maybe all of her. Ask him."

Celeste looked at Morgan, arching her eyebrows. "Really?" she asked.

Morgan reddened further. "She wants me killed, along with Harkon and Taskin," he said.

Celeste studied Morgan's face. "Did you refuse her? Is that why she hates you?" she asked.

Morgan kept his eyes on the floor. "Yes, I refused her. I don't know why she hates me," he said.

Celeste leaned back, folding her arms. Max watched the exchange with amusement. "You don't know much about women, do you?" she asked, then paused. "She must have been quite a woman."

"Don't you have any other questions?" Morgan asked irritably.

Celeste laughed. "Very well. So what happened between you and Wald?" she asked.

"As you've guessed, we were soldiers. Years ago, Wald made a living as a small time arms and ration supplier, and had a contract with . . . our army. He poisoned half of our men with a load of bad beef, and we had to fight with those that were left. We won, but took heavy losses. A lot of good men died that day, because of Master Wald. I believe he'd taken gold from the enemy. I intend to kill him, but he's been avoiding me ever since," Max said.

The tone of his voice sent a chill down Celeste's spine, and she realized that beneath that charming and witty exterior, Max could be a cold blooded killer. She decided to change the subject.

"Why didn't either of you ever get married? Just because you were mercenaries?" she asked.

Morgan looked at her. "We went from one battle to the next, never sure if we were going to live another day. What kind of a life is that for a wife and a family?" he asked.

Celeste glanced at Max, who raised his hands defensively. "Now don't get us wrong. We like women. In fact, I had one in every city, but Morgan was more particular. Women just don't belong on the battlefield. They're soft, sweet, cuddly things, best just before and after a battle. A pleasant diversion . . . ," Max said, then stopped when he saw the expression on Celeste's face. "Well, in general. Nothing personal. I'm sure you're not . . ."

Celeste cut him off. "Not what? Soft? Sweet? Cuddly?" she asked.

Max realized he was trapped. "Uh . . . well, you know what I mean," he finished lamely.

Celeste got up from her bed, and walked slowly toward Max, moving in a way that disturbed both men. She knelt down beside Max, and leaned close to him, stroking his cheek with her fingertips. He sat stiffly, his eyes widening.

She whispered in his ear. "I assure you, Maximilian. I am soft, sweet, and most cuddly. When I want to be. And then again, I can be . . ."

Her other arm whipped up, and in spite of his bemused state, Max managed to catch her wrist, the dagger almost touching his throat. He stared into her exotic eyes, cold now.

". . .quite deadly. My father taught me that," she continued in a low voice. She twisted her wrist free, and slid the dagger back into the sheath as she walked slowly back to her bed.

Max stared after her. "Definitely a woman after my own heart," he said.

Celeste resumed her place on the bed, and continued as if nothing had happened. Morgan hid a smile.

"I have a few more questions. Who is your enemy? Is Wald working for them?" she asked.

Max waited for Morgan, who hesitated, uncertain how much to tell. "I don't know if Wald is working for someone or if he's on his own. Our enemies are very dangerous. That's all I can tell you,"

Morgan said.

Celeste frowned. "And who are you working for? Hopefully, someone equally powerful," she said.

"Hopefully," Max muttered.

"I'm sorry, the more you know about us, the more danger you're in," Morgan said.

"You're planning a trip. Where are you going?" Celeste asked.

Morgan sighed. He hated not telling her. "South," he said.

Celeste raised her eyes to the ceiling, looking tired and lonely. "I can see you aren't going to give me any useful answers. I still don't know anything about you. The only thing I'm sure of is that you fought Wald. You seem to be honorable men, but I've been betrayed before," she said, then lowered her eyes, fixing both men with her gaze. "But I don't see that I have any choice but to trust you. I'm alone, far from my home, with no friends. And after last night, I know I need help. If you two decided to harm me, I couldn't stop you. So here I am, do with me what you will."

Max rubbed his chin thoughtfully. "Should we sell her? She'd be a fine addition to someone's harem," he said. "Or maybe ransom? Do you have any rich relatives?"

Morgan leaned forward, ignoring Max. "You have my word that we'll not harm you. By not answering, I'm only trying to protect you," he said.

Max smiled crookedly. "You have his word. Believe me, his honor means more to him than his life. You're safe with us. I have no honor, so I don't bother swearing oaths. But I like you, you have courage, besides being beautiful. You may be alone, but you are far from helpless," he said, then paused. "But enough about us. What's your story?"

Morgan held up a hand. "No, wait. It's good to be cautious with your trust. Let me tell you what I've learned already, and then you can decide if you want to tell us more. You're Celeste, from Skara Thrae. Your clothes, jewelry, and weapons suggest you're of noble birth . . ." he began.

Max's eyes widened. "You were alarmed when I called you princess. Celeste . . . Celestine? Ryde's daughter, Princess Celestine?"

he asked.

Morgan shook his head. "No. She can't be the princess. What would a Thraen Princess be doing here, without any retainers?" he protested.

When Celeste did not speak, Morgan stared at her. "You really are the Princess Celestine?" he asked.

Celeste sighed, and then nodded slowly. "Yes, I am," she admitted.

"So you thought we knew, when I called you Princess. And we could only know if someone had told us. Like Wald or someone he was working for?" Max asked.

"Yes, but I couldn't imagine why you saved me from Wald, if you were on his side. I was afraid someone else was after me too. I was so tired. I couldn't think straight," Celeste said.

"No wonder you closed up last night," Max said.

"We could have figured it out for ourselves, no one had to tell us," Morgan said.

"I know. But I've been betrayed, chased all over. I have a hard time trusting anyone," Celeste responded.

"But why are you here, alone? And why is Wald after you?" Morgan asked.

"Patience. I liked your idea, first tell me what you know about me and Skara Thrae," Celeste said.

Morgan stared into space, searching his memory. "Skara Thrae is a large island off the coast of Saarland, currently ruled by Warlord Ryde, who oversees the Thraen Confederacy of the Five Clans. His castle is Lugershall, on the small island of Andover, south of the main island.

For the last hundred years, Ryde has discouraged outside contact, and is well known for his isolationist policies. He feels that the Thraens have enough problems of their own, without getting involved in mainland affairs.

Thraen horses are prized worldwide, but they're rarely sold off-island. The only regular export is a breed of dog, the Pomas, small, with long fur, and a poisonous bite. Pomas are intensely loyal to their owners, and royalty often use them as bodyguards for their

91

children," Morgan said, then smiled. "However, it is also said that long exposure to their constant yapping can drive one insane."

Max snorted. "That may explain why so many royal families are crazy," he said, then hastily added, "Of course, the Thraens must be immune."

"Actually, I'm not that fond of Pomas. I don't consider something that small a real dog. I prefer the royal wolfhounds," Celeste said. "What do you know about Ryde and his family?"

"He's married to a woman named Seressa, and has two children, Talbot and Celestine. Ryde is reputed to be a fierce warrior and effective leader, although his temper is said to be legendary," Morgan answered.

"You're a very well educated mercenary. How do you know all this?" Celeste asked.

Morgan shrugged. "I do a bit of reading," he said.

"And he's had the last twelve years with little to do but read," Max added.

"Do they have libraries in asylums?" Celeste asked, and then glanced at the monk's cloak. "Or was it a monastery?"

Morgan ignored the question. "Tell us what happened," he said.

Celeste laid her head against the wall, her eyes distant, the memories obviously painful.

"I was at Lugershall with my family when the Haggas attacked," she said.

"The Haggas?" Max asked.

"An exiled clan, driven from the island years ago," Celeste explained, and then continued. "Some traitor had let the Haggas into the castle, then led them to our arms lockers and troop quarters. Most of our soldiers were butchered in their sleep. Lugershall had fallen while we slept.

Usk the Axminster woke us and we fled through a secret passage known only to my father, then fought our way to the main island. We learned the Haggas had launched a full scale invasion of Skara Thrae. We also heard reports of strangers with the Haggas. Creatures like black mummies, shrouded in coarse fabric, with dark goggles. Gray men that all looked alike. And soldiers in red and black, with plumes on their helmets," Celeste said.

Morgan and Max exchanged glances. Celeste, wrapped in her memories, did not notice.

"Go on. Tell us what happened then," Morgan said.

"Rumor had it that the Sage Regis was the traitor, but we couldn't believe that. Regis was a wise scholar, and my father's closest counselor. But he had disappeared and was nowhere to be found. We rode north to Tantagnel, a small independent outpost on the northwestern tip of the island, where a man named Thuro rules. Thuro and Father share no love and Thuro remained skeptical of our reports until messengers announced the arrival of the invaders at Tantagnel's walls. Father and Thuro agreed to put aside their differences, and fight the Haggas.

The Haggas couldn't breach Tantagnel's defenses, so they settled in for a siege. They evidently didn't know of the caches of food and supplies Thuro had stored in the castle. We finally saw the black mummies and the gray ones for ourselves. They seemed to be advising the Haggas.

Father led night raids that wreaked havoc with the Haggas, while the invaders smashed pockets of resistance elsewhere in Skara Thrae. We heard that the Haggas chief, Kalkin, now ruled from Lugershall.

It was only a matter of time before the Haggas took the entire island and descended on us with all their warriors, so Father decided someone must reach the mainland to get help. As you know, Skara Thrae has few allies, but we hoped that Rulda of Androssar might assist us. If a reliable messenger could reach him. I volunteered, and as much for my safety as anything else, Father agreed.

Tantagnel is on a rocky headland overlooking the ocean, but there are secret ways through caves under the castle that lead to the ocean. One night, I fled the island in a boat with ten retainers, but a strange boat pursued us. It glinted like metal, and moved through the water without sail or oars. We managed to slip away in the swells and the darkness, but had to flee north to avoid other patrols. We made shore just before dawn, but found ourselves two to three days walk north of Androssar.

Thugmonger Wald and his men ambushed us on the beach. Somehow they knew we were coming. My bodyguard fought, and Wald's men killed eight of them. We escaped, but my last two guards died slowing the pursuit.

I finally made it to Androssar and sought audience with Rulda, but he refused to help. He told me Saxhaven and Androssar are on the brink of war, and he couldn't afford to get involved in some Thraen clan dispute. Also, he's still mad at father for cutting off trade with the mainland. He said isolationism works both ways, if Skara Thrae wanted no part of mainland concerns, why should the mainland intervene in Thraen politics?

I tried to convince him that this was more than a Thraen problem, reminding him of the strange creatures we'd seen, but he dismissed that as mere fabrication, an attempt to draw him into the fray. He wished me luck and sent me away.

As I left the palace, Wald's men discovered me. I escaped them, but had nowhere to go. I heard that the Demented Boar was a favorite haunt of sea captains, and I came here to book passage to Kalixalven," Celeste said.

"Book passage?" Max asked. "You told us you were out of money."

Celeste gave him a flat look. "I lied. I didn't know who you were. I still don't. So don't ask about my money," she said.

"Why Kalixalven?" Morgan asked.

Celeste sighed. "My goal was actually Carnac. I think my brother Talbot is there. As children, we were educated by the centaurs at Carnac, and made good friends there, especially Baron Serenus," she said, then paused. "My father and brother have never been close. My father drives him too hard, trying to prepare him for Warlord. But I doubt that Talbot will ever be a Warlord. His heart's not in it. One night they had a terrible fight, and my brother left, vowing never to return. We heard he'd gone to Carnac, to continue his studies with the centaurs."

"How will finding your brother help Skara Thrae?" Max asked.

Celeste shrugged. "I don't really know. I have to do something.

Maybe my brother will come back with me, and help Father rally the other clans to fight the Haggas. Or perhaps the centaurs will help us," she said.

Max laughed harshly. "The Equisapiens are scholars and dreamers; all they care about is dusty books and obscure philosophy. At best, they might come and observe the destruction of Skara Thrae, for the knowledge. But they wouldn't intervene," he said.

"The troops that guard Carnac are skilled warriors, and Serenus was quite fond of us. They might help," Celeste said.

"I guess we'll just have to take you with us," Morgan said wearily.

Max rolled his eyes but said nothing. He knew better than to try to dissuade Morgan.

"Take me with you? What do you mean? I don't even know where you're going," Celeste said.

"We're going to Aquarquff, by sea, once a friend of ours comes into port. From there, you can hire Pathfinders to guide you to Carnac. It's not any farther than from Kalixalven, and our friend won't mind one more passenger," Morgan explained.

Celeste shook her head. "I don't like it. You sound like you have your own problems, without taking on mine," she said.

Max gave Morgan a pointed look, but Morgan ignored him.

"I don't like it either. But I see no other way. You go with us, or we leave you here, for Wald," Morgan said.

Celeste sighed. "I suppose you're right. I really don't have any other choice," she said, then clenched her fists. "I just hate being helpless. Wald and the Haggas are going to pay dearly for this."

Morgan turned to Max, who still looked reluctant. "Don't you want to settle things with Wald? If we take the Princess, he'll come to us. And after hearing the Princess' story, we may have more in common than we thought," Morgan said.

Max rubbed his beard thoughtfully. "There is that. We could annoy both Wald and our enemies at the same time. Maybe that's worth it," he said.

Celeste got up from the bed, putting her hands on her hips. "Since I'm going with you, can't you tell me more? If it's a secret, who am I going to tell?" she asked.

"There's a chance we can get you safely to Aquarquff without our enemies connecting us. If we can do that, you won't need to know what we're doing. Believe me; you're better off not knowing. Getting tangled in our affairs will only add to your problems," Morgan said.

Celeste turned to Max. "I'll try not to cause any trouble, Max. I just don't have anyone else," she said.

"Women are always trouble," Max said with a rueful grin. "Don't worry, Princess. You're one of us now."

Max looked at Morgan. "So what's the plan?" he asked.

"Wald's men are probably still watching the inn, waiting for the Princess to leave," Morgan said.

Max nodded. "I've seen them," he confirmed.

"When is Taurus due?" Morgan asked.

"Probably tomorrow evening," Max said.

"Max, tomorrow you contact Harkon and Taskin. Tell them we're leaving, without them, and sell the horses. As soon as Taurus docks, we'll board. Wald won't want to tangle with Taurus' band of cutthroats," Morgan said.

Celeste sat back down on the bed and yawned. "I'm exhausted. I think I'll take a nap," she said.

"Go ahead," Morgan said. "We'll wake you if anything happens."

While Celeste slept, Morgan and Max talked, of memories and plans for the future. Sometime later, a low voice came from the hall.

"Taskin?" Morgan called softly.

"Yes, sir," came the response.

"*Hostis?*" Max asked, standing beside the door.

"*Solum,*" Taskin said.

"What language is that?" Celeste asked, awakened by the voices.

"An old one," Max said.

Morgan opened the door and Taskin and Harkon entered. They had obviously been in a fight.

"What happened to you?" Morgan asked.

Taskin grimaced, fingering a gash in his leather wrist guard. "Wald's men attacked the stables in broad daylight. We killed several of them, but there were too many, and we escaped before the Guard came. They have the horses. We didn't want to lead them to our relatives, so we came here. We're going with you," he said.

Morgan threw up his hands. "Great! Let's invite the whole city," he said in exasperation.

"Locha! What do you expect us to do?" Harkon asked. "If you hadn't come back and stirred up all this trouble, I'd still be at my brother's inn. This is your fault, so don't complain. I don't like it any better than you do."

Taskin laughed harshly. "Yeah, you could be back at the inn, listening to Dason bluster and waiting for the Sagamore to take the rest of your property in taxes. And I could still be abusing widows and orphans in the name of the crown. Is that what you want? At least now we have the chance to do something worthwhile,' he said.

Harkon walked over to one of the chairs, where he sat down heavily. He pulled out a cloth and daubed at a cut on his cheek. "I know. I know. I'm just too old for all this," he complained.

Max gestured to the newcomers. "Princess, meet our intrepid comrades in arms, Taskin and Harkon," he said.

Taskin bowed and Harkon looked up sharply. "Princess? Oh, Locha, what have we gotten ourselves into? Now we have a Princess to take care of," he said.

"Well met, gentlemen," the Princess said, and then looked at Harkon. "And I will especially enjoy your company, Good Master Harkon. You seem to be an irrepressible optimist. Do you worship Locha?"

Harkon put his head in his hands, muttering something.

"What did you say?" Celeste asked.

"No one worships Locha. I just know his power," Harkon said.

"Poor Harkon seems somewhat unhinged. Must be the strain of traveling," Max commented.

Taskin glared at the other man. "He'll get over it," he said.

"Taskin, guard the Princess. Morgan and I have to talk. Besides, I'm getting hungry. We'll bring back some food and drink," Max said.

Celeste looked slightly worried at the thought of them leaving.

"I trust these men, Princess. We'll be back soon," Morgan said.

Celeste nodded and smiled, then pointed to the pile of clothes by the door. "Could you take my clothes down to Alta? She said she'd clean them for me," she said.

"Tough duty," Max said to Taskin as he picked up the clothes and moved to the door.

"Be careful, Max," Celeste said.

Max bowed in the open door. "Always, Princess," he said.

Taskin bolted the door after them, and turned to face Celeste. He seemed nervous in the presence of foreign royalty.

Celeste studied the two battered soldiers. "Do you have a wound kit? I can tend those cuts and bruises," she said.

Taskin shook his head. "No, Princess, it would not be proper," he protested.

Celeste grabbed Taskin by the arm and dragged him toward the wash basin. "You let me decide what's proper," she ordered.

Morgan and Max sat at a corner table in the dining room, carefully watching the few other occupants. Both of the windows were boarded over now, but they could hear the pouring rain outside. Gunter came over and they ordered lunch.

He looked at them sourly. "How much longer are you going to be up there? And who are those other two?" he asked.

"As soon as Taurus arrives, we're gone. Don't worry about Taskin and Harkon. They're the least of your problems," Max said.

"I know. Wald will be back, and no telling what he'll do," Gunter said.

"Hopefully, he'll follow us and forget about your shabby inn," Max said.

"Thaar preserve us. I hope he does follow you. I don't need his kind around here," Gunter said as he went back to the bar.

Max took a drink of the frothy ale. "Are you sure you want to do this?" he asked Morgan.

"What?" Morgan asked. "Take the Princess, Taskin, and Harkon with us? Of course I don't want to. But what else can I do?"

"Taskin and Harkon can carry their own weight, and will be

good men in a fight. I'm talking about the Princess," Max said.

Morgan sighed. "What do you suggest? Leave her here? Do you think I want Thraen royalty on this trip? I don't even know what to say to her," he said.

"That's what worries me most. You're acting like a lovestruck dolt. A woman is bad enough, but one you love is even worse," Max commented.

"Love? You're insane. She's beautiful and royalty, and that makes me uncomfortable. Besides, you wouldn't know love if you saw it," Morgan retorted.

Max swirled his drink, watching the bubbles. "You're probably right about that. But I still think she's trouble," he said.

Both men were silent for a time and then Morgan spoke. "She described mummies, gray men, and soldiers in red and black. Mhoul, Immortals, and Harriers?" he asked.

Max frowned. "The Mhoul have never left Faerie, and no one has heard from them since the Crusade ended," he said.

"The Monachus suspected the Mhoul were plotting something," Morgan said.

"What could they possibly want with Skara Thrae?" Max asked.

"I have no idea. A base for an invasion of the mainland?" Morgan said.

"Skara Thrae has no harbor or navy. You need ships to invade the mainland. This makes no sense," Max said. "Have you heard of a metal ship like she described?"

"No, but we always fought the Mhoul and the Triad on land. I don't know if they had a navy," Morgan said.

"Could she be mad or lying? Or maybe she serves the Mhoul," Max said.

Morgan stared at Max. "Do you honestly believe that?" he asked.

Max looked away. "No, I don't. You know, if she's going with us, you should tell her the rest. She might need the knowledge at some point," he said.

"Should we tell Taskin and Harkon too? The more they know, the more danger they're in," Morgan said.

Max shook his head. "I don't agree, but I'll leave it up to you. So we wait for Taurus, sail to Aquarquff, say good-bye to the Princess, and someone tells you the next step," he said.

"That's the plan. We better get back upstairs," Morgan said.

"I'll get the food," Max said.

CHAPTER NINE
ANDROSSAR

Max came for them in the late afternoon, dripping from the steady rain.

"You're wet," Celeste observed.

"It's raining," Max said. "One of those miserable coastal storms."

"What's going on?" Morgan asked.

"Taurus arrived earlier than expected, the Windrider just docked. He has a load of raw pelts and they're being off loaded. Harkon and Taskin are waiting out back, and the inn is still being watched. Wald will probably try something between here and the docks," Max said.

Morgan wore his monk's cloak, and had his staff and pack. Celeste wore her Thraen garments, which Alta had cleaned and mended. Max had purchased a long duffel bag, and he put his pack and weapons carrier in the bag. He tapped his side.

"I also invested in a new mail shirt. Seemed like a good idea," he said.

They went down the back stairs, where Gunter waited.

Max nodded at the innkeeper. "Thanks for your hospitality. I'm glad I saved your inn," Max said.

Gunter grimaced and waved toward the back door. "Get out of here. Wald will probably have the place burned down anyway," he said.

"Thank you, Gunter," Morgan said.

Gunter glared at Morgan. "Pacifist monks," he muttered.

Max and Morgan headed for the back door, but Celeste stopped near the old innmaster. She leaned forward and kissed him on the cheek.

"I won't forget what you did for us, Gunter," she said, and then turned to follow the others.

Gunter stared after them, touching his cheek in wonder, and then he smiled and hitched up his apron, sauntering back to the dining room.

Max led the way outside, and then stopped in the entry, scanning the back alley. Rain still poured from the dark, gray sky, one of Androssar's spring storms had arrived. The alley appeared empty and they stepped onto the cobblestones of the street. Celeste and Morgan put up their hoods, but the rain slid unnoticed through Max's black hair. Max did not like hats or hoods; he claimed they interfered with his vision. Taskin and Harkon appeared out of the downpour, flanking them. Morgan nodded to them, and they returned a salute. Morgan smiled to himself. Military habits die hard.

They were near the docks, in the new part of the city. Morgan glanced behind them, the flap of his hood keeping the rain from his eyes. Barely visible through the curtains of rain stood the old city, and he could just make out the palace, looming over the surrounding structures.

Most of Androssar had been built in a series of terraces, clinging to the slopes surrounding the bay of Andros. The croplands lay at the top, almost level with the valley floor above. Descending toward the bay, next came the gardens and parks, then the palace grounds and the rest of the old city. The new part of the city extended into the bay itself, the earth from the terraces filling a portion of the bay, providing more room to build.

The river Saar, with its headwaters above Saxhaven, flowed down the Saar valley, then through Androssar to the sea. In Androssar, the river had been captured and channeled through the terraces, for irrigation, ponds, and waterfalls, and then a moat around the palace. The largest of the waterfalls served as a backdrop for the palace, and today the falls merged into the rain. Below the palace a huge aqueduct collected the river, carrying it through the new city into the bay near the docks.

They reached the waterfront without incident, although they knew they were being followed. The streets lay nearly deserted; few honest citizens cared to brave the storm.

As they approached the docks, Morgan could dimly see the outlines of various ships, and beyond them, the choppy surface of the bay itself. A massive seawall stretched across the mouth of the bay, a gray blur in the rain, and Morgan noticed the Portmaster had closed the huge sea gates against the fury of the storm. To Morgan's right was Rulda's pleasure house, a stone structure clinging to the cliffs above the seawall. Ghostly flickers of yellow light shone in its windows.

Their boots began to sound on the wooden planks of the waterfront itself, suspended on stone pilings over the water. Even though it was still day, the overcast sky and the blinding rain reduced everything to twilight. Max pointed at a pier to their left, a long structure, the far end barely visible. A ship swayed at the end of the pier, tied to a T-dock, its outlines lost in the murk. Cargo boxes and overturned skiffs littered the pier, and light globes mounted on poles stood at regular intervals along the pier. Already lit for the night, the globes created pools of hazy light.

Morgan touched Max's shoulder with the tip of his staff, and Max froze, glancing over his shoulder at the taller man. Morgan searched the pier, with growing unease, and then he stepped close to Max, his face hidden by the dripping hood.

"Stay by the Princess. This is their last chance for an ambush," he said in a distant voice, all his senses straining through the downpour.

Max nodded and moved back to the Princess, his eyes narrowing as he also looked for any unseen enemy. Morgan unslung his pack, and walked on, followed by Max and Celeste, then Taskin and Harkon. The dock waited silently, save for rain pattering on the planks, and the waves slapping against the pilings.

They walked through the boxes, heading for the ship at the end of the pier. They could see a few figures moving about near the ship, the last of the unloading crew, stacking bales of pelts and covering them with tarps.

They had just reached the first light globe when the twang of bowstrings pierced the soggy twilight. Three shafts struck Morgan simultaneously, the force of the impact staggering him. Outlined against the backdrop of falling rain, he spun half around and toppled backwards over the edge of the pier. His pack and staff fell to the boards and his body hit the water below with a splash.

A crossbow bolt imbedded itself in Max's duffel bag. Another skidded from his mailed side, tearing through his shirt. A third shaft gouged across Harkon's forearm, leaving a dark trail that immediately smeared in the rain. Celeste shouted and stepped toward where Morgan had fallen. Max tackled her, throwing his bag clear and shoving her down behind a packing crate. Harkon and Taskin also dove for cover.

Max rolled off the Princess and crouched next to the crate, his swords drawn. Laying down one sword, he picked up a block of wood and pitched it at the light above. The block struck the globe with a popping sound, followed by the tinkle of falling glass. The area around them was plunged into semi-darkness. Two more bolts thudded into the crate. Max could feel the vibration of their impact through the wood.

Celeste crawled over beside him. "Morgan's wounded, and in the water. Help him!" she whispered fiercely.

He shook his head, drops of water flying with the movement. Celeste could barely make out his features in the gloom.

"Don't worry about him. Keep your head down. They want you alive, but anyone that would work for Wald can't be all that skilled," he said.

Celeste grabbed his arm. "But . . ." she began.

"Not now," he hissed. The cold ferocity of his voice choked the words in her throat, and she pulled her hand back. She huddled silently, staring at the dark shapes of Morgan's pack and staff, aching to go to his aid.

Max peered into the rain. "Six bolts, six men. With a spare crossbow each," he said.

He twisted, looking back toward the waterfront. "Probably ordered to kill as many as they could with the first volley, then keep us pinned down until . . . ."

His voice trailed off as spied figures coming from the end of the dock, dark shapes in the rain, moving purposefully toward them. He estimated ten men.

Max gestured urgently at Harkon, who lay behind a coil of heavy rope, and had just finished wrapping a cloth around his wounded arm. Harkon shook his head, and Max beckoned again.

Harkon groaned and rolled to his feet, then took a deep breath and threw himself across the space between them. With an angry whine, a bolt sank into the wood just behind him.

Max caught the rolling man, seizing him with an iron grip. He leaned close to Harkon, his dead eyes boring into the older man. "Don't fear them, fear me," he said quietly.

Harkon laid his head on the deck, the rain splattering across his upturned face. "O Locha, what have I gotten myself into," he breathed.

Max called for Taskin and a moment later he appeared out of the gloom, dodging and weaving. Bolts screamed around him, but somehow he avoided them. When he lay panting in the shelter of the crate, Max faced the two men.

"Stay with the Princess," Max ordered.

Harkon struggled backwards, leaning against the crate. "Where are you going? You can't just leave us here," he said.

Max ignored him, but Taskin silenced Harkon with a threatening glare. Max waved a sword blade above the crate. Almost immediately, a shaft whined overhead in response. Max dropped back, slipping over the side of the pier into the dark water.

Across the pier, one of the bowmen crouched behind a crate, clutching a crossbow. A second weapon lay at his feet, next to a rack full of quarrels. He squinted into the rain, searching for targets. He figured the men would keep the woman down, so he had been firing at any movement he saw. He hoped he did not hit the woman by mistake. Wald would not pay him then, and he would have even more trouble finding work.

The man had positioned himself in one of the shadowy areas between the lights. Without warning, the globe to his left shattered, spraying the decking with glass. Startled, the man turned, bringing his crossbow to bear. Out of the darkness behind him a hand dropped down, jerking the bow from his grasp. He twisted and saw a dark figure standing beside him, holding the bow. It looked like the big monk, the one they had killed. He still had a quarrel hanging from his chest. As the monk flung the crossbow far out over the water, the man screamed and clawed for his dagger. Before the bowman could get the dagger free, Morgan grabbed him by the throat and slammed his head against the crate, knocking him nearly senseless. The stunned man followed his weapon into the water. Morgan kicked the second crossbow after him.

Another assassin crouching nearby heard the scream, but could not see through the rain and darkness. He called out to his companion and Morgan disappeared into the shadows. When there was no answer, the man fired blindly into the gloom, fear overcoming his judgment.

Suddenly a voice bellowed out of the darkness, directed at the distant ship. "ULTIMA RATIO REGUM RAAVS!"

After a pause, with no sound but the water all around, someone on the ship shouted back. "SIC ITUR AD BELLUM!"

Even more fearful now, the assassin fired his spare crossbow at the sound of the first voice. He bent over the weapon, his foot in the stirrup, desperately cranking back the bowstring. Morgan appeared out of the drizzle, kicking the crossbow out of his hands and over the side of the pier. Before the hired killer could straighten up, a fist struck him in the temple. He dropped like a stone.

As the man fell, a bolt lashed out of the rain, thudding into Morgan's side. With a painful grunt, Morgan fell against the crate, sliding to the decking. A third assassin crept into sight, raising his spare bow. He stopped and looked carefully around, then approached the man he had shot.

He bent over Morgan, trying to identify him, then stiffened, shocked to see the form of the twice dead monk. Suddenly, the dead man moved, his legs arcing around, sweeping the assassin's feet from under him. He fell heavily, his head banging on the wood of the dock. Stunned, he struggled to rise. Morgan loomed over him, and his head hit the wood again, much harder this time.

When the light across the dock shattered, followed by the scream, Taskin risked a glance around the crate. He could see nothing. A few moments later he heard the shout, and the response from the ship. He leaned back against the crate, mouthing the words he had heard. Then he smiled.

Harkon saw him. "What're you smiling at?" he asked. "And what was that shouting about?"

Taskin's smile widened. "Help is on the way," he said.

"About time," Harkon mumbled. "I'm too old for this. And I hate the rain. Why didn't I stay in Saxhaven?"

Celeste crawled closer to Taskin, peering at his face in the rain. "What about Morgan? Is he dead?" she asked.

Taskin shook his head. "I doubt Morgan is dead," he said.

Wald's men moved quickly along the pier, knowing they had to work fast, before the men on the ship at the far end became aware of what was happening. It should be an easy task; their quarry pinned down and outnumbered four to one. All they had to do was finish any survivors and collect the woman. Wald had seemed terrified of the men guarding the woman, but so far everything had gone according to plan. The big one that bested Shiva was dead; they had seen him go over the side.

Suddenly, a light ahead of them exploded and they heard the scream, then the shouted exchange with the ship. Slarn, their leader, cursed and urged his companions on to greater speed. Slarn heard a sound from behind them, and as he turned, he caught a glimpse of a man in dark clothing, bearing two swords. The man glided into their midst, the swords carving a path through Slarn's men like a scythe.

Three men fell before they could even turn and fight, but the seven survivors formed a ring around their deadly attacker. Max smiled at them, his eyes pale fire, while his red smeared blades moved restlessly, hungry for more blood.

A third shout came from the ship, another phrase in some unknown language, followed by the sound of boots on the planking. Slarn risked a glance and saw a party of men running toward them, coming from the ship. This was not going well.

Max spoke calmly. "Did you hear what was said? Did you understand it? I can tell you. You have a little time left."

Slarn looked back at him, thinking Max mad.

"*Ultima ratio regum Raavs*. Translated, that means `the final argument of Sagamores---the Raavs,'" Max said, then paused for

107

effect. "And the proper response. *Sic itur ad bellum.* `Thus does one go to war.'"

"Raavs?" Slarn asked, a cold feeling forming in the pit of his stomach.

Max saluted with a black blade. "At your service. And that last phrase. *Bellum longa, vita brevis.* `War is long, life is short.' A war cry of the Raavs. Farewell," he said.

Max whirled, and a man behind him died. The man next to him thrust, but hit nothing. He looked down, shocked to see the sword protruding from his side. Max wrenched it free with a twist, parrying a slash from another of Slarn's men. They tried to reform their circle, to attack from all sides, but Max's blades flickered constantly. Every time he struck, another man went down.

Within moments, Slarn and two remaining men fell back, staring at the bodies all around them. Max waited quietly, watching them, a grim reaper in the rain. Slarn looked down the pier. Reinforcements from the ship approached the woman's location and he could not tell what had happened to the fool crossbowmen. They no longer fired, and he wondered if they still lived. He decided to cut his losses, and ran for his life, his two companions on his heels.

Max let them go. He wiped his blades on the clothing of one of the fallen, and walked back toward the Princess.

A cloaked figure stepped in front of the men from the ship, a hood hiding his features. The leader of the seamen, a burly man with a heavy black beard, skidded to a stop on the wet wood, and raised a strange weapon. The device consisted of three tubes grafted onto a wooden stock, with a trigger in a guard on the underside. The cloaked figure swept back the hood and the heavyset seaman squinted at his face in the sodden light.

"Morgan!" he bellowed. "I heard you were dead."

Morgan shook his head. "No, Taurus, I'm alive. And once again, I need your help," he said.

Taurus grinned, his teeth flashing in the beard. He shoved the weapon into his wide belt, then stepped forward, and engulfed Morgan in his beefy arms, lifting him clear of the decking. Setting

Morgan down, he looked up at the big man.

"You always need my help. What would you do without me?" he said.

"I'm glad you remembered the Raav signals, after all this time," Morgan said.

"I'll never forget three years sailing with the finest mercenaries in the Civilized Nations. And I thought the Raav war cry was a nice touch," Taurus said.

"Yes, it was," Morgan admitted.

"Men, meet Morgan, Commander of the Seventh Raav Legion, an old comrade in arms. He nearly conquered the western continent, with my help, of course," Taurus said, then paused, squinting at Morgan through the rain. "Where's your sword, and why are you wearing that monk's cloak?"

"It's a long story," Morgan said.

Celeste stormed up to them, and struck Morgan on the shoulder. Taskin and Harkon trailed in her wake. "You're alive. I thought you were dead," she said.

"So did I," Taurus said, staring at her.

Morgan stepped back, warding off a second blow. "What's the matter with you?" he asked. "You're mad that I'm still alive?"

"No, of course not, you big oaf. The arrows hit you, you fell into the water . . . ," Celeste said, then clutched at his clothing, looking for wounds. "Your cloak is torn, but you're not even hurt. Why didn't you tell me?"

"Tell you what?" Morgan asked, completely confused.

"About . . . being arrowproof. Why aren't you dead?" Celeste asked.

Max joined them, carrying his duffel, and Morgan's pack and staff. "Oh, that. It's his metasilk cloak," he offered.

Celeste whirled on him. "You knew!?" she asked.

"The first time I touched it. But I don't know how he got it. It's rare and extremely expensive," Max said.

Celeste stuck her finger in Max's face. "Why didn't anybody tell me? I thought he was dead . . . ," she said, then trailed off, realizing that everyone was staring at her.

She took a last look at Morgan, and then turned to face the others. "What are you all gawking at?" she demanded.

Taurus looked at Max. "Maximilian! Great to see you. Who is this?" he asked, nodding at Celeste.

"Princess Celestine, meet Taurus, Master of the Windrider," Max said grandly.

Taurus looked skeptical. "Princess of what?" he asked.

Celeste's flash of anger and embarrassment was subsiding. She put her hands on her hips. "Of Skara Thrae, you dolt. What kind of a sea captain are you, that you don't know that?" she said sarcastically.

Taurus stared at her. "A real Princess. Well met, Princess of Skara Thrae. My ship and crew are at your service," he said, bowing clumsily.

Max leaned over and whispered to Morgan. "I think they'll get along fine."

"Taurus, I do need your help. We have to get to Aquarquff," Morgan said.

Taurus nodded toward Celeste. "The Princess too?" he asked hopefully.

Morgan nodded. "Her too. She's bound for Carnac," he said.

Taurus stepped aside and gestured toward the ship. "I rode the storm south from Skorn, and the Portmaster nearly closed the seagate on my stern. Let's get out of the rain, and talk about the price of passage. We aren't going anywhere until this storm is over," he said.

Morgan took his gear from Max, and they all moved toward the Windrider. Taurus studied Morgan's cloak. "I'll wager there's a strong market for arrowproof coats. Metasilk, you called it?" he asked.

"Forget it, Taurus. You couldn't afford it," Max said.

The Captain glanced at Max's swords. "You still have those ebonite swords?" he asked.

"Yes, and you can't afford them either," Max said.

Taurus sighed. "I guess I'd better find a cargo for Kalixalven. No sense in running with an empty hold," he said.

110

CHAPTER TEN

THE WINDRIDER

Celeste stood near the Windrider's bow, breathing deeply in the night air. The moons Asa and Mora floated overhead, moving across the backdrop of the arch and the brilliant stars. The arch and the moons cast strange reflections on the waters around the ship, gold and silver playing over the mirrored surface. She leaned against the railing and gazed down into the bow wake, but the churning water there disturbed her cursed stomach, and she looked away. She found it refreshing to lean over the rail without throwing up. Androssar had barely slipped below the horizon when she began feeling ill. Her chronic seasickness was a source of great annoyance to her. It was not very regal to spend all sea voyages feeding the fish.

The cool fresh air made her feel better, and in the darkness she could not see things swaying and moving quite so much. She turned and put her back to the rail, looking back along the length of the Windrider. It was a slim, low-riding ship, built for war and speed. Shifting shadows cloaked the ship, highlighted here and there with metal reflecting the night sky. On either side of her rested the bulky shapes of the catapults, covered with tarps against the spray. She looked up, along the sleek lines of the dragon-headed prow, with its short wings spread to shield the catapulteers. Silhouetted against Mora, the grotesque head looked almost alive.

The Windrider carried twin shearing wings, placed just above the waterline on either side of the bow. These wings could snap off oars, leaving an opponent unable to maneuver in battle, helpless before the deadly ram that lay hidden beneath the waves, its metallic beak jutting ahead of the bow.

Shields lined the rail amidships, protecting the crew from missile fire, and the rowing coop filled the center of the ship, beneath the single mast. In the light of the heavens, she could see the defiant bull on the sail, raging against the world. Like Taurus himself, always bellowing and blustering. She looked up to the swaying crow's nest. The lookout appeared as a dark figure huddled against the chill of

111

the night.

Behind the sail stretched the aft deck, with the squat enclosure housing the bridge, four passenger cabins, and the Captain's quarters. The bridge filled the front of the structure, and then came the cabins, arranged on either side of a hallway, with Taurus' cabin at the rear. The bridge had two outer doors, one on each side, and a door leading to the hall. The cabins' inner doors lined the hallway, and each cabin also had an outer door. Morgan, Max and the Princess each had a cabin to themselves, and Harkon and Taskin shared the last cabin.

Through the bridge port, she could just make out the ghostly shape of the helmsman behind the large steering wheel. A metal dragon crouched on the roof, its mouth open and wings spread. The dragon's thick tail forked at the back of the roof and curled over both sides of the stern to drop below the water line. Beyond the aft deck, the high stern reared against the stars.

The crew's quarters lay below decks forward, and then storage areas as one moved aft under the rowing compartment. Below the bridge were the galley and more storage. Due to the Windrider's relatively limited cargo space, Taurus concentrated on small bulk, high value cargo, such as luxury items.

The Windrider carried a crew of twenty-five, including the Captain. Celeste tried to remember the names of the men she had met---Seidon the First Mate, Kevan the helmsman and navigator, and Simon the cook and cabin boy. Simon was deaf, and had been most kind to her while she was sick.

A few crewmen moved across the deck, engaged in various tasks, but most of the crew had retired to their bunks. Morgan was in Taurus' cabin, looking over some maps. She noticed Max sitting amidships under a swaying lantern, polishing a bow of some black wood, his lean features intent under the harsh light of the lamp.

She moved aft, stepping down from the bow deck. Her stomach seemed to have called a temporary truce, and she felt like talking to someone. Max looked up at her approach.

"Evening, Princess. Feeling better?" he asked.

She sighed, leaning against a shield. "Momentarily. The fresh air does me good. Any chance of calling me Celeste?" she

112

asked.

Max tilted his head, considering. "Not tonight. In this light, you are a Princess," he said.

Celeste frowned. "If I thought you were serious about your flattery, I'd be worried. But then, you aren't serious about anything, are you Max?" she asked.

Max looked down at the bow, admiring the black wood as it gleamed in the lamplight. "About some things," he said, and then looked up with a grin. "But not much. Life's too serious already."

He paused, studying Celeste. "Seriously, you are beautiful," he said, and then lifted the bow, squinting along its length, looking for dry spots or blemishes. "But your honor is safe with me, I'm a gentleman. I've never forced myself on any woman."

Celeste smiled down at him. "Thank you, Max. For everything," she said.

They were silent for a moment. Celeste listened to the sound of the waves, the creak of the rigging, and the wind against the sail. Max's polish rag squeaked against the wood from time to time. Then she spoke.

"It wasn't hard to convince Taurus to take us to Aquarquff, although considering what he charged, I can see why. It took nearly all the money I had left," she said.

"We had some good times with Taurus. I think he likes having us around again. Reminds him of the old days. But he's a businessman, with bills to pay, and a ship to maintain," Max said.

"How do you know Taurus?" she asked.

"Taurus captained one of the ships that took us across the Sarlassan Sea to Vaeland. We spent three years together," Max explained.

"Vaeland? I've never heard of anyone going there," Celeste said.

"We were guarding an exploratory party. One of the Sagamores had visions of new wealth and conquest," Max said. "It ended poorly."

"What happened?" she asked.

"Morgan led the first party ashore, and they encountered

113

some natives. The locals seemed friendly enough, until they got a good look at Morgan. Then they attacked. The leader of the expedition died on that beach. Morgan held the savages back long enough for the rest of the men to escape in the longboat.

After that, we sailed along the coast, mapping the area, but no one's heart was in it. So we came home. The Sagamore died the next year, fell off his horse. That ended the western expansion," Max explained.

"What did Morgan do to provoke them?" Celeste asked.

Max looked out over the water. "It was hot that day. Morgan had stripped to the waist, but I don't think it was his splendid physique that set them off. I don't remember him saying or doing anything unusual," Max said, and then shrugged. "Whatever it was, those Vaelings were terrified of him."

"Strange," Celeste said. "What's Taurus really like, under all the bluster?"

"Taurus is a good man, although don't tell him I said that. He runs a tight ship, and is loyal to the death. He's loud and obnoxious, and he has a huge ego, but he's deadly in a fight and fears nothing. In fact, his main problem is charging in when he should be retreating," Max said.

"Is Taurus his real name?" Celeste asked.

"I don't think so. A lot of fighting men take on new names, for a variety of reasons. Taurus fancies certain qualities of his namesake," Max said.

The Princess studied Max. "I heard Taurus call you Maximilian, Le Morte Kahn. Surely that isn't your real name," she said.

Max stiffened, his rag poised over the wood. "I had another name, once," he said quietly.

"What was it?" Celeste asked.

Max hesitated, and then looked up, smiling crookedly. "Sorry, Princess. If you knew that, I'd have to kill you," he said.

"Oh. Well, maybe later," Celeste said.

One of the crew walked by on some errand, and Celeste watched him. "Aside from Seidon, Kevan, and Simon, the rest of this crew makes me nervous. They're a rough looking bunch. Where did he get them?" she asked.

"Seidon and Kevan have served with Taurus for years. I don't know where he found Simon the Deaf. As for the rest of them . . . ," Max said, then looked up at her. "You never heard of the gallows auction?"

"No, what's that?" she asked.

Max looked down, shaking his head. "Thraen isolationists. The gallows auction was started by Rulda, maybe thirty years ago. Rulda saw a means to make money on the condemned men in Androssar. He set up a system where anyone sentenced to death could choose the auction instead, and sea captains from any of the Civilized Nations could bid at the auction," Max explained.

"Bid on the men? How barbaric," Celeste protested.

"Barbaric? As opposed to what? A public hanging? Why waste men's lives, when they could be doing something productive? Let me finish. The highest bidder gets the services of the condemned man for the lifetime of the purchaser. If the buyer dies a natural death, the criminal goes free. The purchaser is called the Redeemer, the convict the Redeemed. Along with the purchase price, the buyer pays a deposit for a bounty. If the redeemed man ever runs off, the bounty goes to whoever kills him. If the Redeemer dies from anything other than natural causes, the death sentence is back in force, to be carried out as soon as possible. If a convict kills his Redeemer, he gets the Cage," Max said.

"The Cage?" Celeste asked.

"A metal cage, hanging over Andros bay. The convict is locked inside. Rainwater keeps him alive for a while, but he usually starves. Not a pleasant death.

The captains get their crews for one lump sum, crews whose futures depend on their Redeemer living a long life. The whole thing has worked so well, the five Civilized Nations entered into a treaty to enforce the Redeemer system.

Most of Taurus' men are Redeemed, but the strange thing about this crew is that their loyalty seems to go beyond self interest. From what I've seen so far, I think these men have really grown fond of their Captain," Max said.

"Where did Taurus get that awful looking weapon of his?" Celeste asked.

"Charon? The Taker to Gaol, he calls it. After the mythical ferryman who takes the evil dead to Gaol. He ran into a weapons maker on one of his voyages, a strange man of no known race or nation, who specialized in those types of weapons. He needed materials rarely found in the Civilized Nations, and so could not mass produce them. He limited himself to specialty work, for a stiff price. After Taurus saw what they could do, he had to have one, bigger and better than anyone else. Hence the three barrels," Max explained.

Celeste glanced down at Max's bow. "Speaking of weapons, that's a fine piece of weaponry you have there," she said.

Max held the bow up to the light. "Is the Princess also an archer?" he asked.

Celeste shrugged. "Father taught me to shoot when I was quite young. I didn't even know you carried a bow. Where have you been hiding it?" she asked.

Max rubbed at a stubborn spot on the gleaming wood. "Stryker stays wrapped in my weapons roll when I'm not using her. A bow isn't very effective in close quarters, so I store her when I'm in town," he said.

"Her?" Celeste shook her head. "You men and your weapons. A strange relationship. Are you any good with it?" she asked.

Max smiled coldly. "I'm very good at what I do," he said.

"You mean . . . killing people?" Celeste asked softly.

Max looked at her with an unreadable expression. "Everyone has some unique talent. This happens to be mine. I was never much good at anything else. At this, I am the best," he said.

"How do you know?" Celeste asked.

"I know. It's a passion of mine, knowing I'm the best. I keep close watch on the competition," Max said.

"What happens when you learn of a rival?" Celeste asked.

"As time permits, I seek them out, and we . . . compare abilities," Max said.

"You kill them?" Celeste asked.

116

"Princess! What kind of a butcher do you take me for? No, I don't always kill them, only if I have to. Skill is the question, not murder or spite," Max said.

Celeste decided to change the subject. "I suppose Morgan has a pet weapon too?" she asked.

Max frowned. "He did, once. *Lex Talionus*, `the law of retaliation.' A fine blade, well suited to his simple, brutal style of swordsmanship," he said.

"But now he won't use it?" Celeste asked.

"No, he's sworn an oath," Max said with a hint of contempt.

"So where is it?" she asked.

"In my bag," Max admitted.

"Just in case?" Celeste said with a grin.

Max sighed. "He'll come to his senses, sooner or later. If he doesn't, we're in trouble," he said.

"You have to admire his dedication to principle," Celeste said.

Max snorted. "No, I don't. He's an honor-bound fool, and he's going to get us both killed," he said, rubbing furiously at the bow.

Celeste had a sudden thought. "You said Morgan's cloak was made of metasilk. What is that?" she asked.

"A type of cloth, woven of metallic fibers. It's nearly impenetrable and even resists compression, acting as a sort of shock absorber. Lighter and tougher than chain mail, but rare and very expensive. Its construction is almost a lost art," Max explained.

"Where did he get it? Is Morgan rich?" Celeste asked.

"No, he's not rich. Few mercenaries ever are," Max said, and then grimaced. "As to where he got it, you'll have to ask him."

Celeste studied his expression. "You want Morgan to tell me. Who you are and what you're doing," she said.

"Yes. But it's his decision," Max said.

Max reached forward, rubbing at another spot, and Celeste was startled to see a glow inside his tunic. "Max, are you on fire?" she asked.

Max glanced down and smiled. "No, that's just something Morgan gave me," he said.

Celeste peered at the soft light. "Can I see it?" she asked.

117

Max looked around. "I suppose," he said, reaching inside his shirt and pulling out the ebonite dagger. "But don't wave it around. Taurus' crew would kill to have it."

Celeste took the dagger and turned her back to the ship, leaning on the rail. The Luminarae in the hilt convulsed and dimmed at first, then settled into a steady, pulsing glow.

"It's beautiful," Celeste breathed. "What is it?"

"A dagger," Max said.

Celeste swatted him with her free hand. "No, this," she said, pointing to the shining globe.

"Morgan called it a . . . Luminarae," Max said.

Celeste tapped the orb, and the Luminarae flared in response. "Poor thing. Is it trapped in there?" she asked.

"I don't know. I haven't heard any complaints yet," Max said.

"How would we even know? Maybe it's lonely," Celeste said.

"My main fear is that Mother will come after it," Max said, then paused. "It seems to like you. Do you want to keep it?"

"No, Max. It's yours," Celeste said as she handed the dagger back to him.

Max put the weapon away. Celeste studied him. "Morgan must be a good friend, to give you such a gift," she said.

Max looked uncomfortable. "Yes, a good friend," he said.

They were silent for a time.

"Morgan has such strange eyes," Celeste finally said. "Gray, with flecks of gold."

Max shrugged. "I never gave it much thought," he said.

"Did his parents have eyes like that?" Celeste asked.

"Morgan was a foundling, raised by an older couple that couldn't have children of their own. No one ever knew his natural parents," Max said.

"That's sad," Celeste said. "Didn't you ever wonder where he came from?"

"Not really," Max said. "Although Morgan is unusual in other ways, not just the eyes."

"What do you mean?" Celeste asked.

"He heals faster than normal, he's incredibly strong, and he has

118

more endurance and stamina than anyone I've ever met. A real freak," Max said. "In fact, some of our more enlightened neighbors in Falmount thought he was a Changeling, a son of Yfel."

"How old is he?" Celeste asked.

Max sighed and looked out over the dark water. "Well, I was born in 5916, so I'll be ninety-six in the fall. Morgan must be about the same age," he said.

"You don't know? When is his birthday?" Celeste asked.

"Some villagers found him. He didn't have any papers on him," Max said. "Since he didn't know his own birthday, we celebrated at the same time."

"You said Morgan was particular about his women. What did you mean by that?" Celeste asked.

Max shifted uncomfortably, taking on a hunted look. "He's too . . . serious about his relationships. He's not shallow and selfish like me. When he falls, he falls hard, and he stays down, if you know what I mean," Max said.

"Oh, I see. Was he ever in love?" she asked.

"I suppose. Once or twice. But it never worked out," Max said.

"What about Malissa?" Celeste asked.

Max laughed. "Don't worry about her. There was no love there," he said.

Celeste spoke slowly, with forced nonchalance. "Doesn't Morgan like me?" she asked.

Max stopped his polishing, and looked at her in surprise. "What makes you ask that?" he said.

Celeste turned around to face the sea, so Max could not see her face. "I don't know. Ever since Androssar, he's been avoiding me," she said.

Max thought for a moment, considering his words. "Morgan thinks this trip is very important. He just doesn't want any distractions right now," he said. "Even very pleasant ones."

"Is that all I am? A distraction?" Celeste said in a tight voice.

Max stood up and stretched. "I've already said more that I should have. It's none of my business. If you want to know how Morgan feels about you, ask him. It's obvious to me," he said.

119

Celeste looked over her shoulder at Max, as he gathered up his things. "Obvious? What do you mean by that?" she asked.

"I think you know. Good night, Princess," he said.

Max moved toward the passenger cabins, then stopped and turned.

"Princess?" he said.

Celeste looked at him. "Yes, Max?" she said.

"Are we friends?" he asked.

Celeste turned around and leaned on the rail. "Well, sure. Why do you ask?" she asked.

"I know you're not interested in me as a lover. Are you just using me to get to Morgan?" Max asked, his voice tense.

"I don't use people, Max," she said. "We both know you don't want me as a lover."

Max pursed his lips, thinking. "You know, you're probably right. You're not my type. I like the frilly empty ones. They're easier to leave in the morning. You have too much . . . personality," he said.

"Friends, then," Celeste said.

Max smiled, and for once it warmed his eyes. "Friends," he said, and then walked away, whistling some raunchy tune.

The Princess remained, alone with her thoughts.

CHAPTER ELEVEN
THE MHOUL

The Windrider slid through the waves under a blue sky dotted with piles of cloud. The ship rose and fell in the heavy swells, a gusty wind rippling the sail. Spray kicked up by the bow flecked the shields lining the rails and occasionally splattered across the deck. The dragon head prow glared to the south across the choppy sea, ignoring the smudge of land on the eastern horizon.

The lookout swayed to and fro in the tiny crow's nest, his eyes slitted against the wind and sun. He had just surveyed the southern horizon, now he swung smoothly around. He glanced at the distant coastline, when something to the north caught his eye. He picked up his watchglass and peered through it. He could barely make out a squat black shape on the line between sea and sky. It appeared to be a ship of sorts . . . but something looked wrong.

The man jerked around, and bellowed for the Mate through cupped hands. As his cry whipped away in the wind another sound reached his ears---a strange chugging murmur, coming from the north. He was about to yell again when the Mate stepped out of the bridge cabin and squinted up from the shade of the dragon on the roof.

"What is it, Tyder?" Seidon called.

"A ship I think, but a strange one. Coming at us from the north," Tyder said.

"What do you mean, strange? A pirate?" Seidon asked as he stepped to the rail.

"Look for yourself, I'm not sure what I see," Tyder admitted.

Seidon pulled out his glass and scanned the north as Tyder leaned over the nest rail, glancing nervously from the Mate to the sea. Seidon looked long and hard when he found the ship, then cocked his head at the throbbing sound, which steadily grew louder.

"Keep your eye on it, Tyder. Yell if it does anything," Seidon said as he moved quickly to the cabin door.

"Captain, you better have a look at this," he said.

121

A thick figure appeared in a doorway at the rear of the bridge. "Look at what?" Taurus asked.

Seidon, unflappable as always, tersely summed up the situation. "A ship coming this way, made of metal, with no oars or sails, and its stomach rumbles," he said.

The Captain looked disgusted, threw his ale mug on a side table and lumbered for the door, followed by Max and Morgan. The heavyset shipmaster passed Seidon without a look.

"If I didn't know you better, I'd bust your head for being drunk on duty. Give me your glass," he growled.

Seidon handed him the glass and pointed to the north, while the Captain steadied himself against the rim of a shield. "Well, you aren't drunk," he said after a moment.

Taurus passed the glass to Morgan. "Have a look," he said.

Morgan studied the ship briefly, and then tossed the spyglass to Max, who caught it deftly. The black ship was moving fast, and getting uncomfortably close. Its throbbing filled the air.

"We should put as much distance between us and that ship as we possibly can," Morgan stated firmly.

Taurus smirked. "The ship has no sail or oars. You afraid of a ship that isn't even all there? Not to mention the fact there isn't any sign that it's manned?" he said.

Morgan looked down at the squat Captain. "I am afraid, and you'd better be. Now let's get out of here," he said.

The Captain laughed. "Don't worry, Taurus will take care of you," he said.

"I agree with Morgan. We should leave now," Max said as he finished his examination and lowered the glass.

Taurus spat in the direction of the black ship and walked toward the cabin.

"Seidon, sound for battle, drop the sail and rig for speed. I'm firing up the draken. We'll show these landfolk what a real ship can do," he said.

Seidon began furiously ringing a bell hanging on the cabin corner. "Look alive, you men," he shouted.

Max turned to Morgan, who was staring thoughtfully at the

black ship. "That looks like the metal ship the Princess described," he said.

"You're right. It has the appearance of Mhoul technology. If it is, we'll have to fight. Why don't you get Stryker and be ready on the forward deck. I'll check on the Princess and make sure she stays out of sight," he said.

"You think she's what they're after?" Max asked as he calmly studied the pursuit.

Morgan shrugged. "I don't know, but after the Demented Boar and the ambush at the docks, I'm beginning to think they want her bad," he said as he turned and headed for the cabins.

"Great, from now on I'll be more careful about who I rescue," Max said as he followed Morgan toward the cabins.

At the sound of the bell, seamen boiled out of hatches and doorways, loosening rigging and taking stations. The sail dropped, its lines singing through the pulleys. Two men ran forward and jerked the covers from the catapults, while others readied oars and laid weapons between benches in the rowing bay.

Inside the bridge cabin, Taurus moved to a console next to the massive helm wheel, closing relays and flipping switches. A sudden roar erupted from the dragon on the bridge roof. A blast of inky exhaust belched from its nostrils and whipped away in the wind. The Captain adjusted a lever and the roar settled. He glanced through the port at Seidon, who was supervising the lowering of the sail. The Mate nodded and waved, and then jumped down to the deck. Max appeared, carrying Stryker and his quiver. He moved forward, and found a place on the bow deck, out of the way of the catapulteers.

The burly Captain twisted a wheel and the water at the Windrider's stern churned into a white froth. Sucked in through the metal dragon's jaws and forced out through the forked tail, a steady blast of air against the sea shoved the Windrider forward. Kevan the helmsman, knowing what to expect, took a white-knuckled grip on the wheel. Taurus shoved a lever up and the Windrider leaped ahead, the sound of groaning timbers mixing with the throbbing of the black ship. Taurus pushed the lever to the last notch and the dragon's roar shook the deck. Max had to step farther behind the shields to get out of the violent bowspray. The Windrider reared up and the stabilizing fins under either side of the bow cut through the water like twin blades. The black ship fell suddenly behind.

Morgan returned to the bridge. "Very impressive. Where did you steal a draken?" he asked.

The Captain folded his arms, keeping a careful eye on the draken's control panel. "I took it from a corsair we sank a few years back. I kept it for nasty surprises like this," he said.

Taurus waved at the door. "See how far behind they are now. You know, we should have faced them rather than running. Makes a bad first impression."

"I wouldn't lay odds on your lifespan with that attitude, my friend. You shouldn't fight something until you know what it is," Morgan said as he looked aft through the door. "We've pulled ahead, but it's still there. Is this as fast as she goes?"

Taurus bristled. "Nothing can catch us now."

"Wrong. Take a look," Morgan said as moved aside.

Taurus scowled out the door. "It isn't fair, they're using sorcery," he complained.

Morgan laughed. "So what do you call your draken?"

"That isn't the same, I'm just magnifying a natural force, but who ever heard of a ship with no sail or oars. That isn't natural," Taurus said.

"I'm sure there's some explanation. Different form of technology, that's all. Don't call the shaman yet," Morgan said.

Taurus checked some readings, and adjusted a dial. "How's the Princess? She feeling any better?" he asked.

Morgan grimaced. "She doesn't take well to the high seas. She's in her cabin, sleeping off the last bout of seasickness. These rough seas make her worse. Simon's taking care of her."

Morgan looked aft again. The black ship was regaining the lost distance, plowing effortlessly through the waves, its throbbing louder now, the beats closer together. There was still no sign of life on the decks.

The Windrider's seasoned crew stood ready for battle. The catapults had been winched back and loaded with fire bombs, although Salk and Fors, the catapulteers, doubted their effectiveness on a metal ship. Max had his bow out, and had already gauged the distance for a shot, should anything appear on the ship's decks to shoot at. The men in the rowing bay kept peering through the shields along the rail, trying to get a glimpse of the pursuer.

Taurus had a satisfied look. "Well, looks like we'll have to fight, whether you want to or not."

He signaled to Kevan, who spun the wheel as the Captain backed off on the power to the draken's engines. The draken's rumble eased and their speed slackened. The Windrider cut around in an arc, leaning heavily from the speed of the turn. The black ship throbbed inexorably forward as spray slid from its metal flanks.

Taurus shut down the sea draken as he shouted orders. "Ready oars! Close quarters battle stations!"

Seidon relayed the commands and the Windrider's crew scrambled to obey. Oars clanked in the rowing bay as men slid them into oarlocks. The sailors not occupied with the final preparations lined the rails, nervously gripping weapons and grappling hooks. The Windrider had turned directly into the path of the oncoming ship, losing momentum rapidly as it plowed through the swells. The draken gave a final belch of smoke and fell silent.

Seidon entered the bridge and moved to Taurus' side. They peered at the black ship through the port.

Morgan stood in the doorway. "Well, now you'll have the fight you wanted. What's the plan, Captain?" he asked.

"Better not ram her, if she is all metal, we'd lose that one," Taurus said, thinking out loud. "No oars to shear . . . or sail to burn . . . no crew to fight . . . "

The Captain shook his head in exasperation. "Guess we'll just warm them up with a volley of fire bombs and see what the heat drives out."

Morgan stepped out to the rail for a closer look at the ship. He could see the rivets in the metal skin and some rust along the water line, and on the deck, a small forward cabin with a view slit and a high sterncastle to the rear. A short mast with a disc rose from the back of the forward cabin, but otherwise the deck was featureless and still deserted. The craft rode low in the water, even lower than the Windrider, which would mean that any boarders from the Windrider would have the advantage of a higher position. Even as he watched, the ship slowed slightly, its throbbing beat easing off.

Inside the bridge cabin, Taurus turned and went to a locker in the corner. Opening it with an ornate key on his neck chain, he pulled out Charon. He opened the weapon, checked the barrels, and loaded it with heavy projectiles from a metal box in the locker. He stuffed more shells into his belt pouch and set the gun next to the control console.

The black ship was still out of catapult range, giving the catapulteers time to make final adjustments. For the first time, there was movement on the ebon deck, and three figures emerged from a hatch near the sterncastle. Two of them towered over the third, a figure wrapped in black.

Seidon turned his glass toward them. "Now we have a black mummy and two giants with bad skin, dressed in armor," he said.

Morgan grabbed Seidon's glass and peered through it. He stiffened.

"A Mhoul, and two trolls," he said softly. "The Princess was right."

"What are you muttering?" Taurus asked as he stepped to the doorway and strained to see more clearly.

"Mhoul . . . from Faerie, to the east. Remember them?" Morgan asked.

"Sure . . . but they never come this far west," Taurus stated firmly.

"They have now," Morgan said. "And the trolls."

"Trolls?!" Taurus exploded. "What have you gotten me into, Morgan?"

"Sorry, old friend. But it looks like they're here, after all this time. The trolls and their masters have entered the Land of Men. According to the Princess, the Mhoul were involved in the invasion of Skara Thrae. They must be after her," Morgan said.

"And you didn't tell me?" Taurus demanded.

"You didn't ask, you just took our money," Morgan reminded

him.

"A bad habit I picked up since the old days. Some of my civilian passengers prefer not to advertise their travel plans. But you still should have told me. You know what the Mhoul are capable of," Taurus persisted.

"Once again, I'm sorry. I didn't think they could follow her across the sea," Morgan said.

Taurus sighed and looked out the port at his men. "Well, I wanted a fight. But my poor crew has no idea . . . I've never fought a troll myself, only heard your stories," he said.

Morgan gripped Taurus' shoulder. "They are mortal. Max and I have killed them. It's just a lot harder. We'll have casualties though," he said. "Their natural armor will turn most sword or spear thrusts, and even arrows. Charon's slugs will probably penetrate, aim for the head or the chest."

"What about the Mhoul? Will it fight us?" Taurus asked.

"They seldom risk themselves in open combat. They don't heal, and any injuries are permanent. Their technology is what I fear," Morgan said.

Taurus turned back into the cabin and picked up Charon, gripping it with his big hands like an anchor in a storm. "Thaar only smiles on the brave. Let's kill some trolls, Morgan," he said.

On the forward deck, Max fitted an arrow to his bow, drew and aimed high. The arrow arched out to meet the black ship, barely falling short.

"Just checking the range," he said to no one in particular.

As if in answer, the disc on the stubby mast swung around to face the Windrider, and a barely audible sound floated across the water. When it reached the men on the Windrider, the strident notes penetrated deep into their brains and immediately made them feel weak and dizzy. For Morgan, the sensation triggered a strange panic.

He shouted frantically, a touch of hysteria in his voice. "Get away from that sound!" he cried, clutching at his ears. "We have to get away!"

Kevan tore the wheel around, while Taurus stared at Morgan. He had never seen the big man show such fear. The Captain lurched for the draken controls, dropping Charon to the floor in his haste. Some of the crew dove into the rowing coop, and shoved oars back into the water. The sound swelled into a terrible keening, and the seamen outside milled aimlessly, hands digging into their ears. Morgan turned toward the Princess' cabin, forcing his body to obey.

The wailing sound suddenly increased in volume, rising and falling in pitch, and with it the numbing pain in their skulls. A deadness spread quickly through their limbs, making it hard to move. Morgan struggled to reach the hall to the cabins, but by the time he had ground out those few steps, all he could do was sag against the doorway.

The screaming sound grew to fill the world, and the Windrider's crew collapsed all over the deck, writhing and clawing at their tortured ears, oblivious to all but the wail from the black ship. Max lay rigid against the dragon prow, Stryker gripped in one useless hand, arrows scattered around him. Taurus hunched over the control console, his face purple with pain, and Kevan hung from the wheel   like a crucified man, his hands locked in agony.

Morgan made another effort, but he lost his balance, falling over backwards. The shock of hitting the floor deadened the keening for a moment, and he rolled over, and then began to drag himself toward the bridge door. If he could make it over the rail, the water should muffle the sound and lessen its effect. With the frenzied wail beating at him, he crawled to the door, his arms and legs like wood. He threw out one arm, trying to grip the side of the door and pull himself up, but his fingers refused to obey and only slapped painfully against the wood. He pushed himself up with his arms, and dragged his legs under him. The effort sapped the last of his strength and he fell back against the doorjamb. He ended up sitting in the bridge door, with his head lolling against the door frame.

As he sat there, helpless, his limbs paralyzed, alone with the sound that drilled into his brain, he realized this torture was somehow familiar. The wailing call began to awaken memories buried for twelve years.

He squeezed his eyes shut, but could not stop the images erupting inside his head. A dead wasteland, all twisted rock and shifting ash, the wind carrying a burnt, metallic stench. Night skies blue with radiation, thirst and hunger, dust and the fatigue of the long march. The black towers of Mogda Thal below him, dwarfed by a huge mountain looming in the background. A sound, a horrible wailing---Morgan could not tell if that was part of his memories or just the screaming from the black ship. Anger, terrible anger, rage and fear engulfing him, carrying him away.

Sergeant Malor, screaming, his eyes bulging, running at him with a bloody sword. Morgan's enraged response, and then the sight of the man he had served with for years laying dead at his feet. Crazed soldiers running blindly, clawing at their faces, and killing anything that came within reach. A man on his knees, sobbing, and a fellow Raav ramming a sword into his back. Imperius being hacked to death by his own troops, and Morgan shouting, urging them on. Gripping his sword two handed, Morgan chopping through his own men, their bodies falling all around him. And surrounding him, filling him, born of the wailing, was the rage, the madness, making him want to kill and kill and kill.

Running through a dead land, the stench of blood in his nostrils, the rage spent, but the madness lingering. Survivors of the butchery stumbling along beside him, all of them nearly oblivious to the others. The waiting line of Immortals, Harriers, and trolls. More insane fighting and the screams of the dying. He knew he took wounds, again and again, but he felt nothing in his madness. Then he was falling, and there was water. He remembered lying exhausted under some brush, while the enemy finished the Raavs. He stared at his nicked and stained sword, hating it and himself.

The rush of memories passed, leaving him empty, shaking, and drenched with cold sweat. In the emptiness, Morgan felt a growing rage, a burning fire in a dead body. A hatred created by what had been done to him, and by what he had done. Morgan forced himself back to the present, made himself aware of his surroundings.

Morgan opened his eyes, fighting back tears of rage and horror. The black ship closed the gap, swinging smoothly around the shearing wing, contemptuously snapping off several oars that hung limply from the Windrider's side. The metal craft came alongside with a slight grating, matching speeds with its helpless victim. The wailing dish turned to bear always on the Windrider.

Four men emerged from the black ship's forward cabin, grappled the two ships securely together with three sets of hooks, and then slid out a boarding ramp that clanged over the rail just forward of the Windrider's bridge cabin.

Another man appeared behind the three figures at the stern. All of the men wore heavy helmets and seemed unaffected by the awful wailing. The trolls and the Mhoul had no such protection, but the sound had no effect on them either. The three nonhumans advanced to the boarding ramp, the central figure stiffly striding along in the swirl of a black cape, and its companions moving with the ponderous troll gait. The men followed.

A troll took the lead and as the boarders clambered over the rail, they passed into Morgan's frozen field of vision. Trolls stood two heads taller than a man, weighing over twenty stone. Jointed plates of natural armor covered most of their hairless bodies, a dark, leathery brown. In the few places where he could see the actual skin, it resembled sun-baked clay, cracked and copper colored. The trolls wore trappings of black leather over the armor.

The lead troll stepped slowly to the deck, its black eyes scanning the Windrider and its helpless crew, the heavy jaw hanging loosely, the spadelike teeth visible in the mouth cavity. Its plated fist gripped a mace of lacquered wood, and a leather helm shrouded the ridged skull. Morgan could hear air being sucked into the breathing holes along the troll's ribs, and caught the first whiff of its sour odor.

The troll turned its head slightly, and a buzzing purr came from its jawline. Morgan could see the speech membrane on the neck fluttering slightly, just before the translator around its neck converted the noise into human speech.

"The humans are down. You may board," it said in harsh mechanical tones.

The troll stepped aside and the Mhoul came into view, swathed in rough black bandages, wearing a black cloak with the hood drawn about its skull. Bandages also muffled the face, the nose making a slight peak in the center. A speaker grille covered the lower part of the face, and large black goggles hid the eyeholes. The Mhoul wore leather gloves and boots, and a belt fitted with loops and pouches encircled its waist. A chain with a complicated medallion, its face covered with blinking lights, hung around the Mhoul's neck.

The Mhoul moved stiffly, its feet thudding on the deck like dead things, and as it moved closer, Morgan smelled it. He had attended cremations before and never forgot that odor of burning flesh. The Mhoul carried with it the same scorched tang.

Something perched on the Mhoul's shoulder, a grayish green toad of a thing, about the size of a cat, with a single eye bobbing on a stalk. Its knobby fingers clutched the black fabric of the Mhoul's cloak possessively and it seemed to be whispering into the Mhoul's ear. Morgan remembered the Mhoul called them riths.

A second troll followed, and the next figure was human---Thugmonger Wald. Four other men climbed aboard and grouped themselves around the ramp head. Morgan could see them out of the corner of his eye. The grayish, hairless skin, strange eyes, and identical features marked them as Immortals. The Immortals all carried drawn swords, and wore light armor.

The Mhoul passed its vacant gaze over the paralyzed crew, the rith clutching and gibbering constantly. The trolls moved to flank the Mhoul, alert and poised, and Thugmonger Wald cowered in the rear. No trace remained of the arrogance he had shown in the Demented Boar.

The Mhoul's sweep ended and it seemed to focus on something in Morgan's direction, and then it turned and stalked toward him. The Immortals remained to guard the ladder, while the trolls and Thugmonger followed the Mhoul. As the Mhoul approached the door where Morgan sat, he noticed a strange red glow leaking from the smoked lenses of the goggles. He felt a strong compulsion to see through the lenses, to discover what burned there. As he looked, the glow seemed to grow suddenly, enveloping him in its redness, sending out crimson fingers groping for his mind. The ruby haze swept over the walls Morgan had raised against his rage and the terrible memories. He lost control, his defenses crumbling.

A tidal wave of raw emotion welled up, driving back the

invading redness. Images flickered at the edge of his consciousness, but Morgan avoided them, concentrating on the rage. The Mhoul faltered in its advance, and then recoiled slightly. The toad on its shoulder screeched, and stiffened, its eye stalk waving wildly. The crimson glow retreated, withdrawn back into the dark goggles. Morgan struggled to contain the surge of anger that still seethed within him.

Through that brief contact, he had definitely attracted the Mhoul's attention. It came closer, moving more carefully now, and all too soon the Mhoul and its escort stood over him. The creature in black tilted its head with a rasp of metallic cloth, as if listening. The rith perched silently, its eye stalk arched downward. The Mhoul stood absolutely still, like a statue, and Morgan remembered they did not need to breathe. The burnt smell, much stronger now, stung his nostrils.

Thugmonger peered over the Mhoul's shoulder. "That's the man who ambushed us at the tavern, stole the Princess, and then by treachery escaped us at the docks," he said.

The Mhoul spoke, flat, metallic sounds coming from the speaker grille. "This man escaped due to your failure . . . as did the Princess. Do I have to remind you of that again?" it said.

Thugmonger recoiled visibly at the rebuke. He paled and cowered further, about to flee in terror at some memory the Mhoul's words evoked.

"No, Dirgelord, never again, I won't fail you again! But that's Morgan Caeda. And Maximillian's here too. They were Raav Commanders. It's not my fault," the fat man said, hatred for Morgan mingled with terror of the Mhoul in his eyes.

The Mhoul turned toward Wald, who backed away. "Morgan Caeda is long dead. Fetch the Princess," the Mhoul intoned in its mechanical whisper.

"Yes, Molid," Wald said. Relieved to have a reason to get away, he eased past the trolls and entered the bridge, stepping over Morgan.

Morgan nearly killed himself straining to move, sick with dread at the nightmare before him, and the thought of the Princess in the Mhoul's dead hands. The rage of his memories still coursed through him, and only the paralysis kept him from screaming. Molid regarded Morgan, impassively observing his struggles, as if he were a dying fish gasping on the shore. The creature on the Mhoul's shoulder also seemed to sense Morgan's effort and slobbered something to its host.

The Mhoul continued searching, trying to re-establish that former mental contact. Probing, it attempted to sense Morgan's thoughts, but Morgan let the rage blot out everything else.

"Rage. But underneath . . ." the Mhoul began, and then suddenly leaned closer. "You are Morgan Caeda! How did you survive the Veil?"

At the Mhoul's words the two trolls began to tremble, their speech membranes trilling, their black orbs fixed on Morgan. O Iosus, what a fate, Morgan thought, to be held helpless in the presence of such monstrosities. He prayed silently. Iosus, set me free, if only to die fighting and not be slaughtered like a helpless babe.

Molid tilted its head oddly, as if trying to see better. The rith stretched forward, its cyclops eye on Morgan. "The Nestbreaker. Should I give you to my trolls? Their vengeance would . . ." it began.

As if in answer to Morgan's desperate prayer, a shout came from somewhere on the bridge roof, followed by three chugging blasts. Molid's chest seemed to explode, the medallion shattered into a cloud of spinning fragments. The impact punched the Mhoul backward and flung it over the rail. A similar sledge hammer blow struck the troll to Molid's left, peeling away the armored plates of its shoulder, and shredding the leather trappings. The troll staggered back, thudded off the rail, and collapsed in a pool of seeping brownish fluid. A gaping hole had also appeared in the wooden rail between the two creatures.

At the first sound from the roof, the second troll had thrown its mace, but even as the mace flew upwards, the troll's companions were struck down. The neighboring violence did not faze the troll, and it quickly brandished a second club of hardened wood. However, the target of its attack seemed to have vanished, and the troll lost a vital moment searching for its assailant.

With the destruction of Molid's medallion, the disc on the black ship's mast drifted loosely to one side. The numbing wail that had filled the air for an eternity ceased. Freed from its awful grip, Morgan went limp with relief. The slight movement attracted the troll's attention and it raised the club.

Morgan wrenched his awakening muscles into action, and rolled backwards through the bridge door. The descending club tore loose a chunk of the door frame where his head had been, showering him with bits of wood. Morgan scrambled away from the troll looming in the doorway. Suddenly, an arrow clattered from its skull plates, tearing the leather skullcap askew. The troll turned toward the new threat, and Morgan knew Max still lived.

Morgan got to his feet, cursing his numb legs. He noticed Taurus dragging himself toward the opposite door, his attention fixed on something just outside. Kevan still hung limply from the wheel, moaning. Seidon was trying to climb out of the corner where he had fallen. Morgan caught a movement out of the corner of his eye and twisted as Thugmonger's sword split the air beside him.

Before Morgan could retaliate, Wald lurched forward, clutching at his back, a shocked look on his face. He toppled heavily, revealing the grim features of the Princess and her stained dagger. Still weak from the sound weapon and her bouts of seasickness, the sudden activity left her breathless. She sagged against the doorway, white-faced.

"Wald burst into my cabin and dragged me up here . . . no strength to fight him," she said weakly.

Morgan staggered to her side and turned her half around. "Go back to your cabin, block the doors, and wait for one of us to come for you. Can you make it?" he asked.

Celeste nodded and turned. "I'll be in my cabin," she said.

The Princess waved her bloody dagger and disappeared down the hall. Thugmonger lay where he had fallen, a crimson stain spreading across his back. While Morgan helped Seidon to his feet, they could hear Taurus roaring somewhere outside. Glancing through the bridge port, Morgan saw that pandemonium reigned on the deck. Taurus shouted again and a chugging blast bloodied two

134

of the Immortals at the ramp. They staggered back, cartwheeling over the rail, as the other two Immortals closed ranks.

Seidon shook his head to clear it and drew his sword. "The Captain sounds angry. I'd better attend him," he said.

On the way out, the Mate grabbed Kevan's collar and pulled him toward the far door. "Time to fight, helmsman," he informed the groggy man.

Morgan looked back outside. Members of Taurus' crew milled around, yelling and waving their weapons, still half dazed and terrified of the trolls and the Mhoul. Even as Morgan watched, their fear focused on the Immortals at the ladder and they surged forward.

Morgan stepped out through the bridge door. Much to his alarm, he could not see the two trolls, although an auburn smear led toward the rear of the ship. He looked forward, and saw Max calmly drawing down on the Immortals.

"Max! Find the trolls!" he shouted.

Max heard him over the din, and swung around, searching the deck over his drawn arrow. Morgan heard a crash of splintering wood and a scream from the direction of the Princess' cabin. We've found the trolls, Morgan thought grimly, as he leaped back inside. He bent over the fallen Wald, hesitated briefly, and then picked up the man's sword. He ran toward the rear cabins as another scream split the air, followed by the sounds of a violent conflict. As he got closer, Morgan realized the screams carried more anger than fear.

He shoved on the door to the Princess' cabin, but as instructed, she had blocked the door. The attack must have come from the outside door.

"Open the door," Morgan shouted.

"I . . . can't . . . come to the door . . . right now," came the Princess' response, mingled with the sounds of a continuing struggle.

Morgan backed up and threw himself at the door. The heavy wood shattered at the impact, and pieces flew across the room. Morgan's momentum carried him halfway across the cabin. He was amazed at what he saw.

The Princess, her anger giving her terrific strength, had the troll with the shoulder wound backed into a corner, battering it viciously

135

with a chair. The troll, who had been trying to capture her unharmed, looked like it was about ready to change its mind. The cabinet that the Princess had shoved against the inner door now lay against the troll's legs, further hindering its movements. Morgan's entrance had thrown the cabinet clear across the room.

Seeing Morgan, the troll glanced toward the outside door, which hung in pieces from its hinges. The troll kicked the cabinet from its legs and shoved the Princess and her chair over backwards, then whirled and leaped out the door. Morgan ran after the troll, but collided heavily with Celeste, who had jumped back up, ready to continue the attack.

"Stinking, foul beast breaks into my cabin and puts its scabby hands on me," she yelled as Morgan tried to untangle himself from her.

"Celeste, get out of the way. Let me handle this," Morgan pleaded.

"Well then handle it! First Wald, and then I have to fight trolls. At least the troll was trying to take me alive, but you nearly killed me. That cabinet just missed me," she raged, then collapsed on the bed, the chair clattering to the floor. "And I'm still sick."

"Please just stay here," he said as he turned and went after the troll.

As he stepped out the door, the waiting troll knocked him to his knees. Fortunately, he had seen the attack coming and managed to roll his head and shoulders forward so the mace skidded down his back. The force was still great enough to flatten him, and without the metasilk cloak, he would have suffered broken bones. He rolled onto his back, trying to suck air into his lungs, gasping with pain and shock. He somehow managed to deflect a second blow with his sword. The troll stepped back for another swing, as Morgan tried to scramble to his feet.

Without warning, the Princess erupted from the battered doorway and pitched a heavy statue at the troll's head. The troll reared back, and the statue struck it squarely in the ruined shoulder. The troll thrummed in pain, and then lurched, half turning. Morgan could see an arrow sticking out of its lower back, piercing the heavy leather plate that covered one of the few weak spots in the troll's armor. Morgan leaped up, and knocked the mace aside with one arm. He rammed his sword into the base of the troll's throat, thrusting half the blade's length up into its head. The troll sagged into his arms, drenching him with its blood. He twisted and threw the dying troll over the rail, leaving the sword protruding from its jaw.

"Thank you, Princess," Morgan panted as he wiped troll blood from his face and leaned against the rail. "Fortunately for me, you're not some frail damsel."

"I am my father's daughter," she said, brandishing a second statue.

"Wonderful. I can't wait to meet your father," Morgan muttered as he turned to rejoin the battle.

Celeste sagged against the rail, the statue falling to her side. "Saving everyone is quite exhausting," she observed.

The second troll had circled around, and attacked the sailors from the opposite side, hoping to create enough of a distraction that its companion could escape with the Princess. The troll now fought in a circle of yelling seamen, while Max stood on the front deck, waiting for an opportunity to shoot it. The Immortals at the ramp had all fallen and Taurus stood over their bodies, encouraging his men in their battle with the troll. Taskin and Harkon stood behind the ring of sailors.

Morgan glanced at the black ship just in time to see a third troll emerge from the forward cabin, lean over the opposite rail and drag Molid from the sea. Morgan expected to see a gaping hole in the Mhoul's chest, but although the medallion chain hung in shattered links, and the bandage strips across the chest were gouged and disheveled, Molid appeared relatively undamaged. The sight reminded Morgan that the Mhoul wove their bandages and cloak from metasilk. The rith had somehow retained its grip and flailed about, hissing and screeching. The dripping Mhoul got to its feet and staggered toward the sterncastle with the troll at its side.

Morgan shouted and waved, getting Max's attention. "The Mhoul, stop the Mhoul!" he yelled.

Max shifted slightly. A moment later the arrow slammed into

137

Molid's chest, staggering the Mhoul. The shaft did not penetrate the black cloth, but bounced off and fell to the deck.

"Metasilk. Aim for the goggles," Morgan shouted.

The troll surged ahead to put itself between its master and the deadly archer. Max reloaded, but could not get a clear shot at the Mhoul's head. He hesitated a moment, then fired again. The arrow plucked the rith from Molid's shoulder like a piece of rotten fruit. The toad creature hissed horribly as it flopped to the deck, the arrow transfixing its hideous form. Molid staggered, clutching at its head as if in pain, then sagged against the sterncastle. The Mhoul drew itself up, its rage projecting like a solid thing. The mental wave was so tangible it caused a lull in the fighting, as men looked around for the source of the sudden black pall.

The Mhoul turned, facing generally in Max's direction, and its metal voice rasped into the momentary silence. "You will die for that," it grated.

Molid then turned away, its arms outstretched, guiding itself down into the sterncastle hatch. The rith lay twitching on the cold deck. The third troll took up a defensive position at the hatch.

The troll on the Windrider still fought. Taurus' men thrust and slashed at the troll, but their swords skidded from the plated skin. The troll stood its ground, the mace lashing into the knot of men. Taskin yelled for their attention.

"Strike at the joints," Taskin directed. "Or the throat or the lower back."

Seeing that the crew ignored him, Taskin sighed. He leaped forward, hacking at the troll's knee. His sword dug in, but the troll shifted its weight, and swung at Taskin, forcing him to retreat.

"What are you doing? Be careful," Harkon urged.

Taskin circled, looking for another opening. "I've fought trolls before, but these fools won't listen. This could go on all day."

Unable to fire without hitting his men, Taurus dropped Charon and leaped into the fray with a double bladed ax. Made bold by their fearless Captain, the hardy sailors redoubled their efforts and finally overwhelmed the troll by sheer weight of numbers. They piled on the troll, forcing it kicking and thrashing to the deck, the mace torn from its grip. Taskin ran forward, stabbing deeply into the throat area. The troll, leaking brown ooze from multiple wounds, finally lay still. The troll had killed two sailors, and several more clutched battered limbs as they staggered back from the troll's body.

The thought that Molid might escape sent a surge of anger through Morgan. He shoved through the sailors, grabbing a fallen sword. Max dropped Stryker and leaped nimbly after the big man, drawing his own swords. Morgan vaulted over the rail to the deck of the black ship. His former rage had been dampened by concern for the Princess, but now it erupted again as he faced the troll. This creature stood between him and the Mhoul, one of those responsible for the horror he had experienced at Mogda Thal. A horror so unthinkable his mind refused to even bear the memory of it, leaving him with tormented visions and nightmares. Because of the Mhoul, seven Legions of Raavs had been massacred, the only survivors half-mad wrecks, their lives destroyed. In Morgan's present state of mind, he saw the troll as just something in his way, something to kill.

The troll stepped forward from the stern well, hefting its mace.

"Molid says you are the Nestbreakers. Come to me and die," the troll said, its grating words barely understandable as they emerged from the translator around its neck.

Morgan immediately took the offensive, hacking and thrusting furiously. His anger doubled his already considerable strength, and the huge troll was actually driven back a few paces by the ferocity of Morgan's onslaught. Morgan's blade struck it again and again, but the tough plates of armor deflected his sword every time. The troll relied mainly on its natural defenses to turn Morgan's attack, and concentrated on smashing the man with its mace. It fought silently, the leather harness creaking as it moved, its breath whistling from its sides. Morgan avoided direct parries, instead he attacked, then twisted away to elude the troll's murderous counterattacks.

Morgan pressed forward, and suddenly Max fought at his side, his slim blades flashing.

"What happened to your sacred oath?" Max asked.

"I vowed . . . to never again . . . raise a sword . . . against my fellow man . . . this is not a man," Morgan said.

Max ducked under the lashing mace and thrust. The black point slid up under a plate on the troll's side. When he pulled it free, troll blood followed, brown ichor staining the copper hide.

"I see . . . a most carefully worded oath," he replied.

They fought on, Max stabbing at joints or openings in the troll's armor, but unable to seriously wound their adversary. Morgan continued to use brute force, half blind with rage. Several of his blows actually damaged the troll's armor; he delivered them with such savagery.

"Molid is getting away. Do you want to keep hacking at the troll like a tree or do you want to kill it, like we did so many times before?" Max finally asked.

Morgan stepped back a pace, glancing at Max. The troll charged, swinging the mace. Both men jumped aside, and almost as one, chopped at the backs of the troll's knees. Morgan missed the joint, his blade merely scoring the armored calf. Max's blade bit in, but not deep enough to disable the leg. The troll turned and its mace was everywhere, smashing and pounding. Morgan dodged one blow, but a second he had to parry, and the mace shattered his sword blade. Morgan staggered back, holding the stub between him and the troll. The troll fended off Max with a back swing, and moved in for the kill. Morgan managed to avoid the first swing, and then Max stabbed at the wounded leg again, forcing it to turn.

"Out of the way!" Taurus' bellow cut through the crash of combat.

Morgan and Max backed off, trying to watch both the troll and the approaching Captain. The troll looked over their shoulders and raised itself defiantly to full height.

"Cowardly man-things," the troll said, any emotion bled from the statement by the translator.

Charon bucked and roared. The troll lurched, its legs blown out from under it. Morgan stepped in and seized the troll's mace arm. Yanking it aside, Morgan shoved the stub of his sword into the creature's throat. The troll sagged to the deck. Morgan released the sword and tore the mace from its dying grasp. Taurus stood nearby, arrogant with his smoking weapon. Morgan did not even look at

140

him, but immediately turned to the stern well.

Taurus waved the gun at Morgan. "What's wrong with him?" he called.

Max shrugged. "The mad monk Morgan," he said.

Max cautiously followed Morgan down the stairs into the ship's dark hold. The interior of the ship was dimly lit by a reddish light emanating from long tubes along the ceilings. Once inside, he crouched defensively until his eyes adjusted to the odd light. Throbbing machinery filled the chamber but he saw no sign of Molid. Hatchways stood to the right and left, leading to more compartments along the outer hull. Max could hear Morgan charging through the ship, knocking things over and shouting for the Mhoul. Max hurried to catch his friend, concerned by his uncharacteristic recklessness.

Max went through the first chamber and entered a second room, which had the look of living quarters. Morgan had strewn beds and bedding across the floor, looking for any possible hiding places. Max caught a glimpse of Morgan's legs as he mounted a steep stairwell at the far end of the room. Max headed for the stairs, but paused at the bottom. A strange angry pulse came from a doorway just beyond the stairs. Max skirted the stairwell and, standing to one side of the door, took a quick look into the next room. By the shape of this chamber, Max guessed he was at the bow of the ship. In the center of the room crouched a squat shape, connected to several heavy cables. It appeared to be the central power source for the ship.

Even as he examined the device, the pulsing sound became louder, the beats closer together, while opaque panels around the top of the object flared red in time to the sound. The intensity of the flashes increased, the harsh light making it hard to look directly at the machinery. Max's instincts warned him that something was very wrong.

Max returned to the stairs and shouted for Morgan. "You better get down here," he called.

Morgan came down the stairs, taking them three at a time, his eyes wild. "Is it down here? Where is the Mhoul?" he asked hoarsely.

"Forget the Mhoul. Listen," Max hissed.

"Listen to what? I want Molid," Morgan said, peering around

141

with a frown.

Max sharply motioned him to silence and Morgan finally stood listening intently. From the next room came the throbbing sound, growing louder all the time, now a deep, menacing rumbling that shook the metal plates beneath their feet.

"We have to get out of here! Something bad is going to happen," Max said.

"I want Molid," Morgan repeated.

Max grabbed the big man's arm and shook him. "Stop it!" Max shouted. "Molid is not here. The power source has been rigged to overload and blow up the ship. We have to leave! Now!"

Max's words seemed to penetrate Morgan's obsession, and he looked at Max as if seeing him for the first time. Morgan shook his head, and rubbed his face, trying to clear his thoughts as Max began to drag him toward the exit. After a few steps, Morgan gently freed himself of his friend's grasp.

The pounding beat took on a new urgency and the two men broke into a run. They clambered up the stairs and nearly collided with Taurus and a knot of men at the top. The deep pulse seemed to reach out after them, deafening and malevolent.

"Abandon ship!" yelled Max as he dove over the rail to the Windrider's deck, not bothering with the ramp.

The sailors on the deck panicked and scrambled across the ramp, certain some new monster pursued them. Morgan vaulted to the Windrider's rail and hauled himself over. He bounced up and managed to get the attention of the milling crew.

"Cast off those grappling hooks or we will go down with her!" Morgan shouted.

Morgan wrenched loose the nearest hook, splintering the rail wood, and several others attacked the remaining grapples. Taurus, suddenly alone on the black deck, darted wildly back and forth like a trapped animal.

"What's going on? . . . Where are they? . . . I'm not running from a fight!" Taurus shouted.

"Get off! That ship is going to explode!" Morgan shouted down to him.

Taurus finally realized the danger and lumbered for the ramp, his crew urging him on to greater speed. Suddenly the black ship leaped in the water like a living thing, a searing flash tearing through the plates on the forward deck. The blast flung Taurus into the air, Charon clutched in his flailing hand. He plowed into the water an arm's length from the Windrider's side, sinking like a stone. Dropping his swordbelt, Max dropped over the side after him. The ramp bounced and fell into the gap between the two ships, spilling the last of the fleeing seamen into the water. Someone slashed through the rope on the last grapple as the metal ship continued to rock violently from the explosion. Almost immediately, the black ship began to dip sharply toward the bow. The blast must have blown the bottom out of the forward sections.

"You men better haul your Captain in before he drowns," Morgan shouted.

A gasping Taurus broke the surface at that moment. Max appeared behind him, holding him up. Two of the sailors in the water swam to help, and they dragged Taurus to the deck, the heavy gun still clutched in his hand.

Max rolled over the rail, spit out some water, and he sat down heavily. "I wish this great seaman would learn to swim. Either that or lose some weight," he wheezed.

A second muffled boom shook the black ship. While the crew of the Windrider looked on, the ship tipped up slowly and slid out of sight, creating a whirlpool that rocked the Windrider and nearly sucked down a crewman still in the water.

As the men stood looking down at the churning waters, Max turned to those around him. "Who fired Charon?" he asked.

The soggy Taurus had recovered enough to speak. "Get Simon out here," he gasped.

Crewmen urged the cook forward, and he hesitantly approached. The man seemed slightly dazed, and Morgan noticed some painful looking bruises showing through his torn shirt. Taurus dragged himself to his feet, and wiped the water from his face and beard with a sleeve. The burly Captain caught up the cook in a bear hug that lifted him from the deck.

143

"He's going to reduce Simon the Deaf to Simon the Cripple," Max commented.

Taurus dropped the gasping crewman to the deck and turned to face the rest of the men, one arm still draped around Simon.

"This is the stalwart soul who saved all our lives," Taurus announced. "He came into the bridge while I lay helpless and took Charon. Then he climbed onto the roof, and blew that Mhoul back into Gaol where it belongs."

"Now I see why his criminals are so loyal," Max whispered to Morgan. "He deceives them with flattery."

"The only problem was, in his zeal, he hit all three triggers at once and who knows which body flew the farthest---Molid's or Simon's. When the sound stopped, I found him unconscious on the opposite side of the ship, Charon at his side," Taurus explained.

Morgan laughed harshly. "Charon's kick saved his life. One of the trolls threw its mace at him even as he fired. If he'd been there a moment longer, he would have been killed," he said.

Morgan walked over and faced Simon. "Are you totally deaf?" he asked, speaking slowly so the man could read his lips.

The seaman nodded vigorously.

"You couldn't feel the sound at all?" Morgan asked.

The man spoke for the first time. "No . . . nothing, " he said.

The Princess now stood nearby. "Simon was with me, giving me some medicine for my stomach. He had just walked to the port and looked out. When the noise started, I grabbed his arm and he saw I was in pain. He carried me to the bunk, and left the room. The sound didn't affect him at all," she said.

Seeing the haunted looks of his crewmen, Taurus climbed up on a crate and addressed the sailors. "It looks like my old friend Morgan has Yfel's hounds after him: metal ships, trolls, and Mhoul. You probably think I should pitch him and his companions overboard, and get as far from here as we can. Well, forget that. Whatever Morgan has gotten himself into, he's my friend and that means I'm with him all the way. And where I go, you go. I am your Redeemer.

But you know I'm more than just your Redeemer. I'm your Captain, and I take care of my men. I've known Morgan and Max for a long time, and I've never seen a better pair of fighters. If I have to face Yfel's minions, I can't think of anyone I would rather have at my side than these two. Besides, they probably know more about these eastern monsters than anyone. And lest you forget, the Mhoul have found us with Morgan and the Princess. They consider us their enemies now. Like it or not, this war has been brought to us. There's no neutral ground or safehaven. We fight or we die.

How have we done so far? They loosed their best on us, and we sent them to the bottom of the sea. We killed the Mhoul, its pet trolls, and those gray men. That cowardly thief, Thugmonger Wald, is dead. The Windrider is still fit for battle, and its crew wiser. I think that's pretty good for a fat old Captain and his band of criminals. I say we stay with Morgan and send the Mhoul back where they came from! What do you say!?"

With little hesitation, the entire crew yelled their answer. "We're with you, Captain! Death to the Mhoul! The Windrider forever!"

Taurus smiled broadly, his teeth white against the black of his beard. He looked like a proud father.

Harkon and Taskin stood nearby. Harkon shook his head. "I should have stayed in Saxhaven. I've fallen in with madmen," Harkon muttered.

Taskin elbowed him sharply, and glared at him.

Max leaned over to Morgan. "Is it something he puts in their food or drink? These men would follow him to Gaol," he whispered.

Morgan smiled grimly. "Before this is over, they may have to," he said.

When the cheering had died down, Taurus gestured contemptuously at the bodies of the troll and the gray men. "Toss this offal overboard!" he said. "And don't forget that traitorous Thugmonger."

Morgan picked up one of the heavy helmets the Immortals had worn. He turned the helmet over, examining the interior. "This honeycomb padding evidently acts as a muffler, deadening the effects of the sound weapon," he said.

"We don't need them, we have Simon," Max said.

Morgan tossed the helmet overboard without comment. While

the crew cleared the decks of the dead, Taurus wiped his soggy brow.

"Seidon, tend to Simon's bruises and then have him see to the other wounded. Prepare our dead for burial at sea. We'll do the service at sundown. Check the ship from bow to stern and get me a damage report. I want this ship moving!" he ordered, then turned to Max and Morgan. "I'll be in my cabin, changing into some dry clothes. Council of war in my cabin tonight. I want more information on what kind of trouble I'm in. Be there or swim to Aquarquff."

Max looked at Morgan and rolled his eyes. Morgan shook his head and sighed.

"You're a mess," Celeste said, as she studied Morgan. "Are you all right?"

Morgan looked down, noting his disheveled clothing, covered with brown stains. "Yes," he decided.

Celeste stepped closer, looking into his eyes. "I'm more concerned about the inside," she said.

Morgan took a deep breath, smoothing back his tangled hair. "I think so," he said, with much less certainty than before.

Celeste studied him a moment more, then hooked her arm into Simon's. "Come along, Simon. I'll tend to those bruises and help you with the others. We don't want to be late for the meeting," she said, smiling over her shoulder at Morgan and Max. Simon smiled too, pleased by the Princess' attention.

The crew of the Windrider went about their tasks, and Morgan and Max moved to the rail.

"The Princess is right. You are a mess," Max remarked.

"I'm fine. Don't worry about it," Morgan said, his annoyance showing in his tone.

"That's rubbish. I know you. What was going on back there? You fought the troll in a blind rage, and tore through the Mhoul ship like a rabid bull. For a man known for his iron self-control, that was a little strange. Do you now have a death wish, on top of everything else?" Max asked.

Morgan sighed and put his head in his hands. "That sound. It brought back . . . memories," he said.

"Memories of what?" Max asked.

146

"Mogda Thal," Morgan said.

"That was twelve years ago. Forget about it," Max said.

Morgan stared out over the water. "I can't. It shouldn't have happened," he said.

"What are you saying? That the massacre at Mogda Thal was your fault?" Max asked.

"Maybe. Partly. I don't know. I can't really remember. The memories were more like visions . . . terrible visions," Morgan said.

Max shook his head. "Your visions were probably hallucinations caused by the Mhoul's sound weapon. Don't flog yourself over some projected fantasies. It's just a Mhoul trick," he said.

"Did you have any hallucinations . . . visions?" Morgan asked.

"Well, no. But you were closer to it, and you would be more susceptible to morbid suggestions," Max said.

"What about the nightmares? Some of these hallucinations were the same," Morgan said.

"What nightmares?" Max asked.

"The nightmares I've been having, ever since Mogda Thal," Morgan said.

"No one knows what happened at Mogda Thal, and after all this time, it doesn't matter. It wasn't your fault," Max said.

"How do you know?" Morgan demanded.

"I know you. I'm sure you were pure and honorable through the entire massacre," Max said.

Morgan pounded his fist on the rail. "If only I could remember!" he said.

"Well, you can't. So get over it," Max said.

Morgan said nothing, but studied the flotsam scattered over the water, the only remaining evidence of the black ship. There was no sign of any survivors.

"I wish we could have studied that ship, to learn more about the Mhoul and their machines," Max said.

"All I want to learn is the location of Molid's body," Morgan responded, as he scanned the debris. "Molid must have decided to sink the ship rather than let us have it."

"Do you think Molid was still inside?" Max asked.

"I hope so, but I didn't see anyone," Morgan said, then rubbed his neck and back, which ached terribly.

"Have Simon put some lineament on that. Can't have you crippled and unable to fight," Max observed.

"I'll see him after our meeting with Taurus," Morgan said as he turned stiffly.

"You better," Max said.

Morgan stopped. "I have to talk to the Princess. Will you come with me?" he asked suddenly.

"Are you finally going to tell her?" Max asked.

"There's no reason to wait any longer. The Mhoul have caught us together and we've done them some serious damage. We can't protect her now. She needs to know," Morgan said.

"Let's go. I want to see this," Max said. "But we can't be late to the Captain's council of war. I have no desire to swim to Aquarquff."

Soon the Windrider turned into the wind, and sailed away. As it moved into the distance, a dark shape appeared in the water, amidst the floating wreckage. It was Molid. The Mhoul stared at the Windrider, the departing ship reflected in the black goggles. While it watched the Windrider, Molid laboriously treaded water, the heavy cloak swirling about the black clad body. The Mhoul's hood was thrown back and the seawater beaded up on the wrapped skull, as if shrinking from the contact. Only when the ship vanished over the horizon did Molid let the weight of its coverings drag it beneath the surface again.

CHAPTER TWELVE
PLANS AND REVELATIONS

They found Celeste below decks, helping Simon bind a crewman's wound. Despite her queasy stomach and the smell of blood and sweat, the Princess had insisted on being there. Between patients, Morgan got her attention and motioned her aside.

"We have to tell you something," Morgan said.

"He should have told you sooner," Max said.

Celeste put her hands on her hips and regarded them. "What? You are married?" she asked.

Her response totally flustered Morgan, who struggled to speak.

Max laughed. "No, he wants to tell you who we really are," he said.

"You're Max and Morgan. I know that already," she said.

"Well, yes. But there's more," Morgan said.

"And I'm telling you I already know. You are the Max and Morgan. The famed Raav Commanders of the Seventh and Eighth Legions, who saved Saxhaven, and fought in the Crusade," she said.

"How'd you find out? Did Taurus or Taskin tell you?" Morgan demanded.

"No they did not. I figured it out myself," she said.

"How?" Max asked, intrigued.

"The Thraens may be isolationists, but I studied at Carnac. There was a detailed history in the centaur libraries and I learned all about you two. When I saw Max's sword and bow, and heard about Lex Talionus, I suspected the truth. Seeing you fight the trolls, the Mhoul, and the Immortals just confirmed my suspicions," Celeste explained.

"She has discovered our secret. I suppose I have to kill her now," Max said.

"Why didn't you say something?" Morgan asked, ignoring Max.

"You were going to tell me, eventually. I wanted to let you choose the time and place," Celeste said.

"I thought it was for the best. I was trying to protect you,"

149

Morgan said.

Celeste gripped Morgan by the chin, and leaned close to him. Morgan's eyes widened. "If I need protecting, I'll let you know. In the meantime, don't keep things from me," she said softly.

Celeste turned toward Max, who was stifling his laughter. "I would have known immediately, except for two things," she said.

"What?" Max asked, sobering.

"Max, you're too short to be a legend, and Morgan is a self-proclaimed pacifist. That confused me," she said.

Max frowned. "Height is irrelevant to the legendary aspect, and Morgan's dementia is of recent origin. He mutates from pacifist to berserker, and that's not the Morgan I knew."

"I did have one more question," Celeste said.

"What?" Morgan asked.

"Who is Malissa, really?" she asked.

Morgan shook his head. "Is that all you think about?" he asked.

"Are you going to answer my question or not?" the Princess countered.

Morgan sighed. "Malissa is the royal concubine at Saxhaven," he said.

"Royal concubine? For a simple soldier, you aim high," Celeste remarked.

"I was arrested for interfering with the city guard, and brought before her," Morgan said.

"She sent for you? Well, well. Where did you meet with her?" Celeste asked.

Morgan hesitated. "Where? What difference does that make?" he asked.

"Where," the Princess repeated firmly.

"Her . . . bedchamber," Morgan admitted.

Celeste raised her eyebrows. "You refused the royal concubine. After you had been summoned to her bedchamber," she said.

Morgan looked at the floor. "Yes. Do we have to talk about this?" he pleaded.

"Was it because of Llorgau? Were you afraid the Sagamore would find out?" Celeste asked.

Morgan grimaced. "No," he said.

"I told you, Princess. He's incorruptible," Max offered.

Celeste just smiled, seemingly satisfied on that point. She stood waiting.

"What?" Max asked.

"Well, you've told me who you are. I'm waiting for the rest," she said.

"The rest?" Morgan asked.

"Why are you going to Aquarquff? Why are you back, after twelve years?" she asked.

"That's a long story . . . " Morgan began.

Simon interrupted their conversation, tugging on Celeste's sleeve. "Princess, can you help me?" he asked.

Celeste patted him on the shoulder and nodded, and the cook returned to a patient. "Taurus wants an explanation too. Join us and we'll tell you the rest," Morgan said.

"I'll be there. Now go get cleaned up. You two are still a mess," Celeste said.

After dinner and a burial service for the two dead crewmen, they all gathered in Taurus' cabin. The burly Captain sat in a heavy wooden chair near his desk, a steaming mug of ale in his hand. The gun Charon lay on a table near the desk, amidst a tangled nest of charts and papers. Morgan sat in another chair, while Max sprawled on Taurus' bunk, hands laced behind his head. Morgan and Max had cleaned up and changed clothes. For once, Morgan did not wear his metasilk cloak. Two bundles lay on the bed beside Max. Seidon stood by a wall chart, and Taskin and Harkon took a position by the door. Celeste leaned against the wall near the open port, staying close to fresh air. She still looked slightly queasy. Taurus had found some spare clothes for her amongst his cache of contraband, and she now wore a silk shirt with flaring sleeves, tight breeches studded with silver, and knee high leather boots.

Taurus waved his mug at Morgan and Max. "One of you is going to tell me the whole story. This is much more than simple passage for five to Aquarquff," he said.

Max nodded at Morgan. "It's his quest," he said.

Morgan leaned back in his chair, and folded his arms. "I haven't told you everything because I was trying to protect you. But it's too late now. The Mhoul won't bother to separate the guilty from the innocent. They'll be after all of us now.

Taurus, you weren't the only one I deceived. The Princess, Harkon and Taskin didn't know either. So now it's time to tell everyone," he said.

"Good. Max had warned me not to tell the Princess anything about you two, and I hate lying to a beautiful woman, especially when she's royalty," Taurus said.

"Thank you, Captain. I appreciate that," Celeste said.

"Where do you want me to begin?" Morgan asked.

"How about trolls, Mhoul, and Immortals? I've heard the stories, but until today I've never had the bad fortune to encounter them," Taurus said.

"Trolls, or Achbor, as they call themselves, serve as the Mhoul's bodyguards and heavy infantry. A race called the Gygax, or gargoyles, provide their air support. The goblins, the Ssin, act as their field generals. They're all part of a military alliance commonly known as the Triad.

The Immortals are a type of artificial human, created by the Mhoul in their laboratories. All Immortals come from the same original stock and are nearly identical in appearance. They are the common soldiers," Morgan explained.

"Why do they call them Immortals? They seem to die easily enough," Taurus said.

"They die . . . but they live again," Morgan said.

"Explain that," Taurus said.

"What he means is that the Immortals collect their dead and use the corpses to make more soldiers. So, in a sense, they are immortal," Max said.

"Locha! We fought the walking dead today," Harkon said.

"As long as they keep dying, I don't really care," Taurus said.

Max laughed. "Imagination never hindered you, Taurus," he said.

"No Harriers," Morgan said absently.

"Harriers?" Taurus asked.

"Arrogant elitists, dressed in red and black, with fancy plumes on their helmets," Max said disdainfully.

"The Mhoul's finest---ruthless, deadly warriors. Raised in the brutal Krang Fere Wilderness. The harsh conditions breed tough fighters," Morgan added.

"That leaves the Mhoul," Seidon said.

Morgan hesitated. "It is said they were human once. Now they're but dead shells, animated by a mysterious force. They wrap themselves in metasilk and are nearly impossible to kill," he said.

"Being dead already," Max added.

"Mysterious force?" Taurus mocked.

"The Lucca," Morgan said softly.

Taurus paled. "Thaar preserve us! The foulest of Yfel's brood, spawned in the heart of Gaol."

"Actually, the Lucca were a race of energy beings from another galaxy. Absolutely evil, and possessed of nearly godlike powers. They caused the Fall of Craig Phadrig and the end of the entire Empire," Celeste explained.

"Oh, that's much better," Harkon blurted out. "What have I gotten myself into?"

Everyone else stared at the Princess.

"How do you know about the Lucca?" Morgan asked.

Celeste shrugged. "I told you. I studied at Carnac. The centaurs know everything."

"Human-Luccan hybrids. How could that be?" Taurus asked. "How can man and demon become one?"

"The details of the process are lost in history. All I know is that somehow the Lucca entered the bodies of men and the result was the Mhoul," Celeste said.

"That's obscene. What person would allow that?" Harkon asked.

"The first subjects had no choice; the Lucca used prisoners of war to perfect the infusion. Later, they had volunteers. Traitors to the human race," Celeste said.

153

"Why would the Lucca want to do this?" Taurus asked.

Celeste shrugged. "Ask the Mhoul. The Lucca were energy beings, maybe they coveted the flesh," he said.

"What else do you want to know?" Morgan asked.

"What was that thing on the Mhoul's shoulder?" Seidon asked.

"They're called rith, and act as eyes and ears for the Mhoul. The Mhoul have lost their normal powers of sight and hearing, so they use the rith. Their minds are one," Morgan explained.

"I haven't seen you since 5985, that time in Androssar, during the Crusade. Later I heard you were killed at Mogda Thal. What really happened?" Taurus asked.

"The Crusade. We were going to drive the Mhoul and the Triad back to Mogda Thal, and reclaim the Land of Faerie," Max said.

Morgan leaned forward, his eyes distant. "You've heard the legends, but we were there. The Raavs formed the spearhead of the Crusade, led by Imperius, the Raav Master-General. The first step was to take the fortresses at Droghelda and Tchoga. That would secure the eastern frontier, and provide a base of operations for an invasion through the forests of Aijalon to Mogda Thal. Max and I led the siege of Tchoga with the Seventh and Eighth Legions. Korl took the Ninth and kept the forces at Droghelda from coming to Tchoga's aid. Tchoga finally fell, and we destroyed the troll Nest in the caverns beneath the fortress. Max and I killed the Sire and the Mother," he said, and then paused, rubbing the scar over his eye.

"A Sire defending its Nest. Thaar smiled on us that day, or we would have both been killed," Max said.

"That's why they called you the Nestbreakers," Celeste said.

"Imperius soon arrived with six more Legions. He'd left the Tenth in Saarland to keep the peace. He planned to divide our forces, leave Max in charge of the siege of Droghelda, and take the rest of the Raavs to Mogda Thal. We advised against it, but he persisted," Morgan said.

"Advised," Max snorted.

"Max was nearly court-martialed for his protests. If Imperius

154

hadn't needed Max so badly, he probably would have. I was ordered to accompany Imperius with the Seventh, while the Eighth and the Ninth were left behind to continue the siege of Droghelda," Morgan said, and then paused. "And then came the massacre at Mogda Thal, which no sane man has any memory of."

"But you survived. So where have you been since?" Celeste asked.

"For the last twelve years I've been in the monastery at Khulankor," Morgan said.

"Khulankor? But it doesn't exist, it's some religious myth," Taurus protested.

"It's no myth. Khulankor was built by survivors of the Fall, who fled there after the destruction of Craig Phadrig. They call themselves the Mons Monachus, and have been in those mountains ever since. They're also the ancient enemies of the Mhoul, and have been secretly waging war with them for centuries," Morgan explained.

Harkon raised his eyes to the ceiling. "Locha preserve us. This just gets worse all the time," he whispered.

Taurus looked at Max. "Is this true? Or is he mad like the rest of them?" he asked.

Max regarded Morgan, who sat waiting. "He believes it. I'm not sure what to believe," he said.

"He seems sane to me," Celeste offered.

Taurus' eyes narrowed. "Now he does. But not earlier today, when the black ship attacked. I feared he'd turned berserker. He fought that troll like a madman, and I thought the monster would kill him before he came to his senses. That's why I used Charon," he said.

Morgan said nothing, so Max spoke. "The Mhoul sound weapon stirred up some memories. He's fine now," he said.

"All right. I'll grant you may be sane. Why did you come back, after twelve years?" Taurus asked.

"The Monachus sent me back. The Mhoul plot something, and I'm to find out what," Morgan said.

"I spoke too soon," Taurus said sadly.

"Let him finish," the Princess insisted.

"So what are you supposed to do?" Taurus asked.

"To protect themselves, the Monachus arranged it so my mission is revealed to me in stages. All I know now is that I'm bound for Aquarquff," Morgan said.

"That's all? You don't know why, or what you're supposed to do when you get there?" Taurus asked.

"No," Morgan said.

"You are mad. How could you agree to this?" Taurus asked.

Morgan shrugged. "I trust the Monachus," he said.

Taurus stared at him in wonder. "You must. By Thaar, I hope you're right," he said.

"I was wrong. It could be worse," Harkon muttered. Taskin gave him a warning look.

"That Mhoul knew you, Morgan. How?" Taurus asked.

"The Mhoul are semi-telepathic and they share memories. I've fought the Mhoul in the past, although I never faced Molid before today," Morgan said.

"So how do you explain the Mhoul attack? Do they know about your mission?" Taurus asked.

Morgan turned to the Princess. "That black ship. Was it like the one at Skara Thrae?" he asked.

"I think so. Although it was dark, so I didn't see the ship very clearly," Celeste responded.

"They were after her?" Taurus asked.

"When you told us about the invasion of Skara Thrae, you described Mhoul, Immortals, and Harriers" Morgan said.

"Those creatures on the black ship were the same beings I saw from the walls of Tantagnel. But why? What do they want from us?" Celeste asked.

"That's the part that makes no sense to me. What would the Mhoul want with Skara Thrae?" Morgan said.

"Maybe they want to use the Pomas as a secret weapon," Max offered.

"Why were they after you?" Taurus asked the Princess, ignoring Max.

"The Mhoul instigated an invasion of Skara Thrae by an

exiled clan, the Haggas. I went to Androssar for help, and they've been following me ever since. Morgan and Max found me at the Demented Boar, and saved me from Thugmonger Wald. He was working for the Mhoul," she explained.

"And you killed Wald. Too bad we couldn't torture some answers out of him," Taurus said.

"He was trying to kill Morgan. I didn't care what he knew," Celeste said.

Taurus laughed. "Good woman to have around, Morgan. Did you get help in Androssar?" he asked.

Celeste frowned. "Rulda refused to assist us. I was at his palace, just before I went to the Demented Boar," she said.

"So why do the Mhoul want you so badly? It's not because you were going to return to Skara Thrae with an army," Taurus said.

"Maybe they want to use me against my father, to break the resistance. He is causing them considerable trouble," Celeste said.

"But how did the Mhoul find us on the open ocean? Unless someone told them where we were?" Taurus asked.

The Princess locked eyes with Taurus. "Are you suggesting I told them?" she asked.

Taurus raised a hand. "No, Princess. I'm just trying to solve a puzzle," he said.

Morgan was rubbing his neck. The troll's mace had left his upper back one large bruise. "We know she's not a spy for the Mhoul. But we need to find out how the Mhoul tracked us," he said.

Max sat up on the bunk, pulling one of the bundles onto his lap. He opened the folds of cloth and held up a strange mechanism. It looked like a thin disc, with hooks on the back. "I think I can answer that question," he said.

Taurus stared at the device. "What is that?" he asked.

Max shrugged. "I don't know. But one of your crewmen was checking the hull for damage, and found this stuck to the wood, just below the waterline," he explained.

Morgan reached over and took the object, examining it closely. "It must be some type of tracking device. Maybe Wald's men placed it when the Windrider was docked at Androssar. This would explain a lot," he said.

"Give me that thing," Taurus said, setting down his mug. He stared at it briefly and held it up. "Is it still working?" he asked.

"It might be. We should destroy it immediately. The Mhoul may be homing in on us right now. I'd like to examine it further, but it's too dangerous," Morgan said, then turned to Max. "You should have told someone about this right away. They've had half a day to relocate us now."

"Hey, sorry. If it wasn't for me, you wouldn't know about it at all. The crewman was just going to pitch it overboard. Besides, I didn't know what it was, and you don't either," Max said in his defense.

"We can't take any chances. We need to break it now," Taurus said.

Morgan stood, taking back the device. He dropped it on the floor and ground his heel into it. He pulled back his foot, to find it completely undamaged by his weight. Taurus grunted with impatience, reaching for Charon. Everyone in the room scrambled away from the device on the floor. Everyone except Max, who lunged forward and scooped up the mechanism. He flung it out the open port, missing the Princess by a mere hand's breadth. The device sailed far out over the water and sank immediately. A crewman passing by outside staggered back, staring after the missile.

"There. Track that, you soulless devils," Max said, then looked at Taurus, who still sat with Charon pointed at the floor. "Didn't want you sinking us, by tearing great holes in the hull with your cannon."

Celeste leaned back from the port, slightly pale. "Be careful, Max. You nearly took my head off," she said.

Max bowed gracefully. "Pardon me, Princess. I merely acted to prevent destruction of our vessel. You were in no danger," he assured her.

Taurus tossed Charon to the table, and took a drink of ale. "So the Mhoul were following the Princess. Do they even know the Monachus sent you, Morgan?" he asked.

"Good question. I don't see how they could," Morgan said.

"Doesn't make much difference now. They'll be hunting all

of us, if only to find out what we know. So what do we do now?" Taurus asked.

Morgan sat down again. "You take us to Aquarquff, as we agreed. Then we part company, and hopefully they forget about you," he said.

"What's next for you?" Taurus asked Morgan.

Morgan shifted uncomfortably. "Celeste will hire some Pathfinders to take her to Carnac," he said.

Taurus poked his mug at Morgan. "Not what I asked. What will you do?" he asked.

Morgan sighed. "Like I said, I don't know. I'll receive further instructions in Aquarquff," he said.

"The Monachus have agents in Aquarquff? There's no Iosian temple there. How will they contact you?" he asked.

Morgan tapped his head. "The information is already here. I just can't retrieve it until the memory is triggered," he said.

"You are mad, old friend. Triggered how?" Taurus asked.

"I'm not sure. Probably by something I see at Aquarquff," Morgan said.

Taurus laughed. "So you're going to wander around town, seeking a revelation? Those religious fanatics at Aquarquff will think you're one of them. Perfect cover," he said.

Max returned to the bunk, picked up the other bundle, and handed it to Morgan. "Since you've rescinded your stupid oath, I thought you might want this," he said.

Morgan held the long, slender bundle as if it were going to burn him. He slowly shook his head. "I didn't break my oath. I . . . just reinterpreted it," he said.

Max shook his head. "Say what you want. Just keep the sword," he said, then walked to the door and stopped. "May I be excused, Captain? I assume we're done."

Taurus waved his mug in dismissal. "This meeting is over," he agreed.

Morgan lay on the bunk in his cabin, bare to the waist, while Simon prepared to put some lineament on his back. The outer door

159

opened, and Morgan turned to look. Celeste stood in the doorway, with the quiet night behind her. The breeze played with her loose hair, and the archlight cast a silver sheen on the silk shirt. Once again, her exotic beauty wove its spell around Morgan. He forced himself to look away.

"Can I come in?" she asked.

"What can I do for you, Princess?" Morgan asked warily.

She said nothing, only moved quietly to the bunk and laid her hand on Simon's arm, nodding toward the doorway. Simon smiled and winked, leaving quickly. Celeste plucked the bottle of lineament from his hand as he passed.

Morgan started to get up. "What are you doing? You shouldn't be here like this," he protested.

Celeste pushed him back down on the bunk, gently but firmly. For a Princess, she was surprisingly strong.

"Shut up and lay down," she ordered.

Against his better judgment, Morgan stretched out on the bunk.

"Like what?" Celeste asked, when Morgan was safely down again.

"Like . . . I mean . . . we're alone," Morgan said.

Celeste looked around the cabin, while Morgan struggled to keep her in view.

"You're right about that. We are alone," she observed. "Is that a problem?"

"Well, it doesn't seem proper. We're alone in my cabin. You're a Princess, and I'm . . . an unmarried man," Morgan said.

"A never married man," Celeste corrected. "Has Taurus forbid such behavior?"

The question caught him off guard. "I . . . don't think so," Morgan said.

"Well, last time I looked we were in open sea, and Taurus' law is all that applies here. Unless you count Iosus. Did Iosus tell you I shouldn't be here?" she asked.

Morgan sighed. One thing his military experience had taught him was when to fight and when to negotiate or surrender. He was not sure which he was doing now. "No, Iosus hasn't spoken of you," he admitted.

"There. You let me worry about what's proper for Thraen royalty," Celeste said.

She studied his bare back, noting the large black and purple bruise spread across his shoulder blades. She touched the area with a gentle fingertip.

"That looks painful," she said.

"It is," Morgan said, his voice muffled in the crook of his arm.

He had given up trying to see what she was doing, but he was still tense, his muscles hard. Celeste opened the bottle of lineament, and poured some into her hand.

"Just relax. I'll take care of you," she said.

"Do you know what you're doing?" Morgan asked.

The Princess warmed the liquid briefly in her hand, and then began applying it to the bruised area. As soon as the lineament was thoroughly rubbed in, she began kneading the rest of Morgan's back muscles, moving her hands in long, slow strokes.

"None of Simon's patients complained. Father made us learn field medicine. How am I doing so far?" she asked.

Morgan closed his eyes, willing himself to relax. "That feels good. I've never had a back rub by royalty before," he said, trying to imitate Max's flippant tone.

"Come to think of it, I've never given one to a soldier before. This is a first for both of us," Celeste said.

Morgan frowned. "Then who have you been massaging? You've obviously done this before," he said.

Celeste dug in a thumb, and he jerked. "Impertinent man. It's none of your business," she said, then paused. "Well, if you must know, Talbot and Father."

"That's all?" Morgan asked.

"Why the sudden interest?" the Princess countered.

"No reason," Morgan said.

It was Celeste's turn to frown. "If you have no reason, then don't ask," she said.

Morgan fell silent, uncertain how to respond. He was not sure why he cared; he just knew the thought of her massaging another

161

man bothered him. In fact, the thought of her massaging him was equally disturbing, but he could not bring himself to stop her.

As she worked on his back, Celeste saw the scars. She traced one of them with a finger. "So many scars," she murmured.

"So many battles," Morgan said, his voice distant.

"And yet you live," Celeste remarked.

"Yes, by the grace of Iosus," he said.

"You're too modest. I've seen you fight," Celeste said, then touched a heavy scar along his right shoulder. "That one looks particularly bad."

Morgan tensed. "It was," he said.

"Don't worry. I won't ask how it happened," Celeste said.

"Good," Morgan said.

Celeste noticed the bandage was gone from his burned hand. "Where's your bandage?" she asked.

"It's healed," Morgan said.

Celeste turned his hand over, examining the palm. Aside from a pattern of new scars, the burn was completely healed. "Amazing. You do heal fast," she said.

She resumed the back rub, and neither spoke for a few moments.

"How did you ever become a mercenary?" Celeste asked.

"I'd heard about the Raavs since I was young. Hodin said they only fought for good, against tyranny and injustice. I always admired that.

Max and I grew up together. We had no interest in farming or the usual trades. When we turned twenty, we went to town and petitioned to join the Raavs. We were both skilled with weapons, and our petition was granted," Morgan explained.

"Who was Hodin?" Celeste asked.

"My father. At least, the only father I ever knew. I never met my natural parents," Morgan said. "I was told they were dead."

"Where are your foster parents now?" Celeste asked.

"Both dead. A fire in their home. I was away on a campaign," Morgan said.

"I'm so sorry," Celeste said. "Was it true about the Raavs? Did you fight only for good?"

162

Morgan opened his eyes, and tensed slightly. "Not always."

"So your father was wrong?" she asked.

Morgan sighed. "The Raavs were just men, better soldiers than most, but even some of them abused their power. So I decided to make the Raavs all that my father thought they were," he said.

"And did you?" Celeste prompted.

"I worked my way up through the ranks to Commander of the Seventh Legion. No one in the Seventh sold their sword without cause. If anyone fell short of my standards, I stripped them of their commissions and sent them away," he said.

"I'll wager you made some enemies that way," she said.

Morgan frowned. "Yes, I did. Several challenged me to combat," he said.

"Did you fight them?" she asked.

"No, duels are a matter of honor. The men I disciplined had no honor," he said.

"An idealist, confronted by cold, cruel reality. That often leads to disappointment and bitterness," Celeste observed.

"So you treat the mind, as well as the body?" Morgan asked, a trace of sarcasm in his voice.

"You'd be amazed at what I can do," Celeste said mysteriously. "What about Max? He doesn't seem like an idealist."

"The people of our village feared him. He had few friends. He'd have left home soon, one way or another," Morgan explained. "And he was very good with weapons, so a mercenary's life seemed natural."

"Max is not his real name," Celeste said.

"He told you that?" Morgan asked.

"Yes, but nothing more. I don't suppose you would reveal his secret?" Celeste asked.

"No," Morgan agreed.

"What about you?" Celeste asked.

"My name? Why?" Morgan asked.

"I don't know. A person's name is a part of them, it tells me something about the person," Celeste said.

"Morgan is the name Hodin and Belov gave me. No one knew

my real name. I saw no reason to take another," he said.

"Belov, your foster mother?" Celeste asked.

"Yes," Morgan said.

"Morgan Caeda," Celeste said, trying out the sounds.

Morgan grimaced. "Not the Caeda part. That came later," he said.

"Caeda. What does that mean?" she asked.

"Killer. Max hung that one on me," Morgan said.

"Morgan the killer and Maximilian, the king of death. What a cheery pair," Celeste said.

"Seems to fit," Morgan said, with a trace of regret.

"Where'd you learn to fight? Mountain villages aren't known for their masters at arms," she asked.

"An old hermit lived near our village, named Cynar. He made some money by teaching the boys to use weapons. He also worked with the smith, and made some fine swords. For some reason, he took a real interest in Max and me, and spent hours training us, but he never asked for any payment. Max practically lived with the man, and worked harder than anyone," Morgan said.

"Tell me more about Max. He's a strange mix---merciless, yet loyal, with the wit of a troubadour. What made him that way?" Celeste asked.

"Max was the youngest of five children, with three brothers and a sister. His father was the village smith, a large, powerful man. There were complications during Max's birth, that left him a frail child, often confined to bed. No one expected him to live for long. His parents thought him special, and doted on him. His father even made him a pair of swords, tailored to his weakness and small size. All the extra attention made his brothers and sisters jealous, and they avoided his company. Max was often alone.

Max surprised everyone, and seemingly by sheer force of will, lived and grew stronger, although he was still small. When he was yet a young boy, his father's kiln-forge blew up and his father was seriously injured. He never recovered. We all watched Max's father dwindle from a powerful blacksmith to a wasted shell. Max took his father's accident badly, and stayed by his side until the end, which took years.

After his father finally died Max began training with weapons. He had to work twice as hard to overcome his childhood weakness. He always used the swords his father had made him. In the meantime, Max's mother died, mainly from grief at her husband's misfortune.

At first, Max and I did things together because there was no one else. I had no family but my foster parents, and Max's siblings still shunned him. In time, the two village outcasts became friends. We'd spend days in the woods, hunting and exploring. But in spite of our friendship, I never really knew Max. He never opened up to anyone, shared his true feelings," Morgan said.

"So you two joined the Raavs, eventually became Commanders, and from what I've read, had a distinguished career. I know about the Targ at Saxhaven, the Crusade and the siege of Tchoga. Do you remember anything about Mogda Thal?" Celeste asked.

Morgan tensed again. "Nothing I want to talk about," he said.

"I'm sorry. I didn't mean to upset you," she said. "And after Mogda Thal, you went into the mountains? To Khulankor?" she asked.

"Yes," Morgan answered.

"Are you a religious man?" Celeste asked.

"I spent twelve years in a monastery. Does that make me religious?" Morgan asked.

"Maybe. Depends on your definition of religion," Celeste said.

"Max used to say I worshipped Momus," Morgan said.

"The god of blame? I can see that," Celeste said, digging in a thumb as Morgan tried to turn and protest. "Answer the question. Don't squirm so."

"I never had much interest in religion, before or after Khulankor. What I found was the Maker, a God that was everything I sought," Morgan said.

"The purity and justice you couldn't find in this world?" Celeste asked gently.

"Yes. Are you religious, Princess?" Morgan asked.

"Officially, Skara Thrae worships the old gods, the Maenor. Privately, my family chose its own way. Personally, I also prefer

Iosus," Celeste said. "What about Max?"

"Many said the only god who would accept his worship was Sett, the goddess of death. Actually, I don't think he gives the subject much thought," Morgan said.

"Tell me more about this oath you've sworn," Celeste said, after a slight pause.

"The oath I've bruised and twisted? I wanted to make a commitment to a better way, to put my killing days behind me. I discovered I may lack the strength to honor my vow. I fought soldiers in Saxhaven, I attacked Wald's men, I've killed trolls. So far I'm a terrible pacifist," he said bitterly.

"You meant well. It may not be the most practical oath, but your motivation is admirable," Celeste said.

"Max thinks I'm a fool," Morgan said.

"You do what you feel is right," Celeste said.

Celeste worked lower on Morgan's back. She noticed a circle of puckered flesh at the base of Morgan's spine, with ridges of tissue spreading out from it, nearly reaching his sides. "What is that?" she asked. "It doesn't look like a scar."

"I obviously can't see what you're looking at," Morgan murmured.

Celeste followed the outline of the mark with her fingers. "Oh, that. It must be a birthmark. I've never been wounded there," Morgan said.

Celeste frowned. "Strange looking birthmark. It's looks more like . . . a tattoo," she said.

"I've never gotten a tattoo," Morgan said. "It's always been there."

"You're somewhat mysterious, Morgan," Celeste said. "I think I like that."

They were silent for a time, and Morgan slowly relaxed, drifting. Celeste's hands felt so good, warm and soft, yet strong. Her clean scent wafted down to him, and her hips brushed against him from time to time. The pain in his back was easing, and he could not remember when he had last felt so at peace, so comfortable.

Celeste broke into his dream with a question that jarred him back to reality. "Have you ever been in love?" she asked.

The question brought a flood of sensations and memories. Visions of Malissa, and his unholy lust for her, and other women he had known, then the urgency and importance of his mission, the likelihood he would not survive, mixed with the ache of lost loves and lives. And through it all swam the sense of Celeste's presence and her beauty, and his growing fondness for her. A Princess from Skara Thrae, totally unsuited for a wandering mercenary with no wealth or title. He did not even know who his real parents were. Then other memories, darker, deeper, unbearable.

Morgan rolled smoothly away, away from Celeste's hands, away from the scent of her. He stood, reaching for his shirt. Celeste was still poised over the bunk, surprised by his reaction.

He could not bring himself to look at her. "I think you should leave now," he said, his voice hoarse.

She straightened, grabbing for the towel beside the bunk, and wiping her hands furiously. "Why? Why should I leave? Because you might feel something for me? I know you want me, why not just admit it? Everyone knows. Max said it's obvious," she said.

Morgan glanced at her, and then lowered his eyes again. His shirt hung forgotten in one hand, and more bruises colored his chest, marks left by the crossbow bolts at Androssar. He looked miserable.

"Max should keep his mouth shut," Morgan said.

Celeste put her hands on her hips. "At least he's honest. He's not afraid to say what he thinks," she said.

"Like you? You always seem to say what you think," Morgan said, finally meeting her glare.

"Yes, I do. I'm attracted to you, Morgan. I'd like to get to know you better, spend some time with you. I'm not asking you to marry me," she said.

Morgan laughed harshly. "The Princess and the mercenary, without a coin to his name," he said.

"You can't hide behind that. I couldn't care less about money or your former occupation. And my lineage means nothing here. Now, how do you feel about me? Are you going to admit what's going on here, or not?" she demanded.

167

"You must think well of yourself, Highness. What makes you think anything is going on? Do you just assume men are attracted to you?" he said, his anger rising.

"Morgan, I'm not stupid and I'm not blind. If I'm wrong, then tell me," she said.

Morgan sighed, his anger deflating as suddenly as it came. "I can't tell you anything. Not now, not under the circumstances. Some other time, some other place, maybe," he said, and then turned away, slipping on his shirt.

Celeste went to him and grabbed his arm, turning him to face her. "Some other time? Some other place? We're here, now. And there may not be any other time for us. The Mhoul may be waiting for us at Aquarquff. All we have is now. Why are you so stubborn? And don't give me that mercenary life nonsense. Thraen women have been fighting alongside their mates for centuries. War and death is a reality we all face. It's no reason not to be together," she said.

Morgan stared down at her, emotions raging across his face, and then he pulled roughly away, walking to the corner of the cabin.

"We only met a few days ago. You don't know anything about me. You asked what I remembered about Mogda Thal. I may have murdered my own men, helped kill my General. I could be a traitor of the worst kind. You don't want to get involved with me," he said.

"I don't believe that. You're just looking for another excuse," Celeste said.

"I just . . . can't. I'm . . . sorry. Please leave," he said.

Celeste clenched her fists, uncertain whether to scream or cry. "At least tell me you feel something. Let me leave with that," she said.

Morgan didn't move or speak. Celeste blew out her breath in a rush.

"Fine," she said. "Be alone, with your self-pity and your sacred mission. I won't trouble you further."

She stormed out of the cabin, slamming the door behind her.

Morgan slumped to his knees, and began to weep quietly, his head against the wall. Years ago, he had failed the men under him, and his general. He had failed the Raavs and all they stood for. He had left his closest friend behind, a friend who had suffered greatly because he had abandoned him. Then he had made a commitment to his God, and as soon as he was tested, he began to fail in that pledge. And now he had failed a woman he realized he wanted to love, to spend his life with. His failure was complete, leaving him with nothing. He knelt---empty, except for one thing.

"O Iosus, have mercy on me," he whispered.

CHAPTER THIRTEEN
MOLID

The two fishermen rowed their small boat just outside the reef, enjoying the calm sea and the clear sky. The men knew the fish would be gathering along the reef, feeding on the bounty brought by the incoming tide. The early morning sun hung over the nearby shoreline, its warmth driving back the chill of the night.

One man worked the oars, his powerful muscles rippling in his tanned arms. The other man stood in the bow of the boat, looking into the water. Through the clear, shallow sea, he located the dim shapes of fish and the jagged outline of the reef itself.

"Here, Jarl. There's a large school just ahead," the man in the bow said.

Jarl lifted the oars, and the boat drifted in the easy swells. The other man climbed around him, going to the net piled in the stern. He collected one end of the net and slipped it over the side. The line of weights attached to the lower edge quickly dragged the net into the water, while the floats on the upper edge held the net open.

"It's down. Quickly, Jarl," he said.

"Hang on, Serge. Here we go," Jarl said, driving the oars into the water.

The muscular Jarl propelled the boat in an arc, swinging the net around the fish feeding along the reef. Serge paid out the net, making sure it did not catch or tangle. A line of floats bobbed in their wake. These men had fished together for years, ever since they were young boys in the village of Connar Bay, and they worked as a capable team, each man sure of his task. Some said they were the best fishermen in Connar Bay. Their catches were certainly among the largest.

A violent thrashing tore the waves ahead of the boat, and fish literally leaped from the water, driven into frenzy by something below them. Jarl heard the commotion and looked around, nearly missing a stroke with the oars. Fish often moved away from the net as it closed around them, but he had never seen them display such blind panic.

Serge noticed the break in Jarl's rhythm. "What is it?" he asked, one eye still on the net.

"I don't know. Something is scaring the fish," Jarl said, drawing on the oars again.

Serge peered down into the water beside them. "Shark?" he asked.

Jarl shrugged his massive shoulders. "I don't know. Whatever it is, it's in our net now," he said.

The boat completed the circle, its hull sliding over the reef, just an arm's length below. The fish still churned in the circle of floats, some throwing themselves out of the net. Serge crouched in the stern, trying to locate the cause of the unusual disturbance. A large shark could tear the net, and would be dangerous if pulled into the boat. Serge cursed silently, they might lose this whole catch if things did not settle down.

He frowned, his sunlined face wrinkling even further. "There is something down there. Doesn't move like a shark," he said.

Without warning, the net jerked, rocking the boat violently. Serge gripped the gunwale to avoid being tossed overboard. A glittering mass of fish exploded out of the water, leaping away from the net.

Jarl pulled in the oars, and stood, bracing himself against the boat's movement. "We better get the net in, before we lose all the fish," he said.

Serge picked up a wicked looking club from the bottom of the boat, and laid it within easy reach. "If that thing has torn the net, I'll kill it," he threatened.

The two men started pulling in the net, first drawing in the bottom to scoop up the fish. As the net came in, they saw they still had a fair number of fish, in spite of their unwelcome intruder. Fish and . . . something else.

A man-sized form flopped into the boat. Jarl stared down at it.

171

"It's a body," he gasped.

The black shape did not move, but lay deeply entangled in the net, half hidden in its folds. Ignoring the flopping fish all around them, Serge and Jarl began clawing at the net, trying to reach the body.

"Some sailor? From a ship off the coast?" Serge asked.

"He's not breathing. I'm sure he's dead. Let's get him out of there," Jarl said.

In a few moments' time, they had the body clear of the net. The men drew back, sudden fear in their eyes.

"What is that? It's no man," Serge breathed, unconsciously reaching for the club.

Jarl shook his head. "It may be a man. And he's hurt, all wrapped up in black bandages," he said.

The two men looked at each other. "What do we do with him? Take him back to the village?" Serge asked.

"I guess. Robar will know what to do," Jarl said.

They heard a slight rustling and both men jumped. They looked down at the figure in their net, which now stirred. Jarl leaned over the body, trying to see through the smoky goggles that covered its eyes. As he bent forward, a bandaged arm shot up and fingers seized his throat. He grabbed the arm, trying to tear the grip loose, but the hand only tightened. Jarl's face colored, and he struggled more violently, realizing he was in serious danger of being strangled.

"Get it off your throat," Serge cried.

"I can't. Help me," Jarl gasped.

Amazed at the black man's strength, Serge grabbed up his club and moved to Jarl's aid. He struck the arm, where he guessed the elbow should be. With a dry cracking sound, the arm bent with the force of the blow, but the gloved hand still clung to Jarl's throat, quickly choking the life from the big man. The thing in black showed no sign of pain, despite the obvious damage to its left arm. Jarl still fought furiously, both hands locked on the bandaged arm, twisting and pulling.

Serge raised the club again, but a black clad leg lashed out, catching him in the stomach. He staggered backwards, his legs hitting

172

the gunwale. Before he could stop himself, he toppled over the side. He lost his club, hitting the cold water with a splash. He went under and bobbed back up, spitting out the briny seawater. Something caught his legs and he realized he had fallen into the end of the net, still hanging over the side of their boat. He kicked, but the net only wrapped tighter around his legs, threatening to pull him under. He sank and then one foot hit the reef and he shoved himself back up. He reached frantically for the boat, and managed to catch hold of the gunwale. The boat was still rocking with the struggle of the two figures inside.

Serge pulled himself higher, until he could see over the side of the boat. Even as he watched, a wet crunching sound came from Jarl's throat and Serge knew his friend had just died. The figure in black reared up, casting aside Jarl's limp body. The thing's head swung toward Serge, tilting back and forth as if the creature had trouble seeing. Moving stiffly, the black man loomed over Serge, and he saw that Jarl's killer now held his club. Paralyzed with fear, Serge could only stare up at the thing as it raised the club.

That evening, the children playing on the beach did not see the boat until it was just outside of the small bay. The waves crashing on the rocks along the bay's narrow entrance covered any sound of the boat's approach. Finally, one of the older children looked up, shading his eyes against the setting sun.

"Look! A fishing boat," he cried.

A smaller boy turned to look. "Is it father and Serge? They're late," he asked.

All of the children now studied the boat, seeing a single figure struggling with the oars. The oarsman seemed strong enough, but the oars flayed the water with no rhythm, at times beating the air instead, especially the left oar. Attempting to reach the safety of the bay, the boat was being washed closer to the jagged rocks. The waves churned and tossed there, throwing spray high into the air.

"Ral, it's father's boat, but where is father?" the small boy asked.

The larger boy shook his head. "I don't know, Dun. That's

173

not him or Serge in the boat. Whoever it is, they're going to crash on the rocks," he said.

Dun began running toward the rocks. "Let's go see," he cried, then started shouting at the oarsman, warning him away from the rocks.

Ral turned to a girl with them. "Sasha, go get Robar. Be quick," he said.

Startled by the urgency in his voice, Sasha asked no questions, but ran for the nearby village. Ral followed Dun. As the two boys reached the edge of the rocks, the boat floundered in the waves just offshore. They could see the boat's occupant clearly now---a nightmare creature, wrapped in black bandages, with dark goggles that covered half of its swathed face. It resembled a monster from one of their parents' fireside stories. There was no sign of Jarl or Serge.

A wave caught the boat and threw it toward the rocks, where it disappeared in a foamy cauldron. With a crash, shattered boards flew into the air as the pounding waves ground the boat into kindling. The two boys stared in horrified fascination, unable to speak.

"Look!" Dun screamed, pointing with a shaking finger.

Ral could not believe his eyes. Somehow, the black man still lived, and dragged himself out of the thrashing surf. Once clear of the water, the figure stood and staggered stiffly up the beach.

"What have you done with my father? How did you get his boat?" Dun shouted suddenly.

At the sound of his voice, the black man's head swung toward them. The goggles passed over them and stopped, as if the man looked past them. Ral wondered if he were blind.

"What place is this?" the figure asked, its voice harshly mechanical.

"Connar Bay. Just north of Port Adele," Ral answered, his voice unsteady.

"Where is my father?" Dun asked again.

The strange man ignored the question, and walked straight for them.

"Wait!" Ral called.

174

The man did not stop, but kept walking. Behind him, the sun vanished behind the waves, the red glow of its passage surrounding the dark figure like an evil halo. As the man came closer, Dun's fear overcame his anger and he fell silent. Ral grabbed him and dragged him out of the creature's path. The black man passed them without a gesture or word. As he went by, Ral could hear the rustling of his black bandages, and the creak of the wet leather boots. The water slid from the slick surface of the wrappings in crystal beads.

Ral thought he could see a red spark behind the dark goggles. A burnt smell stung his nostrils, as if the man were on fire inside those black bandages. Maybe it was a man who had been horribly burned, and still smoldered somewhere inside. He shook his head, that was nonsense. The figure vanished, striding into the trees, and Ral could hear the shouts of the approaching villagers.

Late in the night, Sittle was awakened by a sound from downstairs. His eyes shot open, and he lay there in the dark, listening. He heard another small noise, again from the lower rooms. Moving quietly, the heavyset Sittle laid back the covers and got out of bed, while his wife slept on, only stirring slightly. Sittle retrieved the small crossbow he kept by the bed, and grabbed a handful of quarrels. By feel alone, he slid his feet into the fleece lined slippers and padded to the bedroom door. He knew the layout of his fine home, and did not need a light, not yet anyway. Out in the hall, he eased the door shut, and stood listening in the darkness, but the sounds that had disturbed him were not repeated. Sittle cocked the crossbow and armed it with a quarrel, and then he slid the other bolts into a pocket in his night shirt. He moved toward the stairs.

He suspected a burglar, as something about the sounds had suggested furtive purpose. Mayor of Port Adele, and the richest man in the area, Sittle made a tempting target for thieves. But this thief did not know who he was dealing with. Sittle, a ruthless, cunning man, had won his position by his wits and treachery, and he would not hesitate to kill anyone who tried to steal from him. As he descended the stairs, Sittle glanced at the paintings on the landing, barely visible in the dim light. Sittle was proud of those paintings and the other treasures in his house. Mayor for now, he held even higher aspirations, and had the means to achieve his goal. A few years ago, he had entered a realm most feared, dealing secretly with those the world shunned. But he knew raw power when he saw it, and he wanted what they had, being willing to pay any price.

He paused at the bottom of the stairs, studying the room, the crossbow prowling restlessly. Moonlight leaked through the shutters, the only light in the room. He could see the dim shapes of furniture, but nothing moved. Sittle wondered what had happened to his worthless employees. To reach the house, a thief would have to pass the gate sentries, the grounds patrol, and the house guard. He had no patience with incompetence, and there would be some stiff punishments meted out tomorrow. First, he would deal with the intruder himself.

He turned toward the library. In that room lay his greatest treasures, and would be the likely goal of a thief. Intent on the library, he did not see the still form on the floor until his slipper thudded against it. He jumped back with a silent oath and peered down. Even in the faint light he recognized his house guard, a huge man named Carson. Carson's eyes stared sightlessly, his thick neck twisted at an odd angle.

He padded to the library, his robe swishing around his fat legs, moving with even greater caution now. Anyone who could break Carson's neck was dangerous indeed. From the side of the door, Sittle surveyed the library, and saw a dark figure standing near the bookshelves, its back to him. It appeared to be searching for something, and several books lay at its feet. Without hesitation, Sittle's finger tightened on the trigger. Farewell, thief, he thought.

The twang of the bowstring and the angry burr of the quarrel broke the stillness of the house. The bolt struck its target squarely, and the figure lurched against the shelves. Sittle reefed back the string and loaded a second quarrel, striding into the room as he did so. The thief had not immediately fallen, but still leaned against the shelves, supported by its outspread arms. Sittle walked quickly toward the other man, intending to finish him at close range. He raised the crossbow and squeezed the trigger.

The dark figure spun around, and a gloved hand struck the crossbow, knocking it across the room. Sittle jerked back his throbbing hand, amazed. Before he could move, the intruder stalked toward him, and a hand seized his arm with an inhumanly strong grip. The weak moonlight shone on metallic wrappings, and he found himself staring into smoked goggles, fascinated by the reddish flares in their depths. Sittle sagged with shock, knowing suddenly what type of creature had invaded his home. And he had shot it with a crossbow, possibly angered it.

He fought to form words. "Forgive me. There was no warning of your coming. I . . ." he croaked, his mouth suddenly dry.

Harsh words came from the grille on the Mhoul's face. "You have something for me," it grated.

Sittle tried to think. Something? Oh, yes, now he remembered. The Mhoul's grip tightened and he groaned. A voice came from the stairs.

"Sittle? What are you doing down there in the dark?" his wife called softly.

The Mhoul's head turned toward the sound, and Sittle could hear the rasping sound of its movement.

"Go back to bed," Sittle called gruffly, and then in a gentler voice, he added, "I'll be up soon."

He thought again about the guards, and now he feared for his wife as well. But then he heard her moving back toward the bedroom. Faithful Moffa did not question him in business matters. She enjoyed his affluence and did not concern herself with its source.

The Mhoul's bandaged skull swung back to him, and Sittle spoke quickly. "In the cellar. It's safe, ever since your agent delivered it to me," he said.

The Mhoul released him and stood waiting. Sittle noticed a burnt smell coming from the Mhoul, mixed with the odor of salt and fish. He turned for the door, rubbing his arm, and the Mhoul followed silently on his heels, resting skeletal fingers on his shoulder. As Sittle walked toward the cellar stairs, his mind raced. Always before, he had dealt with Mhoul agents, mere hirelings, but now he had a Mhoul in his very house. Something important must be happening, for a

177

Mhoul itself to be involved. Something too important to trust to a lesser being. Sittle imagined a great profit in this encounter. If he could prove his worth now, he would have a definite advantage.

He stopped at the cellar door. "I'll have to turn on a light," he whispered.

The Mhoul did not reply, only prodded him painfully with its bony fingers. Sittle took that for approval, and opened the door. He touched the light globe by the stairs and a dim radiance flooded the stairwell. Sittle smiled briefly, the globes were another sign of his affluence. Sittle descended the stairs, his eyes adjusting to the light. He moved to the wall to his left, and pushed on a stone block. The Mhoul had followed him down the stairs and remained standing in the center of the room, unnaturally still and silent. The block settled under the pressure of Sittle's touch, and a small panel swung open in the wall, its front covered with false stonework. Behind the panel lay a hidden alcove, and Sittle got down on his knees, reaching inside. He brought out a wrapped bundle, about the size of a man's head. He got clumsily to his feet, and approached the Mhoul, holding out the object.

The Mhoul cocked its head, sensing rather than seeing his offering, and reached out, seizing the bundle and jerking it from his grasp. With one hand the Mhoul tore off the covering and dropped it, revealing a crystalline object, exquisitely carved into the shape of a skull. The stair globe's light seemed to sink into it, causing the skull to glow softly with a greenish light of its own. Sittle stared at the crystal skull with barely concealed avarice. Despite the agent's warning not to even look at it, Sittle had carefully examined the skull as soon as the man left. It was a marvelous piece of work, obviously worth a fortune, and only his fear of the Mhoul kept him from displaying it or selling it. The Mhoul's fingers slid over its surface, while it seemed that the goggled face still had not focused on the object in its hands.

Curious, Sittle took advantage of his first good look at the infamous Mhoul. He found himself somewhat disappointed and concerned by the Mhoul's appearance. He saw a slender, bedraggled figure swathed in black bandages, not very tall, with the remains of a cloak hanging around its neck. Chipped and scored goggle lenses, frayed, disheveled bandages across the chest, and muddy, scuffed boots added to the image. Bits of green clung to its body, that looked and smelled like seaweed, and the burnt fish smell still assailed Sittle's nostrils. The left arm bent oddly, as if the elbow were damaged. This Mhoul had evidently seen some hard traveling. Something major was occurring in the Mhoul's world and Sittle was going to be a part of it.

Finishing its examination of the skull, the Mhoul became aware of Sittle again. "Leave," the Mhoul said in its mechanical voice.

Shrugging, Sittle went up the stairs. These Mhoul may be powerful, but their manners are atrocious, he thought. Oh well, a small price to pay for the wealth, power, and glory he was sure to achieve in their service.

Once the man had closed the door, Molid placed the skull on a small table, pressed on its temples, and then stepped back. With a slight humming sound, the skull's eye sockets began to glow. The rest of the skull's surface turned dark, as if all the energy were being drawn to the eyeholes. A greenish beam erupted from the eyes, spraying across the room. A vague form took shape in the beam and then it cleared. The shaft of light from the skull now held the image of a second Mhoul, one of the toad-like riths perched on its shoulder. The rith's eye stalk swung toward Molid.

"Molid, why are you using an emergency beacon? What has happened?" the Mhoul asked, its voice sounding hollow and distant.

"The ironclad flagship has been destroyed. I require transportation," Molid replied.

"How did this happen?" the other Mhoul asked.

"The flagship was in danger of being captured. I activated the self-destruct," Molid said.

"Captured? By whom?" the image demanded.

"Rukla, I have been shot, deprived of my flagship, cast into the sea, caught in a net, attacked by fishermen, shipwrecked again, and chased by foolish villagers. I would watch my tone, if I were you," Molid grated.

Rukla bowed his head. "Forgive me, Dirgelord. I am merely surprised at your predicament," he said, then touched something

179

invisible to the skull's beam. "You are in Port Adele, near the mouth of the Seir. How did you get there?"

"I walked. Aside from a short trip in a rowboat. When the flagship was destroyed, I found it easier to walk to shore rather than swim. Some great fish tried to eat me, and left with my cloak in its jaws. It was not a pleasant journey and my mood reflects my circumstances," Molid said.

Rukla's image leaned toward Molid. "Where is your rith?" the Mhoul asked softly.

"My rith was killed. I will require another," Molid said.

"We will send someone for you immediately," Rukla said.

Molid paused, and then spoke. "The Thraen woman escaped. She is in the company of Morgan Caeda and Maximilian, the former Raav Commanders."

"The Nestbreakers? They still live?" Rukla asked.

"Yes, they were on a ship with the Princess. The Windrider, captained by one Taurus. They were headed south, but the ship was fitted with a tracking device while docked in Androssar. It shouldn't be hard to find," Molid said.

"We were sure that Morgan had perished with Imperius' troops in the attack on Mogda Thal, and Maximilian disappeared after the siege of Droghelda. Where have they been?" Rukla said.

"More importantly, why do they appear now? And how did they know about the Princess? I want them captured and questioned, and the Princess returned to Skara Thrae," Molid said.

"Yes, Dirgelord. I will attend to it," Rukla said.

"What is happening on Skara Thrae? Has Tantagnel fallen?" Molid asked.

"No, they still resist. The Haggas are pressing the attack," Rukla said.

"Have you heard from Malissa?" Molid asked.

"Yes, Saxhaven is on the verge of war with Androssar. She says it won't be long now," Rukla said.

"Good. We have to keep all attention on the western lands. We cannot afford to have the Mons Monachus guess our true purpose. What progress on the excavation?" Molid asked.

"We have nearly uncovered the Fargate. It was exactly where the Masters said it would be. Once it is clear, it will be made operational," Rukla said.

"And then Kalnaroag will be ours, and we will rule at the side of the Masters," Molid said.

"And our lives will be restored," Rukla said.

"How is Andog?" Molid asked.

"Not good. She was taken to the Guardian for the end," Rukla said.

"The fate of all of us, if we fail," Molid said.

"You mentioned Morgan. Malissa reported he entered Saxhaven, disguised as an Iosian monk," Rukla said.

"She let him leave?" Molid asked.

"She attempted to detain him, but failed. He rode toward Androssar," Rukla said.

"Saxhaven . . . disguised as an Iosian monk. I must return to Skara Thrae immediately," Molid said.

"Another ironclad will be sent and our agents will contact you. Will you remain at Sittle's?" Rukla asked.

Molid turned slightly, and appeared to be listening. Even though the Mhoul could no longer see in the normal sense, it could detect the presence of living beings, such as the man hidden at the top of the stairs. Sittle crouched there, behind the partly closed door, eavesdropping on their conversation.

"I will be outside the town. Come soon," Molid said.

"Soon, Dirgelord," Rukla said.

Rukla's image wavered and withdrew into the skull, seemingly sucked into the eye sockets. The humming ceased, and the greenish light faded, the crystal skull dimming into a uniform sheen. Molid felt for the covering and rewrapped the skull. With the skull under one arm, Molid moved toward the stairs.

Sittle withdrew from his listening post, puzzled yet delighted at what he had just heard. Molid entered the room, the dark goggles glowing. Sittle stared at the reddish flare, which suddenly filled the room, surrounding him. Molid's voice entered his crimson tomb, commanding and powerful.

181

"You will do as I say . . . " it began.

Molid met the men in the trees, at the edge of town. Dawn lightened the eastern sky, a rosy glow that mingled with the flickering light from Sittle's home. The Mhoul agent glanced at the roaring flames that had entirely consumed the Mayor's fine house. No need to ask of Sittle or his family. The agent turned to Molid.

"We are at your service, Dirgelord. The ironclad waits offshore," he said.

"Take me there. I will be returning to Skara Thrae," Molid said, the crystal skull still
under one arm.

CHAPTER FOURTEEN
THE CHAMBERLAIN

Naked in her enormous bed, Malissa lay sleeping, the white web of her tangled hair draped across her pale features. With her eyes closed, she looked almost human. Next to her rested a corpse, its withered arms rigid and half-raised, the fingers still clawed in its death throes. The bent knees and twisted hips made small mounds in the bedding. The head arched against the soft pillows, the eyes wide and staring. A macabre joining of horror and ecstasy etched the sunken face. In her gorged slumber, Malissa had pulled the covers from the upper body, exposing the empty shell that had been a man the night before.

Malissa murmured in her sleep, snuggling deeper into the warmth of the heavy blankets, and then she rolled toward the corpse. Her legs brushed against the body, and she recoiled, her black, soulless eyes flying open. With a grimace, she drew up her legs, and shoved the dead man from her bed. He fell stiffly to the floor, landing on his face. The rigor of his limbs held him up, as if he kneeled at her bedside in supplication. Malissa sat up, the covers falling to her waist, and stroked the hair from her face, tucking it behind her ears. She yawned and stretched languorously, and then slid to the edge of the bed, where she cupped her chin in one hand. Reaching out with the other hand, she ran her fingers through the dead man's hair.

"I'm sorry, Lamod, but you were cold. You know how I hate the cold," she whispered.

The woman's midnight gaze drifted across the large chamber. Vigorous flames leaped in both fireplaces, cloaking the room in heavy warmth. Semi-darkness shrouded the room, relieved only by the flames and a stray shaft of light leaking through a shutter. Malissa frowned at the spot of sunlight.

"Is it day again?" she said. "The nights are too short."

She regarded the two beasts sprawled before the fireplace at the far end of the chamber. They watched her in silent anticipation.

183

"Good morning, my pets. How are you?" she purred.

One of the hairless creatures growled deep in its throat, and ran a tongue over its gleaming fangs.

"Are you hungry?" Malissa asked. "Well, you can't have poor Lamod."

She tightened her grip in the corpse's hair, tipping the body on its platform of frozen limbs. "See? There is hardly anything left of him. Patience, I will feed you soon," she said.

Malissa shivered slightly, and nestled back into the covers. "Anise," she called. "Get those two men in here."

Anise appeared briefly at an inner doorway. "Yes, Mistress," she said.

Malissa pulled the blankets up under her chin, her eyes wandering to the lewd tapestries on the walls. She licked her full lips. "I'm feeling hungry again. I need better men," she said to herself.

Two male servants entered the room, making a wide detour around the cats on the hearth, and kneeled beside the bed. Malissa sat up, the blanket slipping away, and looked down at them. She did not bother to cover herself, and the servants gazed at her with longing. They seemed oblivious to the contorted body between them and the object of their desire.

Malissa tipped her head, her painted mouth twisting into a pout. "Oh, do you want me?" she asked.

The two men nodded, sweat beading their foreheads. Malissa leaned toward them. "Well, you can't. Not now anyway. Maybe later," she said, and then flipped her hand at the dead man. "Take that away."

The servants hesitated, their faces torn between fear and disappointment. One man swallowed and opened his mouth to speak.

"Now!" Malissa said harshly.

The cats growled in response, and one of the men glanced nervously over his shoulder. The other tore his eyes from the woman on the bed, and stared at the corpse, as if seeing it for the first time. With obvious distaste, the servants picked up the body.

Malissa fixed them with her ebon stare. "And burn the body.

Let no trace of it remain," she said.

With a last look at her, the men turned and carried the corpse from the room. The cats sniffed the body as it passed.

"Anise! A bath!" Malissa ordered.

The homely woman hurried into the room, and shuffled to the sunken bath. She lifted a gate, and as steaming water poured into the basin, she lit a small lamp, placing it on a stand behind the bath.

Malissa lifted her white locks, piling them on top of her head. "I think cinnamon and spice will do for today," she said.

Anise searched quickly through a collection of vials in a rack next to the bath. She selected one and poured the reddish contents into the water. The swirling water churned into a mass of pungent foam.

Malissa still held up her hair. "Anise," she said warningly.

Anise almost dropped the vial in her haste to replace it on the rack. She grabbed a hairpin and handed it to Malissa, leaning over the large bed. The servant stepped back, her hands clasped before her. Malissa bound her hair with the pin.

"Is it warm enough?" Malissa asked, as she slid across the bed.

The servant glanced at the steaming water, her face tight. She nodded desperately.

Malissa sat on the edge of the bed, and frowned. "How do you know? Try it," she said.

Anise knelt and reached toward the water. She hesitated, then thrust her hand into the water, and jerked it back. Her hand shone bright red even from that brief contact.

"Good. Shut it off," Malissa said.

Anise closed the water spout, and stood, holding her scalded hand.

"Send for Secondus," Malissa ordered.

As Anise rushed to do her bidding, Malissa slipped into the hot water, the frothy bubbles enfolding her ivory body.

Secondus soon arrived, and stood by the bath. Malissa lay in the water, with her head resting on a cushion at the edge. Islands

185

of foam drifted across the steaming water, hiding and then revealing her pale form beneath. Malissa toyed lazily with one pile of bubbles, pulling it over her breasts. The Chamberlain swayed slightly. He could smell the Hedonae's luring scent, mixed with the spices of the bath. The heat and her fragrance made him dizzy. He tried not to look at her, staring hard at the flickering flames in the fireplace.

"Secondus, what is wrong?" Malissa said suddenly, as she shoved aside the mass of bubbles.

The old man glanced down at her and nearly toppled into the basin. He caught himself with a gasp.

Malissa laughed. "Secondus, you seem unsteady this morning. Perhaps you should sit down," she said.

"Thank you, Mistress," the Chamberlain said, as he collapsed into the nearest chair.

Malissa sat up and beckoned. "Closer. I can't see you over there," she said.

Secondus dragged the chair next to the bath. Malissa laid back, the water swirling over her.

"That's better. What do you have for me?" she asked.

The Chamberlain's eyes flicked across her and away. "Mistress?" he asked.

Malissa slashed her hand through the water, spraying the man seated beside her. Secondus jerked as the burning droplets struck his face.

"The bodies! Did you find the bodies?" she asked.

Secondus took a deep breath, gripping the chair. "Not yet. Soon, I'm sure," he said.

Malissa reached out, and ran her moist hand up his bare leg, under his robe. He trembled, rigid at her touch.

"My dear Chamberlain, you know this palace better than anyone. If you can't find Antony's hiding place, then who can?" Malissa said.

Her cool, wet fingers were like fire on his skin, and Secondus fought to keep his thoughts clear. "I will find them," he said.

Malissa caressed his calf. "You want to find them, don't you?" she asked.

186

"Yes, Mistress," Secondus gasped.

"Do you remember what a stasis chamber looks like?" Malissa asked.

"Yes," Secondus said.

"Tell me," Malissa said coldly.

"A metal box, like a coffin," the Chamberlain said.

"What else?" Malissa asked.

Secondus hesitated, and Malissa's hand shot up his leg. The Chamberlain flinched violently. "A power source. It needs power," he cried.

Malissa relaxed, her hand sliding down. "That's better. Find the chamber, and the bodies will be there. Destroy them immediately. Have the chamber brought to me," she instructed.

"It will be done," Secondus said.

"Have you found my traitor yet?" Malissa asked.

"Antony's retinue is too loyal. I haven't been able to turn any of them," Secondus said, licking his dry lips.

"No one will betray the Ambassador? What have you offered them?" she asked, continuing to stroke his leg.

"Money, rank, the usual enticements," he answered.

"What have you threatened them with?" Malissa asked.

"Threatened?" Secondus asked.

"If greed fails, then try fear," she said.

"Fear," he repeated.

"Yes, Chamberlain. Fear. Family, friends, deep secrets," she said.

"Antony's guards fear nothing. Everyone fears Caestus," Secondus said.

Malissa let him feel her nails. Secondus winced. "Find me a traitor, Secondus. Try harder," she said.

"I will," Secondus assured her.

"The poisons?" Malissa asked.

The Chamberlain's knuckles turned white on the chair. "They are too careful. Everything is tested, and they prepare their own food," he said.

"Secondus, I poisoned the Sagess herself. Surely you can

reach a mere ambassador," she said.

"I just need a little more time," Secondus said.

Malissa rose up, and leaned toward the Chamberlain, resting her elbows on the bath rim. He could not help but look at her, and the sight nearly made him faint. He held on to the chair seat, willing himself not to move. He locked his eyes on a drop of water sliding down her arm.

Malissa traced her fingers across his other leg. "Are you loyal to me, Secondus? Do you want me to win?" she asked.

The cursed drop of water ran toward the inside of her arm, and Secondus shifted his gaze to Malissa's eyes. Those inhuman eyes sometimes helped him maintain control.

"I serve . . . only you, Malissa. You . . . can trust me," he stammered.

The Hedonae settled back, letting the water cover her again. She studied his face. Secondus could see his reflection in her eyes. The sensuous chill in his legs began to subside. Finally, she sighed.

"Chamberlain, could you hand me that robe?" she asked, gesturing toward a fur covering draped over a nearby couch.

Relieved, Secondus released his grip on the chair and stood. He grabbed the robe and handed it to Malissa. He tried not to watch as she stood, but his body betrayed him, and he drank in the glorious image of her wet and naked, with the firelight playing over her creamy skin. He clutched at the chair, bracing himself. Malissa smiled at him, and slowly wrapped herself in the fur. Then she stepped away from the bath and moved around behind him. Secondus tensed again, not knowing how much more of this he could take. Malissa put her hands on his shoulders, and he could feel her breath at his ear. Her intoxicating scent surrounded him.

"Secondus, what am I to do with you?" she whispered.

"Perhaps I should leave, Mistress. I have much to do," he said, his fear mingling with rising passion.

She slid her hands across the back of his neck, and up into the ring of remaining hair. "Out of respect for your age, I have only touched you lightly before. Would you like more, Secondus?" she asked.

Secondus tried to breathe normally. "Oh, yes, Mistress. But I fear I would not survive it," he said.

Malissa pulled at the neck of his robes, baring his chest. She draped her arms over his shoulders, touching the gray hairs on his chest. The old man swayed, his vision blurring.

"Few survive, Chamberlain. But they don't care," she said.

The Hedonae drew back slightly, opening her robe, and then she leaned against him, wrapping her arms around his waist. Secondus could feel her damp softness pressing into his back. He was suddenly cold. Malissa fastened her lips on his neck, her teeth touching his skin. Secondus tottered on the brink of a pit of dark ecstasy.

Suddenly, Malissa pulled away, shuddering. She clutched her robe tight around her, and staggered away from Secondus.

"What is that? What are you doing to me?" she demanded, her face contorted with rage.

Secondus dropped into the chair, dizzy and shaken. He managed to raise his head. "I don't understand. What are you talking about?" he asked.

Malissa rubbed her hands on the furs, as if she had touched something foul. "You are . . . tainted, somehow," she said. "What is wrong with you?"

A wave of terror washed away the last of his passion. She knew! Secondus spun toward her and fell to his knees. "Please! It's not my fault. He did it," he begged.

Malissa took a step closer, although she was careful not to touch him. "Who . . . did what?" she hissed.

"Antony! He poisoned me, and then used the antidote to make me do things," Secondus wailed.

"Antony," she said, the word a curse on her lips.

"If he doesn't give me regular doses, I'll die. I had to do what he said," Secondus said.

Malissa pulled the furs closer around her neck. She shivered. "What did you do for him?" she asked.

"Spied on you. Told him your plans. Please, Mistress. I had to," Secondus said, putting his forehead on the carpet. "I had to."

"Who else did he do this to?" she asked.

"Most of the palace officials. I don't know all of them," Secondus said.

The Hedonae regarded the Chamberlain for a moment. "Rise, Secondus. Do not fear. We will think of something," she said.

Secondus struggled to his feet, tears staining his lined cheeks. "Thank you, Mistress. I knew you would be merciful," he said, reaching out to her.

Malissa retreated a step, shaking her head. She gestured toward a doorway. "Wait for me in there, while I consider the situation," she said.

The Chamberlain hurried toward the door. "Yes, Mistress. It will be all right," he said.

Malissa followed at a safe distance, and pulled the door shut behind him. She leaned against the door, breathing deeply. She was shaken by the venom she had sipped, the slow death lurking in the Chamberlain's body. The cats rose and stalked toward her, their tails twitching. Malissa smiled down at them.

"My beauties," she said.

The felines sat before her, purring deeply. Malissa stepped aside, and threw the door open. "Feed!" she commanded, her voice harsh and guttural.

As one, the cats bounded through the door, and Malissa dragged it shut. She turned the lock, and backed away, listening. The Chamberlain's scream echoed through the chamber, followed by the sounds of his death.

Malissa folded her arms. "Now I need a new Chamberlain," she observed.

CHAPTER FIFTEEN
AQUARQUFF

The Windrider rocked gently with the swells, her sail down. The crew was stowing the sail, and preparing to row into the shallow bay that served as Aquarquff's port. Harkon, Taurus and Max stood in the bow, studying the shoreline.

A brutal sun blazed overhead, and the silver arch shimmered against the clear blue sky. Empty sand dunes lined both sides of the bay, extending as far as the eye could see along the shore. A light breeze stirred the sands, casting a grainy mist from the dune crests. Hardly anything grew on the seaward side of the dunes, save for a few strands of hardy beach grass. The backs of the dunes were more fertile, supporting a thin mix of grass and thorny scrub.

Beyond the dunes reared huge reddish cliffs, looming high into the sky. Sometime in the past, the cliff face had been eroded into strange patterns, by rains that no longer fell. The town called Aquarquff nestled in the shadow of the massive escarpment, consisting of a crowded collection of mud brick and adobe dwellings, extending a fair distance along the shore. The town was surprisingly large, considering the inhospitable location. The houses had roofs of either tile or thatch, depending on the status of the owner, and the walls of the buildings were a uniform reddish-brown, bleached by the sun. Dusty, narrow streets wandered through the town and a strip of brown and green marked the path of a sluggish stream passing from the cliffs to the bay. Small garden plots clung to the banks of the stream.

Several crude corrals stood on the near side of town, holding flocks of skinny goats. Beyond the settlement, next to the cliffs, was a larger, more sturdily constructed enclosure. Several horses pawed the dirt floor of this corral, and small flocks of chickens also scratched in the arid soil, searching for any bits of grain the horses might have dropped. A blue tent could be seen at the base of the cliffs, and beyond that lay the Shah's palace, a large white structure. Near the far end of Aquarquff a windmill towered over a patch of green in the sand, creaking in slow circles in the dry air.

The only other relief from the drab shades of brown was the ragged fronds of lone palm trees scattered throughout the town, and the colorful garments of the few townspeople moving about under the midday sun. The people shuffled slowly through the dust, hunched and faded under the weight of the sun, but their clothing seemed to be a conscious effort to lend some color to the bleached scenery. If not for the relatively cool sea breezes, the town would have long since dried up and blown away.

Harkon mopped his sweating brow. "What a stinking hole," he complained. "Couldn't Morgan have picked a better destination?"

Max leaned on the railing, gazing at the town. "But this is the grand metropolis of Aquarquff. Gateway to the high desert wasteland surrounding Carnac, home to the noble Ha'ashtari nomads, rumored to be the finest horsemen and archers in the known world. Aquarquff is a thriving trading community, serving as an outlet for Ha'ashtari products, and a supply depot for the few outside articles of interest to the Ha'ashtari. Sagamores have journeyed here to purchase Ha'ashtari horses for their war mounts. It is said the nomads' steeds rival those of Skara Thrae.

In fact, it's probably the only place to study the Ha'ashtari culture without risking violent death or slavery. The nomads consider all other races inferior and do not treat outlanders very kindly. The peace pact between the townspeople and the nomads was established to allow trading and has existed unbroken for decades," he explained.

Taurus squinted through the harsh light at the shallow bay with its old wooden dock. The sun glinted like diamonds from the surface of the water. The stream that flowed past the town entered the bay near the dock, its muddy waters staining the sparkling blue of the seawater. Fishing skiffs were scattered on the sand around the dock, and a few nets lay drying in the sun. The unmistakable scent of fish entrails drifted toward the Windrider, coming from the beach.

"I've been here before. This 'hole' carries on a stiff trade, despite its appearance. Although, if the Quffians didn't have a monopoly on the Ha'ashtari commerce, this town would never survive. It has nothing else to offer. The Quffians are a bunch of religious fanatics

192

that regard other cultures as decadent and corrupt. They're also lazy, backward, and arrogant," Taurus said, then paused. "No point in trying to tie up to that dock. It would probably collapse. We'll row in as close as possible and then use the longboat. I've no desire to get stuck on a sandbar and roast in this cursed sun."

Max surveyed the sky, a hand shading his eyes. "It is rather warm here," he admitted, then shifted his gaze to the cliffs. "It's ironic that up there lies a cold desert. What a difference a little altitude makes."

Harkon turned and gazed seaward at two ships anchored farther out, merchant vessels by the look of them.

"Well, there's proof someone does business here. I wonder who they are," he said.

Taurus studied the ships. "Flags with red swords, crossed on a black background. They're from Simperopol," he said.

Behind them, Morgan and Celeste emerged from their cabins at almost the same time. Celeste gave Morgan a cold look, and strode forward, ignoring him. Morgan followed in her wake, his pace slow and listless. He did not look well.

"What's the matter with Morgan?" Taurus asked. "Is the Princess' seasickness contagious?"

Max looked disgusted. "Seasickness. More like lovesickness," he whispered. "I warned the fool."

Taurus stared at Max. "Lovesickness . . . ?" he began, and then stopped short as Max grabbed his arm, shaking his head as the pair came within earshot.

Max noticed something else. Morgan wore the sword *Lex talionus*, and had his staff in his hand. "I see you took my advice on weaponry. About time," Max said.

The Princess turned and looked at the sword, and started to say something, but Morgan brushed past her without a glance.

"It was a stupid oath anyway," Morgan said in a flat voice, and pitched the staff overboard.

Max smiled grimly. "Morgan Caeda is back," he said.

Morgan walked up beside Max and Taurus, looking past them at Aquarquff. At the first glimpse of the settlement, he staggered suddenly, stumbling and grabbing for the rail. Max peered at him, his concern evident. Without thinking, the Princess reached out and laid her hand on Morgan's back. At the contact Morgan stiffened, straightening with a visible effort. Celeste realized what she had done, and took her hand away.

Morgan gripped the rail, his eyes unfocused, sweat dripping from his brow. Max leaned close and started to speak, but Morgan raised a hand for silence. Celeste watched Morgan closely, but did not attempt to touch him again.

After a moment or two, Morgan drew a shuddering breath and looked at Max. "Well, this confirms how the Monachus intend to give us directions," he said, then touched his brow. "They put the information in here, locked away until something triggers its release."

Taurus looked over Max's shoulder. "More likely the sickness in your mind has spread to your body," he said.

Max made a rude gesture. "Be quiet, Taurus. Morgan, what was the trigger?" he asked.

Morgan waved at the town. "The sight of Aquarquff. Now I know the next step," he said.

"The sight of this town gives me nightmares too," Taurus said.

"So what do we do now?" Max asked.

Morgan looked south, squinting at the reddish cliffs. "Hidden in those cliffs is an ancient storehouse, created by the Empire, and filled with weapons and machinery. The place has been sealed since shortly after the Fall of Craig Phadrig and the exile of the Lucca. I am to retrieve certain devices from the cache, and then go to Dragonback," he said.

Taurus leaned close to Max and whispered. "He shouldn't leave the ship. He's obviously mad," he said.

Max frowned. "Dragonback? The mountain at the northern end of Aijalon? That's way east of here, across the Ha'ashtari's Waste," he said.

Morgan nodded. "Dragonback," he repeated.

"Why? What's there?" Taurus asked.

Morgan shrugged. "I don't know. I assume there will be another implant, more information, released by something I see at

194

Dragonback," he said.

"Is that it? Nothing else?" Max demanded.

"Just some information about the cache, and the devices we are to find, nothing beyond that," Morgan said.

Max turned and put his hands on the rail. He stared at Aquarquff, as if the view would tell him something further. "Well, that's more than we knew before," he said.

Taurus stared at Max and Morgan, and then shook his head. "You're both mad," he said.

Morgan took a deep breath. "We'll take the Princess to the Pathfinders, and they'll lead her to Carnac. We'll locate the cache tonight, and then decide the best way to reach Dragonback," he said.

Celeste said nothing, only regarded the distant cliffs, thinking of her brother and happier times.

They pulled the longboat up on the sand beside the dock. The landing party consisted of Taurus, Morgan, Max, Celeste, and two crewmen from the Windrider. Taskin had wanted to come along, but Morgan saw no need. Harkon was content to stay on the ship, muttering something about the heat and the sun.

Celeste wore a long, loose robe with the hood thrown back, her glossy hair shining in the sun. Taurus wore a wide brimmed hat, trimmed with a gaudy feather. Armed only with a cutlass, he had left Charon on the ship, to Morgan's relief. Both Morgan and Max had changed into lighter clothing, more suited to the dry heat, and Morgan had removed the Iosian cloak, to avoid offending the dogmatic Quffians. Morgan wore his sword, and Max carried his bow, in addition to his swords.

Taurus turned to the two sailors. "Stay here and guard the longboat. If it looks like we're in trouble, go back to the Windrider and bring some help," he ordered.

Taurus took a last look at the Windrider, which sat quietly at anchor in the bay, then turned to Morgan.

"Let's get our business done. On top of everything else, there's no liquor to be found in this town. I never liked this place," he said.

"Yes, the Quffians worship the god Korum, who forbids the

use of strong spirits, and illicit sex. There are no public brothels here. Not your kind of town at all, Taurus," Celeste said.

Taurus looked at the ground and shuffled his feet. "Aw, Princess . . ." he began.

Morgan glanced at Celeste. "You didn't have to come ashore, Princess. We could have contracted with the Pathfinders on your behalf," he said stiffly.

Celeste stepped in front of Morgan, put her hands on her hips, and fixed him with a defiant glare. "You may not want me, but I'm coming anyway, whether you like it or not. I studied this area and its inhabitants, especially the Ha'ashtari. I know all about Aquarquff, the Pathfinders, the Waste, and the culture of the Ha'ashtari. You'll probably need what I know, and you should be glad I'm willing to come along. Any questions?" she demanded.

Morgan stared at her a moment, then shook his head. "Lead on, Princess. We'll try to stay out of your way," he said.

With a toss of her head, Celeste turned on her heel and walked toward the town, Morgan following a step or two behind.

Taurus fell in beside Max. "What's going on with those two?" he whispered to Max.

Max frowned. "They're in love, can't you tell? Don't worry about it; if they don't resolve this soon, I'm going to have a talk with both of them. Maybe I'll have to spank the Princess," he said, smiling at the thought.

"I'm worried about Morgan. All that nonsense about the Mons Monachus, mental implants, and hidden storehouses. Do you believe him?" Taurus asked.

"I haven't decided yet. For now, I'll just wait and watch, guard his back, and hope he's not crazy," Max said.

Taurus glanced at Max's bow, which he had slung over one shoulder. "Why bring Stryker?" he asked.

"I hear there are some fine archery vendors in Aquarquff. I may do some shopping, and I might have to try something on," Max said.

"And if you run into the Ha'ashtari, maybe a friendly little game of skill?" Taurus asked.

"I would never think of antagonizing the natives. That could jeopardize our mission," Max said innocently.

Taurus snorted. "I know you, Max. You can't stand the thought of anyone better than you, at anything. And these Ha'ashtari are rumored to be the finest archers in the world. Try to control your obsession, just this once. You could get us all in trouble, if you start something with the Ha'ashtari," he said.

"I'll try," Max said.

They trudged into town through the dry heat, passing the goat corrals and entering one of the narrow streets. The few people they saw showed little interest in the strangers, but shuffled past with their hoods up, shading their faces and heads from the harsh afternoon sun.

As they entered the town, Max took a closer look at the buildings. The Quffians had built their houses to combat the fierce heat, with ventilation slits, narrow doors, and thick walls. The thatch on the roofs appeared to be made of beach grass, and even the tiles on the more expensive houses were crude and ill fitting. Some of the better houses, and the common areas, often had gaily colored awnings stretched out in front of them, and people sat under these awnings, drinking sasich and gossiping.

Celeste seemed to know exactly where she was going, making her way without hesitation through the winding alleys. A group of men, seated in the shade of an awning, called out something to Morgan in Quffian, which he did not speak. Celeste ignored the men, but Morgan could tell by her reaction that she did understand, and that their comment was probably something rude and suggestive.

He caught up with her. "You say you know the customs hereabouts, but it looks to me like you've already offended the locals," he said worriedly.

Celeste shot him a hard glance. "The good people of Aquarquff believe their women should maintain their proper place. Veiled and two steps behind the man, to be exact," she said.

"What did they say, exactly?" Morgan asked.

"They asked if I was your whore, strutting about in the street, with my naked face. There are no public prostitutes locally, so they assume you brought along your own. Hypocrites. It's well known there's a secret harem in Aquarquff that the men visit frequently," Celeste said, her face tight with anger.

Morgan clenched his fists, looking back at the men, who were staring after them.

Celeste noticed his anger. "Are you planning to go back and slay them, to defend my honor? Why should you care?" she said.

Morgan looked at her, surprised by the remark. "Because I do . . . ," he began and then fell silent, thinking of their conversation in his cabin.

They turned a corner, and entered a small square, the town marketplace. A fountain, long dry, stood in the center of the open area, and vendors sat beneath awnings, displaying their wares. Business was slow in the heat of the day, and soon everything would shut down, for the Quffians customarily slept during the torrid afternoons. Celeste did not slow her pace, intending to pass through the square without stopping, but Morgan fell back, giving the displays a brief examination. The vendors were mostly older women, except for the weapons dealers. They called out to the men as they passed; advertising their merchandise, but the women ignored Celeste. Morgan saw spices and salts, dried fruits and vegetables, salted meats, various kinds of cloths, robes, and headware. He saw tables covered with vials of inks, and jars of incense and perfumes. There was also jewelry, daggers, knives, and swords, some of Ha'ashtari make. One vendor specialized in Ha'ashtari archery equipment, including fletching and points.

Morgan glanced over his shoulder, and as he expected, Max had stopped at the archery display, showing great interest in the collection. Taurus just looked hot and bored, and thirsty. Morgan saw several dark skinned Simpero, from the merchant ships, engaged in haggling with some vendors.

Morgan and Taurus passed through the market without incident, but Max remained at the archery table, examining some of the items. Celeste had stopped on the far side of the square at the opening of another street. She pulled up her hood for shade, and stood waiting impatiently.

Morgan and Taurus joined the Princess, and Taurus waved back at Max. "Forgive Max, Princess. He couldn't get past the archery gear," he said.

Celeste started to speak and stopped, listening. Through the still, dry air, Morgan could hear the sound of approaching horses, and he noticed the few people on the street moved quickly to either side.

"Only one race rides horses in Aquarquff. We better get out of the way. The Ha'ashtari are here to trade," Celeste said.

She stepped under a broad awning, wiping moisture from her face with the edge of her robe. Morgan went after her, and then looked back for Taurus and Max. Taurus had followed their example, and was just sitting down on a barrel in the shade. He pulled off his hat, and mopped his brow with a pocket cloth. They were all wishing they had brought something to drink.

Then Morgan saw Max, who walked toward them, studying something that he had purchased from the archery vendor. It looked like a decorated leather arm guard.

Just as Max entered the street, a group of horses and riders burst around the corner, the animals moving in an easy canter. They were on Max before anyone could move, but instead of leaping aside, Max merely looked up and stood his ground. At the last possible moment the lead rider's horse reared up, pawing the air, and the other horses skidded to a stop behind him. Morgan reached for his sword, and Taurus stood and tossed his hat aside. Celeste grabbed Morgan's arm, shaking her head.

Ignoring the flailing hooves that tore the air near his head, Max gazed calmly up at the rider, slipping the arm guard into his belt pouch. Obviously an excellent horseman, the Ha'ashtari on the lead horse sat easily on the rearing horse, returning Max's gaze.

Morgan studied the scene, unconsciously preparing for a fight. He had encountered the Ha'ashtari before, a long time ago, in Kalixalven, on the Seir. The Raavs had stopped in town, and met a group of the nomads on a trading mission, protected by a temporary truce. The two parties of warriors had exchanged insults, but both honored the truce, and they parted without bloodshed. Morgan feared Max's behavior would lead to a conflict with the proud and aggressive Ha'ashtari. He hoped Aquarquff's peace pact would hold this day.

There were four of the Ha'ashtari, three men and a woman, mounted on splendid horses. They held their reins loosely, guiding their mounts mainly with leg pressure. Intricate tattoos decorated their mahogany skins, and the men wore their black hair long, the fronts of their heads shaved, with the remaining hair pulled back. The woman's hair was cut short, a tousled mass of black. They all wore high-necked, sleeveless jerkins, laced up the front, breeches, and moccasins. Their garments were made of supple brown leather, a shade lighter than their skin. Around their necks hung leather pouches, and they wore leather arm bands, and a sort of fingerless glove on their right hands.

The Ha'ashtari all carried horn bows slung over their shoulders, and pairs of wicked looking knives at their belts. Their saddles consisted of simple leather pads, with iron rings for stirrups. A quiver of arrows hung from the right side of each saddle, in front of the rider's leg, and on the opposite side of the saddle were slim lances with crossbars, evidently designed to keep impaled victims from sliding up the shaft. Tied across the backs of the saddles were shaggy garments of hide, necessary on the cold steppes above, but much too warm for the lower elevations. Small round shields, made of metal and leather, had been fastened over the cloaks. Two of the men carried large bundles over their saddles, possibly trading goods for the market.

The man in the lead, a powerful looking individual, had broad shoulders and a barrel chest, a square face with deepset eyes, and a wide nose. His black, shaggy eyebrows nearly met over his nose, and a scar deeply notched his left ear, stretching down to his jawbone. His skin was like the leather he wore, toughened by long days in the wind and sun. A simple headband creased the dark forehead, twisting in the back to secure his long hair.

The man's horse, a magnificent black with a short face and small ears, was of medium build, heavily muscled; yet with legs long enough to cover ground in distance eating strides. The long, flowing mane and tail glistened in the sun. With a light touch to the neck and a low command, the Ha'ashtari calmed his mount, and it dropped to all fours, but it still snorted and pranced, its eyes showing white against its glossy ebon hide.

The woman and one of the other men urged their horses forward, hostile gazes fixed on the offending stranger, the woman reaching for one of her knives. Max ignored them both, still watching the lead Ha'ashtari.

The leader hissed a sharp command, and the other two froze, their horses stomping with the tension. The people of Aquarquff gathered, watching in fearful anticipation.

Max spoke, his calm voice sounding loud in the tense hush. "I am pleased to see that the Ha'ashtari still honor the peace of Aquarquff," he said, using the Trade language.

The woman spat in the dust, and Max glanced at her. He found her quite attractive, in a wild sort of way, with large brown eyes, and full, sensuous lips. The loosely laced jerkin revealed intriguing expanses of dark skin, and the tight breeches suited her supple legs.

"A peace that you seem determined to violate, foolish . . .," she began, in curiously accented Trade.

The leader cut her off with a look, and leaned forward on his horse, looking down at Max. "Most outsiders move aside when we ride through town. Our mounts are bred for battle, trained to trample our enemies. You are either brave or foolish. Which is it, outsider?" he asked.

Max shrugged. "Probably neither. I dislike scurrying, though," he said, then studied the man's fiery mount. "A fine, spirited animal. And obviously under expert control. I see the Ha'ashtari's reputation for horsemanship is not exaggerated. I doubt I was in any great danger."

The Ha'ashtari sat back, his lips curling in a small smile. "I will answer my own question then. Brave, I think. But in other circumstances, foolish. If my daughter had her way . . .," he said, glancing at the woman, "the peace of Aquarquff may not have saved you. Which would have been unfortunate, as both races benefit from the arrangement." He paused again, and his face hardened.

201

"Now would you step aside, and let us pass?" he asked.

Max immediately moved to one side, bowing. "I am honored to meet you, noble Ha'ashtari. May your trading be profitable," he said.

The man nodded and rode past without another look, but the woman glared at Max as she rode by, and Max favored her with another bow. Morgan breathed a sigh of relief, and Taurus bent to retrieve his hat, shaking his head. The townspeople began to move away, relieved that the treaty had not been broken.

Max stood, looking after the riders. Suddenly he called out to them. "Although I wonder if the Ha'ashtari fame as archers has any merit?" he asked.

As one, the Ha'ashtari wheeled their mounts, and the leader stared at Max. "You begin to try my patience, outlander. Was that a challenge?" he asked.

Max rubbed his beard thoughtfully. "I don't know. Was it? I am not familiar with Ha'ashtari challenges," he said.

"Max, no! You don't know what you are getting yourself into," Celeste hissed at Max.

Morgan groaned, and Taurus' hat hit the dirt again as he loosened his saber in its sheath. The Ha'ashtari's daughter whispered fiercely to her father, urging something, and he glanced at the afternoon sun. "We have time. We will do our trading and then you meet us at the windmill. There we will show you the Ha'ashtari challenge of the bow," he said, then paused. "Normally we do not accept challenges from outsiders, considering them unworthy of our skills. But I see fire in your eyes and my daughter thinks you need a lesson in humility."

Max bowed. "We will be there, as soon as our business is concluded," he said, then paused, and everyone tensed again. "May I know your name?"

"Ha'keel," the man responded. "And yours?"

"Maximilian," Max said.

Ha'keel nodded and turned his horse. The others followed.

As the nomads rode off, Taurus walked over to Max. "I warned you," he said.

Max kicked at the dirt. "I'm sorry. I couldn't help myself," he said.

Celeste joined them. "You will regret this," she said.

"You think I'll lose?" Max asked, looking hurt.

"It's not that, you fool. It's the manner of their challenge. I . . ," she said.

Max put a hand on her shoulder. "Don't worry, Princess. Let's go hire your Pathfinders, and then you can explain it all to me as we walk to the windmill," he said.

"That was a tribal chieftain. Didn't you notice the headband?" Celeste asked.

"I was watching his weapons, not his jewelry. Chief Ha'keel. That seems fitting," Max said.

Celeste stared after the departing riders. "I wonder why a chieftain would come to town. Surely not just to trade. Maybe he had some business with the Shah," she said.

As they approached the dark blue tent of the Pathfinders, Morgan was scolding Max.

"Why couldn't you just get out of the way, like everyone else? Then you challenge them to an archery contest. It's not like we want to draw attention to ourselves," Morgan said.

Max pursed his lips. "Like when you took on the city guard in Saxhaven, to help the starving widow? Or when you attacked Thugmonger's men in a public tavern, to save your Princess?" he asked innocently.

Morgan threw his hands in the air. "At least I had a good reason, not just an obsession," he said.

"I don't see what your problem is. We're talking about a simple archery contest here. It's not like I declared war on the Ha'ashtari," Max said.

"We don't have time for this," Morgan said.

"I need a drink," Taurus complained. "Why didn't someone bring a bottle?"

"Oh, that would help. Get us all thrown out of town for violating local taboos," Morgan said.

"Quiet, children. This is it," Celeste said as they reached the tent.

The Pathfinders had pitched their tent at the base of the cliffs, beyond the town. A man sat at a table under an awning near the entry, clad in a blue robe, his face veiled with blue cloth. Celeste walked up to him, and spoke to him in a language the men from the Windrider had not heard before. The Pathfinder half rose, his hand slipping into his robe, and Morgan and the others reached for their weapons. After a moment of tense silence, the man in blue spoke.

"Do not soil the Pathfinder tongue with your lips, woman. You will address me in Trade, or not at all," he said.

"I wish to hire a guide to Carnac," Celeste said calmly in Trade, reaching for her money pouch.

The Pathfinder sat down and his dark eyes flickered toward her and away. "The Pathfinders do not do business with women. Perhaps your escort can . . . ," he said, and then stopped as three gold coins landed on the table in front of him.

Celeste leaned toward him. "Make an exception. I conduct my own business," she said.

The man glanced at Morgan and Max, and then at Taurus, who fanned himself with his hat, looking longingly back toward the Windrider. The Pathfinder regarded the coins, and then raised his eyes to Celeste.

"You wish a Pathfinder, to guide you on the ever-changing road to Carnac. How many will be in your party?" he asked.

"Just myself. And I want to leave as soon as possible," Celeste said.

"And why would a woman such as yourself wish to travel alone to the city of knowledge? Are you to study there?" the man asked.

"My business in Carnac is none of your affair. What is your price?" Celeste shot back.

"Merely exchanging pleasantries. It was not my intent to pry into your affairs," the man said.

He pulled out a form and filled in some information with a quill pen. He looked up at Celeste.

"Do you have a name?" he asked.

"Malissa," the Princess responded quickly. Morgan glanced at her in surprise.

"Malissa," the Pathfinder repeated, his eyes narrowing slightly.

"Do you have a name, Pathfinder?" Celeste asked.

The man in blue frowned. "Our names are not important to this transaction," he said.

The Pathfinder wrote in a price, and then shoved the document toward Celeste. "Sign here, if you can write," he said.

"I can write. In three languages," Celeste said as she grabbed the pen and signed the contract.

The Pathfinder reached for the gold coins. "I think this will be sufficient to cover the toll," he said. He raised his eyebrows as another coin landed beside the first three.

"Here is more, to be swift," Celeste said.

"Be here at dawn. Your Pathfinder will be ready," the man said, then added, "I trust you will not have excessive baggage? We are guides, not porters."

Celeste turned away. "Don't worry. I travel light. I will return at dawn," she said.

The group from the Windrider walked back toward town, while the man at the tent stared after them, absently fingering the coins.

Morgan caught up with Celeste. "Why did you speak to him in his language? Didn't you know it would insult him?" he asked.

"I knew. I did it on purpose. The Pathfinders are as bad as the Quffians. If I didn't need them to get to Carnac, I wouldn't speak to them at all," Celeste said.

"Why Malissa?" Morgan asked.

Celeste shrugged. "It was the first name I could think of. I wasn't going to give that lout my real name. I should have given him the blade of my knife," she said.

Max joined them, Taurus trailing behind. "Killing him would have just raised the price of a guide, Princess. I thought you handled him rather well. Maybe I'll come back and kill him later," he said.

Celeste laughed and hooked her arm in Max's. "That would be nice, Maximilian," she said.

Taurus spoke from behind them. "Tell me again why you had

to hire a guide. You spent years in Carnac. Don't you know where it is?" he asked.

"You don't know about the Pathfinders?" Celeste asked over her shoulder.

"I trade here, but my crew would rebel if I dragged them often to a town with no drink or entertainment. I've never dealt with the Pathfinders," Taurus said.

"The Pathfinders are half-caste Ha'ashtari men, that long ago found a way to profit from their kinship with the nomads. The Ha'ashtari select safe routes to Carnac, the Paths, where they agree to leave travelers unmolested. The Ha'ashtari will attack anyone not on the Paths. The Pathfinders alone are told the routes, and thus they maintain their monopoly on guide services. The nomads change the routes regularly, so having been to Carnac in the past is of little use.

Students and scholars can still reach Carnac, but only with the assistance of the Pathfinders. The centaurs maintain their privacy, as only serious travelers who pay the toll reach their gates, and the Ha'ashtari take a share of the Pathfinders' profits. Because no one else dares raid in Ha'ashtari country, travelers on the Paths can reach Carnac in perfect safety. It's a system that has worked for centuries," Celeste explained.

Taurus nodded in appreciation. "I see. Shrewd business," he said.

"Why do the Ha'ashtari care about the centaurs or their visitors? From what I've heard about them, they would prefer to attack any outsiders that entered the Waste," Morgan said.

"Besides the business aspects, the Ha'ashtari consider the centaurs children of the gods. They nearly worship them," Celeste said.

"Interesting," Max commented.

CHAPTER SIXTEEN
THE CHALLENGE

They made their way back through town, heading for the windmill. As they walked, Celeste explained the Ha'ashtari rite of challenge by bow. Morgan was frowning and muttering by the time they arrived, but Max seemed unperturbed, his dark eyes dancing.

"How long is this going to take? I'm dying of thirst. And I hate walking," Taurus said.

Max looked at Morgan. "Can we send the Captain back to his ship? I tire of his complaining," he said.

Morgan shook his head. "We better keep him with us. No telling what kind of trouble you've gotten us into," he said.

"What trouble? You heard the Princess. It sounds like a simple process," Max protested.

"Simple process," Morgan muttered.

When they reached the windmill, the Ha'ashtari had already arrived, and tethered their horses nearby. A man in an ornate robe and turban stood with the nomads, arguing with the chieftain.

"Please forebear, Ha'keel. The outsider meant no insult. If you proceed with this challenge, there might be death or injury, and the peace of Aquarquff will be a thing of the past. Think of the profitable trade both races enjoy under the pact. We receive your fine horses to export, as well as your tribal weapons and artifacts. You in turn can barter for salt, and metals, and ink for your tattoos, not to mention fine cloths and jewelry, and dried fruits from our gardens. As you told the Shah only yesterday, this arrangement benefits us all," the man pleaded.

Ha'keel stood with his arms folded, and then shook his head.

"Tell your Shah that if there is injury or death, it will be accidental, a mere lack of skill. Of course, a death may be avenged, but I pledge the vengeance will not take place within the town. The pact will remain unbroken, so your fears are unfounded. Now leave us, and let the rite begin. The sun waits for no man," he said.

Seeing the approach of the party from the Windrider, the

official and his retinue turned away, moving back toward the town. As they passed Max, the official stopped and addressed him.

"I am Sherat, a representative of the Shah of Aquarquff. I forbid this challenge," he said.

Max glanced at Sherat. "Shouldn't we discuss this with Chief Ha'keel? He seems inclined to proceed," he said.

"I have. He does want to proceed with this foolishness, despite my warnings," Sherat said.

"Then who am I to violate the challenge? Be off with you, man," Max said.

"Let this be on your head. You will be responsible for what happens this day," Sherat said.

"Fine. Now go away," Max said.

Max went to Ha'keel. "The rite has been explained to me. Who will be your challenger?" Max asked.

Ha'keel nodded toward one of the male Ha'ashtari. "My son, Ha'sim accepts the challenge. He has no equal with the bow," he said.

Max glanced at Ha'sim, a tall, handsome young nomad, who returned Max's look with confidence.

"Until today," Max said. "And who will bear your target?"

The other Ha'ashtari man started to step forward, but the woman blocked his path. Ha'keel gave her a stern look.

"Think hard on this, Sha'lor. There is some danger here," he said.

Sha'lor raised her chin. "I insist, father. This outlander has insulted you, challenged our skills. Ha'sim hits only what he aims at," she said.

"I took no insult. The challenge does not involve you," Ha'keel said.

Sha'lor gave her father a fierce look. "Why? Because I am a woman? I am a Ha'ashtari warrior, the equal of any man here. The challenge was to me, as to any other. Will you deny me this honor?" she demanded.

Ha'keel sighed. "No, daughter. I will not oppose you," he said, then turned to Max. "You will bear the bow, outsider. Who will bear

208

your target?"

Morgan glared at Max, and then started to speak. Celeste had joined them, and was studying Morgan with a thoughtful look.

"I will," Celeste said as she stepped forward.

Morgan closed his mouth, and stared at her. "No," he said firmly.

Celeste regarded him evenly. "Didn't Sha'lor and her father already have this discussion? I know the rite, and Max only hits what he aims at. You know that. Now get out of my way," she said.

Morgan turned to Max. "Don't let anything happen to her," he said.

Max patted Morgan on the arm. "Don't worry. I'll be careful with your . . . ," Max leaned close and whispered, ". . . love. Trust me."

Morgan's face turned several colors, whether from heat or emotion, no one was sure. Taurus led him to the shade of a nearby palm tree.

Ha'keel looked around. "You say you know the ritual. Where is your mount?" he asked.

"Mount?" Max asked, glancing sharply at Celeste.

Ha'keel frowned. "Yes, mount. Your horse," he said.

"Just a moment," Max said, as he grabbed Celeste by the arm and led her to one side.

"Mount?" he whispered fiercely. "You didn't say anything about doing this on horseback."

Celeste rolled her eyes. "This is a Ha'ashtaii challenge. They do everything on horseback. I thought you knew that," she said.

"I guess I . . . overlooked that aspect of their culture. Any chance of changing the rules?" he asked.

Celeste shook her head. "I wouldn't try it. That may be taken as a sign of weakness or fear," she said.

Sha'lor called out to them. "We are waiting, outlander," she said.

Max ignored her, turning to Ha'keel. "Unfortunately, I seem to be without a horse right now," he said.

Sha'lor stepped forward, fixing Max with her dark eyes. "You may use my horse. Unless you are afraid," she said.

Celeste joined Max. "Max, I don't think you should . . . ," she began.

Max interrupted her, studying Sha'lor with a grim smile. "No, I accept. I will use your horse," he said.

Sha'lor turned to her father with a triumphant look. He regarded her for a moment, and then shook his head. "Very well. Let the challenge begin," he said.

"Wait. One more thing," Max said.

"What?" Ha'keel asked.

Max glanced at Sha'lor, intrigued by her fiery spirit. He turned and gestured toward the nearby ridge of dunes. Sparse beach grass covered the back side of the dunes, and a level path of hard packed sand lay at the foot of the dunes.

"Since I am the challenger, I should be able to frame the challenge. Judging from the lay of the land, I suggest that you place your target there," he indicated the top of the dunes, "and have your rider pass along here," he pointed to the area at the dune base. "The rider approaches at full gallop, shooting into the sun, at the target silhouetted against the sky. Is that acceptable?" Max asked.

Ha'keel regarded Max. "That is acceptable," he said.

Max measured the distance from the dunes to where they stood. "I would guess that this windmill is about twice as far from the dune crest as where your rider will pass. Do you agree?" he asked.

Ha'keel squinted into the sun. "Yes, why?" he asked.

"I will ride along here, even with the windmill," Max said.

Ha'keel turned to stare at Max. "No man could make the shot from here. I do not wish the death of your woman. Has she angered you in some way?" he asked.

Max glanced at Celeste with an evil grin. "Well, yes, from time to time. But I don't think her death will be required today," he said.

Celeste began to look greatly alarmed. She was uncomfortable with the thought of Max riding one of the spirited Ha'ashtari mounts, and doubling the distance to the target seemed completely insane, or suicidal, depending on which end of the arrow a person stood. She started to speak, but Max waved her to silence. When

210

Morgan heard Max's proposal, he sat down in the sand under the tree, and leaned his head against the trunk, closing his eyes. He did not want to watch this. He knew Max's skill was inhuman, but the slightest miscalculation could be fatal.

Taurus shook his head. "The man is totally mad, but you have to admire his arrogance," he said.

Morgan sighed. "That arrogance is going to get the Princess killed," he said. "And there is no way I can stop this, without starting a war with the Ha'ashtari."

Ha'keel smiled grimly at Max. "Her death is on your head. Do not seek to avenge her. I agree," he said.

Sha'lor approached with two of the shields from their horses, and handed one to Celeste. She looked at Celeste with something approaching sympathy, and then glanced at Max, trying to judge if he was merely boasting. The Princess looked down at the shield. It looked most inadequate, a pitiful thing made of hide and metal. Celeste pulled Max aside.

"Are you sure about this? Their horses are hard to handle, this shield is very small, and that's a long way away," she said.

Max put his hands on her shoulders and looked into her eyes. "I know how you and Morgan feel about each other, even if he's too stupid and stubborn to admit it," he said, then stifled her response with a hand over her mouth. "Morgan is my oldest friend, and I believe our friendship might suffer if I killed his lady. Besides, I can shoot from a horse, and if I got any closer, Stryker would punch a hole through that buckler and you. I need the distance to lessen the impact. Don't worry. I never miss. Just watch your fingers, in case the point comes through."

Ha'keel called to them. "Are you ready? The sun moves on," he said.

Max turned to him. "I know, I know. The sun waits for no man. I believe you go first, three passes and three shots. Closest to the center of the buckler wins," he said.

Ha'keel nodded and waved to Ha'sim and Sha'lor. "Let the rite begin," he called.

Sha'lor ran for the dune crest, carrying her shield. Ha'sim

mounted his horse and rode off along the dune base. Sha'lor soon reached the top, and stood panting, the shield held high. The afternoon sun was at her back, and all anyone could see was her shape in the glare. At the end of the line of dunes, Ha'sim wheeled his mount, and nocked an arrow. He raised his bow, and Sha'lor lowered the shield, holding it at arms' length before her breast.

Celeste watched in horrified fascination. Max leaned calmly on his bow, periodically testing the wind with a wet fingertip. Morgan still sat under the palm tree, his eyes firmly closed, but Taurus watched intently, shading his eyes with his hat brim, wishing he could toast the challengers. Ha'keel and the remaining Ha'ashtari stood silently, arms folded. A growing crowd of townspeople gathered, in spite of the heat, fearing the fate of their community might hang in the balance. Sherat also lingered, unable to turn away.

Ha'sim urged his mount into a gallop, and the horse charged along the base of the dunes, muscles rippling, sand flying from its hooves. Ha'sim placed the reins under one leg, and leaned over the horse's neck. He kept his bow parallel with the ground, drawing the bow to its full reach. Sha'lor stood motionless, a dark figure on the ridge, the shield nearly invisible in her shadow.

Ha'sim passed Sha'lor, the bow twanged, and the crowd gasped. A moment later, Sha'lor staggered with the impact, then yelled and held up the shield, displaying the arrow sticking there. Celeste remembered to breathe.

Ha'sim turned and made the second pass, galloping back the way he had come. Another shot, and a second arrow imbedded itself two finger breadths from the first. Ha'sim turned and collected his horse for the final run. They thundered closer, the crowd watching in absolute silence. Just as he fired, his horse stumbled slightly in some loose sand, and the bow jerked in response. Celeste covered her eyes, and then dared to look.

Sha'lor still stood, but she had turned slightly, gripping her arm. With a wild shout, she held up the shield. The last arrow had nearly missed, its point tearing through the metal rim. Sharp fragments had cut Sha'lor's upper arm, but the metal had stopped the shaft. Sha'lor strode down the dune face, and threw the shield at Max's feet.

212

Ha'sim rode up, his eyes shining, his mount prancing. Max looked down at the shield and nodded.

"Fine shooting, Ha'sim. Now it's my turn. Sha'lor, will you fetch me your horse," he said calmly.

Ha'sim stared at Max a moment, and then rode over to join his family. Sha'lor's face darkened, and then she turned away. She retrieved her horse and brought it to Max, handing him the reins. Sha'lor's horse snorted at Max's unfamiliar scent, and pulled back on the reins, rolling its eyes. Max grimaced slightly, but maintained his grip.

"Does your horse have a name?" Max asked Sha'lor.

Sha'lor lifted her chin. "Her name is Cha'nu, the Free Wind," she said.

Max nodded, then leaned close to the nervous horse. "Take care, Cha'nu, or my first arrow may pass through your fine withers," he whispered into the flicking ear.

Cha'nu pawed the ground, tossing her head. Max nodded to Celeste.

"Are you ready? Remember to stand still," he said.

"If I move, it will be because I've fainted," Celeste said as she started to climb the dune. Morgan opened his eyes briefly, and then closed them again, refusing to watch. Max watched her, the horse prancing in a half circle, tugging on his arm.

When Celeste was in position, he transferred three arrows from his quiver to the one on the saddle, and then he slung the reins over Cha'nu's neck and vaulted onto her back. Cha'nu immediately reared, and Max nearly slid off. Using mainly the reins, he dragged himself back into the saddle. The pressure on her mouth caused Cha'nu to back up suddenly, nearly trampling Ha'keel, who jumped aside. Cha'nu dropped to all fours, and Max wrapped his legs around her barrel, cursing the lack of stirrups. The grip of his legs signaled the horse to leap forward, which she did, only to stop when Max jerked on the reins. The sudden stop threw Max forward onto her neck, where he clung grimly to the flowing mane. As the horse danced in a circle, Max shoved himself back into the saddle, his bow askew over his back, and his face dark with anger.

213

At first the Ha'ashtari stared in amazement, and then they all started laughing. Max finally got the spinning horse under control, and started to turn her for the first run.

Ha'keel called out to him. "Do you wish to withdraw your challenge? There is no honor in this. You will kill your woman, and then fall from the horse and be killed yourself," he said.

When Cha'nu had spun to face the right direction, Max squeezed with his legs, and the horse lunged forward. Max bounced from side to side for a few strides, then managed to settle into the rhythm of the horse. As the horse flashed by the Ha'ashtari, Max yelled his response.

"My challenge stands," he cried.

Celeste watched from the dune top, any confidence she had fading rapidly. She held the shield as Sha'lor had done, and prayed for a quick, clean death.

"O Iosus, no disfigurement, please," she breathed.

Morgan just groaned. "My only hope is that he can't even get an arrow near her," he muttered.

Max had some trouble getting Cha'nu stopped and turned, townspeople scattering before them. He pulled her head around, and kept her from bolting while he dragged his bow from his back. He got an arrow out, almost dropping it as the horse bounced. The long bow tangled in Cha'nu's mane, and Max tore some hairs out trying to free the bow. He plucked the strands of mane from the bow, nearly falling off while he did so.

Finally, Max had an arrow in his bow, and then got Cha'nu pointed in the right direction and let her go. The horse stretched out, charging back toward the group of Ha'ashtari. Once she was in full gallop, Max did not even try to steer, but shoved the reins under his thigh as Ha'sim had done. Cha'nu's chosen path did not follow any established trail, but led through some of the scrubby brush, and from time to time she would leap the larger clumps. Max's position seemed precarious, and the periodic vaults nearly unseated him.

He appeared to be so engrossed in staying on the horse that he did not raise his bow until he came even with Celeste, then whipped up the bow and snapped off a shot. He hardly seemed to aim, but fortunately he fired between jumps, during a relatively steady gallop. Celeste suddenly sat down in the sand, and someone in the crowd of townspeople screamed. Morgan decided he was going to kill Max, slowly and painfully. Taurus clapped him on the shoulder, cursing in wonderment, and Morgan forced himself to look. Celeste sat in the sand, apparently unhurt, and she held up the shield, the arrow visible in it. Taurus and the townspeople cheered while Celeste got shakily to her feet, and stood waiting.

The Ha'ashtari still stared in amazement at the arrow in Celeste's shield, not realizing their peril until they heard the pounding of Cha'nu's hooves on the harder sand of the trail. Free of any coherent direction from its rider, the horse was returning to Sha'lor. Max hauled on the reins as Cha'nu charged into their midst, forcing them to leap aside.

Sha'lor shouted after them. "Use your legs, fool! Quit pulling on her mouth! You'll ruin her," she yelled.

Cha'nu did not stop but galloped on, with Max clinging to her back. "Ruin her? What about me?" he called back.

"This will be the first challenge where the judges are killed," Ha'keel muttered as he sought a safer position. Ha'sim followed him, torn between laughter and gaping disbelief.

Horse and rider charged past the other horses, who shied away, pulling on their tethers. Cha'nu ran over a small rise and disappeared. The Ha'ashtari stared after them.

Morgan looked around. "Is it over?" he asked hopefully.

Taurus scratched his beard, which itched in the insufferable heat. "I don't think so. He's only shot once," he observed.

Ha'sim looked at his father, who shrugged and shook his head. Sha'lor joined them. "Father, declare Ha'sim the victor. Before that fool kills his woman or himself, or worse yet, injures my horse," she urged.

Ha'keel held up a hand. "Wait," he said, listening intently.

"Here he comes," Celeste called, from her vantage point on the dune.

With the sound of pounding hooves, Cha'nu plunged over the rise, Max still on her back. He leaned forward, legs locked around

215

the horse's barrel, a handful of mane in each fist, and a strand in his teeth. The reins fluttered unheeded in the wind of their passage, and Max's bow bounced wildly over one arm.

As the horse charged toward them, Max spit out the mane and shouted defiantly. "I'm not finished yet!" he yelled.

Sha'lor dove from their path, and then turned, shaking her fist at Max. "Rock brained outlander! Don't you know how to ride at all?" she cried.

Max's voice floated back to them. "I learned to ride . . . on civilized horses . . . not these crazed demons . . . you breed!"

As they charged past Celeste, Max remembered to fire his second shot, once again a quick shot with no apparent preparation. The impact of the arrow knocked Celeste down a second time. Taurus yelled lustily as she scrambled to her feet, holding up the shield. The two arrows stood side by side, with no sky visible between them. Morgan had watched this time, awed in spite of himself at the uncanny skill of his old comrade. Morgan had been praying desperately, but had not expected such a spectacular response.

Cha'nu scattered some more townspeople before Max got her turned for the final run. Everyone watched the woman on the hill. Just as Max fired, Cha'nu leaped over a clump of brush, wringing gasps from the audience. The bowstring twanged, the arrow arced through the harsh light, and then Celeste shrieked and dropped the shield. She lost her balance in the sand and fell from view over the far side of the dune.

Morgan leaped to his feet and charged up the dune, throwing sand everywhere. Taurus waited under the tree, too hot and thirsty to follow. The townspeople waited silently, afraid of the worst. Sha'lor watched, a sobered expression on her face, while the other Ha'ashtari frowned in distaste. Sherat shook his head, muttering.

Cha'nu came running up to Sha'lor, where Max did a flying dismount to land at Ha'keel's feet. His bow went tumbling past the Ha'ashtari. Sha'lor snagged the stampeding horse, and led her aside, trying to soothe her. Cha'nu stamped and pranced, sweating and still wild-eyed from all the excitement. Ha'keel helped Max up, and Ha'sim retrieved his bow.

216

"If your woman still lives, you are chosen of the Gods, outsider," Ha'keel stated.

Sha'lor passed the reins to the other Ha'ashtari man, and returned. Cha'nu fairly dragged the warrior, eager to be away from the madman that had abused her so.

Morgan reached the dune summit, gasping in the heat. Celeste sat on the slope below him, hair disheveled, sand on her face and robe. She was shaking a bleeding hand, and cursing Max in a most unladylike fashion. Morgan plowed through the sand to her side, and helped her to her feet.

He grabbed the bleeding hand. "Are you all right? What happened . . . ?" he demanded.

Celeste brushed the sand from her face with her good hand. "I'm . . . fine. Just a little cut. Do you have something to wrap it with?" she asked.

Morgan pulled out a pocket cloth and gently wrapped the hand.

Celeste looked up at him, her face flushed and her eyes bright. "He did it, he actually did it. I'm still alive," she said, then paused, savoring the worried expression on Morgan's face, as he tended her wound.

"I'm fine. I really am," she said, and then she frowned. "And don't pretend to be so worried. You don't really care what happens to me. We better join the others, and show them that Max won."

Celeste took back her bandaged hand and turned to climb the dune. Morgan stared after her, trying to think of something to say. Failing to find any words, he caught her in two long strides, and grabbed her clumsily. He crushed her to his chest, just holding her without speaking.

Celeste was surprised, but she did not resist, and spent a delicious moment nestled in his arms. Then she gently pushed him back to arm's length, and looked up at him. He glanced down at her, and then turned his head to one side, afraid he would be unable to resist kissing her. Celeste smiled crookedly, a little disappointed.

"What are you doing?" she asked softly.

Morgan squeezed her arms, and then stepped to a safe distance, his breathing ragged. "All right, you win. I care!" he said, then turned

217

and looked at her, like a little boy, afraid and eager, and reluctant all at once. "You have no idea how much I care. But what are we going to do about it?"

For a time they just looked at each other, then Celeste smiled. "They're waiting for us. We have to go now. We'll talk later," she said gently.

Morgan sighed, and then nodded. They climbed back to the crest and picked up the shield. The third arrow had split one of the other two, and penetrated the shield at the weakened area, the bloody point sticking through on the inside.

Celeste looked down at the shield and shook her head. "He warned me. I should have watched my grip," she said.

She took the shield from him and held it up. The crowd below, which had been waiting in tense silence, now cheered wildly. Taurus jumped up and down, waving his hat. Sha'lor studied Max, who was calmly unstringing Stryker. Ha'sim and Ha'keel talked in low voices, their heads together.

Morgan and Celeste climbed down the dune, and Celeste tossed her shield on the ground next to Sha'lor's. The Ha'ashtari approached, to judge the results. Ha'keel confirmed that Ha'sim had struck the shield all three times, two arrows near the center, and one in the rim. He looked to the other shield and his eyes widened. All three of Max's arrows stood in the center ring, with the final arrow splitting the second in half.

Ha'keel raised his eyes to Max. "You are clearly the victor. You have won the challenge. The Gods know you, outlander," he said.

Max smiled lightly. "I accept your decision. The challenge is completed," he said formally.

Celeste gave Max a big hug, and then shook her injured hand in his face. "That's a little too close. Next time be more careful," she said.

Max frowned at the wound. "My apologies, Princess. I thought those Ha'ashtari shields were better made. I will make allowance for the poor quality from now on," he said.

The Ha'ashtari looked slightly offended, except for Ha'keel, who smiled and shook his head. "You would be wise not to visit the

Waste, outlander. In spite of your courage and skill, I do not think you would live long. You are too reckless," he said.

Max bowed, then turned to Ha'sim. "I've seen few better with a bow. If I ever need an expert marksman, I'll ask for you," he said.

Ha'sim stared at him, uncertain whether to be insulted or flattered. He nodded curtly.

"Someday I would like to see you shoot without the horse. If the Ha'ashtari ever need foot archers, we will ask for you. Farewell, outsider. We return to our lands now," Ha'keel said, and then looked around, sweat shining on his brow. "It is too hot down here."

The chieftain and his son moved to their horses, while the other Ha'ashtari retrieved the shields, removing the arrows. He returned Max's arrows with a respectful nod.

Sha'lor lingered, her dark eyes still on Max. "You can shoot, but you cannot ride. I will not forget what you have done this day," she finally said, as she turned to follow the others.

Max watched her walk away. "I have a feeling I won't forget you either," he said thoughtfully.

The Ha'ashtari mounted and rode away, the crowd clearing a path for them.

Morgan turned to Max. "You can ride better than that. What were you doing? You could have killed her. It was just the grace of Iosus that you didn't," he said.

"But I didn't. That was a spirited horse, and if I did embellish a little, there's no harm done," Max said.

Morgan stared at Max suspiciously. "You were showing off for that Ha'ashtari woman. I can't believe it," he said.

"I wouldn't call it showing off. I was just . . . ," Max said.

Celeste had overheard the last of their conversation. "He was doing what?" she exclaimed.

"Never mind. You don't want to know," Morgan assured her.

Some of the townspeople approached Max and his companions, but most wandered back to town, satisfied that their lives would remain unchanged.

Taurus clapped Max on the shoulder, staggering him. "That was a fine piece of work, Max. I've never seen better shooting," he said.

Max rubbed his throbbing shoulder. "Next time I'll let you hold the shield, friend Taurus," he promised.

Max looked at Morgan, who stood silently nearby. "What about you, Morgan? No praise for the skill of your old friend?" Max asked.

Morgan frowned. "The whole thing was stupid, and dangerous, and totally unnecessary. Don't expect any encouragement from me," he said as he turned and walked toward town.

Max leaned over and whispered to Celeste. "He's mad at us, Princess," he said.

Celeste was watching Morgan, holding her injured hand. "But he cares," she said.

"What?" Max asked.

Celeste looked at Max and smiled brightly. "He cares," she repeated.

Max glanced toward Morgan. "Oh, I see," he said.

Max collected his gear, and they all turned to leave, only to find Sherat and his retinue blocking their path, several townspeople standing behind them.

"Your foolish action endangered the whole town. You will leave immediately, before there is further trouble," Sherat snapped.

Taurus stepped up to the Shah's man, until their faces almost touched. "My friend will leave, if and when he chooses, toad face. Unless you want me and my crew to burn down your scurvy little town, and then we'll let Max shoot the vultures off your carcasses. Now get out of our way," he said, his voice rising to a roar.

Sherat staggered backwards in the blast of sound. Gathering up his robe, the man almost ran back to town, his retainers at his heels. The other people melted quietly away.

Taurus shouted after them. "It's hot and miserable, and I haven't had a drink forever. Don't fear the Ha'ashtari, fear the thirst of Taurus!"

Taurus turned to the others and hooked his thumbs in his belt. "Shall we return to the Windrider, before we shrivel in this cursed sun?" he asked.

Max laughed. "Taurus, my friend, you have such a way with

words," he said.

CHAPTER SEVENTEEN
COLD DEATH, GHOST WIND

Morgan and the Princess stood in the bow of the Windrider, which still lay at anchor in the small bay near Aquarquff. Several crewmen worked on deck, but most of them were in the galley, getting ready to eat dinner. The setting sun cast a lurid glow over the cliffs above Aquarquff. Morgan leaned on the rail, watching as lights began to appear in the darkening town. Celeste stood near him, her eyes on the big man beside her.

Morgan sighed. "What are we going to do, Celeste? This is happening at the wrong time," he said.

"Are you sorry you met me?" Celeste asked.

Morgan glanced at her. "No," he admitted.

Celeste turned and leaned on the rail next to him, her shoulder and hip just touching him. "Then be glad it happened at all. We may never have met," she said.

"But you're leaving for Carnac at dawn and we're going to Dragonback," he said, and then paused. "O Iosus, why now?"

Celeste laid her hand on his arm, turning him to face her. "Morgan, let me tell you something. In my life I've met a lot of men. A princess has many suitors. Unfortunately, I found most of them to be little better than beasts---selfish, arrogant, interested only in my body or my title," she said, and then smiled mischievously. "And those were Thraen men, which are the finest of the species."

Morgan laughed, shaking his head. "You are a wonder, Princess. Unlike any woman I've ever known," he said.

Celeste squeezed his arm, her smile widening. "Good. Anyway, where was I? Oh yes. Then I met you and Max," she said.

"Me and Max?" Morgan said with a sudden frown.

"Let me finish. Before I met you and Max, my favorite man was probably my brother Talbot. We had such good times together, especially in Carnac. Of course, I love and respect my father, but I would never marry someone like him. Father used to get so frustrated with me. He couldn't understand why I wouldn't just pick one of the Thraen men and settle down. He even considered arranging a marriage for me, but mother wouldn't have it.

Then came you and Max. You were different. You saved me from Wald and the Mhoul and have shown me nothing but honor. Max is attracted to me, but he wouldn't do anything to hurt you. Besides, he says I have too much personality for a lover. So we have become friends. Max needs friends," she said.

Celeste leaned closer, looking up at Morgan. He lost himself in those exotic eyes. "And you. You've been all over the world, been involved in countless battles and adventures, you've experienced terrible things and seen such tragedy as I cannot imagine, and yet you are somehow . . . innocent. And you treat me like a real person, not just a woman or a Princess. You are a true gentleman," she said, then paused. "And I know you find me attractive, but you've never attempted to take any liberties with me. You didn't even offer to wash my back, that night in Androssar."

Morgan groaned and looked at the sky. The heat had suddenly grown oppressive and he seemed to be having trouble breathing. Celeste's next words brought his gaze back to her.

"So I can wait, Morgan. If we don't have time now, we'll begin again later. After you've defeated the Mhoul, and after Talbot and I have helped Father drive the Haggas from Skara Thrae. But you have to promise me that you will live and come back to me," she said.

"But I . . . ," Morgan began.

Celeste put her hand over his mouth, her soft fingers brushing past his lips. "Promise me," she said firmly.

Morgan took her hand and held it tightly. It felt good. "I promise," he said.

"You'll be back in time to say good-bye?" Celeste asked.

Morgan hesitated. "Yes," he decided. "I'll be back before you leave the ship."

Celeste squeezed his hand and gently pulled hers away. "You better go get ready then. I have some packing to do myself. Until the morning," she said.

She turned and walked toward the cabins. Morgan watched

her, hating to let her go. He could still feel the warmth of her hand, and her scent lingered.

"Until morning. I'll be back," Morgan repeated.

Just as she stepped down to the main deck, Celeste looked back over her shoulder. "We forgot to discuss the other woman," she said.

"What other woman?" Morgan asked.

"Malissa," she said.

"Will you forget about Malissa? She has nothing to do with us," Morgan growled.

Celeste gave a little sigh. "Oh well, I guess that can wait too," she said.

Morgan watched her until she disappeared into the bridge, then he turned and gripped the railing until the wood creaked.

Just after sundown the six men gathered around the Windrider's longboat. Patches of brilliant stars sparkled on the black water of the bay, under the partly cloudy sky. Asa was just rising behind the massive cliffs, and the silver arch glowed coldly overhead. The lights of Aquarquff could be seen in the distance.

A light breeze rattled the rigging of the mast, sending small waves to slap against the Windrider's hull. The ship itself lay dark and quiet, save for the sentries on duty and the six men amidships.

Taurus scratched his beard, staring grumpily at the others, while Seidon stood beside the Captain, watching Max and Morgan put gear into the boat. Morgan wore his Iosian cloak and his sword. Max had his swords, but not his bow. They had packs for each man, and a pile of torches. Harkon and Taskin helped with the loading.

"I don't see the need to skulk around after dark on my own ship. Why don't we get a good night's sleep and find this weapons cache of yours in the morning? After what Max did in town yesterday, none of those cowardly townspeople are going to try and stop us," Taurus said.

Morgan dumped the last of his gear into the boat, shaking his head. "People have been hunting for this cache for centuries. I don't know what we are going to find in there, but I don't want any of it falling into the wrong hands. We have to assume the Mhoul have spies in Aquarquff, and after yesterday's show, they know we're here," he said.

Max held up his hands. "Wait. Back up. You don't know what's in the cache? I thought your memory implant told you all about it," he said.

Morgan stared out over the water, toward the dark mass of the cliffs. Asa cast an eerie light on the reddish stone. "I know there's a cache, and how to find the entrance. And I know the Empire installed certain devices to protect the cache, traps for the unwary," he said.

"Traps?" Max asked. "But you know how to avoid them?"

Morgan glanced at Max, then away. "Not right now. Just this," he paused, and then recited:

CAVE WITHIN A CAVE, HIDDEN FOR THE AGES,
THE HAND, NOT THE EYE, SHALL FIND THE WAY.
WATERS OF THE COLD DEATH.
STAY YOUR EYE ON IOSUS, HE SHALL GUIDE YOU.
THE GHOST WIND.
WILL STEAL YOUR SOUL AND STILL YOUR HEART,
LEST YOU TURN ASIDE FROM ITS WRATH.
THE ABYSS.
FOLLOW THE SHINING PATH.
MOVE TO THE CALL,
OR BEWARE THE BLADES OF DARKNESS.
CRYSTAL OF CHAOS.
SWORDS OF LIGHT WILL SMITE,
LEST YOU BEAR YOUR IMAGE BEFORE YOU.

"Oh good. A riddle. I feel better now," Max said.

"I'm sorry. That's all I know now. I'm sure there will be more later," Morgan said.

"No matter. I knew this quest was suicide when I joined up. Might as well be killed by the Empire as the Mhoul," Max said.

Morgan turned to Harkon and Taskin. "As I told you earlier, you don't have to go. Max and I can do this alone," Morgan told them.

"All right, if you insist . . . ," Harkon began.

Taskin cut him off. "You already made us stay behind when you went into town. We want to go," he said, then looked at Taurus with a grin. "Besides we feel safer with you than here on board, with this drunken captain and his band of cutthroats."

Taurus aimed a kick at Taskin, who jumped out of the way. "Get this bunch of broken down mercenaries off my ship," Taurus said.

"Harkon, does Taskin speak for you?" Morgan asked.

Harkon sighed. "O Locha. Yes, I'll go. But it's against my better judgment. I'm getting too old for this sort of thing," he said.

Max, Morgan, Taskin, and Harkon clambered aboard the longboat, and Taurus and Seidon lowered it to the water. Morgan looked up at Taurus, as he unfastened the lines.

"Keep watch over the Princess. We'll be back before dawn," he called in a hoarse whisper.

"Don't worry. She's safe here," Taurus said, pulling the lines back aboard. "When you get back, we'll discuss the price of passage to Dragonback."

They pulled the longboat ashore, dragging it through the sand to a clump of beach grass. While Taskin and Harkon covered the boat with grass, Max took a clump of brush and swept their path from the water, erasing the drag marks in the dry sand. The incoming tide would finish hiding their trail. Morgan slipped on his pack, staring over the dunes at the cliffs. The men all cast harsh shadows in the moonlight.

When everyone had their gear, Morgan led the way over the dunes. They stayed away from the dune crests, making their way through the shadowy valleys. The cliffs loomed higher as they approached, and they could hear no sound but the hissing of the wind through the sand, and the crash of waves on the beach.

They soon crouched in the darkness near the last of the dunes, studying the area between them and the cliffs. Low in the cliff face, a cave mouth opened in the wall of stone, black on dusky red, with a pile of rocky debris rising to meet it. Low brush covered the ground ahead, feasting on the marshy area behind the dunes.

Max looked back along their route, then touched Morgan's arm. "We're being followed. Should I stop them?" he asked.

Morgan shook his head. "We'll worry about them later," he said.

"Who is it?" Harkon asked.

"I don't know. Maybe I should go back and look," Max said.

"You're not going anywhere," Morgan said.

"What do they want?" Harkon asked.

"Same thing as us, for different reasons," Morgan said.

Max glanced at the cave mouth. "Do we have to go in there?" he asked.

"Yes, the cache is somewhere under the cliffs," Morgan said.

"Maybe I should stay here. Guard the back trail," Max said, his voice sounding strangely tense.

Morgan peered at him in the blackness. "What is it?" he asked.

Max sighed. "I spent three years in a dungeon, underground, with no light, except at feeding time. I just don't like caves anymore. Is that so unreasonable?" he asked.

Morgan put a hand on his shoulder. "You can stay here if you want. But I could use your help in there," he said.

Max was staring at the cave. "No. I can do it. You'll get lost without me," he said.

"Good. Let's go," Morgan said.

Morgan got to his feet, and ran for the cave mouth, skirting some of the brush and vaulting over the smaller clumps. The other three men followed. Morgan did not pause at the cave entrance, but scrambled up the rock debris until he stood inside. Max stayed right behind him, although he did stop at the entrance, taking a deep breath and squaring his shoulders before venturing in. Taskin and Harkon paused behind Max, waiting for him to move on. Once inside, they stood quietly in the blackness of the cave, catching their breath and searching the moonlit dunes for signs of their pursuit. Nothing moved but the waves on the beach.

Max spoke, his voice tight. "Can't we get some light in here?" he asked.

Morgan pulled off his pack, and took out three torches, handing them to the others. "Don't light these until we get around the corner. I don't want anyone seeing the torches," he whispered.

With one hand on the cave wall, Morgan made his way carefully along the rock strewn floor, until they could no longer see the silvery light from outside. Then they lit the torches, blinking in the flare of orange light. Morgan took a torch, studying their surroundings. Before them lay the natural tube of a water worn cavern. It was cool in the cave, and somewhere they could hear water dripping.

Morgan glanced at Max, seeing the sheen of sweat on his face, in spite of the chill. He also noticed Max's white-knuckled grip on his sword hilts, and the twitching muscle in his jaw.

"Are you all right?" Morgan asked in a low voice.

Max's eyes flickered toward him and away. "Yes. Let's get moving," he hissed.

Morgan cocked his head. "I've never seen you like this," he said.

Max turned on him. "Will you move? Or do I have to take the lead?" he asked fiercely.

"Settle down. We're moving," Morgan said.

Morgan led them further into the cave, until they came to a junction of four tunnels. There he stopped and Max moved up beside him.

"I hope you remember this," Max said.

Morgan pointed the torch at the leftmost tunnel. "That way," he said.

Max surveyed the other choices. "Are you sure? I don't want to get lost in here," he said.

"I'm sure. The other tunnels are dead ends or traps," Morgan said.

"All right. Hurry up," Max said.

They entered the left tunnel, which wound back and forth like a snake. Suddenly, they heard a sound behind them, echoing through the darkness.

"Was that a scream?" Harkon asked.

Harkon was in the rear, and Max moved to stand beside him.

228

They listened, but heard no further sound. The crackle of the torches alone broke the stillness.

"Sounded like a scream. Our friends must have taken a wrong turn," Max said.

They started walking along the tunnel again. Soon Morgan paused, studying the right hand wall, and mumbling something. Max joined him.

"What are you muttering?" Max said irritably.

"'The hand, not the eye, shall find the way.' The verse I quoted earlier. There is a hidden cave mouth here somewhere," Morgan said.

Max stared at the solid wall before them. "Here? How do we find it?" he asked.

Morgan held up a gloved hand. "The hand. Feel for it. Everyone," he said.

The men stuck their torches in whatever crevices they could find, and began to search the wall, going over it carefully, running their hands over every surface. A sound came from somewhere in the darkness behind them, and everyone stopped to listen.

"We better hurry," Max said.

"Yes, find the opening," Morgan urged.

Even as they turned back to the wall, a flicker of firelight came from around the bend in the tunnel, and then they heard a strange snuffling sound.

Harkon stared into the gloom. "What was that?" he asked.

"I don't know," Morgan said. "Look, man, look!"

The sounds in the blackness lent speed to their search, and they moved with grim determination, searching every span of the wall. Harkon suddenly gasped, jerking back his hand, and the others ran to where he stood. Harkon's mouth worked, but no sounds came out.

"What? Don't just stand there grimacing. Did you find it?" Max asked.

Harkon was staring at his hand. "My hand just vanished. Into the rock," he said.

"Where? Show us where," Morgan said.

Harkon pointed at a section of rock next to him, but it looked

229

as solid as any other place on the cave wall. Morgan moved quickly to it, and extended his arms. With a faint shimmer, his arms sank into the cave wall. In spite of himself, Morgan hastily pulled back. He looked at the others.

"This is it. Get the torches," he said.

When they were ready, Morgan took a deep breath and stepped forward. The wall rippled like water in a pond, and then the rock swallowed Morgan's form. Max put his head down, and followed. Taskin hesitated briefly and went next. Harkon glanced over his shoulder, seeing the unmistakable glow of torches coming toward him. He could hear the scuff of boots on the rocks and the snuffling sound, louder now. Harkon decided he feared the pursuit more than the mirage before him.

"Locha preserve us," he said as he stepped through.

As Harkon emerged on the other side, he found his companions, standing unharmed in a long straight tunnel. He turned to look at the cave wall behind him. The black, featureless surface reminded Harkon of the back side of a mirror. He noticed two devices on either side of the hidden opening, small boxes with glowing lenses.

Max examined one of the boxes, and then passed his hand in front of the lens. A portion of the blank wall flickered, revealing the tunnel outside.

"Must be projectors of some kind, throwing out the image of a solid wall," he whispered.

Morgan motioned him away from the devices. "Leave those alone. Whoever is following can still hear us, let's go," he said.

They moved down the tunnel at a jog, holding the torches high. Max focused on the torch in Morgan's hand. He felt like the entire mass of rock around them was pressing in, suffocating him. He imagined breathing darkness, and couldn't seem to get enough air.

"The air is bad in here," he said.

"It will have to do. We didn't bring any with us," Morgan said without looking back.

"Very funny," Max muttered.

Something in the tunnel ahead reflected their torchlight. As they got closer, a wall of metal barred their way, gleaming dully in the reddish light. Morgan stumbled, and put a hand to his forehead. Max grabbed his arm.

"What? Don't get sick on me now," Max said.

Morgan shook his head. "Another implant. I don't know if I'll ever get used to this---someone else's memories appearing in my mind," he said.

"So what now? Do you know more?" Max asked.

Morgan nodded and moved closer to the metal barrier. It looked solid, one giant block with no joints or cracks, although dull and tarnished by the centuries, and heavily ornamented with strange carvings. Morgan ran his hand over the surface, tracing the relief with a fingertip.

"The sight of this wall triggered the memory. There is a door here, somewhere. It's coming back to me," Morgan said, his voice distant.

Sounds came from behind them---the snuffling noise again, and low voices.

"They can't know where we are. Unless they heard us," Taskin whispered.

"What is that snuffling?" Harkon asked.

Max's eyes widened as realization struck him. "It's a hound. They are following our scent. It's just a matter of time before they find the mirage. Morgan, hurry up," he said.

Morgan remained absorbed in his examination of the wall, seemingly oblivious to the others. Max stepped closer to him.

"Morgan? Any time now would be fine," he prompted.

Morgan waved him away, impatient with any distractions. They heard a startled cry from the junction behind them, and then a brief silence, broken only by the incessant sniffing noise. Max drew his swords. The black blades showed no reflection, seeming to drink in the torchlight.

"That's it. They've found the opening," he said grimly.

Morgan made a small sound, and then began moving his hands over the metal, touching certain portions in some kind of a pattern.

"Morgan, forget that. We'll have to fight our way out," Max said, peering into the dark tunnel.

231

Morgan stepped back. "Don't be so sure," he said, watching the wall expectantly.

A grinding, groaning sound came from the mass of metal, and everyone turned to stare at it, their enemies forgotten. The center of the wall seemed to collapse in on itself, and the outline of a round opening appeared. A series of plates slowly rotated, like the iris of a human eye, and a doorway formed in the center of the plates as they withdrew, accompanied by the continued protest of machinery that had not functioned for centuries.

As soon as the hole grew large enough, Morgan ducked through, the others quick to follow. They stopped on the other side, looking around. The tunnel continued on, with one major difference. The cavern beyond the door was dimly lit by bluish globes supported by metal stanchions, placed at regular intervals. No longer completely natural, this portion of the tunnel seemed to have been drilled out of solid rock. The shaft extended as far as they could see, fading into blue obscurity.

The door had opened fully, and now stood silent. They could hear movement in the tunnel behind them, and once again, they saw the glow of torchlight.

"Can you close this?" Max asked.

Morgan shook his head. "No, I only knew how to open it. I could try, but if I make a mistake, we could be trapped in here forever," he said.

Max shuddered visibly. "Forget that. What's next?" he asked.

"I don't know. All I got from the last implant was how to open the door. We'll just have to go on," Morgan said.

"This is great. Protect Morgan, boys. If we lose him, we'll never get out of here," Max said.

"Douse the torches, and leave them here. We'll need them on the way out," Morgan said.

They smothered the torches in the dust on the floor, and tossed them in the corner. They heard a cry from the tunnel, as their pursuers discovered the metal wall with its open door.

Morgan signaled and they ran down the tunnel, the sound of their boots echoing hollowly. The floor remained level for a while, but soon it began to descend. The sounds of pursuit faded, as those behind followed cautiously, fearing traps or ambush. Harkon kept looking over his shoulder, wishing he knew the identity of their pursuers, or at least their numbers.

They ran down an increasing slope, and the sounds of their breathing filled the tunnel. Without warning, Morgan skidded to a stop, the others nearly trampling him. They could see something on the floor ahead of them, shining wetly in the light of the globes, a fathomless black, darker than the darkest night. The stygian blotch extended as far as they could see.

"What is that?" Max asked, catching his breath from the run.

Morgan was rubbing his forehead again. "The waters of the cold death. The first trap," he said.

Max studied Morgan's face. "Another implant? They're just giving you bits and pieces, playing with your mind. I don't like this game at all. When this is over, I think I'll take a trip to Khulankor," he said.

Morgan smiled. "If we live through this, I'll go with you. I can get us through this trap, but I have nothing beyond that," he said.

Morgan walked slowly forward, studying the way ahead. As they neared the bottom, they could see that an oily black liquid covered the floor for at least fifty paces.

"That's not water. What is it?" Max asked.

"I don't know," Morgan said.

"How deep is it?" Max asked.

"I don't know that either," Morgan hissed.

"You're so helpful," Max commented.

Morgan drew his sword, and then inexplicably looked up to the ceiling. "Water of the cold death," he repeated. "Stay your eye on Iosus, he shall guide you."

Max was staring at the evil looking pool. "Do we really have time for prayer?" he asked.

The sounds of pursuit drifted down the tunnel. Harkon peered into the dimness, trying to see their stalkers.

"Hurry. They're coming," Harkon said.

"I am praying, but I'm also looking at the path marked on the ceiling," Morgan said.

Max looked up, following Morgan's gaze. He saw a line etched into the rock of the tunnel roof, barely visible in the blue light. The mark twisted and turned, but continued for the length of the black pool.

"Stay your eye on Iosus. Very funny. So if we stay under that line, we will make it across?" Max asked.

"That's the idea," Morgan said.

"You're going to walk across that?" Taskin asked.

Morgan stepped to the edge of the pool, thrusting his sword into the liquid, probing in various places. Twice the sword touched nothing, sliding into the thick substance, but on the third try, the point grated on stone. Morgan pulled back the blade, the black liquid clinging to it like pitch. He jerked it free, and patches of black ooze slid from the blade, to plop into the larger mass.

Morgan stepped out, aiming for the place where his blade had found the path. His boot sank up to the ankle in the pool, but no farther. Morgan brought up his other foot, balancing on the hidden platform. He glanced up at the ceiling, and then probed the darkness again.

"There is a series of stone pedestals, just below the surface, only big enough for one person at a time. The locations of the pedestals are marked on the ceiling. They'll be somewhere along the line above. There's nothing between the pedestals, you have to stay on them. If you fall in, you're dead," Morgan explained, as he found the next step and moved to it.

The black sludge stained Morgan's boots, and made a dull smear on his sword point. Max probed the pool with a blade, locating the pedestal Morgan had used. He stepped carefully onto it, and his eyes widened.

"It's cold, my ankles are freezing already," he complained.

Morgan straightened, now standing on the third pedestal from the edge. "The waters of the cold death. Did you expect it to be warm?" he asked.

Max grimaced, moving to the second column. "Never mind. Just an observation. Move along now," he said.

Morgan and Max slogged through the pool, stepping from one pedestal to the next. Taskin followed them, moving carefully in their wake. Harkon stood at the edge of the pool, thinking he would rather face their pursuers, than step into that oozing mass. The stuff even smelled bad, an acrid odor filled the chamber.

The sound of boots on stone came from behind him, and Harkon twisted around. Turbaned figures appeared on the slope above, outlined against the blue glow of the globes. A man with a large hound led the way.

"Quffians!" Harkon shouted, clawing for his sword.

Taskin yelled back at him. "Get moving. Come on!"

At the sight of their quarry, the men following yelled and charged down the ramp, waving swords and spears. Forgetting his distaste for the black pool, Harkon hastily stepped onto the first pedestal and jumped for the second. He almost missed it, his boot sliding off, and fell to one knee, waving his arms for balance. The waters of the pool covered his left leg, and searing cold clamped down on it. He got his other boot in place and stood, the left leg numb and nearly useless.

"Look out," Taskin yelled.

Harkon whirled, nearly toppling from the shaft, as his frozen leg threatened to crumple. Seeing Harkon standing only ankle deep in the pool, a Quffian leaped for him, spear point extended. Years of fighting experience saved Harkon, as his instincts took over. He brought up his sword, and managed to knock the spear aside, at the same time trying to balance on the pedestal. His attacker missed the first pedestal, and screamed as he slid into the pool. The Quffian dropped his spear and splashed frantically, throwing gobbets of black ooze everywhere. Then he sank, the black liquid sluggishly engulfing his body. Two or three bubbles broke the dark surface, and then it was still. Only the man's spear remained, too light to sink into the heavy mass.

The man's companions perched on the brink of the pool, staring in horror at the fate of their comrade. Their leader, a man in a black turban, turned to face his men.

"Take them alive, or you'll share Hasur's fate!" he shouted.

Max yelled. "Harkon, get out of there. Move, man!"

Harkon glanced over his shoulder at the pool. He had forgotten the location of the next step. "Where is it?" he shouted to Taskin, who now stood four pedestals beyond.

Taskin pointed with his sword point. "Right there, I think. Keep up," he said.

Out of the corner of his eye, Harkon saw movement. The leader of the Quffians leaned forward, straining to reach him, while trying not to step into the pool. His comrades clustered around him, staring at Harkon with fierce eyes.

Harkon thrust at the man, forcing him back, and turned, jabbing his sword into the ooze behind him. His point hit stone, and he jumped in the same motion, landing on the third pedestal, while Taskin showed him the next. He made it to that one, and then risked a look at the pursuit. The leader had found the first step with his sword, and shoved one of his men forward. The man jumped wildly into the pool, expecting to die. He looked surprised when he did not sink, and the leader gestured at him, urging him to find the next pedestal.

Harkon moved on, catching up with Taskin. They could move fastest if they stayed together, trailing in the immediate footsteps of the man ahead. Morgan was half way across the pool now, and finding the pedestals became easier with practice. Max followed him, chafing at having to concentrate on the hidden pathway, with enemies at his back.

The Quffians mimicked their movements, but failed to discover the path marked above, which forced them to search for each pedestal by probing the ooze around them. This took time, and they soon fell behind. Another Quffian lost his footing, and toppled into the pool, to be swallowed by the voracious black mass.

Morgan reached the far side of the trap, and stepped out of the pool onto a sloping ramp. He stood working his feet, numb from the cold. They had felt like dead stumps the last few pedestals. He checked on his comrades' progress. Max was nearly to the edge, moving like a dancer, both swords drawn, with his arms held out for balance. The pool had evidently distracted him from his

236

claustrophobia. Taskin moved more slowly, guiding Harkon, who brought up the rear, about half way across. Sweating and puffing from the strain, the older man was stubbornly making the crossing. The Quffians had not fared as well. They had already lost two men to the pool, and even as Morgan watched, a man lost his balance and leaped for the next pedestal, knocking his companion into the ooze. The unfortunate man clawed vainly at the stone pillar, but the numbing cold sucked away his life in moments, and his limp body settled out of sight. The Quffians still had not located the path on the ceiling, and lost valuable time thrusting spears into the black liquid in search of the next pedestal. But fear or greed drove them on, and Morgan knew it was just a matter of time before the survivors had crossed the trap.

Max soon stood at his side, amusing himself by taunting the struggling Quffians, then Taskin and Harkon finally joined them. Harkon sank to his knees, looking like he was going to kiss the stone at their feet.

"I never thought I would be so glad to see a stone floor. That was awful. I thought we were all going to die," he said.

Seeing that their quarry was escaping, the leader of the Quffians shouted to his men.

"Hurry, fools! They are getting away," he cried.

Max grabbed Harkon, dragging him to his feet. "We'll rest later, my friend," he said, pulling him away from the pool.

Morgan ran up the tunnel, which now began to ascend, the others following close behind. The Quffians redoubled their efforts, and lost another man to the black pool. The hound and its handler stood watching on the far side, the man unwilling to risk his animal to the pool. His fellow Quffians would have to do without his services from now on.

Max jogged up the slope and caught Morgan, leaving Taskin to help Harkon. "What's next?" he asked.

"I told you. I'm getting this one step at a time. I'm empty again," Morgan said, straining to see what lay ahead.

"The suspense is killing me," Max said. "Why did the Monachus do it this way? Give you the information in such small pieces?"

"I don't know. Maybe they knew we might be followed, and if we were captured, I would only have part of the knowledge needed to reach the cache," Morgan said.

"And the Quffians don't know about the implants. They could torture you to death and still not learn anything, because you wouldn't really know," Max said brightly.

"You don't have to sound so cheerful about it," Morgan said.

Max glanced back at Taskin and Harkon. "How's he doing?" Max asked, nodding at Harkon. Harkon was limping, but looked better.

"I'll make it. Just have to get this leg thawed out and catch my breath. You're not leaving me with that pack of murderers back there," Harkon gasped.

They continued up the tunnel. Soon they rounded a slight bend in the cavern and could see a straight incline beyond. This part of the tunnel contained large rings placed at regular intervals up the slope. The rings were inset with yellowish crystals and covered with inscriptions and carvings. Dark niches lay between the rings, inset into the tunnel walls. Morgan noticed the tunnel walls had a scorched appearance, as if a fire had passed through.

Morgan stopped, as the sight triggered another implant. As they stood there, the crystals in the rings began to glow.

"Morgan, tell us what to do now. I don't like the looks of this place," Max said.

Even as he spoke, a strange sound drifted down the tunnel---a howling wail, like the legendary banshee. The crystals began to glow more brightly.

"Morgan . . . ," Max began.

Morgan seemed to wake from a daze. "The ghost wind. We must turn aside," he said.

"What? We can't go back. Not with the good townspeople waiting for us," Max reminded him.

Morgan shook his head. "Not back. Aside," he repeated.

Morgan paused, staring at the tunnel with its rings and niches. The howling grew louder, it sounded like something was coming down the tunnel toward them. Morgan suddenly pointed.

"The niches. We have to get into the niches," he said.

Max shrugged. "Whatever you say. But let's do it before the banshee gets here. She sounds mad," he observed.

Max turned to Taskin and Harkon, who stood white-faced behind them, staring up the tunnel. "Get into those niches. Now," he ordered.

Morgan shook off the fog of too many artificial memories, and moved forward. He passed three niches, leaving them for his companions. Barely deep enough for a man's body, the niches were lined with some black rubbery substance. The crystals in the rings blazed now, the rings themselves vibrating with some rising power. The wailing rushed closer, picking up speed in the descent, and Morgan thought he could see something in the distance, a glowing disturbance racing toward them.

"Hurry up," he shouted to the others. "We have to get into those niches before . . ." He was not sure how to finish and trailed off.

Max stepped into a niche, flattening himself against the back wall, and Morgan entered another, looking back at Taskin and Harkon. Harkon stood safely in a niche, and Taskin was turning to find his own. The deafening wail filled the tunnel. Taskin looked up and stopped, his mouth hanging open, and Morgan followed his horrified gaze. A maelstrom of glowing, twisting fire bore down on them. As the molten chaos passed each ring, it gained in momentum, spurred on by something in the rings. Arcs of blazing power lanced into the walls, scorching and scoring them. The pale fires would reach Taskin in moments.

"It's the ghost wind! Get away from it," Morgan yelled.

Instead of entering one of the niches, Taskin panicked and turned to run. Morgan started to follow, but the ghost wind had reached him. He jerked back into the niche, straining against the back of the hole, while violent energies crackled all around him. His hair stood on end, and his skin crawled as strange forces played across his body. His muscles twitched and jerked, he could hardly stand. His chest felt like an anvil rested on it, and his mouth worked, as he struggled to draw a breath. The howling storm passed an arm's length away, blinding and deafening him. His sword and anything else made of metal sparked and flashed. He closed his eyes and prayed. Then the ghost wind had passed, and Morgan could breathe again.

He leaned weakly against the side of the niche, peering around the edge at the receding mass of glowing fury. He could see Max beyond him, shaken but still alive. The ghost wind had not yet reached Harkon's niche, and through the writhing energies, he could see the fleeing Taskin.

Taskin ran for his life, the ghost wind at his heels. Sheer terror drove him on, faster than seemed possible. He passed the last of the rings, and pounded down the tunnel toward the black pool. He would have leaped headlong in the pool to escape the screaming thing behind him. His straining muscles cramped and his chest was on fire. He was going to die, he knew it.

As the ghost wind cleared the last ring, it seemed to weaken and slow, dissipating. The crystals in the rings that had fed its power were already fading, but Taskin ran on, oblivious to the changes. Through a reddish haze, Taskin could see the black pool at the bottom of the slope. Several Quffians had completed the crossing, and stood staring up at him and his pursuing demon.

Then the remnants of the ghost wind hit him, and Taskin collapsed in a twitching heap, a scream dying in his mouth. His body convulsed and jerked, flailing, as the deadly energies tore through it. He finally rolled into the wall, and lay still. The Quffians backed to the edge of the pool, as the ghost wind blew itself out in their faces. With a dying wail, the pale fires vanished, leaving a shocked silence in its wake.

Taskin lay where he had fallen. The Quffians stood frozen in place, fearing to move. Morgan staggered from his niche and Max and Harkon joined him, their eyes wild and hair disheveled. Harkon rubbed the skin of his arms.

"Something was crawling all over me. It was horrible," Harkon said, and then paused as he noticed Taskin's still form. "Taskin! Are you dead?"

When Taskin did not answer, Harkon turned to Max. "O Locha, he's dead! We're all going to die in this terrible place," he said.

240

Taskin groaned and his eyes fluttered open. He found himself looking at a nearby Quffian, who still stared up the tunnel. Taskin drew a shuddering breath, and tried to move. Guiding his still twitching muscles by sheer force of will, he managed to sit up and lean against the wall. His movement drew the attention of the Quffian, who gripped his sword and glared at him malevolently. But the man still feared the ghost wind, which he thought would reappear at any moment.

Morgan saw what was happening, and drew his sword, determined to see Taskin free of the Quffians. Max and Harkon followed. The Quffians watched them come; certain that the ghost wind would return and strike down Morgan and the others.

Morgan yelled at Taskin. "Get up, man! Get away from there!"

Taskin grimaced and clawed his way up the wall, getting to his feet. Glancing at the poised Quffian, he staggered toward Morgan. The Quffian took a step, and then paused, still half frozen in fear. Taskin forced himself to go faster, focused on Morgan.

Morgan and Max grabbed Taskin, nearly lifting him from his feet. They backed away, watching the Quffians. The last of the townspeople had crossed the pool, and the Quffians slowly advanced, emboldened by their numbers and seeing that Morgan's men were unharmed.

Morgan's group reached the first ring, which sprang to life again as they passed. A familiar wail sounded up the tunnel. The Quffians paused at the sound, and then charged, knowing they had to reach their enemies before the ghost wind returned.

Morgan and the others had no choice but to run straight up the tunnel, toward the growing energies. They could see the fiery turbulence ahead of them, beginning its rush down the tunnel.

"Get as far as you can, then dive for a niche," Morgan yelled over the growing howl.

They forced themselves to run toward the oncoming chaos. At the last possible moment they broke for the nearest niches. The Quffians saw their quarry scatter, leaving them to face the ghost wind. Their leader, observing Morgan's actions, ran to a niche and cowered inside. His men acted on impulse, some heading for niches, some running back down the tunnel, some attempting to climb the walls in a blind panic.

The ghost wind passed again. Morgan crouched in his niche, the experience no less horrible now that he knew what to expect. He heard the screams of the dying, as the ghost wind tore through the Quffians.

When he could move again, Morgan looked into the tunnel. Two bodies lay twitching on the floor, eyes bulging and mouths gaping, while several more Quffians ran ahead of the ghost wind. The storm of twisting lights caught one of the slower men, ending his life in a flash and a crackle of energy, leaving him to roll limply down the slope. One of the fleeing men could not stop in time, and stumbled waist deep into the black pool. Even as he slid from view, his companions cowered on the edge of the pool, as the ghost wind dissipated for the second time. Several of the Quffians had made it to the niches, and now peered out with wild eyes.

Morgan knew they had no time to waste. The ghost wind was triggered by anyone passing the first ring after the black pool. The surviving Quffians would be coming back, and the ghost wind would be unleashed again. The Quffians in the niches would also be after them.

He stepped from the niche and waved to his friends. "Move! Now! We have to get out of here, before it comes back," he yelled.

The others needed no prompting. They jumped into the tunnel and ran upslope. The Quffians were stumbling from niches, and working their way slowly up the tunnel behind them. Morgan passed the last of the rings, just as the energies activated a third time. Set in the floor and ceiling of the tunnel before him were twin jewels, multifaceted red orbs, father and mother of the ghost wind. The orbs glowed with power, and a cluster of pale fires began to form between them.

Max shouted over the whine of the growing forces, trying not to stare at the chaos being born nearby. "What now? We can't stay here!"

Morgan pointed at a side tunnel. "Through there! Move! Move!" he shouted.

They leaped for the second tunnel, even as the ghost wind began to move down the main branch. Their pursuers saw it coming, and most ran screaming back down the passage. Morgan and the others rounded a bend, and stopped, gasping for air. Taskin collapsed, still weakened from his encounter with the ghost wind.

"What next?" Max asked, his hands on his knees, forcing himself to take deep regular breaths.

Morgan shook his head. "All I know is that there are two more traps. The verse called them the abyss and the chaos crystal," he said.

Max cursed. "Two more? I don't know how much more of this we can take," he said.

Harkon leaned against the tunnel wall. "Well I can't take any more. I want out of here now. This is insane," he said.

Taskin sat up, holding his head. "Harkon, shut up! Quit your whining. I have a pounding headache, and I don't want to listen to you right now," he said, with uncharacteristic venom.

Harkon just stared at him, shocked into silence, but Max laughed. "I would say Taskin is feeling poorly right now," he said.

"He's lucky to be alive at all. If the ghost wind hadn't been fading, he would be dead," Morgan said.

Taskin groaned. "I'm not sure I did survive. I feel like l might be dead," he said hoarsely.

Max clapped him on the back and he groaned again. "Good news, my friend, if you feel terrible, you aren't dead. I know that from experience," he said.

They heard a crackle of energies, audible even over the howling of the ghost wind, and a scream. Morgan looked behind them.

"Evidently we're doing better than the Quffians," Morgan said.

Max smiled grimly. "That's true. If this keeps up, we won't have to worry about them on the way out," he said.

CHAPTER EIGHTEEN
ABYSS, CHAOS

They stood at the edge of a vast pit. A thin green line spanned the abyss, a narrow path made of blocks joined edge to edge and coated with some type of emerald phosphorescence. The cavern walls soared up into the darkness, the ceiling hidden somewhere above. In fact, the pathway provided the only light in the chamber, creating a tunnel of visibility through the stygian sea.

Max had dropped a rock over the edge, and finally gave up waiting for it to hit bottom. He turned to the others.

"The abyss," he said. "I like the sound of that."

Morgan grinned. "Feeling better about being underground?" he asked.

"Don't remind me. I'm trying not to think about it," Max said, then looked behind them, at the opening in the chamber wall where they had entered. "No sign of the Quffians. I wonder if they've given up?"

"I doubt it. They probably decided it was easier to just wait for us on the way out. Steal what we found, and torture us for any other information," Morgan said.

"That's a cheerful thought," Max said. "Does the view here bring back any memories?"

Morgan nodded, looking up into the darkness above them. "The abyss. Follow the shining path. Move to the call, or beware the blades of darkness," he recited.

Max glanced at the glowing blocks. "Well, the shining path won't be hard to find. What is the call, and the blades of darkness?" he asked.

Morgan frowned. "The call is some kind of audible beat, you move from block to block in time to the rhythm. If you don't, something happens," he explained.

"What do you mean `something?' Can't you be a little more specific?" Max demanded.

"No, I can't. My brain must be getting tired. Part of the

implant seems to be missing. Maybe that area of my mind has been overstimulated," Morgan surmised.

Max turned to study the path and the darkness surrounding it, looking for hidden dangers. "Yes, your mind. Considering what the Monachus had to work with, we've done surprisingly well," he said absently.

Morgan looked at him sharply. "What's that supposed to mean?" he asked.

"Nothing, nothing at all. Shall we proceed?" Max asked.

Morgan took the lead, moving to the end of the green path. In the oppressive darkness, Morgan could not even see what supported the blocks. He stepped onto the first block. For a moment nothing happened, and then unexpectedly, the block settled slightly with his weight. Morgan tensed, prepared to leap back to solid ground, but there was no further movement.

Morgan peered along the path. He thought he had seen something ahead---like flickering shadows flashing back and forth across the trail of blocks. He could not see them well enough to be sure. He glanced over his shoulder.

"Do you see those . . . flickers on the path up there?" he asked the others.

"Yes, I do. What are they?" Max asked.

"I don't know," Morgan said.

Suddenly, a sound like a gong rang out, echoing through the vast chamber. Without thinking, Morgan stepped to the next block. The sound was not repeated, and he waited tensely.

"Was that the call?" Taskin asked.

Morgan did not look around. "That would be my guess. We go one at a time across the path. Step to the next block only when the gong sounds. I'll try to see what these shadows are," he said.

Even as he spoke, the gong sounded again. He moved to the next block, and the gong rang a second time, and he stepped to the third block. There seemed to be no pattern to the notes, and he had to be careful and not anticipate the sound, and move out of turn. He felt dizzy; the green trail seemed to be hanging in space, although it felt solid enough. The shifting of the first block must have been

245

the trigger for the entire mechanism, as none of the others moved.

He kept on, focusing on the green blocks, and the gong. Twice, something flashed past him, so silent and fast that he could not identify it. He kept his arms close to his sides, and stayed to the center of the blocks. The crossing seemed to take forever, gong, step, gong, gong, step, step. Then he reached the end, and stepped onto the ledge at the far side of the abyss. As soon as he left the path, the gong fell silent.

He turned and waved to the others. Harkon came next, and the man had no sense of rhythm. Several times he almost stepped against the beat, but he finally managed to reach Morgan's side without mishap. The strange shadows had flickered about Harkon, before and behind, but never striking him. When Harkon had crossed, Morgan breathed a sigh of relief, and pulled him away from the edge.

Harkon was shaking, and his breath came in ragged gasps. "As I keep telling everyone, I'm too old for this. When is it going to end?" he asked.

"You should have stayed in Saxhaven. It would have ended by now," Morgan said absently, as he watched the others on the far side of the abyss.

Taskin went third. He had picked up a spear from one of the Quffian casualties, and about half way across, he decided to experiment. Each time the gong rang, Taskin would move, but he would hold the spear over the block in front of him.

"What are you doing? Stop that," Morgan shouted.

"I want to see what would happen if I were in the wrong place at the wrong time. I'll be careful," Taskin replied.

"I don't think you should do that," Morgan insisted.

"I'm the one that's out here. Don't worry," Taskin said.

Taskin had advanced four blocks before anything happened. Then he yelled in surprise, and Morgan could see his arm jerk violently. Something had struck the outstretched spear. Taskin started to examine it, but the gong sounded three times in rapid succession, and he had to keep moving.

When Taskin joined Morgan on the ledge, he showed Morgan

the spear, or what was left of it. Something had sheared completely through the shaft.

Taskin shook his head. "I didn't even see it coming. Something just slammed into the spear, and I almost dropped it," he explained.

"Well, what happened?" Max yelled from the other side.

"You don't want to know. Just follow the gong exactly," Morgan called.

"Or what?" Max insisted. "What happened to the spear?"

"I'll show you when you get here. Hurry up," Morgan said.

Max started across. Morgan strained to see the shadows as they passed, trying to imagine what could have sliced through a spear shaft like that.

Max was only a few blocks away when it happened. He stood waiting on the eighth block, the gong sounded, and he stepped to the next. The block cracked, and fully half of it crumbled away into the abyss. Max lurched, staggered, and fell from view.

Morgan yelled and charged out onto the blocks, all thought of gongs and shadows gone. Something tore through the air just in front of him; he could feel the wind of its passage. He dove headlong onto the next block, digging his fingers into the joint between the blocks and pulling himself forward. When he could see over the edge, he looked down, to find Max clinging to the jagged base of the broken block, suspended over nothing.

Before either of them could speak, a whistling sound split the darkness. Something hit Morgan's pack with terrific force, tumbling him over the opposite edge. As he fell, he managed to grab the lip of the block, and hung there, gasping in shock. His fingers slipped on the smooth stone, and he thrashed with his legs, trying to find some support. One toe dug into a crevice in the rocks below and he shoved himself up, throwing an arm over the edge of the block. He heard something coming at him, and he dropped back to arm's length. A shadow flickered through the greenish glow just above him, ascending into the darkness.

"Morgan! Are you all right? What happened?" Max called, sounding somewhat breathless.

Morgan worked his cramping fingers farther onto the stone,

still searching for something to stand on.

"Yes, I'm fine. It missed me, hit my pack," he returned.

The gong was still sounding, and Morgan could see shadows flashing up and down the path. He looked toward the ledge. Harkon and Taskin stood poised there, looking helpless. The ledge seemed impossibly far away.

"Well, what do we do now?" Max asked.

Morgan rested his forehead against the cool stone, trying to think. He could not hang here much longer.

"We're out of the pattern now. No way to tell what block we're supposed to be on, when to move. We seem safe enough here, at least from the shadows. My arms and fingers are cramping already," he said.

"If you can't climb up, move sideways. Hang onto the edge, and work your way to the end," Max offered.

"Can you make it?" Morgan asked.

"I can. See you at the ledge," Max called.

Morgan took a deep breath and began. He slid one hand, then the next, moving toward the ledge. When he could find purchase with his feet, he rested briefly, and then went on. Once his hand slipped, and he hung for a terrifying moment by one hand, then he managed to catch hold again with the other, and dangled there, quivering with the strain. He forced himself to continue, ignoring the pain in his arms and hands. After a while, his leg hit something to his left, and hands grabbed his pack strap, hauling him upwards. Taskin and Harkon dragged him bodily over the edge. He lay there for a moment, trying to work some life back into his tortured arms, and then he sat up. Max was standing there, rubbing his arms.

"Well, that was fun. Just walking across would have been boring," Max said with an evil grin.

Morgan got to his feet, slipped out of his pack, and stared at it. The pack was sliced nearly in half. A hand's breadth lower, and his spine would have been severed. Most of the pack's contents had fallen into the abyss.

Taskin looked at the pack. "Looks like you need a new pack," he said.

"O Locha, that could have been me," Harkon breathed.

Max walked over and examined the pack. "Morgan is always trying to get out of work. Now he doesn't have to carry anything. What did this?" he asked.

Morgan was staring up into the darkness above the path. "Beware the blades of darkness. Heavy blades suspended overhead, swinging back and forth like pendulums? The mechanism must be geared to the gong somehow," he said.

Max shook his head. "The Empire's artisans were quite ingenious, in a macabre fashion. I'm sort of glad they're all dead," he said.

"The gong has stopped," Taskin observed.

They all listened for a moment, but the cavern of the abyss lay silent once more, and the flashing shadows had ceased.

"Three traps, one to go," Morgan said.

"I won't even bother to ask you for details," Max said.

"Locha preserve us," Harkon muttered.

Taskin turned to him. "I wonder if your god gets as sick of you as I do," he said.

"I can't help it. I'm supposed to be retired," Harkon said.

They laid out what was left of the contents of Morgan's pack, and then divided them between the remaining packs. Max tossed the mutilated pack into the abyss.

Before them lay another tunnel and they went on. This tunnel was again lit by the globes. At the end of a long straight stretch, they came to a large sunken chamber. Stairs led down into it at either end, and mirrored panels covered the walls of the chamber. Several other panels hung from the walls at the top of the stairs.

Morgan hesitated at the end of the tunnel, staring down into the chamber. Max watched his face.

"Getting anything?" he asked Morgan.

Morgan slowly shook his head, frowning. "Nothing. I have no memories of this place," he said.

"Marvelous. What do we do now? Go on through, and hope we survive?" Max said.

"Crystal of chaos, swords of light will smite, lest you bear your image before you," Morgan recited, studying the chamber.

Max glanced into the chamber. "I see no crystal, or swords. Maybe the trap is broken," he said, without much hope.

"Probably just not triggered yet," Morgan said, stepping forward to the head of the stairs.

He froze, as a grinding sound came from the floor of the chamber. One of the iris doors slowly opened in the middle of the floor, its movement labored, as if the mechanism barely functioned. When the door panels had finally retracted, a multi-faceted crystal the size of a small horse rose through the opening on an elevator platform. When the platform was level with the floor, it stopped, and the crystal began slowly turning. The drone of gathering energies came from somewhere under the floor.

"There's your crystal," Max said.

Flashing lights began to appear within the depths of the crystal as the sound of power grew. Suddenly a beam of harsh light erupted from one of the facets, striking the nearest wall. The mirrored surface reflected the light and the beam shot from wall to wall until it finally faded. Another beam lanced out, repeating the process.

"The swords of light," Taskin breathed, fascinated by the flashing beams.

"How are we going to get through that? We're all going to die," Harkon said.

"Morgan, don't forget the smite part. Get away from the door before a ricochet cuts your head off," Max warned.

Morgan backed away. The crystal began turning faster, and soon beams of light leaped everywhere, filling the chamber.

"Crystal . . . swords . . . lest you bear your image before you," Morgan muttered. "Image . . . ."

Morgan's gaze was suddenly drawn to the mirrored panels at the head of the stairs. He moved quickly to the wall, and seized one of the panels. With a grunt he tore it loose.

"Morgan, I know you must be frustrated, but let's not tear the place apart," Max began.

Morgan raised the panel, holding it before him like a shield. He looked around the edge at Max.

"Bear your image before you," he said. "This is what the verse meant."

Morgan turned to Taskin. "Do you still have that spear shaft?" he asked.

Taskin slipped out of his pack. "I kept it, put it in my pack," he said.

Taskin pulled out the spear shaft and handed it to Morgan. Morgan stepped to the top of the stairs. Max was watching him, rubbing his beard.

"Wait," he said suddenly.

Morgan glanced back. "There's no other way. I'm going to have to disable the crystal," he said.

"What about your backside? Those beams are bouncing all over. You're going to catch one in the rear before you get halfway there," Max said.

Morgan looked at the sizzling beams. "It's a chance I'll have to take," he said.

Max sighed. "No, I've been covering your back for as long as I can remember. No reason to stop now. Taskin, give me a hand," he said.

Max and Taskin pulled loose another panel, and Max joined Morgan at the stairs.

"Back to back, just don't leave me behind," Max said.

Morgan nodded. "Ready?" he asked.

Max hefted the panel. "Go. This thing is heavy," he said.

They descended the stairs, trying to watch everywhere at once. If they saw a beam coming, they angled the panels toward it, being careful not to leave too much of an opening for other beams. Scything rays of light struck the panels four times before they reached the bottom of the stairs, reflecting harmlessly away. Max backpedaled as fast as he could, staying literally on Morgan's heels.

They crossed quickly through the maze of slashing beams. Morgan caught two beams on his shield, and Max deflected several more. A spear of light flashed past the edge of Max's panel, striking the back of Morgan's shield near his hand. Almost instantly, it melted a hole the size of Morgan's fist in the panel, spraying him with droplets of molten glass and metal.

Morgan jerked as he was burned in several places. "Watch it. That one almost got my hand," he said.

Max cursed as he deflected a beam. "I'm doing my best. Hurry up," he shot back.

They reached the whirling crystal without serious injury. A beam grazed Max's boot below the panel, and he cursed some more, hopping on one foot.

"Whatever you're going to do, do it fast. This panel is getting hot," he said.

Morgan peered through the hole in his shield, looking for a way to stop the crystal. He considered trying to shatter it with his sword or the spear shaft. A beam struck the back of his panel, just above his head, and Morgan cringed as hot metal spattered him. This close to the crystal, beams lashed across Morgan's panel almost constantly, making his shield uncomfortably warm. He had to do something soon.

He noticed that the crystal rotated on a sleeve with slots in it. As the crystal turned, the slots seemed to open and close, as they meshed with openings in the undercarriage. Leaning closer, Morgan angled his shield just enough and thrust at the sleeve with the spear shaft. The shaft slid off the first time, and a beam seared across the back of Morgan's arm. The metasilk absorbed the heat, nearly melting, and Morgan almost dropped the spear, as the hot metasilk burned his arm. Desperately, he jabbed again, and this time the shaft jammed in one of the slots.

The spinning crystal jerked to a halt, with a snapping sound from underneath. The force of its motion nearly severed the shaft, but it held, the metal edges of the slot digging into the tough wood. The deadly beams still played across the chamber, but they hung motionless now, creating a gridwork of light.

Morgan backed away, looking around the edge of his shield. "Get across the chamber. I don't know how long the spear will last," he called to the others.

Morgan and Max lost no time, stepping over or around the beams. Taskin and Harkon ran down the stairs, and started across the room, carefully avoiding the poised swords of light. Morgan ducked under a last beam, and started up the stairs, covering his back with his panel behind him. Max followed close behind. They reached the top of the stairs, and turned to wait for Taskin and Harkon.

Just as Taskin and Harkon reached the bottom of the stairs, a snapping sound came from the crystal and it shifted.

"Move. Move! The spear is breaking," Morgan yelled.

Taskin and Harkon scrambled up the stairs, casting fearful glances behind them. They were still several steps from the top when the spear shaft broke, and the crystal began to move again. Something in the mechanism had been damaged, reducing the smooth spin of the crystal to a halting, grinding lurch, but it could still hurl beams after them. Shafts of burning light scored the stone steps, and the two men on the stairs dove upwards. They rolled to safety between Max and Morgan's legs, panting with fear and exertion. Morgan held his panel over them, as Max tossed his shield aside and dragged them away from the stairs.

"We made it!" Harkon gasped. "All four traps and we didn't lose a man! Locha be praised."

"Was that the last of the traps?" Taskin asked, trying to catch his breath.

Max looked at Morgan. "I hope so. My implants seem to be failing," Morgan admitted.

CHAPTER NINETEEN
CACHE

As soon as Taskin and Harkon had recovered, the four men proceeded down the tunnel. The passage ended in a small, square room, with a partly closed iris door in the floor. A metal railing encircled the door, with a gap on either side. Morgan leaned on the railing, looking down through the door.

"I can see a large room below. There is a metal catwalk with a railing under the door," he said.

"How far down? I don't see a ladder," Max said.

Morgan got down on his hands and knees, craning his neck to see through the opening. "Twice a man's height. There are catwalks all over down there. The room is huge. I can't even see the walls from here," he said.

"First we have to get this door open. Any idea how to do that?" Max asked.

Morgan studied the door. "It seems to be stuck. I don't see any controls," he said.

Max dropped his pack, and swung under the railing, kicking the door valves with both feet. The plates shifted slightly, widening the opening.

"When all else fails, use brute force," Max said.

Morgan shook his head. "Fortunately, it was opening when it jammed. You might have closed it permanently," he said.

"Well, you had ceased to be much help. Let's get this open," Max said.

Hanging from the railing, Max and Morgan kicked at the door panels. The panels gave way reluctantly, a little bit at a time. Finally, they managed to pry the door open enough to pass a man's body. Morgan climbed back up to squat near the door.

"Get a rope and tie it to the railing. Drop the packs through first," Morgan ordered.

Harkon pulled a knotted rope from his pack. They dropped

the three packs through the door. When Harkon had tied the rope to the railing, Morgan descended and soon stood on the catwalk below. He held the bottom of the rope, urging the others to hurry. Max came next, then Harkon. Taskin was just clearing the opening when a grinding sound came from the door. With a series of jerks, the door cycled completely open, then without any warning, it closed. The metal valves severed the rope, and Taskin landed heavily on the catwalk, coils of rope raining down around him.

Max glared up at the door. "There had better be another way out of here. I am not staying," he said.

Harkon helped Taskin to his feet. "Are you hurt?" he asked.

Taskin grimaced. "A bruised hip. Nothing serious," he said.

"Max is right. We're not staying. Let's get what we came for and find another way out," Morgan said.

Morgan moved to the catwalk railing and looked down. The chamber below was enormous, the walls barely visible in the dim light of the globes hanging overhead. Huge, shrouded shapes littered the chamber's floor, and smaller articles lay on tables scattered throughout the room.

"It looks like someone just dumped all this stuff in here and left," Harkon said.

Morgan spoke softly, his eyes distant. "The Lucca and the Triad betrayed us. I saw Craig Phadrig fall from heaven. Our glorious capital lay in smoking ruins. The Mhoul, the Firstborn of the Lucca, those abominations, led the attack, resulting in more destruction. We fought back, unleashing terrible weapons. When the battle was finally over, the Empire had been destroyed, but the Fargate lay buried under the ruins, and the Lucca killed or driven from our world.

In an effort to save some of the more critical technology, and to protect future generations from the worst of the weapons, we created a series of caches. Various artifacts were placed in the caches, and sealed up, with traps set for the uninvited. We intended to return, and never did. The caches have remained, undisturbed, for centuries."

"Morgan?" Max asked with a worried frown. "You still in

there?"

Morgan shook his head. "Someone else's memories. He actually witnessed the Fall and survived the death of the Empire."

"How is that possible?" Max asked.

"Memories, stored and preserved by the Mons Monachus, generation after generation," Morgan said. "Incredible."

"You're scary," Harkon decided.

"What we came for is here," Morgan said.

Max regarded Morgan. "I have a confession," he said.

"What?" Morgan asked.

"I didn't really believe you," Max said. "Until now."

"And yet you came anyway," Morgan said.

"Someone had to take care of you, if you were insane," Max said.

"You are a true friend, Max," Morgan said.

"This discussion is comforting," Harkon mumbled.

"Shut up, Harkon," Taskin said.

"So let's collect our gadgets, and find a way out," Max said, looking around at the stone walls. He was feeling uncomfortable again, thinking about how this place had never seen the sun.

A gridwork of interlocking catwalks hung from the stone ceiling, and Morgan led the way toward the nearest wall. From there, they descended a spiral staircase to the floor of the vast chamber.

Max studied the huge shapes around them. "How big are these devices you came for?" he asked.

"The Monachus only picked items we could easily carry," Morgan said.

Morgan made his way through the piles of ancient mechanisms, the others trailing after him. Silence shrouded the vast chamber, except for the scuff of their boots. After examining several tables littered with various devices, Morgan stopped and pointed to a cluster of small figurines, carvings of seated men, with blue crystal eyes.

"Taskin, take those," Morgan said.

Taskin hesitated. "What are they?" he asked nervously.

"Don't worry. They're harmless to you," Morgan reassured him.

Doubtfully, Taskin approached the statues, and carefully placed them in his pack. Morgan continued his search, looking over tables and lifting shrouds.

"What are we looking for? If you tell us we could help," Max suggested.

"There it is," Morgan said.

He walked to a large covered object, with a case leaning against it. Morgan picked up the case and carried it to a table. A strange carving etched the face of the container. Morgan opened the lid. The others joined him, peering over his shoulder.

"A sword?" Harkon asked. "They sent us way down here for a sword?"

Morgan lifted it free of the case. It was a sword, with a simple hilt and sheath. "Not just a sword, a sword that can kill a Mhoul," he said.

Max looked skeptical. "Mhoul aren't really alive. How can you kill one?" he asked.

Morgan slowly pulled the sword free of the sheath, and the metal of the blade instantly drew their attention. It looked like congealed gold dust, with thousands of tiny flecks shining in the blade, sparkling even in the dim light of the chamber.

Morgan touched the blade. "It's made of pure aurellium," he said.

"Aurellium?" Harkon asked.

"An element created by Phronesis, just before the Fall. He developed it as a weapon against the Lucca. The metal actually absorbed the Luccan life energy," Morgan said.

"So this sword will kill a Mhoul?" Max asked.

"Enough exposure to this blade would drain a Mhoul completely, killing it," Morgan said.

"Next time we meet Molid, a Mhoul will die," Max said. No one doubted his sincerity.

Morgan replaced the blade in its sheath, and buckled on the sword. "The next thing I need to find will be in a large metal box, about chest high. Why don't we spread out and look for it?" he said.

The four men searched through the vast room, each taking a different route. They stared in fascination and wonder at the collection of artifacts from a lost age. It would take years to catalogue all the devices in the chamber, let alone discover their purpose and function. Some time later Max yelled.

"Look at that!" he cried.

Morgan peered through the gloom, trying to see what Max had found. He saw Max several rows over, running toward what looked like the statue of a warrior on a large pedestal.

"That's not what we're looking for. Don't touch anything else," Morgan warned.

Max had reached the statue and clambered up on the pedestal base. "It's ebonite. A whole suit of it," he said.

Morgan made his way through the maze of relics, knowing better than to try and keep Max away from ebonite. By the time he got to the statue, Max had stripped the figure of its armor. A breastplate and a helmet already lay on the stone floor. Harkon and Taskin had joined them. Harkon picked up the helmet.

"It's ebonite. Do you know how much this is worth? Could I have this?" Harkon asked.

"Is it worth your life? The first Mhoul agent who saw that would kill you for it, after they had tortured you for the location of this place," Morgan said.

Harkon waved the helmet at Max. "But he has ebonite swords. No one has captured or tortured him," he protested.

"Would you try to capture Max?" Taskin scoffed.

"Besides, those swords didn't come from here. I've had them for years," Max said.

"The Mhoul will soon know we've been in the cache. If anyone sees that helmet, they'll know you were with us. Leave it here. It's for your own good," Morgan explained patiently.

"But what about him?" Harkon asked, pointing to Max again.

Max was pulling a light mail shirt over the statue's head. Holding the shirt, he hopped down to the floor. "I'll wear this under my clothes, where no Mhoul agent can even see it," he said.

"You shouldn't take it," Morgan said.

Max eyed Morgan defiantly. "Are you going to stop me? What if a Mhoul agent sees all that junk you've collected?" he asked.

Morgan threw up his hands. "Oh fine. Take whatever you want, take anything you can carry. I don't care," he said, walking away.

Taskin stood watching Harkon, waiting. Harkon read the expression on his face, and threw down the helmet. The metal clanged hollowly on the stone floor. "It's not fair," he complained.

Max rolled up the shirt and stuffed it in his pack. He glanced up at Harkon. "Quit pouting. Just find something small that you can hide, or something that's not obviously of Mercator origin," he said.

Harkon brightened and began examining the table with new interest. Taskin looked disgusted. "Scavengers," he muttered.

It was Taskin who found the box Morgan sought. Made of heavy metal, about chest high and roughly square, the box had a door in the front, but no apparent latch or lock. Morgan studied the box for a moment, and then spoke a single word. Almost immediately, the door on the box grated open.

"What did you say?" Max asked.

"I don't know. I just knew that would open it. I think it was a word from the original Trade language, used by the Mercator Empire," Morgan said.

"You're beginning to scare me," Max said.

Harkon looked inside the box. "It's a piece of rock. First some little statues, then a gold sword, and now a rock. I think your Mons Monachus are as mad as you," he said.

Morgan reached inside the box and pulled out what indeed looked like a piece of rock, roughly triangular, about the size of two fists pressed together, and covered with strange carvings.

"What is it?" Taskin asked.

"It's heavy," Morgan said, hefting the rock.

"But what does it do?" Taskin asked.

"I don't know. I just know it's very important somehow," Morgan said.

Max examined the metal box. "Someone thought it was valuable, to lock it up in this box. If you didn't know the password, you could spend years trying to pry this thing open. What next?" he asked.

Morgan tossed the stone to Harkon. "Since you are so impressed with this, why don't you carry it?" he said.

Harkon put the stone in his pack, grumbling about the weight. Morgan surveyed the chamber, lost in thought. "One last thing," he finally said.

Morgan made his way across the chamber, ignoring the many strange objects he passed, and then stopped before a pedestal that stood shoulder high. A small jewel on a fine chain hung from the pedestal. He picked up the jewel, and lifted the chain over his head, leaving the jewel to dangle on his chest.

Harkon stared at the jewel. "Now that looks valuable. How come all I get is a rock?" he asked.

At Max's questioning look, Morgan waved an arm. "I'll explain later. Now we have to find a way out of here," he said, looking around.

"You still don't know? I thought you remembered this place," Max said.

Morgan looked thoughtful. "I knew what devices to take, but the details of the chamber floor plan are not clear. I think we were supposed to leave the way we came. We'll just have to search for an exit," he said.

They began walking toward the nearest wall. Harkon was still looking at the jewel. Suddenly he pointed at it.

"Look at that. It's glowing. It must be priceless," Harkon said.

Morgan looked down. Sure enough, the jewel radiated a reddish light that pulsated oddly. Morgan lifted it from his chest, and slowly turned, watching the jewel. At first, the light began to fade, and Morgan turned back the other way. As Morgan moved the other direction, the jewel became brighter. At its brightest point, Morgan stopped and looked up.

Max was watching with ill-concealed impatience. "Well, what now? What is it doing?" he asked.

Morgan pointed straight ahead. "This jewel is a Gatefinder. Somewhere over there is a functional Gate," he said.

"A Gatefinder. I knew it was valuable," Harkon said. "What's a Gatefinder?"

Max interrupted. "I'm not going anywhere near a working Gate. You'd have to be insane to even suggest it," Max protested.

Morgan looked at Max. "What's wrong? You've used Gates before," he said.

"Only when we absolutely had to. And only those that were keyed to a specific destination, ones that had been field tested. You said no one has been in here for centuries. You have no idea where this Gate is set for, or even if it still works right. You might just scatter yourself over half of the planet," Max said.

"Excuse me, what's a Gate? That sounds dangerous," Harkon said.

"You don't want to know," Max said darkly. "You only need to know he is insane."

"I'm going to have a look at it," Morgan said.

Without waiting for further discussion, Morgan headed in the direction the jewel had indicated. Taskin and Harkon followed. Max came last, still grumbling.

As Taskin passed a table, something caught his eye. Spilling from a sack were some golden objects. He picked up the sack and tossed it to Harkon.

"There. These look like they might be worth something. Quit complaining, you greedy old wreck," he said.

Harkon caught the sack and peered inside. His sour face brightened. "They look like real gold. I'll take these," he paused, noting Taskin's disgusted look. "For my retirement, you see," he added, carefully placing the sack in his pack.

They found Morgan facing a blank wall. He looked at the jewel, which flared even brighter now. Morgan began to examine the wall, running his hands over it.

"See? There is no Gate. The jewel is malfunctioning," Max said.

Morgan touched a recessed panel on the wall, and a section of the wall next to him lifted, revealing another room. In the center of the room stood a pair of upright stones twice a man's height, capped

261

by a huge block of the same material. The stones were carved with strange patterns, and the air between the stones shimmered and rippled, like heat waves in the desert. A deep, thrumming vibration came from the structure, a powerful sound more felt than heard. Morgan felt his hair stir as if touched by ghostly breezes, and his skin crawled.

Max backed away. "It's a Gate all right. Better get away from it," he warned.

Taskin and Harkon glanced at each other, but Morgan strode toward the Gate, the jewel glowing on his chest.

"Will someone please tell us what a Gate is? I think we have a right to know," Harkon said.

Morgan stood looking at the stones, with their ancient runes and restless energies. "This is the emergency exit," he said finally. "It's our only way out."

Max stopped in his retreat. "Out to where? You don't know where that goes," he said.

Morgan turned. "Well, we can't stay here. Did you see another way out?" he asked.

"No, but we haven't really looked yet. There might be some other way," Max said.

Morgan faced the Gate. "You can stay here if you want. I'm using the Gate," he said.

Without another word, Morgan walked between the upright stones. With a flare of crackling energies, he vanished. A loud pop sounded as air rushed in to fill the void where Morgan had been, and a smell like hot metal drifted through the air. The space between the stones rippled and then stilled.

Taskin and Harkon stood staring, their mouths hanging open.

"Where did he go?" Taskin asked.

"I'm not going through that. It looks dangerous," Harkon said.

Max started forward, cursing as he walked. "Stupid, stubborn, overgrown lout. Because of you I was buried alive for three years. You're not leaving me behind this time. Not in this hole. Never again," Max said as he approached the Gate.

Before Taskin or Harkon could stop him, Max had stepped

into the Gate, vanishing just as Morgan had done.

"What do we do now?" Harkon asked, his eyes wild.

"What choice do we have? We follow them," Taskin said.

"But we don't know what happened to them. I don't even know what a Gate is," Harkon objected. "You were in the Raavs with them. Max said he knew what a Gate was. Don't you?"

"I was in the Raavs and served under them. But I never used a Gate before," Taskin said, then put his head down and walked toward the Gate. "A good soldier doesn't ask questions. He just follows his Commander."

With a blaze of crackling energies, Taskin was gone. "I always hated that part of soldiering," Harkon said.

He heard a rumbling sound, deeper even than the Gate's vibration, and looked around him. Wait for me," he called as he went through the Gate.

Activation of the Gate had triggered a final mechanism, and sheets of dull metal descended over all the exits, sealing the cache like a tomb. Soon, the stillness of the centuries returned, the only sign of the men's passage the footprints in the dust.

Morgan fell to his knees in blue dimness. A single globe lit the small chamber. He felt like vomiting, and did not trust himself to stand. The dim light didn't help his dizziness. His mouth was parched, his eyes dry, and his skin felt hot, like it had been burned. A fine white dust covered his skin and clothing. The dust made him sneeze, and his stomach churned at the sudden motion.

With a flare of light and a crackling from the Gate behind him, Max stumbled out of nowhere, to collapse beside him. He retched once, and pushed himself up to glare at Morgan. Morgan fought laughter when he saw Max's red eyes and powdered features.

They both rolled aside as the Gate surged again, and Taskin fell headlong where they had been lying. They dragged him away from the Gate, as Harkon came through. Harkon rolled on his back, rubbing his eyes, and staring at his skin.

"What in the name of Locha just happened to me? I was on fire, then it was dark and I was freezing, and now I'm here, sick and dried out. Where is here, anyway?" he croaked.

Max leaned over and patted his arm. Fine white dust puffed up. "Thanks to Morgan, you have just experienced the joys of Gate travel. Believe me, you never get used to it," Max said hoarsely. "As for where we are, I have no idea."

Harkon sat up, licking his dry lips. "I don't think I want to ever do that again," he decided.

Taskin groaned. "Me neither. That was awful, almost like the ghost wind," he said.

Max got shakily to his feet, and began brushing off the dust. "I have always maintained that Iosus did not intend for man to travel that way," he said.

Morgan stood up. "Max, you've never cared what Iosus intended, or any other god, for that matter," he said.

Max looked slightly offended. "So tell me, holy man, where have you taken us?" he asked.

Morgan studied their surroundings. "Well, we're alive, and somewhere else, that's all I care about right now," he said.

"Please tell us what a Gate is," Harkon asked plaintively.

Morgan looked down at him. "The Empire used them to travel from place to place. The Gates are nearly indestructible and some of them still work. The Empire could direct where the Gates took them, but no one knows how to control the Gates anymore, so it's just trial and error. Step through, and try to figure out where you end up. Max and I used them a few times during the Crusades, on special assignments. The ill effects are temporary, you'll live," he explained.

Taskin looked at the Gate. "So why didn't we just go in that way, and not through all the traps?" he asked.

"I'm sure this Gate is set to only work one way, from the inside out. I don't know what would happen if you entered from this side," Morgan said.

Harkon shuddered. "I don't want to know. Coming out was bad enough," he said.

Morgan stepped to a small doorway, the only visible exit. Through the door he could vaguely see a long dark hallway, with stairs at the far end. He waited and listened, hearing no sound but the muttering of his companions. Nothing moved in the hall.

Morgan walked down the hall, and the other men followed him. The jewel still glowed because of the Gate, and it shed some light on the hall. Morgan reached the stairs and looked up, seeing a trapdoor at the top of a short stairwell. He climbed the stairs, and pushed slowly on the trap door. It raised with an effort, hinges protesting.

Morgan peered out through the crack of the raised lid. Sand blew in his face, and he could see moonlit dunes, and hear waves crashing in the distance. He looked back at the others.

"It looks like the dunes near Aquarquff," he said.

"Pure, blind luck. We could have been on Vaeland, for all you knew," Max grumbled.

Morgan lifted the trap enough to climb through, and crouched near a clump of beach grass. They were somewhere near Aquarquff, he could see the massive cliffs to his right, and the ocean to his left. He waited and watched, while the others climbed out of the underground chamber. When they lowered the lid, the sand slid into the cracks, rendering the trapdoor nearly invisible. It would be hard to find it again, even though they knew where to look. Small wonder no one had discovered it.

"I don't see anything moving. Let's head for the beach and see exactly where we are," Morgan said.

Max threw back his head, drinking in the open sky. "It's beautiful," he said.

They moved silently through the dunes. A breeze rippled the grasses around them, and blew sand from the ridges, the flow of air cleansing the men of the strange dust from the Gate. The arch hung over them, bathing the beach in silver light. Only the third moon, Damon, remained, riding a moon path over the ocean waves. They reached the water without mishap, and looked for landmarks.

Max pointed. "The longboat is up that way. Not far," he said.

They ran along the beach in the moonlit surf, the waves washing away their footprints. They found the longboat where they had left it. As they uncovered the boat, Max turned to Morgan.

"Wait for me. There's something I have to do," Max said.

"We don't have the time," Morgan said. "It must be close to

dawn, and the Princess will be leaving for the Waste."

"I'll explain later," Max said, as he slipped away into the night.

They dragged the boat to the water, and waited, Morgan impatiently stalking the beach. By the position of Damon, he knew it was nearly dawn. They had been in the caves most of the night. But they had survived the traps, and he had what the Monachus sent him for. And the cache remained relatively secure, even though the Quffians now knew its location.

Max finally appeared, moving through the dunes like a black phantom.

"What were you doing?" Morgan whispered fiercely.

Max pointed toward the cliffs. "Just a hunch. I checked on the cave mouth. Our friends, the Quffians, were hiding in ambush there. The survivors had left the caves, and were waiting for us to return," he said.

"How many were there?" Morgan asked.

"Only eleven. They were relying on the element of surprise to capture us," Max said.

Morgan looked back toward the cliffs. "You killed them," he said.

"Yes," Max admitted.

"You killed eleven men by yourself?" Harkon asked.

"Surprise works both ways. I let the hound go," Max said.

"Probably just as well. They were the only ones besides us who knew where the hidden entrance was," Morgan said.

"Dead men are the most trustworthy," Max said.

"Let's get back to the Windrider," Morgan said.

CHAPTER TWENTY
THE WASTE

Celeste could not sleep; her thoughts and emotions were in turmoil. The prospect of leaving Max and Morgan left her feeling very lonely and vulnerable, although she hated to admit that. She would miss Max's cynical wit, and his twisted flattery. She also realized how safe she felt around him, she had never seen a more deadly fighter. And Morgan, the thought of him frustrated her greatly. Although she had told Morgan she was willing to wait for him, in her heart she did not want to wait another day. What if he was killed, or never came back to her? She tried to be unselfish and brave, and put the needs of others before her own, but it was so hard. She wanted nothing more than to have Taurus leave them on some deserted island and forget about the world and its problems.

Her thoughts drifted back to the flight from Skara Thrae, the fear, the frustration, the miserable sensation of helplessness. She was not eager to repeat that experience. Thugmonger Wald was no longer a threat, but Mhoul gold could always replace him.

On the other hand, she looked forward to the wild freedom of the Waste, the vast open spaces, so unlike the confines of island life. She had such fond memories of the awesome citadel of Carnac, and the gentle wisdom of Serenus, her childhood teacher. And Talbot would be there. She missed her brother terribly. She also worried about her family on Skara Thrae, wondering how they were, and how the war was going. She had been taught to care for the people of the island, and she was concerned for their welfare, especially under the brutal domination of the Haggas.

Celeste turned on her side, burrowing down into the warm bunk, forcing back her chaotic thoughts. She had to get some sleep; tomorrow was going to be a long, hard day. She was actually beginning to settle into sleep when she heard a noise that brought her wide awake again. The deck sentry had passed her cabin several times that night, but this was a different sound---a thud, and a stifled gasp. She held her breath, listening, and could hear the lap of water against the hull, the creak of the rigging, and the dull groan of timbers as the Windrider moved with the waves. For several moments she heard nothing else, and she began to think the sentry had merely stumbled or bumped into something in the dark.

A stealthy sound came from the outer cabin door, and it swung slowly open. A shaft of moonlight spilled across the floor, a shaft that held a shadow. Celeste quietly reached for the dagger near her pillow. The door opened wider, and two figures crept into the room. Celeste knew these men were not from the Windrider's crew. Although several members of that unsavory lot had eyed her speculatively from time to time, all of Taurus' men feared him too much to molest the Princess. She noticed the dark outline of robes and turbans, and recognized the intruders as Quffians.

The men approached from either side of the bed, and the man on her right reached out, to cover her mouth and muffle any cries for help. His hand was nearly touching her face when she moved, slashing with the dagger. The man jerked back his bleeding arm with a curse, staring at the deep gash in his wrist. Celeste flung the bedcover over the wounded man's head, and then swung her legs around, to kick him in the stomach with both feet. With an explosive grunt, the man staggered back, to collide heavily with the cabin wall.

The other man overcame his shock, and lunged, only to twist aside as the Princess' dagger flashed in his face. She rolled from the bunk as the second man dove onto the bed, missing her with his outstretched arms. Celeste grabbed up a chair from beside the bed and backed into a corner. With the chair in one hand, and the dagger in the other, she began shouting.

Cursing, the man on the bed scrambled across and jumped at Celeste, but she shoved the chair into his face. He barely managed to avoid the simultaneous dagger thrust at his groin, and staggered back, realizing that the intended abduction was not going well. His companion finally freed himself of the blanket, and began urging his companion to grab Celeste, while he clutched his bleeding wrist.

A third man appeared at the door. "Can't you fools subdue one woman? She is rousing the entire crew. Hurry up!" he whispered fiercely.

268

The two men made another attempt to breach Celeste's defenses, but were unsuccessful. Outside, they could hear the sound of running feet, and then shouting. With a last baleful glance at the crouching Princess, the two Quffians fled, and Celeste sagged against the wall, weak with relief.

Celeste's two attackers joined the five Quffians outside her cabin, while the Windrider's crew exploded from doorways and hatches, bleary eyed, but ready to fight. Clutching swords and spears, they charged the Quffians from all sides. Taurus burst out of his cabin with a roar, and led the charge. He wore only a rumpled shirt, his hairy legs flashing in the moonlight, and his bare feet slapping on the deck. The first thing the Captain saw was the body of the deck sentry, lying at the feet of the Quffians with his throat cut. The besieged Quffians saw nothing but the massive ax in Taurus' hand and the crazed look in his bloodshot eyes.

Seeing that all was lost, the leader of the Quffians ordered his men to fight to the death, and leaped overboard. He swam for shore, leaving his men to their fate. The flood of seamen washed over the remaining Quffians. Taurus cut a swath through them with his ax, the blade glinting red and silver in the night. Two Quffians crumpled before Taurus' onslaught, then another Quffian fell, cut down by one of the Windrider's crew. The three survivors fought desperately, but before long two more had died. The last man hurled his sword at Taurus with a scream, and jumped overboard. Taurus knocked the sword aside with his ax and ran in pursuit.

Taurus and his men reached the railing and looked over. The unfortunate Quffian had landed in a boat, which waited below, and the force of the impact had sent the man through the bottom of the flimsy craft. A Quffian in the stern stood staring at his comrade, who struggled waist deep in the shattered hull. Water boiled up around the writhing form, and the boat was quickly sinking. Tearing his eyes from the scene, the other Quffian looked up, to see Taurus and his entire crew glaring down at him, their weapons red with the blood of his former companions. Hearing a sound behind him, the Quffian twisted around, and saw the Windrider's longboat coming straight for him. The boat surged through the water, propelled by

Morgan's powerful strokes at the oars. Max stood in the bow, both swords drawn, and a wicked grin on his face.

It was more than the Quffian could bear. With a shriek, he dove out of the boat, leaving his trapped companion to drown with the sinking craft. He swam for shore, fear goading his frenzied thrashing. The longboat ground over the remains of the Quffians' boat without slowing, ramming into the side of the Windrider. Max crouched, trying to avoid being pitched overboard, and Taurus clutched at the railing, cursing violently.

"Thaar, man! Heave to! You'll sink us, not to mention staving in the bow of my longboat. What's the matter with you?" the Captain roared.

Morgan leaped up, throwing down the oars. "The Princess! Is she all right?" he shouted.

Celeste joined Taurus at the rail. She smiled down at the sweating Morgan, relieved by his safe return and secretly pleased by his concern for her.

"Don't worry, Morgan. I'm fine," she said, patting Taurus on the shoulder. "Captain Taurus and his fine crew have seen to my safety."

Morgan relaxed, and then realizing everyone in the longboat was staring at him, began to look slightly embarrassed. He kicked at an oar, mumbling something. Max shook his head, sheathing his swords. Taskin and Harkon still huddled in the boat, slightly unnerved by the wild ride and waiting for Morgan to regain his sanity. Max tossed a line to a man on the Windrider, and the men in the longboat prepared to disembark.

Celeste looked at Taurus. "Nice legs," she commented.

Taurus glanced down at his half clad form, and tugged miserably at his inadequate hemline.

"I agree completely," Max said, as he clambered over the rail.

Taurus whirled, but saw that Max was looking at the Princess, who like Taurus, wore only a large shirt that reached mid-thigh. Morgan appeared at the rail, and stopped, staring at her. Celeste suddenly remembered how she was dressed, and with the eyes of the entire crew on her, the Princess of Skara Thrae turned and ran for her cabin.

Taurus, Morgan, and Max met in the Captain's cabin, along with Taskin, Harkon, and Seidon. Taurus had finished dressing, and held a mug of hot ale. Taurus studied the collection of burns and scrapes on Morgan and his companions.

"Looks like I missed the fun. Did you get your trinkets?" Taurus asked.

Morgan was shuffling through the pile of maps on Taurus' desk. He nodded. "We got what we came for," he said.

"I'm glad you're back. I'm charging you extra for the damage to my longboat," Taurus said.

Max laughed. "When Morgan heard the sounds of fighting on the Windrider, he nearly broke the oars getting us back here," he said.

Taurus lifted his mug. "Here's to love," he said.

Morgan ignored them; pulling out the map he sought. He spread it on the table.

"I'm supposed to go to Dragonback. From Aquarquff we could take one of three routes. First, up the River Seir, past Kalixalven, to this point, then overland to Dragonback. Or, we could go across the Waste, and over Maran pass into Kalixalven, then up the Seir by boat. Finally, we could cross the Waste, enter Faerie, and travel through the forests of Aijalon," he said, tracing the alternate patches on the map with a fingertip.

Taurus and Max exchanged knowing looks. "Why subject ourselves to the Waste, the Ha'ashtari, and a mountain pass, or the dangers of Faerie, when we could just sail up there in the Windrider?" Max asked.

Morgan gripped the edge of the table, his knuckles turning white. "After what happened last night, I'm not going to let the Princess travel to Carnac alone. She's already hired a Pathfinder, we just escort her to Carnac and pay for safe passage on to Kalixalven," he said.

"Exactly. She's hired a Pathfinder, and will soon be in the Waste, where no one will bother her further. What about the mission for the Monachus? Can you afford these delays and detours?" Max asked.

"Obviously, someone working for the Mhoul knows she's here. They want her, and they care nothing about peace treaties or Pathfinder tradition. She's no safer in the Waste than she is here," Morgan said.

"You don't know the Mhoul sent those Quffians. Maybe they just wanted to add the Princess to their secret brothel," Taurus said.

"I don't believe that, and neither do you. Besides, what I plan may throw off the pursuit, give us some time. If we're gone with the Princess by dawn, and Taurus sails for Kalixalven, the Mhoul's spies may think we're still on board," Morgan said.

"Great. Put the Mhoul on my trail, while you run off with the Princess," Taurus said as he waved the mug at Morgan. "I'm charging double for hazardous duty."

"I'll pay whatever you ask. Will you do it?" Morgan asked.

Taurus shrugged. "Why not? I'm bound for Kalixalven anyway. What's a few Mhoul agents skulking at my heels?" he asked. "So I sail for Kalixalven, offload my cargo, and wait for you there. Then you pay for passage on up to Dragonback. Is that the bargain?"

Max laughed. "A bargain, he calls it. You're getting rich at the expense of the Monachus, old friend. I'm just glad it's not my money," he said.

"Hey, I'm running a business here. Friendship doesn't feed the crew," Taurus said.

Morgan held out his hand, and Taurus gripped it. "Bargain," Morgan said.

Harkon stepped forward. "Morgan, I have something to ask," he said.

Morgan turned and sat on the table, folding his arms. "What is it, Harkon?" he asked.

"I'm getting too old for this cross-country travel. I'd like to stay with the Windrider, work for passage to Kalixalven, then I'll join you there. I would just slow you down crossing the Waste, and Taurus has lost several crewmen. He's short handed," Harkon said.

"That's fine with me. I appreciate all you've done for me, Harkon. I'm sorry we disrupted your retirement," Morgan said.

"He complains a lot, but he doesn't really mean half of it,"

Taskin said.

Harkon turned to Taurus. "Will you have me?" he asked.

Taurus grunted. "You seem to be a good man. If you want to join my collection of criminals, I'll not stop you," Taurus said, and then clapped Harkon on the back, staggering him. "Welcome aboard, Harkon."

A soft knock came from the door. "Come in," Taurus called.

Celeste opened the door and entered. She wore riding clothes, with a cloak and hood. She glanced at the others, and then addressed Morgan. "Weren't you going to say good-bye? I'm leaving in a few moments," she said.

"We're going with you," Morgan said, more gruffly than he intended.

The Princess stared at him, and then slowly shook her head. "You can't. What about your mission for the Monachus?" she asked.

"We'll escort you to Carnac. It will only mean a slight detour," Morgan said.

"Slight detour? Remember, I'm familiar with this area, Morgan. You would lose days going to Carnac," she said.

"I don't want you traveling to Carnac alone," Morgan insisted.

"I won't be alone. I have a Pathfinder. That will keep me safe from the Ha'ashtari. There's no one else in the Waste," she said.

Morgan locked eyes with her. "We're going with you," he said firmly.

Celeste turned to Max. "Max, tell him. This is a bad idea," she said.

Max threw up his hands. "I tried, Princess. He won't listen," he said.

Celeste struggled to contain a wave of conflicting emotions. She wanted Morgan to stay with her, but she did not want to jeopardize his mission. They both had others to consider. She began to get angry. Why couldn't he just bid her farewell and leave? Why was he tormenting her with this foolish plan?

"You can't go with me, we both know that. No matter how badly we want to stay together, we can't. Just accept it," she said.

Morgan opened his mouth to speak, when he noticed Max's

hand signal. "I won't . . . ," he began.

Max flashed the signal again, insistently. Morgan closed his mouth, jaw clenched.

Max spoke. "All right, Princess. If that's how you feel, we'll not force ourselves on you. Have a pleasant journey," he said.

Celeste glared at Max suspiciously, and then turned back to Morgan.

"Does he speak for you?" she demanded.

Morgan glanced at Max, who nodded. "Yes," he said in a low voice.

"Men!" Celeste said, and then stormed out of the room.

As the door slammed behind her, Morgan turned on Max. "Why did you do that?" he demanded.

"Relax, friend. I have a devious plan," Max said.

Morgan stared at the door. "Women. I don't understand them. She was mad when we were going, and madder when we weren't," he muttered.

Max laughed. "Women? What about you? We were going to Carnac with her all along. You just used the Quffians as an excuse," he said.

Morgan glared at Max. "Your plan better be good. I don't want anything happening to her," he said.

Celeste turned her mount at the cave mouth, while a Pathfinder waited impatiently just inside the tunnel. She looked down the slope at the town of Aquarquff. The morning sun had not reached it yet, and the buildings lay in cool shadows. She saw the blue Pathfinder pavilion, its walls rippling in the breeze, and then movement drew her gaze to the horse corral at the edge of town. Several figures still gathered there, and she had noticed some type of commotion at the corral on her way to the Pathfinders' tent.

Taurus had provided her with an escort into town. Morgan and Max had not seen her off; Harkon said they were busy with something else. Harkon came with the escort, but there was little conversation. The town had been relatively deserted this early, and they had only seen a few people. No one paid them any attention.

Celeste raised her eyes to the shallow bay. The longboat had returned to the Windrider, and the ship was just turning toward deeper water, banks of oars propelling her into the open ocean. The Princess' eyes blurred with tears, and she forced them back.

She was such a fool sometimes. Morgan had been willing to go with her to Carnac and she had told him no. Now she would probably never see him again. She wished things could have gone differently between them. Although she was disappointed that he had given in so easily, and hurt and angry that he did not even take the time to come to her cabin and say good-bye privately. Maybe she had misjudged him. Maybe he was like other men. Somehow, she could not believe that.

Celeste sighed. She had an obligation to her family, to the people of Skara Thrae. She had to go to Carnac, find Talbot, and somehow help her father to drive the Haggas from her home. She would have to forget Morgan for now.

"Woman, we must be off," the Pathfinder said.

Celeste turned her horse, and nodded sadly. The man in blue rode into the blackness of the cave, holding his torch aloft, and the Princess sank into her own dark thoughts, paying little heed to their surroundings. They rode up a winding slope, the horses' hooves clopping on the stone floor. The remnants of the stream that had carved this cave passage trickled alongside them, reflecting the torchlight and their wavering images. Neither of them spoke, the only sounds the crackling of the torch and the horses' hooves. They moved on, in an island of torchlight, the cave walls sliding silently past. Celeste lost track of time.

A change in the light roused her from her musings, and she looked up, to see a rosy glow from somewhere ahead. They rounded a last bend, and she could see the end of the tunnel. The morning sun poured into the opening, unbearably bright after their time in darkness.

They rode on, and just inside the tunnel entrance, the Pathfinder dismounted, and smothered the torch in the dirt of the cave floor. He leaned the torch against a pile of other torches, and remounted. They emerged from the cave mouth, and Celeste caught her first

275

glimpse of the Waste itself.

A vast, nearly featureless plain stretched away as far as she could see, covered with a carpet of brown grass that bent before the eternal wind. To her left lay the distant smudge of a mountain range, and to her right spread endless steppe. A massive, sloping peak dominated the southern horizon, wreathed in strange formations of cloud. A moving mass of darker brown caught her eye, a herd of wild horses or the Waste antelope.

The Waste. The Ha'ashtari called it Shan'tari, the Land of the Horse. The word Ha'ashtari itself meant the People of the Horse. Celeste smiled, remembering the fierce, proud people of the Waste, and their love of freedom and their horses.

On either side of the cave mouth rose small hillocks, covered with the plains grass and a few scrawny bushes. The stream from the cave wound past, curving around behind her. Celeste turned in her saddle, and looked back. The land there rose in gentle waves, a series of eroded ridges, ending in a large mound with a cap of snow. She knew that beyond that last ridge the cliffs dropped to Aquarquff and the coastal dunes.

An icy blast of wind whipped around her, and she pulled up her hood, tightening the collar of the cloak. The horses' breath made little puffs of steam, torn away by the wind. While those in Aquarquff were enjoying the cool morning hours before the torrid heat of day, on the Waste above any warmth was a precious thing. Celeste appreciated her cloak and warm riding clothes.

Without a word, the Pathfinder rode on, following a path known only to him and his kin. Celeste squinted into the cold air, trying to see some sign of distant Carnac. She knew the effort was foolish, as Carnac lay deep in a river gorge. She also knew the plain was not as featureless and lifeless as it appeared. Hidden gullies, canyons, and scattered oases dotted the Waste, and antelope moved in great herds across the steppes, in their constant search for food and water. Wild horses roamed the Waste, the source of the magnificent Ha'ashtari broodstock. Predators also hunted the rolling plain, packs of hyenas, eagles, and others more terrifying.

Over it all soared the cloudless blue dome of sky, seeming larger here than anywhere else in the world. The silver arch looked close enough to touch, crisp and bright in the thin, cold air, so awesome and grand. Small wonder the Ha'ashtari considered it Heaven, the home of their gods.

A sound drew her attention from the sky, and Celeste saw three riders move out from the cover of a nearby hillock. The Pathfinder reined in his mount, but made no move to draw his sword. No one would be foolish enough to molest a Pathfinder in the Waste. To do so would mean certain death at the hands of the Ha'ashtari. As the three came closer, Celeste was amazed to see Morgan riding toward them, followed by Max and Taskin. Morgan and Max rode easily, swaying with the horses' movements, but Taskin rode stiffly, clutching at the reins. The men had travel packs and saddle bags on each horse. At the sight of them, Celeste was torn between relief and anger. Morgan had lied to her, deceived her, but he was here.

The Pathfinder turned his horse so that he sat between Celeste and the approaching riders. "What do you want, strangers? Are you mad to ride the Waste without a guide?" he called out hoarsely in the Trade language.

Morgan held up a hand. "Peace, Pathfinder. We would pay you to be our guide," he said in the same tongue.

Celeste spoke to the Pathfinder. "I know them. There is no danger," she said.

The man in blue ignored her. "My services have already been retained. You must seek another guide," he said.

The three riders reached them and stopped. Max urged his mount closer, leaning toward the waiting Pathfinder. He held out a handful of gold coins. "We'll pay for the privilege. We go to Carnac as well," he said.

The Pathfinder shook his head. "Return to Aquarquff. Hire your own Pathfinder," he said.

"We're here. You're here. Why not make some extra money?" Max said lightly, still offering the money.

"I don't want your gold," the Pathfinder said.

Max withdrew the coins and slipped them into a pocket, his face hardening. Morgan leaned forward, watching the Pathfinder.

"Will you wait for us? We wish to travel together," Morgan asked quietly.

"No," the man in blue said.

Celeste frowned, and Max grew very still. Taskin tensed, ready to jump off his horse and fight. Morgan spoke again, his eyes boring into the Pathfinder. "Celeste, I think you should come with us," he said.

"Maybe you're right," Celeste said, turning her horse to pass by the Pathfinder.

The Pathfinder reached out suddenly and seized Celeste's horse by the bridle. Max's hands dropped to his swords, and Morgan sat up straight in his saddle. There was a moment of tense silence, while the three men regarded each other. The Pathfinder looked deep into Max's cold blue eyes then shifted his gaze to Morgan's compelling gray stare. He did not see Celeste reach into her sleeve, resting her hand on the dagger hidden there. Finally, the Pathfinder relaxed, releasing Celeste's horse.

"Give me the money," the Pathfinder said gruffly.

Max tossed him the coins all at once, forcing the man in blue to use both hands to catch them. "Good choice," Max said, and then nodded to Celeste. "Greetings, Princess. Good to see you again," he said.

Celeste moved her horse away from the Pathfinder and turned to Morgan. "You lied to me. Then you just let me go, without even saying good-bye," she said. "How did you get here anyway? I thought you were on the Windrider."

Morgan looked mad and embarrassed and confused, all at the same time. He tried to think of something to say, but failed. Max spoke.

"Blame it all on me, Princess. I could see we were getting nowhere by arguing with you, and Morgan was coming along no matter what you said, so I opted for the better plan---outright deception. Sorry, Princess, but it had to be done. We slipped around the town ahead of you, borrowed some horses from the corral, rode up through the cave, and waited for you," Max explained.

"Borrowed some horses? You mean stole, don't you? I

278

saw the disturbance at the corral. Are you a thief, as well as a liar, Maximilian?" she asked.

"Princess, you stab me deeply. Whatever else I may be, I'm not a thief. We paid for the horses, although we didn't have the time to properly bargain with the guards. And I only lie when it serves the greater good," Max said.

"I couldn't let you leave," Morgan finally managed.

"See what I mean? He's totally smitten. Worthless without you," Max observed.

Celeste looked at Morgan. "I'm surprised the noble hero agreed to such measures," she said.

"He sacrificed his honor for love, Princess," Max said.

Morgan's glare would have stricken a faint-hearted man from the saddle, but Max merely smiled innocently back at the big man.

"Will you shut up? You've already made her mad at me," Morgan said, then turned to the Princess. "You needed an escort to Carnac. We'll see you safely there and go on to Dragonback."

Celeste sat straight in her saddle, squaring her shoulders. "Well, since I obviously have no say in this, you don't need my consent," she returned.

Celeste noticed something. "Where's Harkon?" she asked suddenly.

"He stayed with the Windrider," Max said.

The Pathfinder had stowed his coins. "We go. Now. We must be to Tau'kendi by nightfall," he said, urging his mount into the lead.

"Tau'kendi?" Max asked.

The Pathfinder ignored the question, and Celeste answered. "The oasis of Kendi. We must be spending the night there," she said.

"Don't let our guide get away, after all we've paid him," Max said, turning his horse to follow the Pathfinder.

Morgan and Max kept their horses even with Celeste's, flanking her on either side, while Taskin brought up the rear, shifting uncomfortably in his saddle.

"Is that the same Pathfinder you spoke to in Aquarquff?" Max asked quietly.

279

"I don't think so," Celeste said. "But who can tell, with those veils and robes?"

Max leaned close to the Princess. "Are they usually that reluctant to take on new customers?" he asked.

"Your approach was unusual, but he did react oddly, considering how much gold you offered him," Celeste said.

"Yes, we did neglect the paperwork," Max admitted.

"I don't trust him," Morgan said.

"Maybe being ambushed by three lying horse thieves put him off," Celeste said.

"Are you still mad at me?" Morgan asked the Princess.

Celeste regarded him for a moment, and then smiled. "No, you big oaf, I can't stay mad at you. Even though what you did was wrong and you know it. It may be totally selfish, but I'm glad you're here," she said, then glanced at Max. "You too, Max. I would have missed you."

"Did you find what you needed in the caves?" she asked.

Morgan suddenly put his finger to his lips, nodding toward their guide, and the three of them quietly let their horses drift back until they were a safe distance from the Pathfinder. The man in blue apparently did not notice, but Taskin flashed a question in Raav handtalk. Max answered him and Taskin rode around them to close the gap. As Taskin moved in behind him, the Pathfinder glanced back, but did not speak.

The Princess repeated her question. They all kept their voices low.

"Yes, I found what I was sent for," Morgan said, unsure how much he should tell the Princess.

Max frowned at the memory of the caves. "Morgan brought back several things. I'm not sure they were worth all the trouble, though," he answered.

Celeste glanced at Max. "Was there trouble?" she asked.

"Depends on what you mean by trouble. How about crawling through a maze of caverns filled with diabolical traps, with a determined bunch of Quffians on your heels?" Max asked with a wry smile.

Celeste studied Max for a moment. "You three do look a little worn," she observed, and then she turned and looked closer at Morgan's face. "How did you manage to get sunburned in a cave?"

Morgan rubbed his tender skin. "Gate effect," he said, somewhat absently.

"What?" Celeste asked.

"Going in, we went through the caves, but coming out, we used a Gate," he said.

"A Gate? A functioning Gate? Like the Empire used?" she asked skeptically.

"Yes, it was a Gate, still working after all this time," Morgan said.

"We stepped through, and ended up in a buried room in the dunes. I've used them before, with the Raavs, but I've never liked them," Max added.

"That was dangerous. You had no way of knowing what destination it was set for. You could have come out anywhere, or not at all," Celeste said.

"Exactly what I told Morgan. But he was determined," Max said, then paused. "He didn't want to miss your departure."

Celeste glanced at Morgan and smiled. Morgan looked embarrassed.

"Why were the Quffians following you?" she asked.

"They might have been simple thieves or spies for the Mhoul. Who knows?" Max said.

"What happened to the Quffians?" Celeste asked.

"They died," Max said.

"What a night. You must be exhausted. What did you find in the cache?" Celeste said.

"Another sword. One Morgan claims will kill Mhoul. A jewel for finding Gates, a piece of rock with some carving on it, and a set of statues. And I found myself a fine mail shirt made of ebonite," Max said.

"Rocks, jewels, swords, and statues. First, Morgan won't touch a sword, and then he almost gets himself killed so he can have two," she said.

281

Morgan shrugged. "The Monachus thought we would need those artifacts. I didn't question them," he said.

Celeste sighed. "Oh well, you came back safe and you're here now. Although I hope you haven't made a mistake. This detour could jeopardize your mission," she said.

"It was a risk I was willing to take," Morgan said.

"I tried to warn him what love would do. Now I fear for the future of our world," Max said, with mock severity.

"Will you please stop that?" Morgan complained.

Celeste noticed that all three men now wore heavy wool clothes. Max and Taskin had thick cloaks with hoods, and Morgan wore his Iosian cloak. "I see you have brought warm clothes. You'll need them. It gets cold up here," she said.

"Taurus had some on board, for when he goes north to Skorn. They're itchy but hold the heat well," Max explained.

Their conversation lagged, as they all turned their attention to their surroundings. It was nearing mid-morning, the pale sun climbing into the endless sky. On the high plains, the sun shed little heat, and Max pulled the furred collar of his cloak closer, shivering in the chill. An insistent wind found its way into every opening, tormenting him with icy fingers. The silver arch looked frozen solid, and Asa hung near the northern horizon. No clouds marred the blue expanse, only a slight haze to the north.

They passed a cluster of cacti, nearly round and huddled close to the ground, armored with a coat of thick, hollow spines. On the other side of them stood a huge ant mound, its rounded top nearly level with the horse's backs. Max could see the large, reddish insects swarming over the littered surface of the mound. He also noticed that the Pathfinder paused and carefully studied the ground between the cacti and the mound, as if some danger lay there. Evidently their guide did not find what he sought, for he moved quickly on.

Max nodded at the man in blue. "What was he doing?" he asked.

"Those ants will savagely defend their mounds. Even if you cross one of the trails, they'll attack. He was making sure we wouldn't disturb them," Celeste said.

"Wonderful country," Taskin muttered.

After a time they rode through a shallow swale, and then onto a flat area riddled with burrows, marked by mounds of earth. Small, pudgy rodents sat on their haunches and watched them pass. If a horse and rider came too close, they whistled shrilly and disappeared in a flash of brown. The burrows were grouped into two areas, with a space of undisturbed earth between.

Celeste nodded toward the rodents. "Wasterats. The Ha'ashtari call them mus'roo. The males are on the left, and the females on the right. They mate in that area between the colonies. A dangerous time for them---the predators eat well at mating time. They're quite vulnerable away from their burrows and when they're mating, they are . . . distracted," she said.

"I've found the opposite sex is always dangerous," Max said.

Celeste glanced at him, seeing his wicked smile, and laughed.

A shadow passed over them, and Max's hands moved to his sword hilts as he looked up into the sky. A large bird swooped toward the wasterat colony, its dark brown feathers rippling in the wind. The rodents squealed in concert, and suddenly they were gone. The eagle pulled out of its dive with a raucous cry, then circled once and drifted away.

Max leaned on his pommel, flexing cramped muscles. "You seem to know the Waste, Princess," he observed.

"The Waste and the Ha'ashtari were one of my main areas of study while I was at Carnac. I went on several field trips," she said.

"How did the Ha'ashtari react to being studied?" Max asked.

"The Baron Serenus went with me. The Ha'ashtari made no objection," Celeste said.

Max gazed at the endless plain. "There's a sense of freedom here. No cities, no crowded streets. It's too cold though, and I'm not overly fond of horses as a mode of travel," he said.

"You don't like horses?" Celeste asked.

"If Iosus had intended men to ride horses, he would have designed them differently," Max said, then looked at Taskin, who still swayed uncomfortably with his horse's fast walk. "Now there's a gentleman who will suffer before this ride is over."

283

The sun was nearing the western horizon when the Pathfinder turned his mount to the right, winding down an eroded gully. A small canyon opened up before them, and nestled in the shelter of the canyon walls lay an oasis. A spring bubbled from the side of the cliff, its stream of clear water gathering in a stone catchment below. A riot of vegetation clustered around the catchment, and several trees stood nearby. The trees had rough, almost shaggy bark, their tops crowned with a cluster of spiny leaves, and scattered amongst the leaves were dark fruits. Some small animal vanished into the bushes at their approach.

The Pathfinder stopped. "Tau'kendi. We will camp here for the night. You will care for your own horses, and set up your own camp. I am a Pathfinder, not a groom or camp servant," he said, then dismounted and led his horse away.

"Pleasant fellow," Max remarked. "Should I kill him?"

"Not yet, Max. We still need him. With him, we have safe passage through the Waste. Without him, the Ha'ashtari will kill us at the first opportunity," Celeste said.

Max sighed. "I hate it when I have to stifle my instincts. I don't think it's healthy," he said.

Morgan grimaced. "It's your instincts that are unhealthy," he said.

They watered their horses at the spring, and gave them some oats from their supplies. Then they hobbled the horses, letting them graze on the thick grass of the oasis. The Pathfinder withdrew from them, erecting his tent near the base of the cliff wall. Celeste and the others all carried one person tents of the Ha'ashtari style, simple structures of hide, with wooden frames. In Aquarquff, Morgan had taken tents for his group while Max was obtaining their horses. Celeste selected a tentsite and set up her tent with practiced ease. Morgan and the others watched her, unfamiliar with the type of tent used in the Waste. When she was nearly finished, they started on their own and managed to accomplish the task without too much trouble.

By the time it was fully dark, they had a small fire going, and were heating travel rations from their packs. The Pathfinder ate alone, and did not build a fire. After they ate, they sat watching the small fire, listening to the sounds of the Waste at night. The temperature dropped sharply after sunset, and the wind picked up, rushing by overhead, swirling into the canyon. Taskin was glad the canyon sheltered them from the worst of it. He stretched out his fingers toward the feeble warmth of their fire. A strange sound cut through the night, a burst of wild cackling, like insane laughter, and a chill not born of the cold washed down Taskin's spine.

Celeste looked up, the firelight playing across her face. "The hyenas of the Waste. Madstalkers, the Centaurs call them. Hee'ra, in the Ha'ashtari tongue. Cowards, but dangerous to a lone rider, or when they're especially hungry," she said.

The sound came again, farther away this time. "They hunt," Celeste said.

Max got stiffly to his feet, wincing. "I'm going to bed. Thanks to Morgan and his treasure hunt, I got little sleep last night," he said, then stepped out of the circle of firelight.

Taskin glanced at Morgan and the Princess, and then bid them good night as well. He limped to his tent, obviously sore from a day on horseback.

Morgan shifted nervously, realizing he was alone with Celeste. He leaned back, looking up at the brilliant stars. Morgan tried to think of something to say, but the words would not come. He glanced over at the Princess. She was still watching the fire. Morgan studied her beautiful features, and felt even more uncomfortable. Somehow, she felt his gaze and they locked eyes for a moment. Celeste smiled, and then looked up at the stars and the arch.

"This is rather romantic, alone with you under the stars," she said.

Morgan groaned. "That's all I need right now," he said. "Romance."

Celeste looked at him, frowning. "You didn't have to come," she said.

Morgan regarded her. "Yes, I did. I couldn't stand the thought of you alone out here," he said.

"Were you just feeling protective, or was it something deeper?" Celeste asked.

"What do you want from me? I have no idea what my feelings mean," Morgan said.

"What are you feeling? Maybe I can help you," Celeste said.

"Please, Celeste. Give me time. This is hard for me," he said.

"Men. Emotional midgets," Celeste said, then leaned back and looked at the stars. "The stars are beautiful," she said.

Morgan relaxed; glad they were heading back to safer territory. "They are. I haven't spent much time just looking at them," he said.

"All three moons are up. So peaceful looking," Celeste said.

"Asa, Mora, and Damon. The three Fates," Morgan said.

Celeste's gaze shifted to the arch. "Gallinor, the Bridge of the Gods. The Ha'ashtari heaven," she said.

"Hard to believe the Mercator Empire put it there," Morgan said.

"Although they did build the floating city of Craig Phadrig," Celeste observed.

"So it is said," Morgan agreed.

"And they created the Gates---the Landgates, the Worldgates, and the Fargate," Celeste said.

"The Fargate . . . their greatest achievement, and their doom," Morgan said.

"The centaurs teach that the arch is somehow responsible for our long lives and the lack of sickness on Kalnaroag," Celeste said.

"How is it possible?" Morgan asked.

"No one remembers. Not any more," Celeste said. "I wonder what they were like. The people of the Mercator Empire. Nearly gods, it seems."

"And yet they're gone, their civilization ruined. Not gods, then," he said.

"We've lost so much," she said.

"And the Mhoul want to destroy what little is left. We have to stop them," Morgan said.

"Oh Morgan, I hope I haven't made it worse for you. I feel guilty for wanting to be with you. But I can't help it," Celeste said.

"I know how you feel. I shouldn't even be here. I should be on the Windrider, sailing for Dragonback. But I don't care," Morgan said.

"Let's just pray we haven't done something terrible, that we'll regret," Celeste said.

Morgan yawned. "Max was right. I need some sleep. Good night, Princess."

Morgan got to his feet and walked toward the tent. Celeste watched him go.

CHAPTER TWENTY-ONE
BETRAYAL

Morgan woke suddenly, sensing something was wrong, and rolled to his feet, sword in hand. He stepped out of his tent. The rosy glow of dawn lit the eastern sky, smothering the last few stars, and turning the arch into a band of silver flame. The cold air struck him like a blow, and his breath steamed, the small cloud whipping away in the chill breeze.

Max walked toward him from the direction of the Pathfinder's tent, shoving the man in blue ahead of him, each thrust enough to stagger the man. The Pathfinder's veil had been torn away, and he had a welt on his cheek. He was unarmed, his torn sleeve revealing a hidden dagger sheath, and his sword scabbard empty. Max gave the Pathfinder one last push that sent him stumbling toward Morgan. He gestured contemptuously at the man in blue, who stood with eyes downcast and fists clenched.

"You should've let me kill him yesterday. He was trying to sneak off, and take our horses with him. When I stopped him, he tried to stab me," Max said.

Morgan put the point of his sword against the man's chin, lifting. The Pathfinder met his gaze defiantly, his eyes bright in his swarthy face.

"Obviously he was unsuccessful in his attempt," Morgan observed, then pressed his point against the man's throat. "Speak, man. What's the meaning of this?"

The Pathfinder swallowed, the movement shifting the point of Morgan's sword, then he spoke, but in a language Morgan could not understand. The Princess' voice came from behind him, speaking in the same tongue. The Pathfinder's eyes narrowed and he stared at the woman who had appeared at Morgan's side. Her hair was tangled from sleep, and her clothes rumpled, but she held a dagger in her hand, and her eyes were sharp. She asked a question in the Pathfinder's language, demanding some answer.

The Pathfinder's face hardened, and Morgan could tell he had decided something. Morgan tensed; expecting a fight, but the man only clenched his jaw and ground his teeth together. Celeste moved suddenly, reaching out and grabbing the man's chin.

"Stop him," she shouted, pulling down on his mouth.

Morgan lowered his sword, afraid she would cut herself. Max stepped forward. "Stop him from what?" Max asked.

The Pathfinder did not resist the Princess, and his mouth came open, a thin stream of blue trickling from one corner. He eyes rolled up in his head, and he convulsed, his entire body moving in a spasmodic wave. Morgan shoved the Princess aside, uncertain what was happening. The man in blue sank to his knees, and he retched dryly. His arms shook at his sides, his fists clenching until crimson leaked from between his fingers. Then he folded backwards, his legs pinned under him. Max stepped smoothly out of the way as he fell, and stared down at him. The Pathfinder lay twitching, vacant eyes fixed on the dying stars.

"What happened? I didn't hit him that hard," Max said.

Morgan sheathed his sword, scanning the canyon for any other signs of danger. Celeste put her dagger in the arm sheath, and knelt beside the Pathfinder.

"He's dead," Celeste said, and then looked into the open mouth, now stained with blue. "He had a poison filled tooth. Good thing he didn't bite you."

"Why did he do this?" Morgan asked.

"What did you say he was doing when you found him?" Celeste asked Max.

"He was trying to leave, and steal our horses," Max repeated.

Celeste frowned in confusion. "Are you sure, maybe he was just bringing them to water?" she asked.

Max laughed, a short, harsh bark. "Is that why he tried to kill me, because I might help him water the horses?" he said.

Taskin had joined them, limping over from his tent. Celeste studied the Pathfinder, who lay still now.

"Why would he do that? The Pathfinders are bound by years of tradition. To betray someone who's paid the guide price is unthinkable to them. Once passage is purchased, the traveler is untouchable. It doesn't make any sense," she said.

Max rubbed his beard. "Well, he tried to touch me, in a most unfriendly fashion. Perhaps he doesn't think much of tradition," he said.

"Or maybe he was motivated by something stronger than honor or tradition," Morgan said.

"What are you suggesting?" Celeste asked.

"We all have some powerful enemies," Morgan said.

"The Mhoul again? First the Windrider, then the Quffians, and now the Pathfinders. The Princess must really be important to them," Max said.

"It may have been the Princess at first, but now I think they want you and me as well, especially since we entered the cache," Morgan said.

Celeste shook her head in wonder. "They must have spies and agents everywhere. What an organization," she said.

"Well, if the Monachus wanted Morgan to flush out the hidden Mhoul network, he's succeeding at that," Max noted.

"Now all we have to do is survive the flushing," Taskin said.

Morgan frowned. "It still doesn't make sense. What would happen if we were found by the Ha'ashtari, without a guide?" he asked.

"The Ha'ashtari are bound by their law and codes of honor. If you are outside the protection of the Pathfinders, you're at their mercy. Trouble is, they have no mercy. They would probably kill anyone who fought bravely. People they considered cowards, they would enslave. Sometimes outsiders may be taken as slaves even if they showed no fear, if some warrior found them pleasing. They would keep any of our possessions that interested them," Celeste said.

"Why do they want slaves?" Taskin asked.

"The Ha'ashtari are too proud to work, they live by raiding and trading. All menial tasks are performed by slaves, even tending the oases gardens," Celeste said.

"Do they ever sell their slaves or booty?" Morgan asked.

"Well, yes, if the price was right," Celeste said, with a puzzled look.

"That must have been his plan," Morgan said softly.

"So Morgan, Taskin, and I would fight bravely and die, our belongings would fall into Ha'ashtari hands. The Princess, being beautiful and pleasing to any man, would be kept as a slave. Mhoul agents could then purchase the Princess and the things we recovered from the cache. Brutal, but effective," Max concluded.

"Is that what you think happened? Someone paid the Pathfinder to leave us here for the Ha'ashtari?" Celeste asked.

"That couldn't have been the original plan. They didn't know we'd be with the Princess. She was supposed to be alone. At first, they were probably just going to lead her out into the Waste, take her captive, and then deliver her to the Mhoul. When the three of us showed up, their plans had to change. That's why he was so reluctant to let us join you. This Pathfinder must have come up with the alternate scheme last night---a plan born out of desperation. Even so, it would accomplish most of their purposes, except taking Max and I alive," Morgan said.

"I still can't believe the Pathfinders capable of such treachery," Celeste said.

"Maybe it wasn't gold, but some threat that the Pathfinders couldn't ignore. We may never know," Morgan said.

Morgan squatted on his haunches, looking up at Celeste. "You speak the Pathfinder's language. What was he saying?" he asked.

"Just a comment on your lineage, and an assurance that he was not going to answer any questions," Celeste said.

"What did you say to him? Whatever it was, it made him decide to kill himself," Max said.

"I asked him if the Pathfinders had lost all honor and turned to betrayal and cowardice. But I doubt that's why he committed suicide," Celeste said.

Dawn came swiftly in the Waste. The last of the stars had vanished and the rising sun lit the sky. A shadow passed over them and everyone started. Max squinted up into the gash of blue above them. Several large birds circled lazily overhead.

Celeste gestured at the Pathfinder's body. "We should bury

him, before the scavengers gather. Even now, those vultures will signal any passing Ha'ashtari that there's been a death here," Celeste said.

The Princess bent down beside the body and opened the collar. A small leather sack hung around the Pathfinder's neck, which Celeste removed. She opened the bag, and inside laid a smooth translucent stone, with a single mark on it.

"What is that?" Max asked.

"His soul stone. They're a rare agate-like stone, the Ha'ashtari and the Pathfinders search the streambeds for them. They believe the stones are the tears of the gods, and consider them vessels of the soul. The Ha'ashtari give them to their babies at birth, when they believe the new soul enters the stone. They carve each stone with a symbol that identifies the wearer. All their lives both Ha'ashtari and Pathfinders wear the stones in these leather pouches around their necks. Even though they're half-caste, the Ha'ashtari allow the Pathfinders to wear soul stones, as a sign of their heritage," Celeste explained.

Morgan and Max buried the Pathfinder in a shallow grave near the cliff wall while Taskin took down the man's tent and placed it with their gear. Celeste placed the stone from the bag on a flat stone near the grave. Finding a large rock, she smashed the stone to bits. She left the bag near the debris.

"Why did you do that?" Morgan asked.

"When a Ha'ashtari or Pathfinder dies, the soul stones are traditionally placed under the open sky on a rock altar, for easy retrieval by the gods. If a soul stone is shattered before the gods arrive, the soul has no resting place. It wanders, until the Servants of Fear hunt the soul down and imprison it forever. An unthinkable fate, by Ha'ashtari and Pathfinder standards. Destruction of the stone is a penalty reserved for the worst cowards and traitors. By smashing the Pathfinder's soul stone, I've branded him a traitor and coward under Ha'ashtari law," Celeste said.

"Harsh," Max said.

"He deserved it. He violated centuries of tradition," Celeste said.

292

Celeste went through the Pathfinder's belongings, and distributed anything she thought useful to the others. Then they began dismantling their own tents and loading their belongings.

Celeste remembered something. "Taskin, come with me," she said.

"Where are you going?" Morgan asked.

"Each oasis has a cache of food and supplies. We may need more supplies. You two finish here. Be sure and fill all the canteens. No telling where the next water is," she said.

Celeste took Taskin and began searching along the base of the canyon walls. She soon found the cache and returned with grain, field rations, and five tightly rolled bundles.

"What are those?" Max asked, indicating the bundles.

"Horse blankets. Made of hor'gaa wing membrane, light and tough. They keep the heat in and the weather out," Celeste explained.

"Wing membranes? Big enough to cover a horse?" Taskin asked nervously.

"Yes," Celeste said.

"Let's avoid the hor'gaa," Max suggested.

Max and Morgan caught the horses and began loading them, putting the extra gear on the Pathfinder's horse. Morgan wrapped the aurellium sword and tied it beside the pack. As Celeste and Taskin were returning, Max mounted his horse.

"I'll be right back. I'm going to take a look around," he said.

They finished loading the horses, then tethered them, and gathered back at the campsite. The sun rose above the canyon rim, driving away the cold shadows. Max returned, his face red from the frigid wind.

"We had visitors last night," he said.

"How many?" Morgan asked.

"Two. They rode to the canyon rim and then left, heading back toward the coast," Max said.

"Did you see anyone?" Morgan asked.

"Nothing moving but some antelope," Max said.

"Were the horses shod or unshod?" Celeste asked.

Max looked confused. "Shod. Why?" he asked.

293

"More Pathfinders? What's going on here?" Celeste asked.

"That's what I would like to know. Who were they?" Morgan asked.

"Ha'ashtari don't shoe their horses. No one rides the Waste without a Pathfinder, so one or maybe both of them were Pathfinders," Celeste explained.

"They were probably coming to pick you up, to take you back to the Mhoul. When they saw you weren't alone, they left. Did they talk to our Pathfinder?" Morgan asked.

"It looks like he was up there too. Sometime in the night," Max said.

"It's hard enough to imagine one Pathfinder turning traitor, but two or three? This is incredible. No one will believe it," Celeste said.

Morgan studied the Princess. "We'll need your knowledge of this place, and the Ha'ashtari, if we are to live through this. Tell us what to do now," Morgan said.

Celeste squatted down and drew a crude map in the sand with a stick. "Here we are, a day's ride from the cliffs above Aquarquff. Carnac is about here, in the Great Rift. The arc massif is here, an ancient volcano crater that was later fortified in a settlement attempt. To the north are the mountains along the Seir, the Ma'aran Kus. The southern mountains, the Sa'aran Kus, lay along here. Beyond Carnac is the Argurion river, which flows from the Ma'aran Kus into the Nageff, through the Barrier Lift, and down into Aijalon. Kalixalven is here, west of the Argurion, across the Ma'aran Kus. There are oases scattered throughout the Waste, and some marshy areas," Celeste explained.

"Can we make it back to Aquarquff?" Taskin asked.

Morgan shook his head. "I wouldn't recommend that. The Windrider and its crew have left, to meet us at Kalixalven. We have no allies there now, especially with our hasty purchase of mounts and supplies. Not to mention whoever hired the band of Quffians that followed us into the cave, and the men that tried to abduct the Princess. We can't even trust the Pathfinders anymore," he said.

Celeste tapped her chin with the stick. "I agree. Besides, as I said before, no one will believe a Pathfinder turned on his own party.

Most will say we killed him without cause. The Pathfinders and the Ha'ashtari are our enemies now. Reaching Carnac is our only hope," she said.

"Will the centaurs believe us?" Morgan asked.

"Serenus will know I'm not lying. He might be able to convince the others," Celeste said.

"Well, I'd rather die in the wide open spaces, fighting the Ha'ashtari, than go back to that squalid town and kill Quffians," Max said.

"How far is Carnac?" Taskin asked.

"About 900 stadia, maybe five days ride---if we headed straight for it," Celeste said.

"Once you're in Carnac, can we get an escort to Kalixalven?" Morgan asked.

"I think I can persuade Serenus to send someone with you," Celeste said.

"All right then, it's settled. We go to Carnac," Max said.

"So exactly how do we do that, Princess?" Morgan asked.

Celeste pointed at her map. "I see three choices. First, we could ride straight for Carnac, and try to reach the city before the Ha'ashtari catch us. Second, we turn north to the foothills of the Ma'aran Kus, and ride along the edge of the Waste, then turn south again to Carnac. We might be able to avoid the Ha'ashtari if we stay in the foothills. Third, we could loop south in a large arc and approach Carnac from the southeast. The last thing the Ha'ashtari would expect of us," Celeste said.

"I prefer the foothills route. Even if the Ha'ashtari found us, we'd have the advantage of terrain," Morgan said.

"I agree. It might give us a better chance," Max said.

Celeste shook her head. "I say we go south. Running straight for Carnac would be suicide. The Ha'ashtari will definitely watch that route. The foothills will be too slow; the horses won't be able to cover as much ground. South has the advantage of surprise. They can't know we're familiar with the Waste. They'll think us ignorant outlanders, who will choose the easiest route," Celeste said.

"You were here before. Do the Ha'ashtari know you?" Morgan

asked.

"It has been years since I rode these plains. I doubt we'll encounter anyone who remembers me," she said.

"South it is. May Iosus be with us," Morgan said.

CHAPTER TWENTY-TWO
KA'CHI

Morgan and his companions rode out of Tau'kendi and turned south, with Taskin leading the Pathfinder's horse. Celeste guided them; following draws and gullies, staying off the ridges. They all watched the plains around them, searching for any sign of the Ha'ashtari. They passed more of the giant ant mounds, and saw a herd of the Waste antelope, large, shaggy brutes, with wicked looking spiral horns. The antelope moved in a vast herd, the weight of their passage making the earth tremble, and a cloud of dust marking their route.

Celeste and the others stopped to watch them pass. "The Ha'ashtari call them ko'raa. They hunt them in elaborate rituals, and use almost every part of those they kill. The hides and hair are used for clothing, the horns for bows and lance tips. The nomads eat the meat, drying it for meals on horseback. The ko'raa are the lifeblood of the Ha'ashtari," Celeste explained.

Most of the day passed without incident. They kept a steady pace, alternating between a fast walk and a trot, sparing the horses. Celeste showed them how to open one of the cacti, which were filled with fresh, pure water, and they all drank and refilled canteens. They ate while riding, chewing cold rations. The monotonous terrain, gently rolling plains broken only by shallow gullies and washes, stretched to the horizon and the great peak that waited there. The huge sky loomed overhead, silent and cold.

It was nearly dusk when they saw him. A lone Ha'ashtari, on a ridge ahead, outlined by the setting sun.

Max pulled out his bow. "I can kill him from here. He's an easy target, against the sun like that," he said.

Celeste rode over and put her hand on Max's arm. "He's showing himself to us, to let us know we've been found. You can't use the bow, it would be a violation of Ka'chi," she said.

"And why would I care about Ka'chi? Whatever that is," Max asked.

297

Celeste watched the Ha'ashtari, who had not moved. "You have to understand the Ha'ashtari. Courage in battle is everything to them, and they have developed a strict code of honor and bravery, the Ka'chi. It's complex and confusing to outsiders. They'll follow Ka'chi rigidly, unless the enemy violates Ka'chi and shows himself to be without honor.

As long as we comply with Ka'chi, I know the rules, what they'll do next. If we violate Ka'chi, that man's entire tribe will hunt us down and kill us, or worse yet, take us captive. According to Ka'chi, using the bow in battle to kill from a distance is considered cowardly," she said.

"What? These people are experts with the bow," Max protested.

"The bow is used only for the challenge and the hunt, to kill the ko'raa. Within Ka'chi they aren't used to kill human enemies," Celeste explained.

Max looked at Morgan. "These Ha'ashtari are worse than you, with their ridiculous codes," he said.

"So we comply with Ka'chi. What can we expect?" Morgan asked.

"They'll start with equal numbers of hunters and hunted, and add hunters only if the quarry proves itself worthy. They won't use bows; they'll attack with lances and knives. If they can, they'll sneak into our camps and mark us, without killing us. That is the ten'paa, the highest test of courage and skill. In general, there will be a series of feints, and then the kill.

If we violate the Ka'chi, that will invoke the Jinn'she, a type of holy war, and the entire tribe will attack and kill us without further delay. Although if the Ha'ashtari are convinced we killed the Pathfinder without a good reason, they might declare Jinn'she immediately.

If you show fear, they'll make a slave of you, and torment you the rest of your lives. They feel only the brave deserve to die in battle," she said.

"And what will happen to you?" Morgan asked.

"The Ha'ashtari consider their women equals in warfare, and they're treated the same under the law. If I fight bravely, I'll be regarded as a warrior," she explained.

"Promise me you won't fight. Then you will live," Morgan urged.

Celeste glared at him. "I'll live, as a slave, branded a coward, some warrior's plaything. Is that what you want?" she asked.

"I want you to live. If you're alive, there's always some hope of rescue," Morgan said.

"Rescue? By who? The only ones who'll come for me will be Mhoul agents. Besides, I'm Thraen. Our women fight, we aren't cowards," Celeste said.

"Please, Celeste. Don't risk yourself. You're too important," Morgan said.

Celeste locked eyes with him. "If it were you, would you do this?" she asked.

Morgan grimaced. "But it's not me, you are the Princess of . . . ," he began.

"If it were you, would you do this?" Celeste repeated.

Morgan was silent a moment, then slowly shook his head.

"Then don't insult me by asking. Some things are more important than life," she said, then paused. "Now, where was I? If we comply with Ka'chi, it will give us time, time we desperately need to reach Carnac."

"Princess, it is unlikely we'll ever reach Carnac," Max said.

"I've come too far to give up now," Celeste said defiantly.

"I didn't say anything about giving up. I will kill every Ha'ashtari I can. I just don't waste any time on false hopes," Max said.

"Yes, a most encouraging companion in battle," Morgan said absently, watching the Ha'ashtari scout.

As the sun dipped below the horizon, the Ha'ashtari raised his lance in salute, and disappeared. Darkness began to wash across the endless plains, and a cold wind stirred the horses' manes.

"We should continue riding, make as much distance as we can," Morgan said.

Celeste pulled her cloak tighter. "Not a good idea. The Waste is dangerous by day, worse by night. We should find shelter and go on tomorrow," she said.

"And just wait here for the Ha'ashtari? I'd rather move on," Max said.

Celeste chewed her lip. "We can try it. But I still advise against it," she said.

"You make the call. If you say stay, we stay," Morgan assured her.

"No, let's ride on. It might be worth the risk," Celeste decided.

It was soon fully dark, the stars sharp in the cold air. They rode carefully, letting the horses find their way. The arch touched the plains with silver, and Asa lit the northern sky. The wind blew harder, numbing exposed flesh.

Asa hung high in the sky when it happened. The wind shifted suddenly, and the horses sniffed the air, their nostrils widening. Something they smelled made them very nervous, and they started snorting and stomping. Celeste reined in her horse, scanning the moonlit plain.

Morgan rode up beside her. "What is it?" he asked.

"The horses smell something. Do you see anything?" she asked.

They all searched the darkness, but Max was the first to spot the thing. They followed his pointing finger, and saw a dark shape on a nearby ridge, sleek and menacing, about the size of a small horse.

"What is that?" Taskin asked.

"It looks like a sith'gaa," Celeste said.

"A what?" Max asked.

"A sith'gaa. A large black cat, like a panther. It hunts at night, often preying on the wild horses," Celeste explained.

The creature on the ridge raised its head and screamed, a ragged, horrible sound that filled the night. The horses reared in fright, and then Taskin's horse went into a blind panic, running headlong away from the cat, dragging the Pathfinder's horse with it. Taskin hung on grimly, sawing on the reins without effect. He bounced from side to side, but managed to stay on the bolting horse. In moments, Taskin and the terrified horses had been engulfed by the night.

Morgan started to follow, but the cat screamed again, forcing him to concentrate on controlling his own horse. Max pulled out his bow and nocked an arrow. He raised the bow, but the black shape had vanished.

"Where did it go?" he asked.

"The Ha'ashtari believe they're not a mortal animal, but some type of phantom. A guardian spirit for Ha'ashtari heroes," Celeste said.

Morgan stared into the darkness. "We better find Taskin. He may be hurt," he said.

Taskin stood holding the Pathfinder's horse, trying to calm the terrified animal. His horse laid thrashing on its side, in the middle of a Wasterat colony. In the dark Taskin's horse had stepped in a burrow opening, and the badly broken front leg was still jammed in the hole. Morgan dismounted and walked his horse over to Taskin. Taskin, although bruised and covered with dirt, seemed unhurt.

"What happened?" Morgan asked quietly.

"He was running and then we went down. I fell off and plowed into one of the burrow mounds. When I got up, I could see my horse was hurt, broke its leg in one of the burrows. I untied the Pathfinder's horse, and you came. What should we do?" Taskin asked.

"I don't see that we have any choice. We have to kill it," Morgan said.

"We needed that horse," Taskin said. "I'm sorry."

"It's not your fault," Morgan said.

The Princess joined them. "Now you see why I wasn't eager to ride the Waste at night," she said, watching the injured horse.

"I'll do it," Morgan said, reaching for his sword.

"No, horses are sacred to the Ha'ashtari. This is a matter of Ka'chi," Celeste said.

"I'm not going to leave it here to suffer," Morgan protested.

Celeste handed him her reins. "I'm not suggesting that. But it must be done properly, according to Ka'chi. You can't just hack his head off with a sword. Stay here," she said.

Taskin and Morgan watched as Celeste moved around the horse, avoiding the flailing hooves. Max waited nearby, studying the starlit sky.

"What was that thing back there?" Taskin asked Morgan.

"It's called a sith'gaa, some kind of predator. I couldn't see it clearly, but it looked like a huge black cat. Max tried to shoot it, but it disappeared without a trace," Morgan answered.

"It sure scared the horses," Taskin said.

"It was that bloodcurdling scream. I wanted to run too," Morgan said.

Celeste drew one of her daggers, and then stepped close to the horse. Her blade flashed in the moonlight, and the horse squealed in pain. Its jugular vein severed, the horse soon bled to death and lay still. Celeste drew a complicated symbol on the horse's forehead with her bloody knife, then cleaned her blade in the stiff grass and stood.

"Better collect your gear, Taskin. We have to leave now," she said.

Morgan held the horses as Taskin and Max removed Taskin's saddle and gear from the dead horse. Celeste took the reins to her horse, leaving Morgan with the other three. She watched Taskin and Max without speaking.

"I'm sorry. We should have stopped at sundown," Morgan said.

Celeste sighed. "I just hate to kill a horse. They're such noble animals."

Taskin had transferred his saddle and gear to the Pathfinder's horse. He and Max had redistributed the most important items from the pack on the Pathfinder's horse and left the rest. Taskin took a last look at his former mount, and climbed into the saddle again. The cackle of a hyena pack came with the wind.

"Can we go now?" Max said. "I'm freezing."

They rode a safe distance from the dead horse, to avoid the hyenas and any other scavengers that might be attracted to the body. They descended into a shallow swale out of the wind, where Celeste showed them how to dig trenches just big enough for their bodies, and cover them with the tents, forming snug beds. The earth would insulate against the cold, and the tent cover kept out the wind. They tethered the horses nearby and Morgan opened his pack, pulling out the statues from the cache.

"You never did tell us what those were," Max said.

"You create a perimeter with these statues. They're activated by pressing on the head. Then you take this bracelet, and wear it on your arm. If anything approaches the wards, the bracelet will make your arm tingle, and wake you up. Nothing can get past them, and we can get a good night's sleep," Morgan explained.

Max studied the statues skeptically. "It sounds good, but I'll sleep lightly just the same," he said.

Morgan set one of the figurines at each corner of the camp, and kept the bracelet next to his skin. He slipped into his tent and wrapped the blankets tightly around him. The wind carried the sounds of the hyenas feeding on Taskin's horse, a chorus of cackling and snarling that normally would have kept him awake. In spite of the noise, he slept deeply, tired from the long day in the saddle and confident that the wards would alert him to any intruder.

Nothing triggered the wards, and they slept late the next morning. Morgan lifted the tent flap and crawled out. Max squatted nearby, studying a nearby ridge. Morgan followed his gaze and stiffened. Five Ha'ashtari waited on the ridge, sitting on their horses, the morning sun at their backs. Morgan joined Max.

"How long have they been there?" Morgan asked.

"I don't know. I just got up and saw them," Max answered.

A sound came from behind them and Celeste joined the two men. Taskin's head appeared from under his tent flap, and he squinted toward them.

"Five," the Princess commented.

"And how does that fit into Ka'chi? There are only three men in our party," Max noted.

"As I said, they treat women equally. They've sent a warrior to meet me," she said.

Max gestured at the waiting warriors. "But what about the fifth rider?" he asked.

"The fifth is an observer. He will not fight, this time," Celeste answered.

"Will they attack now?" Morgan asked.

"Probably not. They will likely follow us a while, to test our nerves with waiting," Celeste said.

"What if we attack them?" Max asked.

"By the time you rode up there, they would be gone. No, they'll choose the time and place," she said.

"I don't like these rules," Max muttered.

One of the Ha'ashtari raised his lance, turning the point downward, and then he rode toward them, while the other four waited on the ridge.

Celeste frowned. "They want to talk," she said.

"Talk is good," Max observed.

"I'll see what they want," Celeste said.

"I'm going with you," Morgan said.

Celeste shrugged. "If you want," she said, her eyes on the approaching rider.

"Max, you and Taskin stay here," Morgan said.

"Call if you need anything," Max said.

Morgan and Celeste walked toward the Ha'ashtari. Morgan kept his hand on his sword hilt. The warrior stopped a few paces away and regarded them, his tattooed features harsh in the cold light. He was dressed like the Ha'ashtari in Aquarquff, except he wore the hide cloak. He held the lance to one side, still point down.

Celeste greeted him, speaking in Ha'ashtari. The warrior's eyes narrowed, and then he answered in the same language.

"Speak in Trade. I want to know what's going on," Morgan whispered to the Princess.

"I will. I just wanted him to know that I spoke his language," Celeste said.

"You have the Pathfinder's horse. Did you kill him?" the Ha'ashtari asked, using the Trade language. He had evidently overheard their exchange.

"No, he killed himself," Celeste said warily.

"We found his body, in a shallow grave, in Tau'kendi. His soul stone was shattered. Why?" the nomad asked.

"What is your name?" Morgan asked.

The Ha'ashtari studied Morgan for a moment. "I am Ha'korl,

304

of the Meng'tari. Who are you, outlander?" he asked.

"I am Morgan, formerly a Raav Commander," Morgan said.

Ha'korl raised his eyebrows. "Raavs. I've heard of them. They were said to be brave warriors. They never came here," he said.

"There was no evil in the Waste. I fear that has changed," Morgan said.

"What are you saying, outlander?" Ha'korl asked.

Celeste put her hand on Morgan's arm. "Our Pathfinder tried to leave us at the oasis and take our horses. When we stopped him, he killed himself," she said.

Ha'korl swung his leg over the horse and slid to the ground. He stalked toward them and jammed the lance into the ground at their feet. Morgan gripped his sword hilt, but the Princess' hand kept him from drawing it. The Ha'ashtari ignored Morgan, and thrust his face close to Celeste's. She did not blink or flinch, but regarded him calmly.

"You accuse a Pathfinder of treachery?" he hissed.

"I speak the truth," Celeste said, her voice cold.

"You lie! It never happened. You killed him," Ha'korl insisted.

"How did we kill him? Tell me," Celeste said.

Ha'korl frowned. "He was beaten and then poisoned," he said.

"Why would we poison him? Instead of just cutting his throat?" Celeste asked.

Ha'korl leaned back and spat on the ground. "Who knows what outlanders will do? You have no honor," he said.

"I know your ways. I know the Pathfinders are untouchable. I studied at Carnac, with the centaurs. We did not kill him. I destroyed his soul stone, to brand him a coward and a traitor," Celeste said.

Ha'korl shook his head. "I still think you lie. If it were my decision, I would declare Jinn'she and kill you all. But Ha'keel is High Chief now, and he will determine your fate. Until then, there will be Ka'chi, and the gods will decide," he said.

"Ha'keel is High Chief of the five tribes?" Celeste asked.

"You know Ha'keel?" Ha'korl demanded.

"We met in Aquarquff. I would trust his judgment. He'll know we tell the truth," Celeste said.

Ha'korl glanced at Morgan and then studied the Princess, his gaze frank and searching. "When we kill these men, I think I will take you for myself. You have a pleasing body, for an outlander," Ha'korl said.

Celeste stiffened and Morgan stepped between them. "Do you think you can kill me, Ha'korl?" Morgan asked quietly.

Ha'korl met his eyes, although he was forced to look up at the big man towering over him. What he saw in Morgan's eyes made him smile grimly. "You have no fear, outlander. It will be an honor to kill you and take your woman," he said.

"Leave now, or I'll kill you where you stand," Morgan said.

Ha'korl turned and walked back to his horse. He mounted smoothly, and pointed the lance at Morgan. "I'll be back, for you and your woman," he said.

Ha'korl turned his horse and rode to the other Ha'ashtari. Ha'korl raised his lance, turning its point to the sky, and then all the warriors rode into the glare of the sun and disappeared.

Morgan and the Princess walked back to where Max and Taskin waited. "Looked like you had a good talk. Are we free to go then?" Max asked.

"Well, he promised to kill me and take Celeste for his woman," Morgan growled.

"There, you see. That's progress. When is this going to happen?" Max asked.

Celeste looked after the departed riders. "Whenever they decide. At least they didn't declare Jinn'she. They will grant us the honor of Ka'chi. Until Ha'keel makes the final decision," she said.

"Ha'keel? The one we met in Aquarquff? What does he have to do with this?" Max asked.

"Yes, the man whose son you humiliated in an archery contest. He is the High Chief of the Ha'ashtari," Morgan said.

"It was a fair challenge, and the better man won. There was no humiliation," Max said.

"Let's hope Ha'keel feels that way," Celeste said.

"How do the Ha'ashtari choose the High Chief?" Morgan asked.

"Each tribe has a chieftain, chosen for bravery and skill. The most worthy of the five chieftains is made High Chief, who loosely governs all five tribes. If one of the tribes is offended by some action of the High Chief, it can withdraw from the tribal confederacy, and even declare war on one of the other tribes. That hasn't happened in a long time," Celeste explained.

Max licked his lips. "I'm thirsty," he said, starting for a cactus in a nearby draw.

Celeste glanced in his direction, and saw one of the ant mounds to the right of the cactus. "Max, stop! Not that one," she yelled, running towards him.

Max stopped, his swords appearing in his hands. "What? Why not?" he asked.

Celeste caught up to him, and they walked toward the cactus. "I'll show you," she said, bending carefully down beside the spiny plant. She pointed to a mass of white insects that Max could now see crawling through the spines.

"See those?" she asked.

Max squatted down. "Yes, what are they?" he asked.

"Ant cows, for lack of a better term. The ants use them as a source of food and herd them onto these cacti at night, to protect them from insect eating rodents. If anything disturbs them, the ants smell it somehow, and they swarm over to defend their herds. You don't want to be anywhere near when that happens," she said.

Max stood up, eyeing the ant mound with distaste. "Fascinating. I think I will seek another cactus to slake my thirst," he said.

"Good idea," the Princess said.

They broke camp, dismantling the tents and filling the trenches. Max found another cactus and filled their canteens. Celeste fed the horses some grain and then opened a third cactus and gave the horses a drink. The animals seemed familiar with this source of water, and carefully avoided the thorns while they sipped from the cactus. When the horses had finished drinking, they saddled them and loaded their gear and packs.

"Well, which way now?" Morgan asked.

"South," the Princess said.

"Why? They know where we are now. We've lost any chance to surprise them. Isn't Carnac east of here?" Max asked.

Celeste sighed. "It's hard to explain. Ka'chi is very complex. If we turn and run straight for Carnac now, the Ha'ashtari might take that as a sign of fear. On the other hand, if we continue south, at least for a while, it will show them that we don't fear them," she said.

"But is it worth the risk to get any farther from Carnac? How long can we fight them off?" Morgan asked.

"It's a risk. But I'm doing my best to predict how they might react," Celeste said.

"Remember what happened last night, when we didn't follow her instincts," Taskin said.

"You're right. South, then," Morgan said.

Max stood in his stirrups, waving a fist at the sky. "South into glory! Come and get us, Ha'ashtari, if you dare!" he shouted.

The Ha'ashtari followed them all day, showing themselves at regular intervals. Celeste advised that they just ignore the riders, and cover as much ground as they could. She oriented herself by the position of the sun and the arch, still heading south. The Ha'ashtari appeared one last time on a ridge ahead of them, for an evening salute, and then vanished.

Celeste found another oasis, leading them down into a sheltered cleft. She watered the horses from a well built by the Ha'ashtari, then grained them and let them graze. While Celeste tended the horses, Morgan and Max set up their tents. They left the tents above ground this time, as the surrounding cliffs blocked the worst of the wind. Taskin built a small fire and they all had dinner, then Morgan set out the wards again, and they bedded down for the night.

Sometime during the night, Morgan woke with a start, his arm tingling. He grabbed his sword and slipped out of the tent. He went to Max's tent and tossed a pebble against it. Max appeared almost immediately, awake and armed.

"Someone's approaching the camp," Morgan whispered.

Their fire had died to a few glowing embers, and they crouched in the shadows, searching the gloom around them. At first they could see only dark shapes, tinted with silver by the arch, but soon their eyes adjusted and they could make out the individual tents, and the forms of the horses nearby. They saw the well as a column of black, and one of the shaggy trees stood outlined against the night sky. They heard no sound but the wind.

Morgan kept his eyes to the deepest shadows, willing himself to penetrate the darkness. Max touched his arm. Morgan followed Max's gesture and saw a shape move furtively closer, then stop--a flash of movement, almost invisible in the gloom. Another movement caught his eye, and then a third.

Morgan gestured left and then right. Max nodded and gathered himself. With a shout, Morgan and Max charged the intruders, Morgan running to the left, and Max to the right. The black shapes leaped up, taken by surprise. Morgan caught a glimpse of a Ha'ashtari, bearing a stick that gleamed wetly in the archlight. He veered towards the warrior, and recognized Ha'korl. He slashed at the crouching man. The Ha'ashtari attempted to parry with his stick, but the sword severed the tough wood, knocking the stick from his grasp. Somehow Ha'korl managed to duck the blade, which whistled past a finger's breadth above his skull. With a curse, he turned and ran, moving so swiftly that Morgan's next swing missed him.

Max had a similar experience. The Ha'ashtari he faced put up no resistance, only turned and fled into the night. In moments, they were gone, as if they had never been there.

Max looked at Morgan. "These are the people who worship bravery? They just ran away," he said.

Celeste ran up to them, daggers drawn, Taskin at her side. "What happened?" she asked breathlessly.

"Ha'ashtari triggered the wards, sneaking into camp. We challenged them, and they ran," Morgan said.

"Ha'korl?" Celeste asked.

Morgan nodded.

Celeste noticed the pieces of Ha'korl's stick near Morgan and picked one up. She held the stick up, studying it in the dim light. "Ten'paa. I told you this might happen. They were going to sneak into our camp and mark us with the pigment on these sticks. The stain has to wear off, and you bear the sign of their bravery for days. To enter an enemies' camp unarmed and mark him so is considered the highest form of courage," she explained.

Max stared at the little stick. "These people are mad," he pronounced.

Celeste tossed the stick down. "We might as well get some sleep; they won't bother us any more tonight. Tomorrow they'll probably attack," she said.

There was no further sign of the Ha'ashtari the next morning. Morgan and the others ate a quick breakfast and broke camp. Soon they were back in the saddle, still bearing south.

It was mid-morning when the attack came. The party of Ha'ashtari swept over a ridge ahead of them, coming toward them at a full gallop. They held their lances in their right hands, small shields on their left. Four rode abreast, with the fifth bringing up the rear.

Celeste spun her horse, searching the terrain around them, while the men drew their swords and waited. The horses, sensing the tension, began to stomp and snort. Celeste pointed to their right.

"Over this way! Now!" she cried.

Without waiting for a response, she turned her horse and galloped away. With a last look at the charging nomads, the men followed her.

"Are we fleeing? Did you decide slavery wasn't so bad?" Max called out to the Princess.

She ignored him, urging her mount up a small rise to a level area, between a pair of Wasterat colonies. The rodents saw them coming, squealed in alarm, and dove for their burrows.

Morgan smiled grimly. "No, she just narrowed the field of attack to two directions. Remember what happened to Taskin's horse?" he said.

"Impressive. Quite a woman, our Princess," Max admitted.

"Taskin, stay with the Princess. Max and I will hold the front," Morgan said.

They rode into the narrow gap between the two colonies, and Taskin and the Princess moved to the rear. Max's horse spun and reared. He jerked on the reins, and as soon as it came down, he dismounted. He whacked the horse on the rump with a sword blade, sending it toward Taskin and Celeste.

"Kindly tend my rowdy beast. I need both hands free, and I prefer my own legs in a fight," he called.

Celeste caught the horse as it ran toward them. Morgan remained mounted, and the two men positioned themselves between the Princess and the Ha'ashtari. The nomads approached, slowing only slightly as they saw their quarry's defensive position. Lowering their lances, the warriors thundered toward them.

With a wild war cry, the four split, forming two pairs, one in front of the other, leaving two warriors abreast to charge down the gap between the burrows. Morgan waited for them, his blade raised. He noticed that Ha'korl and a woman led the assault.

"Now you will die," Ha'korl shouted.

"Here I am," Morgan yelled back.

Morgan shouted the Raav war cry and spurred his mount forward, between Ha'korl and his companion. The Ha'ashtari on the right attacked with her lance. Morgan knocked it aside with his sword, but Ha'korl thrust from the opposite side at the same moment. Morgan twisted aside, the spiraled head of the lance skidding from his metasilk cloak. His sword came around in a blurred arc, slicing through the shaft of Ha'korl's lance. Morgan aimed his backswing at the woman, but she leaned away from Morgan's stroke, which split the air beside her head. Max ran around the three combatants, circling through the burrows. With a savage yell, he charged the second pair of Ha'ashtari.

Morgan wheeled his horse, being careful to stay clear of the burrows. Ha'korl threw the headless lance and the shield aside, drawing his knives. He was just turning his horse as Morgan pulled his mount into a lunging rear, its hooves thrashing the air. Ha'korl rolled from his saddle as the forelegs of Morgan's horse came down across the back of his mount. The two horses thrashed in a squealing tangle. Morgan fought to keep his seat, and watch both of his attackers. His horse leaped free, driving the other horse to its knees. Ha'korl's horse stepped in a Wasterat hole, further hampering

311

its struggle to rise.

The woman warrior also cast away her lance and shield and moved in, stabbing with her knives. Morgan parried one thrust and dodged the other. He saw Ha'korl coming from the corner of his eye, and swung his horse's rear around. Morgan's horse kicked backwards, forcing Ha'korl to dive aside. As Ha'korl tried to recover his balance, he put one foot in a burrow and nearly fell.

Morgan urged his mount forward, slashing at the woman Ha'ashtari, who parried the first few blows. Morgan suddenly twisted his blade around and cut her deeply across the ribs. The Ha'ashtari lurched in the saddle, dropping one of her knives, and pressing her arm into the wound. She managed to deflect the next stroke, but then Morgan's blade took her in the neck. The headless nomad slumped forward over the horse's shoulder, and then rolled to the ground.

Meanwhile, Ha'korl had remounted his horse and now charged Morgan. Morgan avoided Ha'korl's first knife cut and backhanded his sword into the Ha'ashtari as he rode past, then wheeled his mount, and pressed the attack. Bleeding from a slash across his back, Ha'korl turned to meet Morgan's assault. Morgan chopped at Ha'korl's head, and the Ha'ashtari parried with his right blade. Morgan slashed from the left, and Ha'korl parried with his left knife. Morgan deflected Ha'korl's return thrust, and brought his sword around in a powerful arc. The Ha'ashtari tried to block the cut but Morgan's blow shattered his knife, cleaving through the hand guard and taking off most of Ha'korl's left hand. His face contorted with agony, Ha'korl shoved the bleeding stump under one thigh and stabbed at Morgan with his remaining knife. Morgan knocked aside Ha'korl's extended blade and drove his sword deep into the Ha'ashtari's chest. Even as he was dying, Ha'korl tried to strike again. Morgan caught the man's arm and jerked him from the saddle. He let Ha'korl fall to the ground in a lifeless heap.

Max's adversaries, another male-female pair, thrust at him with their lances, almost as one. His black blades flashing, Max parried both thrusts. As the nomads brought their mounts to a halt, Max rolled to the right under the man's horse, between its pounding hooves. As he came up on the far side of the horse, he thrust at the man. The Ha'ashtari took the blow on his shield, but as he leaned in to thrust again with his lance, he discovered Max had severed his saddle girth. The man threw himself backwards, and landed heavily on the far side of the horse, but still on his feet. Max slapped the horse with a blade. It leaped aside, nearly trampling its former rider, and Max attacked the staggering nomad. Before his companion could assist him, Max had cut down the first warrior.

The other Ha'ashtari charged in and stabbed with her lance. Max parried and whirled, his second blade slicing across the nomad's thigh, but the woman managed to move her horse away before Max could strike again. The Ha'ashtari threw down her lance and shield, and rode in, her knives drawn. Max blocked the first cut, and stabbed with his other blade, but the nomad parried the thrust with the second knife. She turned her horse again, slashing down.

Max spun his blade around the descending knife and cut deeply into the woman's forearm. In the same motion, he thrust at the woman's chest. The Ha'ashtari tried to parry, but Max twisted his sword, sliding past the knife and completing the thrust. Max stepped back and the warrior toppled from the saddle. He turned just in time to see Morgan kill Ha'korl.

The nomads' horses galloped off, avoiding the burrows, their reins flopping. The Ha'ashtari observer raised his lance in tribute, and rode away. Morgan dismounted, and cleaned his blade in the grass, as Max did the same for his swords. Taskin and the Princess came to join them.

"These Ha'ashtari are good. I'm going to enjoy this," Max panted.

Celeste looked at him and shook her head. "You're a sick man, Maximilian," she observed.

Max went to stand over the fallen woman. "But I hate killing women. It's such a waste," he said softly.

Morgan leaned on his horse, catching his breath. "What now?" he asked.

Celeste looked after the departing Ha'ashtari, as he disappeared over a ridge. "They'll be back, next time with more warriors. You've

313

proven yourself worthy of the next level of Ka'chi," she said.

"Great," Morgan said, as he remounted.

Celeste went to the dead Ha'ashtari, taking the leather bag from around the neck of each of them. This time, instead of smashing the stones inside, she placed the bags carefully on top of a large rock nearby.

"The soul stones again?" Max asked.

"I'm just acknowledging that they died bravely, unlike the Pathfinder," she said.

Celeste retrieved the woman's knives and her sheath belt, as the three men gathered around. She held up one of the knives. "The ka'at. In the hands of a Ha'ashtari warrior, very deadly," she said.

"I agree," Morgan said.

Celeste buckled on the belt, and sheathed the knives. "What are you doing, robbing the dead?" Max asked.

She settled the belt on her hips. "I learned to use these as part of my studies at Carnac. Sometimes the Ha'ashtari honor the fallen by using their weapons. They won't take offense if I keep these. Out here, sleeve daggers seem inadequate," she said.

With impressive speed, the Princess drew the knives, and lunged toward Morgan, who backed quickly away. "The grips are designed so the main blade points directly in line with the arms, without having to bend the wrist. The thrust is more powerful that way," she explained.

Celeste squeezed the knife handles and a pair of blades snapped out sideways. She braced herself and then swung both arms, forcing Max and Taskin to dodge the flashing blades. "The crossblades, attached at right angles to the main blade, form a weapon that can stab in three directions," she added.

"You're dangerous," Taskin complained.

"You better believe it," Max said admiringly. "Don't let this one get away, Morgan."

The Princess squeezed the handles again, and the side blades retracted. She sheathed the knives in one smooth motion.

Celeste picked up one of the lances, and held out the spiral point, sighting along it. "The lun'paa, made from the horn of the ko'raa," she said.

"Thanks for the language lesson, Princess. But I used to stutter as a child, and I don't think the Ha'ashtari language is going to suit me," Max said.

Celeste retrieved her horse from Taskin, and mounted, then fastened the lance to her saddle.

"You're taking the lance too?" Morgan asked.

Celeste patted the weapon. "I trained with all the Ha'ashtari weapons. A woman must be properly armed, don't you think?" she asked.

"Want a shield to complete your arsenal?" Max asked.

Celeste wrinkled her nose. "No, they're too heavy," she said.

Morgan gestured toward the nomads' bodies. "Should we bury them?" he asked.

Celeste gazed at the dead, her face turning somber. "The Ha'ashtari don't bury their dead, they merely collect the soul stones and haul the bodies away from the camp, leaving them for scavengers," she said.

CHAPTER TWENTY-THREE
DRIFTERS AND STORMS

They rode hard all day, pushing the horses. Taskin, although miserably sore, did not complain. The terrain began to descend in a series of steppes, and they could see the glint of water in the distance. Morgan reined in his horse, letting it rest. He pointed at the water.

"What is that?" he asked.

Celeste studied the area, and then glanced at the sun, which hung just above the western horizon. The wind blew harder than usual, the southern sky taking on a leaden cast.

"A lowland marsh area. We should seek shelter as soon as possible, I don't like the looks of that sky," she said.

Morgan leaned forward in his saddle. "Princess, we should keep moving. We were lucky last time, but if a large party of Ha'ashtari catch us in the open, I can't guarantee the outcome," he said.

"And around here, there's nothing but open. We need a defensible position," Max added.

Celeste looked around. "I just don't see anything suitable," she said.

Morgan pointed to the marsh. "What about the wetlands themselves? Use them like we did the Wasterat colonies?" he asked.

"No. We don't want to be anywhere near marshlands at night, and I think a windstorm is coming. We have to find shelter up here," she said.

"You know the Waste, but you just don't understand battle tactics. We can't stay here," Morgan said.

Celeste turned on him, her eyes flashing. "Fine, go ahead and do whatever you want. But I warned you, we should stay away from the marsh," she said.

"We don't have any choice. We have to . . . ," Morgan began, but Celeste kicked her horse into a gallop, heading straight for the marshes.

"Now you've done it," Max said, as he rode after her.

Morgan, muttering something, followed, with Taskin at his side.

Night had fallen by the time they reached the lowland area, and an icy wind whistled around them. Marshes and open water glinted in the archlight, most of it looking foul, tainted and stale. Gasses bubbled up from the depths, erupting from the surface in puffs of glowing mist. Nothing grew around the water's edge; the shorelines lay bare and blackened with residue.

They heard no animal sounds, not even the hyenas' cackling. The wind grew fierce, and heavy clouds blotted out the stars in the southern sky. The four riders huddled in their cloaks, trying to stay warm, and even the horses looked uncomfortable.

"Don't go near those pools, they're poisoned with accumulated minerals," Celeste warned.

"Will the Ha'ashtari be moving in this type of weather?" Morgan asked, his breath steaming and whipping away in the wind.

"No one who knows the Waste will be riding tonight. If we don't seek shelter soon, we'll die," Celeste said.

Morgan looked around. "Shelter? Where?" he asked.

Celeste stood in her stirrups, looking ahead. "Maybe there," she said.

Morgan followed her gaze. Ahead of them a large island rose steeply from the marshes, and he could see a cluster of dark shapes on the rounded summit, too regular to be natural.

"Ruins? Here?" Morgan asked.

"A long time ago, before the Ha'ashtari controlled these lands, several Sagamores attempted to colonize the Waste, offering free land to induce settlers to come here. It seemed natural to build a settlement near all this water. Some of it is drinkable, and the lowlands are somewhat sheltered from the elements.

But the Waste proved too cruel, and all of the colonies failed, leaving ruins scattered throughout the Waste, " Celeste said. "Tributes to failed dreams."

"That's the best shelter I've seen so far," Max said.

Without further debate, they rode for the island. They had to skirt several foul smelling pools, and finally reached the slopes of the island's shores. The incline looked steep and treacherous, especially

317

in the dim light.

"The water must have been higher when this settlement was built. The marshes are probably all that's left of a large lake. We'd better lead the horses up this," Celeste said.

"What's that?" Taskin yelled, pointing upwind around the shoulder of the island.

Several strange objects bobbed toward them, bouncing along in the rising wind. They looked like luminous globes, with constantly shifting shapes. From time to time, large sail-like fins would flare out, catching the wind and propelling them forward. They moved without any sound, phantoms in the night.

Celeste leaped from her horse, gripping the reins. "Drifters! We have to get under cover," she shouted into the rising wail of the wind.

Morgan dismounted, and leaned close to her. "What are they?" he asked.

"No one knows for sure, but they're deadly. Another reason the marshland settlements failed," she said.

They all got off their horses, and started up the slope, dragging the nervous animals after them. Hidden beneath the dried crust lay a deposit of slick clay, and when they stepped on the crust it crumbled, leaving only the clay. They made slow progress, climbing up and sliding back. All the while, the mysterious drifters bounded closer, now heading straight for them.

Morgan stopped, and gauged the distance between them and the drifters. "We aren't going to make it this way. Taskin, take my horse. I'll try to slow them down," he said.

Celeste stopped above them, slipping and catching herself. Slimy earth caked her boots. "You can't fight them. We have to run," she called.

Max handed his reins to the Princess, and slid down the slope toward Morgan. "Not alone anyway. I'll stay with you," he said.

"Don't let them get above you. That's how they kill," she said.

Morgan waved his arm urgently. "Go! Get to the top and wait for us," he shouted.

Celeste and Taskin struggled on toward the summit with

318

the horses, leaving Morgan and Max to face the drifters. Morgan counted five of the creatures, quite close now, still rolling silently and formlessly across the ground. The sails flared again, catching the wind and increasing their speed.

Max and Morgan braced themselves, trying to find firm footing. As the drifters came closer, Max realized he could see through their filmy bodies. The ghostly outlines of internal organs were clearly visible, and one sac contained a blot of reddish liquid.

"What do these things eat?" Max shouted after the Princess, struck with a sudden thought.

"It is said they feed on blood," she called down to them.

Morgan and Max glanced at each other, gripping their swords.

The first of the drifting globes reached them. They could see a glowing mantle containing most of its organs, and something coiled at the base of the mantle. The gossamer sails snapped open and the creature soared aloft, over their heads. A mass of glowing tendrils dropped from its underside, spreading out in a shifting curtain.

Morgan and Max dove aside, Morgan sliding down the slope with his efforts. The writhing tentacles swept past them, tracing tortured lines in the muck at their feet. One of the tendrils slapped across Morgan's bare hand, and he nearly screamed with the pain. An angry red welt immediately flared on the back of his hand.

The drifter sensed it had missed its prey. The sails flattened, the shapeless mass of its body settling to the earth, but the raging wind caught it again, rolling it farther down the slope. Morgan dug in his heels and stopped his descent, just as another drifter made its deadly pass.

With the treacherous footing, Morgan could not move fast enough to avoid it completely. He crouched down at the last instant, covering his face with his arms. The tentacles struck him, dragging across his metasilk cloak. The venomous spines lining the tentacles could not penetrate the tough fabric, but more lines of fire lashed his exposed hands. He almost dropped his sword with the pain.

As the thing landed behind him, Morgan whirled, sliding to one knee. He chopped at the glowing mantle, but it collapsed beneath his stroke. The tough membrane resisted his blade, his sword sliding off without cutting it. The drifter slipped from under his sword, and then attempted to crawl back to him, dragging itself through the mud with its flimsy tentacles. Morgan got to his feet and backed away, glancing over his shoulder for further attackers.

Max shouted down to him. "Their attack is mainly downwind. Once they're past, they can't maneuver very well."

Morgan looked up at him, seeing the pattern of welts that marked Max's face. Another drifter rolled downwind of Max, leaving a pile of severed tentacles at his feet.

"Look out," Max shouted.

Morgan turned to face a bounding globe. He set himself and swung his sword in a savage arc. The blade tore into the deadly curtain of tentacles, slicing through them or forcing them aside. A few tendrils raked across his body, but he suffered no serious injury.

The drifters downwind of them had given up their clumsy upwind pursuit and sailed out of sight around the shoulder of the slope. Max scrambled up the slope, avoiding the last drifter. The shining killer landed behind them and rolled silently on.

Morgan climbed up beside Max. "Are you all right?" he asked.

Max nodded, touching the welts on his face with a fingertip. "I hope these marks aren't permanent. It would mar my handsome features," he said.

Max and Morgan resumed their mad scramble up the side of the island. They could see Celeste and Taskin above them, just below the summit. Clouds whipped by overhead, sending hurtling shadows across the slope. Taskin had tied three of the horses at the top, and was turning back to help Celeste with her horse. They did not see the two drifters floating silently toward them.

"Watch out! Drifters!" Morgan yelled, lunging up the incline.

His shout was lost in the wind, and the first drifter launched its attack. It flowed upwards and settled on the rump of Celeste's horse, clinging there with its poison tentacles. The horse screamed and surged forward, nearly flattening Celeste in the mud. She struggled to hold the reins, and keep the maddened horse from trampling her.

She was so intent on the horse that she did not see the second drifter, which gathered itself to pounce on her. Morgan yelled again, still plunging up the slope, but she could not hear him. Taskin saw her danger, and without thinking he leaped. He landed on top of the oncoming globe, clutching for a hold on its slippery surface. His weight crushed the fragile creature to the ground at Celeste's feet.

Taskin rolled clear of the fallen drifter, sliding downslope. The drifter bobbed up again, whirling its tendrils angrily. Celeste backed away from it, still holding her reins. Its hindquarters weakened by the drifter's poison, the horse suddenly sat down in the mud, jerking Celeste from her feet. The drifter opened its sails, swooping toward her.

Morgan charged out of the night, leaping completely over the fallen horse. With one hand he grabbed Celeste and dragged her downslope, out from under the descending drifter. He struck the drifter with the flat of his sword, knocking it sideways. The thing landed in the mud, missing both Celeste and the horse.

Max arrived and attacked the drifter on Celeste's horse, shoving both swords under the creature's mantle and lifting it to expose the tentacles underneath. He slashed grimly at the clinging tentacles, sending pieces of glowing tendrils flying everywhere. To save itself from further injury, the drifter released the horse and raised its sail, lurching off into the darkness.

Taskin climbed up to help Max with Celeste's horse, while Morgan pulled Celeste to her feet. She was covered with mud, her hair a wild tangle in the wind. They managed to get her horse up, although the poor brute's hind legs barely functioned, paralyzed by the stings of the drifter. They fought their way to the summit, slipping and sliding, and collapsed at the top.

They lay for a moment, gasping. The horses, frightened by the wind and drifters, neighed and shifted nervously, pulling on their reins. A distant roaring sounded in their ears, getting swiftly louder and closer.

Celeste staggered to her feet, listening to the ominous sound. "Windfall! It's the Windfall! We can't stay here. We have to find shelter," she cried.

Max struggled to his feet. "Now what?" he asked.

Celeste untied the three horses and ran toward the nearest of the ruined buildings. The men followed, leading her horse. The closest building consisted of four stout walls of stone, its roof having fallen in years ago. They got the horses inside, removed their saddles and gear, and covered the shivering animals with the hor'gaa blankets. The horses huddled in the center of the building, neighing in fear, while Morgan and Max blocked the doorway with fallen timbers from the roof.

Celeste led the way to the next building. The roaring grew to a deafening howl, almost overhead. Clouds whipped across the night sky, driven before the raging wind. The gale was strong enough to stagger them, and bits of debris flew past. They leaned into the freezing wind, forcing a path through the storm.

They stumbled into the ruined structure---a mere shell of stone, with no windows or roof. The walls blocked the wind, making it slightly warmer inside. They tossed their saddles and packs in a corner, and then dragged out all their blankets and spare cloaks. The four miserable travelers huddled against a wall, covering themselves as best they could, trying to shut out the shrieking of the wind and the numbing cold.

Then Windfall was upon them, filling the world with howling, icy chaos. The rock wall creaked and groaned and several stones fell from the top of the wall, landing around them. Morgan and Max climbed out of their coverings and braced some timbers against the wall, trying to strengthen it. They were soon so cold they had to return to the others, and pray the wall held. Windfall pounded on the wall like an enraged demon, hurling itself in gusts against the shield of stone that kept it from its victims.

After what seemed like an eternity, the wind finally eased. Exhausted by their struggles, Morgan and his companions fell asleep.

Morgan woke with the sun in his face and something tickling his cheek. He slowly opened his eyes, squinting against the bright sky. He glanced down and saw Celeste snuggled next to him under a pile of cloaks and blankets, a lock of her hair across his face. She always seemed beautiful to him, even travel worn and disheveled. He could feel the delicious warmth of her body through their clothes, and closed his eyes again, just enjoying how she felt, not wanting to ever move again.

Max shifted position on the other side of him, and Morgan reluctantly returned to the real world. He gently disengaged himself from the sleeping Princess, who stirred restlessly. Morgan quietly climbed out of their coverings, and got to his feet. He stepped over his sleeping companions and looked around the interior of the ruined building.

One wall leaned precariously, with several layers of stone missing from the top. Deciding that its collapse was not imminent, Morgan stepped out through the doorway. Max watched him leave, and then closed his eyes again. Morgan walked slowly through the abandoned settlement, a collection of stone structures of various sizes and shapes. Few roofs remained, and the wind played through the empty doors and windows. Debris littered the streets, driven there by wind and time. He wondered what kind of people would attempt to tame the Waste.

He prayed while he walked, thanking Iosus for His protection, and soon arrived at their makeshift stable. Morgan stepped up on a pile of stone, searching the surrounding marshes for signs of life. The wetlands glinted dully in the morning sun, and beyond stretched the endless plain. He saw no drifters or Ha'ashtari, or anything else for that matter. The land seemed swept clean by the wind, and the cloudless sky added to the effect.

Morgan jumped down and moved toward the horses, who nickered at his approach. He peered through the timbers blocking the doorway. Celeste's horse seemed to have recovered, although red welts still laced its rump. The other horses looked fine; they dropped their heads and resumed picking at the few strands of tough grass growing through the floor stones.

Morgan left them and found an old well, complete with a bucket on a rusted chain. He dropped a pebble into the dark interior and heard a splash far below. He returned to the horses and cleared the timbers from the doorway, then led the horses to the well, letting them drink from the bucket. He found a corral on the edge of the settlement, and tied the horses there while he examined the structure.

With a little work, he had the corral ready, and put the animals inside, letting them graze on the grass in the enclosure.

As he worked, he constantly watched for Ha'ashtari, but he never saw one. He found two more buckets that still would hold water and filled them from the well, then returned to his companions. They were awake by now. Max and Taskin had propped some more beams against the leaning wall, and Celeste had built a roaring fire from woody debris she had collected.

They ate a hearty breakfast, sitting close to the fire, soaking up its warmth. After they had all drank, Morgan set the buckets next to the fire, warming the water somewhat. They took turns behind a makeshift curtain, changing clothes and washing off the caked clay, and then they rinsed their filthy clothes and spread them out to dry in the wan sunlight. Celeste found an ointment in the Pathfinder's gear, and treated everyone's wounds, smearing it on the welts left by the drifters.

Soon they sat around the campfire, drinking mugs of sasich, warm, clean, and full. Morgan looked at Celeste. She had combed her hair, and looked clean and relatively fresh, considering their last few days. Max gingerly touched the welts on his face, now shiny with ointment.

"What are the drifters?" he asked.

Celeste gripped the mug, letting its heat warm her fingers. "No one knows for sure. They live in the marshes, lying dormant under the water, until they get hungry. Then they come out at night, drifting with the wind, looking for prey. It is said they can feel your warmth, and it attracts them. The stinging tentacles paralyze the victim, and then the drifter settles over it to feed. When they're full, they head for the nearest water, and return to dormancy," she said.

"Do they really feed on blood?" Max asked.

"That's what I'm told. I've never seen one feeding," Celeste said.

Morgan glanced at the battered wall above them. "What about this Windfall?" he asked.

"It has something to do with the moons. I noticed all three of them were up last night, before the winds came. It's also more frequent in the spring and fall. If you think it was bad down here in the lowlands, you should experience it up on the highland plains. The centaurs have found people and horses frozen solid, those that were unlucky or foolish enough to get caught in the open," Celeste answered.

"You said the Ha'ashtari consider horses sacred," Taskin said. "Why?"

"The Ha'ashtari believe that their original gods took the form of a man and a horse, both intelligent and immortal. The man god, El'atan, and the horse, a mare named El'tari joined once and produced the centaurs. The centaurs lived in Heaven for a long time, circling the world on the silver arch, enjoying incredible freedom and peace. Then one family of centaurs committed some terrible act of cowardice, no one even remembers what it was. But the gods punished that family with separation into mortal man and the brute horse, casting them out of Heaven, to roam the Waste. That's why the Ha'ashtari glorify bravery, they are attempting to atone for the past sins of cowardice. The Ha'ashtari believe themselves the descendants of the man, and that the wild horses in the Waste came from the horse.

The other centaurs could not bear to be separated from their cursed brethren, and descended from Heaven to build Carnac. The Ha'ashtari believe that soul stones are the tears of the gods, shed when the centaurs left Heaven. They still regard the centaurs as children of the gods, and no Ha'ashtari will harm a centaur or allow one to come to harm. They consider horses sacred, to be treated with honor and respect. The Ha'ashtari feel that, even though they're a cursed race, they are still superior to outsiders, who are the offspring of lesser gods," Celeste said.

"Are you still thinking about your horse?" Morgan asked Taskin.

"Yes," Taskin admitted.

"It wasn't your fault," Celeste said.

"I hope the Ha'ashtari feel that way. I have no desire to be branded horse-killer by a people that worship horses," Taskin said.

"After the Windfall, won't the Ha'ashtari think we're dead?" Morgan asked.

"They won't assume that, they will look for us. Fortunately, any sign of our passage would have been erased by the storm. If they find us right away, it will only be our bad luck," Celeste said.

"What's next under the rules of Ka'chi?" Max asked.

"They'll attack again with more warriors, and then more each time we are victorious, until we're dead," she said.

"Is there any point in continuing south? Have we proven our courage yet?" Morgan asked.

Celeste smiled a crooked smile. "Well, we've survived a prowling sith'gaa, two encounters with their warriors, the drifters, and Windfall. I don't think anyone will question our courage, or our blind luck. Maybe Locha stayed with Harkon. We have definitely lost any advantage of surprise. I was hoping we would enter Shen'tari territory," she said.

"What would that mean?" Morgan asked.

"The Ha'ashtari are divided into five tribes, and each tribe has its own territory. You can identify the particular tribe by the color in the pattern of their leathers. The Meng'tari control the lands above Aquarquff, and their color is blue. The Shen'tari territory surrounds Carnac and the Rift. Their color is red. The Ha'ashtari we encountered in Aquarquff were Shen'tari. The Aram'tari hold the lands south of the Meng'tari and Shen'tari. Their color is yellow. The Rif'tari territory lies in the northeast corner of the Waste, where the Nageff canyon descends through the Barrier Lift into Aijalon. Their color is green. The Ko'tari lands are south of the Rif'tari and their color is black.

If we reach Shen'tari territory, custom demands that the Meng'tari contact them, to inform them of the intruders and the appropriate stage of Ka'chi. That would give us some more time," Celeste answered.

Morgan began to look uncomfortable, but determined. Finally, he spoke. "Celeste, I am truly sorry I doubted your decisions. Every time we have gone against your advice, we've met with near disaster. I won't make the same mistake again," he said.

Celeste took a drink of sasich. "Men. You think you know everything, even when it's obvious you don't. I guess you can't help

326

yourselves," she said.

All three men groaned in concert.

Morgan and his companions broke camp mid-morning. Max mounted his horse and took a last look to the south. The mist-shrouded peak swelled into the cobalt sky, looming over the surrounding flatlands. The clouds sheathing its flanks swirled eerily.

"That's huge," Max commented to no one in particular.

Celeste joined him. "The Ha'ashtari consider the mountain sacred. No outlander has ever been there."

"Does the mountain have a name?" Max asked.

The Princess shrugged. "They never speak of it, except to warn everyone to stay away."

"Makes me curious . . ." Max began.

"Forget it," Morgan said as he got on his horse. "You've caused enough trouble already."

They rode back down into the marshy lowlands and turned northeast. The freezing wind had deepened the crust on the slick clay of the slopes, allowing them to descend without much sliding. The wind blew gently under the clear sky, and the drifters lay in their fetid pools, waiting for darkness. The fading welts on man and horse were the only reminder of last night's horror. They had nearly reached the arid plains above when they first saw the Ha'ashtari---ten figures on horseback, outlined against the harsh sun.

"Locha did not stay with Harkon. The god of misfortune has followed us," Taskin commented.

Celeste stood in her stirrups, shading her eyes with her hand. As they watched, one of the Ha'ashtari rode away. "We must be entering Shen'tari territory," she said.

Morgan peered at the figures on the ridge. "How can you tell?" he asked.

Celeste pointed to the departing rider. "That one was the messenger from the Meng'tari. The Shen'tari have been alerted. Eight of those warriors will attack, the last will observe and report," she said.

Max looked around. "Bad location. They have the high ground, and there is no shelter on this ridge," he said.

Celeste sat down in the saddle and urged her horse forward. "They may not attack for a while. They have time to study us," she said.

"All the time in the world," Max remarked irritably.

They rode straight toward the waiting warriors. As they approached, the group of Ha'ashtari split, four riders moving to each side. The ninth warrior held his position until they were closer, then he raised his lance in salute and rode away.

Celeste studied the man. "Definitely Shen'tari. See the red markings on his leathers?" she asked.

"So Ha'keel and his family were Shen'tari?" Max asked thoughtfully.

"Hoping to see Sha'lor? I wouldn't. She may be in the next party that tries to kill us," Celeste said.

"How romantic," Max said.

The flanking Ha'ashtari wheeled their mounts, raising their lances. The observer rode to a small hillock and sat watching.

"Let's get past them," Morgan said, spurring his horse into a gallop.

Celeste and the others joined him. The Ha'ashtari let them pass, turning their horses, and following at a slower speed.

Celeste pointed northeast. "We might as well head straight for Carnac," she shouted.

They guided their mounts in that direction, letting them settle into a distance-eating run. Their pursuers paced them easily, a short distance to the rear. They pounded across the undulating plain, watching for any break in the landscape that would give them an advantage against the Ha'ashtari.

They were approaching a low ridge, the wind in their faces, when a strong, musky odor assailed their nostrils. Celeste yanked her horse to a halt, looking over her shoulder, gauging the location of those behind.

"What?" Morgan yelled.

"That smell is a herd of ko'raa, just over that ridge. Spread out, and ride around them, then do what I do," she called back.

328

Morgan and Celeste rode to the left, just short of the ridgetop, and Max and Taskin broke to the right. The Ha'ashtari slowed cautiously, observing their maneuvers. Celeste angled up the slope, until she could just see over the summit. Morgan rode up beside her.

In a shallow valley beyond the ridge surged a gigantic, heaving mass of brown. Thousands of the shaggy plains antelope moved through the valley, grazing as they went. Their spiral horns glinted in the sunlight, and their breath rose in puffs of steam over the tide of flesh. The sound of their hooves rumbled like thunder, and in their wake laid a wide swath of mangled and shorn grassland.

Celeste topped the ridge, galloping down into the valley, Morgan right behind her. The beasts nearest them threw up their heads, dark eyes fixed on the riders. They milled nervously, grunting and squealing in alarm. The herd began to close in on itself, the outer animals facing the intruders, their horns tossing.

Celeste circled the animals, putting them between her and the Ha'ashtari beyond the ridge. They could see Max and Taskin on the opposite side, coming around the herd. Once they were all on the far side, Celeste turned toward the herd. The ko'raa backed away, stomping and blowing steam.

"Stampede?" Morgan shouted.

Celeste nodded and pointed to her left. "We spread out along this side, and drive them over the ridge. The ko'raa will usually run rather than fight," she said.

Morgan signaled Max, and the others moved into position. Just as the Ha'ashtari appeared on the ridgetop, Celeste yelled and charged the milling herd. For a moment, the beasts stood their ground, then with a swelling rumble, the whole herd turned and fled. The shaggy wave surged up the slope, straight for the Ha'ashtari, the four riders driving them on.

The nomads took one look at the oncoming mass, and then turned their horses and disappeared. Celeste and the others kept up the pressure, shouting and waving their arms, crowding the animals in the rear of the herd. The ko'raa put down their heads and ran.

As Morgan reached the ridgetop, he saw an incredible sight. Unable to reach any form of shelter, the Ha'ashtari had dismounted and stood in a compact group, calmly waiting for the stampeding animals. Morgan reined in his horse, expecting to see the warriors trampled into the earth. At the last moment, the avalanche of brown split, passing within arm's reach on either side of the Ha'ashtari. The warriors watched them pass, steadying themselves against the movement of the trembling earth. The Ha'ashtari held their horses' heads low, speaking firmly into their ears. The horses shifted and stomped, their eyes rolling, but they did not bolt or rear.

Morgan waved at Celeste, who sat staring at the island of warriors in the torrent. "We've gained some time, at least. Let's use it," he shouted, turning his horse back in the direction of Carnac.

Celeste tore her gaze away from the stampede and followed, while Max and Taskin hurried to catch them. The rumble of the herd faded into the distance.

Despite the fact that the Ha'ashtari had obviously survived the stampede, no one saw them the rest of the day. The fugitives slowed their pace, sparing the horses. Toward nightfall, Celeste led them into a rocky defile, where they made camp for the night. They found no water in the valley, but it was a defensible site. They hobbled their horses in a small grassy area surrounded by rocky cliffs, and fed them the last of the grain. They set up camp beneath an overhang in the cliffs, spreading their bedrolls at the rear of the niche, and then built a fire just outside and cooked dinner.

As the setting sun touched the cliffs, Max nudged Morgan and pointed. Nine figures stood on the bluff opposite them.

"Our friends are back," Max observed.

"Will they attack tonight?" Morgan asked Celeste.

She shrugged. "It's impossible to tell. They may want to mark us in our sleep before the real fighting begins, achieve ten'paa where the Meng'tari failed" she said.

Max rubbed his beard. "I think we should prepare to receive guests," he said.

The arch cast its silvery mantle over the rocks and cliffs, but none of the moons had yet risen, and the cold, clear air made the shadows sharp. Morgan crouched on a ledge, deep in one of those shadows, the dying campfire below him and to his left. He held a coiled rope in his right hand, a noose ready to cast in his left. After it was fully dark, he had placed the wards around their camp and in the walled meadow where the horses grazed. The tingling of the bracelet told him the Ha'ashtari had arrived.

Morgan saw something to his left, beyond the overhang, a flicker of movement in the shadows. Once he focused on the area, he could see their gliding forms. Noiselessly, the warriors crept closer to the camp. Morgan tensed, waiting; hoping everyone else was in place. Two Ha'ashtari slipped across the band of silver light marking the canyon floor, and took up positions on either side of the overhang, one of them just below Morgan's ledge. He could just make out the man's features in the dimness.

Four more figures crossed the canyon and moved toward the overhang. They carried their knives unsheathed. No marking the enemy this time, these warriors came to kill. The four vanished from view, entering the niche. Morgan waited a moment more, and then moved.

His noose drifted down, settling around the neck of the Ha'ashtari below. Morgan yanked on the rope, dragging the man upwards, choking off his cry. Once he lifted the man clear of the ground, Morgan jerked violently on the rope. The crack of neckbones shot through the still night. Morgan let the body fall, and leaped down after it, drawing his sword.

As planned, Taskin had engaged the warrior on the other side of the overhang, but even with the advantage of surprise, Taskin had not been able to kill the Ha'ashtari immediately. The warrior blocked Taskin's furious sword strokes with his flashing knives. Celeste circled the pair of combatants with her own Ha'ashtari weapons, looking for an opening.

Realizing it was a trap, the four Ha'ashtari in the niche charged back out, their knives ready. Morgan caught the first man with a mighty stroke. The warrior tried to parry with his knife, but the force of Morgan's swing snapped the blade and Morgan's sword bit deep into his shoulder and chest. Morgan kicked the dying man aside, and charged between the next two warriors. He deflected a thrust from

331

his left, but a knife blade grated across the metasilk on his right side. He lashed out with a counterstroke, and felt his blade strike flesh. Then he was past them, and he backed against the wall of the niche, preventing an assault from the rear.

Meanwhile, Celeste reached down, grabbed a handful of sandy soil, and flung it in the face of their opponent. The man staggered back, shaking the grit from his eyes. Both Taskin and Celeste attacked at the same time. Taskin's sword cut clanged off the Ha'ashtari's knife, but Celeste's thrust went in under his right arm. The Ha'ashtari slashed down with the knife in his right hand, but the wound slowed him, allowing Celeste to block the stroke with her other knife. Taskin slashed again, low this time, and cut the man's leg from under him, then killed him as he fell.

Another warrior turned to help the Ha'ashtari fighting Taskin and Celeste, but he was too late, his companion went down before he could reach them. He leaped at Taskin, slashing with his knives, and Taskin fell back before the vicious assault. Celeste continued with her strategy, staying clear and biding her time.

Two warriors still stalked Morgan, one bleeding from a shoulder wound. Morgan now faced four Ha'ashtari knives, their wielders attacking with deadly precision. They would thrust, and then slash sideways, using all three blades. Grimly Morgan dodged and parried, hard pressed to keep those blades from his flesh. He aimed a cut at the head of the man to his left, kicking out at his knee at the same time. The man ducked the sword, but could not avoid the kick. His knee buckled, but he managed to slice Morgan's thigh before the big man could move. Morgan parried the second man's attack with a backstroke, and then the man's other knife skidded from his shoulder. Without the metasilk, he would have taken another wound.

Morgan moved his sword in a whirling defensive pattern. He pressed his back against the stone, easing the weight from his bleeding leg. While not immediately serious, the cut would hamper his movements, and he was losing blood. The man on Morgan's left staggered, his damaged knee unable to bear any weight. The man on his right favored his wounded shoulder, the blood spreading across his leather jerkin. Morgan set himself, and then attacked. He slashed

332

to the right, at the Ha'ashtari's bleeding shoulder. When the man tried to parry, Morgan twisted his blade around the knife and severed the man's left hand at the wrist. Morgan's backstroke opened the man's throat, and he fell. Before the other warrior could reach him, slowed by his injured knee, Morgan whirled. The man stared down at the gaping cut in his stomach, and then folded, hugging himself with bloody arms.

Morgan turned, to see how Taskin fared. The Ha'ashtari had Taskin backed against the cliff, savagely windmilling his knives. Taskin had several minor cuts, and was tiring, as he attempted to fend off the furious attack. Celeste lay in the sand, clutching a bleeding arm, one of her knives lying beside her. Before Morgan could run to their aid, a black figure flashed into view. The Ha'ashtari toppled over backwards, the tendons at the backs of his knees slashed. Before he struck the ground, his throat erupted in a red ruin.

Gasping for breath, Taskin leaned against the rock at his back, his bloody swordpoint resting in the sand. Celeste sat up, staring at the dead Ha'ashtari. Max calmly wiped his blades clean on the dead warrior's leg and sheathed them. Despite his relaxed demeanor, Morgan noticed Max was bleeding from a leg wound.

Morgan cleaned his sword in the sand, and walked toward his companions. "The two by the horses?" he asked.

Max gripped his wounded leg and grimaced. "I took care of them," he said.

Celeste scrambled to her feet, still holding her injured arm, and then turned to face the cliff across the canyon. She searched the clifftop, outlined against the night sky, but could see no one there. Celeste called out in Ha'ashtari. After a brief silence, a response came in the same language. A figure moved from the shadows above and vanished.

"The observer?" Morgan asked.

Celeste nodded. "I told him we'd won. There will be no more attacks tonight," she said wearily.

Morgan glanced at Max. Even in the dim light, he could tell something was bothering his friend. "What happened?" he asked softly.

Max spoke without looking at Morgan. "One of the Ha'ashtari by the horses was a woman," he said.

"Is that how you were wounded?" Morgan asked.

Max's cold blue eyes flicked toward him. "I hesitated. She looked like . . . ," he began, and then caught himself.

Celeste joined them. "Sha'lor?" she asked.

Max looked away, his jaw clenching.

Morgan sighed. "At least the woman I want is on our side. You're falling for the enemy," he said.

"I'm not falling for anyone. I just don't like killing women," Max said fiercely.

Celeste touched his arm. "Max, she is Ha'ashtari. If she comes, she'll be trying to kill you," she said.

"And Morgan thinks his love life is complicated. Not that I'm admitting any feelings for that Ha'ashtari savage," Max said, then smiled ruefully. "Morgan, my friend, we are getting old and soft."

"Yes. And we can't afford that luxury right now," Morgan said.

They treated each other's wounds, then dragged the Ha'ashtari dead out into the canyon. Celeste removed the warriors' soul stones and placed them under the night sky, where they bathed in the light of the arch. Then they tried to sleep, even as the sounds of scavengers drifted through the rocky defile.

The battered group woke early and Celeste put some fresh disinfectant on their wounds and replaced their bandages. They were all stiff and sore, and their wounds ached. After eating a quick, cold breakfast, Morgan collected the wards, while the others packed their gear. They had the horses saddled before the sun appeared over the canyon wall.

As they left, they rode past the scattered remains of the Ha'ashtari warriors. Small, furry things scampered away from the bodies, to hide in the tall grass, and a vulture flapped lazily to the cliff tops, where it sat waiting for them to pass. Several more of its kind circled overhead. Max would not look at the dead woman.

They reached the plains above and continued on toward Carnac. The sun hung high in the sky when Max first spotted the Ha'ashtari--

-thirteen of them this time, riding along a distant ridge.

Taskin stopped his horse and studied the other riders. He shook his head. "They just keep sending them, more each time," he said.

Max joined him, leaning forward to ease his injured leg. "They won't stop until we're in Carnac, or dead," he said.

"Dead is more likely," Taskin said gloomily.

Max glanced at him. "Wish you'd stayed in Saxhaven?" he asked.

"No, if I have to die, this is as good a place as any," Taskin said, then turned to Max and smiled. "Here, with good friends, doing something worthwhile."

Max clapped him on the shoulder. "That's the spirit. Let's hurry up and get to Carnac, where we can brag about these adventures over a drink," he said heartily.

"Agreed," Taskin returned, as they spurred their horses to catch up with Morgan and Celeste.

They rode for a while longer, their Ha'ashtari escort keeping their distance. Then Celeste stopped, studying the grass before them.

"A herd of horses just passed here," Morgan said.

"I know," Celeste said, as she turned her horse to follow the tracks.

"We don't have time for this," Morgan complained, as he rode after her.

As if disturbed by the change in direction, the group of Ha'ashtari turned directly toward them and began approaching.

Max rode up beside Celeste. "Our friends are joining us. Can I ask what we're doing now?" he asked.

"We have to find this herd. Before the Ha'ashtari attack," she said, urging her horse on to greater speed.

Max kept even with her. "Forgive me for bothering you, but one more question. Now that I know what we're doing, can I ask why we are doing it?" he pressed.

"No time to explain. Find the herd," she yelled.

The four of them rode along the spoor of the horse herd, their pursuers gaining rapidly. They broke over a low ridge, and there before them, grazing in a valley, stood a herd of twenty to thirty horses. Celeste reined in, studying the herd intently. The rest of the group was studying the approaching warriors.

"We've found the herd. Can we go now?" Morgan asked.

"The herd stallion isn't here. He is probably scouting for fresh range. So where is she?" Celeste asked, and then pointed at a large horse to one side of the herd. "There. The lead mare. Follow me!" she called as she rode off.

Max gave Morgan a questioning look. Morgan shrugged. "She knows the country and the people. We have to trust her," he said.

The herd parted as they rode toward the horse Celeste had chosen. As they approached, the mare threw up her head and snorted, then bolted, running away.

"Stay with her. Keep her going the way we want to go," Celeste called, as she gave chase.

They all rode after the mare, keeping her from turning back to the herd, and guiding her in the direction of Carnac. The mare slowed, and Celeste eased back, concerned only with the mare's course and not her speed. Morgan heard the sound of hooves, and looked over his shoulder, surprised to see the rest of the herd following the mare. Behind them came the pursuing Ha'ashtari.

Celeste waved. "Let the herd join her, but keep them moving in the right direction," she said.

Morgan and the others swung wide, letting the herd reach the mare, and then they rode in the fringes of the group, only moving if the mare strayed off course. The wild horses snorted and rolled their eyes, but seemed content to follow the mare. Their herd instinct overcame their fear of the humans.

The group of Ha'ashtari split, warriors pacing the herd on either side, but they did not approach. Celeste joined Morgan.

"As long as we don't hurt the horses, they won't attack," she explained.

Morgan nodded. "Horses are sacred. They won't take a chance on any of the herd being injured in an attack. The perfect shield," he said admiringly.

Max rode closer, weaving through the herd, and nodded toward the Ha'ashtari. "How long will they wait?" he called.

"A while. They don't want to risk the horses. They have time, time we need," Celeste answered.

They rode on, letting the herd choose their own pace. Some time later another horse appeared on a nearby ridge, following them. Celeste noticed the horse first. "The herd stallion. He wants his herd back," she said.

Morgan glanced in the stallion's direction. "He'll have to wait. We need them right now," he said.

The sun swung low in the western sky. Storm clouds began to gather, and Morgan could see flashes of lightning in the distance. The Ha'ashtari held their position.

"The colts in the herd are tiring. We're going to have to let them go soon. And a lightning storm is coming. We'll have to take cover," Celeste said.

"Do we dare stop? What will the Ha'ashtari do?" Morgan asked.

"If that storm comes this way, they'll seek shelter. You've never seen a lightning storm in the Waste," she said.

"No," he admitted.

"The lightning doesn't just flash prettily across the sky, it strikes the ground, again and again. Anything in the open, especially on high ground, is in danger of being hit," she explained.

The storm grew closer, building in fury, an angry mass of clouds boiling across the sky. Jagged streaks of light stabbed the ground beneath it, and the thunder shook the ground. The wind began to blow harder, carrying the storm with it, and Morgan could see a curtain of rain beneath the black clouds. The herd began to falter, turning this way and that, neighing in fear. The stallion began to move closer, his concern for the herd overcoming his caution.

"We have to let them go," Celeste decided, breaking away from the herd.

Morgan and the others followed Celeste, while the herd immediately turned and raced through a pass to their right. The stallion galloped down to join them. The Ha'ashtari stopped, looking back at the storm, and then they too rode out of sight, leaving the four riders alone.

Celeste shouted over the sound of the storm. "Everything sane is heading for shelter right now. Let's go," she said.

Morgan shook his head. "If the Ha'ashtari catch us in the open, we die. Can't we stay low in the valleys and keep moving? We could take advantage of the storm to gain some distance," he said.

Celeste shrugged, glancing up at the churning clouds and the spikes of lightning. "Either way, we die. Ride on," she said.

They rode furiously down the valley, fleeing ahead of the storm, but the raging elements gained on them. The lightning crashed into the hills behind them, and the thunder sounded almost instantly after the flashes. They crossed a low rise, and ahead of them they could see a massive shape on the horizon, indistinct in the growing murk.

Max pointed and shouted. "What's that?"

"The arc massif, an old volcano crater. The Ha'ashtari call it the Bora'tran. Nothing left but part of the rim rising above the plain. There's an abandoned outpost in the cliffs. If we could reach it, we could hold the Ha'ashtari off for a while. And we might survive this storm," Celeste said.

The curtain of rain swept toward them and they could hear the heavy drops splattering into the ground. A shaft of light arced overhead and thunder crashed.

"Ride for your lives," Morgan shouted.

Their world became a nightmare of raging wind, drenching rain, and constant lightning. Waves of thunder beat at them like a hammer. The horses went insane with fear, they were barely controllable. They tried to stay in the valleys, away from any high ground, but at times they had to cross low ridges to stay on course for the massif.

They were just racing over one of these rises when a bolt of lightning shattered the air beside them. The horses reared and plunged, and Taskin slipped from his wet saddle, landing in a heap in the mud. His horse tore the reins free from his hand and galloped away, up the ridge.

Morgan went after the horse, while Max pulled the staggering Taskin to the back of his horse. Another shaft of light exploded before Morgan, and he dragged his horse to a halt. The instant crash

338

of thunder came so loud and close it almost knocked Morgan from the saddle. Through the downpour, he could see where the bolt had struck. The lightning had blackened the soaked grass in a large circle, leaving Taskin's horse a smoking mass of charred flesh. Ears ringing, and half blinded by the lightning flash, Morgan turned and fled from the ridge.

He rejoined the others and they rode on, Max's horse laboring under the weight of two men. The storm raged and the massif grew closer. Once, Morgan's horse slipped and almost fell, nearly pitching him from the saddle, but he hung on grimly, and dragged himself back into place. The rain continued to lash at them, and a stream of water dripped from Morgan's hood, pouring down his face.

Finally, they rode between walls of black rock, looming stark on either side in the flashes of lightning. The horses scrambled over the remains of an old stone barricade, and then Celeste led them to the left, around the nearest wall of the ancient volcano. Here, the full force of the wind could not reach them, and the fury of the rain had slackened. They rode up a slope, picking their way between rocks and streams of runoff from the storm.

Lightning struck the cliff somewhere above, and after the thunder had died away, they could hear the clatter of rocks dislodged by the blast. Scrawny brush clung to the slope, spidery branches thrashing in the wind, and to their left loomed the black cliff, rising almost vertically. Ahead and to the right rose a jumbled mass of lava, surrounded by a cascade of cinders and ash, the last efforts of the dying volcano.

They came to a second fortification, hewn blocks forming an inner wall between the cliff and the lavadome. Skirting the wall, they found an entry, its wooden gate rotting in the mud. Dismounting, the soggy riders led their horses through the stone arch in the wall. Max and Morgan dragged the gate across the opening, leaving it leaning against the rocks on its side. It was not much of a barrier, but it should keep the horses from wandering.

The rocky arena screened out most of the wind and driving rain, and muffled the crashing of the storm somewhat. They led the horses up the hill, until the cliff swung in to meet the rear of the lava dome. Here, a series of stone steps had been chiseled out of the rocks, leading upwards into the chaotic night.

Stripping the saddles and gear from the exhausted horses, they stowed the tack in an alcove in the rocks, protected from the rain. They covered the horses with the hor'gaa blankets, and left their mounts huddled against the cliff, where an overhang gave them some shelter. Morgan and the others shouldered their personal gear and mounted the steps. The stairs ascended to a wide ledge about halfway up the rear wall of the crater. On the ledge stood the main outpost building, built of stone blocks, with a sagging wooden roof.

Celeste pushed open the door, and they stepped inside. They stood by the door, dripping on the old floorboards. The roof leaked in places, but it was relatively dry inside. A lightning flash revealed a large room littered with debris and rotting furniture. Doorways in the rear led to other rooms.

"I didn't believe we would survive the storm, especially when we lost Taskin's horse," Celeste said, shaking her head.

"Have faith, Princess. Morgan's quest can't be thwarted by a little storm," Max said, then paused. "Now an entire nation of Ha'ashtari . . . maybe . . . but we don't have to face them until morning."

"Perhaps even later, if they try to track us after this storm," Morgan remarked.

"It won't take them long to figure out where we are, there aren't many places to hide in this open country. But you're right, Max; we'll worry about that in the morning. Right now, I'm freezing, soaked, and exhausted," Celeste said.

"Right now, this looks like a palace," Taskin decided.

CHAPTER TWENTY-FOUR
SKARA THRAE

Sage Regis hobbled down the stairs, leaning heavily against the damp stones of the wall, his old knees protesting. The circular stairway was lit by globes in iron stanchions on the walls. He wished the Mhoul had set up their headquarters in the higher parts of Lugershall, instead of down in the dungeons, where it was so dank and cold. He stopped at a landing to rest, his thoughts wandering back to his first encounter with the dark ones.

A man had come to him, bearing a strange piece of intricate technology, and said that someone wished to see him, to share more of the devices with the Sage of Skara Thrae. Intrigued with the artifact, so far advanced beyond anything the Thraens possessed, he agreed to the meeting. The messenger warned him to keep the meeting secret, as the other party feared thieves and spies. Telling no one, he went by night to an old ruin called Draken Cor. Surrounded by fetid swamps and shunned by all, it was rumored to be haunted. Scoffing at the legends of black demons, he had previously explored the ruins but found nothing of interest except for one of the ancient Gates, long silent. He had examined it, but the structure remained stubbornly dormant, and Regis had all but forgotten the discovery.

But on this fateful night, much to his amazement, the Gate crackled with energy, and beside the Gate waited a Mhoul, with two trolls as bodyguards. On the Mhoul's shoulder crouched a hideous toadlike thing. He had almost fled at the sight, no sane person had anything to do with the Mhoul, and the huge trolls looked like something out of a nightmare. But the sight of the Gate, brought mysteriously back to life, held him. He spoke with the Mhoul, who did not seem like a monster of ancient legend, but a rational being that had access to unlimited knowledge and technology. They talked long into the night, and the Mhoul, whose name was Molid, promised him access to all the knowledge of the Mhoul, in return for one small service.

Molid's request was not exactly small and could cost Regis

341

his life. Molid wanted the Sage to betray Ryde and open Lugershall to invading Haggas. At first Regis flatly refused, and Molid did not press him, but asked if they could talk another night, as long as Regis told no one of the meeting. Against his better judgment, Regis agreed, the lure of the Mhoul technology irresistible.

Sage Lang Regis was a scholar in a land of unschooled warriors, and few Thraens understood him or shared his passions. Ryde respected his knowledge, but often ignored his advice. The stocky Warlord, a simple fighting man, had little use for mechanical devices and technology. Ryde's policy of isolationism left Regis effectively cut off from any scientific progress on the mainland, and he felt even more alone.

Ryde's son Talbot, unlike his father, respected learning and education, and had been an able pupil. Unfortunately, the deep differences between father and son had led to an angry parting and Talbot's departure from Skara Thrae. Regis missed the keen, restless mind of Ryde's only son. The Princess Celestine had been the only other one that showed any interest in him and his books, now that Talbot was gone.

He met Molid again, and this time the Mhoul assured him that the change in leadership would be better for Skara Thrae. The island would no longer be at the mercy of Ryde's rages and moods and reason would prevail. Molid promised Regis an influential position in the new government, where he could direct the country into an age of enlightenment. Ryde's isolationism would be a thing of the past, and Skara Thrae would take its rightful place among the nations. With the Mhoul advising the Haggas, Molid said that the invasion should be relatively bloodless, a swift, efficient strike and it would all be over.

Finally, Regis agreed to assist the Mhoul, although a part of him still did not trust the dark ones. On the night of the invasion, Regis opened a secret gate in Lugershall that only he and Ryde knew of, and let the Haggas enter. He directed them to the arms lockers and the soldier's quarters and the deed was done.

Regis wiped the sweat from his brow and leaned back against the stones. Once he had let the Haggas in, Molid's agents had taken him to the Gate, and he went through. He spent the next few days in paradise, examining rooms full of strange devices, and having the Mhoul's technicians explain their purposes and workings. He did not even ask where he was, afraid the dream would burst like a bubble. All too soon he had to return, and when his dream ended, the nightmare began.

He came back to a Skara Thrae in bloody chaos. Lugershall had fallen, most of her soldiers killed in their sleep. Ryde and his family were fugitives, Usk the Axminster had nearly been killed, and Haggas ravaged the countryside. Tantagnel remained the last holdout, where Thuro and Ryde had joined forces. The two long time enemies had been brought together by a common foe, their differences swallowed by a love for their country.

Strange gray-skinned men, called Immortals, accompanied the Mhoul. Lean, wolfish soldiers in red and black served as the Mhoul's personal bodyguards. Krang Fere Harriers, he learned, brutal, ruthless killers, hard men from a hard land. Since his betrayal, Regis had encountered several more of the Mhoul. Shrouded by the black wrappings, they were distinguishable only by their size and shape. The trolls were still present, guarding the Mhoul, and Regis had also seen fantastic metal ships anchored off the coast.

He had confronted Molid about the Mhoul's broken promises, but the dark creature had brushed him aside. Seeing the cold, inhuman way the Mhoul dealt with events, Regis had feared to press him further. He was beginning to realize his mistake. Most of what Molid had told him was lies, but he had betrayed his country, and his life of loneliness had been made permanent. He had no country now; his only hope lay with the Mhoul. Fortunately, Molid still felt a need for the Sage, and Regis felt safe for the time being. But he now knew that, should he become useless to the Mhoul, they would not hesitate to dispose of him.

After his confrontation with Molid, he learned that the Princess had fled to the mainland, where the Mhoul's agents searched for her. Then Molid had departed for a while, and when it returned, the Mhoul was injured, its arm damaged at the elbow. The Mhoul's rith was also absent. Without the rith, Molid seemed to have trouble seeing and hearing. Regis had offered to treat the injured arm, hoping mainly to learn more about Mhoul physiology. Molid had refused him, and had been attended by another of the Mhoul. When he next saw Molid, the arm appeared completely restored. As the whine of small motors accompanied any movement of the joint, Regis suspected that the damage had been repaired mechanically. Molid soon acquired a new rith. In spite of all that had happened, the Sage remained fascinated by Mhoul and their technology.

Now Molid had summoned him to the dungeon headquarters, and Regis had no choice but to respond. He continued down the stairs and finally stood in front of a large, brass bound door. Harriers guarded the door. No one announced him, but the door soon opened, and Molid stood there.

The Mhoul's rith fixed its cyclops gaze on Regis, and Molid beckoned for him to enter, closing the door behind him. Regis shuddered in the damp cold, looking around at the endless array of Mhoul technology. If Molid kept only a small part of his promise, it might be enough, with these wonders as the reward.

Molid went to a large desk and sat down behind it. Regis recognized the desk as being from Ryde's library. Regis found a chair and sat in it, resting his tired legs. Molid studied him for a moment, and then spoke, the harsh mechanical voice echoing in the stone chamber.

"What can you tell me of Tantagnel's defenses?" Molid asked.

"As you know, Thuro and Ryde were rivals, and we seldom visited Thuro's castle. I have no knowledge of its defenses, aside from what I've observed in my visits," Regis said.

Molid leaned forward. The Mhoul did not seem to notice the cold, or heat, or any other physical discomfort. Regis wondered what the Mhoul did feel.

"Then tell me what you observed. You've been inside the castle," Molid said.

Regis rubbed his wrinkled brow, trying to remember what Tantagnel's interior looked like. It had been a long time ago. "The castle was built on a rocky headland, at the north end of the island .

. ." he began, just to fill the silence.

Molid interrupted him. "I know where it is! Tell me what I don't know," it said.

Regis held up a frail hand. "I'm trying . . . to remember. We went up a steep road that led to the gates. There was no moat. We went through an outer gate, down a walkway between walls, and then through an inner gate to a large courtyard inside, with large buildings all around. Thuro gave me a room in a tower, where I could look down the cliff into the sea," he said.

"Was there any access from the cliff side?" Molid asked.

"I don't think so. I didn't see any roads or trails," Regis said.

"Go on," Molid prompted.

"The banquet hall was in the main keep. We had dinner there," Regis said.

"How many soldiers are quartered there? Did you see the storerooms, water sources?" Molid asked.

"I don't know how many soldiers. I remember a fountain in the courtyard. The water tasted good, fresh and cold. I didn't see any storerooms. The food was good," Regis said.

Molid continued to interrogate the old man for a long time, probing his memory with sharp questions. Regis answered as best he could, but he knew the Mhoul was not satisfied.

"For a scientist, your powers of observation are pathetic," Molid finally said.

Molid stood, and then leaned forward, resting bandaged arms on the desk. Regis could see his image reflected in the Mhoul's lenses, and a deep spark of red stirring there. The rith sensed a change in mood, and gibbered, moving restlessly on Molid's shoulder. The motes of crimson flared from Molid's goggles, enveloping Regis like a bloody cloak. Regis stiffened as he felt the Mhoul roaming through his mind, searching. He fought down a surge of panic at the cold, alien contact. Then Molid's suffocating presence withdrew, leaving Regis weak and shaking.

"Unless you are keeping something from me. You wouldn't do that, would you, Sage Regis?" the Mhoul asked, as the fire in its lenses dimmed.

345

Regis hastily rose and tore his eyes from the Mhoul . "No. I tell you I don't know anything else about Tantagnel," he said.

Molid turned away, waving an arm in dismissal. "Then this is a waste of time. Leave," the Mhoul ordered.

Regis started for the door, but something made him stop. He knew it was foolish, but he had seen some horrible things in the past few weeks, and he had to speak. "Molid, you said the invasion would not be a blood bath, but an efficient change in governments. But the Haggas butcher our people, and they are ravaging the countryside. If they're not controlled, there will be little of Skara Thrae left. Can't you make them stop? There's no need for what they do now," he said.

Molid's rith swung its eye stalk to face the Thraen, and then the Mhoul slowly turned. Molid studied Regis, as if considering what to do with him.

"The Haggas are savages, like the rest of you. What I want is Skara Thrae subdued, and under my control. It matters little to me if there is anything left," Molid said, then waved an arm at the dungeon walls. "I don't intend to stay here."

"But Kalkin has taken the throne. He is Warlord now. The Haggas control Skara Thrae," Regis protested.

"If you think that, then you are a fool. Now leave," Molid said.

From somewhere, Regis found courage. "Then it was all lies," he said.

Molid seemed surprised by the challenge. "Not all of it. But I owe you nothing . . . traitor. Now, will you leave, or do I have my Harriers throw you out?" the Mhoul asked.

Regis left, his head down.

Even as the door closed behind the Sage, an insistent throbbing light began to pulse in the room, coming from a crystal skull, on a table to one side of the desk. The rith noticed it immediately, and Molid moved to the skull. The Mhoul placed a gloved hand on the crown of the green crystal, and an image leaped into the room, held in place by a beam from the skull's eyes.

Another Mhoul stood in the beam. "A report, Dirgelord,"

the figure said, its voice distant and strange.

"Taglar. Where are you?" Molid asked.

"On the ironclad, off the coast near Aquarquff," Taglar said.

"What do you have for me?" Molid asked.

"At first, we could not locate the Windrider; the tracking device had evidently been destroyed. We proceeded south along the coast, and finally found the vessel in the harbor at Aquarquff," Taglar said.

"What were they doing there?" Molid asked.

"We contacted our agent in the town. The Princess hired a Pathfinder to lead her to Carnac," Taglar said.

"Why would she go there?" Molid asked.

"It is said she searches for her brother, Talbot, who was at Carnac," Taglar said.

"Go on. What else happened?" Molid asked.

"The mercenary Maximilian engaged some Ha'ashtari in an archery contest," Taglar said.

"Why?" Molid asked.

Taglar shrugged. "Who knows? He won, though, and they returned to the Windrider. Our man kept watch on the ship, and discovered Morgan and Maximilian leaving during the night," he said.

"Where did they go?" Molid asked.

"They took a longboat south along the coast, and then walked inland to a cave in the cliffs," Taglar said.

"A cave? What did they do there?" Molid asked.

"Our agent sent men to follow them . . . " Taglar hesitated, and then continued. "They never returned."

"Did our agent investigate further?" Molid asked.

"Yes, he found eleven dead near the cave. The rest of the men remain missing. The cave was searched thoroughly, but they found nothing. Quffians were also sent to kidnap the Princess from the ship, but they failed," Taglar said.

"You know of the Empire cache?" Molid asked.

"I know the legend. A cache somewhere near Aquarquff . . . filled with devices placed there by the Mercator Empire, after the Fall. Our people have been searching the area for years, but have not discovered it. How could they know?" Taglar asked, and then suddenly his rith became greatly agitated.

"What?" Molid demanded, as if sensing the disturbance. Molid's rith also grew rigid and intent.

"Late that night, our instruments registered a Gate, cycling and delivering," Taglar said.

Molid made an unconscious gesture, like someone brushing back a strand of hair from their face. Taglar knew Molid did that, when deeply concentrating, but made no comment. They all had leftover habits from their human lives, which for some reason refused to die. It was a quirk they had all gotten used to.

"A Gate? These men used a Gate?" Molid asked.

"It is uncertain. The signal faded before we could locate the source," Taglar said.

"Morgan and Maximilian knew of the Empire's cache. They went there. What did they do then?" Molid asked.

"Our agent lost them after the cave. They were next reported in the Waste," Taglar said.

"The Waste? Did they take anything from the cache?" Molid asked.

"Our people observed nothing unusual," Taglar said.

"I want those men taken, and I want what they took from the cache," Molid said.

"Dirgelord, we don't know that they found the cache, or took anything from it," Taglar said.

"How else do you explain the Gate? I want those men," Molid said.

Taglar hesitated. It was obvious the Mhoul did not want to speak further. Molid noticed.

"What? What are you not telling me?" Molid said.

"As you know, Dirgelord, no one moves freely through the Waste except Pathfinders and the Ha'ashtari. Our agents knew you wanted the Princess. They had no orders regarding the two men," Taglar began, and then stopped.

"Yes, continue," Molid prompted.

"Our agent instructed the Pathfinder to turn the Princess over after they left Aquarquff, but the two mercenaries joined them, and the plan had to be changed. Our people followed them to an oasis, where they discussed the situation, and decided to abandon the outlanders, leave them without a Pathfinder. That way, the Ha'ashtari would kill the men and take the woman as a slave. Then our agents could contact the Ha'ashtari and purchase her at the first opportunity. Unfortunately, the Pathfinder never returned, and it was later learned that he had been discovered and killed himself to avoid questioning. In the end, it will be the same. The Ha'ashtari will find them and we will recover the Princess from them," Taglar said.

Molid walked over to the desk and sat down. "This plan is fraught with risk. The Ha'ashtari are violent barbarians, and they cannot be depended on to act reasonably. They may kill the Princess or decide they want to keep her.

I wanted those men alive, to question them. But it is too late now. When you recover the Princess, locate and purchase any articles from the cache as well," Molid said. "And send men to find that cache. Stay there to supervise."

"The Windrider is leaving Aquarquff. What should we do about that?" Taglar asked.

"Nothing. We will deal with them later," Molid said.

"Yes, Dirgelord, it will be as you say," Taglar said.

"Oh, and Taglar?" Molid said.

"Yes?"

"Have our agent in Aquarquff killed. He is incompetent and I do not reward failure," Molid said.

"Yes, Dirgelord," Taglar said as his image faded.

Almost immediately, the skull cycled again, and another scene replaced Taglar's transmission. Molid studied the caller. It was Malissa, wearing her mask, with her colorless hair pulled back. She wore a high necked gown, studded with jewels.

"What is it, Malissa?" Molid asked.

The Hedonae lifted her head slightly. "You asked me to report directly to you. I am doing so," she said.

"So, report," Molid said flatly.

"The Chamberlain has been replaced. If I can keep Antony's poisoners away from him, he will last longer than the old one," she said.

"Are you certain of his loyalty?" Molid asked.

Malissa smiled. "Certain," she said.

"I won't ask how, lest you launch into another of your sordid accounts," Molid said.

"My methods are effective, however base you consider them," Malissa said.

"This Antony has caused you endless problems. Why have you failed to kill him?" Molid asked. "Do I need to do it for you?"

Malissa leaned closer, until her bottomless eyes filled the skull's image. "I came to you, and offered you Saxhaven and war with Androssar. Both tasks are nearly completed. Don't fault me for minor hindrances like Antony," she said.

Molid steepled gloved fingers. "Yes, you came to me. I still don't know why. As I don't know who you really are or where you came from. Don't expect me to trust you. I will trust your results," the Mhoul said.

"And results you shall have. I have found my traitor," Malissa said.

"One who will betray the Ambassador? Good," Molid said. "When will it happen?"

"In due course. I have many plans, that must be carefully coordinated," Malissa said.

"Such as civil war with Androssar?" Molid asked.

"What I plan will ensure war between Saxhaven and Androssar," Malissa said.

"Someday you will tell me the price for your services," Molid said.

"Someday," Malissa agreed.

"And what if I find the price too high, or not to my liking?" Molid asked.

"You will pay, one way or another," Malissa said.

"Don't threaten me, Hedonae," Molid warned.

"Part of my price is the life of the brat Maelin. Does she still live?" Malissa asked.

"Yes. She remains in Carnac, under surveillance," Molid said.

"If she finds a defense against me, you lose Saxhaven. Why risk that?" Malissa asked.

"The centaurs think their city secure from us. I will not show my influence there, unless it is absolutely necessary. If Maelin discovers anything, I will know, and act accordingly," Molid said.

"See that you do. I'll not be responsible for your neglect," Malissa said.

"Just make sure Llorgau remains under your control," Molid said.

Malissa sighed. "I tire of toying with him. Maybe I will finish it," she said.

"You will not. We need him for now. Beware, Hedonae. Your appetites will be your destruction," Molid said.

"But a girl has to eat," Malissa said.

"Well . . . feed on someone else," Molid said.

"Yes, my larder is quite full. Saxhaven still has many . . . " Malissa began.

Molid held up a hand. "Enough. I do not care to hear this," he said.

"Llorgau will live. For now," Malissa said.

"Do you have any other information?" Molid asked.

"One last thing," Malissa said.

"What?" Molid asked impatiently.

"I want Morgan when you are done with him," the Hedonae said.

"Morgan? Why?" Molid asked.

"He is not like other men. He is . . . a feast in a land of famine. I want him," Malissa said.

"If there is anything left, you can have it. Farewell, Malissa," Molid said.

"Farewell, Mhoul," Malissa said.

CHAPTER TWENTY-FIVE

CALLIS

Ka'lur sat at the low table in his tent, writing on a parchment with a quill pen. It was night in the valley of the Pathfinders, and an ornate lamp on the table lit the tent. A breeze rustled the walls of the tent, the sound accompanied by the scratching of Ka'lur's pen. Incense wafted from a brazier on the corner of the table, and Ka'lur paused to inhale the fragrant scent. A larger brazier provided some warmth against the chill of the night.

A gong sounded softly, at the door of the tent, and Ka'lur frowned. He was not expecting visitors. With a sigh, he put down the pen, and reached for his headgear. When he had the blue turban and veil properly arranged, he called out.

"Enter," he said.

The hangings at the front of the tent parted, and a second Pathfinder entered the tent. The newcomer bowed. "Forgive the intrusion, Callis, but two Ha'ashtari wait outside---one is a woman. They wish to speak to members of Ka'nas' cell. They were most insistent," the man said.

Ka'lur placed his elbows on the table, and put his fingertips together. "What tribe?" he asked.

"Shen'tari, Callis," the other answered.

"Shen'tari? What would bring them all this way? Who sent them?" Ka'lur asked.

"They claim to act on the orders of Ha'keel himself," the man said.

"High Chief Ha'keel? To inquire after those associated with Ka'nas. Intriguing," Ka'lur said, then paused. "Send them in, Ka'rek. And see if any of Ka'nas' cell are presently in the valley. Make your inquiries discreet."

Ka'rek bowed again. "On my life, Callis," he said, as he backed from the tent.

Ka'lur regretfully set aside the parchment. He had so little time for the things he enjoyed most---philosophy, literature, and poetry, the jewels of life. Instead, the duties of leadership constantly beset him.

Ka'rek returned with the two Ha'ashtari. The brown-skinned warriors wrinkled their noses at the sweet incense, but Ka'lur took refuge in the scented cloud, he had no desire to smell sweat and horses. Ka'rek made a sweeping gesture toward the seated Pathfinder.

"The Callis of the Pathfinders. Callis, Ha'set and Sha'for, of the Shen'tari," Ka'rek said, making the formal introductions.

The male warrior, Ha'set, brushed past Ka'rek to stand over the Callis. Ka'rek opened his mouth to protest, but Ka'lur waved him away, and Ka'rek left without a word. Ka'lur looked up at the Ha'ashtari, the whitening of his steepled fingertips the only sign of his displeasure.

"How may I be of service, noble Ha'ashtari?" Ka'lur inquired politely.

"We have questions for those close to the dead Pathfinder," Ha'set responded.

"Have you found those who murdered him?" Ka'lur asked.

Ha'set paused, as considering whether the question was worth answering. "We know where they are. The Shen'tari are investigating the incident," he said finally.

"Why the Shen'tari? The man was murdered in Meng'tari territory," Ka'lur said.

Ha'set sighed and folded his arms. "The outlanders are now in Shen'tari lands," he said.

Ka'lur pushed the table away, and stood up from the pillows in one smooth motion. Ha'set did not move, but Sha'for dropped her hands to her knife hilts.

"Bring them to us. We should mete out the required punishment," the Callis said, his eyes sharp over the veil.

Ha'set met his gaze without reaction. "The Shen'tari are well able to find the truth of the matter, and punish the outlanders," he said.

"The murdered man was a Pathfinder. We have the right," Ka'lur insisted. "These outlanders killed their Pathfinder! It is an atrocity, a violation of centuries of tradition. Their punishment

353

must be swift and sure."

Ha'set shrugged. "But the Pathfinder was killed in Ha'ashtari lands, and the outlanders remain in our territory. I am not here to dispute jurisdiction with you. Are you going to take us to his fellows or not?" he asked.

The Callis took several deep breaths, calming himself. To leave such an important matter in the hands of these barbarians seemed a grave injustice, but he really had no power over the Ha'ashtari, and the Pathfinders existed and moved through the Waste at their sufferance. Better to swallow his wrath, and assist. He had no doubt that the Ha'ashtari would find the truth and those guilty would suffer the severest penalty. The fierce nomads may not be cultured, but they were extremely effective.

"Very well," Ka'lur said, and then raised his voice slightly. "Attend."

Ka'rek appeared immediately, bowing as he entered.

"What have you found?" the Callis asked.

Ka'rek glanced at the Ha'ashtari before he answered. "Two of those you seek are in the valley. Shall I send for them, Callis?" he asked.

Sha'for addressed Ka'rek. "Take us to them now," she said.

Ka'rek did not move or speak, his eyes flicking to the Callis. Ka'lur grimaced slightly, and then nodded. Ha'set saw the gesture, and turned to Ka'rek, waiting.

Ka'rek stepped aside, motioning to the door. When the Ha'ashtari made no move toward the door, he sighed, and went ahead. The Ha'ashtari followed, leaving Ka'lur alone in the tent. The Callis resisted the impulse to go with the others. However, it would not be seemly for the Callis of the Pathfinders to follow at the heels of Ha'ashtari visitors. He could trust in Ka'rek to bring him any news.

Ka'lur sat back down, folding his legs under him, and repositioned the table. He reached for the pen and parchment, but could not concentrate. It disturbed him that Ha'keel bothered to investigate Ka'nas' death; the High Chief should have declared Jinn'she and killed the outlanders on sight. Had Ka'lur missed something? Was there more to the matter than the murderous whims and treachery of the outlanders? The outlanders had stolen three horses and supplies from Aquarquff. They obviously had no morals, and murder would not bother them. But Ha'keel was a wily leader, well respected by those he led, his reputation as a cunning warrior legend. The Shen'tari chief obviously suspected more than a simple murder. The Callis had heard of the incident in Aquarquff, one of the outlanders besting Ha'keel's son in an archery challenge. Had Ha'keel been somehow biased by that display? Ka'lur doubted it; part of the Shen'tari's reputation was his calm decision-making. Even if he was biased, the logical reaction would be to kill the outlanders at the first opportunity, to erase the blight on Ha'ashtari prowess.

Ka'lur thought of another recent death, this one in Aquarquff itself. A prominent member of the Shah's retinue, a man named Sherat, had been found dead in his chambers. The outlanders had already left Aquarquff when it happened, but could there be some connection?

Ka'lur picked up the pen. No, he would leave the matter in the hands of the Ha'ashtari. If Ha'keel was wrong, the blame would fall on him. If he was right, the outlanders would be dealt with, and the Pathfinder system would be protected. After Ha'keel had finished, it would be a long time before anyone molested a Pathfinder again.

Ka'rek led the two Ha'ashtari through the tent city. The warriors had not allowed him to bring the lamp, forcing him to peer through the darkness to find his way. He stumbled on the dim path, and one of the Ha'ashtari poked him in the back with a cruel finger. He gathered up his robes, and increased the pace, trying to put some distance between him and the barbarians.

He finally found the right tent and pointed it out. The Ha'ashtari motioned for him to remain on the path, and then moved silently forward. Ka'rek was slightly alarmed. Did they intend to murder the tent's occupants? Why the stealth, if they only wished to question them? One of the warriors crouched by the front of the tent, while the other slipped around the back. It was eerie how they moved, like some kind of predatory animal.

The Ha'ashtari at the tent door stepped inside, and a moment later, Ka'rek's fears returned, as he heard the sounds of fighting, and the sound of a body falling. Knowing he had no chance against the Ha'ashtari, Ka'rek drew his dagger, and shouting the alarm, ran toward the tent. He burst through the hangings, and almost impaled himself on Ha'set's knife point. He drew back, and the Ha'ashtari slapped the dagger from his hand. As his blade fell to the ground, the warrior turned away, resuming a crude search of the tent.

Hearing others approach in response to his shout, Ka'rek stood motionless, studying the scene. The Pathfinder Ka'lok lay dead in the middle of the floor, his veil cast aside. His features were strangely twisted, with a trail of blue spittle at the corner of his mouth. Ka'rek could see no sign of a knife wound. He knelt and examined the body closely.

Sha'for stepped through a slit in the back of the tent, and Ka'rek stood. She was wiping her knife on a piece of blue cloth, evidently torn from a Pathfinder robe. Ha'set paused in his destruction of the tent's contents, and frowned at her. She shrugged and sheathed her knife.

"Ha'keel wanted answers, not bodies," Ha'set commented.

"He attacked me. None of us are skilled at taking prisoners," she responded.

"Help me search. I don't want to face Ha'keel with empty hands," Ha'set said.

That thought spurred Sha'for to join the search, and the two Ha'ashtari continued searching through everything in the tent. They merely glanced up as other Pathfinders entered the tent, their swords out, drawn by the noise. Ka'rek stopped them, shaking his head.

"Send for the Callis," he said, ignoring their questions. "And wait outside."

For the second time that night, the Callis had been torn from his precious parchments. As he strode through the tents with his retainers, his anger was tempered only by his curiosity. Two Pathfinders dead at Ha'ashtari hands. Even the savage nomads did not kill without reason. What was going on? Had some sort of dark dealings infected the Pathfinder ranks? He would find out, and soon, before the whole system came unraveled.

Ka'rek met him outside the tent. The Callis knew that Ka'rek's sharp eyes would not miss much, and he waited for his report.

"Ka'lok and Ka'en are dead. Ka'lok at his own hand, or tooth I should say—a poison tooth, extremely potent toxin, of unfamiliar origin. Ka'en evidently attacked the Ha'ashtari while he was attempting to escape out the back of the tent. Ka'en lost the fight," Ka'rek said.

Ka'lur pulled the collar of his robe tighter against the chill of the night. "Why?" he asked simply.

Ka'rek spread his hands. "I cannot say. Perhaps they feared the Ha'ashtari's questions. I was not in the tent when they entered. The Ha'ashtari are searching the tent now," he said.

"Ka'nas was murdered by the outlanders," the Callis said. "Who contracted with them for passage?"

"Ka'lok contracted with the woman. The two men entered the Waste without escort," Ka'rek said.

"And now both Ka'nas and Ka'lok are dead," mused Ka'lur. "I care not for this mystery."

"Perhaps the Ha'ashtari will solve the riddle," Ka'rek said, without conviction.

Fortunately, they did not have to wait long, as the icy breeze did nothing for the Callis' mood. The Pathfinder's valley lay nestled in the foothills of the mountains at the northern edge of the Waste, and shared the cold of the plains. Ka'lur enjoyed his infrequent visits to Aquarquff, if only to soak in the blessed warmth of the lowlands.

Ha'set emerged from the tent. "May I ask what happened here? Why have you killed my people?" the Callis asked.

Ha'set studied the Callis' face in the torchlight, reading his mood. "One killed himself, and the other attacked us. We acted in self-defense. We did not come here to kill," Ha'set said.

"Why did they do this? What did you do to provoke them?" Ka'lur pressed.

Ha'set stepped closer to the Callis, and the other Pathfinders tensed. "We did nothing. They feared us. Why did they fear us, Callis?" the Ha'ashtari asked quietly.

The Callis frowned, more disturbed by the possibilities than the accusation. What was going on amongst his people? "I don't know. But I will find out. You have my word on that," Ka'lur said.

Ha'set studied the Callis' face a moment longer. He seemed satisfied by what he saw there. Sha'for came out of the tent.

"There was nothing else," she said, her dark eyes sweeping over the group of armed Pathfinders. Ha'set nodded, and turned back to the Callis.

"One last thing. What do you know of a blue poison, hidden in a false tooth, that kills like the na'dred?" Ha'set asked.

The Callis glanced at Ka'rek, and shook his head. "As potent as the dreaded grassadder? We know of no such poison. I will have it analyzed, and the results sent to you," the Callis promised.

"Yes. Do what you will with the bodies. Their souls should wander, but that is your concern," Ha'set said.

Ka'lur frowned, and then spoke. "You should know that the poisoned man, Ka'lok, was the one who contracted with the woman for passage through your land," he said.

Ka'rek stared at the Callis, startled by the admission. Ha'set regarded the Pathfinder.

"And the third man? Did he have any contact with the outsiders?" Ha'set asked.

"Not that I know of," Ka'lur said.

Ha'set nodded, and the two Ha'ashtari walked away without another word. Their dusky skins and leathers made them nearly invisible in the dark valley.

"Savages, rude and uncivilized," Ka'rek hissed with uncharacteristic venom.

The Callis glanced at him, forcing back a smile. "We share their blood, Ka'rek, and live at their mercy. Never forget that," he said.

Ka'rek lowered his eyes. "Yes, Callis. Forgive me," he said.

"There is nothing to forgive, old friend. You often say what I feel. But that is the way of things. We have been given our role in this life by the almighty Korum," the Callis said, then lowered his head and whispered. "Now, find me the truth. I want to know what evil lurks among the Pathfinders."

Ka'rek nodded. "On my life, Callis," he said.

"On all our lives this time, I'm afraid," the Callis commented absently.

CHAPTER TWENTY-SIX
THE ARC MASSIF

Morgan stood near the eroded crown of the arc massif, peering through the tangled rocks at the surrounding landscape. The silver arch sparkled in the clear, cold blue of the sky, and Mora and Damon hung low on the southern horizon. The crisp morning breeze tugged at the big man's hair and cloak. He could hear the far-off cries of birds, and the wind in the ragged stone of the summit.

Morgan turned and examined their backtrail. Nothing moved there, and he was reasonably certain that last night's heavy downpour had erased all trace of their passage. He searched for the scorched patch where Taskin's horse had met its fiery death, but he could not find it. Hopefully, the Ha'ashtari would think they had all suffered a similar fate. Somehow, he doubted they would give up so easily.

He turned to the north, toward Carnac, favoring his injured leg. In the hazy distance, he could see the Rift, the canyon that sheltered the city of the centaurs. It looked about a day's ride away, although the flatness of the Waste made distances hard to estimate.

He took one last look around, searching for any sign of the Ha'ashtari. Aside from several circling birds of prey, and the smoky blot of an antelope herd, the plains appeared lifeless this morning. Settling down on a rock, he spent some time in prayer. When he had finished, he pulled the small book from his cloak pouch and read a few passages.

He was so engrossed in his reading that the slight sound behind him made him jump and reach for his sword. Max stood nearby, having scaled the narrow trail leading up from the outpost building.

"Thought I had better make some noise, or you would suddenly wake up and try to take my head off. Any word from your god? Are we going to live through this?" he asked with a wry grin.

Morgan sighed, and put away the well worn book. "I can only ask. Iosus often answers with events. Is everyone awake?" he asked.

Max glanced down at the outpost. "Yes. Celeste went down to check on the horses, and Taskin is trying to prepare a meal without a fire. He was grumbling, but the Princess wouldn't let him start a fire. She was worried the Ha'ashtari would see the smoke," he said.

Morgan stood, wincing at the pain in his leg. "That was wise. I'm sure they are searching for us this morning, although I haven't seen any movement out there," he said.

Max scanned the plains around them. He was also limping slightly from his wound. "And you probably won't, until they ride over the ridge after you. They know how to use the land," he said, with a hint of admiration in his voice.

"Well, old friend, what do we do next?" Morgan asked.

"We should stay here until nightfall. If we move now, they would find us easily. Let's do some exploring while we're waiting for breakfast," Max answered.

They did a quick survey of the southern rim. Nearby stood a crude lookout post, a half circle of rocks piled up to shield the observer from the wind and enemy missiles. They examined the post briefly, and then climbed along the narrow rim, staying just below the summit to avoid silhouetting themselves against the sky. They found a dim trail weaving through the rugged terrain, and followed it. Incredible heat had fused the rocks at their feet into a jumbled mass, remnants of the lava that formed the massif. A few tufts of hardy grass sprouted from pockets of soil in the rocks, and greenish-yellow lichens coated the ancient lava. The air had a strange smell, a burnt, dusty odor that seemed to come from the rocks themselves when heated by the sun.

The summit narrowed near the end of the arc, with a vertical cliff descending on the outer side and a steep rocky slope on the inside. Centuries of wind and infrequent heavy rains had flattened the summit area, and the arc of stone terminated in a series of natural steps, leading up to a jagged pinnacle. Morgan and Max climbed up the ledges, studying the area, unconsciously thinking in terms of attack and defense. At the very end of the ridge, large fissures rent the rock at their feet, dark fingers reaching across the arc. Max dropped a pebble into one of the cracks, and listened as it fell. Then he climbed to where the cliffs fell away to the plains below, studying the rocky face. Finally, the two men ascended to the very top, and stood looking through a gap in a wall of rock that rose on the southern side.

"This is where I would choose, if we had to fight the final battle here. We could harry attackers at each level, then withdraw, put this wall at our backs," Max said.

Morgan looked through the notch in the wall. "And rather than surrender, we could leap to our deaths," he remarked.

Max shrugged. "From what I hear of the Ha'ashtari, that might be preferable to capture," he said.

"They value bravery, I can't imagine they would mistreat captives who fought bravely," Morgan said.

"They probably consider capture and cowardice nearly the same. I don't want to find out. No surrendering for me," Max said.

"I'm not going to think about that just yet. Let's go back down and discuss our plans," Morgan said.

While they ate a cold breakfast, they talked. Celeste's arm was stiff, but her salves had eased the pain.

"Well, Princess, what should we do now?" Max asked.

"The Ha'ashtari have probably found Taskin's horse by now, but the storm should have hidden our tracks. They will circle from the horse, searching for sign of our passage. When they don't find anything, they will start looking for likely hiding places. It won't take them long to come here.

If we move now, a search party will either see us or come across our tracks. We are one horse short, and riding double, we won't be able to outrun them if we are discovered. I would suggest we stay here for the day, rest as best we can, and proceed under cover of darkness. We can only hope they don't find us before dark. How does that sound?" Celeste asked.

Max and Morgan exchanged glances. "Good plan," Morgan said. "I would add only that we should post a watch at the lookout to keep track of any Ha'ashtari movements."

"Agreed," the Princess said.

The day passed slowly, the fugitives expecting to be discovered at any moment. They took turns in the watchpost, and actually observed two nomad search parties. The Ha'ashtari did not approach

362

the massif, and were only briefly visible.

The horses seemed to have survived the storm without any permanent effects. Celeste gave them a thorough examination, checking their feet and legs, and leading them to water in a cistern still half full from the storm. She had no more grain, but there was enough grass in the crater to keep the horses content for now.

They discovered another cistern near the outpost building and Taskin found some clay buckets and hauled some water for dinner. Max and Morgan cleaned and sharpened their weapons and did some practice drills. They all took turns sleeping, knowing they faced a long night.

Night came without any obvious signs that they had been discovered. Max remarked that the Ha'ashtari were probably just setting up an ambush, and waiting for them to leave. They ate dinner just after dusk, risking a small, smokeless fire. When they had finished eating, they packed up their gear, and Celeste sent Taskin down to saddle the three horses.

They were just collecting the packs when they heard the commotion, and Morgan stepped out of the stone building to listen. The arch cast its silver mantle over the twisted rocks around them, and the stars shone brilliantly in the clear sky, with the wind still for once. Morgan could see the light of Taskin's torch below, where grotesque shadows played on the cliff wall. Morgan heard the squeal of terrified horses, then Taskin shouting, and a deeper, more savage sound.

Max and Celeste joined Morgan, bearing torches.

"Hear that?" Morgan asked.

Max nodded, picking up his bow. "Yes, and I don't like it," he said.

Celeste pushed past them, and charged down the steps toward the sounds. "A hor'gaa," she called back. "Attacking the horses."

"At least it's not the Ha'ashtari," Max said, as they ran after the Princess.

At the bottom of the steps, they came upon a nightmare scene. Taskin's torch lay guttering on the ground, throwing a dim, twisting light. A large winged hulk crouched over one of the horses, now a bloody shape thrashing in the trampled grass. The other two horses darted back and forth at the far end of the meadow area, neighing in terror. Morgan stared at the intruder. A ropy tendril of saliva dangled from jaws filled with jagged yellow teeth, and a large flap of wrinkled skin hung from beneath the jawbone. The naked, ribbed wings flapped sluggishly and the thing's flattened tail thrashed the earth behind it. Morgan caught a whiff of the thing's heavy scent, and he could see its slick oily fur rippling as it moved. Bony ridges protruded from the fur, outlining breastbone and ribs. The hor'gaa crouched possessively on the torn body of the horse, which still struggled feebly. The cruel talons of its hind legs gripped the horse, and small forelegs pawed the air.

As Morgan and the others ran down the last of the stairs, Taskin charged the hor'gaa. The ratlike head swung toward him, its eyes gleaming in the torchlight. The hor'gaa croaked harshly as Taskin swung a cut at its leg. With surprising quickness, the beast leaned away, drawing its leg out of the sword's reach. Snarling, the hor'gaa snapped at Taskin, who ducked beneath the foul mouth, and backed away. The hor'gaa hopped after the retreating man, spreading its wings for balance. Without warning, the beast lashed out with one powerful wing, knocking Taskin from his feet. Before he could scramble away, the hor'gaa bent down and seized his leg in its jaws. Shouting in pain and anger, Taskin chopped at its snout, his sword slashing the hor'gaa's nose. With an explosive grunt, the beast reared up, lifting the struggling man into the air. It shook its head violently, tossing Taskin like a broken doll. His sword went flying and he screamed horribly.

Morgan heard the thrum of Max's bow from behind him, and an arrow sprouted from the hor'gaa's stomach. Squawking in surprise, the thing dropped Taskin in a heap, and turned to face its new enemies. Max put another arrow in its chest, and the beast bit at the shaft. Celeste never slowed, but ran across the grass, straight for the massive hor'gaa, her only weapon a torch.

"Celeste, no! Stay away from it!" Morgan yelled.

The Princess ignored him, raising her torch. The hor'gaa snapped at her, its forelegs raised against the fire in her hands. Celeste veered, dodging the bite, and flung her torch against the hor'gaa's gleaming side. The oily fur ignited instantly, flames forming a halo around the hideous beast. The hor'gaa screamed in pain, snapping its wings. One wing caught Celeste with a glancing blow, knocking her from her feet. The fire spread across its body, and the hor'gaa launched itself into the air, flapping blindly toward the horses. The terrified beasts bolted, running for the low stone wall. Without slowing, they leaped over the wall, and disappeared into the night.

The hor'gaa gained altitude, thrashing and twisting in mid-air, then streaked like a comet through the night sky. The wind of its passage fanned the flames into an inferno, engulfing its entire body, and its mortal screams echoed through the night. Suddenly, it fell from the sky, landing in a gout of flame near the open end of the arc. The thing's body rolled down the slope, smothering the fire that engulfed it.

Celeste picked herself up, as Morgan ran to her.

"Are you hurt?" Morgan asked.

She brushed the grass and dirt from her clothes. "I'm fine. How's Taskin?" she asked.

Max crouched by their wounded companion, setting aside his bow. "He took a bad bite on the left leg, but it doesn't look like the bone is broken," he said.

Celeste and Morgan ran to their side. "A hor'gaa bite is poisonous. We have to treat this wound," she said.

Morgan looked after the vanished horses. "We have plenty of time for that. It doesn't look like we're going anywhere," he said.

"So that was a hor'gaa?" Max said.

"Yes," Celeste said.

"And the Ha'ashtari kill these things to make horse blankets?" Max asked.

"They prey on horses and the ko'raa, so the Ha'ashtari hunt them. They remove the wing membranes, and sew them together into blankets," Celeste explained.

Max shook his head. "Speaking of the Ha'ashtari, flaming banners in the sky will probably attract their attention. We'll have visitors soon," he said.

Max and Morgan carried the wounded Taskin back to the outpost building, the Princess staunching the flow of blood with a cloth in one hand, and carrying a torch in the other. Once in the building, they quickly built a fire and heated some water while Celeste cut away the shredded pant leg, exposing the bite. Celeste cleaned the wound, and applied some medicine from her pack. The bleeding soon stopped, and Celeste wrapped the wound with bandages. Taskin endured the treatment silently, sweat running down his face. When she had finished, Taskin relaxed and closed his eyes, slipping into restless slumber. Celeste covered him with a blanket, and joined Max and Morgan near the doorway.

"How is he?" Max asked, his voice low.

Celeste studied the sleeping man. "The leg bones aren't broken, but the muscles and tendons are badly torn in the lower leg. He will heal with time, if the poison doesn't kill him. Hor'gaa bites are notoriously foul, something in their saliva. We can only wait, and keep him off the leg," she said.

Morgan sighed, looking out into the night. "In the meantime, we have to assume the Ha'ashtari will investigate the hor'gaa's death, or find our horses. We can't go any further, without horses and with Taskin injured. Our only choice is to stay here and prepare to defend ourselves," he said.

Max slid one of his swords free, and studied the dark blade. "The Ha'ashtari will soon be in mourning," he said.

Celeste, seeing the look on his face, shuddered slightly.

While Celeste stayed with Taskin, Max and Morgan climbed to the arc summit, carrying jugs filled with water from the cistern. They left the jugs at the lookout, and walked toward the end of the ridge, picking their way through the jagged rocks in the archlight. Asa had just risen, adding its silvery light to the scene. They did not use torches, to avoid alerting the Ha'ashtari to their activities. As they went, they studied the ridge and the cliffs, planning their defensive strategy. When they reached the pinnacle, they stood gazing over the moonlit landscape.

Max sighed, fingering his sword hilts. "This may be the end of a glorious career. Will the Ha'ashtari sing songs of us around the campfire?" he asked softly.

"It's not over yet. Only Iosus knows the outcome," Morgan stated firmly.

Max raised his eyebrows. "Has your god spoken? Is there something I should know?" he asked, then paused. "Does Iosus ever intervene directly, if the need is great enough?"

"Not usually. But one never knows. We'll prepare as best we can, and wait and see," Morgan said.

"Is that faith or fatalism?" Max asked.

Morgan shrugged. "We have work to do," he said, as he walked away.

They made several trips from the outpost to the summit, carrying more water jugs, weapons, and supplies. Next, they fashioned a makeshift stretcher for Taskin. Dawn lightened the eastern sky by the time they finished. Sweating despite the early morning chill, Morgan and Max labored up the slope, the stretcher swinging between them. Taskin barely stirred, mumbling in fitful sleep. His face was hot and the leg looked red and slightly swollen. They finally ascended to the highest level of the pinnacle, and placed Taskin in the shade of the southern wall. Around them lay the water stores and other supplies.

Max stood and flexed aching muscles, wincing at the stab in his leg. The sun appeared at the rim of the world, spreading its harsh light over the Waste. He walked to the inner edge of the arc, and looked down into the ancient crater. He motioned for Morgan, who quickly joined him. A group of Ha'ashtari surrounded the blackened area where the hor'gaa had died. Morgan counted fifteen riders. The Princess came over.

"They've found us," Morgan said. "And our horses."

"What happens next, according to Ka'chi?" Max asked.

"If the enemy is worthy, and brought to bay, the warriors will attack until we are dead," she said.

"No more limits on numbers?" Morgan asked.

"Oh, they'll come in appropriately sized groups, but the others will be ready and waiting. The rules of Ka'chi are different when there is a siege, instead of an open country hunt," she said.

Several of the Ha'ashtari turned their horses and rode closer, studying their surroundings, then one of the warriors raised his lance, and the entire group rode out into the Waste.

"They're leaving?" Max asked.

"I don't know. Run out there and ask them," Celeste said.

Max shook his head. "Maybe later," he said.

Morgan rubbed his neck. "We should rest, with one person on watch," he said.

"Care to toss a coin for the first shift?" Max asked.

"I'll take first watch. I slept while you two were climbing around this morning," Celeste said.

"Wake us if you see anything," Morgan said.

"You wouldn't rather die in your sleep?" the Princess asked.

"Not today, Princess," Max said with a laugh.

Morgan and Max settled into their rocky perch, and when Celeste finished her watch, Max took her place. Despite Celeste's efforts, Taskin's leg continued to swell and his fever increased. Celeste kept him in the shade of the southern wall, and bathed his face with a damp cloth. Taskin seemed exhausted, often drifting into restless slumber, his body evidently conserving energy to fight the poison. Morgan and Celeste took turns resting, but neither of them could really sleep. The morning passed with no sign of their hunters, and around noon, Morgan climbed up to Max's post. After making Taskin as comfortable as possible, Celeste climbed up to join the two men. She squinted into the mid-day sun, the wind tossing her hair.

"See anything?" she asked.

"Sure," Max said. "Sun, sky, wasteland, some antelope, a bird or two. A lizard scuttled by just a moment ago."

Celeste grimaced, shading her eyes with her hand. "Morgan, do you see them?" she asked, ignoring Max's response.

Morgan turned around and leaned against a rock. "Nothing so far. I wonder what they're waiting for," he said.

"I'm not sure. There's no obvious rule of Ka'chi that would explain the delay. But as I've said before, only the Ha'ashtari really understand Ka'chi. I'm sure they know we're up here," she said.

"Maybe they got tired of losing warriors and gave up," Max said hopefully. At the expressions on his companion's faces, he added. "I don't think so, either. Should I go down and take a look around?" he asked.

Celeste shook her head. "I wouldn't advise it. Even if we can't see them, they're out there," she said, then regarded the two men evenly. "Do we have a chance?"

"No, but they'll pay dearly for our lives," Max said grimly.

Celeste studied their position. "How will we defend ourselves?" she asked.

"We'll wait for them, up here on the ridge. See that narrow stretch of rim? A single man can defend that area, the Ha'ashtari will have to attack one at a time. Max and I can take turns, and hold them there for a long time. If we lose that position, we fall back to the first step, and fight again as they try to climb up. We defend the first level as long as we can, then retreat to the second level, and finally make our last stand on the third level, at the very end of the arc. But Max is right, barring a miracle, our best hope is to delay the inevitable," Morgan said sadly.

Celeste turned toward Carnac, gazing wistfully at the gorge, a great gash in the plain to the north. She grimaced with frustration. "If only we could reach Carnac," she said, and then paused. "We have another problem."

Max looked down at the sleeping Taskin. "Our wounded comrade?" he asked.

Celeste nodded. "If he doesn't get some proper treatment, he'll die before the Ha'ashtari can kill him," she said.

Morgan squared his shoulders, looking defiant. "Something will happen. We aren't dead yet," he said.

"I could go for help, while you hold them off," Max said suddenly.

"Can't you be serious for once?" Celeste demanded.

Max looked thoughtful. "I am serious. If we engage them, and I slip away at night, I might reach Carnac," he said.

"It would take you two days to reach Carnac on foot. Do you think you can avoid the Ha'ashtari that long?" Celeste asked. "Or are you going to steal a horse?"

Max shrugged. "Those four footed hay burners are a nuisance. A good man on foot can run a horse into the ground. And alone, traveling at night, I might just make it," Max said.

"If anyone could, it would be you. But it's still suicide. Let's save desperation measures for later," Morgan said.

"All right. But you think on it. That may be our only hope," Max said.

"You're both crazy. I'm going to get some more rest," the Princess said, as she climbed down.

Max regarded Morgan, who was watching the descending woman. "Has your attitude toward a glorious death in battle changed? Do you want to die of old age, or get killed in some stupid accident? What happened to the old Morgan?" Max asked.

"It's not me I'm worried about. I've lived a long time and have made my peace with the Maker. I just . . ." Morgan stopped, frowning.

Max nodded toward the Princess. "It's her, isn't it? Now you have something to live for," he said.

Morgan shook his head stubbornly. "No . . . she has something to live for. To see her brother, see her country free of its invaders, her people at peace again. I just hate to see it end like this, with her so close to her goal," he said.

"Go. Spend your time with her," Max said.

"I'll take the next watch," Morgan said, turning to follow Celeste.

CHAPTER TWENTY-SEVEN

SIEGE

The sun was slanting toward afternoon when Max climbed down from his perch, and whistled to Morgan, who lay resting in the shade next to Taskin. Morgan and the Princess both jumped up, running to meet Max.

"They're here. In fact, it looks like the whole tribe," Max said.

They went to the edge and looked down into the crater. Ha'ashtari outriders moved cautiously into view, easing their mounts up the slope. They spread out into a thin line, sharp eyes surveying everything around them. Behind the scouts came a larger body of riders. Morgan estimated over a hundred.

Max pointed at the main group. "What is that? Have they declared Jinn'she?" he asked.

"We haven't violated Ka'chi. They have no cause to do that. No, I think something else is going on. But I have no idea what," Celeste answered.

Several of the scouts reached the cinder cone, and three warriors dismounted, their fellows holding their horses. The three on foot climbed swiftly up onto the cone, until they could see into the hidden meadow where the hor'gaa had attacked the horses. Crouching in the rocks, almost invisible even from above, the warriors signaled to their comrades, who advanced along the lava arm, nearing the stone wall. A pair of them rode through the arch of the gateway, stopping just inside to study the valley. The main group waited downslope, the only movement their horses kicking and switching their tails against the flies.

Morgan frowned, looking down at the mass of Ha'ashtari. "Look who is down there," he said.

Max looked, and then lowered his eyes with a strange expression on his face.

"What? Who is it?" the Princess demanded.

"It's Ha'keel, and his son and daughter," Morgan said.

"Really? Why would he be here?" Celeste asked.

371

Max looked again at the Ha'ashtari. "Why did she have to come?" he muttered.

Morgan glanced at Max with a wry grin. "Has your attitude toward a glorious death changed?" he asked.

Max spit on the rocks, his face wrinkled with distaste. "No, I just won't enjoy killing her," he said, turning away abruptly.

Morgan stared after his friend. "That woman will be the death of you," he said softly.

"What are you two muttering about?" Celeste asked.

"Oh, nothing," Morgan said with a sigh.

The Ha'ashtari scouts worked their way up the valley, and then stopped briefly at the steps. The three observers slipped down out of the rocks, remounting, and then the whole party urged their horses up the steps. They stopped at the outpost building, and two warriors dismounted. They disappeared out of sight around the front of the building, and Morgan noticed Max seemed to be waiting for something. Suddenly, a piercing scream came from inside the building. The rest of the scouting party slid off their mounts, vanishing into the rocks around the structure. The riderless horses danced away, but did not bolt. For a moment, nothing moved, and then a warrior emerged, dragging the body of his comrade. The others cautiously emerged from their hiding places, and went to investigate.

Celeste looked at Max. "What did you do?" she asked.

Max shrugged. "Just left them a welcoming gift, a portent of things to come," he said.

"That may have been a violation of Ka'chi," Celeste warned.

Max shrugged. "So what? What else can they do? They've got the whole tribe after us now," he said.

"If they decide we're not worthy of Ka'chi, they'll fill us full of arrows. Don't forget, the only reason we're still alive is because the Ha'ashtari have accorded us the honor of their warrior's code," she returned hotly.

"Are traps a violation of Ka'chi?" Morgan interrupted the exchange.

"It depends, Ka'chi is subject to interpretation, depending on

372

the circumstances," Celeste admitted.

"Well, then, we'll know soon enough. It doesn't make any difference. I doubt that any of us are leaving this ridge alive. Now we have one less enemy to contend with," Max said.

Two of the Ha'ashtari scouts tended their injured comrade, while the rest finished their search of the area around the outpost building. The main party of warriors entered the meadow, riding single file through the gate, almost directly below Morgan and the others. Morgan glanced around, and then quickly moved to a large boulder near the edge.

"Help me with this. If traps aren't a clear violation of the code, we should reduce their numbers even further," he said, as he squatted and gripped the stone. Morgan's efforts actually moved the huge rock, and Celeste was again amazed by the big man's strength.

Max joined him, while the Princess kept track of the warriors below. Grunting and puffing, the two men managed to slide the boulder to the edge of the cliff. Once it teetered on the brink, they turned around and braced their backs against the rock, shoving with their legs. With a grinding crunch, the rock went over and bounced down the slope, gaining momentum as it crashed downward. It struck several other outcroppings, smashing loose more rocks that joined in the plunge. At the first sound from above, the wary Ha'ashtari scattered, some seeking shelter at the cliff base, others hugging the lava ridge, and a few riding back for the gate. With a noise like dry thunder, the growing avalanche of stone poured into the narrow valley, rocks bounding in every direction. A cloud of dust boiled up, hiding the meadow from view. The clatter of rocks became less and less, and finally all was still.

The dust whipped away in the afternoon breeze, and Morgan peered down into the valley. Rocks of various shapes and sizes lay scattered in a fan shaped pattern across the defile. Some of the larger boulders had rolled completely across the valley and shattered themselves on the wall of lava on the other side. Two horses were down, still forms in the battered grass, and a third horse stood nearby, too frightened to move. One of the riders had managed to leap to safety on the mound of lava, but two others lay crumpled amidst the fragments of rock. Morgan could not see the base of the cliff, but the gestures and shouts of the surviving warriors indicated more casualties there. Somehow, most of the Ha'ashtari had avoided the deadly cascade, and were regrouping at the base of the steps. Without hesitation, they urged their mounts up the stone steps, eager to be away from the cliff.

Meanwhile, the scouts had climbed the path above the outpost, reaching the lookout station. It did not take them long to spot Morgan's party on the pinnacle at the end of the ridge. They signaled the warriors below and waited. Seeing that the path to the top was too steep and treacherous for horses, the warriors at the outpost dismounted, leaving their horses in the care of a rear guard. They swiftly ascended the ridge and soon moved along the summit. As they approached, Morgan could see that the lead warrior held his lance aloft, point down.

Celeste noticed the gesture. "They want to talk. No one will attack as long as the lance head faces the earth," she explained.

Morgan headed for the lower ledges. "Well, then we talk. Any delay is in our favor," he said. Max and Celeste followed him.

Morgan met them at the narrowing of the summit. He stood with his legs braced, hand on his sword hilt. Max stood to his right, nonchalantly positioned at the brink of the steep slope, and the Princess to the left, uncomfortably close to the cliff. She wanted to move away from the edge, but she could not see past Morgan's bulk, and she did not want to crowd Max.

The frowning warrior with the lance of truce was Ha'keel, covered with the dust of the avalanche. On either side stood his children, Ha'sim and Sha'lor. Another man crowded close behind them, his face ugly with dark rage. The rest of the Ha'ashtari waited patiently behind the four facing Morgan. Max smiled at Sha'lor, who shot him a hard look.

Ha'keel began to speak in Ha'ashtari, and Morgan raised a hand. "Use Trade. Only Celeste speaks your language," he said.

The Shen'tari chief switched smoothly to the Trade language. "You press the bounds of Ka'chi, with your traps and ambushes. And you have killed horses," Ha'keel said sternly.

374

Celeste responded, looking over Morgan's shoulder. "We thought we faced Jinn'she, since you bring out the entire tribe's warriors. Has Jinn'she been declared, or does Ka'chi still govern?" she asked.

Ha'keel's frown deepened as he studied Celeste. "It was said you knew our ways, that you had followed the tenets of Ka'chi like warriors. Is this woman the source of your knowledge?" he asked.

At a nudge from Celeste, Morgan turned sideways on the trail so she could see better. "I am the Princess Celestine of Skara Thrae, and I studied under Baron Serenus as a child, living in Carnac. I am well versed in Ha'ashtari law," she said.

Ha'keel drove the lance into the sand at his feet. "Then why do you break one of the greatest laws, and murder a Pathfinder!? Your actions make no sense, outsider," he said.

The warrior behind him spoke. "The person of the Pathfinder is untouchable, protected by centuries of honor and tradition. You will die a coward's death for your treachery," he growled.

Celeste studied the warrior. "I see by your colors that you are Meng'tari. Was the Pathfinder sired by your tribe?" she asked.

"The man you murdered was my cousin's son, and I claim blood vengeance," he cried.

Ha'keel raised a hand, cutting off any further outburst. "We have discussed this already, and until I decide otherwise, Ka'chi rules here," he said.

"What gives you the right? They deserve vengeance, or Jinn'she," the man persisted.

Ha'keel half turned to face him, and the warrior closed his mouth. "Ha'serl, lest you forget, this is Shen'tari territory and I am High Chief of the Ha'ashtari. I have the right, unless you would challenge my right," Ha'keel said softly.

Ha'serl quickly lowered his eyes. "No, I offer no challenge. Do as you will," he said.

Celeste took advantage of the distraction. "As I explained to the Meng'tari already, we did not murder the Pathfinder. He sought to betray us, and committed suicide when he failed. We have done nothing to deserve vengeance or Jinn'she. We have defended ourselves bravely, within the bounds of Ka'chi. I have respected the fallen's soul stones, except for the traitor's, which I destroyed," she said.

"See, she admits it. She not only murdered the man, she condemned his soul to wander," Ha'serl said.

Celeste ignored him and continued. "If you will take us to Carnac, Baron Serenus will vouch for our honor, and we can investigate the death of the Pathfinder further," she said.

Ha'keel shook his head. "The centaurs care little for such matters. We see to it that their privacy is respected. No, I do not think we will be escorting you to Carnac," he said.

Morgan broke in. "So why are you here?" he asked.

"The woman has spoken the truth. You have fought well, and bravely, and have come further into Ha'ashtari lands than many others. You survived Windfall and storm. You have shown respect for our ways, and have followed our traditions. The death of the Pathfinder troubles us, but at present we will extend Ka'chi to you. As a further honor, the best warriors of the Shen'tari will be present when you die, to observe your courage and skill, and sing songs of the battle.

As chief of the Shen'tari I declare that we will fight only with the sun, and that we will not consider the traps a violation of Ka'chi. A warrior should be alert and cunning, as well as brave, and your attempts should hone our skills and make us better warriors. However, I will not condone any further traps or the use of bows," Ha'keel said, then paused and glanced at Max. "Although we acknowledge your skill with the bow. This battle will be face to face, blade to blade, as the gods intended warriors to fight. When my lance returns to the sky, the end will be upon you. As for the Pathfinder, I will find the truth. Die well, outsiders."

Ha'serl grabbed his knife hilts. "I will kill them myself," he said.

Ha'keel did not even turn. "Ha'serl, you will attend me. Your blood runs too hot for you to fight well. You would likely dishonor your clan. The Meng'tari mourn already, no reason to add to their pain needlessly. My warriors will be sufficient," he said.

Ha'serl ground his teeth, but did not speak further. His hands dropped from the knives. Sha'lor, who had been regarding Max, spoke. "Father, I ask that I be allowed to face the outsiders. They have killed a Pathfinder, and horses," she said, her dark eyes flashing.

"Allow me also, father," Ha'sim said. "Maximilian has bested me with the bow, and I would test his skill with the blade."

Ha'keel faced his children. "You will come with me, and not speak further," he ordered, then stalked away. With a last look at Max and Morgan, Sha'lor followed him, along with Ha'serl and Ha'sim.

Morgan backed away, shoving Celeste behind him. "Stay with Taskin. Max, I'll take the first attack," he said.

Celeste retreated, and then paused. "Morgan?" she said.

"Yes, Princess?" Morgan said, his eyes on the Ha'ashtari.

Celeste turned away. "Nothing," she said.

"Save some for me," Max said, his eyes glowing.

The Ha'ashtari tensed, ready to draw their blades. Ha'keel passed the last of the warriors and turned. The lance point swung to the sky, and he shouted one harsh word.

Morgan's sword flashed in the sun. He had positioned himself at the narrowest point of the trail, forcing the Ha'ashtari to face him one at a time. He dug his feet into the sand, gripping the sword with both hands, ignoring the ache of his wounded leg. Max waited behind him, his black blades moving restlessly. Celeste moved to the rear, and drew her knives.

The first warrior charged with a wild cry, and stabbed low. When Morgan parried, the Ha'ashtari slashed at Morgan's head with his other blade. Morgan jerked his head aside and aimed a heavy stroke at the Ha'ashtari's head. The warrior raised both blades to catch Morgan's attack. The three blades came together with a sharp clang, the force of the blow driving the warrior to one knee. Morgan kicked at the man's chest, but the Ha'ashtari threw himself backwards out of reach. The warrior attacked again, more cautiously this time. He used the point and the cross bar, one blade and then the other. His blades moved constantly, weaving in intricate patterns of slashing and thrusting. Morgan parried calmly, using his strength and longer reach to counter the attacks. After a few moments, Morgan swept aside one of the Ha'ashtari's blades, and thrust at the man's throat. The Ha'ashtari tried to parry with his other knife, but Morgan's blade pierced his right shoulder. Morgan grabbed the man's left hand, while still pinning the Ha'ashtari's other arm with his sword. Morgan kicked the man's knee with bone breaking force, and then threw him sideways from the trail. Morgan's sword wrenched free as the man tumbled down the steep inner slope in a cascade of blood and gravel.

The next warrior attacked immediately, and Morgan met her, hacking at the Ha'ashtari with vicious abandon. After a few strokes, she toppled to the left, cartwheeling down the outer cliff. Another fighter took her place, and the struggle swayed to and fro, Morgan retreating a step, and then pushing the Ha'ashtari back. The narrow trail restricted their movements, and the smaller blades of the Ha'ashtari could not prevail against Morgan's strength and reach. Morgan lost count of the warriors that fell, focusing only on the next opponent. Despite the cool breeze, sweat streaked his body, and his muscles began to ache with the strain, especially those in his wounded leg. A knife blade raked across the metasilk on his upper arm, and Morgan stepped inside the stroke. The man's other blade came up, and then he screamed as Morgan took his arm off at the elbow. Morgan grabbed the man by his jerkin and lifted him into the air, then threw him backwards, into the men behind him. While the other warriors fought clear of the momentary tangle of bodies, Morgan stepped back and motioned for Max to take his place.

Max slid smoothly forward, and the battle resumed. Four blades lashed in a constant exchange of blows. The Ha'ashtari defended themselves better than most, but Max killed warrior after warrior with cool precision. When he began to tire dangerously, he would trade with Morgan. The struggle wore on into the afternoon, the Ha'ashtari unable to break through the two men's defense, but the line of waiting warriors seemed endless. Vanquished warriors usually fell from the cliff or rolled down the inner slope, leaving the dying ground clear, the gritty sand stained red and gouged from the struggle. The sun sank lower in the western sky.

Celeste brought Max and Morgan food and water when they were not fighting, and treated the new wounds as best she could.

Max was nearing exhaustion, in spite of the brief rest periods. As Morgan tired, he began relying more on strength than skill in his swordplay. He chopped ruthlessly at the Ha'ashtari, breaking blades raised in defense, severing limbs, and battering warriors over the cliffs with his blows. The Ha'ashtari never faltered, preferring violent death to any show of fear. Those warriors in the rear took up a war chant, extolling the virtues of bravery and honoring the fighters on both sides. Ha'keel watched from the lookout post, his dark features impassive. Sha'lor also watched closely, especially when Max fought. Ha'sim joined in the chant, recognizing the skill of the outsiders.

Morgan and Max switched positions yet again, and the big man retreated to stand with chest heaving, leaning on his sword. The metasilk cloak protected him from the most serious wounds, but the Ha'ashtari were deadly, tenacious fighters, and it was only a matter of time before a knife blade penetrated his defense. The nomads had soon discovered the cloak would turn their blades, and now concentrated on his head and legs. He had two oozing cuts on his legs, which did not help his mobility.

Morgan walked upslope a few paces, and cleaned and sheathed his sword. He took a long drink from the canteen Celeste handed him, watching the battle. They did not speak, absorbed in the life and death struggle. Max took a cut along the forearm, and twisted savagely, killing the man who had drawn his blood. Morgan made a decision and whistled, at the same time motioning Celeste to withdraw. With a last flurry of attack, Max drove the warriors back, and then turned and ran.

Morgan covered his retreat, attacking the warriors on Max's heels. As Max passed him, Morgan chopped down the first man in pursuit, then they both raced for the first ledge. Celeste climbed onto the ledge, and then Morgan and Max scrambled up the slope after her, reaching the ledge just ahead of the pursuing nomads. Max grunted as a knife sliced his calf. Morgan slashed down into the climbing warriors, and three of them fell back in a tangle of arms and legs. Morgan kicked another climber in the face, ignoring the knife that gouged the leather of his boot.

Morgan and Max held the lip of the ledge, striking at anyone within reach. Finally, the surviving warriors fell back, leaving the slope below littered with bodies. The Ha'ashtari had lost six in the first rush, with several others wounded. They staggered away, clutching cuts or smashed limbs, and regrouped. Morgan leaned on his sword, while Max checked his calf wound.

The sun touched the horizon when the Ha'ashtari charged again. Morgan and Max stood side by side, methodically cutting and thrusting at the warriors below them. A wounded man grabbed Max's ankle, jerking him from his feet. Max severed the offending arm, but before he could get up, several warriors leaped for him. A knife skidded from his ebonite mail, and another gashed the side of his neck. Max smashed a sword hilt into one man's face, and rammed the other blade into an unprotected throat. An attacker tried to stab him in the thigh, but Max kicked furiously, and the thrust missed, the knife gouging the rock under him.

The warrior raised her blade again. Morgan's foot caught her in the side of the head, sending her flying down the slope. Morgan's sword felled a second Ha'ashtari. A third man reeled back, staggering from the impact of a rock thrown by Celeste. Max kicked another warrior away, and stabbed one in the chest, then rolled free. He jumped to his feet, to see warriors appearing at two places along the lip of the ledge. Morgan attacked those closest, while Max charged the others. As Max ran forward, he noticed the sun sinking below the western hills. Suddenly, Ha'keel gave a piercing cry, and the warrior facing him slid back down the slope out of reach. Max looked around. Morgan's opponents were withdrawing as well. The chanting had ceased.

Ha'keel stood near the lookout, his lance point downward once again. He grounded the lance, and cupped his hands around his mouth.

"Until tomorrow. You fought well today," he called.

Then the Shen'tari chief turned and began to descend the crater wall. Most of the remaining warriors followed him, without a backward glance. A small rear guard took up a position at the base of the lower ledge, to prevent the defenders from regaining the lost ground.

Max cleaned his blades and sheathed them. Morgan and Celeste stood next to him, watching the departing warriors.

"Well, we survived the first day," Max said.

"Yes," Morgan said,"but it's unlikely we'll live through a second."

The two men and the Princess walked back to where Taskin laid waiting. Celeste dressed their wounds, and then made some dinner. Max built a roaring fire against the cold night, using half of their meager wood supply. After dinner, Morgan brewed some sasich, and they settled down around the fire. Taskin had rallied somewhat, although his leg was still badly swollen and he looked flushed with fever. He lay on his side, propped up on a field pack, holding a steaming mug of sasich with slightly trembling hands. Morgan sat with his back to the rock wall, his arms around his knees. Max had squatted down nearby, sitting on his haunches, and Celeste sat with her legs folded under her, huddled in her cloak. Asa and Mora floated overhead, blending silver with the reddish glow of the flames. For a while they sat silently, watching the flickering flames.

"What about tomorrow?" Celeste asked, breaking the stillness.

Morgan grunted. "What about it?" he asked.

A gust of wind stirred the fire, sending up a shower of sparks, and Celeste pulled the collar of her cloak tighter. "Our defense. What's the plan?" she asked.

"They hold the path to the first ledge. We'll hold them at the second ledge as long as we can, then fall back to here," Morgan said.

"That's it? That's the plan?" Celeste asked with a note of wonder in her voice.

Morgan looked at her. "Do you have any suggestions?" he asked.

Celeste looked up at the cold stars. "Not really. I just thought, with all your experience, you two would come up with something more elaborate," she said.

Max grinned. "It seems our reputation has inflated our abilities. Sorry, Princess," he said.

Celeste shrugged. "Just hoping, I guess. We've come so far," she said, then gave Morgan a defiant look. "Tomorrow I fight by your side."

"Yes, Princess. Tomorrow we'll all fight, we won't have any choice," Morgan said. "I'm sorry too. We did our best. Our fates are in the hands of Iosus now."

Max raised his mug for a toast. "Here's to tomorrow, and many Ha'ashtari fallen," he said.

They all raised their mugs and drank. Celeste shook back her hair. "Don't be so gloomy. We have made it farther than almost anyone else. Ha'keel said so. They'll definitely remember us. That's more than most people leave behind," she said.

"We used most of the water today. We only have enough for another day or so. And our field rations are running low," Morgan said.

"Well, if we're dead, that shouldn't be a problem," Max offered.

"Princess, you shouldn't fight tomorrow. Then at least you would be taken alive. Maybe your father or brother could rescue you later," Morgan said.

Celeste gave him a hard look. "We've already had this discussion. I would rather die," she said firmly.

Max chuckled. "And knowing you, they'll be forced to kill you anyway, when you gut the first man that touches you without permission," he said.

"Yes, I'm not practiced in submission and obedience. I would make a lousy slave. Too much of my father in me," Celeste said.

"Could we try a night attack? Take back the ground we lost?" Taskin asked.

"No, Ha'keel's conditions work both ways. If we did that, they would show no mercy," Celeste answered.

"Mercy? The Ha'ashtari play with their victims, like cats. This Ka'chi is a cruel game. Better to fight, and die, rather than draw it out like this," Taskin said bitterly.

Celeste reached over and laid her hand gently on Taskin's shoulder. "It may seem like a game to you, but they're deadly serious about it. It's their way of life, a way to bring some order into the savagery of the Waste," she said.

"I know. I just feel worthless, laying here while they try to kill us," Taskin said.

They were quiet for a while, and then Max spoke suddenly. "Princess, tell me about the Ha'ashtari mating customs. I think Sha'lor likes me," Max said.

Taskin choked on his drink. "She wants to kill you, fool! Your ego has blinded you," he said.

Max wagged a finger at Taskin. "For women, the line between love and hate is very fine," he said.

Celeste glanced at Morgan, then answered Max's question.

"The Ha'ashtari are relatively promiscuous until they find someone worthy of bonding. Once bonded, they are faithful until death, which for a Ha'ashtari in the Waste, may not be that long a union. The bonding is a matter of honor and trust. In fact, after the bonding ritual, the woman fights at the man's side," Celeste said.

"What happens when the women get pregnant?" Morgan asked.

"They go to a birth camp for the pregnancy. They are attended by midwives, older women. Once weaned, the baby stays with a communal group of children, cared for by men and women too old to fight. The older folks are responsible for child rearing and most teaching. Able-bodied warriors teach the fighting skills," Celeste said.

"Do they know who their parents are?" Taskin asked.

"Yes. And the parents visit when they're able," Celeste said.

"Practical and efficient. I like these people. Although it would be hard to fight with women," Max said.

Celeste glared at him and he hastily added. "Except for you, Princess."

"I don't understand something," Taskin said. "You said no one comes into the Waste without a Pathfinder."

"Yes," Celeste confirmed.

"So where do these slaves come from?" Taskin asked. "Who is being captured and enslaved?"

The Princess looked slightly embarrassed. "Well, normally no one crosses the Waste without a guide. But there are a few exceptions."

"Such as?" Morgan pressed.

"Would be horse thieves from Kalixalven. Miners and gemstone seekers from the south," Celeste admitted.

"Why didn't you mention these before?" Morgan asked.

"I didn't want you to worry," Celeste said. "Besides, it's a big Waste, what are the odds of encountering outlander bandits?"

"You lied to me," Morgan said.

"And what about the children of these slaves?" Max asked, changing the subject.

"As I've told you, the Ha'ashtari make slaves of cowards, and any captives they find particularly attractive. The cowards are kept for torment only, and no Ha'ashtari would think of lying with one of them. However, dalliances with the other slaves sometimes produce children.

The male half-breeds, as soon as they are weaned, are sent away to the Pathfinders, and the females are kept as servants. Remember, Ha'ashtari warriors perform no menial labor, so they need servants to do their work," Celeste explained.

"There are no female Pathfinders?" Max asked.

"No, the Pathfinders have taken on the biases of the Quffians, and do not allow women to become Pathfinders," Celeste said.

"But they have women around for other reasons?" Morgan asked.

"Other reasons?" Celeste asked, raising an eyebrow.

"Well, you know . . . offspring," Morgan said.

"And recreation," Max added.

"The Pathfinders fear further dilution of the Ha'ashtari blood, and remain celibate, at least officially. They consider outlander women to be unworthy of them, but no Ha'ashtari woman would have them, so they're left with nothing. But being men, I'm sure they have their . . . recreation, whether they admit it or not," Celeste said.

"So how do they keep their population up, if they don't have children?" Taskin asked.

"They don't. The Pathfinders' population has been steadily dwindling, which will eventually create a shortage of guides, and may bring the whole system to an end," Celeste said.

"They're being slowly strangled by their own prejudices,"

Morgan observed.

Max drained the last of his drink. "We better get some rest. I'm going to take a last look around," he said.

Max tossed his cup down by the fire, and vanished into the surrounding gloom. Taskin finished his sasich and lay back down, the poison having sapped his strength. Morgan collected the cups, and went to wash them. Celeste followed him.

"How is Taskin?" he asked.

"Right now, he seems better. But his leg looks awful, and he still has the fever. He needs medicines and treatment I can't give him," she said.

Morgan set the cups aside to dry, and then turned to Celeste. He studied her for a moment in the moonlight, as if he wanted to remember what she looked like. "Celeste . . . I wish we would have had more time," he said softly.

She looked away, up at the stars, her eyes suddenly moist. "Me too," she said.

"I don't know what else to say," Morgan said miserably.

Celeste looked down and shook her head.

"I have to talk to Max," Morgan said and walked away.

Celeste started to say something, and then stopped, watching him leave.

Morgan found Max kneeling near one of the fissures at the end of the ridge. "What's on your mind?" Morgan asked.

Max stood. "What makes you ask that?" he asked innocently.

"I know you. What are you plotting?" Morgan asked.

Max folded his arms and looked up at the big man. "We both know we'll never leave this place alive. Unless something happens," Max said.

"Like what?" Morgan asked suspiciously.

"Like someone goes for help. To Carnac," Max said.

"Someone being you?" Morgan asked.

"I am the logical choice," Max said.

"How do you plan on getting off this ridge?" Morgan asked.

Max dropped a rock into the fissure at his feet. They could hear it clattering in the darkness for several minutes.

"Down there?" Morgan asked.

Max squatted next to the crack, and pointed down into it. "In here, the walls are narrow enough I can brace my feet against one wall and my back against the other. Then I just sidle down, and no one can see me," he explained.

Morgan peered into the dark fissure. "Does it go all the way to the bottom?" he asked.

"Yes," Max said, pointing toward the end of the ridge. "Several of these cracks extend to the cliff. You can see the opening all the way down."

"All right, then what?" Morgan asked.

"I run to Carnac, and get help," Max said.

"Why you?" Morgan asked.

"You're too big to fit in these fissures, and you're not built for running. Don't worry, I'll make it," Max said.

"Will you? You hate small, dark places," Morgan reminded his friend.

"I can do it," Max said fiercely.

"How long would it take you, assuming you survive the climb, and aren't immediately killed by the Ha'ashtari?" Morgan asked.

Max shrugged. "A day or two. Could you last that long up here?" he asked.

"I don't know. We'd have to, I guess," Morgan said. "What if the centaurs won't listen to you? They're notorious for hoarding their privacy. I'd hate to have you run all that way, and then get killed at the gate."

"That would be up to Celeste. She's the one who claims the Baron as a personal friend. Maybe she can give me some kind of token or password. Something to get their attention," Max said.

Morgan stood thinking, rubbing his chin. "Well, how about it?" Max asked.

"I hate to say it, but this looks like our only hope. We can't fight the whole tribe," he said.

They returned to the fireside and explained Max's plan to the Princess. Surprisingly, she agreed. She gave Max her signet ring as a token and whispered a phrase to him.

"Otium cum dignitate? What does that mean?" Max asked.

"It was the Baron's favorite saying when I was in Carnac. It means 'leisure with dignity,'" she said.

"Sounds like a centaur," Max said.

"When you arrive at the Rift, avoid the main road into Carnac. As soon as the Ha'ashtari know you're heading that way, they'll probably set a trap there. You should come down the cliffs and circle around to the main gate," Celeste said, then paused. "But watch out for the satyrs."

"Satyrs?" Max asked.

"You know. Satyrs. Half human, half goat," Celeste said.

"Satyrs," Max repeated heavily. "I don't suppose they're friendly?"

Celeste shook her head. "That's why visitors to Carnac travel on the main road. The satyrs attack anyone not using the road. Another one of the centaurs' defenses," she said.

"So I have a choice between Ha'ashtari ambushes or being stoned by goat people, assuming I even get to the Rift," Max said.

"Sorry," Celeste said.

Max went over to bid Taskin farewell. He gently shook the wounded man awake.

"What? Is it morning already?" Taskin asked blearily.

"No, I'm leaving. Just wanted to say good-bye," Max said.

"Leaving?" Taskin asked.

"I'm going to Carnac to bring some help. I'll be back in a couple of days. Keep these other two alive for me, will you?" Max said.

"I'll do my best. Although I'm not much good in this condition," Taskin said.

As Max turned to leave, Taskin grabbed his arm. "It was good to know you and serve with you, Maximilian," Taskin said.

Max patted Taskin's arm, somewhat uncomfortable with the display of friendship. "We'll talk about these days over a mug of ale in Carnac's best tavern. See you soon," he said.

Max collected his gear. He took a small pack with one canteen, and some field rations. He reluctantly decided to leave his swords and the bow Stryker behind. As an afterthought, he threw in one of the horse blankets. He checked his various hidden weapons and pulled out the dagger Morgan had given him. The Luminarae flared warmly, somehow comforting Max.

"I'm glad you gave this to me," Max said to Morgan.

"I hope you find it useful. I hear the Luminarae make good companions, and ebonite is, well, ebonite," Morgan said.

Max touched his thumb to the black blade. "A marvelous substance. Extremely hard, holds an edge, and black. I like black," Max said with a smile.

Soon, Morgan, Max and the Princess again stood by the fissure. Max sat down on the edge, and dangled his legs into the darkness. He had arranged his pack so it hugged his chest, and would not be crushed in the descent.

"May Iosus be with you and see you safely to Carnac," Morgan said.

"Be careful, Max," Celeste said.

"Take good care of Stryker, and the swords. I'll see you later," Max said, then paused. "Princess, can I have a moment alone with Morgan?"

"Certainly, I'll be back at the fire," she said.

Max watched her leave.

"Well?" Morgan said.

Max looked up at him. "Remember what old man Cynar used to say, back in the village. If you care, you'll die. That's our secret. We don't think about dying, we just fight. Don't let your feelings for the Princess distract you. It could be fatal," he said.

Morgan looked after the departing woman. "I finally have a real person to fight for. Not just money or some abstract cause. Maybe that's just as good," he said.

Max raised his eyebrows. "Novel concept. Either way, stay alive," he said.

"This caring. Does that apply to a certain Ha'ashtari woman?" Morgan asked.

"No. I'm not a sentimentalist like you. I would never let my feelings interfere," Max said.

"Oh. I see. Like out on the Waste, when you let that woman cut you?" Morgan asked.

"Do you want to sit here and talk all night, or do you want me to get on with my rescuing?" Max asked irritably.

Morgan looked down into the small, dark fissure. "Are you sure about this?" he asked.

"Pray for me," Max said, his face tight.

"I will. See you soon," Morgan said.

Max nodded, then he swung down into the crack, and slipped from view. Morgan could briefly hear the scrape of his boots on the rocks, and then nothing.

The Princess walked back to the fire, where she saw Taskin was sitting up, gripping his swollen leg. She ran over to him.

"What's wrong?" she asked.

"I'm worthless like this. I'm not going to lay here tomorrow and wait for those savages to take me," he said.

"You're wounded. You have to stay off that leg," Celeste said.

"No, I don't. I want you to lance the swelling and drain it, then make me some splints. I will fight on my feet in the morning," he said.

"More likely, you'll be dead by morning, if I do that," Celeste responded.

"I don't care. I would prefer that, over lying here helpless," Taskin insisted.

Celeste heard Morgan approach, and turned to him. "Tell him, Morgan. It will kill him," she pleaded.

"Morgan, please. You understand," Taskin said.

Morgan nodded sadly. "Yes, I do. You better do what he asks, Princess," he said.

Celeste stood up. "I will not cause this man's death, just to satisfy his foolish pride. If you want to butcher him, do it yourself," she said.

Taskin clutched at her leg. "Princess, I beg you. Grant a dying man his last request. I've been a soldier all my life, I can't die like this. Please," he said, and then somehow, he smiled. "If that clumsy Morgan does it, I'll never see another day. You have to be the one."

Celeste sighed and shook her head. "Men," she muttered.

CHAPTER TWENTY-EIGHT
DEATH AND DARKNESS

Max eased himself down into the fissure, bracing his legs against one wall and his back against the other. He moved by sliding his feet down one at a time, and then pushing against the wall at his back with his arms, allowing his body to slip downwards. He alternated between moving his feet and then his upper body, slowly lowering himself into the darkness. Max descended a couple of body lengths, and then stopped to rest. The constant pressure on his legs was tiring, a cramp had formed in his shoulder, and his various wounds ached, reminding him of the long day of fighting. To counter the fatigue, he relaxed one leg at a time, holding himself in place with the other. He worked his arms, keeping his back pressed firmly against the rock.

Now that he did not have to concentrate on the climb, the feeling lurking at the edges of his mind swelled. The darkness and the close confines of the crevice triggered old memories, and the walls closed in on Max, suffocating and oppressive. The blackness weighed down, threatening to crush him. With a muttered curse, Max closed his eyes, and willed himself to breathe with deep, regular breaths. He could not afford to panic now. He had to do this. He forced down the growing terror, clenching his fists. He focused on anger at his weakness, using it to fight back. He fed the rage, and the helpless fear receded, overwhelmed by an even greater passion. If there was one thing Max hated, it was any sign of weakness or fear in himself.

With sweat beading his brow, Max opened his eyes, and stared defiantly into the shroud of darkness. He began to feel better, and his hammering heart slowed. He could do this. He leaned his head back against the rock, looking up at the wedge of night sky above him. A portion of the arch was visible, leaking silver light into the fissure. He stared longingly at the bright stars, bidding them farewell, for now.

"Find another victim, Phaub. You can't have me," Max hissed, imagining the god of fear hovering nearby.

He reached into his shirt and pulled out the dagger. The Luminarae stirred and brightened, pulsing like a living thing. The golden glow cast a soft light on the stone around him and drove away the last of Max's fear.

"Thanks for the light," Max said.

The Luminarae flashed, almost as if responding, and Max stared at the glowing mote, wondering. Then his injured leg cramped, forcing him to put away the dagger. He took a last deep breath, and resumed his climb. Left foot, right foot, push back, slide down, left foot, right foot . . . again and again. When the cramping grew too severe, he would stop and rest, sometimes dangling one leg into empty space to shake out the pain. He was grateful for his leather gloves, without them the tortured rock would have rubbed his hands raw. Even through his heavy tunic and mail, the rough surface wore on his back. Sweat dripped down his face, and he could feel it soaking his clothes. He could also feel the cold, creeping in from the night air everytime he stopped to rest.

At one point the fissure widened, and he had to move deeper into the crevice to maintain his grip. Then it narrowed, and he had to crawl out again. Sometimes the rock bulged, arching his back painfully, but he kept on, one move at a time, each bringing him closer to the bottom. The slice of sky above had dwindled, and he could barely distinguish it from the surrounding blackness.

Suddenly, something interrupted the endless descent, bumping gently against his shoulder. A knife flashed in Max's hand, his back braced rigidly against the walls. He reached out with one hand, keeping the knife ready in the other. His palm collided with a soft mass. He could not identify it through his glove, but the thing clung to his hand, and he jerked it free.

Max cursed the blinding darkness, sheathed his knife, and pulled out the ebonite dagger. The rosy light revealed a fuzzy object dangling next to him, fairly large, oval, and covered with what looked like rough wool. He could see something inside. Max shoved at the thing, and it swung away, then back, suspended from a ropelike strand. He could see similar objects hanging nearby, of various sizes and shapes.

Deciding the cocoons offered no immediate threat; Max sheathed his dagger, and resumed his descent. He had not gone far when he encountered an obstacle. As he slid his back down, his buttocks pressed against something below him. He jerked his rear up, and the barrier clung to his pants, threatening his fragile hold. He clutched at the object, and tore it free. It felt like a sticky rope, which now clung to his glove. He twisted his hand loose with an effort, and drew the Luminarae dagger again. Below him lay a rough strand, stretched taut across his path, and still quivering from his contact. Max gripped the dagger in his teeth, slid sideways, and then climbed down past the rope.

He tried to descend faster, but all too soon, he encountered more of the clinging lines. This time he saw three of them in the Luminarae's light, criss-crossing in the narrow space below him. He could not get past them this time, and reluctantly drew his knife. Max moved around until he hung sideways in the shaft, feet and back jammed against the cold stone. Reaching down, he grabbed the nearest strand with one hand, and started to cut it. The tough, resilient fiber dragged across his blade, leaving a sticky residue. The first one finally parted, and the severed ends sprang apart and fell away into the blackness. He sawed through the second. He had just started on the third when he felt something. The strand throbbed with a heavy regular pulse, as if something crawled along it.

Max stared at the strand. With a surge of primal fear, he hacked at the throbbing line. The movement in the strand quickened, heaving beneath a rapidly approaching mass. The line snapped, and some weight tore it from Max's hand. In the empty darkness, beyond the Luminarae's light, Max could hear a falling body. Then a soft thud against the rock wall. Next, a brief scrabbling sound, like sticks dragged across the stone. Finally, silence.

Max strained to hear more, but there was nothing. Had the thing fallen to its death, or was it still down there, waiting for him? Ramming the soiled knife into its sheath, Max took the dagger from his teeth, and held it as far down as he could reach. As if sensing his need, the spark of flame grew brighter. Below him, he saw more of the strands; the crevice seemed thick with them. He caught a brief glimpse of something clinging to the rocks where the crack widened, a rounded thing that scuttled away from the light.

"Oh, fine. Now something's in here with me," Max muttered.

Max shifted his weight, trying to ease the cramping in his left leg. His other leg trembled slightly, even though his rest periods had grown longer and longer. The constant strain was taking its toll on his tired muscles. He did not want to drop any closer to the thing below him, but he actually doubted he had the strength to climb back up. Maybe the fall and the light had frightened the crawler away. He clenched the dagger in his teeth once more, faced the inevitable and started down.

When he reached the next strands, he changed his strategy, and grabbed the nearest rope. He swung his weight onto it, hoping it would hold. The tough line bore his weight, although it stretched slightly, easing him down. Max kicked with his legs, reaching for another strand. He braced a foot against it, and then peeled his hands free, dropping to the lower line. He dangled from the new rope, alert for any sign that the crawler was returning. He felt nothing but his own bobbing, and swung for the next. He had descended several strands, when his flailing legs hit several strands at once. The strands formed a rough square, and Max perched on them, the glow from the dagger revealing an intricate web all around him. The webbing stretched across the entire fissure, anchored to the glistening rock on either side. Max peered into the shadows beyond the sphere of daggerlight, but saw no signs of danger.

"I don't like the looks of this," he breathed.

Max dropped down through the web, clutching at the sticky strands as he fell. He hung from the web, searching the gloom for any more strands below. Suddenly the web thrummed with movement, and he tilted his head back, the dagger casting its golden light across the web. He heard a clicking, grinding sound to his right, accompanied by a strange rustling. A dark shape skittered toward him, moving delicately along the strands. Max swung his body frantically, kicking out into empty space, reaching for the next strand below. Then his leg hit the strand, and Max grabbed out for it, nearly loosing his grip entirely in his haste. The strand angled down into the darkness, and he let go of the main web, swinging onto the new line. He could still feel the pulsing of the thing above him.

He slid down the strand as fast as its sticky surface would allow, not caring where it led. Then his feet struck the rock wall, and he stopped. The strand was anchored there and went no further. He thrashed around until he was perched on the line. He heard a scrabbling sound above him, and he looked up. He saw a bloated body surrounded by a halo of sticklike legs, just above him. The thing dropped swiftly, suspended from a web spinning out from its abdomen. Several bulging eyes reflected the light, and he caught a glimpse of complicated mouthparts, and fang tipped jaws.

"Iosus, Thaar, Sett!" Max cried, calling on all the deities that came to mind.

His prayers complete, Max drew his belt knife and hurled it, aiming for the center of the descending monster. He heard a squishy thunk, then a sudden rush of air that wailed eerily. The spider's abdomen convulsed and the supporting strand parted. The spider fell, and landed on Max's perch. The force of the impact spun him around the strand, until he hung below it. The spider toppled from the line of webbing, and settled on Max's back. Its scrabbling legs enfolded him, and Max felt something strike his back, piercing his tunic to scrape against his mail. Max hung on desperately, the spider's weight dragging on his arms. He kicked backwards, sinking his heels into the thing's abdomen. With a lurch, the spider lost its grip and fell clear. Max hung limply, his teeth grinding on the ebonite blade, sweat dripping into his eyes. A spot on his back burned fiercely, and the area around it began to feel numb.

Max climbed into the angle between the strand and the wall, trying to relax his dangerously tired arms. He found himself shuddering violently, his skin crawling. His jaw cramped, and he reluctantly sheathed the Luminarae dagger. The darkness rushed in, and the old panic threatened to well up again. He fought it down, gasping the cold night air.

"Roast in Gaol, Phaub. You . . . can't . . . have me," he panted.

He started to slip, and he clutched at the web, but his exhausted arms refused to obey. He pitched backwards into the black and fell. He twisted around, getting his feet under him, and then slammed into another web. The web sagged under his weight, and then rebounded, rolling him back and forth over the strands, entangling him further.

Max quit struggling, reaching for his second belt knife, but the scabbard hung empty. He must have lost it in the fall. He reached for his boot knife, but the clinging strands hampered his movements. He felt something moving on the web, and he grabbed for the ebonite dagger instead. He held it out like a shield, the warm light driving back the darkness. At the very edge of the light crouched a second spider, its button eyes shining. Just behind it laid the body of the first spider. Its legs thrashed feebly, the knife still protruding from its body. Max's arrival had interrupted a cannibalistic feast. The second spider poised on its stick legs, unwilling to leave its prey.

Max froze, the dagger held high. The Luminarae swelled brighter and brighter, spinning angrily in the orb. The spider instinctively backed away from the light. With a decisive click of its mandibles, the thing turned and dragged its kin away into the shadows. Max lowered the dagger and surveyed his position. He lay across three or four interlocking strands, at the edge of the web. An anchoring strand stretched away into the darkness nearby.

Judging by the sounds he heard, the spider had returned to its feast, somewhere in the gloom at the other end of the web. Still holding the dagger in one hand, Max eased his other hand toward his boot knife, straining against the clinging web, trying not to attract the spider's attention. His hand closed on the hilt, and he drew it out. Sweating in the silence, he gently cut himself free, severing the clinging tendrils without cutting the main strands. Once he could move again, he put the ebonite dagger away and began to crawl across the sticky web. He reached the edge of the web, and felt for the anchor line. Suddenly the web began to thrum, the second spider was returning.

"Not again," Max said.

He rolled over the edge of the web, sawing at the anchor strand. Max felt a probing foreleg touch his shoulder, then the strand parted, and Max swung into the darkness, spinning wildly. He slammed against the rock wall, the impact driving the air from his lungs, and nearly tearing free his grip. The boot knife fell from his other hand, and he clutched at the strand with both arms, bouncing repeatedly from the wall. Finally, Max hung motionless, his shoulders aching from the strain. He kicked out for a foothold and realized he hung in a narrow part of the crevice. He lifted his legs and shoved, driving his back against the opposite wall, just as his arms gave out. He let go of the strand, and it swung away. He perched there for a moment, only his trembling legs keeping him wedged in. Then he resumed his torturous descent.

Max did not trust his aching jaw, so he left the dagger in its sheath, and climbed in darkness. He encountered no further webs, and the second spider did not follow him. His climb melted into an endless agony of cramping limbs and rough rock. He thought only of the next move, the next slide down. He lost all track of time in the total blackness. The crack widened and narrowed, and twice he almost fell.

Then Max realized his back was getting even wetter, chill moisture mixing with his hot sweat. His boot slipped on the wall, and he ground his heel into the stone, fighting for a hold. Cold water dribbled into his glove, and when he ran his hand along the wall it came away covered with damp ooze. He moved down again, and his foot slid across the treacherous wet surface.

"Great, just great. This was a stupid idea. What else could happen?" Max grumbled, as icy water dripped down his collar.

The answer to his question came a moment later, when his feet slipped again, and he fell headlong into the dark. Max tumbled over and over, struggling to get his feet under him. He did not quite succeed before he hit the bottom, and the blackness roared over him completely.

Max awoke with a low groan, lying prone on a slight slope. The surface under him was relatively soft; at least he had not landed on bare rock. He had no idea how far he had fallen, or how long he had been unconscious. Max lay on his back, and he could still feel his arms and legs. His pack had slid up until it nearly covered his face, but he had not lost it. Despite his woolen clothes, he was soaked with sweat and seepage and chilled to the bone. He hurt all over, and his head pounded, but he did not seem to be seriously injured. Max sat up and looked around. Blackness still surrounded him, and he felt for the Luminarae dagger. It lay safe in the sheath under his tunic, and he slipped it out. By the dagger's light, Max could see he sat on a mound of debris that had collected at the bottom of the fissure.

He had no desire to remain in the crevice. Putting away the dagger, he struggled to stand, but his legs folded under him and it took two more attempts. He staggered weakly forward, and his outstretched hand hit a wall, which he followed, leaning on it heavily. He came around a bend in the fissure and could see the night sky again. Max stumbled toward the opening and collapsed there. He rolled over and sat up, leaning back against the wall. Before him lay the Waste, gold and silver in the night.

"I made it," Max said, with a note of wonder in his voice.

Mora hung near the horizon. The night was about half gone. He should be up and moving, he still had to reach Carnac. But he was cold, and so tired. Max's legs trembled constantly, and muscle cramps rolled over his body in waves. A hand-sized area of his back was still numb from the spider bite. The Waste's chill air swirled into the fissure, and the shock of the cold alarmed him. He was going to freeze if he stayed here like this. He would be no good to Morgan and the others if that happened. He just needed a short rest. He wished he had some of Morgan's superhuman energy.

He looked back into the fissure. At the edge of the moonlight, he could see a pile of sand, blown into the crevice by the endless wind. Max crawled over to it, and managed to remove his pack. The Luminarae in his tunic flared suddenly, nearly blinding him. He quickly covered the orb with a hand.

"Stop that!" he whispered. "You want the Ha'ashtari to find me?"

The fiery mote only grew brighter, warming his hand. Max nodded, smiling. "Good idea," he murmured.

Max removed the dagger and its sheath, keeping the orb

covered, and put it under his pack. He pulled off his soggy clothing, and spread the garments over the mound. Then he dug a shallow trench, and placed the dagger in the bottom. Max climbed into the hole, settling down over the glowing Luminarae, and covered himself with sand. The orb dug into his back, but its gentle warmth spread through his battered body, and he soon fell into an exhausted stupor.

Sometime later Max forced himself awake. The short rest had done wonders, and the Luminarae's heat had driven away the chills. His muscles had stopped twitching and cramping. Max rolled free of the sand, and stood, brushing the clinging grains from his skin. He picked up his wet clothes, shrinking from the cold contact.

He piled the clothes on top of the Luminarae. "Here, make yourself useful," he said.

The little being in the orb responded immediately, pouring its energy into the sodden garments. Max huddled nearby, watching the glowing pile of clothes. After a few moments, he began dressing.

"Thank you. That's much better," he said. "They're still wet, but warm."

He retrieved the Luminarae and picked up his pack, slinging it over his back. Max looked briefly for his fallen knives, but could not locate them. Working to erase all signs of his presence, he moved toward the opening. Once there, Max searched the night sky, judging dawn was near.

Max knew he still did not have the strength to run to Carnac, and it would be day before he had crossed half the distance. He had to devise another plan, and hope that Morgan's party could survive the delay. The day of fighting and the climb down the fissure had sapped too much of his energy. He needed a day to rest.

Max studied the dim plain around him, and then jogged away from the cliff. As quickly as he could, he laid several false trails, and then doubled back to the cliff. The exercise had warmed him, loosening his stiff muscles. Now he had to find a safe place to hide for the day. He had no desire to spend any more time in the dank crevice. Scanning the cliff face, he noticed a dark shadow above him, a cave. He moved along the cliff base, and then climbed up the rough rock. Just as the eastern sky began to lighten with the dawn,

399

Max scrambled up into the shallow cave where he would spend the day.

Morgan left his bedroll before dawn. Taskin still slept, exhausted by last night's ordeal, but miraculously, he was still alive. Blood and fluids oozing from his lanced wound soaked the bandages on his leg. Morgan and Celeste had fashioned splints from a Ha'ashtari lance, and the pieces of wood lay ready to tie to Taskin's leg.

Morgan woke Celeste and they ate a cold breakfast. Morgan gazed out over the crater, bathed in the growing light of day, his face somber.

"What are you thinking?" Celeste asked.

Morgan sighed. "I'm wishing we had ignored our duty, and made love with wild abandon. Then ran away forever," he said.

Celeste's eyes softened. "How romantic. We have a few moments, at least for the wild abandon part," she said.

Morgan reddened. "Wouldn't it be a little hard to concentrate? With a dying man lying beside us, and a band of bloodthirsty nomads waiting to kill us?" he asked.

Celeste frowned. "Reality is rough on romance, isn't it?" she remarked.

Morgan studied the Princess, taking a long look at her hair, her eyes, her beauty. "I could have loved you, Princess of Skara Thrae," he said softly.

Celeste smiled, looking even more beautiful. "I could have loved you, Morgan," she said.

Taskin groaned, and they both glanced at the wounded man. "We better wake him. The Ha'ashtari will be coming soon," Morgan said.

Celeste roused Taskin and offered him some field rations. He refused the food, but drank deeply. They arranged the splint and bound it up, then helped him to his feet. He swayed, but stayed upright, and asked for his sword. They walked to the edge of the upper shelf. Below them, in the dim morning light, the Ha'ashtari waited.

Max awoke with a start, sunlight bathing his face. The sun blazed nearly overhead.

"Old and soft. Sleeping half the day, while enemies hunt you," he groaned.

He rolled over and unwrapped himself from the horse blanket. He peered out onto the plain, wincing at his wounds and aching muscles. Another clear day in the Waste, the arch split the seamless blue. Aside from a few circling birds, he saw nothing moving. Max crawled forward and peered over the lip of the cave entrance. He saw no tracks in the sand at the base of the cliffs.

The Ha'ashtari would be hunting him by now. They would have attacked Morgan's party at dawn, and soon discovered his absence. The false trails should buy him a little time, and he intended to remain hidden until nightfall. Barring treachery of some kind, he felt that Morgan and the others could hold the Ha'ashtari at least another day. They had a defensible position, and few could face Morgan when he had a sword and a cause. Being unable to fight at his friend's side frustrated Max, but he could do nothing but wait and hope. To move now would expose himself to almost certain discovery.

His clothing was still damp, and Max slipped out of everything but his underclothing and the ebonite mail. He spread the garments out on the sunny stone to finish drying, making sure they were not visible from below. Crawling back into the rear of the cave, Max took stock of his weapons and supplies. In his pack, he had field rations and a water bottle. He had lost both of his belt knives, and the boot knife. That left his two throwing knives in their forearm sheaths, the garrote cord looped around his belt, and the spike in his other boot. And the ebonite dagger. He felt nearly naked with that few weapons. It was an uncomfortable feeling that he did not care for.

Max drank a little water and chewed on some of the field rations. He had sweat so much the night before, he was very thirsty, but Max knew he had to conserve the precious liquid in his canteen. He did not want to take the time to hunt for cacti or springs to refill it.

The day passed slowly, with Max moving only to loosen abused

401

muscles. He took several short naps, resting and regaining his strength. The sun hung low in the western sky, when he heard a noise below. He peered over the edge, to see a group of Ha'ashtari riding slowly along the base of the cliff. He counted twelve of them.

Suddenly, one of the riders raised a hand, and the others stopped. They stared intently at the ground near the fissure where Max had emerged last night. A Ha'ashtari dismounted, and examined the ground. They spoke briefly, and then the warrior on foot cautiously entered the crevice opening. Max hoped he did not find the lost knives.

The warrior soon returned and mounted his horse. The man looked up at the cliff and Max recognized the Meng'tari Ha'serl. Ha'serl motioned and the riders began to follow Max's false trail, leaning down to study the faint traces on the ground.

Max had laid a faint but discernible trail, one that a good tracker could find, but not so obvious as to raise suspicion. The Ha'ashtari turned directly toward Carnac, moving slowly. Max watched them until they rode out of sight over a low ridge, and then glanced at the setting sun. It would be dark soon, and he would leave then. Max fought the urge to go back and determine Morgan's fate. He would do them no good that way; he just hoped Iosus still favored his friend.

Morgan and Taskin fought shoulder to shoulder on the upper ledge, with Celeste guarding their backs. The two outlanders had the advantage of height, and they were fighting for their lives. A knife skidded off Taskin's splint. He winced, chopping at the Ha'ashtari below him. With his injured leg, Taskin could not move very fast, but his years of experience and grim determination still made him a dangerous foe. Again and again, the two men forced the Ha'ashtari back, but they kept coming, a tide of brown.

Two warriors leaped at Morgan. He killed one of them, but the second wrapped his arms around Morgan's legs. Morgan staggered back, bringing his sword hilt down on the back of the man's neck. With a crunch of bone, the man's grip went slack. Morgan kicked free of the limp arms, but the defensive line had been broken. The

Ha'ashtari rushed in. Taskin valiantly tried to stem the flow, but the Ha'ashtari were everywhere.

Celeste rammed a knife into the side of a warrior facing Taskin, and leaped back to avoid the man's dying stroke. Taskin hacked to his right and left, knocking two warriors from the ledge. A third man leaped up the slope, and his blade took Taskin in the thigh. Taskin brought his sword around, and the warrior staggered back down the slope, clutching at a gash across his chest.

Taskin's wound was in his good leg, and he found he could barely stand. Morgan fought his way back to Taskin's side, driving several Ha'ashtari before him. Morgan thrust, and his sword went deep into a warrior's chest. The blade stuck in the man's ribs, and Morgan tried to yank it free. Another warrior came at him from the side, and Morgan kicked her away. The weight of the impaled warrior pulled him off balance, and when he kicked, he fell down the slope. Morgan managed to land on his feet, but he lost his sword. Three Ha'ashtari charged him, determined to finish him before he could recover his blade.

Morgan spun away from the first thrust. A second knife grated across the metasilk covering his back. He grabbed an attacker by wrist and throat, and spun him around, knocking the others back. He twisted the man's arm around, and drove the blade into his own heart, the Ha'ashtari helpless in his powerful grip. Morgan threw the body at his attackers, and dove for his sword. Jerking the sword from the dead man's chest, he rolled. He parried a thrust at his head, and then kicked out at two other warriors who were trying to stab him.

When Morgan had fallen down the slope, Taskin had cried out and stumbled after him. Taskin knocked aside a thrust and stabbed a woman warrior trying to reach Morgan. Two Ha'ashtari blades entered his back. He whirled, and his attackers fell back from his blade. Ignoring his peril, Taskin turned away and chopped at another warrior facing Morgan. Taskin's blade lodged in the joint between neck and shoulder, and the warrior sank to his knees.

While Taskin tried to free his sword, a Ha'ashtari stabbed him high in the side. Taskin punched the woman in the throat, and staggered away, leaving his sword. He coughed and blood came from his mouth. Then he saw Morgan on his back, fighting off three assailants. Taking another knife thrust in his upper arm, Taskin leaped toward the ring of warriors around Morgan. Shouting the Raav war cry, he threw himself on two of them, and all three tumbled over the edge of the outer cliff. Their bodies tumbled down the cliff face, bouncing and spinning through the air.

"Taskin!" Morgan roared.

He brought his sword around in a furious arc, severing a warrior's leg at the knee. He grabbed another warrior's leg and yanked the man's feet from under him. Morgan surged to his feet, laying about with his sword. Two Ha'ashtari fell, and Morgan grabbed a third by the arm, throwing her over the cliff.

Celeste had not been idle. As Morgan and Taskin fought below, she stabbed a climbing warrior in the face, and kicked his body away. Taskin's death and Morgan's plight filled her with rage, the same rage that had made her father famous. Another warrior gained the ledge and advanced on her. She met him with a snarl and flashing knives. Celeste thrust and slashed; using every trick she had been taught. The warrior's eyes widened at her ferocity and skill, and he backed a pace or two, trying to stay alive. He blocked several thrusts, and then aimed a cut at the Princess' head. She ducked and spun, catching the man in the back with one of her cross blades. He staggered forward, at the same time slashing at her. Celeste deflected the knife with one of her blades, and cut the tendons at the back of his left knee with the other. The man sagged to one knee, and Celeste kicked him in the back. The man tumbled down the slope, landing on top of one of Morgan's opponents.

Morgan took advantage of the confusion to fight his way to the slope. He backed up it, thrusting and parrying. As he reached the top of the slope, a signal came from the rear of the swarm of Ha'ashtari, and the attack ceased. The warriors retreated, leaving Morgan and Celeste alone with the dead.

Morgan leaned on his sword point, breathing heavily. He had a gash over his left eye, and blood streaked his face. On his sword hilt, red smears trailed from another cut across the back of his hand. He had taken several wounds in the legs, which now shook from pain and fatigue.

Celeste remained relatively unharmed, despite her torn clothing, covered with dirt and blood. She was staring at the cliff where Taskin had fallen.

"He's gone," she said unbelievingly.

Morgan wiped blood out of his eyes. "I'm sorry. One more rush like that and we're finished," he admitted.

Celeste stared at him, her fists clenched. "I don't want it to end this way. It's not fair," she said.

"I can't do any more," Morgan said.

"If you die, I'll kill myself. I won't be their slave," Celeste said.

Morgan touched her arm. "Please don't. Live, Princess. Someone will come for you," he said.

She ignored him, looking at the Ha'ashtari. "What are those butchers waiting for now?" she said.

Morgan followed her gaze. The Ha'ashtari had withdrawn to the lower ledge, where they stood waiting. Ha'keel stood near the lookout, conferring with two warriors. The three of them turned and descended the trail to the outpost.

"It looks like we'll have to wait a while. Let's get a drink, and tend our wounds," Morgan said.

Celeste looked at his battered body, as if seeing it for the first time. "You're a mess. Let me clean you up," she said.

Morgan and Celeste sat in the shade of the rock wall, sipping water and eating rations. The Ha'ashtari still waited below and Ha'keel remained at the outpost. Celeste had bound Morgan's wounds, washing them and administering a disinfectant.

"Do you think Max made it?" Celeste asked.

"If anyone could, it'll be Max. We can only hope and pray," Morgan said.

Celeste looked down at the Ha'ashtari. "Rest. I'll keep watch."

Morgan leaned back, and relaxed, closing his eyes. He drifted, almost sleeping. After some time, Celeste nudged him.

"They're coming," she said.

Morgan stood. Ha'keel was climbing back to the rim.

"Farewell, Princess," Morgan said, as they walked back to make their last stand.

Ha'keel spoke to the waiting warriors, who seemed confused and unsettled, as if their chief ordered some strange thing. Finally, they turned and advanced along the rim. Ha'keel raised a lance, point down. He approached Morgan and Celeste, alone.

"What now?" Morgan asked.

"Maybe we live," Celeste said.

Ha'keel stopped at the base of the slope. He looked up at them.

"I have a proposal," the chief said.

"Why don't you and I fight, and let the gods decide?" Morgan suggested.

Ha'keel regarded the big man intently. He seemed surprised. "I am tempted to accept your challenge, if only to keep you from further decimating my tribe. However, that is not to be," he said.

"What's your proposal?" Celeste asked.

"If you surrender, I will take the woman to Carnac, and you will undertake the Ru'atan," Ha'keel said simply.

"You would guarantee the Princess safe passage to Carnac?" Morgan asked.

"Morgan," Celeste whispered warningly. "Don't even think it."

"Yes," Ha'keel said.

"Why would you do this? We're accused of killing a Pathfinder," Morgan said.

"When I first heard your story, I sent warriors to the Pathfinder camp to investigate. They have returned," he said.

"What did they find?" Morgan asked.

"They sought to question some of the Pathfinders. One man killed himself and the other fought and died as well," Ha'keel said.

"What does that tell you?" Celeste asked.

"It tells me they had a secret, more important to them than honor or tradition. If one Pathfinder committed suicide to avoid the truth, would another, as you have said?" Ha'keel said.

"Do you believe us then?" Morgan asked.

"I am a cautious man, outlander. I would not have the blood of the innocent on my hands. Let the centaurs decide the fate of the woman," Ha'keel said.

"And mine?" Morgan asked.

"The Ru'atan will decide yours," Ha'keel said.

"What exactly is the Ru'atan?" Morgan asked.

"You will have until tomorrow, while your needs are tended to. Then, you will face the Fist of El'Atan," Ha'keel said.

"No," Celeste said.

Morgan held up a hand. "What is the Fist of El'Atan?" he asked.

"Holy executioners. It's suicide, Morgan. Refuse," Celeste said.

Morgan looked around, at the rocky rim, and the waiting warriors. "This is suicide," he said.

"The Fist of El'Atan consists of five Ha'ashtari warriors, chosen for their prowess and piety. In certain matters, they decide the will of El'Atan," Ha'keel said.

"How do they decide?" Morgan asked.

"Trial by combat. The survivor is chosen by El'Atan," Celeste said.

"What are the terms of this combat?" Morgan asked.

"Ha'ashtari weapons only. You will be given a span of time to choose your place. Then it is just you and the Fist, under the Arch," Ha'keel said.

"Any chance of just letting us go?" Morgan said.

Ha'keel frowned. "Even if you were not accused of killing the Pathfinder, the penalty for entering the Shan'tari without escort is also death. I am bound by law, tradition, and honor. My will is not unfettered," he said.

Morgan had been leaning on his bloody sword. Suddenly, he straightened. "We accept," he said.

Celeste stared at him. "Are you mad?" she demanded.

"You'll be taken to Carnac. You will live," Morgan said.

"But you'll die, and I don't want to live without you," Celeste said.

"You will live," Morgan repeated.

"No, I refuse," Celeste said.

Morgan's arm flashed and his sword suddenly quivered in the

ground between Ha'keel's feet. Ha'keel's warriors surged forward, but the High Chief did not flinch. "We surrender. Keep your word, chief of the Shen'tari," Morgan said.

"Morgan!" Celeste cried.

"Princess, he loves you. Grant him the ability to save that which is most precious to him," Ha'keel said.

Morgan and Celeste stared at the Ha'ashtari chief.

"Besides, El'Atan may yet spare him. The gods are inscrutable," Ha'keel added.

"You better live," Celeste said, throwing down her knives.

"I will try, Princess. I will try," Morgan said.

Ha'keel picked up Morgan's sword and regarded it admiringly. "Come down," he called to the pair above.

As Morgan and Celeste descended the slope, Ha'keel gave orders to his waiting warriors. "Collect their belongings," he said.

Ha'keel's warriors retrieved their packs and other gear. They carried Max's bow like it had fallen from heaven. Ha'serl joined them. He had been searching the end of the rim for Max.

"He is not there!" Ha'serl said.

"I knew he wasn't. Did you think he was hiding while his friends fought, like a coward? I sent patrols to search for him, as soon as the fighting began this morning" Ha'keel said scornfully.

"He is a coward, and a murderer," Ha'serl said, turning to Morgan. "Where is he?"

Morgan shrugged. "He went to Carnac, to bring Celeste's friends," he said.

"Carnac? How? Did he fly?" Ha'serl demanded.

Morgan said nothing. Ha'serl moved to strike him, and then thought better of it. He had seen what the big man could do.

"We have searched the inside of the crater, and found no one. When he did not join in the defense this morning, I assumed he was moving down the inner slope, to attack us from the rear. That leaves the cliffs. No man could scale those," Ha'keel said, then turned to Ha'serl. "You searched the upper levels. What lies there?"

"Nothing. The ledges, the south wall, the end of the rim. Some crevices at the very end," Ha'serl said.

"Crevices? Big enough for a man?" Ha'keel asked.

Another warrior spoke. "The tet'rik wait there. If he did enter the dark of the rocks, he is dead," she said.

"Tet'rik?" Morgan whispered to Celeste.

"Large spiders. That build their webs in the crevices of the massif. If your friend did encounter one of them, he is most likely dead," Ha'keel explained.

"Poor Max. I didn't know about the spiders," the Princess said.

"Don't worry. It would take more than some overgrown insect to stop Max," Morgan assured her.

"You may be right. Ha'serl, search the place again. Find out if those crevices lead to the bottom of the cliff," Ha'keel ordered. "Ha'mok, bring these two to my camp."

Ha'keel's warriors led the captives down the slope to the main Ha'ashtari camp, just outside the inner wall where Morgan's party had pastured their horses. Ha'serl soon entered the camp.

"Some of the cracks reach the bottom. He could have descended through them," he said.

"Ha'serl, you want to kill the outlander. Take eleven warriors, and search the base of the cliff. Find his trail and follow it. I give you the man. Take his life, if you can," Ha'keel said.

"I will find him, and kill him," Ha'serl said, then looked at Morgan and Celeste. "He is not worthy of the Fist. That honor is reserved for Ha'ashtari, not murdering outlanders. And she should be given to the Meng'tari as a slave."

"Do as you are told. Ha'drak, go with him," Ha'keel ordered.

Ha'serl and Ha'drak selected ten other warriors. Sha'lor approached her father, but Ha'keel held up his hand.

"Don't even ask, daughter. I want you here," he said firmly.

Sha'lor turned and walked stiffly away. Ha'keel watched her, shaking his head.

"Foolish girl," he muttered.

Ha'serl's warriors collected their mounts and rode away. Ha'keel had the prisoners brought to his tent.

CHAPTER TWENTY-NINE
NIGHT RUN

Max jogged through the flowing plains grass, following the Ha'ashtari's faint trail. In the darkness, the Waste appeared as a restless sea beneath the silver arch. Asa lay just below the horizon, casting her light across the northern sky. Max came to the crest of a ridge and slowed, then crouched and moved carefully through the tall grass, making sure he did not outline himself against the sky. He parted the curtain of stalks and peered down into a valley. A small cinder cone laid to his right, a distant cousin to the great volcano that had formed the arc massif. A stream of lava had flowed from the vent, moving down the valley as it cooled. The twisted mass extended out of sight to Max's left.

Max recognized the place from the night before. He had marked his trail to this point, and then created three false paths, each going in a slightly different direction, but all generally toward Carnac. Doubling back on each of the three trails, he had finally moved along the lava flow, the jumbled rock not leaving any sign of his passage. When the flow had finally ended, Max had circled back to the massif, using all his skill to mask his return.

Max noticed movement in the valley. The Ha'ashtari rode along the far side of the lava flow, searching for his trail. They had evidently found where he climbed into the lava, and had ridden around the cinder cone to pick up his tracks, not willing to risk their horses in the jagged seam of rock. They found the first of his three trails and turned to follow it. When they were a safe distance away, Max slipped down into the valley and made his way to the lava flow. He climbed carefully through the twisted rock, knowing a fall would prove fatal now. When he reached the crest of the flow, Max settled down in a crevice to wait and watch. He knew the Ha'ashtari would probably double back when the false trail ended, and he did not want to run into the return party. The safest place for him now was right here, although he chafed at the loss of time.

410

Asa rose, a sliver of ivory against the brilliant stars. The moon's light cast a ghostly pall over the dark plain, and the arch hung overhead, silent and eternal. Gazing at the arch, so majestic in the wide open spaces of the Waste, Max could see why the nomads thought their heaven lay there. Where else would the Ha'ashtari gods dwell, but on that massive band of silver that dominated their sky? The crevice sheltered Max somewhat from the chill night air, but he still huddled for extra warmth.

The Ha'ashtari finally returned, spread out now to scan for side trails. They must be excellent trackers, to be able to follow that faint trail at night. They reached the edge of the lava flow, and turned to move along it. Max sat motionless, a part of the rocks around him. He studied the party below him. Eight men and four women, evidently led by Ha'serl. The Meng'tari had probably demanded the privilege of tracking and killing Max. Max peered at the women in the dim light. He did not think any of them was Sha'lor. He was genuinely relieved at the thought and that disturbed him slightly. Morgan was a bad influence on him. A warrior could not afford such feelings.

The group of riders stopped. They had found the second trail. They sat just below him now, and Max could hear their low voices. Ha'serl pointed along the flow and gave some command. Six of the Ha'ashtari split off and rode along the flow, while Ha'serl and the others turned onto the second trail. The Meng'tari was crafty. The first false trail had made him suspicious and he was trying to avoid losing any more time if the second trail proved to be a lure also.

Max settled back against the rough stone. He did not care what they did, as long as they concluded in the end that he was still back at the massif. Then he would have the head start he needed. Max half dozed, saving his strength for the mad dash to Carnac.

Mora had joined Asa in the night sky by the time Max again heard the sound of horses. He looked down and saw Ha'serl's party returning at a full gallop. The Ha'ashtari angled along the lava flow, heading for the other group of trackers. Max smiled grimly. He could imagine Ha'serl's thoughts about now. The Meng'tari must be furious at having been duped twice.

411

After the riders had passed, Max moved higher in the flow, trying to locate the other Ha'ashtari, who by now had undoubtedly found the third trail. He could see Ha'serl's warriors but the other group was out of sight. Max returned to his niche. They would be back.

After a time the warriors did return, and Max watched them from the rocks. What they did next he found disturbing. He had assumed the Ha'ashtari would think he had returned to the massif, after finding that all three trails were false. Instead, Ha'serl rode along the flow, stopping from time to time to dispatch a warrior, on foot, to search the lava itself. Max's plan would come unraveled if they found him in the lava, so he turned and moved quietly, searching for a better hiding place. He found a deep crack in the tortured rock, and he slipped into the opening. He laid there, the boot spike in his hand, listening intently. Before long, he heard the soft scrape of a hide boot on the lava, and he tensed. He could kill any searchers, but their absence would eventually bring the others. He knew he could not kill twelve Ha'ashtari, alone, under these conditions. His life, and those of Morgan's party, depended on Max remaining undiscovered.

He heard another slight sound, and a shadow flitted across the rocks in front of him. A warrior poised momentarily, not two body lengths above him. It was a man, and Max could see the deadly knives ready in his mahogany fists. Then he moved on, and Max let his breath out through clenched teeth. Twice more he heard movement around him, and then silence. Max waited a while longer, and then eased himself out of the crevice. He was just in time to see the entire group of Ha'ashtari galloping madly out of the valley, heading back to the massif. Max sheathed his spike, and watched them go. That was too close; he would not underestimate the nomads again.

Now the game was speed. He would run directly for Carnac, hoping to reach the city by dawn. With any luck, he could make it. He tried not to think about his comrades. Such thoughts would only be a dangerous distraction. He had to focus completely on the task ahead.

Max climbed carefully down out of the lava flow, and began the run to Carnac. He quickly oriented himself, using the position of

412

the arch and the stars. He picked the upper limits of a pace he could maintain for the distance, and ran. The arch and two moons lit the way, impassive and aloof.

Ha'serl reached the massif, his horse sweating heavily from the long gallop. The outlander had tricked them, and his death would be cruel.

"Spread out along the cliff base. Find his trail!" he shouted, his rage nearly boiling over.

The Ha'ashtari split up, moving in both directions along the foot of the massif. Ha'serl waited impatiently, fingering his knives. The other warriors finally returned. Ha'serl addressed one of the warriors in the party that had gone to his right.

"Ha'col, where is he?" Ha'serl demanded.

"He did return to the massif. We found a trail back there. He came this way, along the base of the cliff," Ha'col said.

Another warrior, from the second group spoke up. "We went back to his original trail, and then searched the cliff foot more carefully on the return. We found a very faint spoor. He was following us, using our trail to mask his own," the warrior said.

Ha'serl wheeled his mount toward the speaker. "He did what?" he asked.

The warrior, a woman with a scar across one cheek, shrugged. "He was following us, while we searched for him," she said, then pointed toward Carnac. "He must still be out there somewhere."

"Fools! He could be halfway to Carnac by now. If he reaches the city, you will answer to me. This devious outlander has blackened the honor of all Ha'ashtari. We will hunt him down and kill him," Ha'serl said, as he urged his horse into another long run.

"Shouldn't we get fresh horses? These are nearly spent and will slow us down," Ha'drak said.

"We don't have time. Do you want this man to reach Carnac?" Ha'serl shouted back over his shoulder.

"His hatred has driven him mad," Ha'drak muttered, but he turned his horse to follow the Meng'tari.

As Max ran, he constantly checked his back trail, watching for pursuit. He concentrated on speed, not trying to cover his tracks. The chill night air sawed at his lungs, sweat dripped in his eyes, and his sleeves were wet from wiping his forehead. His feet and legs ached from the constant pounding, especially his injured leg. He had actually tripped and fell a ways back. The pack added extra weight, but he was not ready to abandon it yet. He had to slow slightly, and try to control his ragged breathing.

Max ran on, numb to everything but keeping his legs moving. Time passed, and soon he noticed all three moons floating above him. Dawn was not far off. He glanced over his shoulder, quickly scanning the plain behind him. He stopped, panting, his breath steaming. Two Ha'ashtari came over a low rise, riding hard, coming straight for him. Ha'serl must have split the group, so they could cover more ground in the search. On horseback, with Max's obvious trail, they were gaining rapidly. Max turned and searched the plains ahead. He could see the dark gash of the Rift, too far away with his enemies so close. More irregular terrain lay to his left, and he ran that way, looking for a place to fight.

He sprinted over a low rise, and nearly over the edge of the cliff hidden behind it. He plowed to a halt, sinking to his knees. He knelt on the brink of a narrow canyon, etched into the face of the Waste by some long vanished watercourse. To his left a wash of sand and rocks tumbled down into the gorge, through a gap in the cliff face. Max heard a shout behind him. The Ha'ashtari had seen him, and he could hear the pounding of the horses' hooves. He forced himself to his feet, and scrambled for the landslide. He took a last look at his pursuers. Another pair of riders appeared on the horizon, following the first. Max smiled grimly, and ran down the slope.

He reached the bottom in a cloud of grit and tumbling stones. He looked both ways, searching for cover. A labyrinth of eroded rock stood to his right and he headed that way. Behind him came the sound of hoofbeats. He ran into the darkness under an arch of stone. Once through the arch, moonlight flooded a small opening in the twisted rocks. Max twisted to one side and almost plunged headlong into one of the squat cacti. He staggered back; noticing the mass of white insects huddled among the thorns. He glanced to the left, and saw a huge ant mound.

Ha'jek and Ha'fors plunged down the slope into the canyon, scattering sand and rocks. At the bottom they reined in, searching for the outlander. They soon found him, leaning against an arch of rock to their right. He looked exhausted, although a knife glinted in one hand. The Ha'ashtari charged toward him, and the man looked up, and then disappeared into the rocks.

Ha'jek took the lead, and slowed slightly as he approached the rocks, suspecting a trap. He could see nothing in the shadows of the arch. He heard a slight noise his left, and rode forward through the arch, his knives drawn. He emerged into the moonlight, seeing the ant mound just as the thrown rock struck his temple. The Ha'ashtari crumpled from the saddle, falling heavily onto the cactus. The wicked spines pierced his leathers, drawing blood in a score of places. The horse leaped ahead, then stopped and spun, hemmed in by the maze of rocks.

The pain of the spines in his back compounded the agony in his head, and Ha'jek dropped his knives, thrashing free of the cactus. He landed on his hands and knees, staring blearily at the white insects that now crawled over his arms. Remembering the ant mound, his head snapped up, and he saw the ants swarming toward him. He staggered to his feet, and tried to run. His horse, seeing the ants, and no opening but the arch, bolted toward the stumbling Ha'ashtari. Ha'jek heard it coming, and reached for the fleeing animal, but the horse's shoulder struck him a glancing blow, and he fell. Before he could rise again, the ants were on him.

Ha'fors had waited a moment, to give his companion time to clear the arch. Suddenly, he heard a commotion, and then the sound of a running horse. He was preparing to charge to Ha'jek's aid, when the screams began. He hesitated, wondering what would make a Ha'ashtari warrior cry out so. Ha'jek's horse burst through the arch, its eyes wild. Ha'fors' mount reared, as the other horse plunged past without stopping. The horrible screams went on and on.

Ha'fors fought to control his mount, which now spun and thrashed, terrified of something beyond the arch. He could see the animal's distended nostrils, and caught a whiff of a strange tang in the air. Then the source of the screams stumbled through the arch. It was Ha'jek, covered with a writhing mass of stinging, biting ants. The poor man staggered blindly, arms outstretched, barely visible beneath the living shroud. His cries became garbled, as some of the insects crawled into his gaping mouth. A black tentacle uncoiled from the arch, more ants scrambling angrily after Ha'jek, pursuing the intruder.

Ha'jek fell and rolled, slapping wildly at the clinging insects. The river of ants on the ground joined their fellows, flowing over him. Ha'fors' horse backed away, and the Ha'ashtari did not stop it, knowing his tribesman was doomed. Ha'fors saw motion to his right and turned. A dark shape flashed past him, and sudden pain exploded in his side. He clutched at the wound, his vision darkening. As he fell from the saddle, dying, he stared in wonder at the blood on his hand.

Max stepped aside as the second horse ran away, his stained knife gleaming dully in the moonlight. Ha'fors lay in a heap at his feet. Ha'jek's awful sounds had finally ceased, the body still, except for the heaving layer of insects. Max shook his head, wrinkling his nose at the sharp scent of the ants.

"What a death. I'm sorry, warrior," he whispered.

The sound of approaching horses came from beyond the rim of the canyon, and Max turned, melting again into the shadows. The ants slowly retreated, leaving the chewed, swollen corpse behind.

Ha'serl and the scarred woman, Sha'kre, forced their horses into a sliding rush down the landslide into the gorge. They slowed as they reached the bottom, small rocks tumbling in their wake. They had seen two horses running down the canyon, and had heard the awful screams.

"Look there," Sha'kre said, pointing.

Two bodies lay on the canyon floor, near an arch of stone. The Ha'ashtari rode toward them, cautiously, their knives drawn. Their mounts began to tremble, smelling something. The last of the ants crawled into the shadows of the arch. Ha'serl directed his horse to the first body.

416

"Ha'fors," he said, his face hardening.

At a gasp from Sha'kre, the Meng'tari turned. The riddled flesh of the second corpse made it unrecognizable.

"Maybe we should wait for the others," Sha'kre said.

"I do not fear this one. I will have his life. Wait here if you want," Ha'serl growled.

Sha'kre drew herself up. "I am not afraid. Find him, Meng'tari," she said.

Ha'serl took the lead, his eyes scanning the walls of the gorge, and probing every bush and mound in the narrow defile. They did not venture through the arch, knowing the death that waited there, but circled the maze of stone. Sha'kre rode just behind, looking everywhere. Two Ha'ashtari dead, and still no sign of their quarry. It was uncanny how the outlander had disappeared. This man is dangerous, she thought, they should have waited for the others.

It was almost her last thought. She followed Ha'serl past an eroded rock wing, jutting from the cliff face, and she heard a slight sound. Sha'kre turned in her saddle as something hit the rump of her horse, and pain erupted in her throat. With a wet gasp, she clutched at the spike in her throat, and then slid heavily from the saddle.

Ha'serl wheeled at the sounds behind him, to see Sha'kre slump to the ground. Max rolled to his feet, and stood waiting, his face chiseled marble in the moonlight. Ha'serl ignored the death of his companion, his hate filled eyes only for Max. He slammed his knives into their sheaths and pulled out his lance. His horse reared.

"Kin killer! I swear blood oath for your death," Ha'serl screamed.

Max stood before him, apparently unarmed, but without fear. "Are you a coward, Ha'serl of the Meng'tari, that you would come against an unarmed man with horse and lance? Climb down from there, and fight me hand to hand. Or is your fear too great?" he taunted.

Ha'serl threw down his lance, and vaulted from the saddle. "I fear no man, outlander! I will crush the life from you with my bare hands," he said.

With a harsh cry, the Ha'ashtari flung himself at Max. The

smaller man sidestepped, and struck Ha'serl a sharp blow across the back of the neck. Stunned, the Ha'ashtari went to his knees, and Max moved in to finish him. Ha'serl leaned on one arm, and kicked out at Max. Max barely had time to shift his weight before Ha'serl's heel drove into his knee. Max hopped back out of range, his knee throbbing. Ha'serl leaped to his feet, and circled Max, more wary now, his rage under control.

Max studied the way he moved, realizing this was not going to be an easy victory. The Ha'ashtari had their own forms of unarmed combat, patterned after the movements of animals in the Waste. Max was extremely tired, his strength sapped by the long descent from the massif and the brutal run for Carnac. He had lost his spike in Sha'kre's throat, something he would never have done when rested. Ha'serl, driven by his anger, would show no mercy.

Ha'serl leaped forward, striking at Max's head and bruised knee. Max deflected one blow and dodged the other, and before Ha'serl could back away, Max lashed out with a foot. The Ha'ashtari managed to partially avoid the kick, but it still skidded painfully from his thigh. Ha'serl staggered backwards, blocking two more of Max's punches.

Max kept moving. He was too tired to draw this out. His first mistake would be his last, against an opponent like Ha'serl. He still had his throwing knives, but Max wanted this man bloodied under his own fists. Besides, tricking Ha'serl into throwing down his weapons and then killing him with a concealed knife would probably be a violation of Ka'chi. Although he doubted that it really mattered at this point. What else could the Ha'ashtari do to him?

Ha'serl came after him again, this time with a series of kicks. In spite of his numb thigh, the Ha'ashtari was fast. Max retreated, countering the attacks. Suddenly, Ha'serl whirled, swinging his leg around in a sweep. As Max fell, Ha'serl kicked him in the side, and then dropped down on top of him, an elbow aimed for his throat. Max twisted away, although Ha'serl managed to land a flailing blow as he moved. Rolling to his back, Max lay still, apparently stunned.

Ha'serl leaped to his feet and tried to drive his heel through Max's head. Max caught the descending boot, and levered it up.

Before Ha'serl could twist free, Max drove a foot into his groin, and the Ha'ashtari folded. Max shoved on the foot, and Ha'serl fell over backwards. Max got stiffly to his feet, as Ha'serl tried to do the same. Max kicked him in the head, and the Ha'ashtari went down again. Ha'serl crawled away, and Max followed. He waited while Ha'serl got to his feet. The Ha'ashtari was dazed, but not finished. The pain from his damaged groin kept him bent half over, but he kept his hands up.

"I was going to kill you, Ha'serl. But I think a sound thrashing suits me better," Max said.

"Kill me if you can, outlander. But I will suffer no further dishonor at your hands," Ha'serl gasped, blood running from his nose.

Without warning, the Ha'ashtari kicked a spray of sand at Max's face. Max turned his head, but Ha'serl kicked him in the stomach and aimed a vicious blow at his head. The punch missed, and Max managed to catch Ha'serl's wrist. He jerked the arm straight, then rammed the heel of his hand into the elbow. With a loud pop the joint gave way, and Ha'serl roared in pain.

Max kicked him in the knee, and as the man went down, Max drove his fist into Ha'serl's lower back. Max backed away, wiping the sand from his face, and drawing in great lungfuls of air. His stomach spasmed, and the cramping threatened to double him over.

Ha'serl should have been finished, but he managed to get to his feet. His injured arm hung limply, and he shifted his weight to his good leg. Without warning, he dove and rolled, then kicked up at Max. Max could not get clear, and the kick skidded from his side. Ha'serl brought his leg around and swept Max's feet from under him for the second time. Max landed hard.

Before he could move, Ha'serl dove on top of him, striking at his throat with the edge of his hand. Max caught the descending hand, and elbowed the Ha'ashtari in the face. Ha'serl tried to knee him, but Max pulled his legs up and rolled, dragging Ha'serl with him. Max punched Ha'serl in the face twice, and twisted free.

As the Ha'ashtari tried to rise, Max settled on his back, one forearm pressing into his throat. Ha'serl thrashed madly, nearly shaking Max off. Max kept the pressure on his throat, and Ha'serl began to weaken. Finally, the Ha'ashtari slumped. After a moment, Max released him, and Ha'serl collapsed in the sand.

Max sagged to his knees, his chest heaving. As soon as he was able, he staggered to his feet. The horses stood nearby, watching him warily.

"No ants to scare you off. Good thing," Max said.

Speaking gently and moving slowly, he managed to catch Ha'serl's mount, and tied him to a bush. The other animal moved closer, curious. Max caught the second horse, and stripped it of saddle and bridle. He used the reins to bind Ha'serl hand and foot, and left him lying beside his saddle. After removing all of Ha'serl's weapons, Max turned to Sha'kre. He retrieved his spike and cleaned it.

He went back to Ha'serl's horse, and leaned against it. "I think it's time to ride awhile. My legs are all used up. Forgive me any offense I've given to your breed. Horses have their place as well," he said softly.

The horse danced nervously, uneasy at the presence of a stranger. Max walked the horse to where he had hidden the pack and retrieved it. He slipped into the pack, then gripped the horse's mane and climbed into the saddle. He urged his mount up out of the gorge, and turned once again toward Carnac.

CHAPTER THIRTY
TA'HODA

The eastern sky burned with the dawn as Max approached the great Rift. He glanced behind him. Dots on the horizon marked the location of the pursuing Ha'ashtari. Sweaty foam flecked Max's tired horse and its body steamed in the chill air, he had ridden hard since leaving Ha'serl in the gorge. He slowed his mount, and stopped at the summit of the cliffs surrounding the Rift. Max looked down into the great canyon, still half in the shadow of night.

The Rift had once been a gigantic cavern, with an underground river running through it. At some time in the distant past, there had been a great upheaval in the planet's crust, and a portion of the cavern roof had collapsed, forming the canyon. A large mesa rose from the floor of the Rift, its top worn flat by the passing centuries. The river still flowed, now called the Stark. He could see it emerging from the mouth of the massive cave at the far end of the Rift. The Stark meandered through the canyon until it reached the mesa, where it split into two channels, completely encircling the plateau. Once past the mesa, the channels merged again, and the river continued its journey into the cave mouth at the opposite end.

Scattered trees covered the valley floor, with an understory of grass and tough shrubs. Max could see a herd of goats, their herdsman curled up in the grass nearby. Any flat ground near the river had been tilled for crops. Warm air caressed his face, and Max shivered. Thermal activity heated the lower valley, which made it considerably warmer than the frigid plains above. Patches of mist whipped past him, formed by the clash of temperatures.

The city of Carnac had been constructed on the mesa's summit, its builders taking advantage of the natural defenses. The city was built of great blocks of reddish sandstone, carved from the surrounding cliffs. A massive wall encircled the summit of the plateau, thick enough for several riders to pass abreast, with squat stone towers spaced evenly along the wall. From his vantage point, Max could see into the city itself, a great mass of monolithic structures, crowded within the protecting walls.

On the downstream end of the mesa, sediments left behind by the river had formed a large point of land. A lesser wall bounded this area, with a massive gate at the very end. A ramp led from the lower gate to the mesa summit and the main gate of the city. Two wooden bridges provided access from either side of the river.

Max studied the surrounding cliffs, their copper heights tinted crimson by the rising sun. Vertical near the summit, rocky slopes covered the lower elevations, littered with debris fallen from the cliffs above. The hardy vegetation of the Waste had claimed portions of the slopes, brownish green patches dotting the rock fields. The upper cliffs were broken here and there, allowing a descent to the valley. On the opposite side of the Rift, a stone roadway ascended to the plains above.

Max looked back. He could see nine Ha'ashtari, much closer now. He wondered how they had reacted to finding Ha'serl, bruised, tied, and helpless. Max imagined Ha'serl was still angry with him. It did not matter. He had made it to Carnac.

Dismounting, Max leaned against the horse until the feeling came back into his abused legs. Then he stepped back, giving the horse an affectionate slap on the rump. The horse ran a ways, and then stopped, staring back at him.

"Farewell, horse. And thanks for the ride," Max called.

The horse snorted once and trotted toward the Ha'ashtari. Slipping out of his pack, Max drank the last of his water, watching the approaching warriors. He stuffed a packet of field rations in his tunic and left the pack lying in the grass.

Max turned and began to descend into the Rift. He moved quickly, but carefully, not certain how close to the city the nomads would pursue him, and not wanting to be caught on the slopes. He worked his way down through one of the gaps in the upper cliffs, half climbing, half sliding on the steep incline.

He stopped to rest his weary legs, the rocks disturbed by his passage clattering on ahead of him. Over the sound of the rocks he heard something else, a strange, staccato call, that echoed eerily through the cliffs.

"Satyrs," Max groaned, as he resumed his climb down the slope.

He heard an answering call, then the sounds of movement in the rocks around him. Max increased his pace as much as possible, but the treacherous footing limited his speed. He was about half way down, scrambling sideways around a huge boulder, when a shadow fell across the rocks beside him. Max looked up to see a strange creature perched on the boulder. Silhouetted against the glare of the eastern sky, it looked like a half-naked man wearing wool pants. Then he saw the delicate hooves, and knew it was no man.

The face appeared human, except for the small horns protruding from its brow. The satyr carried a pouch and a sling, with a stone knife at its waist. Max had heard of satyrs, but never seen one. Now he would likely have to fight one, or several, judging by the sounds all around him.

The perching thing cried out to him, evidently some form of challenge. But the stuttering tongue was completely alien to him, and he had no idea how to respond. He did not speak satyr.

"Just passing through. Don't mind me," he called reassuringly.

The satyr squawked and spat threateningly, obviously not reassured. Max decided to leave, and leaped down the slope in great bounds. He heard a whirring sound behind him, and a small stone shattered on the rocks to his left. He moved even faster, dancing across the shifting debris. He heard more gabbling cries, and risked a look at his attackers. Several more satyrs clung to the cliffs, whirling slings overhead. He put his head down and ran, relying on momentum to carry him to safety. Max began jumping along the tops of the larger rocks, trying to ignore the jagged terrain waiting if he missed a step.

Missiles buzzed all around him like angry hornets, striking the talus and spraying him with stone fragments. A rock glanced off his ribs, further scoring his tattered tunic and mail. If he did not get out of range soon, he was dead.

He jumped down to another rock, and his weary legs buckled. He toppled forward and fell into a jumble of boulders. He landed on a heap of smaller stones that slid downslope, and then slammed feet first into a large rock. As he lay there, stunned and bruised, the barrage continued. Sling stones ricocheted around him. Holding his arms around his head, Max got to his feet. He stumbled around the rock, and huddled against the lower side, seeking temporary shelter from the missiles. He scanned the slope below him, looking for the fastest way down. To his right the slope ended in a cliff, with the sparkling river at its base.

Desperate, Max bolted toward the cliff. A rock struck his shoulder, and he staggered, almost falling. He forced his feet to keep up, and ran headlong. Another missile hit him in the back, and only his mail kept his ribs from cracking. Wheezing with pain and exertion, he took a last look behind him. Satyrs scampered through the cliffs above him, their hooves making them incredibly sure-footed on the rocky slopes. Their warbling cries mingled with the whir of their slings.

A rock dug into the back of his leg, and Max went down. He rolled down the slope, adding to his collection of cuts and bruises, blinded by a cloud of dust and grit. Fortunately, the finer debris above the cliff gave under his weight, preventing serious injury. However, the smaller rocks also made it harder to stop his downhill tumble. He stuck out his legs, digging into the rubble.

Suddenly, there was nothing under him but air. He had slid over the edge of the cliff. His streaming eyes cleared, and he saw the river rushing up at him. He fell feet first, and barely had time to straighten his legs before he hit the water. With a tremendous shock, he plunged into the cool water, and a moment later, he slammed into the sandy bottom of the river. His breath erupted from his lungs in cloud of bubbles. A haze of sand swirled up, which the current immediately caught and pulled away. He fought the urge to inhale, and ignored his screaming lungs. Max kicked toward the surface, but the weight of his clothing and mail threatened to drag him back down. He fought for his life, clawing at the water with all he had left.

Max's head finally cleared the water, and he drifted, gasping and choking. Paddling weakly, he struggled to keep his head above water, not caring where the current carried him. After sucking in several lungfuls of air, he shook the water from his eyes. He had fallen into the river about halfway past the mesa, but the current had swept him nearly to the end of the plateau. Angling through the water, Max paddled for shore. Soon he was nearing one of the bridges, and he reached out for a support piling. He caught it, spun around in the swift flow of water, and then his kicking feet hit the bottom.

Staggering to the edge of the river, Max collapsed under the bridge, and lay there for a few moments, amazed he was still alive. His clothing was tattered and torn, and watery blood leaked from several areas of his body, but the river had washed him clean of the rock dust from the cliffs. Max wiped the water from his eyes, and slowly got up. His injured leg buckled under him, and he almost went down again. He kept upright by sheer force of will.

"I didn't make it this far, to stop now," he grated.

Scrambling up the slope, Max reached the bridge deck. He bent over, hands on his knees, gasping. Finally, he straightened and staggered toward the gate. After a step or two, he forced himself to walk almost normally, not wanting to approach the gate of Carnac like some stumbling drunk. He walked down a well used road, flanked by waist high grass, leaving a wet, red trail. Max could see the guards on the top of the wall, watching his approach curiously.

A Ha'ashtari stood up from his hiding place in the grass to his left. Another appeared on the right side, then another and another. In a moment's time, seven nomads ringed the exhausted Max, their knives held ready. Max glanced at the city guards, but they did not seem inclined to intervene. Carnites prided themselves on being isolationists, and the centaurs simply did not care, unless there was something to be studied or learned.

Max sighed, facing his fate calmly. He only wished he had been able to help Morgan and the others. He had failed them. Now there was nothing left, but to die well. Actually, he was too tired to care. He tensed his forearms, feeling the comforting pressure of his throwing knives in their hidden sheaths. Taking a last look at the open sky, Max dropped his gaze to the waiting enemy. The Ha'ashtari met his gaze appraisingly, as if they were deciding something.

Max shook the water from his eyes, and broke the tense silence.

"It was an honor to fight you, Ha'ashtari. But be warned. I plan on taking two or three lives in my passing," he said, as he reached for

425

a blade.

A dull sound came from behind him. Max whirled, a throwing knife poised on his fingertips. The Ha'ashtari were plunging their knives point first into the dirt at their feet. He turned around slowly, seeing that all warriors had done the same. He lowered his knife, wondering if they intended to beat him to death with their fists.

A warrior stepped out onto the road and approached him. Something in the man's eyes made Max slip the knife back into its sheath and wait. When he was close enough, the warrior reached out with his right hand and touched Max lightly on the forehead.

"Welcome home, ta'hoda," the man said simply.

The other warriors nodded in agreement, and the man withdrew his hand. Max knew something significant had just happened, but what? He only knew they no longer seemed inclined to kill him.

Hooves clattered on the wooden bridge, and Max turned. The nine pursuing Ha'ashtari had arrived, Ha'serl in the lead, his arm in a sling. At the sight of the knives in the dirt, the new arrivals dragged their mounts to a plunging halt.

"What is this?" Ha'serl spoke to the warriors around Max. "Who sent you?"

The man who had touched Max spoke. "Ha'keel sent us, as soon as he realized the ta'hoda was missing. He left you to waste your time following his trail. We all knew he would come here," he said.

Ha'serl slid from his horse, and stalked closer, furious. "This is no ta'hoda. He is a kin killer, and I want him dead, Ha'dros," he shouted.

Ha'dros studied the Meng'tari's bruises, and his sling. "Why did you not kill him yourself, when you had the chance?" he asked.

At the look on Ha'serl's face, Max started laughing. Giddy with fatigue, the question struck him as hilarious. One of the warriors with Ha'serl smiled.

"We found him, beaten and bound like a slave," the man said. At that, all of the Ha'ashtari joined in Max's laughter.

Ha'serl stared at them, turning purple with rage. He whipped out his knife. "I will kill the outlander, right now!" he said.

426

As Ha'serl stepped toward Max, Ha'dros moved between them. He stared into the Meng'tari's eyes.

"We have accepted this man as ta'hoda, a lost one. He is Ha'ashtari now. If you try to harm him, I will kill you," Ha'dros said softly.

Ha'serl hesitated, then stepped back, slamming his knife into its sheath. "You are all fools. This man comes amongst us, kills a Pathfinder, kills our warriors, dishonors me, and you accept him as a brother. Don't you know this could mean war between the Meng'tari and the Shen'tari? I am brother to the chief of the Meng'tari, and I have influence with him. Tribes have warred for less than this in the past" he said.

Ha'dros shrugged. "That was the past, before Ha'keel. All Shen'tari know that the Meng'tari have been tainted by constant contact with the outlanders. Your honor may have been lost long ago. Take your complaint to Ha'keel, but we stand by our decision. Anyone who can do what this man does must be a lost one. He wields a bow like a Ha'ashtari born, he fights like a sith'gaa, he made it past you and your warriors, then he survived the cliffs and the satyrs. The gods know this one," he said.

Ha'serl looked around him, but saw no sympathy on the faces of the other Ha'ashtari. "This is not finished," he snarled, mounting his horse and riding off.

Ha'dros watched him go. "He is right. This is not over. Watch your back with that one," he said.

Without another word, the Ha'ashtari retrieved their knives, and began to walk back across the bridge. Max stared after them, speechless for once. Finally, he spoke.

"What about Morgan and the others?" he called after Ha'dros.

Ha'dros spoke without turning. "I don't know. When we left the massif, they still fought. Farewell, ta'hoda," he said.

The warriors crossed the bridge and vanished into the trees. They soon appeared on horseback, galloping up the road to the plains above. Max stood motionless, too tired to move, then he sat down in the road.

From the city wall, a man in a white robe with a shaven head, an older sergeant, and three soldiers had observed the entire scene. The man in the robe had been taking notes on a board with paper clipped to it.

The bald man waved his stylus. "Fascinating. Unprecedented. And to think I was present to witness this historic event," he rambled.

The sergeant shook his head. "Been a long time since I've seen Ha'ashtari pass up a chance to kill. Who is that man?" he asked no one in particular.

"What happened?" the robed one exclaimed. "He has been declared ta'hoda! A rare and momentous occurrence."

"Ta'hoda. What's that?" the sergeant asked.

The robed man waved his arms. "No time to explain. I must make my report. The Academy will be astounded," he said as he walked swiftly away, his robes flapping.

One of the soldiers spoke, still watching Max. "Poor wretch. He's just sitting there in the middle of the road," he said.

"He's getting up," another soldier remarked.

The men on the wall waited as Max slowly approached the city gate. The Carnites saw a small man, soaking wet, his clothing in rags, covered with cuts and bruises, limping heavily, with no horse, sword, or possessions. A sorry figure, and yet the Ha'ashtari had spared him.

Max stopped at the gate and looked up. "Open the gate," he called. "I would speak with Baron Serenus."

The sergeant considered Max. In spite of his tattered appearance, the man had courage, to demand entrance like royalty. "What about?" the sergeant asked.

"I have a message from the Princess Celestine of Skara Thrae," Max answered.

"Be off with you. No one comes uninvited into Carnac," one of the soldiers said.

The sergeant rubbed his chin. "There was a Princess here by that name, twenty or thirty years ago. I remember her, a real beauty. And one of the Baron's favorite students. What is your message?" he asked.

"The message is for the Baron. Don't keep me standing out

428

here like a beggar," Max said impatiently.

"Either I take your message to the Baron, or you'll stand out there until you rot. You're in no position to bargain," the sergeant responded.

Max sighed. "Oh, all right. But I have something to give him as well. You'll have to come down here and get it," he said.

"Stay there. I'll be right down," the sergeant said.

One of the soldiers touched his arm. "Are you sure about this? You know how the centaurs feel about being disturbed. You could get demoted, or worse," he asked.

The sergeant shook his head. "And if something happens to one of the Baron's favorites? I'll take the chance," he said.

"May the gods be with you, sergeant," the soldier said.

Max waited until he heard the gate begin to open, then he dug out the Princess' ring. The huge gate opened a crack and the sergeant slipped through. He approached Max warily.

"Give me the message, stranger," he said.

Max considered taking him hostage, and trying to force the gate open. He decided that would fail, and then no one would take the message to the Baron. He curbed his impatience and anger, and handed the ring to the sergeant.

"This is the Princess' signet ring. Tell the Baron, the Princess is at the arc massif, under siege by the Ha'ashtari, and she needs help immediately. Oh, and pass on this phrase to the Baron. 'Otium cum dignitate' " Max said.

The sergeant stared at the ring, and whispered the strange words. "I'm a simple soldier and know nothing of royalty or secret passwords, but I'll carry this to the Baron. At no little risk to myself, stranger," he said, starting to turn.

Then he stopped. "What's your name?" the sergeant asked.

"Just call me Max," Max said, too tired for titles. "And your name, sergeant?"

"Balt, just Balt," the sergeant said with a smile.

He entered the gate, and it closed firmly behind him. Max sat down and leaned against the gate, soaking up the warmth of the valley and the rising sun. He might even sleep, if he was not so concerned about his friends.

Sergeant Balt soon stood on the porch of a massive building. He had just pounded a huge ring against the door, announcing his presence. Presently, the door swung open, and a servant stuck his head out.

"What do you want?" the servant said peevishly.

Balt glared at the man. "I have an urgent message for the Baron," he said.

The servant blinked at him stupidly. "Did the Baron send for you?" he asked.

"No, I have a message. An urgent message," Balt said, his patience wearing thin.

"I don't think . . . ," the servant began.

"Obviously you don't think. Step aside, man, or I'll walk over you. Do you have no idea what urgent means?" Sergeant Balt said.

The servant backed away, pulling the door open. "Sure. Disturb the Baron. But I take no responsibility for this," he said.

Balt shoved past him. "The day I hide behind some simpering servant is a long time coming," he growled, with more conviction than he felt.

The servant led him through endless halls and rooms, to the heart of the great building. The entire place was constructed of reddish stone, and filled with strange wonders. The servant left him standing in front of a large door, with a grille over it.

"Remember, I'm not to blame for this," the servant whined.

Balt ignored him, wondering what to do now. After several moments, he cleared his throat and spoke loudly.

"I have an urgent message for Baron Serenus, from the Princess Celestine of Skara Thrae," he said.

Silence followed. Balt was about ready to try again when a deep, powerful voice came from the grille. He almost turned and ran at the sound of it. Only his years of military training kept him rooted to the spot.

"Celeste, is she here?" the voice said.

Balt swallowed. "No, Equo, she is at the Arc Massif, in danger

430

from the Ha'ashtari," he managed.

The voice came again, even louder this time. Balt's heart raced. "Celeste in danger? Who is this?" the voice demanded.

"Sergeant . . . Balt . . . on duty at the gate. There's a man there . . . from the Princess," Balt said.

The large door slid suddenly aside, and Balt went to his knees. The Baron Serenus stood in the doorway. Even though he had seen the Centaurs many times, the Baron was overwhelming. The centaur stood nearly twice the height of a man, his powerfully muscled torso tapering to the equally massive equine body below. A giant sculpture of black and bronze, the Baron wore no clothing or ornamentation except a waist pouch, with an unruly mane of black hair flowing down his back. The Baron stared down at the man, stamping a hoof in uncharacteristic agitation. The sound rang through the reddish halls, and Balt flinched. He forced himself to look up at the Baron, to meet those strange brown eyes, pools of liquid autumn, strangely compelling and hypnotic. The Baron spoke, and Balt could see the large, flat teeth in the wide mouth.

"How do you know this . . . man . . . is from the Princess?" the Baron asked in his booming voice.

Balt fumbled in his pouch for the ring. He almost dropped it.

"Here. He gave me this and . . .," he said, and then stopped as the Baron's massive hand engulfed his and took the ring. It looked like a fleck of gold in the centaur's grip.

"This is her ring," the Baron said.

"Otium cum dignitate," Balt blurted out, hoping he got it right.

The Baron stared at Balt for a moment, and then reached down with his free hand. He grabbed the sergeant by the tunic, lifting him effortlessly from the floor. Balt squeezed his eyes shut, then opened them when the Baron swung the sergeant onto his huge back, almost gently.

"Hang on to my mane," the centaur said. "I would see this man."

The morning sun had nearly lulled the exhausted Max into slumber when he heard a commotion inside the gate. People were shouting and running, and he heard the heavy sound of hooves on

431

stone. He was thinking about getting up, when the gate suddenly opened behind him. Numb with fatigue, he fell over on his back in the gateway.

And found himself staring up into the face of a centaur. The creature was leaning over him, concern obvious on its face. A massive arm came down and plucked him up. The hand went away and he stood, weaving slightly. He noticed a crowd of onlookers, soldiers and citizens. His message had evidently created quite a stir.

"Celeste is in danger?" the centaur boomed, the powerful tones nearly toppling the weakened Max.

He winced, but answered quickly. "Yes, Baron. We must go to her at once," he said.

Sergeant Balt stood nearby, looking slightly shaken. Max wondered what had happened to him. He supposed the mere presence of the majestic centaur was enough to disturb most people.

The centaur studied Max. "Your appearance bespeaks a long and arduous journey," he commented.

Max laughed weakly. "Yes, Baron. Most arduous. I can see why you get few visitors," he said.

"We prefer it that way," the centaur said.

The Baron reached into the pouch at his waist. He pulled out a bluish globe and handed it to Max. Max peered at the object. It had a small nipple at one end, and seemed to be a clear envelope filled with a blue fluid.

"What am I supposed to do with this?" Max asked.

"Bite the nipple and drink the fluid. It will make you feel better," the centaur said.

Max hesitated, and the Baron gestured impatiently. "You're too tired. You won't make the journey back. And then what will become of your friends?" the centaur asked.

Max shrugged, and did as the centaur directed. The fluid burned like fire in his throat and the blaze spread throughout his body. He dropped the empty sphere, and coughed.

"I came all this way, and now you poison me?" Max gasped, clutching at his stomach.

"Be patient. The restorative effects are almost immediate," the

432

Baron said.

Max realized he was feeling better. The fire had purged him, and then faded, the fog in his head was clearing, the pain from his abused body eased, and he felt much stronger. He straightened, and took a deep breath.

The Baron nodded with satisfaction. "Sergeant, follow us with a squad. We will be at the arc massif," he ordered, then turned again to Max.

He reached down and tossed Max onto his back. Max clutched at the Baron's muscular torso, and then grabbed handfuls of mane to steady himself.

"Sorry to pull your hair. I'm still a little dizzy," Max said.

"Hang on to my mane if you like. I won't mind. We are going to Celeste," the Baron said.

The Baron trotted through the gate and down the road, Max clinging to his back. The centaur moved quickly for such a massive creature. The clatter of his hooves on the stone pavement rang through the valley, while the people of Carnac stared after them.

Balt shook his head. "Who was that man? And why's the Baron acting like that?" he asked.

The robed man stood nearby. He shook his head. "The Baron has a reputation for unseemly passion. I must inform the Academy," he said softly.

Morgan and Celeste walked toward the waiting Ha'ashtari. After the pair's surrender, their captors had taken the outlanders' weapons and Morgan's metasilk coat. They had been allowed to bathe and rest, and Celeste had tended Morgan's wounds. As always, his injuries were healing at an incredible rate. The nomads had fed them well. For most of the day, the Ha'ashtari had left them alone in a tent, and they talked some, but could not bring themselves to say good-bye again.

Morgan had asked for permission to bury Taskin. Celeste and Morgan laid him to rest beneath a pile of stones, while the Ha'ashtari watched curiously.

Five warriors stood near the High Chief's tent, hooded and

clad in red leather. Their clothing matched the ruddy afternoon sky. Even the warriors' weapons had been stained crimson. As they approached, Celeste explained what Morgan faced.

"The Fist of El'Atan. Five warriors, chosen by lot from each of the tribes, and trained from birth to judge the will of the gods. Probably the finest warriors of the entire Ha'ashtari race. Like I said before, suicide," she said.

"Your encouragement is most appreciated," Morgan said wryly.

Ha'keel came out of his tent and stared at the big outlander. Despite the days of pursuit and fighting, the man had seemingly regained his strength in a single day. Too bad he must kill this man, he was a formidable warrior.

"Are you prepared for the Ru'atan?" Ha'keel asked formally.

"I have prayed that Iosus' will be done," Morgan replied.

Ha'keel raised an eyebrow. "Then your fate is in the hands of the gods. Die well, outlander," he said, handing Morgan a pair of Ha'ashtari knives.

"You'll escort the Princess to Carnac?" Morgan asked, slipping the weapons into his belt.

"I have given my word," Ha'keel said.

"That's enough for me," Morgan said, then turned to Celeste.

"Farewell, Princess," Morgan said.

"Live, Morgan," she said, her eyes moist. "And come back to me. Or I'll never forgive you."

Morgan bowed. "As you command, Princess," he said.

Morgan faced Ha'keel. "I'm ready," he said.

Ha'keel gestured toward the open Waste. "Choose your place, warrior. After a time, the Fist will join you. El'Atan will be your judge," he said.

Morgan nodded and walked past the warriors in red. "Beware, Fist of El'Atan. I've been commanded by my Princess to live. I will do so," he remarked in passing.

Several of the Ha'ashtari laughed at the outlander's boldness, and the Fist acknowledged Morgan's challenge, their hoods rustling as they nodded silently. When Morgan reached the perimeter of the camp, he broke into a slow run.

434

"Live, Morgan," Celeste whispered. "Live."

The Baron raced across the plains, the late afternoon sun highlighting his muscles as he ran. The centaur seemed tireless, he had not slowed or broken stride since they left Carnac. Max could see his ribcage expanding with deep, regular breathing, his skin still dry despite the rigorous pace. Max shifted his weight, his legs cramping from being stretched across the centaur's wide back. It was like riding a draft horse, without the ridge of backbone. He let go of the mane with one hand, flexing stiff fingers. The effects of the blue draught were fading, and his fatigue crept in again. Max just hoped he did not fall off before they reached the massif.

They came over a low ridge, and the arc massif lay in the distance, across a wide valley. At the sight of the massif, the Baron increased his speed. A herd of antelope grazed in the valley. At the centaur's approach, the beasts threw up their heads and stampeded over a hill, the dust of their flight whipping across the centaur's path.

After they left Carnac, the Baron had plied him with many questions, which Max answered without hesitation. Somehow he knew the centaur would see through any deception, and they could not afford this creature's ill will. Also, Max figured if anyone remained free of the Mhoul's taint, it would be the centaurs. The Baron seemed mainly interested in the Princess, and most of his questions had centered on her. However, when Max mentioned Morgan and Khulankor, the centaur was equally intrigued.

Max twisted around, and looked behind them. Far away, he could see a party of soldiers from Carnac, trying in vain to catch them.

"You've been running for most of the day, and you show no sign of tiring," Max commented.

The Baron shrugged. "Hybrid vigor," he remarked vaguely, intent on his goal.

Max pulled his collar tighter, trying to shut out the chill air. "Aren't you cold?" he asked the naked centaur.

"We seldom feel the cold, or suffer from the heat," Serenus replied.

Max stared down at the man-horse he rode, shaking his head in wonder. He could understand why the Ha'ashtari considered them children of the gods.

Without warning, the centaur stopped. Max's head slammed into the broad back, his face buried in the flowing mane.

"Mmmffffph," Max said, spitting out a mouthful of coarse hair. "Why did you do that?"

The Baron lifted his head. "Look there," he said, pointing.

Max leaned around the centaur's massive shoulder, searching the plain before them. He spotted six figures, one loping ahead of the others. The lead runner was headed for a low hill, crowned with eroded pillars of stone.

"That's Morgan. He's going to make his stand on the hill," Max said.

The centaur nodded, and charged toward the mound. Max had to grab a handful of mane to keep from flying off the Baron's back. They pounded down into a long swale, losing sight of the runners, and then Serenus galloped across the valley and up the other side. The centaur's powerful hind quarters bunched and launched them over the ridge, where they almost trampled Morgan, who stood just over the crest. He had heard their approach, and skidded to a stop, thinking them some new threat. The Baron reared up, bringing his great mass to an abrupt halt.

Max clung to the centaur's back, gripping the mane. He did not want to fall off now. After all, appearances were important. The Baron twisted sideways and came down. Morgan crouched before them, a Ha'ashtari knife in his hand, his eyes wide. When he saw Max on the centaur's back, his eyes widened even further.

Five Ha'ashtari dressed in red ran up to them. They stopped and lowered their crimson knives, staring in silent awe at Max and the Baron.

"Morgan, I bring you the Baron Serenus. He was inclined to assist us," Max said nonchalantly.

Morgan bowed. "I'm honored to meet you, Baron," he said, breathing heavily.

The Baron nodded, and regarded the Ha'ashtari. "What is

this?" he demanded.

"We are the Fist of El'Atan," one of the warriors said.

"We judge the will of El'Atan," added another.

"Today, I speak for El'Atan. You will not harm this man," the Baron said.

The Fist nodded and sheathed their weapons. "As you command, Equo," they said in unison.

"Has Celeste been harmed?" Serenus asked abruptly.

The warriors hesitated. Morgan shook his head, startled by the timbre of the centaur's voice. "No, Ha'keel promised he would bring her to you," he said.

Max looked at the Ha'ashtari. "And you? Were they escorting you to Carnac as well? " he asked Morgan.

Morgan grimaced. "I was given the honor of Ru'atan. Trial by combat," he explained.

"Maybe we should let you finish," Max said. "After all, it was an honor."

The Baron interrupted, his booming voice silencing any further talk. "Enough of this. I would see Celeste," he said.

Serenus gestured to Morgan. "Approach," he said.

Morgan stepped toward the warriors in red, offering his knives to one of them. "I won't need these anymore," he said.

The hooded man took the weapons without comment. Morgan walked over to the centaur and looked up at him. Before he could move, the Baron reached down and pulled him from his feet, depositing him on his back behind Max. Then the centaur turned and galloped from the hill, leaving the silent Fist. The Baron slowed, cantering smoothly toward the massif.

Morgan clutched at Max, almost sliding from the centaur's massive back. "You're quite a sight. You look like trolls have been playing with you," Morgan said.

"Satyrs and Ha'ashtari, no trolls," Max said, then glanced over his shoulder at Morgan's abused features. "I don't look any worse than you. What happened after I left?"

"We fought again in the morning. Celeste had lanced Taskin's wound, and we made him a splint. He only had one good leg, yet he

437

killed several of them. He died trying to save me, took two warriors over the cliff with him," Morgan said.

"He was a good soldier. I'll miss him," Max said. "What happened then?"

"A short time later, the Ha'ashtari stopped attacking. They knew you weren't with us, and sent out search parties. Then Ha'keel offered us a deal. He would take Celeste to Carnac, and I would be judged by the Fist," Morgan said.

"And you agreed," Max said.

"Yes. Celeste would live, and I would fight the Fist. It seemed best," Morgan said.

"I'm sure Celeste thought so, too," Max said with a smile.

Morgan shook his head. "No. She was mad," he admitted.

"I'll bet," Max said.

"The Meng'tari Ha'serl wanted to kill us both, but Ha'keel sent him after you. Told him if he wanted to kill someone, to try his skill against you. Did he find you?" Morgan asked.

"Yes," Max said.

"Is he dead?" Morgan asked.

"No. I killed three of his companions, but Ha'serl I left alive," Max said.

"I'm surprised," Morgan remarked.

"Dishonor is worse than death to these people," Max said, and then nodded toward their mount. "I told him everything."

Morgan lowered his voice. "Everything?" he asked.

The Baron spoke, startling both men. "Yes, everything. We will discuss this further when we return to Carnac," he said.

"So is there anything else you want to tell me, now that our secret is out?" Max asked.

Morgan sighed. "Ha'keel has the artifacts from the cache. Did you tell the Baron about the cache too?" he asked.

The Baron answered for Max. "Yes, he did. I would examine those devices, and hear more about the cache," he said.

"Did you tell him about the Pathfinder? I still think the Mhoul were involved. If they have spies among the Pathfinders, what about the Ha'ashtari?" Morgan said.

"That was the most incredible part of your friend's story. And I refuse to believe the Ha'ashtari have been corrupted. They may be a simple, barbarous people, but their devotion to Carnac and my race is complete," Serenus said.

"I apologize, Baron. I didn't mean to leave you out of our conversation, and I had no intent to insult the Ha'ashtari. Considering what's at stake, I just felt I needed to be cautious," Morgan said.

"That's probably wise, especially when the Mhoul are involved. I took no offense. I merely wished to point out the error in your reasoning," the Baron said.

Max looked behind them. The Fist followed at a distance, running lightly through the grass. Farther back, Max could see the soldiers from Carnac.

They entered the ancient crater by the light of the setting sun. Ha'ashtari outriders had spotted them, and now rode a respectful distance to either side. The main Ha'ashtari camp lay just beyond the inner wall, and they could see Ha'keel striding towards them. Awe and amazement etched the faces of the Ha'ashtari around them. A centaur, child of the gods, had appeared to them. Seeing Max and Morgan riding their demigod, they stared even harder.

Serenus stopped, waiting for Ha'keel. Max and Morgan quickly slid from the broad back, and stood beside the Baron, massaging sore muscles. Several of the Ha'ashtari pointed at Max, whispering.

Ha'keel approached, and saluted the centaur. "Bring me the Princess," Serenus boomed without preamble.

Ha'keel nodded and signaled. "Immediately, Equo. We are honored by your presence," he said.

"It is not for honor I come, but rebuke. Why do you mistreat my friends?" the Baron asked, looming over the chief.

Ha'keel lowered his eyes submissively, but displayed no sign of fear. The warriors around him shifted uncomfortably. "Their Pathfinder was dead. I had nothing but their word," he said evenly.

"Wasn't that enough?" Serenus asked.

Ha'keel frowned. "The word of a stranger, especially an outlander, means little to the Ha'ashtari," he said.

"Yes, I suppose," the Baron admitted. "Your people have been

439

most useful to us, but this time you almost went too far."

The arrival of the Princess interrupted further conversation. "Serenus!" she cried, running toward the Baron, her arms outstretched.

Serenus reached down and lifted her up, holding her out at arm's length. "Has it been so long? You are grown. A woman now," the Baron said.

She patted his arm, her feet dangling. "It's been almost thirty years," Celeste said.

The centaur hugged her carefully, and then set her down. "Are you well, Princess? Did they harm you?" he asked.

"I'm fine, Baron. You saved us," she answered.

Celeste quietly turned to Morgan, and held him for a long time. Serenus raised his eyebrows at the display of affection, watching the pair in amused silence. No one else dared to speak.

"You just keep coming back," Celeste said.

"You told me to," Morgan said, enjoying how she felt.

Celeste noticed Max, and ran to him next, hugging him. Then she examined him, observing his battered condition. "You look terrible, Max. Was it awful?" she asked.

Max shrugged. "I've had better times. But I think I survived," he said.

"Do you know about Taskin?" she asked softly.

Max nodded. "Morgan told me," he said.

"He was a brave and kind man. I'll miss him," she said, her eyes glistening.

"So will I. He owed me a drink in Carnac," Max noted.

The Fist arrived, and one of them nodded toward Morgan. "The Equo judged him, on behalf of El'Atan," he said.

Ha'keel regarded the Baron. "Do you judge them all innocent?" he asked.

Serenus rubbed his chin, thinking. "Let's call it a temporary pardon. I realize there are serious allegations," he said.

A warrior stepped forward from behind Ha'keel, and Max saw it was Ha'dros. "He is ta'hoda, a lost one," he stated, pointing at Max.

440

"A lost one?" Morgan asked Max.

Max rubbed his beard. "I'm not sure what it means, but it saved my life at Carnac," he said, then pointed to Ha'dros. "This fine gentleman and his companions decided not to kill me, because I was ta'hoda."

"It means you have the spirit of a Ha'ashtari, a spirit that was lost and inhabited the body of an outlander by mistake. If the spirit is great enough, it will manifest itself to the Ha'ashtari, even though it is trapped in the body of a lesser being. Something has convinced them you are one of their lost spirits," Celeste explained.

"Obviously my stalwart courage and superhuman fighting abilities. These people are fine judges of character," Max said.

"I fought beside Max. Why am I not ta'hoda as well?" Morgan asked, curious.

"I don't know," Celeste said.

Ha'keel spoke. "Morgan fears nothing and is a great warrior, but he doesn't have the Ha'ashtari heart. He kills because he has to, not for the kill itself," he said.

"You're right. That's one difference between them," Celeste said, studying Morgan.

Max frowned. "I never thought about it that way," he said.

Ha'serl rode up and dismounted. He knelt before the Baron, pointing at Max. "The outlander has killed a Pathfinder, violating the laws of the Equo and the Ha'ashtari. He has dishonored me as well. He should die," he said.

"You told me a Pathfinder had died," Serenus said, looking at Max. "But did you kill him? That is a serious charge."

"It's not true. The man betrayed us and killed himself," Celeste protested.

"You lie!" Ha'serl hissed. "Be silent, woman."

Serenus loomed over him. "Take care how you address the Princess, little man," the centaur said, his voice wilting the Ha'ashtari.

"It's not certain they killed the Pathfinder. There is evidence to the contrary," Ha'keel said.

The soldiers from Carnac finally arrived, escorted by a ring of Ha'ashtari riders. Sergeant Balt led the troop.

441

"Sergeant, I trust you brought extra horses. We will return to Carnac. Princess, ride with me," Serenus ordered.

Celeste touched the centaur's arm. "Baron, you forget the limits of lesser beings. Max is exhausted, and your own troops have ridden hard. Night is falling. May we spend the night here and return to Carnac in the morning?" she asked.

The Baron frowned. "I suppose," he said. "Ha'keel?"

"We will prepare quarters immediately, Equo," the High Chief said.

Early the next morning, they assembled at the edge of the camp. Celeste was already mounted on the Baron. Ha'keel and the other Ha'ashtari stood nearby.

"Balt, bring the horses," the Baron ordered.

"Baron, we had our own horses," Morgan said.

"We'll leave those horses here," Serenus decided, then turned to Ha'keel. "I would know the truth of the Pathfinder's death. Come to Carnac in three days, and I will hold court."

He turned to Ha'serl. "You can make your accusations then. But once I have pronounced judgment, do not question it," he warned.

"Yes, Equo," Ha'serl said.

Ha'keel saluted again. "In three days time, I will be at the gates of Carnac," he said.

Ha'keel gestured and several warriors came forward with the outlanders' packs and possessions, including Morgan's cloak and swords. Ha'sim carried Max's swords and bow. He handed them to Max.

"Fine weapons," he said. "Worthy of a ta'hoda."

"You're a good judge of weaponry, Ha'sim. Thank you for returning them," Max said.

The soldiers from Carnac brought horses for Morgan and Max. Ha'dros stepped between Max and the horse from Carnac. He held the reins of his own horse.

"You're one of us now. You should ride a warrior's horse," he said.

Max nodded and took the reins. "I am honored, Ha'dros. I'll take good care of him," he said.

As Max mounted, he noticed Sha'lor standing nearby, watching him. He urged the horse over to her.

"Now that we're family, we should get to know each other better," he said, leaning toward her.

Sha'lor said nothing, but put her hand on a knife hilt, her face hard and defiant.

Max laughed. "A fine spirited woman, this one," he said.

As he turned away, Sha'lor's expression changed, softening. Ha'keel noticed the shift, and frowned.

CHAPTER THIRTY-ONE

CARNAC

Upon arriving in Carnac, Morgan's party had been given quarters in the Baron's compound, where they luxuriated in hot baths before having their wounds treated and sleeping for what seemed like forever. Their clothes had been taken for cleaning or replacement, and Morgan now wore simple soldier's attire. The servants had also taken his metasilk cloak. Max refused to let the ebonite mail out of his sight, and still wore it under his clean clothes. Ignoring Morgan's protests, soldiers had confiscated the other articles from the cache. The Baron had said they would be safer with him.

The next day, Morgan located the Iosian temple, and paid his respects. None of the monks approached him with any messages from Khulankor. Morgan was getting very frustrated with the lack of communication from the Monachus, or any other kind of support, for that matter. After he left the temple, Morgan had gone in search of the Princess. Since their rescue from the Ha'ashtari, they had both been tense and uncertain around each other. Morgan was determined to find Celeste and have a talk with her. Part of him wanted to take her away and forget about the world, and the rest of him knew that was not possible. Everytime they faced death or separation, he regretted not opening up to her more, but then they would be thrown together again, and he would realize they had no time for a relationship at this point in their lives.

Morgan's main problem was the kind of relationship he wanted. Were he more like Max, he would take Celeste and enjoy her to the fullest in the short time they had together. But he could not do that. If he loved a woman, he wanted to marry her, and commit himself to her for the rest of his life. And that was impossible for him and Celeste right now, which left him with his aching desire to be with her.

Women had always been a mystery to Morgan. He had no idea how to relate to them. His few attempts at love had been disasters. Morgan knew he was often attracted to the wrong kind of women, the glamorous, frivolous type that would walk into his life, bedazzle him, and leave just as quickly. After those experiences, Morgan had withdrawn, unwilling to let himself be hurt again.

Not that he had ever been given much time to devote to the subject. There had always been another conflict, another cause, another evil that needed his attention. Before, it had only been a particular city or people, now he battled something that could threaten their entire world. His sense of duty would not let him be distracted from that responsibility. And he had chosen this life, no one forced him to join the Raavs, or even leave Khulankor, for that matter. It was something he had to do; he would have no self-respect if he ignored the plight of those around him, when it was in his power to help them.

Morgan was walking along an open balcony when he found her. Celeste wore a floor length dark green dress, sleeveless with a modest neckline, and had her hair pinned up in a tousled mass of brown. She leaned on the balcony railing, looking down at the street below. Morgan paused for a moment, admiring her beauty in the golden sunlight. This was the first time he had seen her in a dress, and she was a glorious sight.

With a sigh, he went to her side. She glanced at him, and he saw she had been crying, and noticed the soggy cloth in her hand. When she saw him, she turned her head away, wiping furiously at her tear-streaked face. Morgan just stared at her; he could not imagine why she would be crying now.

"What's wrong?" he finally asked.

She finished drying her face, and gave him a forced smile that did not reach her red eyes. "Nothing. I'm fine," she said.

Morgan folded his arms, and leaned on the rail, waiting for an answer. After a while, she looked at him again. "What?" she asked. "Oh, all right, I'm not fine. Talbot isn't here."

"Where is he?" Morgan asked.

She spread the cloth out on the railing to dry. "He was here, but he went on to Aijalon," she said.

"Why did he go there?" Morgan asked.

Celeste shrugged. "He was bored. He went to find the

445

elves," she said.

"The elves. What for?" Morgan asked.

"While he was here, he studied the races of Faerie, the trolls, goblins, gargoyles, and the elves. He became fascinated by the elves. When he learned no one had seen an elf for nearly two thousand years, he went to find them," she said.

"How long has he been gone?" Morgan asked.

Celeste frowned. "Serenus said he didn't pay much attention. He doesn't know for sure when Talbot left. It's been a while though. Time means little to the centaurs. I need to have someone search the gate records; no one leaves Carnac without it being recorded. He had a guide though, so he wasn't alone," she said.

"What are you going to do now?" Morgan asked gently.

"I don't know. I just wanted to get here and find Talbot. Now I don't know what I'm going to do," she said.

Morgan studied her. This was a new side of Celeste, one that he had not seen before. She seemed so lost, so vulnerable, not the determined Princess he had been traveling with. He took her in his arms and held her. She nestled into his embrace, and almost started crying again. They stood without speaking, and then Morgan forced himself to let her go, turning to face the street. Maybe it would help if he changed the subject.

"Tell me about the Baron. You seem to know him well," he said.

Celeste was silent for a moment, remembering, and then she smiled. "I was only sixteen when my father sent me here. I had never been off the island, and it was an incredible adventure. Talbot was here already, and we loved being together again. Serenus frightened me at first; he was so big, and so strange. But he was kind, gentle, patient, and seemed to know everything. I grew to love him, almost like another father. There was so much to learn here, and I couldn't get enough. My love of knowledge impressed Serenus, and he made a special effort to tutor me. The Waste, and the Ha'ashtari, drew me. The Waste was so big, so different from Skara Thrae. It seemed to go on forever, with a sky so close you could touch it. The Ha'ashtari were fierce, and wild, and free. They reminded me of

446

the best qualities of the Thraens. Those were wonderful times," she said.

"The Baron doesn't act like the centaurs I've met. Most of them are reserved and distant, they never get involved, they just watch. I couldn't believe it when Serenus dropped everything and ran to your rescue," Morgan said.

"Where did you meet a centaur? I thought you had never been to Carnac before," Celeste asked.

Morgan shrugged. "As you know, they leave the city from time to time. I've encountered them in various places over the years," he said.

"Serenus isn't like most centaurs. He cares, and he does get involved. That has caused trouble for him at the Academy," she said.

Morgan smiled. "I can imagine," he said. "What about this trial the Baron spoke of?"

"Serenus knows I would never murder a Pathfinder. But the charge is serious, especially to the Ha'ashtari, and Serenus respects that. Holding a formal inquest, and hearing all the evidence, is his way of showing that respect," Celeste said.

"As long as he comes to the right conclusion. I would dislike having to flee Carnac," Morgan said.

"I trust him," Celeste said. "He'll find the truth."

"Tell me about Carnac, the city, the people," Morgan said.

Celeste looked up at the huge buildings around them, squinting into the sun. A cool breeze drifted by, and Morgan caught a whiff of her perfume. He forced himself not to look at her. It would be so easy to go to her room right now.

"Carnac was built long, long ago, and it's never been conquered," she said.

Morgan gestured at the figures in the street below. "What about the people who live here?" he asked.

"The centaurs rule the city, although it practically runs itself. The closest thing to a government is the Academy. People are sent here from all over the world, to be students at the Academy. Royalty usually have a personal tutor, as I did. The other students attend classes at the Academy. The libraries and laboratories of Carnac

447

are incredible. All the knowledge in the world seems to be gathered here. On rare occasions, a centaur will leave Carnac on a special assignment, or to teach someone who can't come here. They use those excursions as opportunities to gather more knowledge about the world, and to reclaim artifacts and relics. The museums are full of things they brought back. The centaurs also have agents everywhere, looking for old knowledge or objects of interest.

Sometimes, in return for their services, children are brought here and raised to be the soldiers and servants in Carnac," she explained.

Morgan interrupted. "They barter with their children?" he asked.

"Many of the children receive better treatment here than they ever would at home. When they are adults, they're given the choice to leave if they want. Most stay. It's a beautiful, peaceful city," Celeste said.

"But what about their families?" Morgan asked, still not satisfied.

"Their parents make the choice. No one forces them. They choose to give their children a better life, an education, a future. They can even visit if they want. It's not so bad," she said.

"So all those soldiers were sent here as children," Morgan said.

"Most of them. They're fiercely loyal to the centaurs, and love Carnac. A few others come here, and seek to serve the centaurs. Some are tested and accepted, the others are turned away. It's good, steady work, and there's little risk. No one has attacked Carnac for centuries," she said.

"So those that show little aptitude for soldiering become servants?" Morgan asked.

"That's usually how it works," Celeste said.

"What about the satyrs?" Morgan asked.

"There's some ancient connection between the centaurs and satyrs, some strange kinship. No human knows for sure what it is. The satyrs are allowed to live in the cliffs and they forage on leftover crops in the valley and whatever they can find in the cliffs. They'll attack anyone without proper escort, and serve as another line of defense for the city," she said.

"Poor Max. He had to come right through them," Morgan said.

"It's almost as if he has a pact with death herself. Maybe he bribes Sett with the lives of others, to keep her from coming after him," she said.

"You're not the first to say that. That's why they call him Le Morte Kahn, the Lord of Death. It is said that he worships Sett, and that in return for his service, she has spared him. But I've been with him long enough to be painfully aware of his mortality. And I think this last adventure with the Ha'ashtari has disturbed Max, reminded him of his age and vulnerability. He's spent most of the time since we arrived in the taverns, in the company of a Sergeant Balt. Do you know him?" Morgan asked.

"I remember Balt from before. A good man, a veteran soldier. And I wouldn't worry about Max, he'll be his old self in no time," she said.

Morgan laughed. "I gave up worrying about Max a long time ago," he said.

The sound of running feet interrupted their conversation. Morgan and Celeste turned around, and a woman threw herself into Morgan's arms. Celeste stepped back, her eyes narrowing. Morgan gently disentangled himself from the mass of blond hair and the ivory arms, pushing the woman back far enough to see her face.

"Morgan, it's me, Maelin!" the woman cried. She had a child's voice, in spite of her obviously adult body.

"Maelin?" Morgan responded, incredulously.

Maelin pulled free and spun around. "It's me! I'm all grown up now, but it's still me," she said, then grabbed Morgan's hands. "Oh Morgan, it's so good to see you. I heard you were dead."

Morgan stared for a moment. Maelin's head barely reached Morgan's chest. Her long blond hair, clean but wild, framed her big green eyes and fine delicate features. She wore a loose yellow garment and no shoes. With her pale skin, she looked like a porcelain doll.

"Maelin, you have grown," Morgan remarked.

They heard a yapping sound and two animals came running toward them. The first was a dog, a little ball of reddish hair, with stubby legs, and a short face with enormous black eyes. It was doing the yapping, its pink tongue visible between oversized canines. The second was . . . also a dog, but the ugliest beast Morgan had ever seen in his life. Larger than its companion, it had long, knobby legs, and a skinny, almost hairless body. A motley collection of colors blotched its hide, from the stub tail to the horribly deformed face. Wrinkled naked skin covered the truncated, twisted features and stiff hairs protruded from various parts of the face, waving around like antennas when the dog moved. The lower jaw hung askew, a black tongue lolling from one corner, leaving a trail of spittle on the floor. The bulging eyes were particularly disturbing, the left cloudy and rolling aimlessly, while the right darted to and fro. In fact, the violent movement of the right eye caused Morgan to fear it would pop out of the animal's head at any moment.

Maelin scooped up the yapper, and Morgan grabbed her, swinging her around so that he stood between her and the second dog. He regretted being unarmed. The hideous beast skidded to a halt, its clawed feet raking across the smooth stone. The dog tilted its head, staring up at Morgan with its good eye. The other eye rolled up, until only the white showed.

Morgan pointed at the animal. "What is that?" he asked, watching the thing carefully.

Maelin peeked under Morgan's arm. "Oh that's just Clavius. Morgan, meet Clavius Dementus. He was brought here for the centaurs to study, because he's so . . . unique. He's really quite sweet, once you get used to how he looks. In fact, I think he's so ugly he's cute," she explained.

"'Crazy nail?' What kind of a name is that?" Morgan asked.

Maelin laughed, a sound like tinkling bells. "No, Morgan. 'Demented spike.' That sounds much better. Don't you think it fits him?" she asked.

Clavius jumped up on Morgan, his skinny toes digging into Morgan's leg, a rope of spittle now dangling precariously close to

450

his knee. Morgan could not bring himself to pet the creature. He glanced over his shoulder, at the bundle of fur in Maelin's arms.

"I see you still have Brutus," he said. Brutus yapped in greeting.

Celeste stifled a laugh. "Brutus?" she asked, looking at the tiny beast. "I've been around a lot of Pomas, but I never heard of one called Brutus."

Morgan stepped aside, and Clavius slid off and staggered away. He gestured to Celeste. "I'm sorry. You haven't met. Maelin, this is Princess Celestine, from Skara Thrae," he said.

Maelin beamed at Celeste. "We have a lot in common already. I'm a Princess too, and we both know Morgan," she said.

Morgan compared the two women. "But that's about all. You two are completely different," he observed.

Celeste also studied the tiny Maelin. "A Princess, you say?" she asked.

"She is Llorgau's daughter, from Saxhaven," Morgan said.

Celeste nodded. "And you obviously know Morgan," she prompted. Something in her tone made Morgan nervous.

Maelin grabbed Morgan's arm possessively, looking up at him. "Yes, we were supposed to be married," she said.

Morgan groaned at the look on Celeste's face. He tried to think of something to say, some way to explain. He could see the storm clouds gathering.

Maelin let go of his arm, and slapped his shoulder playfully. "I was only a child then, but when Morgan saved Saxhaven from the Targ, my mother wanted to pledge me to Morgan. When I grew up, of course," she explained.

Celeste folded her arms, raising her eyebrows. "And what did Morgan say?" she asked quietly.

Maelin frowned, her pretty face in a pout. "He said no, a mercenary was not worthy of a Princess. Mother was disappointed, but what could she do? Father gave him a reward instead. I was crushed. Morgan was a hero, and he didn't want me," she said.

Celeste's face softened slightly. "Not worthy of you? Seems I've heard that before. You didn't want her, Morgan?" she asked.

451

Morgan searched for a way out. "I didn't say that . . . I just . . . ," he stammered.

"So have you changed your mind, now that she's all grown up?" Celeste asked.

Both women were watching him closely, waiting for his answer. Clavius' hindquarters collapsed, and he sat down, drool running down his chest. His good eye bobbed back and forth.

Morgan backed away, his hands out. "Will you women stop tormenting me? It's cruel," he said.

"Morgan, we're so different. You're always running around, fighting, and saving people. I don't like travel, I hate violence. I don't even like to get dirty. My books are what I love now. How could we be married?" Maelin asked.

Celeste stared at the childlike Maelin. "Books?" she asked skeptically.

Maelin nodded, her tangled locks bobbing. "Books, libraries, laboratories. Carnac is heaven for me, although I miss my father," she said, her face clouding at the mention of her father.

"Maelin was a child genius. Even when I knew her, she was brilliant. It was inevitable she would end up here," Morgan said.

"Yes, I have the Baron Serenus as my personal tutor. He likes me," Maelin said.

Celeste frowned. She felt big and clumsy next to this petite doll, and a woman from Morgan's past was the last thing she needed right now.

"Well, I'm sure you two have a lot to talk about. Good to meet you, Maelin. Morgan," Celeste said.

"I wanted to talk to you about something, but . . . ," Morgan began.

"Yes?" Celeste asked.

Morgan glanced at Maelin. "I guess it can wait. Never mind," he said.

"Enjoy your evening," Celeste said.

"You as well, Princess," Morgan returned formally, while Maelin waved, hugging Brutus.

Morgan watched the Princess leave, and then turned to find

Maelin studying him.

"What?" he asked.

"She likes you, she would prefer to be jealous of me, but hasn't quite made up her mind. You want her, and don't know what to think about me, now that I'm . . . a woman," Maelin observed.

Morgan started to argue, but knew better. "You're dangerous," he finally said.

Maelin just giggled. "Walk with me," she said, hooking her arm in Morgan's.

They moved down the walkway. Morgan heard the scrabble of claws, and looked down, flinching at the sight of Clavius walking beside him.

Maelin followed his gaze. "He likes me. Don't be mean to him," she chided.

"Sorry. It will take me a while to get used to him," Morgan said.

"He's very loyal," Maelin added.

"I'm sure he is. How have you been?" he said, trying to change the subject.

"Like I said, it's been wonderful, except I miss father. Where have you been all these years, Morgan? I heard you were dead," she said.

"I went to the mountains for a while. On my way back, I stopped in Saxhaven," he said.

"How was he?" she asked quietly.

Morgan shook his head. "Not good. I don't know what to do for him," he said.

"Did you meet Malissa?" Maelin asked.

Morgan took a deep breath. "Oh yes," he said.

Maelin glanced up at him. "But you didn't . . . ," she began.

"No," Morgan said firmly. "Well, almost. But Antony came in time."

Maelin smiled. "Dear, faithful Antony. He sent me here, to keep me safe," she said.

"He'll do everything he can for your father. But it's hard. Llorgau is beyond wanting help anymore," Morgan said.

"I'm still looking for a cure, here in Carnac," she said.

A group of people passed them on the balcony, giving Clavius a wide berth. The poor dog seemed oblivious to their reaction.

"Have you found a cure?" Morgan asked.

"We've just discovered something. It's harsh though, and may be quite a shock to his system," she said.

"How would it work?" Morgan asked.

Maelin smiled ruefully. "Well, it . . . causes total impotency," she said.

Morgan blew out his breath. "That is harsh. But it would work, if they couldn't . . ." he trailed off, not sure how to say it to Llorgau's daughter.

Maelin squeezed his arm. "I'll keep trying. Maybe I can find something else, something to counteract her poison," she said, then paused. "Saxhaven is so different now. My city, and my people, are . . . dying. It was horrible to watch, the loss of my mother, the changes in father, the old retainers being replaced by Malissa's puppets. I wish it could be like before, when you came riding in and fought the Targs. Our city was proud then, our people noble, the leaders wise . . . it's all gone now."

"I'm sorry about your mother, about everything. I wish there was more I could do," Morgan said.

"You couldn't stay and help Antony? Father admired you . . . once," she asked.

"No, I couldn't. There's something else I have to do," he said.

"I understand. Why are you here?" she asked.

"Max and I are heading east. We made a detour to help Celeste reach Carnac," he said.

"I heard Max was here too. I can't wait to see him. He always made me laugh," she said. "I heard about Taskin too. I'm sorry. It would have been nice to see him again. I'm just glad he was able to leave Saxhaven, and not be killed by Malissa."

They walked in silence for awhile. "How long are you staying?" Maelin asked.

"I have to appear before the Baron on another matter. When

454

that is resolved, we'll be leaving," he answered.

"The Pathfinder business?" she asked.

"You don't miss much, do you? Yes, it's about the death of the Pathfinder," Morgan said.

"What about Celeste? What's she going to do?" Maelin asked.

"I don't know. She came here to find her brother, and he's gone," Morgan said.

"To Aijalon, in search of the elves. He was nice, even flirted with me for a while, then lost interest. Restless, though. He didn't seem happy," Maelin said.

"I'm glad you're here. Seeing you brings back good memories," Morgan said, and then glanced down at the Princess of Saxhaven. "Even though I can't believe how grown up you are."

"Let's make the most of our time together," Maelin said.

Two days later, the Baron held court in a huge stone amphitheater, open to the sky. Serenus stood on a dais in the center, his arms resting on a marble lectern. Ha'keel, Ha'sim, Sha'lor, and Ha'dros represented the Shen'tari, and Ha'serl and Ha'ral the Meng'tari. The Ha'ashtari, Morgan, Max, and Celeste all sat in the front row of the tiered steps. Maelin sat farther back, the Poma in her lap. She had insisted on attending, and the Baron could not refuse her. Ha'serl still had his arm in a sling, and bore the bruises from his fight with Max. Max had a hangover, and looked terrible. There was even a Pathfinder present, sitting alone with a veil hiding his features. A second centaur stood near the exit, observing the proceedings. He watched Serenus, seemingly more interested in his actions and words than anything else.

The Baron raised a hand, and the muted conversations ceased. "I am here to judge the matter of the murdered Pathfinder. Three outlanders stand accused of the crime. I could just pardon them, but out of respect for Ha'ashtari law and the concerns of the Pathfinders, I have called this hearing. I have questioned the accused individually, and have spoken to all interested parties.

This shall be the order of the proceeding. The accused will

present their version of the events, with orderly questioning by the other parties. Then the Ha'ashtari will produce their evidence. I will allow the Pathfinder representative to submit any evidence in his possession. At the conclusion of the presentations, there will be closing statements, and then I will make my decision.

The accused may begin," the Baron said.

Morgan let Celeste do the talking. "At Aquarquff, we contracted for passage to Carnac. We stopped at the first oasis, and spent the night there. Early in the morning, the Pathfinder tried to steal our horses and leave us alone in . . ." she began.

Ha'serl stood up. "The outlander woman lies! The Pathfinder was of Meng'tari blood, of my family, and would do no such thing. These outlanders murdered their Pathfinder, and they should die," he said.

The Baron regarded Ha'serl sternly. "If you have a question, ask it in the appropriate fashion. Otherwise, be silent. The Meng'tari will have their turn to speak. Let the woman finish her story," he said.

Ha'serl hesitated, glaring at Celeste and Morgan, and then finally sat down.

"Continue," Serenus said.

"As I said, he was trying to steal our horses and leave, knowing what that would mean, for us to be caught in the Waste without him. But Max stopped him. The Pathfinder then tried to kill Max, but Max disarmed him, and brought him back. When I tried to question him, he killed himself. Later, we found that two other Pathfinders had met with him the night before. That's what happened," Celeste said.

"How did you know there were other Pathfinders?" Ha'keel asked.

"Who else rides shod horses in the Shan'tari?" Celeste countered. "Max found tracks of two shod horses above the oasis," she said.

"Two Pathfinders," Ha'keel said thoughtfully, then looked hard at Celeste. "Why would a Pathfinder do such a thing? Escorting travelers is their livelihood. Why would a Pathfinder jeopardize their very existence?"

Ha'serl spoke again. "You see? Her story makes no sense. It is a lie," he said.

"Meng'tari, you have been warned. If you will not respect this proceeding, you will be removed. Is that understood?" Serenus said, raising his voice only slightly.

Ha'serl nodded mutely, as the Baron's echoing tones faded.

"How do you explain your claim?" Ha'keel asked Celeste.

"I can't. Our Pathfinder must have been paid to do it. He couldn't have had any personal grudge against us," Celeste said.

Ha'serl opened his mouth, glanced at the Baron, and then closed it slowly. The other Ha'ashtari stirred and muttered.

"Paid!" Ha'keel said, his tone harsh.

"Ha'keel," the Baron warned.

The High Chief took a deep breath and continued. "The Pathfinders are half Ha'ashtari. Woman, you don't know anything about us if you say these things. Even a Pathfinder would spit on blood money," he said.

"How would you explain it then? It happened, just as I said," Celeste said.

Ha'keel studied Celeste for a moment, rubbing his chin. "You are the Princess Celestine, of Skara Thrae," he stated.

"Yes, I am," Celeste said.

"Why do you enter our lands, Princess of Skara Thrae?" Ha'keel asked.

"I sought my brother in Carnac," she answered.

"Why?" Ha'keel pressed.

"Because I haven't seen him for a long time. Why would you want to see your brother?" Celeste said.

Ha'keel ignored her rising anger, methodically continuing his questioning. "Why is your brother in Carnac?" he asked.

"He's not. He left," Celeste said.

"But he was here?" Ha'keel asked.

"Yes, he was here," Celeste said.

"Why did he come to Carnac?" Ha'keel asked.

"What difference does that make? Wanderlust, seeking adventure . . . he couldn't stand my father, if you have to know,"

Celeste said.

Ha'sim chuckled at that remark, and Celeste glared at him.

"Again, why do you seek your brother? If he had wanted your company, he would have stayed in Skara Thrae," Ha'keel asked.

"Skara Thrae has been invaded. My father has been driven from his throne, and I barely escaped with my life. I came to ask my brother's help," she said.

"And why is he here?" Ha'keel asked, pointing at Morgan.

Celeste looked at Morgan. "He can speak for himself," she said.

Morgan frowned. "My friends and I encountered the Princess in Androssar. She needed help, so we agreed to escort her to Carnac," he said.

Ha'keel raised his eyebrows. "That was generous of you. What did she pay you for your services?" he asked.

"She didn't pay us. We were traveling east anyway, and we wanted to make sure she arrived safely," Morgan said.

"Why do you travel here?" Ha'keel asked.

Morgan hesitated, grimacing. He glanced at the Baron, who watched impassively.

"I was sent," Morgan said.

"By who?" Ha'keel asked patiently.

"I won't lie, but I cannot tell you," he said.

Ha'keel's eyes narrowed. "You will not answer?" he asked.

"Why won't you answer? What do you fear?" Ha'ral demanded.

"Betrayal. Traitors and cowards. The same treachery we faced at Tau'kendi. I have powerful enemies, whose influence reaches even here. If the Pathfinders have been corrupted, how can I trust the Ha'ashtari?" he asked.

The Ha'ashtari looked shocked. Ha'serl was speechless, for once. Max sensed the tension, and his foggy gaze cleared.

"If your accusation wasn't so outrageous, I would kill you," Ha'keel said. "You actually believe the Ha'ashtari would serve the interests of outsiders?"

"Would the Pathfinders? The evidence is right before you. I served for years with the Raavs, and one thing I learned in that time

458

was that any mortal can be turned, no matter what the race," Morgan said.

"The Raavs," Ha'sim said softly. "So that is where he learned to fight like that."

"The Ha'ashtari would die rather than serve outsiders. Only the Equos have earned our obedience," Ha'keel said.

"It doesn't make any difference why we are here, or who sent us. All you want to know is who killed the Pathfinder, and we're telling you it was suicide," Celeste said.

"But you have no idea why?" Ha'keel asked, and then frowned. "How exactly did the Pathfinder kill himself?"

"He had a poison tooth. When we tried to question him, he bit on the tooth, and the poison killed him," Celeste said.

Ha'keel looked intently at the Princess, as if the next answer were very important. "What kind of poison?" he asked.

"I don't know," Celeste said. "It was blue, and he died quickly."

"Blue," Ha'keel said, as if to himself.

Ha'ral stepped forward. "When you were captured, you held certain artifacts. What were they?"

"I can't tell you," Morgan said.

"There was a sword, a large stone, a jewel, and several small idols. You will not tell us where you got these things?" Ha'ral asked.

"No," Morgan said.

"I say they are sorcerous talismans, and that you came to the Waste to work some evil magic. When the Pathfinder discovered your plans, you killed him," Ha'ral said.

"That's ridiculous," Celeste said.

Ha'serl turned to the Princess. "Isn't it true that you destroyed the Pathfinder's soul stone?" he asked Celeste.

Celeste faced him. "That is true. I did it to show . . . ," she began.

Ha'ral cut her off. "Not only did they betray and murder their Pathfinder, but they destroyed his soul stone, condemning his soul to wander. What other penalty can there be but death?" he asked.

"Do you have any further questions?" the Baron asked.

"No," Ha'keel said.

"These outlanders killed a Pathfinder. There can be no doubt about it. Their stories are lies, or madness at best. They claim the Pathfinder betrayed them, because he was paid to. That a Pathfinder would violate centuries of tradition and doom his own people by his acts. Who would believe such nonsense? They should die. There is nothing more that needs to be said," Ha'serl said.

"We will now have closing statements. Ha'serl of the Meng'tari, since you have already begun your statement, do you wish to finish it?" Serenus asked.

Ha'serl addressed the Baron. "The woman intended to enter our lands, to travel to Carnac, supposedly to seek her brother. As required, she contracted with the Pathfinders for passage. These others," Ha'serl paused to point to Morgan and Max, "must have forced her guide to take them along, breaching the woman's contract. They had also stolen horses from Aquarquff. At the first oasis, these outlanders murdered their Pathfinder, and then shattered his soul stone. In their defense, they speak madness. They are guilty and their punishment should be swift and just. That is all I have to say," he said.

Ha'serl sat and Serenus motioned to Ha'keel, who stood to speak. "All that the Meng'tari speaks seems to be true. Although they paid for the horses in Aquarquff. The circumstances indicate guilt, and the outlanders refuse to answer many of our questions. Morgan gives no explanation of his mission or motives, and he possessed strange objects, the like of which we have never seen before," Ha'keel said, and then paused. "But consider this also, Equo. I sent Shen'tari to question the Pathfinder's fellows. One of them killed himself with a poison tooth, a blue poison, that is not from the Waste. My warriors found out later he was the same who contracted with the Princess for passage. Another Pathfinder died to avoid questioning, a member of the same cell as the other two. Was this mere chance?

I know these outlanders to be brave and honorable, that they followed the tenets of Ka'chi. Are they lying? Are their tales madness? Or is there some deeper evil here? That is a question I gladly leave to the Equos, who in their wisdom will find the truth."

Ha'keel sat and Serenus turned to the Pathfinder. "Do you

wish to speak?" he asked.

The Pathfinder stood and bowed. "The important issue here is the entire Pathfinder order, and not the lives of three outlanders. From time immemorial, the Pathfinders have been the guides to Carnac. This is a system that is vital to the Waste and all its inhabitants. Anyone who molests a Pathfinder should be dealt with severely. Their persons must remain inviolate. If there is the slightest doubt of the innocence of these outlanders, take the safe course and have them killed. Think of the greater good, Equo. I have spoken," he said.

The Baron folded his massive arms, and studied the speakers, weighing their words. "Do the accused have anything further?" he asked finally.

Morgan stood. "Only briefly, Equo. We all paid for our passage with the Pathfinder, and for the horses from Aquarquff. Even if our situation forced us to unusual methods, there was just compensation. The Meng'tari steal horses all the time, it's sheer hypocrisy for them to cast blame for that. Our Pathfinder betrayed us, and when we caught him, he killed himself. We did him no mortal harm. His soul stone was shattered as testimony to his dishonor. Our stories are true. I believe there are traitors among the Pathfinders. The Pathfinder order should focus on that, and not seek the death of innocents. You know who and what we are, and why I cannot answer some of the Ha'ashtari's questions. You know the nature of my 'sorcerous talismans', and my true purpose. Judge for yourself whether we are capable of this crime. We trust our lives to you, Equo," he said.

The Baron got to his feet, towering over the audience from his dais. His powerful voice echoed from the ranks of seats and the columns above. "These people stand accused of a heinous crime. If they are guilty, they should be executed. First, I consider the character of the accused. The Princess I know well, she tutored at my side for five years. Morgan and Maximilian I know by reputation. Commanders of the Seventh and Eighth Legions of the Raavs, the finest fighting force ever assembled. None of these three are the type to commit a cowardly murder.

461

Next I consider the circumstantial evidence against them. A Pathfinder died in their presence. Is this enough to convict them? I think not. Two other Pathfinders perished rather than be questioned by the Ha'ashtari. The Princess purchased guide services from one of them, who later dies the same death as the guide. There is some deeper evil here, beyond a mere murder.

I have other evidence I cannot share. When I consider it all, there is only one conclusion. I find the outlanders innocent," Serenus said.

The Meng'tari looked quite displeased, but none dared challenge the Baron's decision. In spite of his aching head, Max clapped Morgan on the back, while Celeste sighed and put her head in her hands. Maelin squealed and jumped up, clapping her hands. Ha'keel seemed satisfied, and Ha'sim smiled. Max caught Sha'lor gazing at him, and blew her a kiss. She turned away.

"Meng'tari, I grieve with you for your loss, and I share your outrage at the death of a Pathfinder. But I suggest you look elsewhere for your vengeance," the Baron said, and then regarded the Pathfinder. "And I suggest you return to your order, and tell your Callis this. Look deep within your ranks. If you find the evil I suspect, root it out, without mercy. If you fail to cleanse yourselves, the Equos will do it for you."

"High Chief, Ha'keel. I appreciate your wisdom and honesty. May you find honor and good hunting," Serenus said.

Ha'keel nodded. "I will, Equo," he said.

The Baron turned to look at the other centaur, his gaze defiant, daring the centaur to question his logic. The other centaur returned his gaze impassively, and then left the auditorium.

CHAPTER THIRTY-TWO

ASSASSINS

That night, Maelin walked through the dark rooftop garden, praying for her father. Brutus and Clavius frolicked in the shrubbery, the rustle of vegetation marking their paths. Suspended globes, scattered throughout the garden, lit the moonless, still night. Beyond the garden wall, other buildings rose into the darkness, their stone sides tinged with silver in the faint archlight. The trees and shrubs cast tangled shadows across the stone path, and somewhere a fountain gurgled. Statues dotted the garden, dark figures in the wan light.

As she prayed, she began to have the strangest feeling, a sense of imminent danger. She suddenly knew that she was not alone in the garden. Maelin stopped and turned slowly around, her eyes searching the rooftop. She saw nothing but the dark skeletons of trees and shrubs, which now stirred in a cold draft that swirled through the garden. The dogs seemed to sense the intruder, and fell silent, their play forgotten. They sat unmoving, invisible in the rustling foliage.

Maelin walked toward the nearest light, trying not to panic and run headlong. As she moved, her eyes continued to sweep the garden, and she constantly cast glances over her shoulder. Despite her efforts, she could discover no tangible reason for her uneasiness; she could not even tell where the dogs were anymore. Even so, the feeling of danger remained, if anything it grew stronger. The cold wind blew harder, filling the garden with menacing sounds.

She thought she heard something else, and stopped to listen. A brief stirring came from the vegetation behind her, and then it was gone. She held her breath, wanting to scream, but fearing to do even that. After a few agonizing moments, she hurried on, making it to the pool of light beneath the globe. She huddled in that small island of safety, the icy breeze tossing her hair. Where were those dogs? She still saw no sign of them. She looked ahead to the next light, but it seemed impossibly far away, a river of darkness barring her path. She heard another slight sound in the shrubbery, closer this time. The breeze was becoming fierce, almost a shrill wind. The light blinded her to anything beyond, and she realized she had to move.

With a deep breath, she stepped away from the light and walked briskly down the stone path. The way narrowed, arms of greenery reaching out from either side. She studied the vegetation as she approached; peering into the tangle of leaves and branches. She stubbed her toe on the edge of a stone in the path, and looked down. As she did so, something crashed through the foliage behind her, and before she could turn, a cruel hand clamped onto her arm and dragged her from the path. Thrashing, she tried to cry out, but another hand smothered her scream, settling firmly over her mouth.

She fought grimly, but found her resistance futile against the strength of her attacker. Branches raked her arms and neck as the assailant pulled her into the brush. Stumbling and twisting, Maelin was dragged through the screen of vegetation and thrust into the deeper darkness under a large tree. Then she was spun about and shoved against the bole of the tree, the hand over her mouth now pinning her head to the trunk with brutal force. In the blackness, she saw her assailant as only a large shape; she could make out no features. The wind now rushing through the garden blew aside a limb overhead, and a wash of silver light revealed an upraised arm, clutching a black-bladed dagger. The light vanished, and Maelin fought harder, knowing that blade was about to descend. She clawed at the arm that held her, and kicked at the dark figure. She might as well have attacked one of the garden statues, her struggles had little effect. In resignation, she asked Iosus to receive her spirit, certain she was going to die.

A rustle came from the brush to their left, and her attacker paused. Once again, the wind opened the canopy to the night sky, and the ghoulish light fell upon a hideous face thrust from the leaves. Maelin's assailant was so stricken by the awful sight that he backed away, the hand falling from her mouth. Maelin sagged, sliding along the rough bark to the ground. The apparition in the leaves twisted, one eye fixed on the dark figure, the other eye rolling aimlessly, the contorted lips drawn back from a tangle of yellowed teeth. The assassin crouched, holding the dagger before him, frozen in shock. Then the branch overhead swung back into place, and the darkness rushed in. Maelin heard a sharp crash in the vegetation, and the assassin backed another pace, trying to locate the ghastly newcomer.

As he stepped back, something closed on his ankle, and two points of sharp pain blossomed there. He twisted and the pressure ended, but fire swept up his leg, numbing, terrible pain. Grinding his teeth to keep from screaming, the man dropped the dagger and clutched at his leg, staggering into the tangle of brush. He forced his way through, and stumbled onto the path. He gasped, sucking in the cold air, the wave of agony now reaching his chest. He tried to take another breath, but his lungs would not work. A great roaring filled his head, and he collapsed on the path. The last thing he heard was a chorus of barking, a strident, yapping sound.

Drawn by the shrill barking, a guard arrived a moment later.

"Princess, are you here?" he called.

The guard saw the dark figure on the path, and heard a weak response to his call, coming from the brush beside the path. The barking seemed to be coming from the same location. The guard shouted for help, then ran to the fallen man. The soldier crouched over the assassin, scanning the shrubbery for the source of the sounds. Maelin pushed through the foliage to his right, and almost fell. The guard caught the disheveled woman, who clung to him frantically.

"Help me," she cried. "I've been attacked. He was going to kill me, he had a knife."

The guard started to say something, to comfort her, when he heard a noise in the brush. Clavius burst through the leaves, his bulging orbs glinting in the archlight. The guard recoiled, his sword coming up. He dropped his point, even though he recognized the hideous beast, his reaction was almost instinctive.

Maelin pulled free, and fell to her knees beside the ugly dog. She threw her arms around the misshapen head and hugged him. The wayward eye completed another orbit, and the lolling tongue slapped against the woman's tangled hair, the stub tail attempting to wag.

"Clavius, you saved me," she said.

Brutus quit barking and wriggled through the brush, his little tongue curling around the oversized canines, and his button eyes bright. Maelin saw the Poma, and reached over to hug him.

"And you too, Brutus. I love you both," Maelin declared.

The guard heard the sound of the alarm, then the pounding of boots on stone. As he turned to look, several more soldiers came charging down the path, light wands held high and their swords drawn. Behind them ran a large man the guard recognized as a personal guest of the Baron.

Maelin scooped up Brutus and stood. Clavius peered around her dress with his good eye. The guards slowed as they approached, and the big man shoved past them. He grabbed Maelin by the shoulders, looking down at her.

"What happened?" Morgan asked. "Are you hurt?"

Maelin held up the Poma. "No, Brutus and Clavius saved me. Clavius scared him and then Brutus bit him," she said.

Morgan brushed a twig from the Princess' tangled locks, and touched a scratch on her cheek. He noticed the other cuts and scrapes, and a bruise already forming on her arm.

"I have no doubt that Clavius scared him," he said, then paused, seeing the black stain on the Poma's teeth. "Brutus bit him?"

Maelin looked up at him and smiled brightly. She seemed to be recovering from her ordeal. "It was good of you to come to my rescue. How did you know?" she asked.

"I was walking Celeste back to her room, and we heard the alarm," Morgan said.

Maelin squinted mischievously. "Sorry for the interruption," she said.

Morgan reddened slightly. "It's not . . . we weren't . . ." he started to explain, but Maelin's attention had wandered already. She was looking at the dead assassin.

Morgan turned to look at the fallen figure. The guards had turned him over. Dressed entirely in black, a hood covered his face, the dead eyes visible through holes in the hood. A guard reached down and pulled the hood off. Agonizing death had contorted the man's features.

Maelin turned away, burying her head in Morgan's shoulder. He put his arms around her, looking down at the dead man. He noticed that the cold wind had faded, the trees growing quiet around them.

"Who is that? Do you know him?" Morgan demanded.

The guards shook their heads. "We will find out," one man assured Morgan. "No one enters Carnac without their presence being recorded."

Maelin burrowed deeper into Morgan's chest. "It was awful. Why would anyone want to hurt me?" she murmured.

Morgan stroked her hair. "I don't know. But it won't happen again," he said firmly.

Maelin remembered something. "He had a black knife," she said in a small voice.

Morgan turned to one of the guards. "Find that knife. It may tell us what the dead man cannot," he said.

At the entrance to the garden, Celeste watched, her attention focused on Morgan and Maelin. Then she turned away.

Another pair of eyes observed the scene. A dark figure crouched on the garden wall, hidden in the shadow of a tall tree. Seeing that his accomplice had failed, the watcher turned and disappeared over the wall. He hurried away, reluctant to convey the bad news to their cruel mistress.

When Celeste got back to her room, she found Max sitting by the door. He smelled of liquor and smoke. She looked down at him, her hands on her hips.

"Well, where have you been? I've hardly seen you since we got here," she chided.

Max looked up at her with bloodshot eyes, fingering the Luminarae dagger. "You know where I've been. Let's take a walk," he said. "I feel like talking."

"Since you asked so nicely, why not? I think we need to talk," Celeste said.

Max put away the dagger, and held out his hand. "Help me up," he said.

Celeste reached down and pulled him to his feet. He smelled even stronger up close. "Are you drunk?" she asked.

Max nodded, weaving slightly as he stood. "Probably. I seem to remember a lot of drinking. I need some air," he said.

Celeste hooked her arm in his. "Let's walk on the balcony," she suggested.

They made their way to the balcony without speaking. Max leaned on the railing, looking up at the night sky. The arch hung overhead, cold and silent, its ghostly light washing over the red buildings. It was late, and no one walked the street below.

"I love the open sky," Max remarked.

Celeste leaned on the railing beside him. "What's wrong, Max? Why are you acting like this?" she asked.

Max sighed, itching his nose. "I almost died out there in the Waste. Those Ha'ashtari nearly had me. Would have, but for that 'lost one' nonsense. The whole thing reminded me of something that I constantly try to forget. That I'm human after all, mortal. Just another man, getting older and slower every day. Soon I'll face someone better than me, and they'll kill me, like I've killed so many others.

When I'm drunk I still feel invincible. So I stayed drunk for a few days. It was nice to spend time with Sergeant Balt, to talk about the good old days, when we were young and fearless," he said.

"You're human, Max. Why does that scare you?" Celeste asked.

Max let out his breath slowly. "Deep down, I'm afraid of dying, like any sane person. But I fear other things more. I can't face being helpless, useless," he said, shuddering.

"Like your father?" Celeste asked.

"How did you know about that?" Max asked.

"Morgan told me. On the Windrider," she said.

"It was a horrible way to die, to slowly rot away, with everyone watching, unable to stop it," he said.

Celeste laid her hand on his arm. "Max, you're going to die. It happens to everyone. How you live is more important than how you

468

die," she said.

"Not to me. I want to choose my death. And I choose to die fighting, not because of old age or . . . some stupid accident," he said, then turned to face her. "Want to know a secret?"

"Sure," Celeste said, leaning closer.

"You asked once about my real name," Max said.

"Yes, Max, I did," Celeste agreed.

Max looked around. "Elrod," he whispered.

Celeste's jaw twitched, and Max frowned. "If you laugh, I'll be forced to slay you where you stand, Princess," he said.

Celeste rubbed her face furiously, and took a deep breath. "I won't laugh," she said.

"Good. I don't want to slay you," he said.

"I wouldn't want that either. Your secret is safe with me," Celeste said.

Max peered at her, his eyes sharp. "I'm really drunk. I won't even remember this in the morning," he said.

"Remember what, Max?" Celeste asked innocently.

Max sighed. "Enough about me, how are you?" he asked.

Celeste stared down into the empty street. "Does Morgan love Maelin?" she asked.

Max snorted. "Why ask me? I've only seen her twice since I came here," he said, then stopped, reflecting. "Although she has turned into quite a woman. Pretty, great body. But too smart for me though. What makes you think Morgan is after her?"

"He almost married her. They seem so close," Celeste said. "When she was attacked, Morgan . . . ."

"Wait! Someone attacked Maelin? I have spent too much time in the tavern. Is she all right?" Max asked.

"Yes. She had the dogs with her. Brutus bit him," she said.

"So he's dead," Max said. "Who was it?"

"I don't know. I just saw a body, all in black. Maelin said he carried a black knife," Celeste said.

"Sounds like a professional. Any idea why he was sent for her?" Max asked.

"Who knows? Maybe the Mhoul, or Malissa, or just some city

intrigue. You didn't answer my question," she said.

"Your jealousy has made you cold, Princess," Max observed.

Celeste glanced at him. "I'm sorry. You're right. The poor girl was almost killed, and all I can think about is her in Morgan's arms. Never mind," she said.

"She was a child when her mother tried to give her to Morgan, maybe fifteen. We were heroes, Llewelyn just wanted to show her gratitude. Knowing Morgan, I would say he sees her as a sister," he said.

"The sister he never had?" Celeste asked.

"Could be. I wouldn't worry about it though," Max said.

"I don't know. She's very attractive. And she acts so cute and helpless. Men like that. They like to feel needed, protective," Celeste mused.

Max straightened. "All right, now I'm tired of talking about Morgan. When are you going to find me a good woman?" he asked.

"You don't want a good woman, Max. You just want someone to sleep with, once in a while," Celeste chided him.

"Like I said. A good woman," he laughed.

"Why are you like this? Don't you want to really love someone?" Celeste asked.

Max sighed. "You know, I think I'd like that. Trouble is, no one would ever love me," he said.

"What makes you think that?" Celeste asked.

"I see it in their eyes. People fear me, they see something . . . dark. With my enemies that's fine, but even my friends get that look sometimes. Especially women," he said.

Celeste frowned. "I can't deny it. I know what they see. But that doesn't mean no one could love you, in spite of your dark side," she said.

"You would have to share that dark side, to love me. It's not really evil, just dark, smells of death. But no one else has it," he said, and then paused. "Except maybe the Ha'ashtari."

"Sha'lor?" the Princess asked.

Max grabbed her arm again. "Only in my dreams. Let's walk and move to less dangerous ground," he said.

They walked down the dimly lit balcony, arm in arm.

"Have you decided what you're going to do now?" Max asked.

"I'm going to follow Talbot. Find him," she said.

"To Aijalon. That's no place for a Princess. Trolls, goblins, gargoyles, deep, trackless forest. And worse, if the Mhoul find you," Max said.

"I'll ask the Baron for an escort. I can take care of myself," Celeste said firmly.

"You've read about Faerie in books. To actually go there is something else," Max said.

"I'm going. What else would I do?" Celeste said.

"You could stay here. The Baron will take care of you," Max said.

"Stay here? With the Haggas in Skara Thrae? With my mother trapped in a castle, under siege? With my brother in Faerie?" she protested.

"You can't do anything about Skara Thrae, and your brother chose to leave home. He chose to go to Aijalon, to look for the elves. Let him go, Celeste. He's not much of a brother anyway," Max said.

"You don't know him. You don't know the first thing about him. How can you say that?" she asked fiercely.

"Oh, come on, Celeste. I know he's your brother, but face the truth. He's selfish and irresponsible. He's a lot like me that way. He won't be any good to you," Max said.

"You have no right to say that! It may be true, but you have no right," Celeste said.

"Let's call a truce on that one. My head hurts," Max said.

They walked in silence for a while. Suddenly Max turned to the railing, pulling the Princess with him.

"What now?" she said.

Max put a finger to her lips. "Don't turn around, but we're being followed. Stay here and I'll see who it is," he said.

Max walked slowly away. "Good night, Princess. See you soon," he called.

Celeste glanced around, and when she looked again, he had vanished, swallowed by the shadows. She leaned tensely on the rail, her ears straining for any sound. She knew Max well enough to not think him mistaken. First the attack on Maelin, and now this. Carnac had changed, for the worse.

Time passed, with no sound, and no sign of anyone. Celeste watched out of the corners of her eyes, scanning the balcony constantly. She kept her arms crossed before her, her hands within reach of the hidden daggers. She would not be a helpless victim, like Maelin.

Suddenly, Max appeared at her side. She had not heard him return, and she flashed a dagger in his face.

"Easy, Princess. The enemy is gone," he said, holding up his hands.

"Who was it?" she demanded, sheathing the dagger.

Max looked around at the darkened walkway. "I don't know. There was someone following us, but he was good. I couldn't catch him. He's gone now," he said.

"Why would someone follow us?" Celeste asked.

"Let's get you back to your room. I'll ask Balt to put a guard on your quarters," Max said.

"See, I'm no safer here. I might as well go after Talbot," she said.

"Whatever you say, Princess," Max said, still scanning the area.

Max was quiet as they walked back toward her room. He glanced at the Princess.

"You love Morgan, don't you?" he asked.

"I'd like to, if we had the time," she said.

"Go talk to him. You shouldn't be alone, like me. If you find someone, don't wait," he said.

"We have talked. And we don't have any choice but to wait," Celeste said.

Max shrugged. "Well, talk again. Decide what you're going to do. You two are driving me crazy with your lovelorn looks and long sighs," he said.

"You're right. This is killing me inside. I need to do something about it," she said.

"Good girl. Now, go. I'll arrange for the guard," he said.

Celeste smiled at Max. "Thank you, Max. And don't give up, you'll find someone," she said.

Max waved an arm toward Morgan's quarters. "Go, woman," he said.

Morgan awoke instantly at the pounding on his door. He pulled on his pants and went to the door, with his sword.

"Who is it?" he asked warily.

"Let me in. We have to talk," Celeste said.

Morgan unlocked the door and swung it open. He glanced at her, and then scanned the hall behind her. "What is it? What's wrong?" he asked.

She entered the room, brushing past him. "Us. That's what's wrong," she said.

With a last look down the hall, Morgan closed the door and turned to face the Princess. "Us? Can't this wait until morning? I've had a long day," he said, leaning the sword against a chair.

Celeste's eyes flashed. "Did you wear yourself out comforting Maelin? I saw you," she said.

"Saw what? She was scared, that's all," he said.

"I saw you holding her," Celeste said.

"Someone had just tried to kill her. She was terrified. What was I supposed to do?" he asked.

"And you didn't notice that she's a beautiful woman? Did she feel good in your arms?" she asked.

Morgan finally realized what was bothering her. "I wondered where you went, after we heard the alarm. You're jealous of Maelin?" he asked.

Celeste's anger faded and she walked over to the bed and sat down on it. She looked miserable, her eyes moist. "I'm sorry. I'm doing it again. I don't mean to be so selfish and petty. I just don't need another woman in your life right now," she said.

Morgan walked over and collapsed on a chair. He rubbed his tired eyes. "There is no other woman. I've told you that. Not Malissa, and not Maelin. Maelin is just a friend that I haven't seen for a long time. She was afraid and needed someone to hold her," he said patiently.

Celeste looked at the ceiling and drew a deep breath. "I know. I know. This is not what I came to talk to you about," she said.

"Then what's so important?" Morgan said.

Celeste looked at Morgan. "I can't keep on like this. I can't just open and close my heart at will," she said.

Morgan leaned forward, frowning. "I don't understand. What are you saying?" he asked.

"I told you how I felt on the Windrider, and you . . . ," she began.

"But later I . . . ," he protested.

Celeste held up her hands. "No, let me finish. Later, you did say you cared, and then we talked. We had feelings for each other, but both of us realized the timing was wrong. When I found out you cared for me, my heart opened. You were leaving for Kalixalven, but I could wait. So I closed my heart until later. Then you showed up in the Waste, and I couldn't help it, being with you opened my heart again.

At the massif, I thought we were going to die, and I regretted waiting and wished I could have another chance. But we lived, and came to Carnac, and still I knew we couldn't be together. You have to go to Dragonback. So do I close my heart and wait some more? I just can't take any more of this. I'm an emotional wreck," she said.

"I'm sorry. I hate it too. It's so frustrating. But what can we do?" Morgan asked.

"This is what I have to do. I have to control my feelings, not let them out, until we can really be together. We need some distance, emotionally. Then, whatever happens, I can deal with it," she said.

Morgan looked at her sadly. "Can you do that?" he asked.

"I have to. Let's just be friends. No more for now," she said.

"Well, if that's what you think is best," Morgan said.

Celeste started to cry. "Is that it? Whatever I think is best? What do you want?" she asked.

"I want to love you. But if you need to . . . ," Morgan said.

"Don't blame me. You need to make your own choices," Celeste said, then stood up. "I think I should leave now."

Morgan jumped up. "But . . . ," he said.

"No, I have to leave. Now," she said, her voice tight.

She almost ran for the door, but Morgan caught her there. He took her arm and turned her towards him. "Can I have one last kiss?" he asked.

Celeste looked up at him, and then touched his face with her fingertips. With a visible effort, she turned her face away. "I don't kiss my friends like that," she said.

Morgan took his hand from her arm. Celeste opened the door and left the room, closing the door firmly behind her. Morgan let her go. A few moments later, the sound of breaking furniture came from his room.

CHAPTER THIRTY-THREE

EQUISAPIENS

The next day, Morgan and Celeste followed Maelin into the inner courtyard of the Baron's private residence. The servant at the door had protested, but few could refuse Maelin when she really wanted something. A small scratch on her cheek and another on her neck were the only signs she had almost died the night before. Of course, her long sleeved gown hid the other bruises and scrapes.

Celeste had been quiet and withdrawn this morning, and Morgan felt very uncomfortable around her. He was still not sure what had happened last night. He wished someone could explain it to him. He considered asking Max or Maelin, but that did not seem right.

Maelin had awakened them early, apologetic but insistent. She said the Baron needed their help, but was in such a hurry she could not explain fully. They stopped for Max, but he was not in his room. Morgan decided he needed to have a talk with him. He had been acting strangely ever since they arrived in Carnac.

The morning sun filled the open courtyard. A fountain splashed playfully, the water cascading down a rocky slope and then flowing along a channel to disappear under another arrangement of stones. A well tended square of grass surrounded the fountain and channel. Square pillars of reddish stone ringed the area, and lined the entry hall.

Five centaurs rested on the cool grass, their legs folded under them. They sipped on steaming drinks, brought by the attentive servants who now hovered in the shadow of the pillars. One of the centaurs was a female, the first Morgan had seen. She had the same statuesque appearance as the male equisapiens, only with a slightly lighter build and skin tone. A medallion hung between her breasts, which were covered by a plain leather harness.

As the humans entered the courtyard, four of the equisapiens looked up, apparently disturbed by their presence. One of the centaurs gestured toward the trio with his drink.

"What are they doing here? Did you send for them?" he asked, his powerful voice filling the courtyard.

The fifth centaur, the Baron Serenus, shook his head, but smiled. "No, but they are my friends, Canto. They may remain," he said.

Canto looked at one of the other centaurs. "This only underscores my point. Serenus calls them friends. An equisapien has no friends outside of his own race, there are only study subjects," he said.

"Maybe you have no friends, Canto. I am surrounded by them, and it hasn't interfered with my duties in any way," Serenus retorted.

Maelin and the others sat on the stone border surrounding the grass, leaning back against the pillars.

"Good morning, friends," Serenus said. "How are you feeling, Maelin?"

"I'm fine, Equo. Thank you for asking," Maelin said.

"Have you found out . . . ," Morgan started to ask, but Maelin grabbed his arm and shook her head.

She leaned close and whispered in his ear. "We're guests in the Baron's home. When other centaurs are present, we shouldn't speak without permission," she explained.

Morgan grimaced but sat back without speaking. The centaurs ignored the exchange.

"Marlenus, I believe this attack on the woman is only further evidence of Serenus' indulgences. He must be censured, be made to cease acting this way," Canto said.

Marlenus ran a hand through her reddish mane. "I'm not sure I see the connection. Please explain," she said.

"Yes, please do. I want to hear this," the Baron remarked dryly.

Canto hesitated, realizing that he should have laid a better foundation for his accusation. "Serenus befriends these humans, becomes involved in their affairs, and this violence within our city is the inevitable result. His behavior is not customary," Canto said.

"Maelin was sent here by the Sagamore of Saxhaven, to study. How is that not customary, Canto?" Serenus asked.

"Her presence is not the issue. Your conduct with her is the problem," Canto said.

"What conduct? What have I done?" Serenus persisted.

Canto waved a large hand, as if the question was foolish. "It's obvious. She is not just a student; she's more like a pet, a plaything. You like her, even call her friend. It's unseemly. And this is not the first time," Canto said, then pointed to Celeste. "He did the same thing with that one, years ago when she studied here. There is a dangerous pattern of excess developing here."

"Excess," the Baron smirked. "You must not have enough to occupy your time, Canto, to concoct such nonsense."

"Not nonsense, Marlenus. He left here like a raging beast when he learned of the woman's peril in the Waste. He brought her friends into the city, even though they are not students or legitimate travelers. Then he held court, and pardoned these strangers, even though the Ha'ashtari sought to punish them for murdering a Pathfinder. Are these acts of calm, objective rationality?" said a third centaur. Morgan recognized him as the one who watched their trial before the Baron.

"How would you respond, Serenus? Does Marcus speak accurately?" Marlenus asked.

"I did go to her aid. She is the Princess of Skara Thrae, an old student and . . . friend. I brought her companions back, a mere act of hospitality. The Ha'ashtari had accusations against them, and I heard the evidence and decided the issue. Marcus was there and I defy him to dispute my logic and reasoning. The matter of the Pathfinder concerned me; there was evidence that someone has infiltrated the ranks of the Pathfinders. The man who died, killed himself, after being discovered attempting to strand the Princess and her friends. Then two more Pathfinders died when Ha'ashtari were sent to question them in the valley. I have instructed the Pathfinders to search out this evil.

To ignore this corruption in the Pathfinder system is foolish. The attack on Maelin is another example of the naiveté of isolationism. Her attacker was identified as a traveler from the East. No one knows anything else about him.

Are we going to sit by and watch Pathfinders betray their clients,

478

and allow assassination attempts on royalty, in the middle of our city? How much longer can we afford to neglect the rest of the world? We must become involved at some point, or perish," Serenus said.

"What are you saying, Serenus?" Marlenus asked.

The Baron regarded the others, choosing his words. "I believe the Mhoul are involved somehow," he said.

Canto nodded. "More evidence of instability. Complete paranoia," he said.

"If it is the Mhoul, dare we dismiss the Baron's concerns?" another centaur asked.

"Are you defending him, Actus? Do you share this fantasy?" Canto demanded.

Actus shook his great head slowly. "I admit that the Baron is impulsive, and acts with more emotion than is proper. But if there is any reason to suspect the Mhoul, our involvement is justified. The Mhoul are a threat to Carnac, to all of Kalnaroag," he said.

"The question seems to be: are the Mhoul plotting something, some design that is showing itself even in Carnac, or are these disturbances merely the result of Serenus meddling in the affairs of humans?" Marlenus mused.

The Baron indicated Morgan. "Ask him. The Mons Monachus sent him from Khulankor to find out what the Mhoul were doing," he said.

"Now we are going to listen to this . . . human? A possible murderer?" Canto asked.

"Beware, Canto. Lest you display the same passion you fault the Baron for," Marlenus observed. "Speak, Morgan."

Canto fell silent as the other centaurs looked at Morgan, who rose to his feet.

"I thank you for hearing me, Equa. The Mons Monachus in Khulankor have evidence that the Mhoul are planning something. I was sent as a scout, to help discover their true purpose," Morgan said.

"And what have you found?" Marlenus asked.

Morgan decided to be blunt, to make sure he held their attention. "The Mhoul have coordinated an invasion of Skara Thrae

479

by the exiled clan Haggas. That is why the Princess Celestine left the island, to find her brother Talbot, so he could help her repel the invasion. After we left Androssar, our ship was attacked by a Mhoul ironclad, manned by a Mhoul named Molid, several trolls, Immortals, and some renegade humans. The ship was destroyed and we proceeded to Aquarquff, where we penetrated an ancient cache of the Mercator Empire, to recover weapons necessary to stand against the Mhoul. As the Baron said, something is wrong in the Pathfinder order, and the Mhoul probably instigated the attack on Princess Maelin. They are searching for me, and I had just been with Maelin."

Canto waved a hand in dismissal. "A fantastic story. He has no proof," he scoffed.

"Proof of what?" Serenus asked.

"Any of it," Canto said.

"Morgan arrived wearing a metasilk cloak, bearing a sword of aurellium," Serenus said.

The other centaurs stared at Morgan. "Where did you get such things?" Marlenus breathed.

"The cloak was given to me by the Monachus, when I left Khulankor. The sword came from the cache I told you about," Morgan said.

"He also had a Gate finder, a set of proximity wards, and another artifact I could not identify. His friend Max took a shirt of ebonite from there also," Serenus added.

"Where are these things? We must study them," Marcus said, then turned to Morgan. "Tell us the location of the cache."

"I can do that, Equo, but the cache is sealed. We could only leave by the Gate," Morgan said.

"A Gate? You know of a functional Gate?" Canto demanded, and then glared at Serenus. "Why weren't we informed of this earlier?"

Serenus shrugged. "You didn't want to get involved, remember?" he said.

Canto turned to Marlenus. "We must have these things. This is an incredible opportunity," he said.

Marlenus regarded Canto. "Now you believe this man?" he asked.

Canto frowned. "It's worth investigating. Think of the possibilities," he said.

Marlenus drained her drink, and handed the cup to a servant who appeared at her shoulder. "Serenus, I know you. I knew your parents. Fine folk, who hoped the name they gave you would portend great things for you, peace and knowledge. Ironically, you have been anything but serene. You display a dangerous propensity for passion," she said, then leaned forward, fixing Serenus with her large, liquid eyes. "Do not loose the beast, or it will consume you! I am glad your parents did not live to see your indulgences. They would have been sorely disappointed. But despite your excesses, you have proven yourself to be a fine scholar and teacher, and your students are a tribute to the Academy. Your knowledge of the Mhoul and ancient history is without equal. We would grieve the loss of this knowledge if you were sent into exile. Please attempt to restrain yourself in the future."

"Speaking of ancient history, Prefect, hear this, and please do not take offense. I say this only out of concern for our city and our race," Serenus said, then paused. "I know we must subdue the beast within, that self control is the key to our survival. But there is danger in traveling too far down that path as well.

Let us learn from the Yggda, who regarded the galaxy as their laboratory, and worshipped only science. Consider their lack of compassion, their ruthless pursuit of knowledge, their cold brutality to other species. Remember how they enslaved any living thing that interested them, regarding them as mere specimens for study. Remember it was they who created the chimera, another interesting experiment. What about the horrors of the Specimen War, when their collection of playthings rebelled and drove them from Kalnaroag?

Consider what evil was spawned by the passionless objectivity of the Yggda. When you strive for pure logic and rationality, you leave behind love, honor, loyalty, hope, and joy. Without these things, what are we? Can we survive? Or will we become like the Yggda?

481

Remember their fate," he said.

"This is ridiculous. We are nothing like the Yggda, and never will be. You would have us descend to the beast, to scamper through the rocks like the satyr. That is one reason why we allow them to live in our cliffs, to remind us of our peril. Keep your foolish emotion, Serenus. I will have none of it," Canto said.

"May I speak one last time, Prefect?" Morgan asked.

Marlenus looked at him and shrugged. "Why not? We have been slandered by one of our own this day, compared to the Yggda. Why would we take offense at your words?" she said.

"The Mons Monachus shares your problem. The single minded pursuit of knowledge, or even academic spirituality, without using the knowledge to better the world around you, has a price. You become distant, isolated, and uncaring. Objectivity becomes apathy, rationality becomes cruelty. Knowledge alone cannot feed the soul. When the soul dies, there is nothing left but evil.

This may be heresy, but I will say it anyway. Khulankor is dying. The Monachus have separated themselves from the world of man; they desire only to meditate on heaven. That is not what Iosus intended, He meant for us to share our treasures, to pass on the gifts He has given us. When we attempt to hoard these things, the treasure tarnishes, the gifts decay, until we are left with nothing. I realize now that there is a slow death creeping over Khulankor. It even affected me. When I found Khulankor, I abandoned the world below, and did not care what sufferings occurred there. I see the same malaise in Carnac. Beware, Equa, you are not immune. The Baron's passion may be the only antidote to your disease," he said.

Marlenus rose gracefully to her feet, and the other centaurs stood as well. "Well, an interesting day. We have been compared to the Yggda, and now to the Mons Monachus of Khulankor," she said.

The Prefect looked down at Morgan, her red mane draped around her ivory shoulders. "Be thankful, human, that we do not yield to our passions when insulted. You will provide us with detailed information on the location of the Empire cache, and I will consider whether or not you may keep the articles you have retrieved from

482

there. While I do not want to interfere with matters the Monachus consider important, to leave such things in the hands of humans troubles me. Your vaunted lack of rationality makes it dangerous to trust you with too much knowledge. That is another reason we have chosen to be the teachers of the lesser races. Our teaching is a form of prevention, to save you from yourselves," she said.

Marlenus turned to Serenus. "I will not take action at this time. But be warned, we will not tolerate your excesses forever. Thank you for your hospitality," she said.

"What about the Mhoul?" Serenus asked.

"We will leave them to the Monachus and their minions for now. We will continue to study and observe, as always," the Prefect said.

The four centaurs left the courtyard. Maelin jumped up and ran to the Baron, grabbing his arm. He looked down at her and smiled.

"I'm so sorry. We've gotten you in trouble," Maelin said.

Serenus patted her unruly locks with his free hand. "Don't worry, little one," he said, then looked at Celeste. "I had a similar discussion with them when Celeste was here."

Celeste got up and went to the Baron. "I just wanted to be your friend. I had a wonderful time here, because of you," she said.

"We did nothing wrong. But they just can't see it," the Baron said, gazing after the departed centaurs. He turned to Morgan. "So the Monachus suffers from the same malady, do they?"

"That's how I see it. Although I didn't realize it until just recently," Morgan answered.

"I fear for them, then. Apathy will defeat us, when strength of arms could not. A sad fate," the Baron said.

"But not a certain fate. They have you to warn them," Morgan said.

"You heard them. They will not heed my warnings, until it is too late. If I persist, they will merely cast me into exile, remove the ember from their eye," Serenus said.

"They wouldn't do that, would they? Kick you out of the Academy?" Maelin asked.

"They would. And exile me from Carnac as well," Serenus said.

"What would you do then?" Celeste asked quietly.

Serenus gently freed himself from Maelin's grip. "I don't know. Continue to travel, and learn. Help when I could," he said, then looked around at the courtyard. "And try to forget."

"Oh, how sad. I hope it never happens," Maelin said.

"What did they mean about controlling the beast?" Morgan asked suddenly.

The Baron regarded them for a moment. "What I am about to tell you is the great mystery of the Equisapiens, their heritage and their curse. Few humans have ever learned our true nature. I tell you this in confidence, as friend to friend. The centaurs and the satyrs are a joining of man and beast, created by the Yggda in one of their heinous experiments. The early centaurs realized the threat of our bestial side, how it could overwhelm us if not contained. Our brothers the satyrs did not, nor did they heed our warnings. They acted as they felt, letting the beast grow, until now their human half is almost submerged, consumed by the animal nature.

Our race decided the only way to overcome the beast was to rigidly control any of its manifestations: passion, anger, rage, almost any emotion was suspect. Our ancestors turned to rationality, to pure intellect, for our salvation. They felt those qualities were the finest elements of human nature, the things they would cultivate and preserve. Logically, we became the teachers of the world, the observers, the collectors, distant and aloof. We came to Carnac, built this city in the middle of the Waste, allowed the Ha'ashtari to isolate us further, and settled down to slowly rot.

We were too successful, in my opinion, and in our efforts to kill the beast, we have lost a part of our human half as well. Perhaps I am too passionate, too involved, but I have these feelings. I cannot stand to just watch the world go by. I must act," Serenus said.

"Why you? Why do you have these feelings?" Morgan asked.

"There is much speculation about that. Marlenus believes I am some kind of genetic throwback, a ghost of our ancestors. Canto considers me mentally ill, and a threat to our entire race," Serenus said.

"I'm glad you are this way. I wouldn't change you for anything,"

Maelin said.

Serenus sighed. "Unfortunately, little Princess, you do not rule in Carnac."

Two days later, Morgan stood before a massive door in the Baron's home. The servant had left him, without saying a word. Morgan looked around. The hallway lay empty, save for some statues and wall hangings. He faced the featureless door, searching in vain for a handle, lock, or knocker. He saw only a small grille above the door. After a moment or two, Morgan began to feel rather foolish, so he called out.

"Baron Serenus? It's Morgan. You summoned me," he said, hoping no one overheard him talking to a door.

Almost immediately, the Baron's powerful tones boomed from the grille. "Morgan! Forgive me, I was distracted and didn't see you on the scanner. Come in, please," he said.

As the echoes subsided, the door slid smoothly to one side, revealing a long, dimly lit hallway, with another door at the far end.

"Straight down the hall," the Baron said.

Morgan entered the hall, and the door closed behind him. He walked quickly to the inner door, which opened at his approach. He stopped and gazed in wonder at the fantastic room beyond. An opaque band circled the chamber near the ceiling, filled with a glowing, swirling liquid. The strange light it cast filled the room with shifting half shadows, as if Morgan had plunged beneath the sea and looked up at the sun. Strange devices and elaborate mechanisms filled the room, lying on the floor, on large tables, hanging on the wall. A sturdy looking crane system hung from the ceiling, suspended over one of the workbenches.

The Baron stood by one of the tables, a piece of machinery in his hand. More pieces lay scattered on the table. Serenus gestured for Morgan to approach, and Morgan joined him, stepping carefully around several artifacts.

"My play room. Sorry for the mess," the Baron said, still studying the metal object in his hand.

Morgan waited while the Baron probed the device with a tool.

485

He had amazing dexterity for someone his size.

"I have spoken with Sebastian," the Baron replied offhandedly.

Morgan stepped closer, staring up at the centaur. "When? How? Is he here?" Morgan burst out.

Serenus waved the tool. "Peace, human. Just a minute," he said.

The Baron laid down the tool and the mechanism, and moved to a control panel. He touched a glowing square. Immediately, the sounds in the room took on a hollow, echoing tone. The echoes and the swirling light gave the room a dreamlike aspect.

"A sound dampening field. Just to be safe. Carnac has obviously been infiltrated with Mhoul agents," the Baron said.

Morgan tried to curb his impatience. "You said you spoke with Sebastian," he said.

"Oh yes, he contacted me this morning. I had sent him a message that you were here," Serenus said.

"You can contact him, whenever you want? Why didn't you tell me? I need to talk to him, to tell him what's been happening," Morgan said.

"I am afraid that is not possible," the Baron said.

"Why not?" Morgan demanded.

"It is too dangerous. The Mhoul may be able to monitor our communications and we cannot risk that. My original message was a single code phrase, and my later discussion with Sebastian lasted only a few moments," Serenus explained. "It's very frustrating. We have been unable to penetrate the Mhoul codes and distortion fields, leaving them to transmit at will, while we are forced to keep our communications to a minimum."

"The Mhoul probably know I'm here already. Can't I speak with him?" Morgan persisted.

The Baron shook his head, his mane dancing down his spine. "The very fact that we can and do communicate is a closely guarded secret. Even if the Mhoul detect our transmission, it takes them a while to trace the origin and the destination. That secret is too important to compromise by giving them enough time to trace the contact to Carnac," he said.

"But you called Sebastian anyway?" Morgan asked.

"Yes. I took the risk. Without Academy approval. I felt it necessary to update Sebastian on your progress and recent events. Ironically, he already knew most of it," Serenus said.

"What did he know?" Morgan asked.

"He knew your route: Saxhaven, Androssar, Aquarquff, the Waste, Carnac," the Baron said.

"They told me to go to Aquarquff. Through Saxhaven to Androssar would be the logical route. You told him I was in Carnac. I guess it's not surprising he knew the route. Except for traveling through the Waste," Morgan said.

"He knew you were in Carnac before I sent him the message," Serenus said.

"How did he know that?" Morgan asked.

"He did not say," the Baron answered.

"Evidently the Monachus have their spies as well. I wish I could contact one of them," Morgan said. "What else did he know?"

"He knew you had encountered the Mhoul, and that you had successfully penetrated the cache at Aquarquff," Serenus said.

"Did he know about the Princess, and Skara Thrae?" Morgan asked.

"He did not mention that. We focused mainly on you. There was not time to chat," Serenus said.

Morgan had a sudden thought. "You knew Sebastian, before . . ." he said.

"Before what?" Serenus asked.

"Before I met you. Before I told you about him," Morgan said.

The Baron smiled, his liquid eyes luminous in the dancing lights. "I have lived a long time, and have traveled far, Morgan. I have dealt with those at Khulankor in the past. Including Sebastian," he admitted.

"Did he tell you I was coming?" Morgan asked.

"No, I have not talked to Sebastian in a long time," Serenus said.

"Did he leave me any messages?" Morgan asked.

"He said to be careful, and to trust in Iosus. That's all," the

Baron said.

Morgan clenched his fists, controlling himself with a visible effort. "They send me out, with nothing but someone else's memories locked in my head, and never bother to speak to me again. Until now, and then he leaves some cryptic message. I've been attacked at every turn, in constant danger, then chased all over the Waste. We've nearly been killed several times. I still don't know what the Mhoul are planning, and I don't even know what I'm supposed to do. What do they want from me?" he grated.

Serenus regarded him, as one who watches a child in a tantrum. "Are you finished?" he asked calmly.

"Yes," Morgan said.

"I have something for you," the Baron said.

The Baron turned and moved to a large cabinet on the wall. As he passed a control panel, he touched a button on the console. The cabinet had a depression on its face, shaped like a hand. The Baron placed his hand in the molded hollow, and the cabinet opened. The Baron removed a wrapped bundle and placed it on the table before Morgan.

"Your artifacts. Marlenus has graciously decided to return them," the Baron said.

Morgan unwrapped the bundle and studied the objects inside— the aurellium sword, the Gatefinder jewel, the carved stone, and the wards.

"Most gracious of her. Why?" Morgan asked.

"She isn't sure about you, but the Monachus, despite your alleged 'stagnation,' can be a powerful ally or an equally powerful enemy. In the past, the Monachus and the centaurs have been allies, and she has no desire to alter that arrangement. Now that she knows the location of the Empire cache, Marlenus figures she can retrieve her own technology. Canto is even now mounting an expedition," the Baron said.

"I told her the cache is sealed. The location won't do them any good," Morgan said.

"Closed to foolish humans, not the great Marlenus, Prefect of the Academy at Carnac," Serenus remarked sarcastically.

"Is she going to help us?" Morgan asked.

"You heard her. The Mhoul are your problem. At least for now," the Baron said.

Morgan picked up the aurellium sword, and drew it out a ways. The golden blade sparkled in the fluid light. "Will this really kill a Mhoul?" he asked.

"It appears to be pure aurellium. The Histories tell us that substance could draw out the life force of a Mhoul and kill them," Serenus said.

Morgan replaced the sword, and regarded the other artifacts. "The wards I have used, and the jewel. I know how they work," he said, then picked up the carved stone, and turned it over. "But what is this?"

Serenus frowned. "I must confess that I have not divined its true purpose. The tests show it is made of Gate material. Maybe it is just a fragment of a Gate, one that was destroyed in the Fall. So much of the Gate technology has been lost to us. The Mhoul are the only real Gate experts left," he said.

"A piece of a Gate? What would I do with this?" Morgan asked.

Serenus patted him on the shoulder. "You will know, when you need to," he said.

Morgan laid down the rock. "Faith is hard," he observed, then turned to the centaur. "Have you seen Max's dagger?"

Serenus nodded. "An ebonite dagger, with a Luminarae in the hilt," he said.

"You listed the other artifacts at our trial, but you didn't say anything about the dagger," Morgan said.

"I instructed Max to tell no one of the dagger," Serenus said.

"Have you told anyone?" Morgan asked.

"No," the Baron said.

"Not even the Academy?" Morgan asked.

"No," Serenus said.

"You are a rebel. Why not?" Morgan asked.

"It's hard to explain. Perhaps because of the Luminarae's nature," Serenus said.

"I don't understand. What do you know of the Luminarae?"

489

Morgan asked.

Serenus folded his arms across his bulging chest. "An ancient form of life. Intelligent, somehow. Rumored to be on this planet, even before the Specimen War, when the Empire builders won their freedom from the Yggda. They were first observed sometime after the Yggda arrived and constructed the Gates. I have read the Yggda even attempted to study them, but could devise no method of holding them prisoner. It is said they withdrew from the world while the Yggda ruled, and appeared again at the arrival of the Lucca," he explained.

"And you know of the Luminarae at Khulankor?" Morgan asked.

"Yes," the Baron said.

"I still don't understand why you kept Max's dagger a secret," Morgan said.

"The Luminarae go where they please. I felt it best their presence in Carnac be known to few," Serenus said.

"This one didn't have much choice. It's attached to the dagger Max carries," Morgan said.

"No Luminarae can be held against its will. If that sprite didn't want to stay with Max, it would leave," Serenus said.

"Mysterious creatures," Morgan remarked.

A voice came out of the air, startling Morgan. "Baron, it's Celeste and Max," said the Princess, her voice sounding oddly mechanical.

Serenus returned to the control console, and his hands moved over it. He spoke into a grille on the panel. "Enter. Morgan is here," he said.

Morgan noticed the room had lost its echoes. Evidently, the Baron had deactivated the privacy screen. A moment later, the door opened and Celeste and Max walked in. Celeste seemed familiar with the liquid light, but Max stared at it.

"Baron. Morgan," the Princess said.

She still acted stiff and formal around Morgan. He wished he could say something to make her feel better.

"Celeste, you are lovely this morning," the Baron said.

Morgan had to agree. She wore a loose gown, but it did little to hide her athletic curves. Her hair hung in intricate braids, and her tanned skin contrasted with the light fabric of the gown.

"Thank you, Baron. You summoned us?" she asked.

Max nodded at them and began roaming the chamber, looking at the scattered artifacts.

"Max, don't touch anything. Yes, Princess, we need to discuss your plans," Serenus said.

Celeste folded her arms, and glanced at Morgan, as if she expected an argument. "I am going to Aijalon, to find Talbot," she said.

The Baron nodded. "I suspected as much, knowing you. May I send an escort?" he asked.

Celeste smiled. "I was hoping I wouldn't have to ask. Can you spare anyone?" she asked.

"I have made arrangements for fifty soldiers, and a guide," the Baron said.

"Fifty? Do I need so many?" the Princess asked.

"The land of Faerie is dangerous, and the Mhoul seek you. I hope fifty is enough," Serenus said.

"And a guide?" Celeste prompted.

"A student here. Named Diomedes. An expert on the land of Faerie, its dangers and its inhabitants. He can even speak all the languages," the Baron responded.

"Baron, I can never repay you, but you have my sincerest gratitude," Celeste said, then looked at Morgan. "Don't you have anything to say?"

Morgan shrugged. "I've learned not to argue with you," he said, then addressed the Baron. "We will be proceeding to Kalixalven, to meet the Windrider. Do we need a Pathfinder? I want no further trouble with the Ha'ashtari."

The Baron chuckled. "Don't worry about that. In fact, Ha'keel has insisted on sending an escort for the ta'hoda when he leaves Carnac," he said.

Max looked up from one of the tables. "Are they still going on about that nonsense? I hope this tradition of theirs doesn't carry any hidden baggage for me. I'm not getting any tattoos," he said.

"There is one other aspect you will become aware of. But it shouldn't be too much of a burden," the Baron said with a smile.

Max looked suspicious. "What other aspect? Tell me now. I don't like surprises, especially Ha'ashtari surprises," he said.

The Baron spread his hands. "It is not for me to tell. You will know soon enough," he said, then paused. "A word of warning. Do not offend the Ha'ashtari, whatever you think of their customs."

Max frowned. "I know. Thanks for the warning. I'll try not to make them mad," he said.

The Baron regarded Celeste and Morgan. "I would suggest you travel together, at least until you reach the foothills. Then the Princess can follow the Argurion River through the Nageff into Faerie," he said.

Celeste looked at Morgan. "That's fine with me," she said.

Morgan shrugged. "Sounds reasonable," he said.

"Good. I will bid you farewell on your departure," Serenus said.

"Thank you, Baron. For everything," Morgan said as he collected the bundle of artifacts.

As they walked down the hallway, Celeste spoke. "You can't seem to get rid of me, no matter how hard you try," she said.

Morgan did not look at her. "That's the problem. I don't want to get rid of you," he said quietly.

Celeste glanced at him, but could think of no reply. Behind them, Max rolled his eyes and sighed.

CHAPTER THIRTY-FOUR

SHADOWS

They were ready to leave early the next morning. The Baron had provided Celeste and Morgan with horses. Celeste had a prancing roan stallion, and Serenus had given Morgan a massive black, that bore the big man's weight easily. Max rode the horse the Ha'ashtari had given him. They wore traveling clothes, and had stowed their gear in saddlebags. Morgan wore his metasilk cloak again.

The Baron and fifty soldiers waited for them at the gate. Next to the Baron stood a small man in a loose robe.

"Good morning," the Baron called, his voice echoing through the nearly deserted streets.

He waved his arm at the bright sunlight on the towering red buildings. "A beautiful day for traveling. I trust you slept well?" he asked.

Celeste rode over to him, followed by Morgan and Max. Even on horseback, the Baron still stood a head taller than the humans. Celeste gripped the centaur's hand.

"It's a fine day, Baron. Thank you again for everything," she said.

"My pleasure, Princess. Once again, I will miss you," the Baron said, then gestured to the little man beside him. "This is Diomedes. He will be your guide."

Diomedes bowed. "I anticipate most felicitous relations, Princess, and fortuitous transambulation," he said.

Max leaned over to Morgan. "So he's a linguist. What language was that?" he asked.

"Thank you, Diomedes. I'm sure we'll get along quite well. But we won't be walking, we'll be riding," she said with a laugh.

Diomedes frowned. "A disturbing revelation. I prefer non-equine forms of locomotion," he said.

"Sorry, Diomedes. We ride," Celeste said.

A soldier led a pony over to the little scholar and helped him mount. Diomedes rearranged his robes over the saddle, a look of distaste on his delicate features.

The Baron indicated a stocky soldier. "This is Captain Rusk. He will be commanding your escort, Princess," he said.

Rusk bowed. "My life is yours, Princess," he said.

"Thank you, Captain. Your company will be welcome," she said.

As the fifty mounted, Morgan spoke to the Baron. "Are the Ha'ashtari here?" he asked.

"Yes. They were outside the gate at dawn. There are about thirty of them," the Baron said.

A shout came from the street behind them. Everyone recognized the voice. "Your bride is here," Celeste remarked dryly.

Morgan glared at Celeste, but said nothing. Maelin ran up to his horse and grabbed his leg. She held Brutus under one arm, and Clavius ambled down the street behind her, leaving a trail of spittle. Even the horses shied at his approach.

"Farewell, dear Morgan. I will miss you," Maelin said.

Morgan ruffled her hair. "It was good to see you again. I hope you find some way to help Llorgau," he said. "And be careful."

"I will. And don't worry about me," Maelin said as she swept a pale arm around to indicate a lean man standing behind her. "Serenus has given me my own personal bodyguard. This is Vasari."

Morgan studied the man, who returned his gaze with dark eyes. Vasari looked like a leather whip in clothes, with a well worn sword hilt. Morgan doubted many would survive a dispute with this man.

"He appears to be quite capable, Maelin. But be careful just the same," Morgan said, then addressed Vasari. "Don't let anything happen to her."

Vasari nodded. "I will protect her with my life," he said.

"I believe you," Morgan said.

Maelin walked over to Celeste's horse and looked up at her. "May Iosus be with you, Celeste. I hope you find your brother. I'm an only child, so I don't know what it's like to have a brother," she said, then paused and smiled in Morgan's direction. "Although Morgan is just like a brother to me."

Celeste looked surprised and grateful. She reached down and

494

gripped Maelin's shoulder, careful not to disturb Brutus.

"Thank you, Maelin," she said. "I wish we had more time to get to know each other."

Maelin grinned and leaned closer. "We could have talked about Morgan," she said.

"Yes," Celeste said, laughing as she glanced at the big man.

Morgan saw them looking at him and laughing, and he frowned. Serenus waved an arm and the massive gates began to swing open. Morgan and the others rode through and descended the ramp. Celeste turned in her saddle for one last look at the city, and the Baron raised an arm in farewell. The centaur dwarfed the Carnites around him, and Maelin looked like a tiny doll beside him. At the bottom of the ramp, the main gate parted at their approach, and they rode over the wooden bridge.

Thirty Ha'ashtari stood waiting beyond the bridge, their horses wandering loose, grazing on the lush grass. As Morgan's party arrived, the Ha'ashtari collected their horses, and mounted in one smooth motion. Three Ha'ashtari rode toward them, and Morgan recognized Ha'dros, Ha'sim, and Sha'lor.

Max brightened at the sight of Sha'lor. He leaned toward Morgan. "I really think she likes me," he whispered.

Morgan shook his head, stopping to wait for the Ha'ashtari.

Ha'dros nodded to Morgan, but addressed Max. "We are yours, ta'hoda, until we reach the end of the Waste. And then . . ."

Ha'sim and Sha'lor urged their mounts forward, turning to flank Max. The Carnite soldiers moved out of their way. Ha'sim looked proud, but Sha'lor seemed tense and withdrawn. Max slipped into the calm, loose manner he had just before he fought. He watched both Ha'ashtari out of the corners of his eyes.

"What is this?" Max asked quietly.

Celeste had been studying Ha'sim and Sha'lor, and something about them caused her expression to change, turning into a mixture of wonder and mirth. Max noticed.

"Will someone please tell me what's going on?" he demanded.

Celeste pointed. "Look at their left cheeks," she said.

Morgan and Max followed her pointing finger, Max choosing

Sha'lor's cheek to examine. On each Ha'ashtari's left cheek was a new tattoo, a circle with a symbol inside. Sha'lor lifted her head at Max's scrutiny, refusing to look at him. What a dark beauty, Max thought, with her midnight hair and flashing eyes.

"I see it. So?" Max pressed.

Celeste suppressed a grin. "You're a 'lost one,' Max, and you're leaving the Waste. Ha'ashtari tradition requires that you have an escort. In this case, a very special escort. Ha'sim and Sha'lor are your Shadows," she explained.

"Shadows?" Max asked, looking slightly nervous now.

"Shadows. Constant companions, personal bodyguards, a part of the Shen'tari tribe to accompany you wherever you go," Celeste said.

Max frowned, then looked at Ha'dros. "I truly appreciate this, but . . ." he began.

Celeste interrupted him. "Max, may I have a word with you? Now," she said firmly.

Celeste moved her horse over to Max, and leaned close to his ear. "To be a Shadow is a great honor, and to be rejected as a Shadow is a great dishonor. If you turn them away, Ha'sim and Sha'lor will be obliged to kill themselves, and if the dishonor is too great, it may mean Jinn'she. I recommend you accept your fate quietly," she whispered.

"But they are Ha'keel's only children, and he is sending them away. And . . . Sha'lor really doesn't like me. Besides, I don't need any escort or bodyguard," Max protested.

Celeste shrugged. "You are ta'hoda. Maybe you should have been a little less impressive on the battlefield," she said.

"We were fighting for our lives! I wasn't trying to impress anyone," he said.

"It's too late. Live with it," she said, walking her horse away.

Max grimaced, glancing at Sha'lor. Then he faced Ha'dros, who sat waiting patiently, his face expressionless. "I am greatly honored, Ha'dros. These two will make worthy Shadows," he said carefully.

Ha'dros smiled and nodded, and Sha'lor relaxed slightly, glancing at Max when he turned away. Ha'sim sat even straighter in his saddle.

Ha'dros looked at Sha'lor, and she reached into her belt pouch, urging her horse toward Max. Max watched her warily. She pulled out a small bag on a leather thong. Without a word, she leaned close and slipped the thong over Max's head. As she did so, she looked straight into Max's eyes. He could smell her scent, fresh and wild, mixed with leather. Her bare arm brushed his cheek and he shivered at the feel of her skin. Max barely resisted a sudden urge to kiss her, but all too soon she leaned away. Max took a deep breath, trying to clear his head. This woman was dangerous in more ways than one.

Max hefted the pouch. He could feel a hard, smooth shape inside.

"Your soul stone. You are Ha'ashtari now," Sha'lor said.

Max studied the pouch, with its strange symbols. "I'm not sure I have a soul," he said absently. Then he gently placed the bag inside his shirt, next to the ebonite mail.

"Well, Shadows, the sun waits for no one. Let's be off," Max said, as he kicked his horse into a gallop toward the cliff road.

Ha'sim and Sha'lor followed him easily, the rest of the Ha'ashtari falling into place behind them.

Morgan looked at Celeste. "Would you mind telling me what that was all about?" he asked.

Celeste shrugged. "Max approved of his escort," she said simply, and then rode off.

Morgan stared after her a moment, then he joined the soldiers from Carnac as they followed the Princess of Skara Thrae.

On the wall of Carnac, a lone watcher turned away. He must report to his masters, that the ones they sought had left the city.

CHAPTER THIRTY-FIVE
MONS MONACHUS

Gregor climbed the stone steps to the observatory, two Luminarae floating behind him. Despite his age, he was breathing evenly when he reached the top. The Saan guarding the entrance nodded respectfully and pulled the door open for him. The Elder of Khulankor stepped into the observatory and studied the room for a moment. He had been in this chamber many times in his long life, but he still wondered at the awesome technology that lay before him, at the same time humbled by the power and responsibility that came with it. From this room, he could survey the entire planet, tracking the intrigues of nations, observing the movements of armies, the building of cities, the ebb and flow of civilization itself. The ancient orbiters, the eyes and ears of this network, still circled overhead, sending a constant stream of information to the observatory.

A huge viewscreen covered the opposite wall, and the blue green light from this screen colored the entire chamber, casting a strange hue across the faces of the technicians and other devices that filled the room. An image of Kalnaroag hung there, complete with mountains, valleys, seas, and rivers, as if seen from a great height. Clouds obscured various areas, and near the edge of the scene, where night had fallen, Gregor could see the twinkling lights of a city. Rows of monitors and instrument panels stood between Gregor and the planetary display, their screens and graphs closely observed by the operators. A series of ledges, descending toward the front of the room, created a large amphitheater, with the viewscreen as its stage. Five technicians currently worked in the room, and a large man sat before a control console near the foot of the massive screen. Absorbed in the play of lights and readings on the panel before him, the man seemed unaware of Gregor's arrival. A Luminarae hovered over his left shoulder.

Gregor descended the steps toward the screen, acknowledging the greetings of the technicians. As he neared the forward control panel, the man seated there spoke, his powerful voice rising above the hum and click of the instruments.

"Blessings on you, Elder. Thank you for coming," he said.

"How is our pilgrim faring, Brother Sebastian?" Gregor asked.

Sebastian turned his chair to face the Elder, and pulled another chair toward him. "Please sit down. I know it's a long climb up here," he said.

Gregor sat in the offered chair, arranging his red robes more comfortably. "We can observe the entire world from this room, but we can reach it only by an ancient stone stairway. An interesting contrast," he observed.

"Exercise is good for the soul, the humble surroundings keep us from pride, and the long climb gives us time to reflect," Sebastian said with a smile.

Gregor frowned. "Didn't I say that once?" he asked.

Sebastian's smile widened, splitting his heavy beard. "Yes, Elder, that was wisdom from your own lips. Has your philosophy changed on that point?" he asked.

"No, I merely remark on one of the paradoxes of our world, the blending of old and new," he said.

The behavior of the Luminarae distracted the two men, their attention drawn to the fiery motes above them. When Gregor had arrived, Sebastian's Luminarae had risen to join the other two, and now the three Luminarae circled overhead. Their colors and pulsing rhythms settled into mirror images, their slow dance somehow peaceful and reassuring.

"I wish I knew why they did that," Gregor commented.

Sebastian squinted up at the Luminarae. "Evidently they are communicating. I wish I knew what they were saying," he said.

Gregor lowered his eyes to Sebastian. "I guess we have to accept their presence and good will on faith, without being able to fathom their secrets. A gift from the inscrutable Iosus. Anyway, back to my question. How is our man Morgan?" Gregor asked.

Sebastian clasped his hands over his massive torso. "Much better than some here had hoped, or feared," he said.

"The man was your disciple. Do I detect a note of pride in that statement?" Gregor asked.

Sebastian waved a hand dismissively. "Pride is a sin. I am merely stating facts," he said.

"Well, then make your report," Gregor said.

Sebastian glanced at the large screen, noting the area currently displayed. He turned his chair to face the panel, and his large hands moved over its surface.

"Please direct your attention to the main viewscreen," he said.

Sebastian touched another button, and a red dot appeared on the screen, deep in a mountain range. "Here is Khulankor, Morgan's point of departure," he said.

His hand moved again, and a second dot appeared, in a patch of green surrounded by the brown and white of the mountains. A red line connected the two points.

"From here he went to Saxhaven, where he met with an old friend, Antony, the Sagamore's ambassador. He also encountered Malissa," he said.

Gregor leaned forward. "The Hedonae? Did she discover his true nature?" he asked.

"I doubt it," Sebastian said. "She let him leave Saxhaven."

"Did his virtue remain intact?" Gregor asked.

"With the Hedonae, more than your virtue is at stake. But yes, somehow he managed to resist her charms. Perhaps Antony assisted him; my reports are sketchy on that point. He then had audience with Llorgau, who promptly exiled him from Saxhaven," Sebastian said.

Gregor raised his eyebrows. "What did Morgan do?" he asked.

"I have no information on that. He probably made some comment about Llorgau's new consort, or the state of affairs in the realm," Sebastian said.

Sebastian punched in another command, displaying a third point of red, this one near the blue of a sea. The red line extended to connect the three dots.

"From Saxhaven, he traveled to Androssar. Somewhere along the way, he picked up Maximilian, another old companion from the Raav days. In Androssar, by some whim of Iosus, he came into contact with the Princess of Skara Thrae, who had fled the Haggas invasion and sought Rulda's help," Sebastian said.

"Will Rulda come to their aid?" Gregor asked.

"Evidently not, for the Princess left the palace almost immediately after her audience with Rulda. She was being pursued by Mhoul agents, when rescued by Morgan and Maximilian," Sebastian said.

"Mhoul? Are you certain?" Gregor asked.

"Reasonably. This is further evidence of my contention that the Mhoul are involved in the invasion of Skara Thrae. We have detected Gate activity on the island, and I doubt that the Thraens have regained knowledge of Gate technology. The Mhoul must be involved somehow," Sebastian said.

"Whim of Iosus indeed. Morgan runs afoul of the Mhoul almost immediately," Gregor observed.

"That was our main reason for sending him. To draw out the Mhoul, and cause them to reveal their purposes," Sebastian said.

"What did the Mhoul do in response to Morgan's interference?" Gregor asked.

Sebastian frowned. "Unfortunately, I do not know what happened next. Our next report comes from Aquarquff," he said.

Sebastian displayed a fourth point on the screen, located on a ribbon of yellow next to an ocean, a considerable distance south of the third point. "For some reason, Morgan kept the Princess with him, and booked passage on the Windrider. The Windrider is captained by one Taurus, another of Morgan's old comrades," he said.

"Morgan appears to have quite a collection of old friends," Gregor said.

"Yes. One of the reasons he was the best choice for the assignment. He has many contacts in the world below. The Windrider left Androssar, after a severe storm, and arrived at Aquarquff. We have little information on what occurred during the voyage. However, we do know one thing. Our orbiters detected an explosion along their route. We couldn't identify the source, but the Windrider did not appear to be damaged when it reached Aquarquff. The type of explosion suggests advanced technology, with a significant release of refined energy. My guess is that the Mhoul pursued them and one of their vessels was destroyed," Sebastian said.

"But you have no proof of that, only the explosion?" Gregor asked.

"No, it's mostly conjecture at this point," Sebastian admitted.

"Were they able to penetrate the Empire cache?" Gregor asked.

"Yes. We detected Gate activity, indicating someone used the emergency exit. And I had another contact, which I'll explain later," Sebastian said.

"If the Mhoul were following Morgan, do they now know the location of the cache?" Gregor asked sharply.

"First, we don't know they were able to track him to Aquarquff. Second, the Empire cache is well protected. Without knowing how to evade the defenses, I doubt that even the Mhoul could reach the cache. Even so, I have agents attempting to determine the status of the cache. All we know for sure is that Morgan left Aquarquff and headed into the Waste," Sebastian said.

"The Waste? Why did he go there? He was supposed to go to Dragonback. He had access to the Windrider, and the best route from Aquarquff to Dragonback would be along the Seir, not through the Waste. If the Mhoul don't kill him, the Ha'ashtari will," Gregor said.

"I don't know Morgan's reason. The Windrider did leave Aquarquff and travel up the Seir. It is now docked at Kalixalven," Sebastian said.

"But Morgan was not aboard?" Gregor asked.

"No, our tracking devices place him here," Sebastian said, as he manipulated the controls once more.

A fifth dot appeared on the screen, this one in the middle of a vast brown expanse, near the edge of the screen. The red line extended to this point, along a circuitous route. Gregor peered at the screen.

"Why, that's Carnac, isn't it?" he asked.

"Yes, Morgan was in Carnac," Sebastian said.

"Why did he wander so, on the way to Carnac?" Gregor asked.

"He was being pursued by the Ha'ashtari," Sebastian said.

"Why? Didn't he know enough to hire a Pathfinder?" Gregor asked.

Sebastian paused, and then spoke. "I hesitate to tell you this, but I contacted the Baron Serenus in Carnac," he said.

Gregor stared at him. "I am finding your recklessness harder and harder to defend. How do you justify an unauthorized transmission?" he demanded.

"The Baron had sent me a message, notifying me that Morgan had arrived in Carnac. I needed to know what was happening with Morgan. Our communication was brief and untraced," he said.

"You will not make any more such transmissions without my express permission. Do you understand?" Gregor said sternly.

"I understand," Sebastian said.

"Well, what did the Baron tell you?" Gregor asked.

"The Baron had rescued Morgan's party from the Ha'ashtari. There was some matter of a Pathfinder being killed. The Princess remained with Morgan. Evidently, her brother had been in Carnac and the Princess came there to find him. The Baron confirmed that Morgan had penetrated the cache, and had the devices with him. He also confirmed that Morgan had encountered the Mhoul at some point and they appeared to be pursuing him. We didn't have time to discuss the details," Sebastian said.

"Pathfinders, Mhoul, Ha'ashtari. I see you didn't select Morgan for his discretion," he said.

"A lightning rod that doesn't attract lightning is of little value, wouldn't you agree?" Sebastian said.

"You said Morgan was in Carnac. Where is he now?" Gregor asked.

"He just left the city, and is traveling north to Kalixalven, presumably to rendezvous with the Windrider," Sebastian said.

"Well, at least he's going in the right direction. Did the Princess stay in Carnac?" Gregor asked.

"No, her brother had left Carnac, and was rumored to be heading for Aijalon. She now intends to travel there," Sebastian said.

"Was there any sign of Mhoul activity in Carnac?" Gregor asked.

"Unfortunately, there may have been. An attempt was made to kill the Princess of Saxhaven," Sebastian said.

"The Princess of Saxhaven? What does she have to do with Morgan?" Gregor asked.

Sebastian smiled. "More old friends. They spent some time together in Carnac. However, I believe the real reason is Malissa," Sebastian said.

"Malissa?" Gregor asked.

"I suspect the Hedonae may be a Mhoul agent. One of the reasons the Princess of Saxhaven went to Carnac was to seek a defense against the Hedonae. It seems logical the Mhoul, or Malissa herself, would seek to stop her," Sebastian said.

"Especially if they knew she'd been talking to Morgan. This is a complicated affair you have thrust us into, Sebastian," Gregor said.

"And I believe we need to delve even further into this matter. We should investigate the invasion of Skara Thrae," Sebastian said.

"Why do we care that the Thraen clans are at war again?" Gregor asked.

Sebastian looked pained. "You sound like one of our Brothers from the Insular Order—afraid to soil himself with worldly affairs. You know the Mhoul were involved in that invasion. Why? What is their purpose?" he asked.

Gregor fingered the gray tassel of the Praesian Order. "You know I'm not of the Insula. But I am responsible for the safety of everyone here, and I can't afford to let idle curiosity endanger Khulankor. Because we sent Morgan out, the Mhoul now know the location of the Empire cache at Aquarquff, and there are devices there that could be used to attack us. Once Morgan penetrated the cache, the Mhoul would know we sent him. And then you make contact with Carnac, further putting the monastery at risk. Where does it end?" he asked.

"I would also have our agents contact Morgan. Let him know we have not abandoned him," Sebastian said.

Gregor shook his head. "Now I know you're not being objective. You've let your feelings for Morgan cloud your judgment. I faced considerable opposition when I proposed Morgan's mission.

504

If this adventure of yours causes any more trouble, I may be hard pressed to continue my support. My position is precarious enough. The Insula are outraged we even considered such a thing, and the Feran Order see this as an opportunity to rush into a war with the Mhoul. Would you have civil war in Khulankor?" he asked.

Sebastian stood, his anger evident. "Look around you, man! Have you forgotten what our agent died to reveal to us? The Mhoul have somehow contacted the Lucca after all these centuries, and are now excavating a site in Doomdroth. A site in the area where Craig Phadrig fell to earth. We all know what lies buried beneath the ruins of Craig Phadrig! The Fargate! The Lucca's doorway to Kalnaroag. If the Mhoul are attempting to reach the Fargate, dare we sit idle and worry about our petty internal squabbles? The entire world is at risk. We must act," he said.

Gregor gazed calmly at Sebastian, who towered over him. The Luminarae had ceased their dance, and now hovered over the two men, their pulsing quickened.

"Sit down," he ordered quietly.

Sebastian slowly sank into his chair. "Forgive me, Elder. My passion has caused me to sin," he said.

"Now you are sounding like a Feran. Do you wish to abandon the Praesian Order?" Gregor asked.

"No, Elder. Feran militancy is not the answer. But I am concerned for the fate of Khulankor, and Kalnaroag, if we continue on our present course," Sebastian said.

"We have taken action. All that is reasonably required at this point. Does Morgan have the keystone?" Gregor asked.

"Yes. The Baron saw the stone, and described it to me. But he didn't know what it was," Sebastian said.

"And have the dwarves been contacted?" Gregor asked.

"Yes, they were made aware of our plan through their agents in Carnac," Sebastian said.

The two men were silent for a time, watching the screen, lost in their own thoughts.

"We should have told Morgan of his ancestry," Sebastian said.

Gregor laughed harshly. "Reveal that his ancestors were the

hated Borrigan? How would that burden have helped him?"

"But for the Borrigan, we might still suffer the cruelties of the Yggda," Sebastian reminded him.

"The world does not remember the betrayal of their masters, but the horrors later inflicted by the Borrigan themselves," Gregor said.

"The madness was not really their fault, it was their nature," Sebastian said.

"When the Yggda fled with the Hedonae, they were doomed," Gregor said.

"It is rumored some remnants of the Borrigan still inhabit Vaeland," Sebastian mused.

"Morgan is living proof they still exist somewhere," Gregor agreed.

"You also should have told me about the tracking device you planted in Morgan's head," Sebastian said.

"We felt it best that he did not know," Gregor said.

"And you knew I would tell him," Sebastian said.

"Yes," Gregor admitted.

"I led him to believe he would be contacted by our agents," Sebastian said.

"There has been no need," Gregor said.

"Morgan doesn't know that. He must feel alone and forgotten in the enemy camp. Is that what you want?" Sebastian asked.

"His feelings are irrelevant. He has the memory implants. He lacks nothing necessary to his mission," Gregor said. "Besides, he has your transmission to cheer him."

Sebastian regarded Gregor. "I fear your high station has made you cold, old friend," he said.

Gregor stood. "We've done all we can for now. Do not take any further action without consulting me. Thank you for the report," he said as he turned to leave.

The two Luminarae drifted after him, while the third settled to hover near Sebastian's head.

"I was beginning to think you wouldn't come. I had asked several times before," Sebastian said.

The Elder of Khulankor stopped on the steps. He looked tired. "I have many matters to deal with. Your request was only one," he said, then resumed his ascent.

Sebastian watched him for a moment, and then spoke. "I am reminded of a scripture, from the Codex," he said.

Gregor stopped and turned to face him. "And what is that?" he asked impatiently.

"May those who curse days curse that day, those who are prepared to rouse Leviathan," Sebastian recited.

The man in red regarded the stone at his feet, as if it would give him insight. "Are the Mhoul truly mad enough to 'rouse Leviathan,' to bring back the Lucca? Don't they remember what happened last time those beings walked this world?" Gregor asked.

"The Mhoul are a dying race, born of the Lucca. They feel the Lucca's return is their only hope. Would we act differently?" Sebastian asked.

Gregor sighed. "I pray we would. We should prefer death, rather than sacrifice Kalnaroag to those creatures," he said.

"I will pray that Morgan succeeds. For now, only he can give us the information we need," Sebastian said.

"Yes, pray for him. If he survives what must come, it will only be at the grace and mercy of Iosus," Gregor said, as he resumed his climb.

Sebastian swung his chair to face the screen. He regarded the fifth dot, and the expanse of deep green beyond it.

"Iosus be with you, Morgan," he said quietly.

507

Look for the Second in the Return of the Lucca Trilogy,

To Rouse Leviathan

In this sequel to the Lost Warrior, Morgan Caeda continues his quest to uncover the secrets of the Mhoul.

Accompanied by Maximilian and Celestine, Morgan enters the mysterious forests of Aijalon where he is captured by Mhoul soldiers and taken to the ancient castle of Ragoulgard. After escaping the castle and the cruel experiments of the Mhoul scientist Dragoslav, Morgan and his companions journey to the underground dwarf city of Shieldaig.

To reach Mogda Thal, the Mhoul capital, Morgan must survive the labyrinth of Cnoc Thor and its deadly guardian. In the end, Morgan faces his worst fear... *the return of the Lucca.*

For updates visit our website at http://publishing.fearnought.net

GLOSSARY

Academy: the centaur learning center in Carnac.

Achbor: race name for the trolls.

A.F.: landmark for computation of time on Kalnaroag. Literally, After the Fall.

Aijalon: forested region east of the Waste.

Alta: Gunter the innmaster's wife.

Andog: a female Mhoul.

Andros: bay at the mouth of the Saar River.

Androssar: port city in Saarland, located at the mouth of the Saar River.

Antony: (Ambassador of Saxhaven) man who served with Morgan and Max in the Raavs. Nicknamed Glossauric (golden tongue) by his friends.

Aquarquff: settlement along the coast, between the Waste and the Sarlassan Sea.

Aram'tari: one of the five Ha'ashtari tribes, holding the southern portion of the Waste.

Arc massif: an old volcano crater in the Waste, called Bora'tran by the Ha'ashtari.

Argos: god of the sea.

Argurion River: a river flowing south and east through the Waste into Aijalon.

Argyle: soldier who served under Morgan in the Raavs.

Asa: the first moon of Kalnaroag.

Aurellium: metal that absorbs Luccan life energy, discovered by the Mercator Empire scientist Phronesis.

Balt: a soldier from Carnac, stationed at the gate when Max arrived.

Baron Serenus: a centaur, tutor of the royal family of Skara Thrae.

Barrier Lift: a line of cliffs separating the Waste from Aijalon.

Belov: Morgan's adopted mother.

Borak: new Captain of the City Guard in Saxhaven.

Borrigan: Yggda defensive force. Genetically altered humans, bred for aggression.

Bridge of the Gods: common name of Gallinor, the silver arch.

Brutus: Llorgau's favorite dog, a Poma.

Caestus: eunuch who serves as Antony's bodyguard.

Callis: the leader of the Pathfinders.

Carnac: capitol city of the centaurs, located in the Waste.

Celestine: Princess of Skara Thrae.

Cha'nu: (the free wind) Sha'lor's horse.

Charon: (taker to Gaol) one of Taurus' weapons.

Civilized Nations: confederation of western nations, including Saxhaven, Androssar, Kalixalven, Skorn, Simperopol, Cannes.

Clavius Dementus: a deformed dog that Maelin befriends in Carnac.

Codex of Khulankor: a sacred writing, thought to be the autobiography of Iosus the Maker.

Connar Bay: a village just north of Port Adele.

Craig Phadrig: a great floating city, the capitol of the Mercator Empire.

Crusade: a military campaign organized by the Civilized Nations, intended to recapture territories held by the Mhoul.

Cynar: old hermit who taught Morgan and Max the use of weapons.

Damon: the third moon of Kalnaroag.

Demented Boar: a tavern in Androssar.

511

Diomedes: a scholar from Carnac, sent by Serenus to guide Celeste into Aijalon.

Draken Cor: swamplands containing the Gate on Skara Thrae.

Dragonback: a mountain at the northern end of Aijalon.

Drifters: a predator of the Waste, living in the marshy lowlands.

Droghelda: troll fortress, located in the Barrier Lift.

Ebonite: a black metal, light and very hard.

El'atan: the man god of the Ha'ashtari.

Elixin: race name for the elves.

El'tari: the horse god of the Ha'ashtari.

Equisapiens: the centaurs.

Equo/Equa: title of respect used for centaurs.

Fall: (also the Fall of Craig Phadrig) generic name for the end of the Mercator Empire. Specifically, it refers to the destruction of the Empire's capitol city.

Falmount: Morgan and Max's childhood village, in the foothills of the Perpetual Mountains.

Fargate: experimental Gate intended for travel between galaxies.

Feran: the militant order of Khulankor.

Gate: Mechanisms developed by the Yggda and the Mercator Empire, allowing the instantaneous movement of persons and objects from place to place.

Gallinor: the silver arch that encircles Kalnaroag.

Gaol: place of punishment for the wicked in the afterlife.

Great Rift: the canyon in which Carnac was built.

Gregor: the Elder of Khulankor.

Guardian: a sentient beast created by the Mhoul and used to perpetuate their existence.

Gunter: the innmaster of the Demented Boar.

Gur-Ban: rock apes that inhabit the Perpetual Mountains.

Gygax: race name for the gargoyles.

Ha'ashtari: (people of the horse) a nomadic race of warriors who inhabit the Waste.

Ha'drak: a Ha'ashtari warrior of the Shen'tari tribe.

Ha'dros: leader of the Ha'ashtari sent to Carnac to intercept Max.

Haggas: an exiled Thraen clan who invade Skara Thrae.

Ha'keel: High Chief of the Ha'ashtari.

Fist of El'atan: five Ha'ashtari warriors, chosen to conduct the Ru'atan.

Ha'serl: a Ha'ashtari, of the Meng'tari tribe.

Ha'set: a Ha'ashtari, sent by Ha'keel to investigate the death of the Pathfinder Ka'nas.

Ha'sim: Ha'keel's son.

Harkon: Argyle's brother.

Hedonae: an ancient race of beings who feed on the life force of others, attracting male prey with their scent. Created by the Yggda to control the aggressive impulses of the Borrigan.

Helmsdale: village between Saxhaven and Androssar.

Hodin: Morgan's adopted father.

Hor'gaa: a winged predator living in the Waste.

Immortals: breed of artificial humans created by the Mhoul, used as the common soldier.

Imperius: General of the Raavs. He led the Crusade and died in the massacre at Mogda Thal.

Insula: order of priests at Khulankor, devoted to holiness and separation from the world.

Iosus: the Maker, the creator god worshipped by the monks of Khulankor.

Jinn'she: Ha'ashtari holy war.

Ka'at: the Ha'ashtari knife.

Ka'chi: the Ha'ashtari code of honor and bravery.

Kalixalven: a city on the south bank of the Seir.

Kalkin: the chief of the Haggas.

Kalnaroag: Morgan's homeworld.

Ka'lur: the Callis of the Pathfinders.

Ka'nas: Pathfinder who escorted Celeste and killed himself.

Ka'rek: a Pathfinder, personal assistant to the Callis.

Kevan: Windrider's helmsman and navigator.

Khulankor: monastery in the Perpetual Mountains, built by survivors of the Fall, and birthplace of the worship of Iosus on Kalnaroag.

Khundlu Mata: (Passage of the Sagamores) the road between Saxhaven and Androssar.

Ko'raa: the Ha'ashtari name for the Waste antelope, large shaggy animals with spiral horns.

Korum: the god of the Quffians and the Pathfinders.

Ko'tari: one of the five Ha'ashtari tribes, whose territory lies in the southeast corner of the Waste.

Krang Fere Harriers: elite soldiers of the Mhoul army.

Lang Regis: (Sage of Skara Thrae) scholar and advisor to Ryde.

Landgates: Gates used for travel on Kalnaroag.

Land of Men: generic name for the region west of the Barrier Lift.

Land of Faerie: generic name for the region east of the Barrier Lift.

Llorgau: Sagamore of Saxhaven.

Lex talionus: (law of retaliation) Morgan's sword.

Llewelyn: Sagess of Saxhaven, Llorgau's wife.

Locha: god of ill fortune.

Lucca: race of energy beings that brought about the Fall of Craig Phadrig.

Lugershall: Ryde's castle.

Luminarae: (the fire of God) energy beings that dwell in Khulankor.

Lun'paa: the Ha'ashtari lance.

Luras: goddess of lust.

Ma'aran Kus: a range of mountains, between the Seir and the Waste.

Madstalkers: the hyena of the Waste.

Maelin: Princess of Saxhaven, Llorgau's only child.

Maenor: (the elder gods) the deities worshipped by most Thraens.

Malek: a bandit, leader of the hillmen who planned to attack Max's caravan.

Malissa: one of the last of the Hedonae, the Royal Consort of Saxhaven.

Marlenus: a centaur, the Prefect of the Academy.

Masters: term of respect used by the Mhoul, when referring to the Lucca.

Maximilian, Le Morte Kahn: (Maximilian, the Lord of Death) retired Commander of the Eighth Raav Legion.

Meng'tari: one of the five Ha'ashtari tribes, controlling the western portion of the Waste.

Mercator Empire: trading empire formed by several alien races, including humans, after they regained their freedom from the Yggda.

Metasilk: fabric woven of metallic fibers, nearly impenetrable.

Mhoul: human/Luccan hybrid, created by the Lucca in their quest to return to physical form.

Mithredath: formal name for the Perpetual Mountains.

Mogda Thal: Mhoul capitol city, located near the ruins of Craig Phadrig.

Molid: Dirgelord (leader) of the Mhoul.

Momus: the god of blame and guilt.

Mons Monachus: Iosian monks living at Khulankor.

Mora: the second moon of Kalnaroag.

Morgan Caeda: (Morgan the Killer) retired Commander of the Seventh Raav Legion. Nicknamed Caeda by his friend Maximilian.

Nageff: a canyon splitting the Barrier Lift, through which the Argurion river flows.

Pathfinders: half-caste Ha'ashtari who serve as guides across the Waste.

Phronesis: Mercator Empire scientist who first opposed the Lucca.

Poma: a small breed of dog from Skara Thrae, with a poisonous bite.

Port Adele: a town on the north side of the Seir, at the mouth of the river.

Praesian: order of priests at Khulankor that stress moderation in all things.

Quffian: inhabitant of Aquarquff.

Raavs: mercenary military force based in the Civilized Nations, divided into ten Legions.

Rif'tari: one of the five Ha'ashtari tribes, residing in the northeast corner of the Waste.

Rith: a toad-like telepathic creature, used by the Mhoul to aid their sight and hearing.

516

Ru'atan: the Ha'ashtari trial by combat.

Rukla: a Mhoul involved in the invasion of Skara Thrae.

Rulda: the Sagamore of Androssar.

Rusk: a soldier from Carnac, leader of Celestine's escort to Aijalon.

Ryde: Warlord of Skara Thrae, Celestine's father.

Saan: defensive force of Khulankor.

Saar: river that formed the valley of Saarland.

Sa'aran Kus: a range of mountains along the southern border of the Waste.

Saarish: language spoken in Saarland.

Saarland: wide river valley between the Perpetual Mountains and the Seir.

Sagamore: ruler or king.

Sagess: queen, the Sagamore's wife.

Sarlassan Sea: the sea between Saarland and Gaeland.

Sasich: a bitter drink, served hot, similar to coffee.

Saxhaven: a city in Saarland.

Sebastian: a priest of Khulankor, Morgan's mentor and friend.

Secondus: Chamberlain of Saxhaven.

Seidon: First Mate of the Windrider.

Seir: a large river flowing between Saarland and the Waste.

Seressa: Ryde's wife, Celestine's mother.

Sett: the goddess of death.

Shadow: an honor guard for the ta'hoda.

Sha'for: a Ha'ashtari, sent by Ha'keel to investigate the death of the Pathfinder Ka'nas.

Sha'lor: Ha'keel's daughter.

Shen'tari: one of the five tribes of Ha'ashtari, controlling the central region of the Waste.

Sherat: official of the Shah of Aquarquff.

Shieldaig: subterranean capitol of the dwarves.

Shiva: a former wrestler, now in the employ of Thugmonger Wald.

Simon the Deaf: cook and cabin boy of the Windrider.

Simperopol: a southern city.

Sith'gaa: large feline predator that inhabits the Waste.

Sittle: mayor of Port Adele.

Skara Thrae: an island kingdom off the coast of Saarland.

Skorn: a city north of Androssar.

Specimen War: revolt that led to the freeing of the Yggda specimens.

Ssin: race name for the goblins.

Stadia: a unit of distance measurement on Kalnaroag, approximately 600 feet.

Stark: the river that flows through the Great Rift, and encircles Carnac.

Stryker: Maximillian's bow.

Taglar: a Mhoul involved in the invasion of Skara Thrae.

Ta'hoda: (the lost one) according to Ha'ashtari belief, a person in whom resides the lost spirit of a great Ha'ashtari warrior.

Talbot: the Prince of Skara Thrae, Celestine's older brother.

Tantagnel: Thuro's castle.

Targ: tribe of mountain savages, living in the Perpetual Mountains.

Tari'shan or Shan'tari: (horse land) the Ha'ashtari names for the Waste.

Taskin: soldier who served under Morgan in the Raavs, later employed as a Guardsman in Saxhaven.

Tau'kendi: (oasis of Kendi) an oasis in the Waste.

Taurus: Captain of the Windrider, an old friend of Morgan and Max.

Tchoga: troll fortress in the Barrier Lift.

Ten'paa: Ha'ashtari ritual of marking the enemy, a display of courage.

Tet'rik: large cave spiders that inhabit the Waste.

Thaar: the god of war.

Thugmonger Wald: an old enemy of Morgan and Max, now working for the Mhoul.

Thuro: a Thraen clan leader.

Trade: a common language used on Kalnaroag.

Trang: new general of Saxhaven's armies.

Triad: a military complex consisting of the trolls, goblins, and gargoyles. The Triad now serves the Mhoul.

Usk: the Axminster of Skara Thrae.

Vaeland: largely unexplored continent west of Saarland, across the Sarlassan Sea. Somewhere in this land lies the abandoned city of the Yggda.

Vaelings: primitive inhabitants of Vaeland.

Vasari: Maelin's bodyguard in Carnac.

Viras: goddess of love, twin sister of Luras

Waste: the high desert inhabited by the Ha'ashtari and the centaurs.

Wasterats: small colonial rodents that inhabit the Waste. Called mus'roo by the Ha'ashtari.

Windfall: tremendous windstorms that ravage the Waste during the spring.

Windrider: Taurus' fighting ship.

Worldgates: Gates used for travel between planets.

Yfel: the god of evil, arch rival of Iosus.

Yggda: alien race that conquered Kalnaroag and assembled a collection of specimens from various worlds for scientific study.

Neil Lynn Wise

Neil Lynn Wise was born in Oregon in 1955. A lover of books, he was especially fond of science fiction and fantasy novels. At college he dabbled in Military Science and Commercial Art, before meeting the woman of his dreams and settling down to complete a Bachelor's Degree in Wildlife Biology. After a nine year career with a state fish and wildlife agency, he entered law school and now practices environmental law on the wet side of Washington State. Neil and his wife Marcie live in the country with their dogs and horses.